About the Author

Meredith lives in Shropshire with his beloved wife. As well as being a dedicated sports fan, Meredith loves drumming, stand-up comedy, swifts and blackbirds. He began to lose his sight as a teenager but, despite the minor inconvenience of blindness, these days he 'sees' life more clearly than ever.

Gorgeous and Adorable

MEREDITH VIVIAN

——

Gorgeous and Adorable

Vanguard Press

VANGUARD PAPERBACK

© Copyright 2024
Meredith Vivian

The right of Meredith Vivian to be identified as author of
this work has been asserted by him in accordance with the
Copyright, Designs and Patents Act 1988.

A CIP catalogue record for this title is
available from the British Library.

ISBN 978-1-80016-814-5

This is a work of fiction. Names, characters, businesses, places, events and
incidents are either the products of the author's imagination or used in a fictitious
manner. Any resemblance to actual persons, living or dead, or actual events is purely
coincidental

Vanguard Press is an imprint of
Pegasus Elliot Mackenzie Publishers Ltd.
www.pegasuspublishers.com

First Published in 2024

Vanguard Press
Sheraton House Castle Park
Cambridge England

Printed & Bound in Great Britain

For Joanna Lovely

I'm incredibly grateful to so many, for their insights, support and encouragement, but I thank the following in particular:

Nigel Lines
Derek Griffiths
Debs Joy Karim
John Hammond
Robert Hammond
Julia Williams
John Moffatt
Gillian, Ade and Kenton McCusker
Sarah Porter
Roland Casson
Ali Thurm
Adrian Thomas
Pete Godfrey
Stilt Godwit
Holly Vivian

Special thanks to Priscilla Church for her precise 'marking'.

Monday

Chapter 1

Gasping for breath, Tina paused at the top of the final flight. She thought, as she always did, that when they moved out, it would be to a ground-floor flat. This time, though, her exhaustion was way beyond anything she'd felt before. She pulled her keys out of the left-hand pocket of her parka, selected the Yale and inserted it. She paused. What would she tell him? Would she say anything at all? She turned the key, slowly opened the door and went inside.

'Where've you been?'

Tina groaned. 'Don't start, Dad, please.'

'What do you mean? It's six a.m. and you're coming in looking like death warmed up! Where have you been? And don't bother lying.'

Tina put her keys on the kitchen table and looked at her dad. As usual, he was wearing his grey overall; she couldn't tell if he was just up or hadn't gone to bed. He also had his worst face on: half disapproval, half disappointment.

Tina wanted to tell someone what she'd been through — all of it. She wondered what it would be like to tell her dad. Not a good idea. He would blame her and then get into a state. She knew from painful experience that talking about anything upsetting would give him the screaming abdabs. Even if he didn't crack up, he'd ask what she expected if she hung around with scum like the Abbotts. Anyway, he'd be right about that.

She said at last, 'I've been at the hospital.'

Worry etched his face. 'Why? What's wrong?'

'Nothing, Dad; don't get into a paddy. It wasn't me. Someone was really ill.'

'Who?'

Tina turned to the kettle and filled it. 'Want a cuppa?'

'I asked you a question.'

Tina leant against the sink and screwed her eyes tight. The pictures wouldn't go away. 'Brian Abbott.'

'Typical, that old drunk. I suppose he fell over or down somewhere?'

Tina heard again, and felt, the crunching thud of the heavy dish smashing into Brian's head, only inches from hers. She shuddered as she remembered the sickening weight of him crumpling against her, and how she'd had to wriggle free of him. 'Yeah, he fell over.'

'Pissed, I suppose?' Tina nodded. 'Listen to me, love. I know you think I'm a stupid old fool who doesn't know anything. And maybe I don't know much, but that family is a bad one. I don't think Kevin is right for you; and that oaf, Abbott, well — he's more caveman than anything.'

Tina put the kettle on the hob and lit the gas with a match. 'Well, you don't need to worry anymore.'

'Why not?'

Tina thought about the hours sitting at Brian's bedside. It had been like a crazy dream: the three of them — Jenny, Gary and her — just sitting there. To start with, they had rehearsed their story over and over again; then, they'd sat in silence, waiting. And then, the sudden, shallow gasping of the huge, unconscious man; the nurse rushing in, taking his pulse, calling for a doctor; them telling Jenny nothing could be done; and the hideous rattling sound of his last breath. That bit seemed like it had lasted for ever.

She had stared disbelievingly at the still figure, desperate to ask, 'Is he dead?' but hadn't dared. She tried to see Jenny and Gary's reactions out of the corners of her eyes. They were like statues. Fascinated by seeing someone die, she couldn't help but wonder at the enormity of it: a man had been alive and then he was dead. Right there, in front of her.

She heard Gary's voice at last. 'Dad? Dad, are you…? Shit!'

Tina still stared at the man in the bed. Was he going to open his eyes? No, Brian Abbott was dead, all right. She was looking at a man's dead body.

Tina took Jenny's hand. 'I'm sorry, Jenny. I'm so sorry.'

Jenny Abbott's voice was low and monotonous. 'He'll be okay, love. We'll get him home and things will get better. Don't you worry.'

'But, Jenny, I think he's…'

'I'll make some tea; he'll sleep it off and… I know him, he'll come round soon.'

The nurse turned to Jenny and said, 'I'm so sorry, Mrs Abbott.'

Jenny looked confused; she turned to Gary.

'He's gone, Mum. We've lost him.'

Jenny shook her head, 'But, he's… I don't… What about…?'

Tina took two mugs off the draining board and spooned sugar into them. She wasn't quite sure what had happened next. She remembered getting on the bus with Gary and Jenny. They had got off before her. Gary said, 'Don't forget we've got to go to the Cop Shop at nine a.m.'

She'd wanted him to give her a hug. She'd wanted to give Jenny a hug. She definitely hadn't wanted to go home but she had done, and now her dad was giving her gyp.

'Coz he's dead.'

He whistled. 'Flippin' hell!'

'Oh, and I dumped Kev, too.'

'Good riddance.'

Tina poured boiling water into the pot. Why wouldn't her dad ask how she was? All she wanted was someone to give her a cuddle, a loving stroke of her head, tell her that she was a good girl.

'I suppose he got pissed up and crashed his car or something?'

Against her better judgment, Tina brought back the events of last night. Was Brian Abbott really dead? Everything had the ingredients of a nightmare. She wasn't sure about any of it. All that business about the tattoo, and him head-butting a posh bloke, and the police... What was that all about?

'Are you all right?'

She looked up at her dad. He was doing his best. How could he know what she'd been through? In her head she counted off what had happened: being molested by a drunken old man, lying to the police about his injury, then seeing him die in front of her eyes. Was she all right?

'I'm fine, Dad.'

'You going to school?'

'No, I've got to go to the police station to give a statement. I have to say what happened.'

'What did happen?'

'I don't know. He was in the kitchen and fell over. He must have hit his head on something. That's all I know.'

Tina remembered him pressing himself against her, his hands on her breasts, his erection thrusting... Jumping up, she ran into the bathroom, locked the door, knelt in front of the toilet and vomited. She stayed there, sickening images whirling.

'Don't be long. I've got to get to work early today.'

Tina sat back on her heels and silently cried.

Her dad's heavy hand banged on the door. 'Come on, Tina! I'm going to be late.'

She got up, flushed the toilet, rinsed her mouth and opened the door.

'You look terrible. Make sure you tidy yourself up before you go to the police. You don't want them thinking we're like the Abbotts.'

Tina thought about how loving Jenny Abbott was and wished she'd be her mum. She remembered the feel of Gary's arms around her in the car park, too. He'd been so sweet.

'Sorry, Dad. I'm going to go to bed for a couple of hours. I'm absolutely knackered.'

'Tina?'

'Yeah?'

'I'm sorry I'm such a crap dad.'

Tina smiled sadly, 'You're all right, Dad.'

'I'm sorry I was such a crap husband, too.'

She felt sorry for him, all over again. 'I'm sorry I'm not a very good daughter.'

'I've decided: I'm coming with you to the police station. I'm sorry, I'm so selfish it didn't even occur to me.'

Her dad getting involved was out of the question. He'd make everything much more complicated and she couldn't take the risk of him cracking up again.

'Thanks, Dad, you're all right. I've only got to sign a statement; it's all straightforward. I'll see you later. We can have a nice, quiet evening.'

'Hmm... If you're sure.'

When the front door closed, she ran a bath, poured in a load of green bubble-bath and sank into it, waiting for the hot water to purify her. It didn't. Her life was totally shitty. She had fucked up good and proper; now she even had a dead man on her conscience. There must be something wrong with her: awful things happened wherever she went. She let her head slip under the hot water. Everything was suddenly quiet, calm. She felt safe at last. The warmth of the water and the overwhelming relief lulled her. She let herself slip into a wonderful place where nothing mattered and no one knew her.

Through the quickening rhythm of blood hammering in her head came another sound, insistent. She sat up, gasping. The phone was ringing. Reluctantly, she hauled herself out of the bath, wrapped herself in a towel and went into the hall.

'Hello?'

It was Kev. 'Where the fuck are you?'

She couldn't help herself bark a sarcastic laugh. 'Um, you ring me. I answer. I wonder if I'm at home?'

'Jeez, you're a selfish bitch. I mean, why aren't you here? My fucking dad's just died and you're nowhere to be seen.'

'I'm really sorry, Kev. I'm sorry about your dad. I'm sorry about everything. I'm sure everything's my fault. I don't know what I can do. You're better off without me. Everyone is.'

'Tell me the truth — don't bother lying. Have you been screwing Gary?'

'For fuck's sake, Kev. I've had enough. Never ring me again.' Tina banged the phone down and went into her bedroom. She looked for clean pyjamas — nothing clean, just shit everywhere. She picked up a shirt from the floor and put it on, pulled back the blankets and got into bed. Reaching down to the floor, she tenderly lifted the sagging giraffe, its neck broken beyond repair, and held it tight to her chest.

Chapter 2

'I dunno what I ever saw in her. She's a selfish bitch.'

Derek said, 'Let me guess: she let you get your end away?'

Kevin was grudging. 'Yeah, but apart from that?'

Jenny Abbott came downstairs and put her coat on. She looked at herself in the mirror, touching her hair into shape. Gary shrugged on his coat.

Derek said, 'I'll drive you in. I can use Dad's car.'

Jenny checked her bag. 'Thanks, Derek. That's helpful, but what about your work?'

'Sod 'em. I think my dad being dead is a bit more important.'

Gary gulped as his brother's words hit home. His head was completely mashed by everything that had happened. It was only a few hours ago that he'd stood right here in the hall, whispering to Joe as they checked over the 'evidence'. And that had been only a few minutes after he'd seen his kind, gentle mother bash his dad's head so hard it was no wonder he'd gone down like a sack of potatoes. The hours in the hospital had stretched on and on, and when his dad had snuffed it, he'd suddenly felt so many emotions he couldn't pick them apart. His overwhelming response was to keep his mum safe, no matter what. He knew that he must stay in control; for his mum, for Tina, for himself. There was so much at stake, he could not let emotion get in the way. It was probably childish, but he tried to imagine he was a secret agent who had to keep calm, not let on, stay ice cold.

Right now, he wanted to make sure his mum was okay. Derek was going to be in the way. He said, 'We can go on the bus, can't we, Mum?'

Derek was adamant. 'Don't be stupid. I'm taking her.'

They got in the battered Cortina, Gary in the back.

'You all right, Gary?' Jenny Abbott said, looking back at him from the front seat.

'Yeah.'

She stared at him. He looked back, his eyes questioning. She said, 'Once we get this out of the way, we can begin to think about everything.' Gary nodded. She seemed okay.

Derek was wrestling with the gears; the engine cut out. 'Shit! This car is a pile of shit.' He got it going again, then said, 'I still can't get my head around all of this. How can someone die, just like that? I mean, one minute he was being Dad, just — you know, being Dad. Then, he's brown fucking bread. I don't get it. The other thing is, he hadn't been drinking like normal, so he can't have been drunk.'

Gary said, 'There was a glass of whisky on the table, nearly empty. Maybe he'd been knocking it back without us knowing?'

Derek turned to Jenny. 'Mum?'

'I don't know, love. I honestly don't know.'

Gary thought about Tina. He was really worried about her. The whole story relied on her holding her nerve. She'd been really shaky when they'd left her on the bus. He had tried to be reassuring but he wasn't sure how best to help her. One thing was definite: he didn't need to worry about his mum. She was doing fine. When she had hit his dad, she'd gone into some kind of trance but, pretty soon, a woman new to him had appeared. His mum had always been a quiet and hesitant person; now, although quiet, she seemed to have developed a new edge. A hard edge.

Derek said, 'I don't want to go near the Old Bill. I'll drop you off round the corner and wait there.'

'Thank you, dear. I don't know how long we'll be, so please don't wait if you need to get to work.'

'Don't worry, Mum. I'll be here.'

Gary and Jenny got out and walked back to the main street. He said, 'Before we go in, I think we should have a talk with Tina. I hope she hasn't gone in yet. Can we hang on for a minute?'

They only had to wait five minutes. Tina got off the next bus to arrive. Jenny opened her arms in welcome as Tina walked towards them, 'Hallo, Tina. How you doing?'

Tina went straight over and clung to the slight woman. 'I've been better.'

Gary edged them down an alley between two shops. He said, 'Listen, I've been thinking and realised something — something important. Last night they got me to say that Dad had stuck his head into that bloke. They made me think that, if I admitted it, they wouldn't be bothering with whatever happened to Dad in the kitchen. They didn't say that, but that's what I thought they meant. They were really happy with me saying it was Dad. But now that Dad is dead, they don't have anyone to arrest. So, I'm thinking that maybe they'll try and pin his death on us. That way they'll have the conviction of Dad for the attack, and at the same time, they will have us for his death. Do you see? It's a double success for them.'

Tina breathed out. 'Shit…' She lowered her voice, 'But, hang on a minute — it was self-defence. Anyway, we didn't mean to kill him.'

'It doesn't matter. I saw this case on Crown Court, where a bloke had stopped a burglar in his house. He hit him over the head; the bloke died. He got banged up for murder, even though he was the one being robbed.'

Jenny said, 'I did it. I'll own up to it.'

'No, there's no way that's happening.' Gary's voice was so harsh it shocked him. He whispered, 'I'd rather go to prison than you go, Mum. That's the end of it.'

Tina said, 'But they can't prove anything, can they?'

Gary whispered, 'I dunno. My head's gonna explode.'

They stood in silence for a minute, every-day life continuing around them. Gary said, 'We've got to stick to our story and wait and see. We won't say anything other than what we said last night. If they ask us anything new, we say we don't know.'

He looked at Tina, she nodded.

'Mum?'

She nodded.

Tina said, sniffing, 'I'm so sorry about everything. I wish I hadn't come around yesterday. I… well — if only… oh, I don't know. Anyway, I'm sorry. I don't know what else to say.'

Jenny turned and pulled the crying girl to her. 'Shush, don't cry… don't cry. We'll get through this.'

Not used to giving physical comfort, Gary uncertainly patted his mum on the back.

He said, 'Okay, let's get on with it. Mum, you and me go in first. Tina — you follow in a couple of minutes.'

Gary and his mum walked up to the newly built, concrete and glass block and stared through the doors. They hesitated, then continued into the large vestibule and stood waiting in front of the high-topped counter. Behind it stood a red-faced, uniformed copper, his belly straining his buttons. He was speaking on the phone. Gary eyed him up: he looked like the kind of arrogant bastard Gary hated. The pot-bellied copper was repeating sarcastically everything the caller was telling him with a poxy smirk on his face.

Gary looked around. There was a wooden bench along one wall. He took his mum's arm and they went to sit down.

'I didn't say you could sit down.'

They turned around to the copper. His hand was over the mouthpiece as he stared at them.

'Well, we thought we would sit down and wait,' Gary said.

'Listen, son, I'm in charge here. I'm the desk sergeant, not you. You don't do anything until I tell you. Do you understand?'

Gary reddened. No one talked to him like that. He knew he must keep his cool, 'Sorry,' he mumbled.

The pompous fart started talking into the phone again. Gary could hear voices around the building and saw people working at desks, behind the counter. He wondered if the two detectives were here. He remembered their elation as he'd told them that his dad had head-butted the bloke. What would they be like today?

Pompous Fart put the phone down. He was writing something in a register. He didn't look up. Finally, after turning pages, then turning them back, he shut the big book and looked at Jenny and Gary. 'Ah, sorry, I didn't see you there. How can I help you?'

Jenny said, 'We're here to sign statements. I'm Jenny Abbott and this is my son, Gary.'

The copper beamed at them. 'How lovely to see you both. I've been hearing all about you. We're all very pleased to make your acquaintance. I'll let the boys know you're here.' He picked up the phone and dialled. 'Your special guests are here. The wife and the kid. No, not yet. Certainly, of course.' He beamed again, 'Perhaps you'd like to take a seat?'

They sat down. Gary whispered to his mum, 'All right?'

'Yes.'

The main door opened. Gary looked up. Two coppers came in either side of a shabby bloke, his wrists handcuffed. A woman stood outside the door, screaming blue murder. The threesome staggered past Gary and his mum and disappeared through a door opposite. When Gary turned back, Tina was there.

'Hello, dear. I'm so sorry you had to cope with everything last night, and now this.' Jenny patted the bench next to her.

'Hang on a minute, sweetie — over here.' Tina went to the desk. 'You are?' the cop said, peering down his nose at her.

'Tina Castleton. I'm with Jenny and Gary.'

'I'm sure you are but you don't do anything without my say-so, and that includes sitting down. Do you understand?' Tina nodded. 'Do you understand?' he repeated.

Tina's voice was tiny. 'Yes.'

'I still can't hear you.'

Gary watched as Tina seem to slump; her head drooped and for a second he thought she was going to crumple up in front of them. Then, her head shot up and she yelled, 'Well, why don't you clean your effing ears out then!'

The sergeant threw up his hands in defence. 'Don't shoot!'

Gary laughed. Even Jenny smiled.

Tina's hand was over her mouth. She took it away, 'I'm sorry! I didn't mean...'

To their surprise, Pompous Fart was chuckling. He said, 'Don't worry about me, love. I'm all mouth: hot air and trousers. Do take a seat and make yourself comfortable.'

Tina turned around and came to sit next to Jenny. 'I'm sorry, Jenny. I'm really sorry.'

'That's all right, dear. We understand, don't we, Gary?'

Gary looked at Pompous Fart and nodded, 'Yeah, course we do.'

Jenny sniffed. 'Mm, someone smells nice.'

Tina smiled shyly. 'Oh, sorry about that. I nearly drowned in the bath this morning; I went a bit mad with the bubble bath.'

Gary liked how she smelled but he was suddenly really shy around Tina. They had shared so much the night before but now, in the hard light of the police station, it was as if last night hadn't happened. He'd like to hold her hand and reassure her, give her a cuddle — he wasn't sure what. Maybe what he wanted was for her to cuddle him?

'Why aren't you wearing your glasses?' Tina asked, looking at him.

As soon as they'd left the hospital last night, he'd taken them off. He didn't want people to see him looking weak. 'Oh, I left them at home.' Without his glasses, Gary's sight was blurry again. He looked around. There were notices on the walls but the only one he could read was about a police social.

One of the doors opened and there stood the one Gary had named 'Dickie Davies': the copper with the white streak in his hair. He was unshaven and looked like he hadn't slept which, Gary thought, like them, he probably hadn't.

'Ah, here you all are. Come this way, please.'

They followed him down a corridor. Gary sniffed. There was a rotten smell coming from somewhere nearby. He squeezed his nostrils closed. Jeez, this place stank!

Dickie showed them into a tiny room and indicated they sit on the far side of a plain, metal table. When they were seated, he called down the corridor, 'Chris, get five cups of tea with sugar and then get yourself in here.' He shut the door, sat down opposite and looked at them in turn. 'I am so sorry. I cannot say how sad this situation makes me. You must all feel gutted by the loss of Brian. Please accept my sympathies; mine and all of us here.'

The door opened and the detective with the Kevin Keegan perm came in, carrying five mugs of tea. He'd made a bad job of the task. Tea was dripping from every mug.

'Jesus, what's wrong with a tray?' Dickie snapped. He turned back to Jenny. 'Mrs Abbott, how are you doing?'

'Trying to cope. It's all very difficult to take in.'

'I know. It must be. How about you, Tina? It must be so upsetting.'

Tina nodded.

'Gary, I'm so sorry you've lost your dad. How are you feeling?'

Gary was edgy. He knew this copper was a crafty bugger. What was he up to? 'I'm coping.'

Dickie smiled. 'Well done, team! You're doing brilliantly well.' He turned to Keegan, 'Serve the tea, then.'

Keegan pushed wet mugs around the table and then sat down next to Dickie. They all picked up their mugs and slurped in unison.

Dickie said, 'I really appreciate you being here. We've got to go through a few procedural matters. We'll do it as quickly as possible, then you can all go home and start to come to terms with what's happened. We're going to ask each of you to tell us exactly what you remember from last night. We'll write it down. You can read it, then, if you agree with what we've written, you can sign it. Does that sound okay?'

They nodded. Gary had been thinking a lot about this moment. He had to keep his eye on two separate problems. His first job was to make sure that their story didn't break down. Last night, in the hospital, they had kept the lie going pretty well: as far as anyone knew, his dad had caught his foot in the iron's flex and he'd pitched over and struck his head on the edge of the sink. Jenny, Tina and he had remained constant and definite about all the details. They had gone over it again and again last night; they'd become word perfect. As far as Gary knew, the investigation of the kitchen had not suggested any other explanation for what had caused his dad's death. They must stick to their story. The second part of it all was the incredible conversation he had had with Dickie and Keegan in the car park. They'd said they were looking for someone who had attacked a bloke: the attacker had been driving a blue Cortina and had a tattoo on his arm. Gary had confirmed that his dad did drive a Cortina, had Jailhouse Rock tattooed on his arm, and that he'd stuck his head into the face of a posh bloke three weeks ago.

Gary wasn't sure why they were here now. What were these bastards up to? Would they try and weasel out a confession from Tina or his mum? He knew he wouldn't give in to them, but — he glanced at his mum. She had relaxed: Dickie's kindness was working. He looked at Tina. She was smiling at Keegan. Fuck.

Chapter 3

Terry Castleton lit his mid-morning cigarette and settled back into his sagging armchair. He picked up the plastic cup of his Thermos and sipped the thick, sugary tea. Outside his shed, he could hear the excited sounds of children letting off steam. Some voices came near to the shut door. He listened.

'He's in there. I can smell his fag.'

'Oi, Baldy!'

Terry ignored them.

'What you doing in there, Baldy?'

'He's doing a poo.'

Shrieking laughter.

'Oi, Baldy, I'm going to tell Mr Dixon you're doing a poo in your shed.'

'Maybe he ain't pooing. Maybe he's picking his nose and eating it.'

Silence.

'Why can't he be doing all of it at the same time? I can.'

'No you can't.'

'I can.'

'Well, I can have a poo, pick my nose, eat it and — erm… go cross-eyed all at the same time.'

'Baldy, we know you can hear us. Are you having a poo?'

Terry swigged his cooling tea, took one last drag from his roll-up and sighed.

A ball crashed against the wooden side of the shed. Terry got up, opened the door and glared at his persecutors. They stared back.

He said, his voice flat, 'Clear off, lads. Let me get on with my work.'

The three boys stared in silence. One of them said, at last, 'Give us one of your fags, Baldy.'

'Hop it.'

One of them started hopping around in a circle; the other two cheered him on.

Behind them, Terry could see a teacher coming out of the school with the bell in her hand. He said, 'Hop it,' again and went back into his shed.

The bell rang. The boys yelled 'Bye, Baldy' and he was alone.

There was a load of grass to be cut today but he just wanted to sit and stare. He rolled another cigarette and tried to bring back happy memories. He thought of his little girl; he always did when he needed something to cheer him up. Tina had been a pupil at this school. He used to come and pick her up on his days off. He pictured her in the little group of girls emerging from the main door, engrossed in chit-chat, twirling, laughing, being herself. When she saw it was him, rather than Diane, her face would fall. He never let on that he'd seen her disappointment or how much it hurt him. To be fair to Tina, she did her best to appear pleased it was him, rather than Diane. Usually, by the time they reached home, he would have managed to get her to tell him what she'd done that day, what had upset her, what had made her happy.

He remembered the awful moment he'd told her about Diane. Thinking back to it now, he found it impossible to believe that he'd had the courage to tell her. His own pain had been a searing knife wound; having to inflict even greater agony on his beautiful little girl had been too much for him. Tears rolled down his cheeks as he remembered it.

He had watched her peel away from her friends and walk towards him. Her long, blonde hair was being blown in the breeze, her blue eyes wide and questioning.

'Where's Mum?'

'Um — you've got me. Sorry.'

'What's wrong? You look funny, Dad. Where's Mum?'

'Come on. Let's go.'

'What's wrong with you, Dad?'

'I'll tell you when we get home.'

Tina stopped walking, 'I'm not coming.'

Terry was struggling. 'Come on, Tina, please.'

'What's wrong, Dad? Tell me.'

'Come on, Tina; let's go home.'

'No.'

'I'm not going to say it again: come on, Tina.'

'No.'

Terry grabbed her arm and tried to drag her; she went dead. He picked her up and began to walk down the main road. Tina started screaming. Terry put her down. He was beginning to panic. What was he supposed to do?

He knelt down in front of his ten-year-old daughter and said, his voice catching, 'I'm sorry, Tina. I'm really sorry. Your mum has left us.'

Tina was silent. He looked at her face: it was blank.

'She left us a note.'

She stood still. He watched her eyes glaze.

He went on. 'She's decided she would rather live somewhere else, with someone else.'

Tina was trembling.

Terry couldn't stop himself now. 'She has found someone else to live with: Ronald Simpson. He's a bloke at her office. Apparently, they really like each other and although she loves us, and especially you, she wants to be with him. I didn't know she was going to leave. I came home and there was a letter. I'm so sorry, Tina.'

He bowed his head, unable to prevent his daughter seeing him fall to pieces.

Now, as he relived those awful moments, the sobs came again. His daughter hadn't cried, screamed, or refused to come home. No — his beautiful, brave, little girl had wrapped her skinny arms around his neck, hugged him with all her strength and said, 'Don't cry, Daddy. I'll look after you.'

And, ever since that day, she had.

Chapter 4

Gary had been waiting in the pokey interview room for at least an hour. Tina had gone first, then his mum. Dickie had explained that they would be interviewed separately and then they could either wait in the reception area or go home; they couldn't be together until the statements were signed.

Gary had willed Tina and his mum to keep calm and stick to the story. Now, it was his turn. Here they were, Dickie and Keegan, sitting opposite him.

Gary was alert. He didn't trust these coppers. He could see through their sympathy: their sheer joy last night had told him everything he needed to know. They had thought they had solved a serious crime with the culprit bang to rights. Now that Brian Abbott was dead, they'd lost their big prize. He thought back to the moment he'd overheard them in the hospital car park. Dickie's voice was jubilant: 'What a result. I can't fucking believe it. This is medal time, fucking hell!'

Dickie said now, his voice dripping with concern, 'Gary, can I say again how sorry we are about what's happened to your dad. It's a terrible business.'

'Yeah, it is.'

Keegan said, 'I can't believe it. We were just chatting last night and we thought he'd pull through.'

Gary looked at him: what a tosser. The younger cop was very obviously trying to look like something off the telly. He had a huge bubble perm and wore his shirt undone at the neck, its enormous collar spread wide atop the jacket of his navy suit.

Ignoring his colleague, Dickie said, 'We want to make this business as quick and painless as possible. All we need to do is run over the facts. We've done the same with your mum and Miss Castleton. We'll be done in a few minutes.' Dickie was older, maybe in his forties. He had a suit and tie but he looked rough around the edges. He pulled out a packet of cigarettes. Bensons. 'Want one, Gary?'

Gary was gasping for a fag but refused; he wasn't going to be drawn into their little game.

Keegan looked sulkily at the other detective when the cigarettes were put back in his pocket. He got out a packet of his own: Dunhill. *Wanker*, thought Gary.

Not wishing to be outdone, Gary reached into his jacket pocket: no fags. Shit. Instead, he felt the hard plastic of his glasses case. Reluctantly, he pulled it out and put on his new glasses. The difference in his vision startled him again. He looked at Dickie and saw him properly for the first time. The detective was definitely the worse for wear. His eyes were red; he badly needed a shave; his collar was frayed... He looked more like a tramp than anything. Keegan was younger than he'd realised. Early twenties. Suddenly, Gary didn't feel so anxious. These were just blokes; stupid blokes.

Dickie said, 'Now, let's get down to business. My name is Detective Sergeant Nott. My colleague here is Detective Constable Armstrong. Can you confirm your name, address and date of birth please?'

'Gary Abbott, 27 Carlisle Road, 16th October, 1959.'

'Thank you, Gary. There are two sets of events we want you to talk us through: those occurring last night and those of three weeks ago. We'll go with last night first, as we want to compare what you said with what your mum and Miss Castleton said. It's interesting, Gary. They had different recollections of what happened. That's funny, don't you think?'

Gary swallowed. Shit. He controlled himself. He said nothing.

'Gary?'

'Yeah?'

'Don't you think that's funny?'

'I dunno. I didn't hear what they said, did I?'

'Hmmm, that's right: you didn't hear them.'

Gary was pretty sure Dickie was trying to wind him up. His mum, Tina and he had gone over it so many times: surely they hadn't got it wrong?

Dickie said, 'So, talk me through it. Detective Constable Armstrong will write it all down.'

Gary told them what they'd rehearsed: him and Tina being in the front room and hearing a crash; them rushing into the kitchen as his mum had come in the back door; seeing his dad unconscious on the floor; the oven being on to heat up the apple crumble; the crumble dish on the floor next to Abbott's body; apple crumble absolutely everywhere; his dad's foot caught up in the iron's extension lead...

Dickie said, 'So, you all arrived into the kitchen at the same time?'

'That's right.'

27

'A bit of a coincidence, wasn't it?'

'What do you mean?'

'Well, all three of you getting to the same place at the same time?'

'Well, Tina and me were already in the same place. It was my mum who arrived separately.'

'Hmmm. Chris, any questions?'

Keegan had been yawning. 'Er, well, um.'

Dickie looked annoyed. He said, 'Can you take a look at what Mrs Abbott said, and Miss Castleton? I think they told us different things to what Gary here has just told us.'

Keegan made a show of reading through his papers. At last, he said, 'Yeah, you're right.'

'I thought so.'

Gary almost laughed out loud: they were a couple of bungling pricks.

Dickie said, 'Okay, I've got a question, Gary.'

Gary had relaxed. He nodded in readiness.

'You saw your dad on the floor. He was unconscious. You were extremely concerned, I imagine?'

'Yeah, I was.'

'So you rang for an ambulance?'

'Yeah.'

'I would have done that, too. I would definitely have rung for an ambulance when I'd seen my dad on the floor as a result of this awful accident.'

Gary nodded. This was easier than he'd expected.

Dickie paused for a long time then said, 'I tell you what, Gary. I would definitely have called for an ambulance, but I definitely would not have requested the police, as well. You did, Gary. Why did you ask the police to come?'

Gary's heart and stomach lurched into each other: shit, fuck, bugger. What had he done? Was it reasonable to have asked for the police? Had he inadvertently indicated that it hadn't been an accident? He looked at Dickie, who stared back. He caught a glimpse of Keegan; he was smirking.

Gary said, 'I just thought it was a good idea.'

'Why? Why would the police be needed?'

Gary's brain was racing. He grabbed at the nearest thought, 'Well, I saw something on the telly once: the police came along when someone got hurt in an accident.'

Dickie smiled, brown teeth showing. 'Did you? What did you see? What programme was it? When was it on? What happened? Did the police find that it wasn't an accident after all?'

Gary clenched his fists under the table. He was losing this. 'I can't remember any of that. I panicked last night. I was really frightened. When I rang 999, I just said ambulance and police without thinking.'

Dickie said, 'Yes, it's funny how we can't think straight sometimes; we kind of panic a bit.'

Gary was silent.

'Gary?'

'What?'

'We can't think straight sometimes; we kind of panic, don't we?'

Gary tried to work out what was going on. Was Dickie laying another trap? He said, 'I don't know about that. All I know is that I was bricking myself last night. I didn't know if my dad was alive or dead. I can't be sure of anything.'

'Of course. I do understand, you know.' He looked at Keegan. 'Any other questions?'

Keegan asked, casually, 'Did you speak to anyone else at any point between this terrible accident and the ambulance and uniformed police arriving?'

Gary swallowed — was it audible? He had rung Joe. Joe had come around. Could the police know that? He said, 'No, no one.'

The two of them looked at each other.

Dickie said, 'We want you to identify someone for us.'

Keegan picked up a folder and pulled out a large photograph. 'Do you know this man, Gary?'

Gary looked: it was a classic black and white 'mug shot'. His mouth went dry.

'Gary?'

'Yeah?'

'Who is it, Gary?'

'It's Joe. Joe Marshall.'

'And this is the man you were with, along with Victoria Court, Anthony Alexander, Frank Gordon, Katy and Susan Walker, all day yesterday?'

'Yeah.'

'When were you with him 'til?'

'About five p.m.'

'Thank you, Gary. We'll corroborate that, of course.'

Keegan shuffled the statements together.

The coppers smiled at each other. Dickie said, 'Okay, I need another statement from you. This one is to describe for us precisely what happened on 20th March when your filthy shit of a father decided to attack an innocent man. I want all the details, including who else was there.'

Gary told them. Everything. Keegan wrote furiously to keep up.

Dickie got his cigarettes out. 'So, Gary, old lad, this is the situation: your dearly-departed father stuck his head into a pillar of the community. That man now has brain damage. However, your father is on his way to a better, or worse, place. He is on his way to that place because, unbelievably, he fell over in his own kitchen and smashed in his own head. What's your thinking on the matter? You can tell me. We're old pals now, aren't we?'

'I've told you everything I know. There's nothing else.'

Dickie lit up. He blew smoke up at the nicotine-stained ceiling; he seemed to be weighing something up. Finally, he said, 'You know I said my name was Nott?'

Gary nodded.

'Well, that's not what my colleagues call me.'

Gary wondered what the fuck he was on about this time.

'No, they call me Detective Scunt. S for sergeant and — well, I'm sure you can spell. You can spell, can't you, Gary?'

Gary didn't answer.

'Do you know why they call me that?'

Gary relaxed. This was his kind of conversation. 'I can guess. Shall I call you Detective Scunt from now on?'

Dickie smiled thinly. 'Very good. Very good, Gary. You're a tough guy. Let's see how tough you really are, shall we?'

Gary stayed silent. He was nearly through; he wasn't going to mess up now.

Dickie turned to Keegan. 'Is Mr Flanagan coming in today?'

Keegan shook his head, 'He's off today, back tomorrow.'

Dickie turned back to Gary, 'You're in luck, Gary. My boss will want to talk to you. A word of warning: he makes me look like Andy Pandy.'

Gary stared back and kept shtum.

Chapter 5

Gary opened the door and got in behind his mum. The last few minutes with those shitheads had brought the events of three weeks ago flooding back. At the time, it hadn't really registered with him. Everything that had happened since had relegated it into a general blur. Describing it to Dickie and Keegan, or whatever their names were, had brought it back. Sitting here, in this car, in the same place, made it even starker. He'd been a bit drunk, but the images were clear enough.

He, Steve, Phil and Paul had been at a bus stop when a car had screeched to a halt beside them. He looked through the open window: it was his dad. They'd got in, and the old Cortina had skidded around the corner and pelted up Theobald Street. His dad had been really pissed; he'd even said as much to Paul. When they'd been held up behind the flashy car at the temporary traffic lights, his dad had got into a right strop and had started shouting and swearing, then held his fist down on the Cortina's horn. When the bloke in the suit had come over, his dad had gone all meek and mild; but suddenly he'd jumped out of the car and smashed his head into the face of the bloke. Even now, three weeks later, Gary could almost hear the man's wife screaming, 'You bastard, you've killed him! You're a lunatic!' Well, his dad hadn't killed the man; Brian Abbott had been the one to die.

Derek started the car. 'You took your time.'

Gary said, 'Where's Tina?'

His mum said, 'She wanted to go home by herself.'

'Why so long?' Derek asked again.

Gary wondered if now was a good time to tell his brother that he'd dobbed his dad in. He decided against it; he needed to talk to his mum first.

'They wanted to know what I was doing yesterday.'

'Why?'

'They're ruling everything out.'

Gary saw his older brother eyeing him up in the mirror. He didn't look convinced.

Derek said, 'What's with the glasses?'

Gary felt self-conscious. 'Oh, I've been told I gotta wear 'em.'

'Since when?'

'Since I got my nose broken.'

Derek was grinning, 'You look like a right square. Who are you? Joe 90 or Brains?'

Gary ignored him. He wanted to take them off but wasn't going to show Derek he was embarrassed.

Derek said, 'I'd better get to work. I'll drop you home and go straight off.'

When Gary and his mum went in, the house was empty.

Gary said, 'Mum, we need to talk about stuff.'

'I know. Before we do, let's clean everything up.'

They worked together in the kitchen. Jenny hoovered up the mess from the apple crumble; Gary mopped behind her. They wiped down all the surfaces, including the bloody edge of the kitchen sink. They put everything away, back in its normal place. Order was restored.

'Cuppa?' Jenny asked.

'Yeah.'

Finally, they sat down at the kitchen table.

Gary went first. 'How you doing?'

'Numb.'

'Me too.'

'I can't believe what's happened.'

'Nor me.'

'I keep thinking he's going to turn up, any minute.'

'He's not going to.'

'I know, Gary. It's just that I can't get it into my head.'

Gary nodded. He said, 'I think I should be sad. I should be really upset, shouldn't I? My dad's just died.'

'I'm feeling the same. My husband's dead; I killed him! I'm not sad, though.'

'Listen, Mum: I would have done the same thing. Anyone would have.'

'I know. Actually, I'd do it again. Isn't that terrible? I meant to kill him, you know.'

Gary nodded.

'Gary?'

'What?'

'I'm really sorry, love. I have to tell you something.'

'Yeah?'

'I've wanted to kill him for years.'

Gary looked at his mum. Her eyes were on him, waiting for his answer.

'Well, I'm sorry you had to wait so long.'

Jenny reached across the table and gripped her son's hand.

'Gary?'

'Yeah?'

'There's something else.'

'What?'

'Something odd happened the other day.'

'What?'

'Well, it was Thursday, I think. This man came to the door. He was an insurance salesman. In fact, you saw him, do you remember? You were upstairs and you came down and he was here in the kitchen.'

Gary did remember, only too well.

'Anyway, he was nice and friendly, but it was really weird how the conversation went. To start with, he was going on about some special policy, apparently, I had been picked out. I wasn't really paying attention. To be honest, I was more worried about Dad coming home and finding a strange man in the house! Anyway, we were talking about insurance, and all of a sudden, we were talking about other things: about Brian, the family, the future. I was listening to him, without really paying attention, and I started to drift off, and if I'm honest, I think I fell asleep. Can you believe it? With a strange man in the kitchen?'

Gary could believe it.

'Anyway, then Brian came home, and this bloke went into the front room, and they were in there for a while, chatting. The point is that, after he'd gone, I felt different. It was like I'd taken a drug or something. I felt much better about everything. To be honest, I felt like I'd had a really good night's sleep and had woken up a new woman.' She laughed. 'Listen to me! What do I sound like?'

'Mum, I have to tell you something.'

'Yes?'

'I know who he is.'

'Eh? How do you know him?'

'Er, well — he's the bloke organising the party for the old lady at The Beeches.'

'But he came here selling insurance policies. I'm sure he said his name was Peter something — Peter Gregory, I think. But you met him here! You didn't say anything.'

'I know. The thing is, Mum, he's a very clever bloke. He's helped me a lot. I don't know what that visit here was all about. I know that we can trust him, and he was trying to help us.'

Jenny said, 'I thought at the time he wasn't quite what he said. What's going on, Gary?'

'I'm sorry, Mum. I mentioned to him that I was scared. I thought Dad was going to — well, I was scared, scared for you. He must have thought he could do something to help. I dunno.'

'Hmm. I'm not sure that an insurance policy was going to be much help.' They considered this. 'Gary, don't get too involved with him; he sounds a bit dodgy. Also, we need to look after Tina. I don't like to think of her coping on her own.'

Gary had been thinking exactly the same.

Chapter 6

Tina couldn't help herself smiling at the desk sergeant as she walked out of the station. He saluted smartly.

'Carry on, Officer,' she called back.

'Thank you, Ma'am.'

She said goodbye to Jenny, who was waiting for her interview, and made a beeline for home. She wanted — no, she needed a safe haven right now. She looked at her watch; it was nearly eleven a.m. Dad would be home for lunch in an hour. As usual, however upset she was, she felt compelled to look after him. He never had a proper lunch: she would make him something nice today. She nipped into Sainsbury's and bought a Fray Bentos steak and kidney pie, a tin of garden peas and a packet of Smash: his favourite dinner. Suddenly excited at the idea of treating him, she put a tin of cling peaches and a can of evaporated milk into her basket. As she queued to pay, she picked up a Marathon for herself.

'That'll be two pounds and five pence, dear.'

Tina put her shopping into a carrier bag and rummaged in her pockets: damn, she had only two pound notes.

She said, 'Oh, blast it. Er… I won't bother with the Marathon.'

She hurried out of the shop to cook her dad his feast before he got home. She'd do anything for her dad. When her mum had left, she had known it was her job to protect him: he couldn't cope on his own. He'd taken a load of time off work, then got himself sacked. He had tried to kill himself but couldn't manage that properly. She grimaced as she remembered coming home from school to find him on the floor of the kitchen, his head inside the oven. He was unconscious, but hadn't put enough money in the meter to finish himself off. He'd spent a few weeks in the loony bin: that had been the worst time. She had gone to live with her auntie in Watford. All she had wanted was to get back to her dad — for them to be together again.

When he came home, he had started to pick up a bit and, after a year out of work, had got the caretaker job at her old primary school. After his previous work as Head of Security at the big electronics company, it was a come-down.

But she had to give him credit: he had stuck it out. Her love for him flared in her as she thought about him at work, putting up with the little shits who did their best to make his life a misery. She had done the same regarding the old caretaker when she'd been at school and knew exactly what he was having to face.

Now, she pushed her way through the heavy door of their block and began the trudge up to the third floor. As she started the final flight, Tina looked up and saw someone sitting at the top. It was Kev. She stopped.

'Watcha,' he said.

'Watcha.'

'I've been waiting for you.'

'So I see.'

'Where've you been?'

'Kev, you know I've been at the police station.'

'Oh, yeah.'

'Then I went into Sainsbury's. Now I'm here.'

Tina started up the stairs again. She sat down next to him.

'Kevin, I'm so sorry about your dad.'

'Me too. I can't believe he's... not here anymore. I didn't see him yesterday and I wish I had. I mean, I could have said goodbye, or something.'

Tina nodded.

'What was he like yesterday? When you saw him? I mean, was he happy?'

Tina's head filled with the grotesque memories but she said, 'Normal, you know.'

'I know he was a drunken bastard, but he was my dad.' Tina nodded. 'Can I come in?'

However much Tina didn't want to be with Kev, she still felt sorry for him. 'Just for a few minutes. I want to get my dad's dinner ready.'

They went inside. She emptied the bag's contents onto the worktop.

Kev said, 'Tina, I really miss you.'

'What do you mean? You saw me last night.'

'Yeah, but earlier you said you didn't want to see me again and I thought — you know, I thought you were dumping me.'

Tina took her coat off and sat down at the table. 'I'm sorry, Kevin, I really am. I don't want to be your girlfriend anymore. You'll find someone much nicer than me. I'm a right cow most of the time. You should find someone who's a bit more... I dunno, more — er, nicer.'

'I like you, though. You're pretty and sexy and we have fun, don't we?'

'But, Kev, life's not just about sex and fun.'

Kev was narked. 'I know that. I'm not stupid.' He paused. 'Go on then, what do you want? What do you want that you're not getting now?'

She knew she couldn't explain and that, even if she could, he wouldn't understand. She didn't answer.

He moved up behind her and put his hands on her shoulders. She tried not to cringe.

'Come on, Tina; give me another chance.' He began to massage her shoulders. 'Maybe we could think about it, in a few days?' He carried on stroking her. 'Why don't we think about it now? You like it when I do this, don't you?'

Right now, Tina was feeling nothing but panic. She didn't want to hurt him, but he was beginning to frighten her. She didn't want any man touching her, let alone anyone connected with Brian 'sleazebag' Abbott.

He said, his voice coaxing, 'You're so sexy, babe. All I want to do is make you feel good.' She felt his fingers inch towards her breasts. She closed her eyes and prayed he'd give up. 'Why don't we get into bed? You know we always have a nice time.'

She was close to screaming now, or puking. Possibly both.

He took his hands away; she breathed again. Then, in horror, she heard his flies being undone and him fumbling. 'Oh, Tina, look how much I need you...'

She recoiled, shoved back her chair and screamed, 'Get out! Get out. Fuck off now! Fucking hell — first it's your dad; now it's you. Get out now!'

Kev's face was red with fury. He put himself away. 'What do you mean? What do you mean, "first my dad"?'

Tina's brain was about to burst. She couldn't bear it; she wanted the world to just go away and leave her alone. Out of the corner of her eye she saw the tins of food. She picked up one of them and threw it at Kev with all her might. It missed by miles. She picked up another and threw it. He had his arms over his head and was retreating towards the door. The pie was next; she whirled it at him like a discus. It thudded into the door behind him. He yanked the door open and fled down the stairs.

She screamed after him, 'Never, ever, come near me again! You're a worthless pile of shit!'

Breathing hard, Tina shut the door, gathered up the ingredients for her dad's dinner and turned on the oven.

Chapter 7

Terry opened the shed door and stuck his head out. It had started to rain. 'Shit!' The plan had been to mow the lawns outside the front of the school this afternoon; he'd run out of indoor jobs. Peering towards the heavens, he wondered how best to use his time. What was the time? It was only 11.27 a.m. Too early for dinner. He put his coat on and went into the school.

'Hey, Terry! Can you come and have a look at the boys' toilets? We've got a blockage.'

He looked down the main corridor to see one of the teachers waving at him. It was Miss Ratcliffe. Terry really liked her. She was young, maybe mid-twenties. She reminded him of Tina: blonde and full of life. He hoped his girl might be a teacher one day. She'd have to work a lot harder than she had done in the last year or two and, more importantly, keep out of the way of trash like the Abbotts.

He puffed his chest out and walked towards Miss Ratcliffe. 'Of course; which one is it?'

She gestured towards the side corridor. 'Those. Second cubicle. I suspect someone's put something down it; something not designed for such treatment.'

'Leave it with me: my middle name's Clark Kent. Now, where's the nearest phone box?'

She smiled at him as he adopted the one-armed flying pose.

Terry looked in at the toilet and satisfied himself that it was a suitable job for the afternoon - if it carried on raining - then went to the headmaster's office.

'Good morning, Terry. How's you?' Jim Dixon called.

'Fine, I'm waiting for the rain to finish. I want to do the front lawns today. What do you reckon? Will it ease up?'

Dixon looked out. 'Hmm, not sure. Why don't you take an early lunch?'

'Yeah, if you're sure?'

'Sure. Terry?'

'Yeah?'

Dixon coughed. 'Shut the door will you?'

Terry closed the door and stood in front of Dixon's desk, anxious: what was this all about?

'Er — ahem… I'm glad you've popped by. You weren't too friendly with any of the pupils during break this morning, were you?'

'Meaning?'

'I'm sure it's nothing, but three boys spoke to Mrs Dutton after break. They said you called them over?'

'No, not me. Three boys were trying to wind me up, but I ignored them.'

Dixon nodded but picked up a sheet of paper and read out, 'The caretaker called us over and asked us if we wanted to come inside his shed. We said no. Then he asked us if we wanted a cigarette. He opened his packet of cigarettes and showed them to us. We said we didn't want any cigarettes. Then he got angry and told us to eff off and leave him alone.' Dixon looked up at Terry.

Terry could feel his face reddening. His heart was bibble-bobbling. 'That's rubbish, Mr Dixon. I couldn't get rid of them. They were bothering me, not the other way around.'

Dixon was impassive. Surely he didn't believe those little liars?

'But did you tell them to — Well, did you swear at them?'

Terry thought back. Had he? He had certainly got wound up. 'I'm not sure. I suppose I could have said "sod off". I don't think so. I definitely did not eff and blind. Oh, also, I don't smoke tailor-mades; I smoke roll-ups.'

Dixon nodded at last. 'I didn't think it could be true, but I have to follow up what the children report to us.'

'Of course. I understand.'

'See you later, then. Good luck with the weather.'

Terry walked out to his car. He got in and rolled a cigarette. He wanted to lock those little shits up in his shed and throw away the key. Why couldn't people leave him and Tina alone?

He drove back to the flat and squeezed his Hillman Imp between a motorbike and a van. He opened his door to find someone standing near the bike: Kevin Abbott. 'What do you want?'

Kevin spat, 'Your daughter's a right little bitch!'

Terry got out of the car and straightened up. No one was going to talk about Tina like that.

His face contorted with rage, Kevin threw a punch. Terry leaned back and watched the leather-gloved fist sail past his chin. Kevin stumbled forward into Terry and the pair lurched back into the open door of the Imp. 'You little fucker' hissed Terry as the sharp edge jammed into his lower back. Before he could react, Kevin had shoved on his helmet and was pushing his bike out towards the main road. He leapt on, kick-started the machine and roared off. Terry slumped against the car and waited for his heart to slow. He was beginning to feel that overwhelming sense of dread. Shutting his eyes, he whispered, 'Not again. No more. Please... no more.'

Terry straightened, feeling his heart lurch and his back twinge, then walked slowly to the entrance to the flats. Grasping the banister for support, he pulled himself up the three floors and unlocked the front door. Tina was there, smiling in welcome.

'Ah, here you are! Ready for your special treat?'

Terry sniffed. Something was in the oven. 'What's going on, love?'

'Come on. Your table awaits.'

Tina led him to the Formica-topped table. It was laid: knife and fork, a lighted candle stuck to a saucer and a bottle of Pepsi next to two glasses.

'What's going on?'

'Oh, I dunno. I thought it'd be nice to have a cooked dinner. Sit down.'

Terry took off his overall and put it on the back of his chair. He pulled out his tobacco and papers. He was calming down. All he wanted was here: his little girl and their sanctuary.

Tina came over to him. 'Sorry, sir, I can't offer you wine but here's a bottle from the cellar.'

He smiled as she placed the ketchup reverentially between their places. He picked it up and studied it closely. 'Ah, you're right, an excellent year.'

'You all right, Dad? You're really pale.'

'I'm fine, thank you. How about you? You're looking very pale, too.'

'Oh, I'm fine. It was horrible last night at the hospital: I've never seen anyone die before.'

'Were you actually there when he—? Oh, I'm sorry, love! I hadn't realised.'

'Yeah. Then I had to go to give a statement to the police, with Jenny and Gary Abbott. We were at the house when Brian fell over, and we had to say what happened and what we saw.'

Terry looked closely at her. Here she was, telling him, like it was a normal occurrence, about death, the police, giving evidence. He knew rationally that she was getting older, growing up, but he hadn't properly come to terms with the fact that she was no longer his little girl.

'I'm sorry.'

'Why? What for?'

'Not being very nice this morning.'

'Don't be silly. Now, time for your dinner, my lord. Oh, one thing: I'm afraid it's got a bit battered and bruised. I'm sure it tastes all right though.'

Ten minutes later, they were scraping their plates clean. 'Beeeautiful! Thank you very much.' Terry said, smacking his lips.

'I'm glad you liked it; it's nice to have something special now and then.'

Terry rolled a cigarette. 'Want one?' he asked.

'Ta.'

As he rolled the fag, he plucked up his courage, 'Tina?'

'What?'

'I think I'm beginning to go down again. I'm scared.'

Tina looked at him sharply. 'No, come on, Dad. You're all right.'

'I don't want to, but I feel a bit wobbly: life's getting to me. I'm sorry.'

'No, come on. We can handle things. I'll make everything all right, Dad. You don't need to worry: I'll look after you.'

He stared at her face, the worry etched into it. 'Thing is, I don't want you to have to look after me. I'm your dad: I look after you. Thank you, but I'm worried about you, too.'

She snorted. 'Me! I'm tough as old boots. Nothing's going to get me down. Nothing.'

He made himself say, 'I'm sorry about Brian Abbott, and you and Kev.'

'Don't be. They're worthless maggots. I'm better off without them.'

Terry said, casually, 'I saw Kevin when I got back. You two didn't have a row or anything, did you?'

'What did he say?'

'Nothing much.'

Tina looked down, uncertain. And looked up, grinning. 'I threw our dinner at him: peas first, then peaches, then the pie. It was brilliant. Lucky they weren't open!'

Terry laughed. 'I'm sorry I missed it. I'd have joined in. I can't stand that little 'maggot'.'

They smoked their fags.

'I'd better go back to work.'

'You can't. Not yet.'

'Why not?'

She smiled delightedly, that little girl again. 'Because, your highness, it's peaches and cream for afters. Well, Vapo, actually, but that's close enough.'

'Fantastic! I thought I heard "peaches".'

She got up and went back to the kitchen area. Terry pulled a handkerchief out of his coat pocket and wiped his eyes before she could see his tears.

Chapter 8

Gary got up from the table. 'Mum, I know we've got loads of stuff to do, but I need to pop out for an hour. Do you mind?'

'No. Actually, I'd like to be on my own for a while. I wouldn't mind a little lie down. When you come back, we can do a list. We need to organise a funeral; tell Dad's work... Loads of things. Do you want me to ring up school?'

Gary was putting his coat on. 'Nah, don't worry; I'll do that.'

'Don't be long.'

'Don't worry, Mum. We'll be all right.'

Gary shut the door quietly behind him and lit a fag. He thought he should be feeling something — sadness, depression, fear, anger? He didn't read much, but he watched a load of films and telly and knew that you were supposed to feel all kinds of things when someone died, especially your dad. Right now, he didn't feel anything except the urge to protect his mum from what had happened. No, there was something else: he was worried that Tina was going to snap. He didn't really know her. She'd been coming around a lot recently, but she and Kev spent most of their time giggling, up in the bedroom he and Kev shared. Although Tina was also sixteen, Gary had always thought of her as older than him. She seemed really confident: make up, perfume, clothes that showed off her body. That had been until last night. When she'd turned up at the hospital with no make-up on, in a big coat and jeans, he had realised that she was just a kid, like him. He had always found her really sexy. Now, he thought of her more as a friend he wanted to look after.

He turned into the car park of The Beeches. He didn't want to have to go in, so skirted around the side of the concrete building to see if Joe was out the back. He breathed a sigh of relief: Joe was cutting branches off a tree, or bush, or something. Gary approached, uncertain.

Joe turned and smiled. 'Am I pleased to see you!'

Gary smiled back.

Joe put his loppers down, rubbed his hands on his trousers and shook Gary's hand. 'Come on, let's have a case conference: how about this bench?'

Gary's mood lifted the moment he saw Joe. Although he'd told his mum that things were going to be all right, he wasn't sure he believed it. Now, sitting side by side with Joe, his confidence was coming back fast.

Joe said, 'I knew something serious must have happened: the police came around here to see me this morning. They wanted to check if I had been with you yesterday. Tell me everything.'

It all spilled out of Gary: the lies they'd told, the long night, his dad's death; the police and Gary's admission to them that it had been his dad who'd nutted the posh bloke; that morning's interview at the station. Joe put his arm around Gary and held him really tight. No man had ever done this before. Gary liked how it felt: male, strong, understanding. Before it felt awkward, Joe let go.

'I'm so sorry, Gary. What a terrible thing — all of it. You must be done in.' Gary nodded. 'Are you worried about the — er... the fabrication?'

'The what?'

'You know, the "evidence" we set up.'

Gary thought over the way he and Joe had arranged the kitchen to support the lie that his dad had fallen when his foot caught in the flex of the iron; he pictured Joe pressing the unconscious man's fingers against the crumble dish. 'Well, to be honest, I don't know. I don't think the police believe us, but I don't know if they can prove anything. What do you think?'

Joe was silent for a minute. At last, he said, 'There are two risks. The first one is controllable: you, your mum and Tina have to stay completely with the story you've already given the police. As soon as you vary from what you've said, or you vary from each other, they'll start to drive you apart.'

Gary nodded. That made sense to him. He'd already thought that. 'The other thing?'

'This is trickier, I think. There is bound to be a post-mortem. Because your father died as a result of an accident, or, as you say, because the police may suspect it's the result of an assault, they'll be examining your dad's body to see if the injury is consistent with what you've told them.'

'Shit.'

'I know. We can't do anything about that. Although him bashing his head against the edge of the sink may result in an injury that's like a heavy dish cracking his skull, we can't know if a doctor will think the same.'

Gary groaned. 'Shit, shit, shit...'

Joe went on. 'Did the police tell you to keep out of the kitchen?'

'No. Why?'

'Well, that means they think they've got everything they need from a possible crime scene. Is it like the way I saw it last night?'

'No. My mum and I cleaned it up. Blood stains and everything.'

Joe nodded. 'I think that's a good thing.'

'How long will it take them?'

Joe breathed out. 'I don't know, Gary. His body was already in the hospital, so I guess that speeds things up. If the police have suspicions, then they might try and push it through quicker. Honestly, I don't know.'

Gary said, 'I didn't tell you what happened... I mean — what led to it.'

Joe looked at him.

'Dad was — um... attacking Tina. My mum came in and saw it. She lost her rag and BAM! Smashed the apple crumble into his head.'

'Blimey,' Joe thought for a while. 'Do you know if Tina punched or scratched your dad? If she did, then there may be signs on his body. That could be tricky.'

Gary shook his head. 'I dunno.'

'I reckon it would be a good idea to find out.' Gary nodded. 'How's the rest of your family doing, Gary?'

'We're still trying to get our heads around it.'

'Your mum?'

'She's really strong. She went into a daze last night when she hit him, then again when he died. Now, she's amazing.'

'When I met her, I had the impression that she had a lot of hidden strength.'

'Joe?'

'Yep?'

'Did you tell her to do anything? I don't mean did you tell her to kill my dad. Nothing like that. I wondered if you... gave her something, um — something... oh, I dunno.'

'I did say something, Gary.'

'I thought so. What was it?'

'I told her that she had a choice; that she had choices.'

'Is that all?'

'That's all.'

'Oh.'

'You've got choices, too.'

'Such as?'

'Well, this one for a start: you can choose whether to tell the police about me, about my involvement.'

'Well, I can't do that. If I do, I'll be admitting it's all a lie.'

'That's true. I've got a choice to make.'

'What's that?'

'There is something I think you ought to know. I was talking to Victoria last night; she made me promise to come clean about stuff.'

Gary remembered the "mugshot" that Dickie and Keegan had shown him. 'Joe?'

'Hmm?'

'Dickie and Keegan — sorry, that's what I call them, in my head — showed me a picture of you. A police photograph.' Gary looked at Joe.

Joe smiled. 'Well done, Gary: you're doing a Joe Marshall!' he told him.

Chapter 9

'Mum — this is my friend, Joe.'

Jenny Abbott looked up from her papers at the man with Gary. He was the same man who had come around the other day: Peter Gregory. This time, though, he wasn't wearing glasses or carrying a load of brochures.

'Jenny, it's really good to meet you again. Gary has told me everything. He wanted me to join you both for a chat about — well, everything.'

Gary nodded.

She said, 'I don't understand. The other day you were pretending to sell me insurance. Now you're here to talk about what has happened to us. Gary, what's going on?'

Joe sat down opposite Jenny. 'I'm sorry about the subterfuge. Gary, his pals and I are arranging a birthday party for an old and dear friend at The Beeches. Gary mentioned that things were really difficult at home. He told me that he was scared that you were going to get hurt. Badly hurt. I took the liberty of coming to visit you and seeing if I could help in any way. I know — I had no right to do that and I'm sorry. I have a very bad habit of getting too big for my boots and wading into peoples' lives without asking them. I should have come clean with you. I'm really sorry I wasn't straightforward with you.'

Jenny opened her mouth to speak. Joe held up his hand. 'May I? There's a bit more to say and I want you to hear it all.'

Jenny looked at Gary again; he nodded his assent.

'Okay. Gary has asked me to say this bit, too. Last night, when your husband received his knock on the head, Gary rang me to come over. When you were waiting for the ambulance, I nipped in and Gary and I looked at the kitchen to see if the story he had planned to tell would stand up to scrutiny. I helped him sort out one or two details and then I left.'

Jenny was open-mouthed.

Gary said, 'I needed someone to help me, Mum. I couldn't be sure that everything would look legit when the Filth turned up.'

Jenny looked at Joe. She said, 'What did you do? What details?'

'Nothing, really; well, there was one tiny thing,' Joe responded. 'We had to get your husband's fingerprints onto the crumble dish. I just about managed to do that.'

Gary said, 'I'm sorry, Mum. I should have told you, but everything was so mad. I didn't know what I was doing or what you'd think.'

Jenny looked at Joe. 'But — who are you?'

Joe smiled. 'I'm Gary's friend; he's my friend. I work at The Beeches; I'm a gardener there. I'm a friend of Victoria Court, the headmistress of Gary's school.'

'Oh. Does she know about all of this?'

Gary looked at Joe. That was a good question. Gary had been so involved in the fine detail of family life, he'd had no time to think about everyone else in his life — his new life.

Joe said, 'Not yet. I had to talk it through with you; and Gary, of course.'

She shook her head, wearily. 'I'm going mad. Nothing ever happens to me. I don't think I can cope.'

For the first time, Gary felt the start of panic. His mum must stay in control! She had to.

Joe reached across the table and took Jenny's hand. 'May I?'

She looked down.

Gary watched as his mum's face lost its anxiety. He felt his own stress begin to subside.

'Jenny?' Joe's voice was quiet, gentle.

Jenny's face cleared. 'Yes?'

'I'm going to tell you something about me. You might find it hard to hear. Gary knows about it; he wants me to tell you.'

Joe paused for a minute. Jenny's eyes were on him.

'I killed someone — a long time ago. My mother was being treated incredibly badly; she was being abused. I decided to take action. I felt I had no choice. The police caught me, and I went to prison, for a long time. I don't believe you should have to be punished for anything. From what I understand, you have been punished already. I will do everything in my power to help you and Gary get through this. We're all going to stick together: you, Gary, Tina, and me. We're all in this together and we'll pull through. If you're worried, or unsure, talk to Gary or give me a call. I'll keep out of the way, too. After all, we don't want my involvement complicating things, do we?'

Jenny looked at him. He looked back. She nodded. He gave her hand a final squeeze then sat back.

Gary said, 'We need to talk to Tina. Mum, do you have a number for her?'

'No, Kev will have it.'

Gary didn't want to ask his brother for Tina's number. That was a seriously bad idea. 'Hmm. Any other way of getting in touch with her?'

Jenny shook her head. 'I don't even know where she lives.'

Gary pressed. 'You must have heard her say something?'

'Um, er… not really. The only thing I know is that her dad is a caretaker at one of the primary schools.'

Chapter 10

'Hello? Victoria Court.'

'It's Gary. Gary Abbott.'

'Oh, Gary, I've been wondering about you.'

'Yeah, well… sorry.'

'What's going on, Gary?'

'My dad's dead. He died last night. Well, this morning really. In hospital.'

'Oh, Gary, I'm so sorry. May I ask what happened?'

'We're not sure. We think he tripped over in the kitchen and hit his head.'

'How awful. How's your mum coping?'

'She's doing all right.'

'I had a call from the police last night. They wanted to know if I'd been with you yesterday. I told them, obviously. They didn't say what it was about and, well, I thought it wasn't really my business. I have been worrying, though, with you not being in today.'

Gary felt bad he hadn't told her; she'd been so nice to him over the weekend. 'Sorry, Miss.'

'Don't be silly. This is awful news; I'm so sorry.'

Gary wasn't sure what to say next. He'd wanted to tell her but talking to the headmistress wasn't something he was used to doing. He said, 'Erm… I had a chat with Joe. He knows about it.'

Gary heard a pause, then, 'Ah, that's good. He's a — er… a good person to talk to. Was he… um… good to talk to?'

Gary felt she was trying to say something; or trying not to say it. 'Yeah, really good. Why?'

'Oh, I — well… Oh, nothing. Can I help in any way, Gary?'

'Thanks. No, thanks. I wanted to say that I'm sorry I didn't come to school today. Will you tell people? Wilson? The other teachers?'

He heard her smile. 'Of course I will. Thank you so much for ringing.'

'That's okay.'

'Gary?'

'Yeah?'

'Have you spoken to Anthony today?'

'Nah. I've been sort of busy.'

'Well, the thing is: I'm not sure of anything, but I understand his father has also… Mr Alexander is dead.'

'Fuck!' Gary clapped his hand to his mouth. 'Oops, sorry, Miss. Flip! I don't believe it. What happened to him?'

'I don't have any details. Anthony's mother rang in this morning.'

Gary shook his head. What was going on? He said, 'Is Anthony all right?'

'I'm afraid I don't know. I hope so.'

'I'll ring him up. I think Joe should call round, don't you?'

Again, the long pause before, 'Yes, I suppose so.'

'Miss?'

'Yes, Gary?'

'I don't know if you're worried about Joe or not, but I just thought I should tell you that he's a good bloke. I think you can trust him. He's looking out for my mum and me.'

'Oh, Gary, that's really kind of you. I know he's terribly helpful and understanding. Thank you for reassuring me.'

The key in the front door turned and Kevin burst in. 'Oi, you — I want a word with you!'

'Excuse me, Miss. I'd better go.'

'Thanks for calling, Gary. Good luck with it all. Keep in touch, won't you?'

Gary put the phone down and turned towards the furious face of his older brother. 'What?'

'Jeez, you look like a fucking knob. What are you wearing those for?'

Gary remembered his glasses. 'Er, guess what? To help me see better?'

'Take them off.'

'Why?'

'So I can beat your fucking head in!'

Gary wasn't one to back down from a fight but, right now, he did not feel like a scrap. He asked, 'What's eating you?'

'You know.'

'No, I don't.'

Kev shoved Gary's chest, forcing him back. 'You've been screwing Tina. I know you have. She told me.'

Gary thought quickly. He and Tina had nearly got off a couple of days ago but he'd thought better of it, just in time. Since then, they'd been through

51

the nightmare of last night and this morning, and he was sure she wouldn't have said anything to Kev. There again, Gary didn't really know Tina: would she have said something? He said, 'That's a lie.'

Kev was shoving him again. 'You and her are up to something; I know you are. She's gone all Little Miss Princess on me.'

Gary didn't know what he was on about. Kev's face was inches from his and he stank of beer.

'Do you know what she said to me this morning?'

'No.'

'She said, '"First your dad, then…" me! What's she mean by that?'

Jenny came down the stairs. 'What's going on? Kevin, stop shouting.'

'No, I won't stop shouting! Fucking hell, what did Dad do?'

Jenny said, 'Be quiet, Kevin. What are you talking about?'

Kev's voice had lost its aggression; it was more pleading now. 'Tina said Dad had done something to her. What did he do?'

Gary shook his head at his Mum.

Jenny said, 'I don't know, Kevin. I don't know what she meant.'

Kev was crying now. 'What's going on? Someone tell me what's going on.'

Jenny put her arm around her distraught son and said, 'Come on, love; let's have a cup of tea.'

Kevin's anger boiled over again. 'I don't want a fucking cup of tea; I want my dad back. I want my dad back and I want to kick the shit out of him.'

Jenny wasn't to be shrugged off so easily. 'Come on, Kev. I'm having a cup; you might as well have one, too. How about you, Gary?'

Kev spun around and pointed a finger at his brother, 'You piss off! I don't want to see your ugly face again, ever!'

'Fine by me.'

Gary turned to go upstairs. The phone rang; he picked it up. 'Yeah?'

'It's Joe.'

'Yeah?'

'I've got it.'

Chapter 11

'Don't tell me you're still at it?'

'Well, you know I said my middle name was Clark Kent?'

Miss Ratcliffe smiled. 'I wasn't sure if it was really you?'

'Yeah, well, it's not that Clark Kent. I've had my arm down this bog for hours now and, put it this way, it's not as easy as lambing.'

'I'm sorry. You are rather — um, covered.'

'I found the offending article.' Terry pointed at a plastic toy: limbs at rakish angles and uniform in need of some serious spit and polish.

Miss Ratcliffe stepped away from the body. 'Oh dear. Not much action left in that man.'

'He's probably someone's best-ever Christmas present. I'll give him some medical attention and see if I can't get him back for one more tour of duty.'

'I'll put a notice up. How about, er.... "Unknown soldier found, urgent medical attention needed. Contact War Office?"'

Terry smiled. He really liked Miss Ratcliffe. He wondered if she'd be prepared to have a word with Tina.

She said now, 'Do you mind if I leave you to it? I really must fly: my boyfriend's taking me to White Hart Lane tonight. It's Spurs against Liverpool.'

'Good luck with that. Er — Miss Ratcliffe?'

'Call me Louise. That is my name, after all!'

'Thank you, Louise. I hope you don't mind, but I'd really welcome some help with something but — I know you're rushing so, perhaps… when you've got a bit more time?'

Louise Ratcliffe looked at him and smiled. 'You can't keep me dangling! Tell me now; and then I can go away and think about it?'

'Actually, there are two things. Let me say both of them… You let me know when you can spare five minutes.'

She was looking at him carefully. Her expression had altered slightly: was there a hint of nervousness?

Terry blurted, 'I'm worried about my daughter. I'm worried about myself. That's it.'

'Oh. Um…'

'Don't worry, Louise. I'm not a nutter. I'm not going to embarrass you. I need some friendly advice.'

Louise smiled. 'I'll come and see you in your lair tomorrow, during morning break. Will that be okay?'

'Thank you. That'll be smashing.'

She jogged down the corridor. 'See you tomorrow.'

'Come on, you Lily-Whites!' Terry called after her.

As he mopped up the mess he'd made, Terry felt better. Asking for help was not his style and he was relieved that Louise had not rebuffed him. He wasn't sure what a young teacher could do to help them, but he had a good feeling about her. Gingerly, he picked up the Action Man. 'Come on, old lad. I'll look after you.'

Outside, the sky had cleared. There was a glimmer of sun from beyond the block of flats. He breathed in deeply. Were they going to be okay?

'Excuse me.'

Terry looked around to the voice. A tall youth was walking towards him: scruffy, glasses, surly.

Terry said, 'How can I help you?'

'You don't know me, but you do know my brother: Kevin Abbott?'

'Don't tell me: you've come to say sorry. Well, you can tell your brother that he'll never, ever see my daughter again. If I see him, I'll have him arrested for assault. You can sling your hook an' all.'

'I don't know what you're on about. All I want is to get a message to Tina, that's all.'

'Hop it.'

The youth stood his ground. Finally, he said, 'I'm doing my best to help her, Mr Castleton. Honestly. I need to talk to her about something important. If I don't, then she might be in trouble.'

'What trouble?'

'I can't say.'

'You'd better say, sonny Jim. If my daughter is in trouble and the bloody Abbotts are involved, then I need to know about it.'

The lad was looking desperate. He said, 'Look, I'm not like my brother. I need to get a message to Tina. It's about…'

'What? What is it about?'

'My dad dying.'

Terry took pity on the wretched lout. His dad had just died, after all. 'What's your name, son?'

'Gary.'

'Stay there. I'll ring home. If she says she doesn't want to have anything to do with you, then that's it. Get it?'

'Yeah.'

Terry muttered under his breath as he walked back into the school, 'Bloody Abbotts'. In the staff room, Mrs Dutton was talking to Mr Dixon. When they saw Terry, the conversation stopped dead.

'Sorry to interrupt you both. I was wondering if I could use the phone?'

The headmaster and teacher looked at each other. 'Of course, Terry, help yourself,' Dixon said.

Terry sat down and picked up the phone. As he dialled, he waited for them to start speaking again: they didn't. Terry looked around at them. They were watching him. He put the phone down and said, 'What's up?'

Dixon cleared his throat. 'Nothing, Terry, nothing at all. I'd better get on with, er — ha, paperwork. Always paperwork.'

Terry looked at Mrs Dutton. He liked her. She was about his age, maybe a bit younger, and a real beauty. She was always smiling, seemingly a naturally cheerful person. The children loved her. She didn't look so cheerful right now: her expression was distinctly disapproving. She said, 'Yes, I'd better get off home. Dinner won't cook itself.'

Terry waited for them both to leave, then rang home.

'Hello?'

'It's me.'

'Watcha.'

'Tina, one of those Abbott boys is around here. He says he needs to speak to you. I don't want them infecting our lives: they're rotten to the core. I'm happy to tell him to go forth and multiply, if you want?'

'Who is it?'

'Why are you whispering, Tina?'

'Er… someone's here.'

'Who?'

'No one.'

'Tina!'

'I'll tell you later. Now, who is it with you?'

'Gary.'

'Oh, I do want to speak to him. Did he say it was urgent?'

'Yes, it is, apparently.'

'Dad, will you bring him back with you?'

'Are you sure?'

'Yes, sure.'

'All right. We'll be there in a few minutes.'

'Okay. Give me ten minutes.'

Chapter 12

As the tiny car puttered along the streets, Gary tried to think of something to say. He knew nothing about Tina's dad. Mind you, he didn't really know anything about Tina. The fact that they had shared, with his mum, in the killing of his dad did not really equip him for a cheery chat with Tina's father. Also, as Mr Castleton had made clear, Gary and his family weren't his favourite people. After five minutes of silence he said, 'Wanna fag?'

'No.'

Gary put a cigarette in his mouth.

Terry said immediately, 'I don't allow smoking in this car.'

Gary put the cigarette back. He was tempted to light up anyway but didn't push his luck. He said, 'I don't know what Kev's done but I'm not like him.'

Silence.

Gary looked out of the window and worked on keeping his temper.

The car pulled into a car park outside a block of flats. Gary knew this area. He used to come and lob bricks off the flat roof with Steve. He grimaced: what a prick he'd been back then.

Tina's dad turned to him. 'Listen, son. Tina told me your dad died; I'm sorry for you. That makes no difference to what I'm going to say. I will not allow my daughter to have anything to do with low-lifes like you and your family. She is way above you and your brother: she's in a different league. If I find that you have done anything to harm her, I will kill you. I want you to believe me: I will kill you. Do you understand me?'

Gary looked at the man sitting inches from him: he meant it.

'I won't, Mr Castleton. I promise.'

Tina's dad heaved himself out of the car. Gary was about to get out, when he saw someone exiting the door to the flats. He swore under his breath.

'Are you coming or not?'

Gary awkwardly reached down to tie up his laces. After a few seconds, he peered out of the window and saw Keegan get into a two-door Avenger. The flashy copper checked himself in his mirror, revved up and skidded out into the main road.

'Sorry, I was doing up my laces.'

Mr Castleton grunted, 'Come on. The quicker we get this out of the way, the better.'

Gary followed him up the stairs. When they got to the top, the older man was huffing and puffing like he'd run a marathon. 'Remember what I said?'

'Yeah, don't worry.'

Tina got up from the table when they went in. She looked really tired. She smiled though — first at her dad, then at him. 'All right, Gary?'

'Yeah, not bad.'

'Gary's not staying long, are you, son?'

'No, well, I just — the thing is, well… um.'

Mr Castleton stood there, staring at him, suspicious.

Gary raised his eyebrows at Tina.

She said, 'Tea?'

'No. We don't want tea. Gary here wants to leave as quickly as he can. Isn't that right, Gary?'

Tina looked angrily at her father. 'Come on, Gary. Come with me.'

Gary followed her as she led the way into her bedroom. She closed the door after him. He'd never been into a girl's bedroom before. He looked around for somewhere to sit: there was nowhere except her bed.

She said, 'Sorry. It's a terrible mess in here.'

Gary nodded. Everywhere he looked was discarded clothing, including underwear. He felt his face redden.

'Sorry about my dad. He's a bit protective of me.'

'It's all right. I'd be protective of you if I turned up.'

'You have been protective of me, Gary. You've been wonderful. Last night was so…' Tina shuddered.

'Tina?'

'Yes?'

'I saw that copper leave a few minutes ago. What did he want?'

Tina slid clothes and what looked like a giraffe off her bed and sat down, her back against the wall. 'Are you going to sit down?'

Gary shyly sat down next to her. Not sure what to do next, he pulled his fags out of his coat and offered them to her.

'Ta.'

Gary struck a match and lit their fags.

'He said he needed to check a few details.'

'What details?'

'Don't worry, I was really careful. I told him exactly what I said in the police station. He said he wanted to know what we were doing in the front room when we heard the crash in the kitchen.'

'We told him that. Didn't you tell him, when they interviewed you?'

'Yeah, but he said he needed to check again.'

'What did you say?'

'The same thing, that we were talking.'

'Is that all?'

'He wanted to know what we were talking about.'

'And you said?'

'What we agreed. That it was ordinary stuff but mostly that I was telling you that I didn't want to go out with Kev and what he was like.'

'And…?'

'He wanted to know why I was telling you all of that?'

'Jesus — the nosey bastard! What did you say?'

'That I was really pissed off, that you asked what was wrong and that I blurted it all out.'

Gary nodded. This all fitted with what he'd said. 'Did he ask anything else?'

'Yeah, it was sort of funny. He wanted to know if I'd dumped Kev. Then he asked me if I was going out with you.'

Gary reddened again. 'What did you say?'

'Yes, and No. Then — can you believe it? — he said that he didn't have a girlfriend at the moment and would I like to go for a drink!'

'What a fucker!' Gary was outraged.

'Well, actually, he's quite nice looking.'

Gary felt a flare of jealousy. 'He's a total prick. Who does he think he is — Kevin fucking Keegan?'

Tina laughed. Then, remembering everything, wiped her eyes. 'God, Gary. I forget for a few minutes, then it all comes back. I'm so sorry about your dad. I know he was horrible most of the time, and he was disgusting when Jenny came in and… but he was your dad.'

Gary saw his father assaulting Tina again and felt an overwhelming desire to wrap his arms around her. He didn't. Instead, he said, 'I'm sorry, Tina. I wish I could wind back the clock. I should have stayed in the kitchen with you and him. If I had, none of this would ever have happened.'

He thought — yeah, but then his dad would still be alive and they'd be stuck with him.

Tina got up, took a mug off the windowsill and wedged it between them. She flicked ash off into it; he did the same.

'Listen, Tina, the coppers told me that we said different things from each other when we gave our statements. I've gone through it all with Mum and we think we said the same things. Can you think of anything you said that wasn't the same as what we agreed?'

Tina thought for a long time. She shook her head, 'I don't think so.'

'I think they were trying to wind me up. That's what they do on the telly — make the suspects get nervous; make them say stuff even if it's not true.'

Tina said, 'Did Kev tell you where my dad works?'

'No, I didn't want to ask him. He thinks you and me are — well, he's suspicious of me.'

'And me. We're over, anyway. I've dumped him properly now.'

Gary was relieved. 'My friend found out where your dad works. I need to tell you about him. He's on our side and he'll help us.'

Mr Castleton's voice bellowed outside the door, 'Time for you to go.'

Tina turned to Gary, her face close to his. 'Gary, thanks for looking after me. You're a nice bloke. I know I've got a terrible temper, and you probably think I'm a bit of a scrubber, but I'm quite nice really. You won't turn out to be horrible like — well, you'll be nice to me, won't you? Please be nice?'

Her face was turned up to him, her eyes wide and searching. Gary felt himself harden; he wanted to hold her, feel her. He croaked, 'We'll look after each other.'

She smiled then dropped her cigarette butt into the mug. It sizzled.

A heavy fist bashed the door.

'Listen, Tina, my friend said something important to me. Did you scratch or claw at my dad last night? The thing is we need to know, coz if he's got marks of fingernails on him then the police will realise our story isn't true.'

She looked at her fingers. 'No, thank God. Blimey, your friend is pretty sharp.'

'He is. Anyway, that's good. Well done. By the way, can I have your phone number? We'll need to keep in touch, just in case.'

'Of course. What do you think will happen next?'

'My friend says they'll do something called a post-mortem. It's a kind of medical investigation. Doctors will be able to tell if Dad died from it being an accident or not. We'll probably know in the next day if they've found us out.'

'Oh, no! I can't bear it.'

Gary wanted so much to hold her. 'Can I ask you a question?'

She smiled up at him, "Course.'

'What did you say to that copper, when he asked you out?'

'I dunno. I think I said I'll think about it.'

'You don't want to go out with him, do you?'

'Well, he's good looking and he's got a job, and a car.'

'Yeah, but he's a copper, and a knob, and he might arrest you for — well, I don't know — being involved in killing somebody.'

'Oh, yeah, I hadn't thought of that.'

Gary looked around the room. 'Er, he didn't come in here, did he?'

'God, no! This room is disgusting, I wouldn't ask a tasty bloke in here!'

Gary felt his confidence slip away. He'd tried so hard to be the strong man throughout. Now he just felt like a kid out of his depth.

Tina didn't seem to notice. 'My number is 4416; do you want me to write it down?'

'Nah, I'll remember it.' He got up. 'If you hear anything, ring me. If Kev answers, put the phone down. I'll ring you back.'

'I will. Thanks for everything, Gary. I couldn't cope without you.'

She stood. They faced each other, uncertain. Again, her dad's fist hammered. 'All right, Dad. Gary's off now.' She looked back up at Gary. 'There's one more thing, Gary. It's important.'

'What?'

'You know the other day, whenever it was, when we were in your bedroom and I — well, we… you know?'

Gary remembered it, all right. He hadn't been able to get the pictures out of his head. What had possessed him to tell her to leave his room was impossible to remember: what had he been thinking? What she had offered him that day had been the realisation of his waking dreams. He licked his lips, 'Yeah?'

'I'm so sorry about that. I don't know what got into my head that day. Please forgive me. I know you're a decent bloke and I — well, I thought you were like all the other blokes. You won't hold it against me, will you?'

Hopes of her repeating that moment dashed. Gary mumbled, 'Course not. It's all forgotten.'

Her face relaxed. She smiled — a beautiful smile. 'You're a true gent, Gary Abbott. I'm lucky to have a friend like you.'

Gary gritted his teeth and inwardly cursed his luck.

Chapter 13

Terry had been getting wound up ever since meeting Gary outside the school. Those bloody Abbotts! He'd thought they'd seen the last of them when Tina had got rid of that oik, Kevin. Now, another of them was in her room. To be fair to this one, he did seem a bit more respectable; at least, he had some manners. Still, it was his little girl in there with a boy — a grubby, common boy who would have only one thought in his head.

Terry banged again. This time the door opened, and Gary came out. 'Thank you, Mr Castleton. I'm off. Thanks for the lift.'

Terry eyed them up: they looked shifty. 'On your bike, son.'

'See you soon,' Tina called as the lout left.

Once the door was closed, Tina said, 'Honestly, Dad — why can't you be nice sometimes?'

'Why do you think?'

'I know Kev's awful, but Gary has been really kind to me. I wish you'd be a bit more friendly.'

Terry didn't want to be horrible; he simply couldn't relax when it came to his daughter. 'I'm sorry, love. I'm not having a very good time at the moment.'

Tina went into the little lounge and slumped on the sofa. Terry followed her in and sat down opposite. He wanted so much to talk to her but how could he? Once again, he pictured telling Tina the truth about her mother. He'd been determined to protect her from that. Since Diane's leaving them, Terry had never given Tina any reason to think badly about her mum — well, apart from the small issue of her having run off with another man. Terry wanted Tina's life to be a happy one: free from upset, pain or misery. She was watching him now.

'What?' he said.

'You're covered in muck, Dad.'

Terry looked down at his overall, 'Ah, sorry. I saved a man's life today.' He pulled the bag out of his pocket and gently eased the broken soldier off his makeshift stretcher.

'Bog?' Tina asked.

'Yep.'

'Classic.'

'You know that teacher, Miss Ratcliffe; the young one I told you about?'

'Yeah?'

'I'm going to talk to her tomorrow. I thought she might have some ideas about what kind of jobs you could do.'

'Yeah?'

'She's nice. I might ask her if she'll speak to you about it.'

'Dad?' Terry looked at her. 'Don't worry about me. I'll be all right. What are we going to do about you, more's the point?'

'What do you mean?'

'Well, you're not getting any younger, are you?'

'Charming.'

'You're forty-six; you're not very fit; you never do anything. When are you going to find someone nice to go out with? You haven't had a girlfriend — well, lady friend — since Mum left.'

'Because… well, the thing is,' he cleared his throat, unnecessarily, 'I'm fine as I am. Anyway, I haven't met anyone nice, have I?'

'Of course not: you never go out! Dad, please take that overall off: it's covered in shit.'

'Sorry.' He stood up, took it off and went into the bathroom and stuffed it into the large, plastic laundry basket. He needed to get Tina off the subject of his love life as quickly as possible. He went back into the lounge. 'Anyway, never mind me. What about you? You're going to leave school in a couple of months. What are you going to do?'

'I've got my exams first. I need to get some qualifications.'

'For once we agree; are you doing any revision?'

''Course I am.'

Terry looked hard at her. He had never seen any evidence of it. 'I was thinking you could be a high-powered secretary.'

'My typing's rubbish.'

'What about working in accounts?'

'I can't add up more than my fingers.'

'Telephone operator?'

'Dad, give me a break!'

Running out of ideas, Terry searched through his head for suitable jobs.

Tina said, 'I'm thinking of becoming a nun.'

Terry looked at her face; she wasn't smiling. 'Has anyone done anything to you?'

Tina shook her head, 'Oh, it's nothing, Dad. I'll get a job at *Woolies* — Pic n' Mix, or selling records. I'm not bothered.'

'Well, I think you should try for something more ambitious. I'm going to ask Miss Ratcliffe for some ideas.'

'Dad, do you fancy her?'

'Of course not. She's not much older than you. She is nice though; you'll like her.'

Terry picked up the newspaper to check what was on the box.

'Dad?' He looked up. 'Um, I need to tell you something.'

He put the paper back down. His heart was thumping again; he didn't like the way it was pounding these days. 'Yeah?'

Tina seemed to be grappling with something.

Terry couldn't stand the suspense. 'Go on.'

He nervously watched his daughter. She closed her eyes, shook her head, then said, 'Er, well — a copper asked me out today.'

'What? You're only a girl. I'll have him arrested!'

'Dad, I'm sixteen, for God's sake.'

'Yeah, but how old is he?'

'I don't know — twenty something?'

Terry thought about the worthless Abbotts. Maybe a policeman wasn't a bad option.

'Hmm. Well, don't rush into anything, will you? You don't have to do anything you don't want to. Why don't you go for a walk together? How about you ask him back here for tea?'

Tina smiled.

'What are you smiling at?'

'Oh, it's what Gary said about him.'

'What was that?'

'"Who does he think he is? Kevin effing Keegan?"'

'How does Gary know him?'

'It doesn't matter, Dad.'

'What were you and Gary talking about earlier?'

'We were just going through what we said to the police this morning?'

Terry remembered. 'Sorry, love, I'm a selfish bastard. I'll go and get fish and chips. Let's watch the telly and forget about the rest of the world. It's

"This Is Your Life". Then at eight p.m. it's "The Rockford Files" or "Man About The House"; apparently it's the last ever episode tonight.'

Tina smiled at him. 'Thanks, Dad.'

'Is that all right then?'

'Lovely.'

'Cod or plaice?'

'Cod.'

'James Garner or Richard O'Sullivan?'

'I don't mind. Whatever you want, Dad.'

Chapter 14

As Gary neared his house, tiredness finally began to get the better of him. He hadn't slept for God knows how long. In the last day and night, so much had happened he wasn't sure he could bring it all to mind. He tried to get it in order: the trip to Anthony's father in prison; then the strip club in Soho to see Katy's mum; then home to see his own mum smash in his dad's head with the dishful of unbaked apple crumble. Was that all of it? Yes, apart from his dad dying, of course. And today — was it still only Monday? — it had all been madness. He was desperate to eat something, then fall asleep for a very long time.

He saw someone cross over the road as he got his keys ready. He smiled. Anthony Alexander, looking like a prick.

'Hello, Gary.'

'Watcha.'

The two boys stood together, uncertain. Anthony put out his hand. Gary said, 'What is this? An interview?'

'No, I thought it would be nice to greet you, you know, with an eye to formality but with a nod to close friendship, too. I wasn't sure how best to… I wanted to let you know that — these situations are awkward, aren't they? I mean, we're not exactly long-standing friends but notwithstanding that, I felt compelled to offer—'

Gary cut in. 'For fuck's sake, Anthony: you don't half talk a load of shit.'

'I think that's rather unfair of you.'

Gary remembered the reassurance and kindness he'd felt when Joe had gripped his shoulders earlier. He said, 'You're a wanker, Anthony,' then gave him a bear hug.

'Get off me, you great oaf!'

Gary laughed and shoved him away. 'Despite you being a knob and a tit, I'm quite pleased to see you.'

'What are you doing?'

'Right now?'

Anthony nodded.

Remembering what Victoria had told him, Gary said, 'Anthony, Victoria Court told me about your dad. I'm really sorry. I don't know if you know, but — can you believe it? — my dad's fucking pegged it, too!'

'What? I don't believe it. Gosh, I'm so sorry, Gary. May I ask what happened?'

'I was going to ask you that.'

Anthony looked around him, 'Shall we go somewhere? I don't want to be at home right now; my mother's — er, a little the worse for wear. Do you think we should go inside or…?'

'Fuck, no. My house isn't exactly receiving guests right now. Where can we go?'

'Let's go to the café in the high street; where we went last week?'

The unlikely confidants walked away from Gary's house: one tall and powerful, the other short and quick.

Gary glanced down at Anthony's blackened, short-cropped hair. Antony looked up. 'What?'

'I think I prefer the old look.'

'What, even though I looked like someone you wanted to beat up all the time?'

Gary felt bad all over again. It was true, the moment he'd seen Anthony's wispy blond hair, then heard his posh, smart-arse voice, he had wanted to give him a good kicking. 'Yeah, well now I wouldn't risk it; you look like the kind of kid I'd run away from.'

The bright, neon lights of the Italian café washed over the pavement. Anthony pushed open the door and went inside.

'What would you like?' Anthony was pulling cash out of his pocket.

'I'm starving. I'm going to have the mixed grill and chips.'

Anthony looked at the greasy menu. 'Hmm, I think I'd rather have something authentically Italian. I wonder what their Spaghetti Bolognese is like.'

'You don't want that foreign shit, do you?'

Anthony smiled, 'You're right. I'll have the same as you. You can be my guide into the world of gourmet cuisine.'

Gary pulled out his fags and looked disconsolately at the single Number 6 in the packet. 'Shall we share it?'

Anthony shook his head, 'No, thank you. I'll join you for cigars and brandy after the meal.'

The elderly proprietor shuffled to their table. 'Well, wadda you want?'

They ordered. Anthony said, 'Tell me, Signor, how would you describe your cellar?'

Gary snorted; the owner shuffled off.

Anthony was indignant. 'Well, really! I'm not surprised this place is empty, manners like that.'

Gary looked around; they weren't quite on their own. In the far corner was a middle-aged couple with two teenage boys. Gary recognised them; they were younger kids at school. He remembered his glasses and went to take them off, then thought better of it.

From behind the counter came sounds of frying, chopping and a monotonous whistling. Every now and then they heard the rat-a-tat-tat of Italian: grumbling man, shrill wife. The air was thick with smoke, fat and hopelessness.

'God, Anthony, this is a dump.'

Anthony was wiping his side of the table with a handkerchief. 'Do you think so? I quite like it. It's got an earthy charm. I feel as if I'm in touch with everyday life for the first time.'

Gary looked at him. It didn't seem possible that only a few days ago he would have happily beaten that stupid, ugly face into a bloody pulp. Now, he was very pleased to be in the company of Anthony Alexander, even if he did look like a ferret and sounded like Lord Snooty.

'I'm sorry about your dad.'

'I'm sorry about yours.'

'What happened?'

'I was going to ask you that.'

'You first.'

Antony paused. 'When I got back yesterday evening — do you remember the police being at my place?'

Gary nodded.

'They came to tell us that my father was dead. They wouldn't say how. My mother and Granny went with them to Lewes to identify the body. I stayed behind. When they came home — hmm, maybe ten thirty p.m. — my mother went straight to bed. Granny poured herself a large whisky, sat down and told me what they'd found out.'

'Yeah?'

'My father had been strangled.'

'Fuck! How? Who by? Why?'

'Exactly. That's what we want to know.'

'But — that means someone killed him!'

'Not necessarily. You see, he was found in the showers, hanged. A bit of washing line was attached to the bars across the window, and he was found hanging. There was a bucket by his feet; he could have jumped off it. But the police don't know if he killed himself or if someone did it to him.'

'Bloody hell.'

'I know.'

Gary wasn't sure what to say next. He tried to picture the scene. He remembered seeing a film in which a body had been found dangling limply from a rafter. The body had looked like a dummy in a shop window, entirely unlike a real person. He wondered what had been in the mind of Anthony's father before he decided to kill himself. He wondered what he'd done to make someone else kill him. Was it worse than what had made his own mum attack his dad?

'Are you sad?' Gary ventured.

Antony was thoughtful for a minute. 'I'm not sad, but I suppose I'm nonplussed.'

Gary couldn't remember what it meant. He racked his brains; he'd read it recently. He shook his head.

'Remind me: what's that mean?'

'Er, well — being so surprised, shocked, that it's hard to work out what to think, or feel. I mean, I know I'm supposed to feel things, but I'm not sure that I feel anything at all.'

Gary had been hunched over the table, mirroring Anthony. He sat back and stared. 'That's it. That's exactly it. It's as if something has happened to someone else and not me. The only thing I'm really bothered about is making sure my mum is safe.'

'I hope you don't mind me asking: what happened to your father?'

Gary told him everything.

'My goodness! Oh, my word.'

Their dinners arrived.

'Would you like something to drink?' Anthony asked.

'A cuppa, ta.'

'May we have a pot of tea, please?'

Gary laughed. 'Anthony, you are such a... "A pot of tea"? This isn't the Ritz, you know.'

'Oh. Two teas, please, Signor.'

They silently worked through their piles of greasy food. The teas arrived.

Gary called to the retreating back of their waiter, 'Oi, Mussolini, do you sell fags?'

The old man pointed at a cigarette machine on the wall behind the fizzy drinks cabinet.

'Got any change, Anthony?'

Anthony dug in his pockets. '75p.'

'That'll buy us a packet of ten.'

Gary scraped up the last few chips on his plate, crammed them into his mouth and went over to the machine. One of the boys looked up and nudged his brother. They sniggered. The cocktail of poison Gary had bottled up over the last twenty-four hours erupted. Blindly, he reached for one of the plastic chairs and was about to crash it into the family's table top.

'Gary!'

He looked round. Anthony had a thumb in each ear, fingers waggling; his protruding tongue was flapping wildly.

Gary coughed, put the chair neatly back under its table and carried on to the cigarette machine. The boys' father turned around to see what was going on. 'You all right, mate?'

Gary carried on to the machine, fed in coins and made his choice. 'Yeah, ta. My dad died today and I'm a bit upset.'

'Oh. Sorry about that.'

Gary nodded at him and walked back to Anthony. 'Shit, that was close. Thanks for getting me out of trouble.'

Anthony smiled. 'Well, I thought for one horrible moment there was going to be another death on our hands. Also, there seemed to be a growing possibility that my post-prandial cigarette would not reach me in time to accompany my digestive.'

Gary smiled. 'You knob; you're an absolute knob.'

'One day — although I accept it won't be soon — you're going to be kind and respectful to me.'

'Have a fag and shut up.'

Anthony took a cigarette from the new packet. Gary lit it and his own. He said, 'I went to see Joe today.'

'How was he?'

'Brilliant.'

'I was thinking I might have a word with him.'

'Anthony, I've suddenly realised something. You know I told you that Joe had come around last night to help me set up the crime scene? Well, that's obviously secret. You must never tell anyone what I said about him being involved. In fact, everything I told you has to be secret. You can never tell anyone. I mean it, Anthony: you must never breathe a word.'

'It's all right. I won't. I promise.'

Gary thought about what Joe had told them about murdering someone. He felt a tremendous weight of responsibility bearing down on him. All he wanted right now was the simple life of a few days ago where nothing mattered. He said, 'I'd better go. My mum will be worried. She's got to try and keep herself together, too.'

'Me too. Shall we meet up tomorrow? Do you want to meet the others? They'll want to help you if they can.'

Gary thought about Frank and the Walker sisters. He did want to be with them. He liked their kindness: it was what he really wanted right now.

'Yeah, let's do that. Are you going to school?'

'I am. I know it sounds strange, my father having just died, but I'd like a bit of normality right now. Also — you won't be bothered about it, being an ignorant thug — but I'd quite like to pass a few exams.'

'Watch it, mate. I've got a place lined up at Oxford or Cambridge; I'm not sure which I'll take. Anyway, I'll probably go in, too. Maybe we can have another fight in the bogs. This time I'll break your nose.'

They put out their fags and got up. Anthony went to the counter and paid. Gary looked over at the two boys. They were watching him. He pointed at them and mouthed, 'You're fucking dead.'

Chapter 15

'Goodnight, Dad.'

'Night, love.'

Tina shut her bedroom door. She looked around her room: it was disgusting. How did she let it get into this kind of state? What must Gary have thought? She stooped and began to pick up her clothes, one by one. At first, she checked each item — clean or dirty? She soon stopped bothering. The fact that everything was either on the floor or mixed up with dirty stuff meant that it could all be put in a huge pile ready for washing or, better still, burning. She went to the kitchen for some carrier bags, came back and stuffed whites into one, mixed colours into another. After a few minutes, the floor, bed and chair were clear of clothes. She started on the rest of the detritus. Several minutes later she had another full bag. This one held wrappers, fag ends, dead matches, hair clips, tissues, receipts, empty boxes, lipsticks — a pile of rubbish. Just like me, she thought, as she scrabbled under her bed for more of the crap. She pushed the bags up against the door, sat down on the floor and looked around. The room was tidier, but it was in a terrible state: dust, stains, burns, cracks, splinters, greasy remains: further evidence of her pathetic, shitty life.

She reached up to the pillow end of her bed and pulled the giraffe down. Her voice was low, reassuring. 'Come on, it'll be all right. Come on, don't worry. I'll look after you.'

The injured creature looked trustingly back at her. Tina felt her heart begin to burst. She clutched the giraffe to her chest and through her hot tears, she pleaded, 'I'm so sorry. Please forgive me. I'm sorry about everything.' She pressed her face into the old material, inhaling its familiar mustiness.

'Tina?'

She jumped. 'What?'

'Er, I wanted to make sure you're okay?'

She wiped her nose and eyes on her sleeve. 'Yeah, thanks, Dad.'

'Good girl. Tomorrow's another day. We'll knock 'em dead, won't we?'

'You bet your arse we will.'

'Goodnight.'

'Goodnight, Dad. Thanks for the fish and chips and everything.'

She heard his door close. Looking down at the giraffe, she whispered, 'We are going to be all right, aren't we? You'll help me, won't you?'

Tina smiled when she saw the love in his eyes; she hugged him hard.

Chapter 16

When Diane left, Terry knew he must protect Tina from any semblance of the truth. He felt the oh-so-familiar panic return as the pictures flashed back into his head. There seemed to be some kind of switch that got flicked; all he could do was watch the scene through again. He didn't want to: he'd do anything to turn it off. Terry screwed up his eyes and shook his head in a futile hope of deleting the nightmare.

He'd come home early that day; his assigned job had been cancelled at the last minute. He came in, took his coat off and leafed through the post on the kitchen table. Terry sniffed: Diane's perfume — very strong. Her handbag was on the coffee table. There were cigarette butts in the ashtray. He heard sounds from upstairs. He listened: yes, she was in their bedroom. He smiled; she'd be really pleased to see him. They had all afternoon before it was time to collect Tina. Perhaps they could have a bit of uninterrupted fun?

'All right, Gorgeous?' There was no answer, but the sounds of movement continued. He went up the stairs, confused. As he neared the top, the nature of the sounds became clear. He knew what he was going to see. Despite the agony he was about to feel, he couldn't help himself looking. The bedroom door was ajar; he looked in through the crack. On the floor was a pair of shoes: men's shoes. Not his shoes. He could see trousers too, and underpants.

A man's voice suddenly blurted, 'Fuck, oh, fuck!'

Diane's voice, deliciously encouraging, answered, 'That's it, babe, let me feel you; that's it, yes, yes…'

Terry put his ear close to the half-inch gap: creaking bed springs, groans, gasps, slapping flesh. Sick with horror, but consumed by a ghastly fascination, Terry silently inched open the door and peered in. Diane, naked and on all fours, was being fucked from behind by a stranger. The man, haughty, like a senior officer, had his eyes half closed, focused on his task.

Numb with shock, Terry backed away. Something in him — perhaps love for Diane — made him feel ashamed. Whatever it was, his only thought was to get away. Back downstairs, the evidence was obvious. Diane's open handbag had pound notes spilling out of it. There was a leather briefcase leaning against the coffee table. Flung over the armchair was an overcoat. Terry was going from hot to cold, then hot again. His breathing was shallow. He had to get out now. If he stayed a second longer, he would kill them both. The drive to destroy them was already building. He had to get out — now. He rushed through the hall and threw open the door. Gasping, he ran down the path and out into the street. Where could he go? Blindly, he ran.

Lying in bed now, six years later, his breathing was as shallow, his heart hammering, the panic as real. He got up, went out to the kitchen and made himself a cup of tea. On the table lay the Action Man. He wondered which of the boys it belonged to. Had one of the older boys stuffed it down the lav, cheered on by his bully-boy friends? Terry felt his blood boil at the injustice of it. He'd make everything all right again; it was his duty. He opened the broom cupboard and found his sewing kit. He smiled to himself as he remembered the day he'd been issued with it: way back, in Catterick, twenty-four years ago. He hoped the Quartermaster would be pleased that, all these years later, the kit would be used to get a man back into the front line.

The camouflage uniform was on the storage heater, drying after the boil wash. Within minutes, the badly-torn fatigues were in one piece, albeit in need of pressing. The soldier's right leg, which had sustained a nasty fracture at the knee, was repaired with some wire, and taped firm. Finally, Terry glued the broken neck as securely as he could.

'There you go, son: you're ready for action.'

The soldier, his face determined, looked up at his surgeon. Terry looked back.

Chapter 17

Jenny Abbott, Derek, Kevin and Gary sat around the kitchen table. The boys were smoking in brooding silence.

Jenny said, 'I'm going to have to go to bed. I'm wrecked.'

'Yeah, me too,' Gary said.

The other two looked at each other. Derek said, 'Hang on a minute, Gary.'

Gary looked at his brothers. What was going on?

'Goodnight, I'll see you in the morning,' Jenny said.

The boys were silent.

Jenny said, 'No shouting or aggro, you lot. We're all tired. It's been awful for us all. Please don't get worked up.'

Gary said, 'Nah, don't worry, Mum. We're fine.'

When their mother's footsteps had reached the bathroom, Kevin said, 'Come on, Gary, cut the crap. What really happened?'

'Exactly what we said. Honestly, Kev, there's nothing else to say.'

'But to die in his own fucking kitchen. I don't believe it.'

'He didn't die in the kitchen.'

'You know what I mean.'

Derek said, 'Look, Gary, if he was giving Mum a belting and you belted him, then that's fair enough. You and him have been getting ready for a scrap for a while now. If you did it, say so.'

Gary was tempted. The weight of the truth was making him so tired. Maybe it would be easier if they knew the truth. He looked across at Kevin. His eyes were narrowed: he did not look like he was going to be sympathetic. 'No, I didn't do it. He must have tripped over the lead and hit his head. I can't think of anything else that could have happened.'

Derek said, 'Maybe it's for the best, anyway. I found out today who Dad did in, that night.'

Gary and Kevin looked at him.

'It was the owner of that big factory down past the cinema. Apparently, he's still in hospital.'

'How do you know?' Gary asked.

'When you told me the Filth had identified him for the assault, I asked around at work. Apparently, it was in the newspaper. One of my mate's brother is a fork-lift truck driver at this bloke's company and they were all talking about it. He used to be the mayor.'

'What, your mate's brother?' Kev asked.

Derek and Gary sniggered.

Kev's face went red. 'Fuck off, you two. Jeez, I've had enough of being made to look fucking stupid.'

'Why, who else has?' Derek asked.

'That fucking bitch, Tina.'

Gary felt his face redden.

Derek asked, 'Yeah?'

'I went round to her place this morning. I thought she'd probably want someone to look after her. So I go in, check she's all right. I even gave her a massage, you know, to relax her. She only tells me to fuck off. What a slag.'

Gary kept his head down. He was relieved that Tina had told him to get out.

Kev went on. 'I got my own back. When her old man turned up, I gave him a thorough beating. You should have seen him: he went down so hard, it was like he'd been shot.'

Gary now realised why Mr Castleton had been so against him, earlier. Thinking about Tina's dad now, though, he doubted Kev could have beaten up someone that big. 'Wow, you're a big hero, Kev, beating up caretakers. You're a real tough guy.'

Kev leapt to his feet. 'You fuck off, you little cunt. I know you've been slipping Tina a length. Do you think I'm fucking stupid?'

Gary had had enough. He'd spent the whole day being sensible, staying calm and in control. He stood up, went around the table and piled his fist into his brother's head. Kevin flew backwards against the kitchen work-top, his hands went to his face as he sank to the floor.

Gary looked down at Kevin. For a moment he wasn't sure what to say: 'Sorry' or 'You had that coming'.

Derek said, 'Kev, I think you can assume that Gary did not slip Tina a length.'

Gary felt bad now. 'I'm sorry, Kevin. I'm really wound up. There's nothing between Tina and me. Honest.'

He bent down to his brother and put his hand on his shoulder.

'I miss Dad,' Kev was crying.

His brothers were silent.

Derek said, 'So what happened that night?'

Gary said, 'All of a sudden, he got out of the car, went up to this posh bloke and stuck his head into his face. Really hard. To be honest, he was so drunk he probably didn't even know what he was doing. How we stayed on the road after, I don't know. It was sort of funny, but I knew he'd gone overboard.'

'And how did the cops know it was him?'

'Because he'd rolled his sleeves up and the posh geezer saw Jailhouse Rock tattooed on his arm.'

Derek whistled. 'Poor old Dad: grassed up by Elvis.'

'Yeah, I know. The funny thing is that, when he went down in the kitchen, he was listening to his poxy Elvis records.'

Kev got slowly to his feet. 'My fucking head — shit, it hurts.'

'Look, Kev, I'm sorry. I lost my rag. There's nothing going on between me and Tina. I promise you there isn't.'

Kev grunted and went upstairs.

Derek leered at Gary. 'If you aren't giving her one, and Kev certainly ain't, I'll give it a go.'

Gary made himself smile.

Tuesday

Chapter 18

Geraldine Dutton lifted the lid on the first tin: the cake looked delicious. She fought off the urge to try a crafty morsel. Instead, she replaced the lid and reached for the biscuit tin. She swallowed. They looked even better. This time, she couldn't resist and took a bite, then another.

'For God's sake, Geraldine. No wonder you look like a whale.'

She felt her face redden, why did he have to sneak around like that. There he was, leaning against the door jamb, his expression accusing. No, it was worse than that: there was disgust.

Guiltily, she wiped crumbs and saliva from her lips. She laughed, 'Well, I had to check they were edible before offering them around, didn't I?'

'Oh, it's up to you what you do. The thing is, I don't think you realise that you've put on a lot of weight and, well, you know, you are looking a bit ...'

'Like a whale?'

'All right, not a whale, more walrus.'

Geraldine knew she had put on weight, of course she did. In the last few years, she had gone up a size or two; but that was what happened to middle-aged women, wasn't it?

Maybe Edward was right, but why did he have to be so cutting all the time? His constant finger-wagging was getting to her. He used to shower her with compliments — eyes, complexion, figure. He always used to tell her how much he loved her body and what it did to him. When had the compliments turned to caustic comments: maybe it was years ago? She couldn't remember when he'd last told her that he loved her — all of her.

He said, 'You're not going to school like that are you?'

She'd been a bit worried that her lovely, silk blouse might be on the tight side, but she knew that young men liked curvaceous women. 'Yes, why not?'

'Put it this way, if any of those buttons pop you could be liable for some extensive damage to unsuspecting colleagues, not to mention vulnerable children.'

She sniffed, 'Not funny Edward.'

'Well, don't say I didn't warn you.'

She opened the cupboard under the sink and pulled out a carrier bag.

He said, 'Make sure there's some left by the time you get to school. It won't be much of a birthday party if there's no cake. Oh, and by the way, you've got chocolate crumbs on your blouse. I'd get rid of the evidence, if I were you.'

Geraldine looked down; damn, he was right. She brushed them off and went into the hall. The mirror beckoned to her; she ignored it. Seeing the overnight bag by the door she said, 'Will you be home tonight?'

'I'm not sure yet. I plan to be but there's a big bash tonight for Tony Curtis; I may well get roped into that. Elton and Rod are coming along, and, all being well, Pan's People are surprise guests. So, I'm not sure. I'll come home by taxi, if I do.'

Geraldine thought about her life compared to his — she loved the children, her colleagues, her work. Plus, a new development, she now had her Daniel. Edward would have to put up with vacuous celebrities, shameless hangers-on and skinny dancers.

He said, 'How about you? Will there be drinks after the party?'

Geraldine doubted it but didn't want him to think she was going to be on her own this evening. 'Oh, probably, I'll see. It might be nice to go out and let my hair down.'

Edward was shovelling papers into his leather briefcase. He looked over at her, his eyes curious. 'Good, have a lovely time.'

She was pretty sure he could see through her but kept up the façade, 'Oh, I will. We all have such a laugh these days. Jim's made such a difference.'

'Jim? Since when has he been Jim?'

'Oh, he insists we all call him Jim.'

Edward's look pierced into her head, poked around, then left: she knew he knew she was bluffing. He nodded, 'Have a great time.'

'You too.'

'I'm hardly going to have a nice time, am I? I don't think you quite understand the pressure I'm under right now.'

Geraldine felt bad. Edward did have a very demanding job. It was because of his work that they had such a comfortable lifestyle — well, apart from the house, of course. But it was true, his success meant that they could have foreign holidays and new cars whenever they wanted them. She said, 'I'm sorry. I hope it all goes well. Let me know if you're coming home as soon as you can, and I'll have a nice meal waiting for you. How about a bottle of something with it?'

'I'll do my best to get back. It's out of my hands.'

She kissed him on the cheek. Did he shrink away? She heard his clipped 'bye' and then the door close. She went into the sitting room, opened the drinks cabinet, chose a bottle of Riesling and put it in the fridge. Idly, she wondered whether Daniel liked wine.

As she drove along the suburban streets, Geraldine speculated again if Edward were having an affair. They'd been married for eighteen years; most of that time they'd been happy. She couldn't put her finger on when things had cooled off: was it when she'd started putting on weight? Their everyday time together had become formal rather than the easy, playful way they used to be. Edward spent a lot of time at work and increasing amounts of his weekends playing golf. It felt like a sit-com cliché: him becoming a predictable, middle-class, middle-aged professional; she the dutiful wife who ran the house. Thank God for her job. The traffic lights changed to red; she put on the handbrake. Before she knew what was happening, the lid was off and another biscuit was on its way. What was wrong with her? She felt her face redden again, this time with shame. No wonder they didn't have sex anymore. Why would he want to make love to a walrus? She didn't fancy sex either. Well, that wasn't true. She didn't want to have sex with him, only with Daniel. She put the biscuit back. As the tall young man appeared in her mind, she found herself licking her lips. Ever since he'd started at the school, she'd found herself fantasising. It was ridiculous: he must be twenty years younger and probably had loads of girlfriends of his own age. It didn't matter though; she couldn't stop herself imagining him taking her in any number of after school situations. Sometimes it was in the stock room, urgent and rough. Other times she pictured him watching her as she took off her clothes, offering herself to him. Now, driving along the dual carriage way, she was chalking fractions on the blackboard. She felt him press against her, his hands on her breasts, his voice whispering in her ear, his firm body insistent. Up ahead, she saw Mrs Rumney walk into the road, lollypop brandished. Geraldine braked and waved. As she waited, she mopped her face with a tissue. She knew she ought to get a grip on these thoughts. But what was wrong with a bit of fantasy, now and then? She drove slowly into the school drive and manoeuvred into a space. Opening the glove compartment, she fished around for the little perfume bottle and dabbed behind each ear. As she did so, some boys appeared in the rear-view mirror; they reminded her of yesterday's problem.

She had always liked Terry Castleton. When Tina had been at the school, the teachers had known a bit about the breakup of the family and how it had affected Terry. Until then, Tina had been a terrible handful. Geraldine smiled as she remembered the tantrums Tina had regularly got into: she was like a volcano but, somehow, her mother leaving had made the little girl much more responsible. When Terry had started work at the school there had been some disquiet: would he be able to cope after his nervous breakdown? He'd soon reassured them all. He was hardworking, and, despite what had happened, always seemed to be cheerful. Both she and James Dixon had been disbelieving when they'd heard the accusations from Ian Sadler, Duncan Barr and Philip Cox. However, when Ian's mother had rung up yesterday afternoon, it had suddenly become a serious issue.

Geraldine picked up the cake and biscuit tins and heaved herself out of the car: Edward was right, she did need to lose some weight.

'Morning, Mrs Dutton.'

Geraldine coloured as Terry approached her. 'Oh, ahem, hallo, Terry, how are you?'

He looked at her, weighing her up. 'I'm fine, thank you. Are you all right? You look a little, um?'

She put aside her suspicions and smiled broadly, 'I'm very well, thank you. It's Daniel Jenkinson's birthday today; I've made a cake for him. Will you be joining us to sing Happy Birthday?'

'What time?'

'Lunchtime.'

'Er, well, that's very nice of you, but I normally go home for dinner.'

She looked at him closely. He was different somehow. Yes, he wasn't wearing his usual grey overall. Instead, he wore a dark blue shirt and a tweed sports jacket. She said, 'You're looking rather smart, Terry. You're not going for an interview, I hope?'

He blushed. 'No, I, well, um, no.'

Geraldine hadn't looked properly at Terry Castleton for years. He was nice-looking, in a hefty sort of way. Maybe that's what people thought about her?

He said, 'Would you mind giving this to Miss Ratcliffe?'

She took the box from him, her eyebrows raised.

He smiled, 'I saved someone from the trenches yesterday; she's going to make sure he gets safely back to barracks.'

Puzzled, Geraldine took the box. 'See you later, Terry. Do come along for your slice of cake, won't you?'

She went into the staffroom and looked around for Daniel.

Chapter 19

'Gary, are you awake?'

He didn't recognise the voice. Was it one of the coppers'? Gary had been wrestling with them all night, mostly Dickie but there had been several others including Cilla Black and David Coleman, both of them in uniform.

'Gary, are you all right?' At last the fog began to clear. He reassured his mum, 'Yeah.'

'Do you want some breakfast?'

He groaned, 'What time is it?'

'9 o'clock.'

Gary stretched and sat up.' Yeah, I'll be down in a minute.'

He heard her make her way downstairs. Kev's bed was empty. He must have got up and gone to work. Yesterday's events were properly coming back to him now. Today might be the day that they all got arrested. He wondered how Tina was. He flopped back and imagined her in her bed; would she be frightened? Perhaps she'd like him to get in with her, to hold her again, like he had in the hospital car park. The thought of cuddling her, whispering to her, was incredibly arousing. Gary felt shame flare: she needed looking after, not to be taken advantage of by someone like him.

He got up, put on his jeans and went down to the kitchen.

His mum smiled at him, 'Hello, Sleeping Beauty.'

'Morning.'

'What do you want to eat?'

'Bacon sarnie?'

'Coming up.'

'According to Joe we might hear from the police today.'

Jenny put bacon on to fry, 'I'm going to tell them everything; I've decided. It's for the best. I did it to protect Tina. You know that; she knows that. Why are we pretending?'

'I don't trust them, that's why. They're not interested in why it happened. All they want to do is bang someone up. I've seen it on the box. Their boss will be on at them to put someone away for murder. That's how it works, Mum.'

'You don't know that, love. Why would they do that? They're just ordinary people. The police are people, just like us.'

'No! That's just it. They're bastards. You don't join the police if you're like us. They're out to get us; believe me, Mum.'

Jenny flipped the rashers over then buttered two white slices. She said, 'I don't like all this lying, Gary. We're going to get caught out: then it will be much worse.'

Gary had been thinking the same, but they were in it now. They might as well keep going. He said, 'The thing is, if we tell the truth then we'll have to say that he was attacking Tina. I dunno why, I just don't want to tell them that. It's bad enough that he was doing it, never mind telling people, and 'specially not the bloody police.'

Jenny poured tea into a mug and spooned in sugar. 'Here you go. I know; it's all so humiliating.'

Gary said, 'After breakfast I'm going to ring Joe. He'll know what to do.'

Jenny picked up the tongs, lifted out the sizzling rashers and laid them side by side on the bread, 'Ketchup?'

'Naa.'

'I know you like that man, but I can't help thinking that he's a bad influence. Honestly, love, he's killed someone and been to prison. He's not exactly a pillar of the community, is he?'

'In case it's slipped your mind, we've killed someone and we might be going to prison.'

They stared at each other.

Gary said, 'Sorry, Mum. I know he's got a dodgy past but I'm sure he'll look out for us. Anyway, he's just as much caught up in this as we are. If we go down then we can take him with us.'

'It's not 'us', is it? It's not 'we'. It's me. I'm the one that did it; I'm the murderer.'

Gary drained his tea and banged the mug on the table. He shouted, 'No, Mum, you are not taking this one. I won't have it. If anyone is getting done it's me. That's the end of it.'

He picked up his sandwich and took a massive bite. 'Mmm, lovely, thanks.'

Jenny smiled at him.

Chapter 20

Tina had four machines going. As well as the bags she'd filled last night, she had pulled off her bedsheets this morning and gathered up some towels. She'd fed in her coins, then rushed home to hoover the flat from end to end. She had looked into her dad's room but already knew that it would be spick and span. He had tried to instil order and cleanliness in her but, unlike him, she was lazy and — what was the word he always used? — slovenly.

Tina had opened all the windows, mopped the kitchen floor and bleached the bog. She looked at her watch: quarter to eleven. There were a few minutes left before the washing machines finished. What should she do next? She wondered how Jenny and Gary were doing. She jumped up and went to the phone-box down the road.

'Gary, it's me, Tina.'

'Oh.'

Tina thought he'd be pleased. He sounded pissed off. 'Is it a bad time?'

'No, sorry, we were just thinking about you and how you were doing. I — um, well — I wasn't sure what to say, that's all.'

She pressed him. 'But you don't mind me ringing, do you?'

'No, I'm glad you have.'

Reassured, Tina said, 'Have you heard anything? You know, from the...'

'No. You?'

'No. Nothing.'

Gary said, 'Not even from your new boyfriend?'

'Listen, he's not my boyfriend. Mind you, I have to admit, he is rather dishy.'

Gary was quiet.

'How's your mum?' Tina pressed on.

'She's okay. She wants to tell the Filth everything. I told her that's a stupid idea. We're going to keep on saying nothing.'

'Good. Me too. They can't prove anything, can they? The mortem thing can't prove anything. Even if they think we did it, how can they say for certain?'

Gary said, 'Yeah, you're right. The only thing they can do is to try and get us to start disagreeing about what happened. Tina, you're brilliant — well done.'

Tina flushed. 'Am I? Really? Oh, good. Thanks, Gary.'

She remembered her laundry. 'Listen, I've got to rush. You shamed me into it: I'm doing my washing, down the launderette. Give me a ring as soon as you hear anything. You will, won't you?'

'Sure, I will. You ring me too, won't you?'

'Yeah. Bye then.'

She put the phone down and ran to the launderette. Two women had arrived and were filling up machines. Beyond them she saw an old man pulling her own washing carelessly out of its machine into a plastic basket. Items were spilling out: her dad's overall on the dusty floor.

She roared at him. 'What the bloody hell are you doing?'

The old bloke looked at her. 'I'm using the washing machine, sweetheart. Your stuff is in my way.'

Tina ran over, picked up the overall and flapped it furiously. 'Jeez, it's covered in dust now, you dirty old tramp.'

The women were shocked. One of them said, 'That's no way to talk, young lady. You say sorry, now.'

Tina rounded on them, 'Keep out of it, you old bag!' She turned back to the man. 'Look at my nice, clean washing: you've ruined it!'

The old man looked at her with contempt, 'Who do you think you are? Look at you! Look at you — you're nothing but a cheap tart.'

Tina felt hot tears spring to her eyes. This was so unfair. She was trying her hardest to get herself cleaned up. She was trying to be respectable, like her dad wanted her to be.

'Are these yours, too?'

She looked up. The old man was opening the next machine.

'Get your filthy hands off my stuff!'

He grabbed hold of a sheet and started pulling it out. Tina rushed up and began punching him in the back.

'Get off me, you bitch! If you don't get off me, I'll swing for you.'

A door opened at the back of the launderette. An Asian man came out. He stood watching the odd couple, one throwing ineffectual punches, the other wrestling with sheets. Another customer came in. Tina and the old man carried on scuffling. She was yelling, 'They're my sheets! They're my dad's sheets. Get off them, you bastard!'

Tina felt someone take her flailing arms and gently pull her away. She watched as the stranger put his arm around the shoulders of the old man and said, 'Come on. Let's put those sheets into a basket, shall we?'

The proprietor returned to the back room.

Grumbling, Tina got three more plastic baskets and emptied the rest of her washing into them. She stuck her tongue out at the old man, took her loads to the far end of the launderette and stuffed everything into a drier. She inserted three twenty-pence pieces and got it going. She looked back at the old man. He was sitting down now, wiping his face with a handkerchief. After a few seconds, he entered into a lengthy discussion with the younger bloke, who had sat down next to him. The second man was listening, nodding, shaking his head.

Now that she'd calmed down, Tina felt guilty. The old man must be at least seventy, maybe eighty. She could have killed him. Sighing, she got up and approached them. 'I'm very sorry. I lost my temper. I've been trying to get my life together. Are you all right?'

The men looked up at her. The old man had a nasty, mean face. He said, 'You ought to be arrested. You're a disgrace. Your parents should be shot.'

Tina felt her temper flare again but this time she kept it under control. 'Well, I'm sorry, anyway.'

She looked at the other bloke. He was looking back. He smiled. There was something really nice about him: he had lovely, kind eyes. He said, 'Hello, Tina, my name's Joe.'

Chapter 21

Terry took off his overall and hung it on one of the nails by the door. He lifted his sports jacket from its hanger and shrugged it on. Hmm, it was definitely a bit too tight these days. He tried to remember when he'd bought it: it must have been ten years ago. Diane had always supervised his clothes and, apart from socks and underwear, he hadn't bought anything new since she'd gone. The jacket was too good to get rid of, though. Anything Diane had been involved with was bound to be good. She'd been stylish, modern; she'd always scrubbed up and made sure he did, too. Thinking about it now, Terry couldn't work out what a beautiful young woman like her could possibly have seen in him. Yes, he'd been in better condition and so, soon after he'd come out of the Army, maybe he had had a few prospects. But he should have realised: a stunner like her was always going to get bored with him.

He combed his short back and sides and sucked in his belly: he wanted to look good for Louise. Tina was relying on him. He'd brought a larger flask today and an extra cup. Remembering the Penguins, Terry fished them from his overall pocket and put them on the little plastic table he'd set up. He was ready.

The distant bell signalled the start of morning break. He hoped she'd be able to get here quickly; they had only fifteen minutes. Terry had popped a note in with the Action Man. 'Hope you're still able to join me for a chat this morning. The kettle will be on and you'll think you're at The Savoy.'

He heard movement outside. He laughed silently at himself: he was nervous!

'Oi, Baldy, what are you doing in there?'

Terry's heart sank. What did those little shits want this time? Still, they'd scatter as soon as Louise came along. He ignored them.

'He's pretending he's not in there.'

'We know you're in there, Baldy.'

'We're going to tell on you.'

'My dad's going to punch you.'

'Oi, Baldy, you're a fucky.'

Terry looked at his watch: where was she?

The boys' football crashed against the shed wall, right beside his ear. Terry jumped. He got up and opened the door, 'Clear off! You've had your fun. Go on. Run along like good little boys.'

'You gonna make us?'

Terry had a good mind to do just that. He knew better. 'Miss Ratcliffe is going to be here in a minute. She won't be very pleased to see you here, will she?'

'Ooh, is she your girlfriend, Baldy?'

'Yeah, I bet she is. Look! That's why he's got his smart clothes on. Do you want to kiss Miss Ratcliffe, Baldy?'

'Of course she isn't his girlfriend. He's more like her grandad, you idiot!'

Terry looked past them towards the school building: no sign of Louise.

'Give us one of your cigarettes.'

'On your bikes; go on, sod off.'

'You swore at me. You're in trouble now. I'm gonna tell Mr Dixon on you.'

With that the boys ran off, giggling.

Terry knew the minute he'd sworn that it had been a mistake.

Where was Louise? His mood had plummeted. Minutes earlier, he'd been hopeful; cheerful, even. In a matter of minutes, life was returning to its usual dark, shitty reality. He looked across the field to the playground: there was no sign of her. Terry turned back to his hastily-constructed 'Savoy' and sat down at the 'table for two'. He stared at the Penguins placed neatly next to the flask. What had he been thinking? As if a teacher like Miss Ratcliffe was going to come and talk to a fat, old caretaker in his shed! He let his head loll, closed his eyes and prepared to give up.

Chapter 22

'It's none of my business, but do you think it might be a good idea to split all that washing into two dryers?'

'Probably, but I've run out of change.'

'I've got change. How much do you need?'

'I can't take your money.'

'Borrow it, then.'

Tina looked at the man. Was he a perv? He didn't look like a perv; he had such a friendly face. But maybe some pervs didn't look like pervs.

'No, thanks. I'm fine.'

They were sitting at the dryer end of the launderette, staring at the clothes going round.

Joe said, 'Gary told me you were here. I was with him when you rang.'

'Oh?'

'Yes, we're good friends. I think he's told you about me?'

'Oh, he said he'd spoken to someone. That's you?'

'It's me. I know everything about what happened. I came around to the house when you were there. Gary asked me to check over the kitchen before the ambulance and police came.'

Tina looked at him, her eyes wide. Joe nodded.

He said, 'Come on, here's some change. You'll be here forever, otherwise.'

Tina stopped the dryer, pulled out half its contents and bundled them into the neighbouring machine. She took a fifty-pence coin from his outstretched palm and got the new one going, then restarted the original. She sat down next to Joe but not before waving cheerily to the group of muttering wrinklies at the far end.

Joe said, 'I hope you don't mind me appearing like that. I wanted to have a word with you, to introduce myself. You don't mind, do you?'

Tina looked into the man's face. He seemed genuine. In fact, she thought he looked really nice. There was something reassuring about him. 'No, I don't mind. Actually, it's good to have the company. I hate this place.'

'Gary told me that you haven't heard anything from the police.'

Tina shook her head.

'Nor me.'

They sat in silence. Tina wanted to say something but wasn't sure what. Joe was a few inches away from her on the plastic bench. He was still. She wondered what he was looking at, what he was thinking. She risked a glance: he was staring straight ahead at the dryer. She took the opportunity to get a better look. He had short, dark hair, almost like an army cut. He was big — well, not really big — strong. His face was tanned, as if he'd been on holiday. She looked at his hands; they were brown, too, and big, like her dad's. She wondered if this man had a daughter, too.

Joe said, 'By the way, that old git up there needs a good pasting. Well done, you!'

Tina laughed out loud. 'Yes, you're right. Thank you, Joe.'

'I'm really sorry about what happened. Gary didn't go into detail, but I understand Mr Abbott was behaving extremely badly towards you. It must have been very frightening: being there when he got hit; then being with him when he died. Honestly, Tina, you've been through a terrible ordeal — really traumatic. Then, all this business with the police. How are you standing up to it?'

Tina had been watching the clothes and sheets go round and round. Joe's words were bringing tears to her eyes. She pulled a tissue from her pocket and blew her nose. She nodded, 'Yeah, it's been horrible. All of it.'

'Is there anyone at home looking after you?'

'My dad. He always looks after me. He's not very good at it but he does his best. It's just me and him.'

'Have you told him what happened?'

'God, no. He wouldn't be able to cope with it. He knows Brian died but that's all. My dad's really kind, but he's not very strong. Well, he is really strong, you know, at lifting things, that kind of thing. I mean, he's a bit, um — fragile.'

'You two look out for each other?'

'Yeah, we do.'

Joe nodded. He looked at Tina. He said, 'There's something I need to say. Gary told me that one of the police officers showed an interest in you yesterday. Is that right?'

She nodded.

Joe went on. 'The thing is, he may be really charming and kind, but he might be trying to catch you out. I know you've got your feet on the ground, but I think you ought to be wary. I hope you don't mind me saying that?'

Although she'd been flattered by the policeman asking her out, she had thought it was a bit funny. It was a pity in a way: he was good-looking and a much better catch than that shithead, Kevin Abbott. She felt grateful that this man was thinking of her safety. She said, 'I don't mind. You're probably right.'

Joe smiled. 'Good. I'd better be on my way. I'm supposed to be at work. Can I give you my phone number, just in case?'

'In case of what?'

'In case you need to call me.'

'About what?'

'Probably nothing, but in case there are any developments?'

'Oh, I see. Okay, have you got a pen?'

Joe wrote on a scrap of paper. He pressed it into her hand. 'It's been lovely meeting you. I don't know if we'll see each other again but I shall certainly remember you, especially your pugilistic skills!'

Tina wasn't sure what he was on about but knew he was being nice. She smiled and said, without thinking, 'Will you talk to my dad?'

'What about?'

'Oh, I think he could do with a friend. He's had a tough time. Would you mind?'

Joe said, 'I tell you what: why don't you mention the idea to him and let me know if he's interested? Is that fair enough?'

Tina put out her hand. 'Deal!'

She felt his fingers wrap around her hand: a crackle of static fizzed up her arm.

'Oh! Did you feel that?'

Joe laughed. 'I shouldn't have worn my nylon slippers! Hang on to this in case you need it. Bye, Tina. It's been fun.'

She watched him walk back through the Oldies. He stopped to shake hands with the crabby bastard and they shared a word or two. At the door, Joe turned and waved. Tina raised her hand and smiled, then saw that the old man and the two women were waving to him, too. She opened the other hand: he'd put a ten-pound note in it.

Chapter 23

Gary had watched Joe jog down the street. Although he wanted to see Tina, he thought that she would feel a lot more confident about everything if Joe, rather than he himself, spent a bit of time with her.

Joe had calmed Gary and his mum this morning. There was something about him that made everything seem manageable. He wished he could be more like Joe. Gary's trouble had often come from his temper: it invariably got the better of him and that was not helpful right now. He was sorry he'd lost it with Kev last night. He loved his brother, really. Sometimes, though, he was a complete prick. Last night was one of those times. He'd almost punched Derek, too. Gary didn't want his brothers lusting over Tina. What he wanted was for her to have a nice, kind boyfriend; someone decent and respectable. He wanted to be that person but knew, regrettably, that he was as much of a bastard as his brothers.

When he went back into the kitchen, his mum was putting papers into a bag. He said, 'I'm going into the garden for a bit. I need some fresh air.'

'Gary?'

He turned around.

'I think you're right,' his mum said. 'Joe is a good person. I think he's all right.'

'I agree, Mum. I know he's got form, but he'll look after us. The thing is, though, I don't think we should tell Derek and Kev about him. I dunno why; I think they might not... Anyway, what do you think?'

'You're right, love.' They nodded at each other.

Then Gary said, 'Do you know where the key to Dad's shed is?'

'No, why?'

'I've been thinking about him. I suppose I wanted to be close to him for a few minutes. I thought that being in his shed might bring back some memories, as it's where he went to be on his own. I thought it would be nice to be there with him. Do you mind?'

'I don't mind. But I would like to look in it myself. Do me a favour, Gary: can I do it first?'

'How will you get in?'

'I'll ask Derek to take the door off.'

'I can do that.'

Jenny turned to look at him, her face suddenly stern. 'No, I want to look around the shed first.'

Gary put his hands up. 'Okay, sorry.'

Jenny smiled. 'Don't be silly, there's no need to say sorry. I don't mind you looking around. I want to go first, that's all.' She went into the hall and put on her coat. 'I've got to go to the funeral people and sort out all the arrangements. I'll be back in an hour or so. What are you going to do?'

'Er, not sure. I'm thinking I might go to school.'

'Well, if you want to, then that's a good idea. Don't feel you have to, though.'

Gary waited until he saw her hurry up the street, then went out of the kitchen door and down the short concrete path to the brick-built shed at the bottom of the garden. He tried the handle — it was locked. This wasn't a surprise: his dad's shed was absolutely out of bounds to everyone. Gary clambered around the back of the shed, forcing his way into the thick laurel bush that pressed against the little window. He peered inside; it was almost pitch black. He could make out a workbench and some shelves. He thought about smashing the window. Too risky: he wasn't sure if he'd be able to fit through, even if he could open the window from the outside. He struggled back to the door and considered his options. He reckoned he could smash the lock and force his way in. Why would he do that? It was a shed, nothing special. Maybe he should leave it alone and get on with something else? No, his imagination had got hold of him: there was something urging him to do it and he had to get in there. He gripped the round handle hard, turned it and kicked at the door: nothing moved. He pressed his back to the rough wood, turned the handle again and this time smashed his heel against the bottom of the door. It shuddered in its frame but was never going to give.

Gary's mind was made up now. He walked over to the greenhouse. As far as he knew his dad had never grown anything in there — it was where he 'put stuff'. Gary looked around. There were bits of timber, old engine parts, empty bottles, broken deckchairs, a load of bricks, a plaster statue of some politician — was it Churchill? — his mum's old sewing machine, bike wheels and chains, and a ton of useless shit. Gary wondered why on earth his dad had bothered building a greenhouse: there wasn't even a plant pot in here. He picked up one of the bricks and forced his way back to the shed window. He hefted the brick, took a couple of practice swings then closed his eyes and whacked the brick against the glass. The brick bounced back. He knew he hadn't put enough effort into it: the thought of glass flying into his face had made him tentative. He went back to the greenhouse and pulled a rotting sack from under the timber. Repositioning himself by the window he gripped the brick hard, held the sacking against the glass and swung properly: there was a satisfying, dull breaking.

Gingerly, Gary put brick and sack down and inspected the damage. He was pleased: the glass had cracked through rather than shattered. He poked at it; a piece fell into the dim interior. Gently, he reached in and lifted the window catch. Gary guessed the window hadn't been opened for years and was going to be set in its frame. He picked up the sacking again and gripping the edge of the broken glass, he pulled. The glass came away, but the window didn't budge. He grasped the edge of the frame with the sacking and pulled hard; he felt it move slightly. Gary breathed slowly and evenly then, with a mighty effort, heaved. The window opened. He shot backwards into the tender arms of the laurel bush.

Catching his breath, Gary prepared for the bit he'd been dreading: squeezing headfirst into the shed. His own bulk and the laurel prevented light entering the window and he could see nothing beyond the cluttered worktop. He leaned in — at least he could get through — but he guessed he'd have to go full length and topple off the worktop onto — what? He'd got this far: he launched himself in, slithered across the worktop and crashed down.

For a few seconds, Gary lay still. His head was ringing from a solid hit, his arm was twisted against God-knew-what and his back was pressed up against something sharp. Slowly he dragged himself to his knees, then his feet. The first thing he noticed was the smell: it smelled of his dad. Years of cigarettes, oil and damp, dirty clothes filled the small space with such associations it was as if his dad had just walked in. For a moment Gary felt an overwhelming wave of sadness. He wanted his dad back, so he could say sorry; so his dad could say sorry. Gary shook his head. No, his dad had been a bad-tempered, violent man who hadn't given a shit about his wife, his sons or anyone else. Gary stretched out a bruised arm and ran his hand up and down the wall beside the locked door. His fingers found a switch. Light filled the little space at last. He looked around.

By the door was a splintered, old cabinet with fishing rods standing to attention. Gary remembered the one time he'd gone fishing with his dad: it had not gone well. Gary had tried to get the net under the large fish as his dad had brought it close to the dam wall. Gary hadn't quite got the angle right and the fish had taken the opportunity to wriggle free of its hook and escape to freedom.

'You total idiot, Gary! Jeez, you're a dozy tit. Bloody hell, that was a seriously, big carp and you've let it go. Come here, you little bleeder.'

Gary had been grabbed by his collar and flung into the lake. He could still feel the panic as he'd gone under, his feet taking an age to hit the sludgy lakebed. There had been a moment of horror at the thought of what might be down there waiting for him before he bent his knees and pushed back up. When he'd surfaced his dad was roaring with laughter.

'Bloody hell — it's Nessie! Where's my camera? Did you meet any other monsters down there?'

Gary had walked home on his own, vowing that one day he would kill his dad. Seeing the fishing rods now brought back that pledge. He hadn't really meant it then, but maybe his subconscious mind had absorbed it as a firm commitment.

On hooks on the wall opposite the rods were a rake, spade, garden fork, hoe, pickaxe. The shelves lining the wall behind the door were loaded with tobacco tins, cardboard boxes, string and wire, batteries, an old hurricane lamp, light bulbs. In the corner was a teetering tower of paint pots, and next to them, wellingtons and old walking boots. Hooped to the ceiling were landing- and keep-nets and tucked into the eaves were rod rests. The big, fishing umbrella his dad had bought last year hung from a nail in the wall.

The cause of the bump on his head was a steel box sticking out from under the workbench. Next to it was the old fishing umbrella, its snapped spokes pointing upwards. Gary looked at the scattered mess of stuff on the workbench. There was a vice at one end, a full ashtray, pencils, several cardboard boxes, torch, a toolbox. He opened one side of the toolbox — spanners, screwdrivers, pen knife, assorted screws and nails. Leaning against the wall under the spade and fork was a folding chair. Gary opened it up and sat down at the bench. He pulled over one of the cardboard boxes. Inside was a load of tattered girlie mags. Gary idly flicked through them. Suddenly aware that his dad must have done the same, he stuffed them back in the box and put the flaps back down hard. His mum probably knew about the porno: that was why she didn't want him rifling through the shed. He pulled the other boxes towards him. The first held hooks, tangles of line, split shot, a variety of spinners, treble hooks and colourful floats of all shapes and sizes. The other box was full of old cigarette cards, wads of Green Shield stamps, and half a dozen Green Shield books with the stamps stuck in.

Gary bent down to the steel box and tried to haul it out. Something was in the way. He got down on his haunches to free it; a bag of old sand was jamming it against the wall. He shoved the sand aside and eased the box out. It had a handle on its lid and a lockable catch holding it fast. He clicked the catch; it opened. Inside were more mags, match-day programmes, coupons, more cards, folded newspapers, and a bulky, brown envelope. Gary turned it over. There was nothing on either side. He slid out the contents — more photos, a letter, and a rolled-up tie. The first photo was a man staring unsmiling into the camera: it must be Gary's grandad. Gary wasn't sure if he could remember him. He knew, but not sure how, that he had been really frightened of him. The only thing he could remember was his grandad's voice: deep and harsh, like a bear. In the picture, he saw him as a younger man, dressed in a suit, white collar and the same tie as the one in the envelope. Gary looked at it now. He guessed it must be some kind of military tie. The other photos were of Grandad with Gary's dad, one with Grandad much younger, standing next to a tiny bird of a woman — was it his Nan? The others were of strangers, except the last: Gary's dad, his arm around Gary's mum, a scowling Grandad, a smiling young woman and a vicar. Gary examined his mum's face: she looked so pretty and innocent. Gary touched her face; he wished he could make it all better for her. Unfolding the letter, he read.

7th October
Brian
This is my last letter to you.
Thank you for your recent help. It's worked out nicely, everything's under control.
Now that Dad and Ray have gone, I can see no need for us to have further contact. We've got nothing in common. You can live your life how you want. Your way isn't my way and I want to get away from all the horrible memories.
I send best wishes to Jenny and the boys and hope that you all do okay.
Remember, this is my final word. I'm sure you understand.
Maureen

Underneath, scrawled in his dad's heavy hand…

Fuck off you bitch

Gary knew that he had a relative called Maureen. He had never given any thought to her. He'd wondered if she was a distant cousin of his mum or dad but never bothered to find out. It now appeared that she was his aunt. Was she the young woman in the picture? He looked at her. She was jolly-looking, in a fatty kind of way. He could see a resemblance to his dad, but she looked happy: his dad, and his dad's dad, looked more like a couple of villains off the telly.

Gary scanned the shed again. There didn't seem anything worth investigating. It was dank, dirty and depressing. He put the envelope in his pocket, closed the steel box and shoved it back under the workbench. Carefully, he picked up the one piece of glass that had fallen into the shed and flicked it out into the laurel then, reaching across, pulled the window shut. Looking around one more time, he switched off the light, turned the latch, slipped out and shut the door behind him.

Chapter 24

Tina stumbled up the final flight, her lungs, as usual, burning. One of the bags of laundry had burst. Cursing, she put down the intact bags and hugged the split one to her chest. Somehow, she managed to fish her keys out of her pocket and struggle inside the flat. Whether it was her drive to get everything clean or her shortage of breath but, for the first time ever, she noticed the stench of the place. Opening the windows one by one, Tina wondered how their lives had become so seedy. Her dad was a respectable man. He'd had a good career in the army; he had done well in security. Her mum had been a really successful secretary — Tina remembered her beautiful clothes and glittering jewellery — and she'd always have money in her purse. Now, they were living in a dump, like trash. At least it looked cleaner after her morning's frenzied attack. She went into her bedroom. It was a hell of a lot better. But it was still really horrible. She pulled the bed away from the wall. Damp stained the yellowing paintwork. She sniffed the curtains, her nose wrinkling in disgust. God, no wonder Kevin Abbott treated her like a slut: she was one. Eyeing her from his normal place on her pillow, the giraffe tried to cheer her up.

'You're right,' Tina said, 'I know you are. We've made a start; I won't give up.'

Tina went back into the lounge and started pulling laundry out of the bags. She carefully folded each item and made neat piles. One of her dad's shirts was grubby. In her head, she told the old man in the launderette to piss off, all over again. She ran the hot water for a few seconds, wetted the kitchen cloth, dabbed it against the coal tar soap in its dish, then wiped the marks from the shirt. She held it up to the light; it was better, but she doubted it would pass her dad's critical eye. Still, everything else was clean, and now it was folded and put away. Time for a cuppa and a fag before Dad came home for dinner.

As the kettle heated up, she checked cupboards and the fridge. She wasn't going to be able to do a nice dinner like yesterday; there wasn't much she could do with a few cans, half a loaf of Mother's Pride and a block of cheddar. She went through the cans: tomato, mushroom, chicken soups; baked beans, three Ambrosia creamed rice puddings, a tin of custard and, because she'd always wanted to try Italian food, a can of ravioli. She looked at the label and wondered if Dad would like it. Wanting to make it like a proper Italian meal, she cut a lump of cheese, and in the absence of a grater, began to chop it into tiny pieces. The kettle boiled. Tina glanced at the kitchen clock — nearly half-past twelve. He was late. She made a pot of tea and laid the table.

Chapter 25

'...Happy birthday, dear Daniel! Happy birthday to you!'

There was cheerful laughter and applause.

'Blow out the candles,' Geraldine urged the tall young man, his face pink with embarrassment. He sucked in a long breath and blew ineffectually; half the candles remained lit.

James Dixon was scornful. 'Come on, you can do better than that.'

Daniel tried again; this time he made a better fist of it.

'What's it like to be twenty-two? It's so long ago, I've forgotten,' Geraldine said, standing inches from him.

She couldn't keep away from Daniel; there was something so sweet and innocent about him. Compared with cynical, jaded Edward, Daniel seemed eager for the world to be good, kind and decent. She touched his arm.

'Let me cut you a slice, Daniel. I promise you it's extremely moist.' She looked into his eyes as she positioned the knife before sliding it deep into the creamy depths. Daniel swallowed loudly and looked away.

Geraldine handed around cake and biscuits, basking in her colleagues' compliments.

'Mmm, Edward's a lucky chap, having you to make such delicious fare,' Jim Dixon said.

Geraldine nudged Daniel. 'Tasty?'

'Delicious, Geraldine. You have gone to a lot of trouble. Honestly, I wish you hadn't.'

'It was nothing. Anyway, I thought you looked as if you could do with fattening up a bit.' She rubbed her knuckles up and down his ribs. 'You're all skin and bone.'

Daniel blushed, 'Excuse me, I must catch up with Louise. I missed her this morning.'

Louise Ratcliffe had arrived. She was looking harassed, but smiled as she saw Daniel moving towards her. Geraldine knew that her own flirting with Daniel was ridiculous and that anyone watching must be cringing with embarrassment. Even the birthday cake was looking back at her, its expression disapproving. Geraldine gave it a ferocious glare, gathered up another slice and crammed it into her mouth. She looked around, ready to challenge any critical eye. Gazing over at Daniel, she saw him and Louise whispering. They looked very close. Never mind. She'd carry on with her fantasies; they were all she had to spice up her life.

'Have you got a second, Geraldine?'

She turned to the headmaster. 'Of course.'

'Bad news, I'm afraid. I've had Duncan, Ian and Philip back today. They said they'd been sworn at and chased by Terry. I don't want to believe them, but we have to take it seriously. What do you think?'

Geraldine was watching Daniel. He'd turned around to his desk and was bending over, writing something. She found herself licking her lips as the black nylon of his flares tightened over his neat buttocks. Louise, standing next to Daniel, looked across the room at her. The two women's eyes locked for a second. Then, feeling childish and, finally, embarrassed, Geraldine looked at Jim.

'Sorry, I was distracted for a minute. Well, you're right. We need to make sure we follow up the complaints. I've known Terry for years; his daughter used to be a pupil in my class. She was a terrible handful, especially when her mother, Terry's wife, ran off with another man. I think Terry is harmless but, to be on the safe side, I'll keep my eyes open. Now, time to get ready for my next class.' She started gathering up cake, biscuits, serviettes and tins. She felt a tall presence next to her.

'Thank you very much, Geraldine. It was so kind of you to make such an effort.'

She looked up into Daniel's shy, smiling face. It was more like an overgrown pupil's than a teacher's.

'You're very welcome, Daniel. You will let me know if I can ever do anything for you; you know, anything at all.'

She saw his eyes move over her face, then down to her straining buttons. Geraldine smiled.

Chapter 26

When Gary went back into the house, his mum was still out. He was glad; it gave him a chance to see if he could find any photo albums. He had a vague idea that there were some, somewhere, but he certainly hadn't seen any pictures recently.

Gary had never been bothered about family history. He knew that he had one, but for whatever reason, it wasn't something that interested him — until now. Seeing the photos in his dad's shed had made him wonder about the past. His dad had certainly never talked much about his own family, other than to go on about what a bastard his father had been. Gary couldn't remember anything about his dad's mother. He would ask his mum about them. He wondered if she had been in touch with Maureen. Would Maureen be upset by her brother's death?

There was a light knock on the front door. Gary's heart thumped: the cops? He sucked in a deep breath and opened the door a crack. It was Steve, Paul and Phil. They stood on the step looking unsure. Gary stared at them. Ever since their first day of primary school, they had been friends. They had had countless adventures together, most of them involving stupid, reckless acts that, at the time, were brilliant but now seemed childish and embarrassing.

'Watcha,' Gary said.

'Watcha,' Steve said.

Silence.

'Um, we heard about your dad,' Paul said.

'Yeah.'

Steve said, 'Thing is, we're sorry about — you know. That's it, really.'

'Ta.'

Paul said, 'Yeah, he was a brilliant bloke. We're really sorry and all that.'

Phil chipped in. 'Yeah, we was just saying, the last time we saw him was when he gave us a lift home. You know, that time he head-butted that arsehole up Theobald's Street.'

Gary said, 'Well, actually, that wasn't such a big joke after all.'

Steve said, 'Yeah, we know.'

Surprised, Gary looked at him.

'The Filth came to school today. We had to go into old Earnshaw's office and answer a load of questions. Honestly, Gaz, we had to tell them everything that happened. We didn't want to, but we had to. I'm sorry, mate.'

Phil was looking anxious, 'Yeah, we was going to get into all sorts of shit if we didn't tell them. Sorry, Gaz.'

The three friends were looking sheepish. Gary did his best to stay calm. He needed to know what the police had said but he didn't want to alert his friends.

He said, 'I guess they wanted to know about that night?'

Paul said, 'Yeah. We told them about your dad picking us up. We didn't say he was pissed or anything. I said the arsehole had been swearing at us, that he was really aggressive. I thought that would put the blame on him. What do you reckon?'

Steve said, 'I thought of saying something like that, but I wasn't sure.'

Gary didn't care what they said about that night. He wanted to know what else the police were after. He muttered, 'Who were they? Did they say their names?'

'Er, not sure. Why?'

'It doesn't matter.'

Steve said, 'The one doing the talking looked like Dickie Davies. The other one looked like a prick, all flashy. It was funny, he tried to light a fag but old Earnshaw told him to put his stinking cigarettes away. It was fucking hilarious.'

Gary didn't laugh. He was shit-scared of Dickie and Keegan. He said, 'Did they ask anything else?'

Paul said, 'They wanted to know if we ever visited your house.'

'What did you say?' Gary tried to stay casual.

'I said I'd been a few times.'

Steve chipped in, 'I told them I'd been plenty of times, over the years.'

'Anything else?' Gary said.

'They wanted to know if we ever saw your mum and dad having an argument or getting angry.'

Gary turned to Phil. 'And what did you say?'

Phil laughed. 'I said that I'd only ever seen your dad angry; that was what he was always like.'

Steve and Paul nervously laughed with him.

Gary said, 'It's all right. Thanks for telling me. I'm sorry, I should have let you know last night. It's all been fucking mental.'

Steve opened his mouth to say something then shut it. He looked at Phil and Paul. He plucked up his courage.

'What happened?'

Gary wanted them to go. Their stupid, nosey faces were getting on his tits.

He said, 'I don't really know. We think he fell over in the kitchen and bashed his head. He pegged it at hospital yesterday morning.'

'Shit!'

Phil smirked. 'You sure you didn't crack him one, Gaz?'

Gary's blood boiled over. He lunged towards his friend and grabbed him around the neck. 'You say that to anyone and I'll fucking kick your stupid, ugly face in.'

Steve and Paul dragged him away. Steve said, 'He was joking, Gaz. Leave him alone. He's a cretin, that's all. Come on, let him go.'

Gary allowed himself to be levered off Phil. He pulled himself together; this was not helpful. 'Sorry, Phil. I'm really sorry. This has all been a fucking nightmare. You lot are better leaving me on my own. Thanks for coming around. I'll see you soon, yeah?'

Looking nervously at him, the three edged away.

Gary stepped forward; they flinched. 'Listen, don't worry about me. I'm all right. It's my mum I'm worried about. You're better off leaving us alone for the time being. If anyone asks, just say my dad got drunk and bashed his head when he fell over. That's what we think happened.'

The three friends had backed out to the pavement. They nodded their understanding. Gary went back into the house and shut the door. He looked out from the window and saw them in a huddle. He wished he'd kept his temper: bloody typical! Only a few days before, he would have sought out Steve, Paul and Phil; well, Steve, anyway. Now, the only person he really wanted to talk to was Tina. He went into the hall and dialled her number.

'Hallo?'

'Er... It's me, Gary.'

'Oh, hallo.'

'You all right?'

'Ummm, sort of all right. You?'

'I'm all right. Well, sort of, I suppose. I don't know what I'm doing half the time. Thing is, I'm in a mad place. My dad is dead; that's bonkers. My mum killed him; that's double bonkers. We're in it up to our eyeballs with the police. I had a fight with Kev last night; he's never going to forget that. I keep thinking the police are going to arrest us any minute. I sort of miss my dad — sort of. But at the same time I'm really glad we've got rid of him. Then, well — you and my mum, and me… well, we've got a massive secret and I dunno how we're going to keep it. It's all fucking weird.'

'I think that about sums it all up.'

Gary was pleased to hear her smile. He said, 'Did Joe find you?'

'Oh, Gary, he's such a nice man. It's just as well he came along. I was in the middle of a punch-up with this horrible old man. Joe came in and broke it up. We sat by the dryers and had a chat. He's so calm and — well, I'm not sure really. He had all the old dears eating out of his hand. I really like him.'

'Did he say anything about anything?'

'Not really. He told me that we'd be all right and to keep in touch with him. He said I ought to — er, nothing much.'

'What? What were you going to say?'

Tina paused. 'Oh, it's nothing really. The thing is, he thinks I should be careful if I go out with that young copper.'

'Jeez, of course you should. Honestly, Tina, you're not going to, are you?'

'He's probably forgotten he even mentioned it.'

Gary doubted that very much. He was pretty sure the police hadn't finished with them. Also, Tina was a really pretty girl; sexy, too. He felt certain Keegan would try and get his end away.

He said, 'Well, Joe's right. Make sure you don't let him… just don't let him, that's all.'

'Don't worry. I'll be careful. I can handle blokes; I'm an expert. By the way, what was the fight with Kev about?'

Gary thought back to the incident. He was ashamed of himself. He said, 'It was nothing, as usual. He was saying stupid stuff and I lost my rag.'

'Was he being nasty about me?'

'Not really. The thing is, he thinks you and me, well — he thinks we're… you know.'

'Oh, well… ah. I see.'

'I told him there was nothing going on, but he won't let it go. In the end I walloped him.'

Tina laughed. 'Good. Thanks, Gary. You're my knight in shining armour, defending my honour. Not that there's much honour left.'

Gary felt his face flush. He saw his mum coming towards the front door. He said, 'Mum's back. Listen — keep in touch, won't you?'

'Yeah, I will. My dad should be home soon. Actually, I'm a bit worried about him. He should have been here ages ago. I hope he's all right.'

Gary thought back to Terry Castleton. He thought he'd be able to look after himself, a big lump like that. He said, 'Bye then. Look after yourself. I'm here if you need anything.'

'Thanks, Gary. You're such a nice bloke.'

Gary felt his heart flutter. He liked being a nice bloke. He went into the kitchen and put the kettle on. 'Want a cuppa, Mum?'

'Oh, lovely. Thanks, Gary.'

He watched her put some shopping away and then flop down at the table. She looked exhausted. The kettle boiled. He filled the pot and sat down opposite his mum.

'How did you get on at the funeral place?'

'It's all fixed. It's going to be a week tomorrow. We're going to have him buried at St Michael's.'

'Why? I don't think I ever saw him in a church in my life.'

Jenny Abbott took off her glasses and put her hands over her face. Through her fingers he heard her say, 'He might not be bothered, then or now, but if we want God to look after us, we should respect him a bit more than we've done in the past. Also, I think burial is always better than cremation.'

The words jolted Gary. He blinked back tears.

Jenny said, 'Nothing from the police?'

'Naa.'

Jenny took her hands away and looked at her son. She seemed to be weighing up something.

'What?' Gary said, nervous.

'No more fights with your brothers. We need to pull together right now.'

'Sorry, Mum. I'll be as good as gold from now on.'

She smiled at him. 'You're doing brilliantly. Please don't fight with your brothers, especially not Kev.'

She got up and poured the tea.

'Mum?'

She turned around.

'When did Grandad die?'

Jenny turned back to the mugs. 'Why?'

'I was thinking about who would come to the funeral. I couldn't think of anyone except us. Then, it occurred to me that I couldn't remember a funeral for Grandad. I know Nan died before I was born.'

Jenny said, 'There wasn't a funeral.'

'Why not?'

His mum was silent for a long time. She spooned sugar into the mugs, added milk and stirred. She sat down and pushed his mug towards him. 'Coz he disappeared. We don't know what happened to him.'

Gary stared at her. 'What do you mean, "disappeared"?'

Chapter 27

Tina finished the ravioli. She wondered what all the fuss was about — wasn't Italian food supposed to be delicious? What she'd had was slippery gunge; even the cheese hadn't helped. She should have had cheese on toast. That would have been much nicer: maybe the Italians should try it, then they'd realise how food was supposed to taste. Part of her was glad that her dad hadn't been forced to eat it. He obviously wasn't coming home for dinner today. Normally she'd be at school, so wasn't sure how often he stayed at work for dinner — maybe it was often? She realised that there must be stuff that she didn't know about her dad and his life, but she was pretty sure there wasn't much.

When Mum was with them, her dad had been livelier. He used to take her away on day trips to the seaside or off on camping weekends. They'd had real adventures together on their long walks: building camps, flushing out Germans, finding their way through the countryside without being observed. What she'd enjoyed most about those times was that it was just her and her dad. They'd been a team, a platoon. He taught her everything about being in the army and how to be the perfect soldier. The nights before their expeditions, they sat down together to plan where they would go. He got out the road atlas to show her the route they were going to take. Next, he would unroll a great big map of the area and run his pencil along the wiggling lines. He sometimes gave her the coordinates of their destination so that she could plan the route herself. She had learnt all the Ordnance Survey symbols and never had to check the key. Then discussions started about what would be in the rucksack: binoculars, camera, sandwiches (always Dairy Lea and cucumber), two Penguins, the flask of tea, a Pac-A-Mac for her, tobacco for him and, at least in the early days, her faithful giraffe.

When her mum left, her dad didn't take her on any more adventures. Instead, they moved into this crappy flat and festered. She'd discovered boys; that, at least, had got her out of the dump. Her dad? He'd become a recluse.

Tina looked at the clock again — twenty past one. He definitely wasn't coming home now. She hated it when he didn't behave as she expected. She started to worry about him, then she got scared.

Chapter 28

Gary stared at his mum. 'What do you mean disappeared?'

'What I say. He was living here, and he disappeared.'

'I don't remember any of this. Where was I?'

'You were only a little boy, maybe three or four. Um… let me think; it was 1963, I think. You were staying with Maureen. Grandad was living with us; he had Derek's room.'

Gary couldn't get his head around what she was saying. 'But, disappeared?'

'Oh, it's all so long ago, love. He was with us for a few weeks. He went out one day and never came back. We don't know what happened. We looked for him. The police looked for him. He just disappeared.'

'So, maybe he's still alive?'

His mum looked at him. 'Maybe he is. We don't know. We never heard anything about him, ever again.'

Gary racked his brain. His recollection of his Grandad was so hazy he couldn't pinpoint any detail, other than that frightening voice. He certainly couldn't remember ever staying at Maureen's house. He didn't even recognise the woman in the photograph. He said, 'Why don't we ever see Maureen? What happened to her?'

'She didn't get on with Dad. He didn't get on with her. They had a big bust-up. I think she blamed Brian for what happened to Grandad. I spoke to her yesterday, to tell her about — you know.'

'What did she say?'

'Well, put it this way, she said she was sorry but… you know… She didn't sound it.'

'Is she married? Does she have children? Do I have cousins? Blimey, Mum, there's so much I don't know! Where does she live? Honestly, this is doing my head in.'

'I don't think she's married now. She was, but I think she split up with Ray. There weren't any children. She lives in a place called Totteridge.'

Gary pictured the woman in the photograph. Had he really stayed with her? Then he thought about the grim-faced, old bloke. 'You must have had an idea of what happened to him? People don't disappear.'

She took her glasses off again. 'Listen, Gary, there was some talk about him being involved with some dodgy types. I don't know any details, but Dad always told me not to ask any questions.'

'Have we got any photos of him? Of Nan? I mean, there must be pictures of them? There must be pictures of Dad when he was a kid?'

She shook her head. 'I'm sorry, love. Dad got rid of all our photographs. I used to have albums but they accidentally got thrown on to the fire one night. I think you can probably guess what happened?'

'Dad pissed?' She nodded. 'What was he like?'

'Grandad?'

'Yeah.'

'To be honest, I was frightened of him. He made everyone nervous. He could lose his temper, out of the blue. Even Dad kept out of his way when he was in one of his moods.'

Gary thought about the pretty, young woman in the photograph. 'I'm sorry, Mum. Your luck ran out when you got caught up with the Abbotts: jeez!'

'Hmm. Well, I have to admit my mum and dad weren't too pleased. It's not all been bad, though. I've got three lovely boys, haven't I?'

Gary laughed out loud. 'Lovely! You've got three absolute thick, ugly shitheads. Mum, you need to take a look at your life. You married a violent bastard. Your father-in-law was a violent bastard. Your sons are violent bastards. Your sister-in-law refused to have anything to do with us. Your own parents didn't want you to get married into the family from hell. Not too bad!'

She smiled. Gary saw the pretty young woman again. She said, 'Well, if you put it like that — maybe things haven't been perfect.'

Gary smiled, too. He was going to make sure that his mum's life started to pick up — from now on.

Chapter 29

Tina was at a loose end, now. She knew herself well enough to realise that being unoccupied was not good for her. She thought about going into school, but only briefly. Although she hadn't exactly left school, no one there was missing her. Some girls in her class were working hard for the exams, but they weren't close pals. Some of the others had stopped going altogether.

Tina wasn't a model student. She wasn't hopeless by any means, just unbelievably lazy. Was that fair? Perhaps it wasn't laziness; maybe she had a very low boredom threshold. She could easily drift off for a double lesson and not even realise that it had come to an end. She had been one of the best at primary school: very competitive, always anxious to impress her teachers. The day her mum left put an end to any interest in doing well at school.

Tina allowed herself to think about her life with her mother. All her friends had loved Tina's mum. Why wouldn't they? She was young, incredibly beautiful and the most fashionable woman they had ever seen. Tina basked in the reflected glory. Tina's friends would beg to come to her house to play: they wanted to dress up, be a model, learn how to put on makeup.

'You need to look a million dollars,' Diane told her rapt audience. 'That way you'll have your pick of the boys, get a rich husband and live happily ever after!'

Although she had loved having such a glamorous mother, after her mum left, it didn't take Tina long to realise it was her dad who meant everything to her. When he'd begun to cry in the street — despite her own shock at hearing the news — it had been her dad's despair which had at first frightened her, then made up her mind: she was going to look after him.

In the early days, Tina used to wonder where her mum was. She'd known about a man at her mum's work, Ronald Simpson, and knew now that they had shacked up together. That was all, though. Perhaps she should have made some effort to try and find her, but Tina really wasn't interested. If her mum didn't love them, then she wasn't wanted. It was that simple. Also, to have hurt her dad so much was more than enough for Tina to hate her. When her mum had done the runner, the damage to her dad had been instant. He'd gone from a recently serving soldier — big, forceful and impressive — to a doddery old man who wouldn't say boo to a goose.

At secondary school, Tina had, without realising how or why, become a loner. She put on a lot of weight, was spotty and, according to the other girls, 'stank'. The girls steered clear of her; the boys called her 'Fat Arse'. She ignored them all. She and her dad looked after each other and that was all that mattered. Then, as her dad had always predicted, she started to change. As she grew taller, her weight was redistributed, to the great interest and admiration of boys. Her complexion cleared and her hair went from lank and greasy to long, lustrous honey. Suddenly the girls wanted to be her friend again; the boys couldn't leave her alone. Tina enjoyed their attention. It hadn't taken her long to get a reputation for being 'easy'. She lost her virginity when she was fourteen, and since then, had had sex with more boys than she could easily remember. She craved being wanted but, somehow, far from bringing contentment, the sex always left her feeling cheap and grubby.

Kevin Abbott was the most recent in a line of older boys. She had assumed that greater maturity would bring something extra: kindness, consideration, respect. She'd been wrong about that. The only thing any of them had wanted from her was sex and the more she gave them, the less she enjoyed it. She liked to please boys, but it was becoming clear to her that what was more important than anything was to have people's respect. This realisation was very new. Quite how she was going to gain that respect was, as yet, beyond her. She did know that flying off the handle, or jumping into bed (or for that matter, into the backs of cars or behind bus shelters) with boys, were not the most effective strategies.

Groaning out loud, Tina thought back to the time she and Kev had got off. It had been a disco at The Lair on the last night of school before Christmas. She'd got a bit pissed on vodka before getting there and had decided that she was not going to leave until she'd pulled.

'Cor! He's nice,' said Carolyn Jack, Tina's pulling partner, pointing.

Tina looked across at the new arrival. He did look pretty tasty, with his slicked-back hair and centre parting, his leather jacket open to reveal wide-collared shirt in vivid green, and gold medallion. His flares completely covered his shoes but, as he walked, she saw the massive two-tone, crepe wedges. 'He's mine,' Tina announced and started towards him.

Carolyn tutted, her voice just audible over Patti LaBelle, *Voulez-vous coucher avec moi?* 'You bitch! How come you always get in first?'

Tina turned around and smiled. 'Coz I give them what they want. It's pretty simple.'

She wiggled and wobbled around Kev who, much to her delight, was a fantastic dancer. He went through all his moves, clearly keen to show off to anyone watching. It quickly became clear that he'd clocked Tina and very soon they were dancing together.

When the music became slower, Tina said, 'Watcha.'

'Watcha.'

'You with someone?'

'Might be.'

'Well, are you?'

'Well, it depends.'

Tina wasn't going to be pissed around, 'You've got five seconds, mate — you with someone or not?'

'Nope. Why?'

'Well, you look like the kind of bloke that I might want to be with, if you're lucky.'

10CC's *I'm Not in Love* started up, and Tina pressed herself against him. 'I love this song.'

Five minutes later they were outside, Kev's hands all over her; hers all over him. In another five, she was on the back of his bike speeding out of town. She yelled, 'Where are we going?'

'The Ritz.'

She hugged him tight to her, as they roared along the quiet lanes. Reaching around his waist she ran her hand up and down his thigh. He turned his head and shouted, 'This is your lucky night!'

Ten minutes later, she got to her feet and dusted off whatever grub had been on the floor. Kev sat on the edge of the petrol lawnmower and lit a fag. The shed in the cricket ground wasn't quite how she'd imagined the Ritz; the few seconds of urgent thrusting hardly lived up to his romantic claim. However, from that evening, his attentions were persistent, and she couldn't find a nice way of giving him the elbow; not until the other night.

Images of Brian Abbott's assault on her two nights ago flashed into Tina's head. Had she brought it on herself? There she'd been, tight top, short skirt, best make-up, giggling at his innuendos. She knew the kind of man he was: what did she expect? She enjoyed the attention she attracted — it made her feel wanted, even needed. What she hadn't imagined was how it would feel to be forced, overpowered, powerless. Now the horror and panic engulfed her again. She wrapped her arms around herself and, burying her face in the crook of her arms, allowed herself to let go. As the racking sobs subsided, she felt Gary's arms around her as they stood in the dark, hospital car park. That had been what she wanted: someone to protect her and comfort her.

Chapter 30

Gary was nervy. His head was beginning to feel as if it might burst. The pressure was unbelievable. He needed to do something, anything.

The worry about the police turning up and pulling their story apart was a fear that wouldn't go away. He was pretty sure Tina was going to fall into the trap Dickie and Keegan were setting. Even if it wasn't a trap, the chances were that Keegan would get his sleazy hands on her. His mum was so tired she looked like she was going to collapse any minute. All that stuff about his Grandad added another layer of total madness to his life. People didn't disappear, did they?

His mum had told him to stop asking questions. He said he would, but he couldn't get it out of his head. It was the envelope in his dad's shed that had him so intrigued. Why had he kept the photos? Maureen's letter? The tie? His dad was not the kind of bloke to keep stuff for sentimental reasons. Well, Gary didn't think he was but maybe he didn't know him as well as he thought.

After his mum had clammed up, Gary had gone out for a walk. He didn't have anywhere to go, so he slouched around the local streets. He wondered whether Joe had heard anything from the police and altered his meandering course. Perhaps he was at The Beeches?

Gary stood and watched Joe weeding. What was it about this bloke that made life feel so much calmer? Joe looked up and smiled, 'Ah, the man of the moment.'

'Watcha.' Gary suddenly felt a bit shy.

Joe said, 'Are you going to make me sit down and have a chat for a few minutes?'

'If you've got time?'

Joe stood up and walked towards one of the benches. Gary followed.

'So, Gary, tell me your news.'

'There's nothing to tell. I was wondering if you've heard from the police?'

Joe shook his head. 'You?'

'Nothing. Do you think that's a good thing?'

'I wish I knew. What time did your father die?'

'Er, I'm not sure. About six a.m., I think.'

'Okay, so there's been a day and a half to do the post-mortem. I would have thought we might have heard from them by now, especially if they're suspicious.'

Gary said, 'Are you worried?'

'I am. I want this thing to blow over.'

Gary pulled out his packet of Number 6 cigarettes and lit one. He said, 'Can I ask you a question?'

'Of course.'

'I'm worried about Tina. I think she's going to get into trouble with the cops. Did you talk to her about that?'

'I did. Don't worry, Gary. She's going to be fine. I'm very confident in her. She's got a bit of a temper, though!'

Gary nodded, smiling. 'There's something else.' Joe looked at him, alert. 'How can I find out about a missing person?'

'Who's missing?'

'My grandad. I thought he was dead, but my mum said he disappeared years ago, before I can remember him. He was staying at our house and disappeared.'

'Blimey! Why don't you ask your mum to tell you?'

'I did. She doesn't know what happened.'

'Well, you could go and talk to your nice new friends in the police?' Gary snorted. 'Or, how about a chat with the local newspaper? Did your mum say if it was in the public domain?'

'Nah, she didn't say. You think it might have been in the newspaper?'

'Maybe. Is it worth a phone call?'

Gary liked the idea. He'd gone to the newspaper office a few days ago. There was something exciting about it. Walking by, as he had almost every day, it had looked like any boring office. When he'd gone in with Frank, he had been drawn to the reporters, that pretty girl on reception, felt a buzz of energy — it had thrilled him. 'Thanks, I'll go down there now.'

'Keep in touch, won't you?'

Gary stood up and stuck out his hand. Joe shook it hard. He said, 'We'll be all right. I reckon things are going to work out.'

Gary felt much better. He liked being with Joe: he made life simple. He said, 'Have you got any qualifications, Joe?'

'Well, not really. I learned loads of skills in the Army. I did pretty well in insurance. Then I had my bit of trouble and spent a few years in top quality hotels, as you know. I did learn plenty in prison and must have read thousands of books. Why do you ask?'

Gary had grown up believing he was thick, but the last few days with Anthony, Frank and the Walkers had made him realise that he was ignorant, as well. He'd always thought that to rebel against the establishment, and education in particular, was what he ought to do. It was becoming clear to him that he'd thrown away his chances of getting anywhere in life. Maybe he could catch up?

He said, 'Oh, I dunno. I've been thinking that I could learn to do something; maybe go to college or something. I've left it too late to get any CSEs. Exams start after Easter and I've done eff-all work so there's no point in even trying, is there?'

Gary was embarrassed. Who did he sound like? Would Joe laugh at him? He glanced at him; Joe was looking off into the distance. He wasn't laughing.

Joe was silent for a long time. Gary wondered if he'd heard the question. He wasn't sure whether to leave it or ask again. Finally, he wiped his face, opened his mouth to say something — he wasn't sure what — when Joe looked straight into his eyes and said, 'I think you are a clever, strong and resourceful man; you can do anything you like. But don't worry about other people's opinions. What do you think, Gary?'

Joe kept looking at him. Gary said, 'Er... well, I think you're right.'

Joe's expression relaxed. 'Good. We're in agreement then?'

'Yeah,' Gary nodded. 'Yes, we are.'

Joe said, 'Let's catch up later, or tomorrow? As soon as we have any more news.'

'Yep, sure.'

Gary felt Joe's hand on his shoulder. Then The Beeches' odd-job man was off back to his weeding.

Chapter 31

The ball crashing against the shed brought him to his senses. After the boys had gone back into class that morning, Terry had stayed slumped in his chair. Deep depression descended on him. He had so many jobs to do but could not summon up the energy. Gradually, his mind had become so frozen he must have fallen into a trance and then deep sleep. Well, the little shits had done him a favour on this occasion: it was high time he got home for dinner. Heaving himself to his feet, he carefully took off his smart jacket, hung it up and replaced it with his overall. He checked the time, blinked, then shook his head: twenty past two? Could that be right? He'd been comatose for at least three hours. He heard something outside the door: light footsteps, breathing, suppressed giggling. He called out, 'I can hear you. Clear off!'

'We can see you, Baldy.'

Terry tried to ignore them. They persisted, 'We can hear you.'

'Hop it.'

'What's he doing? Can you see?'

Terry heard jumping. 'Nah. The window's too high.'

'I think he's doing a poo again.'

'Yuk.'

'Are you doing a poo?'

'Get lost!'

Terry heard them walk around the back of the shed, evidently trying to gain a better vantage point. They banged on the wall as they went.

'He's not doing a poo.'

'How can you tell?'

'Coz he hasn't pulled the chain, idiot.'

'You're the idiot. He does it in a bucket and then takes it home with him.'

'Yuk, that's disgusting!'

They began to chant, 'Baldy's having a poo, Baldy's having a poo, Ee-Aye-Addy-Oh, Baldy's having a poo.'

Terry sat down in his chair and waited for them to stop. They didn't. Instead, they started the next verse as they danced around the shed. 'Baldy's eating his poo, Baldy's eating his poo, Ee-Aye-Addy-Oh, Baldy's eating his poo...'

Terry reached for his jacket. He heard and felt it tear as it caught on the nail. He pulled it over his head. Tears ran down his cheeks. It wasn't fair — why did he have to deal with this? All he wanted was an easy life. Why couldn't he be left alone?

Suddenly he couldn't control himself. His shoulders heaved as sobs overtook him. He felt his face contort with the agony of his life. The boys continued their chant but Terry couldn't hear them anymore. For some time, he had been worried that everything was going to end in disaster and now he realised, with dismay, that that moment had come. He knew Tina would be upset but she'd definitely be better without him, much better. The jacket over his head cut out the light but now all he could see was black. He tried to rouse himself — Tina might still need him; he had to be around for her, just in case. She wasn't ready to cope alone. It was too late; he could feel his heart hammering; he could hardly breathe. He wasn't breathing. He was shaking violently. He wanted Tina with him — how could he leave her? He felt the chill of dread: he was going. Terry tried to cry for help. He couldn't. He thought his heart was going to explode, was going to burst his chest wide open.

'No, no, please no... Tina... Please, no.'

No one heard him. He couldn't make a sound; he couldn't move a muscle. With a superhuman effort, Terry tried to heave some breath into his lungs. He thought he heard a distant grating noise — was he making it? Then came a monstrous *bang, bang, bang!* in his head. Maybe his head was going to explode before his heart had the chance? Unbidden, Diane's beautiful face was in front of him. He reached forward to touch her, to feel her hair, to hold her again in his arms. She reared back in horror, her face full of loathing. He tried to call her over, his silent voice pleading, desperate. She was backing away, shaking her head. Beside her were men, holding up wads of bank notes. One of them started laughing; they all joined in, voices coming from every angle. He was surrounded by scorn, by their utter contempt. Terry knew he couldn't fight them, had never been able to. The race to explode was won — he felt and heard a monumental crash in his head. Terry knew he was about to die. There was silence. He gave up the fight.

Chapter 32

Geraldine counted out thirty Alpha Beta maths textbooks and remembered the arithmetic lessons she'd had as a little girl. She had always operated on the principle that any child she taught would feel that she was on his or her side and not an enemy. She shuddered inwardly as she thought back to the dreaded Mr Carpenter: he'd been a brute and a bully. The staff room door opened, and Louise came in.

'Hello, Geraldine. How's it going?'

'Very well. Although I'm still regretting all that cake I had at lunch time.'

'Me too. It was scrummy, though.'

Geraldine wondered if she could broach her favourite subject. She looked over at Louise. She decided to risk it. 'Are you and Daniel an item?'

Louise looked sharply at her. 'No, why? What makes you think we are?'

Geraldine shook her head. 'Oh, I thought you two looked very pally earlier. I'm sorry, I didn't mean to be so personal.'

'No, he's a nice bloke but I've got a boyfriend.'

'Sorry, Louise. Please accept my apologies.'

'Of course.'

Geraldine looked away, embarrassed. It was none of her business to whom Louise and Daniel were romantically attached. It was just that, if Daniel were unattached, she could continue to dream. She felt her colleague's eyes on her.

Louise said, 'He is good-looking, though; I have to admit.'

Geraldine nodded enthusiastically. 'Yes. Oh, he is.'

Louise said, 'I think I might see if I can't tempt him in my direction; you know, for a laugh?'

Geraldine felt her blood boil. Louise was young, slim and pretty; she was going to snatch her Daniel away from her.

'Oh, Geraldine, you're so easy to tease,' Louise laughed. 'Of course I won't. I don't want to be a party-pooper, but I think he's got a girlfriend already.'

'Oh. Oh well. Probably just as well. Anyway, I am a happily married woman. That's what I'm supposed to say, isn't it?'

'Not true, then?'

Geraldine had had no intention of sharing her private life with anyone, but Louise was such a sweetie she couldn't help herself blurting it out, 'Oh, I suppose we're all right, but we've become so staid and boring. I know Edward thinks I'm a good wife. You know: meals on tables, clean clothes in wardrobes, dust-free carpets. I know that he provides money for all our luxuries — holidays, good car, all mod cons. But I think he's an intolerant know-all who's become so cold he's almost reptilian. He thinks I'm fat, naïve and an embarrassment in public. I imagine we've successfully entered the middle-aged-couple club. We've met all the eligibility criteria.'

'Oh, I'm sorry. It's up to him what he thinks, but you're certainly not fat, you're not really naïve and, apart from when Daniel's around, you're definitely not embarrassing.'

Geraldine laughed. 'Oh, Louise, that's not really a ringing endorsement! I'm so sorry. What must you think of me?'

'You're a really lovely person, Geraldine. I think you're wonderful and so does everyone else.'

Geraldine smiled wanly. 'Thanks, Louise. The thing is, though, I don't want to be 'nice'. I want to be sexy again. You know — to turn heads like you do.'

'You're very attractive still. I think you probably underestimate your pulling power.'

'Thank you! You are a dear girl, even if you do tell porkies. By the way, did you see the box Terry left for you?' Geraldine pointed towards the pigeonholes. As she thought of that morning's chat with Terry, she remembered that Jim had asked her to follow up the boys' complaints. She looked at her watch: five minutes until the last lesson. 'Excuse me, Louise. Thanks for the chat. Sorry to be such a drama queen. Or — more like it — love-struck teenager!'

Louise was opening the box. 'Oh, blimey! I was going to have a chat with Terry this morning. Flip, he'll be furious with me. I forgot to tell him about my doctor's appointment. Do you know his daughter? He said he wanted to talk to me about her.'

Geraldine smiled. 'Oh, yes, Tina and I had a few run-ins when she was here. I suppose she must be leaving secondary school soon. Poor Terry, he'll have his work cut out there, that's for sure.'

Louise was gently lifting out the Action Man. 'Ah, look! Terry's fixed him up. He's got a neck brace, his leg's fixed, and he's even got bandages.' She brought the figure to her nose. 'There's not a whiff of the trenches at all. Terry's such a kind bloke. I feel a bit sorry for him; there's something terribly sad about him.'

Geraldine nodded and walked down the main corridor to the door to the playground and field. The three boys were little tinkers and of the type likely to make up stories. Nevertheless, the fact that the parents had got in touch did give the allegations a little more credibility. She scanned the groups of children as she marched towards Terry's shed: no sign of the boys. She stepped on to grass. Fifty yards away she heard singing and then the boys popped out from behind the shed. They were throwing a ball to each other as they paraded around, chanting as they went. They were oblivious to her quickening steps. She watched them go around the back of the shed again, singing 'He's washing his face in poo, he's washing his face in poo, Ee-Aye-Addy-Oh, he's washing his face in poo.'

As they re-emerged, Philip Cox drop-kicked the ball hard against the wooden wall. He looked up at her, as did Duncan Barr and Howard Sadler. They stood there dumbly.

Very quietly, Geraldine said, 'Go and sit outside Mr Dixon's office. I shall be with you shortly.'

They scuttled back to the school building in silence.

Geraldine went to the shed door and tapped quietly. She gingerly opened it and looked in. Terry's body was crumpled on the floor. His smart jacket was partially covering his ashen face. She knelt down to him.

'Terry, can you hear me? Are you all right? Terry? Terry... Oh, Terry, please be all right!'

Geraldine began to cry as she felt for his pulse.

Chapter 33

'Terry, can you hear me? Come on, Terry! Come back to us.'

He didn't recognise the voice. Was it Diane's? It was a lovely, kind voice.

'You're going to be all right, Terry. Open your eyes when you're ready.'

He felt a hand on his. It moved to his face, stroking, soothing. He tried to open his eyes; they wouldn't obey him.

'If you can hear me, grip my hand.'

He felt the lovely hand on his again. Was it really there? Maybe it was a dream? He gripped it as tightly as he could.

'Ow, gosh. Good boy. I'll wait here for a minute while you get your strength back. You've had a terrible shock. Take your time, there's a good lad.'

Terry knew he was alive but did wonder, for a split-second, if he might have gone to heaven.

'I'll sort out those little stinkers. I'm so sorry you had to put up with their nasty game. You're all right now, Terry, dear. I'll look after you.'

Terry recognised Mrs Dutton's voice now. He thought he was probably strong enough to open his eyes, even to get up, but right now everything seemed too much effort.

'Do you think you can say anything, Terry?'

Terry did want to say something but couldn't think what. He made himself speak, 'I'm so sorry.'

'Why are you sorry?'

'I'm a total failure.'

'Oh, you dear man. You're not a failure. You're wonderful. Come on, chin up. Let's see the real Terry Castleton.'

He opened his eyes at last. Geraldine Dutton was staring at him. Her face, full of concern, was the kindest he'd ever seen. He felt tears spring into his eyes again.

'Oh, Terry, I'm so sorry. You've had a terrible time, haven't you? You stay still for a few more minutes. Take your time.'

Terry closed his eyes again. Was he all right? He was beginning to feel a bit foolish, lying here like some kind of — what? He was a grown man — capable, experienced. He was ex-military, for God's sake! Pride was getting the better of him now. He made an effort to get into a sitting position.

Geraldine smiled encouragingly. 'Come on. Let me help you up.'

He felt her grip on his hand tighten as she began to pull him up. Something small and hard hit him in the face. Then he heard several small skitterings as others similar flew around him.

'Oh! Gosh! Yikes! Oh no!'

Terry sat up quickly. What on earth was going on? Mrs Dutton had let go of him. She was desperately trying to gather up something from the floor whilst holding her blouse together. She lunged over him to reach whatever it was she was after and let go of her blouse, revealing a creamy bust, only vaguely restrained by a lacy bra.

'Oh, Terry, I'm — oh, blast! What must you think? How embarrassing!'

Galvanised by her distress, Terry found his strength and long-lost operational skills. He struggled to his feet, picked up his jacket and holding it in front of his face said, 'Here you are. Put this on.'

Mrs Dutton stood up, turned her back to him and slipped her arms into the sleeves. She shrugged the jacket on properly, did it up and turned to face him. Although red-faced, she was smiling broadly. 'Oh, my goodness! What a performance. What must you think of me?'

Terry stood back and examined her. 'I think you'll pass muster. Nothing untoward showing. In fact, I think you look rather stylish.'

They stood and stared at each other, uncertain. Terry wanted to hug this woman, to let her know that he thought she was an angel. He realised that she must feel extremely awkward and probably wanted to get away from there as soon as possible. He cleared his throat.

She said, 'I thought for a minute you were — I was so frightened.'

'Me too. I thought I was a goner. I've been having a few funny turns recently but this one was — Phew! Blimey! — in a different league. Tina has been on at me to go and see a doctor but… Well, anyway: all's well now. Still, it scared me a bit. At least I now know what it must feel like to die and go to heaven.'

She laughed. 'I'm so sorry: you pull through, and then I do my best to finish you off once and for all.'

'Don't be silly. Anyway, shock tactics often work. Honestly, Mrs Dutton, you saved me. Thank you.'

'I don't suppose you've got a safety pin?'

Terry said, proud as punch, 'I'm ex-army; I've got everything you can ever need in an emergency situation. Now, let's see.'

He reached over to a ledge and picked up a Golden Virginia tin. Rattling it before opening, he nodded and flipped the lid off. 'Here you are, madam. Top-quality haberdashery at your disposal.'

He held the tin out for her to select a pin of her choice. She reached in and picked a sturdy one. 'Excuse me, I'll just adjust myself.'

She turned around, undid the jacket's buttons and pulled the two sides of her blouse together, fastening them with the pin. She straightened her back and lifted her head to test the security of the temporary adjustment. The pin held but the shirt didn't: it ripped noisily.

'Tarnation!'

'I'm really sorry. This is all my fault. I tell you what, why don't you wear my jacket for the rest of the day. Or, if you prefer, my standard-issue caretaker's overall is also available. What's it to be?'

Geraldine did up the jacket's buttons again and turned to face him. 'The jacket, I think. Do you really think it suits me?'

'You look like a film star, hmm, Elizabeth Taylor?'

They smiled at each other. She said, 'I must go and sort out one or two, or indeed three, disciplinary matters. I'll be back after class, just to make sure you're back to full strength.'

'No, please don't. I'm fine now. Your shock tactics have done the trick.'

They smiled again.

Terry said, hesitantly, 'Erm… I hope you don't mind but I think it might be a good idea to pull up your collar and lapels. You'll be a bit more covered up, if you see what I mean.'

Geraldine looked down and saw that the buttoned jacket was not doing its duty to full effect.

She followed Terry's advice. 'Thank you, Terry. You are a real gent. Now I'm off to see if Jim still has a cane available.'

Chapter 34

The last time Gary had been to the newspaper office, he'd been with Frank. He knew they hadn't made a very good impression. Frank had looked like death warmed up. No, he looked like death. Gary had remembered feeling totally stupid and was certain that the two women in reception thought he was thick as shit. The problem Gary had was that he was pretty sure he was even thicker than that. However, although he'd left the office with a big dent in his self-esteem, he had also come away excited. When he'd witnessed that reporter's triumph at getting an interview with someone down the film studios, Gary's imagination had flared: what must it be like to go and talk to famous people about… films? World championship fights? Cup finals? Robberies, or criminals getting sentenced — big stuff like that? Wouldn't it be incredible to write articles for national newspapers or even the telly? He knew that this paper was only a local one, but even so, he felt the rush of excitement again as he approached the door.

Remembering the previous visit, Gary stopped and got his glasses out. Before putting them on, he glanced up and down the street, in case someone saw him looking like a prick.

'Hello, you back again?'

Gary looked at the woman: yes, the same one as before. This time, though, the tasty girl wasn't here. Never mind. He was here for information. 'Er, yeah, hello again.'

'You look different. What have you done to yourself?'

'Nothing. You must be thinking of my friend.'

'No, I wouldn't forget him. You don't get many zombie giants in this place.'

Gary smiled. That was a pretty good description of Frank.

'Anyway, did you write your article?'

Gary remembered that he'd asked for advice on his article about Grace, the old lady in The Beeches for whom they were organising a hundredth-birthday party. 'Oh, yeah, thanks for your help with that.'

The woman was looking at him expectantly. Beyond her, he could see the main office, with half a dozen people at desks. Some were smoking, two were on the phone. Their desks were piled high with papers, pens, pencils, folders and lever-arch boxes. Every desk had an ash tray on it, some had more than one mug. In the far corner was a small, separate office with glass walls, within which a man in his thirties, smoking a fag, was talking to the tasty girl. Judging from his manner and dress, the man looked like he was in charge of the place. Gary liked his obvious air of authority. What struck him most, however, was that he was wearing glasses; a pair that looked remarkably like his own.

'This isn't a viewing gallery, you know!'

Gary started. 'Oh, sorry, I—'

The receptionist was looking amused at him. 'Yes?'

'Who's that bloke? In the office.'

She turned around to check, 'That's Rob. Rob Mitchum. Like the actor. He's our editor.'

Gary stared through the glass at him. Wow, did he look neat! And with a neat name, too. He shook himself out of his reverie.

He said, 'Sorry, um… I want to find out whether something was ever in the paper; something that happened years and years ago.'

'Do you remember what I said the other day? The Kipling poem?'

Gary smiled. 'Yeah: 'when' is 1963; 'who' is my dad's dad; 'where' is — well, he was living with us at the time; 'why' is because he disappeared; 'how' is, er — well, that's what I'm trying to find out.'

'Hmm, well… that's not exactly fine detail, but it's a start. Well done, so far. Would you like to talk to one of our reporters?'

Gary couldn't help himself grinning. 'Yeah, great! What about Robert Mitchum?'

She laughed. 'I was thinking more of Nigel. He's our crack reporter. Not.'

'Oh, thanks. He'll be fine.'

She called out. 'Nige, I've got an enquiry for you.'

A tall, skinny bloke in his early twenties got up and came over to the desk. He looked at Gary with interest.

'Yes, how can I help you?'

Gary didn't want to be an ordinary member of the public. He said, 'I've got a major story for you. I'll need to tell you in private.'

Nigel didn't look convinced, but asked, 'Eve, is the interview room free?'

Smiling, she said, 'Well, since you've obviously got a major scoop, I'll book it out for you.'

Nigel smiled back at her. He turned to Gary. 'Come on, then. Come through and spill the beans.'

He raised part of the reception desk to allow Gary in, leading him towards a door marked 'Interviews'. Gary followed, his eyes alive with interest and excitement.

Chapter 35

After Geraldine Dutton had left, Terry rolled himself a cigarette and tried to get his equilibrium back. He'd had a few spells recently, where his heart had almost drummed out of control, but today's experience was different. He had been certain that death had arrived. Halfway through his cigarette, he found himself gagging on the smoke he was inhaling. The thought of the tar filling his lungs and straining his heart, clogging them up, started the awful hammering all over again. He got to his feet, opened the shed door and flung the cigarette out into the nearby bushes. He turned back, picked up his pouch, papers and matches, balled them up in his fist and tossed them into the rubbish bin by the door. He had thought about giving up smoking for years but hadn't made any effort to do so; today's humiliating disintegration was his 'wake-up call'. He stood up straight, filled his lungs with clean air and decided to face the world afresh.

Terry looked around the school field to see what he could usefully do in the last hour; nothing caught his attention. He looked back towards the school: what was this? Walking towards him was Mr Dixon, preceded by three boys. Dixon called out, 'Ah, Mr Castleton — the very man we're looking for.'

Terry groaned under his breath: he could really do without any more contact with children. The small group came close and stopped.

'Mr Castleton, Philip, Ian and Duncan have come out to say something to you. Before they do, I would like to say sorry from the whole school for the wretched way you've been treated. I hope you can forgive us and give us a chance to put matters right?'

Terry nodded then looked at the three boys; they were examining, in fine detail, the ground in front of them.

Dixon said, 'Right, Philip: you first.'

The ginger-headed boy mumbled, 'Sorry.'

Dixon barked, 'Duncan?'

The tall, goofy one muttered, 'Sorry.'

'Ian?'

The chubby one whispered, 'Sorry.'

Dixon said, 'Hmm. Not exactly profuse are they, Mr Castleton?'

Terry nodded his agreement to this assessment. He said, 'Mr Dixon, may I make a request?'

'Certainly.'

Terry was sorely tempted to request permission to stick these little gits' heads in their own poo, Ee-Aye-Addy-Oh, but resisted. Instead, he said, 'Would it be reasonable to ask them to tell their parents what they've been doing?'

'That's an excellent question. Let's ask our friends; let's find out from them. Duncan — you first this time. What do you say? Mr Castleton will want to hear you properly this time.'

Duncan swallowed. He risked a quick look at Terry, then looked back at the ground.

'Duncan?' Dixon looked at him for a response.

Duncan's voice was tiny. 'Yes.'

'Yes, what?' The boys looked stricken. Terry couldn't bear it. 'No, it's all right. I've changed my mind. Can I ask for something else, Mr Dixon?'

'Absolutely.'

Terry had a tremendous yearning to be a kid again, to feel that innocence once more. The culprits' miserable predicament reminded him so much of himself and his childhood; he couldn't help being on their side. He said, 'I've got a few minutes free before the end of school. Would it be all right if Philip, Duncan, Ian and I had a game of football together?'

The four faces in front of him brightened in unison. Dixon shouted out, 'Great idea! Can I join in?'

Terry said, 'What about the whole class?'

'I'm not sure the girls will want to play football.'

Terry thought for a moment, then said 'Well, they can play if they want to or play whatever they want? We can call it the Castleton Hour; we can have it once every five years. It's for Mrs Dutton's class, as they're special. What do you think?'

Dixon smiled, 'I don't know. What do you say, boys?'

Ian, Philip and Duncan were looking more cheerful by the second; they were nodding enthusiastically.

Dixon, grinning, said, 'That's it, two teams. I'll be one captain; Terry, you be the other. Teams to line up in five minutes. Boys, you go off and tell Mrs Dutton that the quinquennial Castleton Hour is about to start.'

The boys sprinted off. Dixon put his hand out, 'Terry, I'm ashamed of myself. Please forgive me.'

Terry took the proffered hand. He looked Dixon squarely in the eye and said, 'You've made a very big mistake. You and your team are going to get one hell of a beating.'

They grinned at each other then turned to see a gaggle of excited children streaming past Geraldine Dutton and out onto the field.

Chapter 36

When the perpetrators of Terry's misery burst into Geraldine's classroom, their hysteria had been such that she thought Jim must have used the cane. Their grins soon put her right. When they began yelling that everyone had to go and play football, she felt just as eager to get out onto the field. The excited chatter, as she approached Jim and Terry, was deafening.

'QUIET!' Jim's bellow settled them down.

Geraldine looked at Terry: how was he doing? He was smiling broadly.

Jim called out, 'Right, I want two teams. Team one, captain Mr Castleton; team two, captain Mr Dixon. Anyone who doesn't want to play can play something else. That's right, isn't it, Mr Castleton?'

'Those are the rules.'

Dixon looked around, saw Geraldine, and said, 'The referee is Mrs Dutton. That's right, isn't it, Mr Castleton?'

Geraldine looked at Terry; his face was beaming. He called out, 'If that's all right with Mrs Dutton.'

Geraldine wanted to say that she didn't like football, nor did she know the rules, but Terry's face was so happy she cried out, 'You bet.'

She watched as the 'players' sorted themselves out into teams and took up their places around the pitch. Passing the goalposts on her way to the centre circle she read, etched in black felt tip against the white paint, 'Mr Dixon is a wanker,' and underneath in a different hand, 'And so is Mrs Dixon.' She made a mental note to ask Terry to remove the legend and also wondered whether Jim would be relieved that he hadn't been singled out. When she got to the middle, Jim had the ball and was doing some 'keepy-uppy'. She was impressed: he got up to eight before losing control.

Terry called out, 'Cor, you know what you're doing, Mr Dixon.'

Jim smiled, 'Well, I had a trial for Orient many years ago.'

Geraldine picked up the ball and put it on the centre spot. Suddenly unsure, she said, 'That is right, isn't it?'

Jim Dixon, Terry and most of the players laughed.

'What? Have I got it wrong?' Geraldine looked around for someone to help her out.

Terry said, 'Absolutely right, Mrs Dutton. So far you've got everything right. All you need to do now is blow for the start of the match.'

Jim said, 'Listen everyone, this match is the inaugural playing of the Castleton Cup. It won't happen again for another five years unless, of course, my team doesn't win. In which case we'll be playing tomorrow. What's the name of your team, Mr Castleton?'

Geraldine watched Terry turn around to consult his players, some of whom she saw were his persecutors of only minutes before.

Terry turned back to her, 'Referee, we're the Castleton Crackerjacks.'

As soon as he said it, everyone shouted, 'Crackerjack!'

Jim called out, 'Referee, we're the Dixon Dynamites.'

Still not quite sure what she was supposed to do, Geraldine called out, 'Okay, who goes first?'

Jim took out a coin, handed it to her and called, 'Tails'.

She flipped it high into the sky. All eyes watched it arc through the air and settle heads up. She called, 'Er, I think that means the Crackerjacks go first?'

Everyone shouted, 'CRACKERJACK!'

She was about to whistle when another class started coming out, followed by another. Soon the whole school was at the touchline. She looked over at Terry: he and Jim Dixon were laughing like two little boys.

She yelled, 'Ready, steady, go! Oh, sorry — um, is that right?'

Terry called, 'Put your lips together and blow.'

Her whistle, although feeble, was loud enough to be heard. Cheering started around the pitch as the ball disappeared into the thick of what she could only describe as a melee. For several seconds, Geraldine could see nothing but an unstructured brawl: twenty or so boys, maybe ten or twelve girls, a tall, slim, grey-haired headmaster and a heavy-set, bald caretaker. Slowly but surely order became established, and much to her astonishment, it came from Terry who seemed to have the ball glued to his foot. He was now wriggling through wave after wave of reckless tackles, including Jim Dixon's, and was fast approaching the Dynamites' goal. He reached the penalty box, stopped dead, dragged the ball back, changed direction so completely that he left the hapless defenders rushing towards the place he'd been about to be, then chipped the ball across for Philip Cox to head horribly wide. Philip turned to Terry and cried out in agony, 'Flip! Sorry, Mr Castleton!'

Geraldine looked across at Terry. He was bent double, hands on knees, his face beetroot red, and was sucking in great lungsful of air. He caught enough breath to shout, 'Don't worry, even Kevin Keegan misses sometimes.'

The match continued. Geraldine was relieved to see Terry replace seven-year-old Priscilla Bagnall in goal; his face had returned to its normal, far from healthy colour. Despite his evident lack of fitness, his goalkeeping was as good as his outfield play. Every time the ball came near, he was first to it, at one point, leaping high to punch a cross in spectacular fashion all the way back to the halfway line.

Jim Dixon called, 'Ref, can we have half-time now? We need a team talk.'

Geraldine whistled ineffectually, tried again, then cried with all her might, 'HALF TIME!'

The teams gathered around their captains.

'Oooh, wow! That's a snazzy jacket! Is it official referee issue?' Louise asked Geraldine as the latter mopped her face.

'Oh, do you like it? You don't want to know how I came to be wearing it. Suffice to say everyone would be getting an eyeful if it weren't for Terry's help.'

Louise peeped over the top button of the jacket. 'Crikey! What's been going on?'

Geraldine laughed. 'I said, don't ask.'

'He's brilliant at football; who would have guessed?'

They looked across at Terry, surrounded by at least twenty children. He was a different man: normally, Terry had a downcast air, moving with a listless manner, as if he could barely muster enough energy to get wherever he was going. Now, as he encouraged his troops, he was taller, more forceful, and clearly in charge. The 'Crackerjacks' were listening, nodding and obviously taking in whatever it was he was telling them. The 'Dynamites', to Jim Dixon's evident exasperation, were simply larking around.

'Do you want this?' Louise was holding out a whistle.

'Oh, thank you! At least I can make myself heard now.' Geraldine blew hard and called the teams to order. 'Are you ready for the second half? Wait — where are you all going?'

Louise said quietly, 'They change ends at half-time.'

'That's right. I do know about football, you know.' She blew again; the match restarted. Terry was reading the colourful description of Mr and Mrs Dixon on the upright; Jim spotted him and launched a long-range shot. It bounced uncontested past Terry.

'GOAL!' Jim Dixon went careering around the field, arms outstretched, chased by his teammates. Crestfallen, Terry looked at his Crackerjacks. 'I'm so sorry. Blast! A schoolboy error. Sorry, lads.'

Geraldine blew for the match to restart. Dixon got the ball again and tried for another lucky longshot. This time, Terry caught it, bounced it twice and launched a giant drop-kick over the head of Christine Jennings, the 'Dynamites' six-year-old goalie. The Crackerjacks mobbed their keeper/captain.

Geraldine blew for the restart. Fifteen minutes later, the match was still level. Terry called David Biggs over to go in goal, ran into the scrum of scuffling children, collected the ball, dribbled it into the penalty box and gently tapped it into the path of seven-year-old Sally Matthews. Sally, who, with her friend Patricia Whiting, had been re-enacting a scene from White Horses, was not aware that the match was in her grasp.

'SHOOT!' screamed her teammates.

The bobbling ball bounced off the little girl's shin into the path of Dixon who, having rushed back, sliced it clear. The ball, spinning wildly, ricocheted off Patricia's shoulder. Patricia, not used to the breathless excitement of top-level cup matches, went down like a lead balloon. The ball described an elegant parabola and looped past a bemused Christine Jennings — still furious at the drop kick that had evaded her despairing dive — into the far corner.

Geraldine blew for the goal and, on Louise's advice, for full time. The crowd went mad.

Jim Dixon went madder still, 'Handball! That's handball! Patricia handled that ball. It's a free kick to the Dynamites!'

Geraldine looked at Louise, 'What? I don't get it. What shall I do?'

'Stick to your guns. Shake your head, blow your whistle and say "well done"'.

Geraldine did as she was instructed and that was that.

Terry Castleton knelt down to the still-howling, injured player. 'Well done! You were amazing. Look, everyone's coming over to say well done.'

Patricia looked around: she was surrounded by beaming players.

'Well played, Mr Castleton,' Jim Dixon was begrudging in his congratulations.

'Yes, well done Terry! Well done the Crackerjacks!' Geraldine cheered along with everyone else.

Terry was flushed with the excitement of the match, and with his unaccustomed exertion. He said, 'Well done, lads and lasses. Well played, everyone.'

Geraldine, noticing that the cup-winning goal-scorer was struggling to come to terms with public acclaim and her glory, lifted her up as if she were the cup itself. Patricia, half crying, half smiling, was only now beginning to understand the impact of her brief intervention.

Terry said, 'What's your name?'

Geraldine came to the little girl's rescue. 'This is Patricia Whiting, isn't that right?'

Patricia nodded and sucked her thumb.

Terry said, 'You are a wonderful footballer, probably the best one in the whole match. You are a very special person.'

Uncertain, Patricia looked at him, then at Geraldine, who nodded her agreement.

Dixon came over again. 'Am I right in thinking you've played before, Terry?'

'Well, I didn't ever have a trial for Orient but — yes, I've played before.'

'I thought so. You tricked me, you scoundrel.'

Terry said, 'So — same time, same place, five years from now?'

'Definitely.' Dixon turned to Geraldine. 'Er, Mrs Dutton, you might want to think about checking your buttons?'

Everyone turned to see that the buttons of Terry's smart jacket had become unfastened as Geraldine had hoisted the soon-to-be legend to the skies.

Red-faced, she hastily attended to her frontage. 'Oh, golly! I think it may be time for us all to go home?'

Chapter 37

Nigel knocked on the interview room door. It opened and a shifty-looking, bearded man in his fifties came out.

'After you.' Nigel held the door for his guest.

Gary went in; it wasn't dissimilar to the interview room at the police station. This one had a square table upon which sat a vast, glass ashtray full to the brim with stubs, four unmatched chairs, a desk — one leg of which was propped on a sturdy, hard-back book — in the corner, shelves and shelves of paper, and an overwhelming smell of fart.

Nigel said, 'Blimey! Sorry about the... Want to take a seat?'

Gary sat down and wondered how long he'd be able to hold his breath.

Nigel said, 'Jeez, I'm tempted to light a match, just to see if it explodes!'

Gary's laugh was explosive. He found himself laughing hysterically. It had been a long time since he'd really let go. It felt wonderful. His laugh turned to wheezing giggles and before he could stop himself, he let one go. Nigel's laughter also turned into falsetto giggling.

The door opened. Rob Mitchum stood there.

'What on earth...? Fuck me! That's disgusting!' He backed out and slammed the door shut. Gary and Nigel heard him shout, 'Achtung! Achtung! Geiger counters, everyone. Nigel's pressed the red button.'

Gary wiped tears away with his sleeve. He was beginning to get his breath back. Nigel started wrestling with the window catch. Finally, he opened it: fresh air broke through the fug. 'Phew! That's a bit better.' He pulled out a packet of Piccadilly and offered it to Gary. 'Fag?'

'Ta.'

'Right. Now that we've gone through thick and thin together, how can I help you?'

Gary pulled himself together. This was important. 'Well, I want to find out about something that happened in 1963. I don't really know much about it and it's all a bit funny.'

Nigel had a pad open; his pen was poised. Gary really like the way he looked: attentive, alert.

Nigel asked, 'What date in 1963?'

Gary thought: the letter from Maureen had been dated 7th October, so it must be before then. How much before though? The events must have been fairly recent on that date, otherwise why had she written then? He said, 'I don't really know. Before 7th October. Probably quite near to that time.'

'What happened?'

'I don't really know that, either. All I know is that my Grandad was living with us, and he disappeared.'

'What's his name?'

'Abbott.'

'First names?'

Had Gary ever heard his Grandad's name? His father had always called him 'the old bastard'. Gary racked his brain, yet nothing came to him. 'Sorry, I don't know.'

'Where were you living?'

'Carlisle Road. We still do.'

'Who else was there?'

'My parents, two brothers.'

'How long had he been living with you?'

'I dunno. A few weeks, tops. I was only three. My brothers were five and eight.'

'What do your parents say happened?'

Gary swallowed. 'The thing is, my dad died a couple of days ago. My mum's upset and doesn't want to talk about the past — well, at least, not at the moment. I didn't know about Grandad disappearing until this morning when I found a letter from my aunt.'

Nigel looked at Gary closely. He said, 'I'm sorry to hear about your dad. Was he ill?'

Gary remembered that he needed to be on his guard, especially with a reporter. 'Not ill, he had a sudden accident.'

Nigel was studying Gary. He said, 'Accident?'

'Don't worry about him: what about my Grandad?'

'When you say disappeared, what do you mean?'

Gary was getting edgy. This wasn't quite what he'd been expecting. In fact, it was reminding him of his conversations with the Filth. 'I don't know; that's the point. My mum said that he'd disappeared. Apparently, he went out for a walk and never came home. I don't know any more than that; I wasn't around.'

'Where were you?'

'I was staying with my aunt.'

'Why do you think you were staying with your aunt? I would have thought it might be nice to have your Grandad staying with you?'

Gary had been wondering that. It was probably because his grandad had been a bastard, like his dad. 'Um, yeah. I dunno. We've only got a little house. Well, three bedrooms, but it's not a mansion.'

Nigel was writing stuff on his pad; Gary couldn't read it. He wished he hadn't mentioned his dad dying: that was making things more complicated.

Nigel said, 'Were the police involved?'

'In what?' Gary wanted to kick himself.

'When your Grandad disappeared: what else?'

'Sorry. Yeah, they looked for him. They couldn't find him.'

Nigel put his pad down. 'Hang on. I'm going to ask a colleague if he remembers anything about it.' He got up and went to the door. 'Alan, have you got a minute?'

Gary saw the bearded bloke get up and come over. Nigel said, 'Come in; it's safe, we've cleared the air.'

Alan came in, sat down and lit a fag. He looked at Gary, then at Nigel. Nigel looked at his notes. 'Gary has been asking if there was any coverage of his grandad's disappearance, sometime in 1963. His name was Abbott. We don't know his first name. Sound familiar?'

Nigel and Gary looked at Alan. The older man's eyes were shut, his brow furrowed in concentration. Unbelievably, he farted again. His eyes popped open, 'Flaming Nora! That's the last time I get a kebab from that shithole!'

Nigel got up and stood by the window. He said, 'It's not the kebab; it's the eight pints of Watneys you had before it. Anyway, never mind your effing insides, Alan. What about Gary's grandad?'

Alan said, 'Yep. We covered it. I can't remember the details. It was before Kennedy… Not long before though.'

Nigel said, 'Remember anything about it?'

Alan shut his eyes again, concentrating hard. Nigel said, 'Don't worry: I don't like the look of that expression. Come on, Gary! Let's get out of here before we die of asphyxiation.'

Gary scrambled to his feet and followed the reporter. They went out of a door marked 'Fire Exit'. Nigel was striding up the metal steps of a fire escape, two at a time. He shouldered open a door back into the building. Gary caught him up. They were in a dusty room, metal shelves lining the walls from floor

to ceiling. 'We've got back copies here going all the way to 1896. Now —
over here: sixty-five… sixty-four, here you go. 1963, bottom shelf.'

Gary bent down and saw a row of thick, cardboard folders with a year
printed on the spine of each. There were four for 1963. He looked up at Nigel,
'Can I look through?'

'Sure. I'll leave you to it. Come and see me when you're done. We're
closing up at five thirty; if you're not down by then, I'll come and find you.'

Gary said, 'Thanks! Brill!'

He waited for Nigel to leave, then got down on his knees and pulled out
the first of the '1963s'. He heaved it over to the table in the middle of the
room. Opening the cover, he saw that it contained the editions from January
through to the end of March. He put it back and pulled out the last of the four:
October to December. Gary sat on the office chair and lifted out the first
edition of October. As he turned the pages, an episode of Columbo popped
into his head: he'd watched, spellbound, as the shambling detective had,
within seconds, found the very piece of information he'd needed from a huge
stack of documents. It soon became clear to Gary that Columbo's search had
been assisted by fiction. His own would need to be far more painstaking.

Chapter 38

Terry got stiffly into his car. He generally found it difficult, but this time, for one moment, he thought he actually mightn't be able to manoeuvre his aching limbs behind the wheel. If his 'funny turn' had knocked the stuffing out of him, it was the football match that was now wreaking its revenge. He tried to remember when he'd last played: he couldn't. He and Tina had kicked a ball around their back garden when she was a toddler, and maybe he'd played some five-a-side soon after leaving the army, but that was it. He started up the Imp and was about to release the handbrake when Geraldine Dutton rushed out of the school. He wound down his window.

'Terry, don't forget your jacket.'

He smiled. 'Don't be silly. Hang on to it 'til tomorrow. You'll need it for — well, you need it more than I do.'

'Don't you mind? I was so silly this morning, coming out without a coat. I must give you your jacket; I feel bad hanging on to it.'

'It's fine. It looks much nicer on you than me. See you tomorrow.'

He let out the clutch and drove slowly down the approach road, away from the school. He looked at his watch — quarter past four. There should be enough time. He turned out on to the main road and thought back over the day. It had turned out to be one that he knew he'd never forget. The first half had been excruciating; the second, his best for years. Every single person on that field had smiled at him. Louise had hugged him and had shown everyone how he'd saved the Action Man. She'd then called over Stewart Dillon so that Terry could hand over the soldier: Stewart had been overjoyed to get him back. Jim Dixon had lifted Terry's arm and called for three cheers and teachers and children united in their acclaim for the caretaker many of them had never noticed. After the cheers had died down, Geraldine Dutton brought him out a monstrous slab of cake which, despite his determination to improve his health, he'd shovelled down his gullet at indecent speed. Now, he was edging his little car into a parking place outside the jewellers.

'Yes, sir, can I help you?'

Terry said, 'I'd like a cup or a shield for a school trophy. Have you got anything?'

The middle-aged woman unlocked a cabinet underneath the counter and brought out a variety of trophies in different shapes and sizes. Terry pointed at the classic, silver, FA Cup-shaped trophy.

'How much is that one?'

The woman looked at its base. '£14.99.'

'Hmm. And how much to engrave it?'

'Well, that depends on the number of words, and style.'

'It's for a school football cup. Give me a sec and I'll jot something down. Have you got a pen and paper?'

The assistant passed him over a pad and pen. He scratched his head: what should it say? He wrote, shook his head then, with more confidence, finished with a flourish. He handed pad and pen back.

The assistant read it. 'Hold on, I'll check with Mr Harrington.' She came back two minutes later. 'That would be £19.99 altogether.'

'Hmm. Okay. How long will it take?'

The woman called out, 'How long, Mr Harrington?'

Terry heard a grunted, 'I'll do it now.'

'Wonderful, do you mind if I sit down?'

Anxious, the woman assistant asked, 'Are you all right? You do look rather… are you in pain?'

Terry smiled. 'I am in pain, that's true! I've been playing football for the first time in years and — put it this way — I'm not First Division standard.'

'Please do sit down, before you fall down.'

They both laughed. Terry eased himself on to the straight-backed chair by the window. He wondered what he could buy Geraldine Dutton to say thank you. He wasn't sure now that he had been about to die. Nevertheless, she had helped him come round and then — the most important thing — had made the rest of the day possible. He scanned the cabinets: far too expensive and, in any event, it wasn't really appropriate to give a colleague jewellery. He would ask Tina for some ideas. A high-pitched whine came from behind the door at the back. He hoped they'd be pleased with him. Gingerly, he rubbed his shin: ouch. One of the little bleeders had kicked him bloody hard. He smiled to himself. It might have been Jim Dixon: 'competitive' didn't come close. He wondered how the little girl was doing. She hadn't stopped grizzling by the time everyone's mums had come to collect the children. On one occasion he'd picked up Tina from school, she'd been crying. The cause of her agony was John Blackley: he hadn't wanted to kiss her during kiss-chase!

Mr Harrington emerged from the backroom. He nodded at Terry then disappeared.

'Here you are, sir. That will be £19.99.'

Terry put his hand into his pocket: damn. His wallet was in his jacket. 'Oh, I'm so sorry. My wallet is — What a nuisance!' The assistant was looking at him; there was a funny expression on her face. He realised she must be wondering if he was up to something shifty. 'I'm so sorry. It's all right, I'm not — Anyway, can I come back tomorrow? I'll be back after twelve.'

She smiled. 'It's fine. Don't worry. I'll save it for you. I just hope no one else comes in and asks if we sell Castleton Cups!'

Terry smiled his thanks. She smiled back. For a second, he was lost for words; he wasn't used to attractive women smiling at him. He found some words.

'Er, you've been very helpful, thank you. I'll be sure to tell people about you... I mean, about Harringtons. You know — the shop.'

'Thank you! You're very welcome.'

As Terry drove away, he dared to think, just for one minute, that things might be all right, after all.

Chapter 39

Gary was now working back through September. To begin with, his heart had been thumping; he'd expected to find something immediately but he was starting to feel disheartened. He'd never bothered to read the local newspaper before. His mum always got it and he often found her going through it on a Thursday, when it came out. The only newspaper he ever looked at was the Sun and that was only when his dad brought it home from work. He'd check out page three, look at what was going to be on telly and read the sports news. Apart from that, he wasn't interested — not in the national news, and definitely not in what was going on in his own town. So he hadn't anticipated how easily he would become side-tracked by the exercise he was now undertaking. As he flicked to the last edition of August, he began to worry that he might have been so distracted by some of the other stories, he could have missed the very one he was looking for. He told himself to concentrate. Why was he bothered about a cricket match from thirteen years ago, anyway? Okay, the captain's wife had given birth to triplets the day before the match but so what? He carried on turning pages.

August 16th: 'Mayor's reception for racing driver, Graham Hill'; 'Colleagues killed in car crash'; 'MP says "no" to planned bypass'; 'Police bust brothel' and bottom right, in small type, 'War hero still missing'. Gary's heart jumped. He read on.

'Two weeks after his disappearance, army veteran and retired train driver, Bertram Abbott, who had been visiting his family in Carlisle Road, is still missing. Police are keen for anyone who may have seen the sixty-eight-year-old to come forward with any information. Mr Abbott, a tall and powerfully-built man with grey hair and moustache, has a strikingly deep voice and walks with a slight limp.'

Gary, his mind racing, skipped the contact details and hurriedly turned to the front page of 9th August: this time it was the main headline: 'War hero mystery continues'.

'Bertram Abbott, father and grandfather, hero of the First World War, is still missing. The 68-year-old army veteran, who had been visiting his family, disappeared over a week ago. The police are now asking for anyone who might have any information to come forward.'

Gary looked at the photograph next to the headline. It showed the hard face of his grandad in dark suit, white shirt and the tie Gary had found in the shed. He continued to read.

'Mr Abbott had been enjoying a few days' holiday with his son, Brian and his family, in Carlisle Road. Last week, Mr Abbott senior went out for his daily constitutional walk: he has not been seen since. Police are keen for anyone who might have come into contact with him, or who saw him over the last few days, to get in touch. The detective leading the investigation said, "We would like to hear from anyone who may have seen Mr Abbott on Wednesday 1st August and in the days leading up to that point. You may have valuable information that will help us establish the facts of his disappearance and current whereabouts."

'Bertram Abbott, who received a Military Cross for gallantry during active operations in the First World War, had a long and decorated career in the Royal Engineers. Mr Abbott saw active service again during the Second World War when he took up the duties of an ARP warden in Westminster. After the war he worked as a train driver for Southern Railways, before retiring in 1960. His son, Brian Abbott said, "I'm really worried about Dad. Although he's a tough man, he's got a heart of gold and I really can't bear to think of him in any sort of trouble. If anyone has seen him recently, please let the police know."

'…police have issued the following description: 6ft 1in, powerful build, short grey hair and moustache. Mr Abbott has a slight limp resulting from an injury during his time working on the railways.'

Gary quickly flicked through the issue to check if there was any other coverage: nothing. He went to Thursday, 2nd August. Nothing on the front page. Perhaps there hadn't been enough time to get it into this edition? Gary leafed through, just in case. He got to page seventeen.

'Visitor goes missing.

Bertram Abbott, a sixty-eight-year-old visitor from Lewisham, South London, went missing yesterday. Police contacted the paper just before it went to press and are asking local people to contact them if they saw anything unusual in and around Carlisle Road. The man is described as tall, heavily built, with grey hair and moustache.'

Gary sat back in his chair. He'd discovered what he was looking for but what had he found? It was what his mum had said: Grandad had disappeared. He was none the wiser. He had learned that grandad had been a soldier, was a war hero, lived in Lewisham and had a limp. He looked back at the three articles: something was there but he couldn't see it. He read through the stories again: still nothing. Maybe it was the photograph? Gary pulled out the envelope again and put the pictures of his grandad against the one in the paper. The old man looked like a right sod. It was his eyes: hard, critical. There was still something in the newspaper coverage that he couldn't put his finger on. Whatever it was it had given him the jitters. He looked at his watch — quarter-past five.

Dispirited, he shut the volume and pushed it back into its place on the shelf. He wondered if he could risk a fag before he went back downstairs. Looking around, he thought better of it: it was a bonfire waiting to happen. He thought about speaking to the old bloke, Alan. Maybe he'd remember a bit more about it. There must have been all sorts of investigations at the time, even if they weren't covered in the newspaper. He smiled again as he thought about the poor bloke's dodgy insides and the hysterical laughter of earlier. Then it clicked in his head. He bent down again, pulled out the bound copies and put them on the table. He rifled through to the last article and looked carefully — yes, there it was, underneath the photograph. He'd seen it, but it hadn't registered.

'If you have any information that might be helpful to the police, please contact Detective Inspector Flanagan on 953 5353.'

Dickie Davies' boss!

Chapter 40

Tina was woken by the sound of the key. She looked through the lounge doorway towards the front door.

'Dad, where have you been?'

Terry closed the door behind him.

She said again, irritation in her voice, 'Dad, where have you been?'

'Don't start, Tina.'

Tina said, 'What do you mean? You come in at five p.m. looking like death warmed up!' Both recognising the scene of yesterday morning, they smiled at each other. 'Seriously, Dad. Are you all right? You look like you've been hit by a bus.'

Terry filled the kettle and put it on. 'Honestly, I have had THE craziest day ever. It started off badly, got worse, then it all turned out like — well, lovely.'

'Flip! Let's have the goss.'

Terry told her everything, including the boys' song.

Tina laughed, 'You don't bring it home, do you?'

'You can laugh, mate. You should have seen me. I went down like a sack of potatoes.'

She looked at him. He had come into the lounge and was now slumped on the sofa, evidently exhausted.

'Actually, Dad, I've been a bit worried about you. I know you're big and strong and all that but do you need to see the doctor? I mean, I don't think you could play another game of football any time soon, could you?'

'Don't you worry about me. You're looking at the new, streamlined Terry Castleton. Plus, I've packed up the fags.'

'Really? What for? They say that when you give up smoking you put on a load of weight. I'm sorry, Dad, I think you might need to pack up stuffing your face rather than cutting out a few rollies.'

'Bloomin' cheek! I've got a very healthy diet. Anyway, I'm going to eat less and exercise more, as well as pack up smoking. What's more, I think you should stop smoking, too. It's much easier to stop when you're young.'

Tina picked up her packet of Silk Cut, studied each one with care, then made her selection. She chose a match with equal consideration and lit up, exhaling with exaggerated pleasure. She said, 'You look after yourself. I, Father, shall continue to look after me.'

'Well, put it this way: this property is now a smoke-free zone. That's the last cigarette you're smoking in here.'

'Fine, I'll move out.'

'Fine.'

They sat in silence for a minute. Terry broke it. 'Oh, and the other thing is: smoking makes you look tarty.'

'What? How dare you! Anyway, Mum used to smoke. She didn't look like a tart.'

Terry was silent. Tina looked at him; had she gone too far? He suddenly looked like his balloon had been burst.

'Maybe you're right,' she said. 'I'll give it a go. Yeah, why not? We can give up together.'

Terry smiled at her. 'Thanks, love. You're an angel.' He got up to make the tea. Tina stretched, got up and followed him into the kitchen. Terry said, 'I popped into Harringtons and bought a silver cup to give to the school. It's the Castleton Cup.'

'I hope they're going to pay for it?'

'Nah, it's a present from me.'

'You're too soft.'

Terry smiled, 'Yeah, but, honestly, it was such a great thing. I want to pay them back for it. By the way, I'd like to give Mrs Dutton something for looking after me. What should I get her? I don't want it to be too — you know — too over-the-top. It's got to be something meaningful, though.'

Tina thought back to her time in Mrs Dutton's class. She'd loved that year; it was probably her favourite. Everything in the world was easy back then.

'How is she?'

Terry thought back to the flying buttons and subsequent revelations. 'She's as lovely as ever.'

'Well, how about some chocs?'

'Hmm. That's a good idea but she may be on a similar regime to me.'

'Oh, she's whacked on the weight then?'

'No, she's in pretty good nick; more than, in fact. I heard her say she was trying to cut out cakes and chocolates.'

Tina thought. 'Why don't you make her something? You're so good at knocking stuff up.'

'Any ideas?'

'I don't know. Um... What about a carving? Or maybe a bit of jewellery?'

Terry poured two mugs of tea; he brought hers over. 'Okay, I'll give it some thought. What have you been doing today?'

'Can't you tell?'

'Um — nothing?'

Tina looked around the flat, her gaze returning to him, eyebrows raised. Terry took the hint. He looked around the kitchen, went into the lounge, then bathroom.

She called, 'You can look in my room, too.' He cautiously opened her door, then went in. Tina stood behind him. She said, 'I hope you don't mind. I did some of your laundry, too, and put it away. I would have cleaned your room but since it was spotless, I didn't bother. Honestly, Dad, you're such a swot.'

She watched her dad; was he pleased? He sat down on her bed, his face impassive. Finally, he looked around the room again. Seeing the giraffe, he picked it up and gently held it, as if he were handling an injured bird. In silence, he looked into its face. Tina had a horrible feeling he was going to break down again.

She said, 'Do you remember I bought some ravioli? I had it for lunch. It was disgusting. Honestly, I don't know how those Italians can eat that kind of stuff. I saw all sorts of Chinese and Indian packets in Sainsburys yesterday. I'm definitely not going to try any of that muck. What shall we have for tea tonight? Now that you're on a diet, perhaps you should have some lettuce, and I don't know, a pickled onion?'

She looked at him; he was staring at the giraffe. She carried on. 'Is booze bad for you? Perhaps you should knock beer on the head, as well? I think you can buy non-alcoholic beer these days. Do you want me to nip out and get something for tonight? Dad, what's wrong? Do you want something like one of those Vesta dinners — I don't know, a beef curry? Dad, what do you think? It might be nice. Dad, what's wrong?'

He looked up, his face serious. 'I thought I was going to die today. I don't know if I actually was, but I thought I was. What I kept thinking was that I couldn't die yet; I just couldn't. I couldn't because you needed me. I think I've been kidding myself. You don't need me: it's the other way around. You've been looking after me and I've only now begun to realise. All these years

152

you've kept me going, when I've been a waste of space. Look at your room? It badly needs painting and I didn't even notice. Look at this chap? He's about to lose his head and I haven't noticed. All I do is watch telly, smoke cigarettes and feel sorry for myself. All you do is make sure I'm all right, and what? I don't even know what you do! You lost your mum and you ended up with a fat, old man who doesn't pull his weight. You must wonder what you've done to deserve it all.'

He looked back at the giraffe. She watched him tenderly straighten out its neck. He said, 'I'm sorry about your mum. I need to tell you about what happened. I've been scared to. The thing is—'

Tina cut across him. 'So, what's it to be — beef curry or sweet and sour pork?'

Chapter 41

'What are you doing to celebrate, Daniel?'

'I'm not sure. I daresay my folks will want to serve up more cake. The trouble is: the one you baked made me realise what cakes can taste like. Honestly, Geraldine, everything was amazing.'

She smiled at him; he was such a cutie. 'You're worth it, Daniel. Also, I have to say, you need to put on a few pounds. Look at you — as skinny as a butcher's dog.'

She eyed up his lean frame. What would it feel like naked? She wondered if it was unnatural to want to uncover, reveal, explore, please, satisfy... Sex with Edward had been enjoyable, especially in the early days, but they'd never taken their time over it. Looking back, it had always been a rather hectic activity. Edward was not a passionate man. He was her first and only sexual partner and it had become apparent to her in recent years that there might be more enjoyment in bed to be had than he'd provided for her. Conversations with friends, magazine articles and one or two novels had begun to reveal much more exciting and emotionally fulfilling possibilities. There was something about Daniel's sensitive way, as well as his lithe body, that made her yearn to try sex all over again; this time, with someone more — more what? To her taste? She asked, 'Will you be celebrating with anyone else?'

Daniel was putting on his jacket. 'No, just family.'

He zipped up the jacket.

Geraldine couldn't help herself sounding eager. 'Oh?'

He was blushing. 'Well... er, thing is... um. I'm not sure how to say...'

Geraldine watched him fiddling with his zip. She was finding his naivety really appealing, even arousing. She wanted to take him in her arms, to say, 'Daniel, it's all right. You can trust me to look after you.' In her head she could hear his trembling voice. 'Oh, Geraldine, I've been dreaming that, maybe one day, you and I could—I've been looking at you and I can't help myself... may I undo...? Oh, you're so... Will you? Yes, that's — oooh! Mmm...'

He said, 'The thing is, Geraldine… um, it's a bit—well, may I ask you something? The thing is, you're such a nice person and I was wondering if…'

She stepped towards him, her eyes encouraging. She found herself playing with the buttons of Terry's jacket. She had to stop herself undoing them. 'Yes, Daniel? You can tell me. You can say anything to me, you know that, don't you?'

He smiled. 'Thank you. Well, the thing is, my girlfriend is coming home on Friday and I was planning to propose to her. I was wondering if I could run through something with you. I've got this brilliant idea, but I don't know if she'll like it or not. You know loads of things. You've been through it all before, and you may even have a daughter the same age as her. We're going away on Friday night, driving to this little town in Suffolk…'

Geraldine stepped away from Daniel and busied herself with papers on her desk. She checked that Terry's jacket was securely done up, lapels and collar as high as they could go. Her face was as hot as the sun. She wanted to laugh at herself, but her embarrassment was too acute. She also felt like crying with disappointment. For an exhilarating moment she'd believed her fantasy was about to come true. What was she thinking? Daniel was a handsome, intelligent man; he was a kind and sensitive colleague; he was nearly twenty years her junior. He was, as people often said in such circumstances, young enough to be her son. She was a fat, middle-aged woman who was completely out of touch with his generation, with reality. What was wrong with her? She shook her head to get rid of the ridiculous images that, seconds ago, had been flooding her mind, and her body.

'…and then when she opens the curtains, she'll see it on the beach. What do you think? It's not over the top, is it?'

She looked at him. His face was like a child's: earnest, imploring. Briefly, ever so briefly, she wanted to make him feel as pathetic as she did. The moment passed. She smiled at him.

'Daniel, that sounds absolutely lovely. She'll love it, I'm sure. How could she resist you after that?'

He beamed.

Chapter 42

Gary tapped on the fire door. He heard a chair scrape, then Nigel opened up, and smiled. 'How did you get on?'

Gary stepped into the smoky room. Only Nigel was left, plus, beyond his editor's partition, Rob Mitchum. 'Yeah, I found it. There were three articles, all in August. I didn't learn that much, to be honest. It seems like the mystery was never cleared up. Actually, I was going to ask Alan about it; has he gone?'

Nigel smiled. 'He hasn't gone. Where do you think he might be?'

'Bog?'

'Yep. Do you want to wait for him?'

'Do you mind?'

'Fine by me.'

Gary sat at an empty desk. He looked at the mountain of stuff. He remembered flicking through a book, years ago. He'd come across a picture of a bloke sitting at a desk like this one. He had been wearing a tie, smart shirt; everything about him looked powerful. Gary remembered staring at the picture, wanting to be like that man: in charge, in control. Through the glass window of the office door, he could see Rob Mitchum at his desk. He was reading something, then writing, then reading again. He shuffled through a book then started writing again. Suddenly, he put his pen down and grabbed the telephone. Through the partition, Gary could hear his rumbling voice. Rob slammed the phone down and started writing again.

'Do you want to work for a newspaper?' Nigel asked.

Gary jumped. Nigel had obviously been watching him. 'I dunno. What's it like?'

'It's great. You get to go to loads of places, meet all sorts of people; hear lots of things that aren't obvious to the outside world. It's really hard work, though. Do you like hard work?'

Gary wasn't sure. He couldn't ever remember working hard at anything except getting through the last three days without fucking up. He said, 'I'd like to work hard on something that I was good at.'

Nigel nodded, 'I know what you mean.'

The door opened and Alan came back in, sweating profusely. Looking at Gary, he said, 'Find anything?'

'Yeah, you were right. It all happened before Kennedy; three months before.'

Alan grunted.

Gary said, 'I was wondering: was it ever sorted out? You know, what happened to him?'

'He's your grandad, not mine. If anyone would know, I would have thought it would be you.'

Gary felt stupid. 'Oh, yeah. No — Ha ha! I mean, did anyone ever find anything? Did the... What I mean is, did the paper ever follow it up?'

'I don't think so. I don't remember anything, anyway. Why the interest all of a sudden?'

Nigel chipped in. 'Gary's found a letter. He didn't know what happened to his grandad. That's right, isn't it, Gary?'

Gary nodded. He was disappointed. All his hard work and nothing had come of it.

Alan said, 'Why don't you go and talk to the police? They'll know more about it than anyone, apart from your parents.'

Yeah, a cosy chat with Dickie and his bastard boss, Flanagan, Gary thought. *I don't think so.* He got up, 'Thanks very much for all your help. If you ever think of anything, let me know, won't you?'

Nigel got up, too. 'Of course. What's your phone number?'

Gary called out his number then went through to the reception area. The nice bird was there.

She smiled. 'Hello. You again?'

'Hello. Yeah, it's me.'

'You looking for a job?'

'No. Well — why?'

'We're looking for an apprentice. I thought you might have applied.'

'Really? How do I find out about it?'

'To be honest, I'm not sure. I only started a couple of weeks ago. Want me to find out and let you know?'

'Definitely, thanks very much. Er, my name's Gary. Gary Abbott.'

She smiled at him. The girl was really pretty. Quite long, dark hair; big, brown eyes. She had a cheeky sort of smile.

'Sorry, what's your name?'

She laughed, 'Oh, sorry. Karen Mitchum.'

He looked over her shoulder towards the back office.

'Yeah, he's my uncle. I only got the job because of him. I haven't been doing any work at school and my parents said I could leave if I got a job. I'm not thick; I'm unbelievably lazy. No one else was going to give me a job, were they? Anyway, so far, so good.'

Gary smiled ruefully. 'Well, I haven't done any work at school, either. The problem is my uncle doesn't run a newspaper.'

'Oh, pity. Still, some of the people who work here haven't got any qualifications, either. Alan, the old bloke, his qualification is drinking pints and eating dodgy kebabs. You wouldn't believe—'

Gary held up his hand. 'Yeah, I would. Nigel and me were stuck in the same office with him earlier. Put it this way: I've only just recovered.'

Karen laughed. Gary laughed, too.

She said, 'How's your friend?'

Gary thought of Frank; he'd really like to see him right now. Maybe he'd ring him up when he got home. 'I think he's all right.'

'We were worried about him. He looked so sad. I hope he's going to be okay. He seemed — I don't know; like a lost soul or something.'

Gary nodded. 'I know what you mean. I'll get in touch and find out. Do you want me to let you know?'

She smiled, 'Well, yeah, thanks. I'll let you know about the other thing. What's your number?'

For the second time in five minutes, Gary gave his phone number.

'Thanks, I'll let you know.'

They heard Rob's voice call. 'Karen?'

She jumped up. 'I'd better run. See you again, maybe?'

Gary was surprised: she was tall, nearly his height. 'Yeah, maybe. Well, definitely maybe.'

She smiled at him. Gary felt butterflies flitter through him.

'Bye then, Gary' she held out her hand. He shook it.

She looked down at their clasped hands, 'Gosh, you've got big hands.'

Before he could stop himself, he said, 'Well, you know what they say: big hands, big...'

She looked at him, challenging. 'Yeah, what do they say? Oh, and who's "they"?'

He said, embarrassed, 'Er... big hands, um — big, um...'

She broke in. 'Head?'

'No, I was going to say: big hands, big gloves. And the "they" are experts in the field.'

She laughed. 'Nice recovery. I'd better scram. See you around, Big Gloves.'

Gary watched her walk quickly into Rob's office. She turned as she went through the door and flapped her hands at him. He smiled and nodded.

Chapter 43

Geraldine put her keys down on the hall table. She checked her appearance in the full-length mirror, expecting to cut a ridiculous figure. Relieved, she saw that the jacket covered everything up and that actually, as Terry had told her, she looked pretty good.

'Thank you, Terry,' she said out loud.

She took her bag through to the kitchen, unloaded the cake tins and looked in the fridge for a suitable supper. Would Edward be back tonight? The spectacle (ludicrous spectacle!) she'd made of herself today had made her question how she had been behaving with Edward. Until now, she had thought his increasingly critical attitude towards her — towards what she did and said, the way she looked — so unfair. But what if he was right? Was she going through some kind of mid-life crisis? Perhaps she should be working much harder on her appearance? Had she got staid and predictable? She now realised that all her efforts in fantasising about Daniel ought to have been spent working on her marriage. She'd been asking herself how she could please Daniel, rather than trying to satisfy her own husband's needs.

Digging around, she found a quiche Lorraine, some leaves, a pot of coleslaw, an avocado, olives. She opened the vegetable drawer: yes, new potatoes. How about a pudding? She looked in the freezer. Arctic Roll. That would do.

Happy with her menu, Geraldine went upstairs to change. She carefully took off Terry's jacket and hung it on a coat hanger. Looking at herself without its protection, she reddened again: what did she look like? She angrily wrenched off the tattered silk blouse, unclipped the lacy bra, which she now saw was doing nothing but cause an unattractive bulging, and tried to see herself as Edward might. Her face was all right: no lines, nice dimples. Her hair was still light brown; no grey that she could see. Maybe she needed a haircut? Well, possibly a trim, but no more than that. She liked it long: it made her feel young, even if she was only kidding herself. Many of her contemporaries had gone for the dramatic reduction, either bobs or really short with side partings; she thought they looked older as a result.

Her problems were from the neck down: her arms and shoulders were round and squidgy; her breasts, perhaps her best feature, were now being held up by three tons — of what? Where did all that blubber come from? When did it arrive? Then, her thighs: bloody hell! She turned to look at her rear: double bloody hell! Edward was right. *Damn and blast!* she thought bitterly. No wonder Daniel hadn't been putty in her hands. She laughed out loud: she would have literally felt like putty in his. She said aloud, as if addressing one of her most foolish pupils, 'Geraldine Dutton, you really are a silly, silly girl.'

She found one of her normal Marks and Spencer bras, a big, baggy sweater and some tracksuit trousers. Edward had given her the tracksuit for Christmas, obviously sending her a message that she'd chosen to ignore. Slipping on her moccasins, she went downstairs to prepare the meal. It would be nice to give Edward a treat. The wine was already chilled; how about setting up the dining room, for once? Opening the door, she remembered their most recent dinner party: another embarrassment.

Edward had invited his golf-club friends and their wives, explaining to her that his captaincy next year was dependent on the success of the evening. She'd done a lovely meal: melon and raspberries in port, spaghetti Bolognese, salad; then lemon meringue pie, a cheese board with, what she thought was an ideal touch, Elizabeth Shaw mints with coffee. Edward had bought champagne and had stocked up the drinks cabinet. Everything had run smoothly until they'd gone through into the sitting room. Edward had offered drinks to everyone then said, 'Not for you, Geraldine: I think you've had enough.'

There had been an uncomfortable silence, their guests gazing first at Edward, then at her. She looked at Edward — was he smiling? No, his face was stern. She said, 'Oh? I'd like a glass of port, please.'

'Really, Geraldine, you know you get one of your heads if you drink too much.'

Dick Bentham chipped in. 'Come on, Edward. Geraldine has given us all such a lovely dinner — surely she deserves a drink?'

Geraldine looked gratefully at him; he was such a nice man. His young wife, a blonde bombshell, said, 'I get terrible headaches with port; I never touch the stuff.'

'There you are, Geraldine. Listen to Gloria's advice. Best you don't.' Edward was sitting down with his balloon-glass full.

Ian Stockton looked across at her, his eyebrows raised. What was he trying to convey? She was half-mortified, half-furious. She knew that this was an important evening for Edward: that was why she'd gone to so much trouble.

She wanted a drink, and she definitely did not appreciate being treated like a child. However, if she made a fuss, he'd be so angry with her.

She said, light and airy, 'Do you know, I think Edward is right; I do feel a bit squiffy.'

Jack Stubbs said, 'I have to hand it to you, Edward: you know how to maintain a tight ship. I wish I had your level of control, eh, Brenda?'

They watched for her reaction, then laughed as Brenda stuck two fingers up at her husband.

Dick smiled at Geraldine. 'That was a beautiful meal, Geraldine. Thank you so much.' There was general appreciation. Dick went on, 'I wish Gloria could knock up a spread like that.'

The bombshell said, 'Well, maybe if I did, I wouldn't look the way I do!'

Edward turned to her. 'I was wondering, Gloria: how do you keep so slim? Perhaps you'd give Geraldine a few tips?' There was more nervous laughter and some surreptitious glances towards Geraldine. She felt her hot face burn brightly.

Gloria looked over at her, her smile condescending. 'Stop it, Edward. Geraldine is a very beautiful woman.' More appreciative noises.

Edward got up and walked towards the sideboard, 'Now, anyone for a cigar?'

Geraldine watched as he opened the lid and presented the box to Dick, then Jack, and finally, Ian: they all took one. Edward handed a lighter to Dick who took his time unwrapping, examining, and lighting his. Puffing happily, he said, 'I like a woman with some meat on her bones. You want something to hang on to when — you know. Plus, if the seas are choppy, a bit of ballast is always helpful.' The men laughed.

Edward, now also emitting thick, blue smoke, said appreciatively, 'Well, Dick, you wouldn't get much stability from Gloria; she's a real lightweight. Mind you, I imagine she's pretty good on a choppy sea? You're a lucky chap, Dick!'

Gloria tittered; bashful but pleased, 'Oh, Geraldine, how do you put up with this awful man?'

'With difficulty?' Brenda suggested.

Geraldine smiled at Brenda, grateful for the support. She wasn't very good at the clever chit-chat. She let it all go. The evening would be over soon and her duty would be done.

Edward said, 'What about you, Ian? How do you like your fillies?'

Ian drained his tumbler, smacked his lips, and said 'Short reins, tight bridle, blinkered, and...' he paused for effect, 'and a whip in my hand.'

The men creased up. Gloria and Jill Stockton giggled. Brenda and Geraldine looked at each other, tight-lipped.

'There you are, Gloria. He's the chauvinist, not me,' Edward said, his hand on the bombshell's arm. 'Another whisky, old man?'

Ian looked sadly into his empty glass. 'Oh, go on, then. If you twist my arm.'

Edward looked at Dick and Jack: they proffered their tumblers. Edward refilled them, then his own, and sat down.

Geraldine couldn't bear it. 'Brenda, Jill, Gloria?'

Brenda said, 'Not for me. Why don't I help you with the washing up? I don't suppose you'll get any help from Lord Muck.'

Jack was shocked. 'Brenda, what a thing to say!'

Geraldine was in a fluster. She appreciated Brenda's support, but this was Edward's evening and it had to go well. She looked across at Edward; he was waiting for her to say something.

'Actually, Brenda, you're wrong there, Edward is an excellent kitchen porter. When you're all gone, he'll spend the next hour making everything ship-shape. He's really quite domesticated.' Geraldine felt her face redden again. Surely they'd all see through such an obvious lie?

Edward said, 'Geraldine's not giving me enough credit. I should have it done in fifty-eight minutes, sixteen seconds.' They all laughed, even Brenda, this time.

Geraldine wondered how long it would take her to clean everything up. Maybe more than an hour? Edward would stand and watch for the first few minutes, long enough to finish his cigar. When she finally got to bed, he'd be snoring.

Now, a few months later, Edward was indeed the captain of the golf club. He was happy. And she'd almost got past the humiliation of that evening.

She considered the room. The table was large enough for twelve; she'd lay it at one end, for the two of them to sit opposite each other. Lifting the canteen of cutlery from the sideboard, she thought, for the first time in her married life, that she'd prefer it if Edward had to work late; better still, that he'd have to stay overnight at his club.

Chapter 44

'Here you go, here's the salad stuff. What shall we have?'

Terry was smiling at Tina. She had bullied him out of the flat and down to Sainsbury's. Now, pushing the trolley, like Boadicea, she was daring anyone to get in her way.

They looked at the shelves. As far as Terry was concerned, a salad was lettuce, tomato and cucumber.

'What's an advocado?' Tina asked, picking one up.

'I don't know. They don't look very nice. How about some radishes? Look — spring onions.'

'They've got olives. Do you like them, Dad?'

'Get out of it! They're disgusting.'

'Come on, try and be a bit more daring. What's this? Artichoke?'

'Never mind all the fancy stuff: pick up some of the cress. That'll do us.'

'Dad, you're so boring. I tell you what, to make it all a bit posher, why don't we have mayonnaise? I heard it's really nice; it's what French people have with their salad.'

'Mayonnaise! What's wrong with salad cream all of a sudden? Oh, go on then: if it makes you happy.'

'Okay. So, what shall we have with it? Do you like salmon? The tins are around the corner.'

Terry followed on behind, feeling the way he had as a kid, following his mum around.

'Oh, 'allo, Tina. How you doing?'

Tina had been stopped by a couple of girls her own age. They were all smiles, flares, flicks and highlights. Tina was half-hearted in her greeting. 'Watcha. I'm fine.'

The short one said, 'We haven't seen you for days. You're not ill, are you?'

'No, I've had a bit of a — well... No. I'm fine. What about you two?'

Terry hid behind a pillar. He didn't want to embarrass his daughter with her friends.

'Fine. Nothing much going on. We're all getting ready for exams. We got our timetable today; they start on 21st May.'

'Oh.' Tina did not sound bothered.

'You still with Kev Abbott?'

'God, no — what a total prick! No, I dumped him ages ago.'

'Who you with then?'

'I'm off blokes. They're all — Well, anyway... No one.'

'I heard Steve Bellingham fancies you.'

'Don't make me laugh.'

'We're off to the Mops and Brooms tonight. Do you want to come?'

'Oh. Well, thanks for asking, but me and my dad are staying in tonight. Where is he?' Terry emerged from his hiding place. He smiled at the girls. Tina ticked him off. 'There you are. Honestly, I can't take you anywhere! See you around, yeah?'

She walked on, leaving her friends, and dad, behind. Terry smiled again and followed. He heard one girl say, 'She's such a loser.'

Rage rushed through him. He was about to turn around when Tina called. 'Here it is! Pink or red?'

He hurried over.

'Sorry about that, Dad. Honestly, they're such a couple of losers.'

He asked, 'Who were they?'

'Lynn and Marie. They're not really my type.'

'Who are your friends these days?'

She was looking at the cans. 'I think red might be better. What about tuna? Do you like that? Hang on, they've got sardines here. They're from Italy. Shall we try them?'

'I thought you didn't like Italian food?'

'Well, they're only little fish. They haven't been messed around with, not like some of that other stuff they eat.'

Terry asked again. 'I was wondering who your friends were. You know — best friends.'

'Oh, no one you know.'

'Well, why don't you ask them around and do what girls do. What do girls do, anyway?'

'We play chess, discuss philosophy, argue about the value of the pound in today's economy, plan revolutions... What do dads do?'

Terry stopped asking questions; she was too smart for him. They continued their tour. Tina stopped at the display of beers and lagers and perused their descriptions.

'There's some weak ones but none of them are alcohol-free. I was sure there was such a thing.'

The idea of beer without alcohol didn't appeal to Terry: what was the point? 'Don't worry, love; I'll have a few bottles of Guinness.'

'Sorry, mate, you can have some Shandy Bass.' She put four cans in the trolley. 'Anything else?'

'You used a hell of a lot of cleaning stuff today; do we need to stock up?'

'No, but I tell you what, my hands are wrecked. I'll get some Marigolds.'

It was only when they got to the till that Terry remembered he didn't have his wallet. Out of habit, he patted his pockets, knowing the wallet to be at home with Geraldine Dutton for the night. 'Bugger!'

'What?'

'I haven't got any money.'

'Dad, you idiot.'

'Sorry. What a pain. I don't suppose you...?'

She smiled, 'Well, you're in luck. I was going to pay anyway: my treat.'

'How can you afford it?'

Tina put her finger against her lips, then patted her nose, then winked.

Terry had a flashback to all the times Diane had done that. He knew where her money had come from but, please God, not Tina! He said, 'Look, if you've got the cash that would be great, but we're going to talk about this when we get home. I'm definitely paying you back.'

As they walked past Boots, Tina said, 'Can we take a quick look at the make-up in here?'

'What do you mean, we?'

'Come on, Dad. Don't be a pedandist.'

Terry stood watching Tina as she looked at a selection of lipsticks, mascara, foundation, blushers, eye-liners. He had never paid attention to Diane and the hours she spent in front of the mirror, but Tina evidently had. She was holding up two lipsticks, side by side. She said, 'Shall I go for 'crushed raspberry' or 'cherry cream'?

'Hmm, tricky. How about stewed rhubarb?'

Her laugh was derisive. 'I'll go for the raspberry.'

When they got home, Terry put everything away. Tina was in the bathroom. He called, 'Right, out you come. We are going to have a serious talk.'

Tina emerged from the bathroom and sat down opposite him at the kitchen table. She had applied some of her 'crushed raspberry'. She said, 'What do you think — not too heavy?'

He had to admit she looked stunning. 'It was very kind of you to pay for everything. I will pay you as soon as I get my wallet back. It was lovely of you to do all the cleaning and for making everything look so...' He looked around the flat, '... like a proper home. But you've got to think about your future. It's time we sorted out our lives. I've decided: I'm pulling myself together. I'm going to get fitter; I'm going to lose a few pounds... Okay, a few stone. I think I should be getting a better job. Honestly, when an ex-soldier gets beaten up by three little boys, something's got to change. I've let myself down and, worst of all, I've let you down. I've decided, my time is up. Now, it's your turn. You are going to sort yourself out. I don't want to hear any old flannel; you're either going to go to school and try and get a few exams, or you're going to get a job. I don't care what the job is, as long as it's legal, respectable and makes the most of your talent. You are really clever; you're beautiful; you're funny; you're — well, lots of things. I was thinking, when you were looking at the make-up, you should go into that line of work. I bet there are jobs at the film studios for makeup artists. Or maybe you could go to college and learn it, and then get a job in the West End or something? Anyway, the point is, both of us are on the up and up. You've got me through some horrible times — I don't know how you did it, but you did. I'm going to show the world that Terry Castleton is back in town. Do you know what they called me in the army?'

'Baldy?'

'Well, actually, yeah, they did call me that. They also called me lots of other things. Anyway, what I'm saying is: you, madam, are coming with me. We're going to get out of our prison and we're going to escape. Are you with me?'

Tina had been filing her fingernails. Was she listening? Was she going to give one of her throwaway, wisecrack answers? She looked up. Her eyes were blazing. 'You watch, Dad. You and me — we're on our way!'

Chapter 45

Derek said, 'Where've you been?'

'Out.'

'I mean where, tosspot?'

'Where's Mum?'

'Upstairs.'

Gary went into the kitchen and put the kettle on. He called, 'Want a cuppa, Del?'

'Yeah, go on then.'

Gary wondered about the wisdom of asking Derek about Grandad. It was probably safe, as long as they kept away from anything to do with the other night. Derek would have been eight when the old man disappeared; he'd remember something about it. Gary filled the pot and went into the front room. He lit a fag. 'Want one?'

Derek looked at the packet of Number 6. 'No, ta. They're shit. I'll have one of my own.' He lit one of his Embassy Regals. Looking at Gary through the smoke trickling from his nostrils, he said, 'You're looking shifty. What are you up to?'

'Nothing. I was going to ask you something.'

'Yeah?'

'I always thought Grandad was dead. Mum told me he disappeared. Do you remember it?'

'We weren't here. We were at Auntie Maureen's.' Derek was looking into the far distance, clearly searching his memory. 'He was staying with us. Then Mum got a call from Auntie Maureen asking if we wanted to go and stay with her and Uncle Ray. We were there for a couple of weeks, I think. It was during the school holidays. When we came back, he'd done his runner.'

Gary was trying to get some fragments of memory back but nothing came to him. 'I can't remember any of this. Do you know what happened?'

'Well, we didn't know anything, either. I suppose Auntie Maureen knew, but she didn't say. When we got home, Grandad wasn't here anymore. No one said anything. I remember asking where he was, and Mum just said he'd gone.

I thought she meant he'd gone home. At Christmas, Dad said we wouldn't be getting anything from Grandad. The bastard never gave us anything anyway, so I don't know why Dad even said that. The only other time it came up was when we heard that Auntie Maureen had left Uncle Ray. Dad said, then, that Grandad would have been pleased: apparently, he never liked Uncle Ray. I asked why we never saw Grandad anymore but Dad told me to shut it, so I did. To be honest, I never asked again.'

Gary said, 'I can't even properly remember him. I've got a memory of a horrible voice. What was he like?'

Derek laughed. 'He was awful. He was absolutely massive, like a giant. I know I was only little, but he made Dad look like a kid. He never smiled. He used to stare at me, like he hated me. The only thing that made him laugh, that I remember, was when he threatened to show us his willy. When we ran away, I can remember him laughing this horrible, wheezing chuckle. God, we were glad to go and stay at Auntie Maureen's.'

'So, when you—' Gary looked out of the window; a car had drawn up. His heart lurched as he saw Dickie Davies get out. 'Fuck!'

Derek looked out. 'Who's that?'

'It's the fucking cops.' They peered through the net curtains. Joining Dickie was Keegan and then another man: tall, older, stooped. Gary ran upstairs. 'Mum! Mum, are you there?'

Jenny opened her bedroom door; she looked half asleep.

'Mum, the Filth are here. Are you all right?'

Her eyes cleared. She nodded.

'Listen, Mum. Are you clear about everything? Keep to the story. No matter what they say. Even if they say the post-mortem thing proves this or that, don't change anything.'

'I know, Gary. I understand. I had a chat with Joe this afternoon. He told me everything would be fine.'

'Really? What — did he ring up?'

'No, he popped round for a cup of tea. He's such a nice man.'

They heard heavy raps on the door. Jenny led the way down.

Dickie said, 'Good afternoon, Mrs Abbott. We wondered if we could have a word with you?'

Jenny opened the door wide for them. 'Come in. Go through to the front room.'

The three men entered the hall. They wiped their feet carefully before going through. The older man said, 'You probably won't remember me, Mrs Abbott. My name's Flanagan, Detective Chief Inspector Flanagan.'

Jenny, then Gary, followed them into the front room. They all sat down. The three policemen perched on the sofa, trying to fit between the arms and failing. Flanagan got up and looked around uncertainly. After a few seconds, he bent down and shoved the old, brass fish with the broken tail out of the way, then lowered himself on to the battered, leather pouffe in front of the telly. Gary glanced at his mum: guilt was written all over her face.

Keegan leapt to his feet. 'Here you are, Sir — take my seat.'

Flanagan smiled at him. 'No, you're all right, Armstrong. I'm fine here.'

Gary stared at him. He'd been expecting some kind of monster. Instead, Flanagan looked more like a vicar. He had a large, domed head, tufts of white hair around the sides. He wore wire-rimmed spectacles behind which were kind, gentle eyes. He was wearing a faded blue corduroy suit and a thin, dark-blue tie. His shoes were old, brown suede things — Hush Puppies? Gary glanced at Dickie. He looked edgy, hands bunched into fists, his eyes flicking here and there as if something was about to attack him. Keegan looked like a frightened rabbit.

Flanagan was staring at his own hands. He had long, white fingers which he made into the church-and-steeple thing that kids did at primary school. The room was silent. Gary wondered where Derek had gone — probably a long way off. Flanagan looked up at last.

He said, 'Mrs Abbott, I'm so sorry to learn of your husband's sudden demise. What a terrible shock. When we last met, you were suffering a most upsetting ordeal. Now we meet again, and you're having to endure another awful situation. I'm so, so sorry.'

Gary looked at his mother; she was staring at Flanagan. What was she thinking?

Flanagan turned his kind eyes to Gary, 'Gary, I'm very sorry for you, too. Losing your father so suddenly must be unbearable for you. Please accept my heartfelt condolences. My colleagues and I are terribly upset for you both.' He turned to Dickie and Keegan. They nodded in agreement.

No one said anything. Flanagan sat on his tuffet, like a small child, watching his fingers move. Five minutes must have gone by. Gary knew they were being tested. He kept his nerve.

At last, Flanagan said, 'I remember Brian very well. I think it's fair to say he was a character? Yes, quite a character. He was very upset when his father disappeared. I remember that distinctly.' He turned to Gary. 'Gary, when your grandfather went missing, I was in charge of the search and investigation. I have always been troubled by that sad business. I've often felt as though I let the Abbott family down. I'm sure I should have been able to establish the whereabouts of the old fellow, or at least find out what happened. I failed. I'm so sorry.' He looked down again, then, 'Mrs Abbott, may I call you Jenny?' Jenny nodded. 'Jenny, Detectives Nott and Armstrong have told me everything that happened on Sunday night. I can't believe the tragedy of it. I mean, I do believe it, but it's so unbelievable. Poor Brian. You must be struggling to come to terms with it?' Jenny nodded again. 'Same for you, Gary?' Gary didn't trust himself to speak. He nodded.

Flanagan said, 'Detective Constable, would you be kind enough to pass me your folder?'

Keegan handed over a cardboard wallet. Flanagan opened the flap and pulled out a load of papers held together by a giant paperclip. He slowly flicked through the wadge. Dickie and Keegan looked like they were sitting on drawing pins: what was wrong with them? Finally, Flanagan put the papers back in the folder and handed it over to Keegan. He looked at Jenny, his face kind and concerned. 'Do you mind if I take a very quick look at the kitchen, Jenny? I need to understand how it all fits together.' Jenny Abbott got up and led the way into the kitchen. Dickie and Keegan got up to follow but Flanagan said, 'Just Jenny and me, if you don't mind, gentlemen?'

Gary cursed under his breath. He wanted to be with his mum, to correct her if she got anything wrong. Now that they were on their own, Dickie and Keegan relaxed. Dickie said, 'How's it going, Gary?'

'Fine.'

'We've been busy since we last met.' Gary said nothing. 'We got a call, out of the blue, a couple of hours ago?'

Gary tensed. Were they going to arrest them?

'Yeah, it was funny; out of the blue it was.'

Gary knew Dickie was going to dangle him by the short and curlies. He sat back and folded his arms.

'Yeah, out of the blue. I was surprised. Not much surprises me, but this did.'

Behind their heads, Gary saw Derek in the street talking to Kev. Kev looked toward the house, then they both walked quickly away.

'Do you know who rang me up?'

Gary shook his head. 'I've no idea.'

'It was your friend, Nigel Philips, at the local rag.'

Gary looked at him sharply. Delighted by the reaction, Dickie smiled at Keegan. Gary swallowed. What had Nigel done that for? He seemed like such a nice bloke.

Dickie said, 'Yeah, he said that you were trying to find out about your missing grandad. Nigel looked up the old copies and saw that Mr Flanagan had been the investigating officer and thought he'd have a word. What he didn't know was that I was also working on the case. I was a DC then, like Armstrong is now. Anyway, Philips was interested in the story and thought he'd do a bit of digging around. Of course, what he also didn't know was that your dear father — the man who stoved in John Eustace's head — died early yesterday morning. He was terribly interested in that. He was even more fascinated to learn that we were waiting to arrest him once he woke up; but of course, your dear father slipped away before we could get the chance. So, you see, it's all been incredibly busy, hasn't it?'

Gary didn't understand: how had Nigel been able to do that? He must have rung the police whilst Gary had been looking through the old copies. Why hadn't Nigel told him that he'd rung the police? Gary made up his mind there and then. Fuck apprenticeships: Nigel was going to get a beating. He said, 'Yeah, very busy.'

Dickie was smiling. He turned to Keegan who was grinning like a lunatic. Gary could hear Flanagan talking through the closed door. His voice was low, gentle. Every now and then his mum's higher tones; she sounded all right.

Dickie said, 'Guess what, Gary?'

'What?'

'We're getting the report of the post-mortem this evening. Might even be waiting for us when we get back to the station.'

Gary gulped.

'I bet you're looking forward to the doctor's confirmation, aren't you?' Dickie grinned at Keegan, who was now nodding like one of those dogs in the back window of a car.

The kitchen door opened and Jenny came back in. Flanagan's hand was on her shoulder. She looked calm. The old man said, 'May I have a word with you, Gary?'

Gary looked at his mum. She smiled; was she trying to reassure him? He got up and went into the kitchen. Flanagan shut the door behind him. He sat down at the table and gestured to Gary to sit opposite him. Gary did as he was instructed.

'As I said, Gary, this is all a most horrendous time for you. The last thing I want to do is make it worse. All I want you to do is tell me what you saw and did. I'm not interested in what you think might have happened. Does that make sense?'

'Yeah.'

'Also, I'm not the kind of police officer who tries to catch people out. I'm interested in the facts; that's all.'

Gary nodded. He didn't believe him, but he'd go along with the pretence.

Flanagan said, 'The other thing I need you to understand is that I knew your father. When his father, your grandfather, went missing all those years ago, I spent some time with him. I understood him a bit. Then, when my colleagues told me that it was your father that had carried out the assault three weeks ago I — well, put it this way — it was in keeping with the kind of man I knew him to be. So you see, anything that may or may not have happened here on Sunday night would not be a surprise to me. Do you understand what I'm saying, Gary?'

Gary wasn't quite sure but nodded, anyway.

'So, take your time, Gary. You tell me what happened here on Sunday night.'

Once again Gary explained that he had been next door with Tina, talking. His mum had gone out to buy a bottle of wine from the corner shop. His dad had been in the kitchen. Tina and he had heard a crash. They dashed into the kitchen as his mum had come in through the back door. On the floor was his dad, unconscious. His foot was caught up in the iron's lead which itself had got wrapped around the legs of the ironing board. He had rung for an ambulance and the police.

During his description, Flanagan had got up and was walking slowly around the room. He was now looking out of the window, his back to Gary.

He said, 'I remember your father being a very sociable man. Would you agree?'

Gary thought about this. Yes, he was: he liked being with his drinking pals. He liked his sons to be with him, so he could show off or put them down. Flanagan was right, his dad was very rarely on his own. So what was behind the question? Gary was ahead of him — Flanagan was going to ask why he'd been on his own in the kitchen? That was a good question, especially when Elvis was playing in the front room and it had been his dad who had put on the record. Gary's brain raced; what would he say?

Flanagan asked again. 'By sociable, I mean he enjoyed other people's company.'

'Oh, I see. Yeah, he did.'

'I was picturing him in the kitchen, by himself, with you and Tina Castleton next door. I understand you were listening to an Elvis Presley record. Do you like Mr Presley's music?'

Gary saw there were some traps here; at least two, possibly three. He said, 'I'm not a big Elvis fan. He's a bit old-fashioned.'

'Your father admired his work?'

'Yeah.'

Flanagan moved away from the window and came to sit down again. He took off his spectacles, pulled out a handkerchief and cleaned the lenses. He looked across at Gary. His eyes were so kind and gentle, Gary almost blurted out everything to him. Flanagan put his glasses back on and smiled. 'Thank you, Gary. I think I've got everything I need. You and your dear mother have been so helpful. I'm terribly sorry we've had to bother you at this sad time. I shall leave you now to begin to come to terms with your loss.'

He got up and put his hand out. Gary shook it. Flanagan's hand was cool and firm.

'After you?' Flanagan said, stepping back from the door. As Gary moved past him, he saw the detective looking around the kitchen once more: quick, darting glances.

Gary stepped back into the front room; although silent, the atmosphere was electric. He sat down in the armchair again. Flanagan didn't come through. What was he up to? Dickie and Keegan were back on their hot coals. Were they scared of Flanagan? Finally, the old man came back in and held out his hand to Jenny.

'Thank you, Jenny. We're off now. You and Gary have been so kind and helpful. I think everything's becoming clear. It has been so difficult: shocking and sad at the same time. One of us may have to be in touch again, to sort out formalities. In the meantime, please accept my condolences once more, from all of us.' He looked towards his colleagues, who nodded emphatically.

The three men went to the door.

Flanagan said, 'We'll let ourselves out. Good day, both.'

Gary stayed in his chair until he saw them get into their car and drive away. He turned to his mum. 'What did he say? What did you say? Was it all right?'

'He was the same as last time. He is a gentleman. I trusted him before and I do now. He's not like the others; he's a respectable man.'

'Oh, Mum, he's a bloody copper. Don't be fooled by him. He was trying to catch you out. Didn't you see the other two? They're shit-scared of him.'

'No, I don't think you're right. Not all policemen are like that. He's what they call "old school".'

Gary was sure he could see through the act but he didn't push it. 'What did he ask you though?'

'He asked me to say what I saw. I told him what we always say.'

'Did he ask any clever questions?'

His mum thought for a minute. 'The only thing he asked that was different was how long Dad was in the kitchen by himself.'

'What did you say?'

'Well, I said it had taken me about twenty minutes to go and buy the Blue Nun. I said I didn't know if he'd been on his own or not, coz I wasn't there.'

Gary nodded. That's right. His mum couldn't have known that. Gary thought that Flanagan was on to something. Why would his dad be sitting on his own in the kitchen for twenty minutes when he and Tina were in the front room listening to Elvis? Gary knew that this wasn't evidence of anything, but it was enough to make Flanagan suspicious. He said, 'Listen, Mum, I know Flanagan seems to be a nice bloke but he's really, really clever. Don't let him trick you.'

'I understand, love. Joe said that we need to be on our guard right now.'

Gary remembered the surprise visit. 'Did Joe say anything else?'

'He said that if he were the police, right now he'd be trying to make us nervous, to see if we started to forget our own lies.'

Gary nodded. 'He's right, he must be. So let's not fall for Flanagan's little game. The other thing is, the other two were saying that they're expecting the result of the post-mortem — any minute, they said. I don't know if that's true, but whatever it says, we're not changing anything.'

His mum said, 'We'd better ring Tina, to let her know what's going on.'

Gary leapt to his feet, 'I'll ring her now.'

Chapter 46

She put the phone down and thought about it all: there was a dreamlike quality to everything at the moment. The phone rang again; she jumped.

'Hallo?'

'Hallo, can I speak to Tina, please?'

'This is Tina.'

'Oh, hello, Tina. This is Chris Armstrong. Do you remember me?'

Tina laughed, 'Of course! It was only yesterday that I saw you.'

'Yeah, of course. I never know how much of an impact I make.'

Although he was a copper, and she was deep in the shit, Tina really did quite like this bloke.

She said, 'Oh, don't worry, you did all right.'

'Good, that's a relief. Some people don't like coppers; it's as if they're allergic to them.'

'"Can I help you with your enquiries?" That's what they say, isn't it?'

He laughed. 'That's right! Actually, though, I'm having the evening off and I was wondering… you're probably busy and…but, anyway, do you want to go for a drink? Don't worry, nothing about work or anything. Just as friends.'

'We're not friends, are we?'

'Well, not yet, but I was hoping that we could become friends.'

Tina could feel her heart thumping: should she? Could she?

'It's terribly kind of you. The thing is, I don't want to talk about what's been happening. It's been so awful, seeing Mr Abbott in hospital, then — well, you know. If we went out, you wouldn't talk about any of that, would you?'

'No, definitely not. Scouts Honour.'

'What does that mean?'

'I mean, no: you and me, going out together. You know — mates.'

Tina giggled. 'Going out with a policeman! What would Kevin say?'

'Going out? Well, I was thinking more just going for a drink, rather than going out.'

Tina laughed again. 'Oh, yeah. Sorry, I was getting carried away!'

Armstrong said, 'Don't get me wrong. Everything's on the table. It's just that, well — you know. I didn't want to scare you off.'

She squealed. 'Everything's on the table! What on earth do you have in mind?'

'Oh, sorry. No. I meant… a friendly drink. I didn't mean to alarm you.'

'Don't you worry about me. I can handle myself.'

He said, 'Oh, I'm sure of it. Okay, tell me: what time? Where do you want to go?'

Tina looked at the kitchen clock: twenty to seven. 'How about you pick me up at half seven? Do you know the Mops and Brooms?'

'Sure. That's great, that's smashing. I can't wait. I'll come up to your door.'

'No, don't worry about that. I'll be down by the front door. Yeah, it'll be nice to get out after everything that's been happening. Thanks, Chris. Can I call you Chris? You are a policeman, after all. In fact, you're a detective, aren't you?'

'Tonight, I'm an ordinary citizen going out with a pretty girl.'

Tina giggled. 'Flattery will get you everywhere. See you later.'

She put the phone down and went into the lounge.

'You're popular tonight.'

Tina still wasn't sure she'd done the right thing. She made up her mind: she wouldn't tell her dad. He'd get anxious and make everything much worse. 'Not really, it's girl stuff.'

Her dad looked up from the paper. 'Yeah, what stuff?'

'Oh, you know those girls in Sainsbury's we met? Well, they persuaded me to go out with them this evening. It's nothing special: just a drink. I know. Don't say it: "The Mops and Brooms is a dump." Well, it might be a dump to you, Dad, but for young people it's the place to go.'

'I wasn't going to say anything about The Mops and Brooms. No, my concern is that you're off to a pub and you're only sixteen. Honestly, when I was your age, I was still collecting stamps and reading the Beano!'

Tina laughed, 'You still read the Beano.' He buried his nose back into his paper and grumbled.

Tina went into her room and looked through her freshly laundered clothes. She needed to look good, but not too obvious and definitely not tarty. She held up her white, denim loon pants: creased but otherwise perfect. She rummaged through her tops and decided on a tight, white, nylon polo neck. Something else on top, a bit of class? Her wardrobe was crammed full of stuff but after some vigorous hanger-sliding she saw the crimson waistcoat Alice Thorpe had given her last year. She pulled it out of her wardrobe; yes, a good match with her new lipstick. Which shoes? Her two-toned platforms would be best with the loons, but they were agony; was Chris Armstrong worth the risk of long-term damage? What was the time? Ten to seven: time for a quick bath. Tina stripped off, put on her dressing gown and went out with her loons. 'Dad, you wouldn't iron these, would you, while I have a quick bath?'

'Certainly, me lady; your wish is my command. Do you want me to blacken the steps, polish the silver, sweep the parlour?'

'Never mind your grumbling, Cinders, get on with it.'

Her dad heaved himself up and pulled the ironing board out of the cupboard. Tina went into the bathroom and turned on the hot water. As the bath filled, she brushed her teeth. She was excited about the evening. Nervous, too. She was pretty sure it was a good idea, but he was a total stranger and — well, he was a flipping detective. Still, it was definitely worth a try.

She poured some of the bubble bath in and watched it froth up. She turned off both taps, took off her dressing gown and gingerly lowered herself into the foam. Which perfume should she go for? From her position she could see the bottles: Tramp, Charlie and the pink, French one that Auntie Mary had given her for Christmas. What about a necklace? Yes, if she wore the gold pendant it could draw his attention to her chest: ideal. The gold earrings would match the pendant, too. She stretched out and imagined how the evening would turn out. Tina smiled. This was going to be fun: risky but fun.

'Your ladyship's gown is prepared and hanging on the door to her chamber. Any other services?'

'No, thank you — you may go now.'

She sat up, cleaned her face with a flannel then hauled herself to her feet. Stepping out of the bath, she reached for a towel and patted herself dry. She used the towel to wipe condensation from the mirror and looked at her face: not too bad. She'd look fine once the war-paint was on. Sniffing each bottle in turn, she decided on the French one: it was definitely more refined. Dressing gown back on, she hustled out of the bathroom and into her bedroom.

Her dad called out, as he always did, 'Cor, Turkish brothel or what?'

She looked at her watch: ten past seven. In her dressing gown, she sat down in front of her mirror. She'd have to be quick —foundation, blusher, blue eye shadow, highlighter, eye liner, mascara and, finally, her new 'Crushed Raspberry'. Thanking God for Rimmel, she pressed her lips together and stared at her face. She smiled, 'Not bad, not bad at all.'

A quick look at the time: only five minutes. Her hair was a bit all over the place, but thirty seconds of furious brushing made it shine. She put on underwear, squeezed into the polo neck, and sucking in her breath, pulled on her loons. Now the platforms: as she'd thought, they were excruciating. They gave her the extra height, though, and it made her loons look great. She looked in the mirror: yes, she needed the waistcoat. Digging around in her bedside drawer, she found the earrings and then the pendant. She looped the thin gold chain over her head and looked again: it shone like a beacon; no, far too obvious. She took the pendant off and viewed herself from all angles. She smiled again: tasty.

Tina opened her bedroom door and sashayed out, 'What do you think, Dad? Any good?'

He looked up, 'Well, apart from the fact that you look like something from outer space, not bad. Really not bad.' This was rare praise. He added, 'Those shoes are ridiculous. How high are they?' Tina pulled up one trouser leg to reveal five inches of stack.

He tutted. 'Ridiculous. If you get home in one piece, I'll be amazed.'

'Thanks for your encouragement, Dad. Now, I must fly. See you later.'

'What time?'

'Hmm, when the all-night-drinking dens chuck us out.'

'Not too late, please. Tina, do you hear me?'

She was putting on her long, wet-look coat. 'See you later. Thanks for doing my ironing.'

'Thanks for the nice tea, and the chat. Be safe, please.'

She slammed the door and tottered down the six flights to the front door. A car's red lights shone through the glass. She paused. He could wait a minute or two.

Chapter 47

'Shall I get fish and chips?'

'No, it's fine. I'll do some liver and bacon. That'll build us up a bit.'

As his mum fried onions, Gary flicked through the local newspapers she always saved. Every issue had Nigel Philips' name against various articles. Gary had really liked Nigel but, right now, he would happily have cracked his skull open with an earthenware dish. Why had he played a trick like that? One minute he'd been friendly and helpful; the next, he'd been blabbing to the police.

'Cabbage or cauliflower?'

'Neither, ta.'

'Cabbage it is, then.'

Gary ventured a casual enquiry, 'So, you know that old bloke, Flanagan?'

His mum was quiet for a minute. She carried on pushing onions around the frying pan. At last, she said, 'He investigated Grandad's disappearance.'

'Mum, do you mind if I ask you about that?'

'Oh, I suppose you can... But it was all so horrible, I've always tried to forget it.'

'What happened?'

'Well, he went out after dinner one day and that was the last we ever saw of him. We contacted the police and they spent ages trying to find him. All our neighbours were interviewed. We were all interviewed. No one saw him at all. It was really strange. Even the local newspaper covered it for a few weeks. Anyway, Inspector Flanagan kept coming back and asking questions. He was like a dog with a bone.'

'He's a clever bugger. I thought he was a bit of a joke to start with, but I can tell he's a crafty sod.'

'I think he wants to find out the truth, love.' Gary snorted. 'Do you want mash or boiled?'

'Mash.'

Gary pushed a bit further. 'Derek said we went off to stay with Auntie Maureen.'

Jenny looked off into the distance. 'Yeah, that's right. I'd forgotten that. You must have gone for a week or two. It's funny: I thought you went on your own. That's right, though. She brought you all back after he went missing. I should have remembered that: it must have been lovely and peaceful.'

'What do you think happened to him?'

Jenny was silent again, thinking. 'I have absolutely no idea. Dad always said the old man knew some bad people. I don't know about that. To be honest, I didn't want to know.'

'What, gangsters?'

Jenny smiled at him, 'No, not gangsters. Unpleasant types.'

Gary pictured the grim face of his grandad and thought he could hear that awful, harsh voice. If he were alive now, Gary was pretty sure he'd keep out of his way. He said, 'So, he never turned up then?'

'No, we never heard anything again. The police always said they'd keep the investigation open, but nothing ever happened. I'd forgotten all about Flanagan 'til he turned up this afternoon.'

'Why didn't we keep in touch with Auntie Maureen?'

Jenny served up their dinners. She clattered knives and forks down, picked up the ketchup and gave it a hard shake. She undid the lid and looked inside. Turning to the larder, she picked up the vinegar bottle, dribbled some into the ketchup then, replacing the lid, shook it again. 'There you are: two more meals out of that.'

'Mum?'

She looked up. 'Mm-hmm?'

'Why did we lose touch with Auntie Maureen?'

'Oh, it's all in the past now. Let's leave it, shall we?'

Gary had already got more out of her than he'd expected. Anyway, he'd decided. He was going to take a trip to Totteridge in the morning.

Chapter 48

Chris Armstrong was holding open the passenger door for her as she approached. He said, 'You look nice. Mmm, wow! You smell nice!'

Tina smiled at him. 'Thank you, you're a proper gentleman.'

She settled into the car and let him shut the door. The radio was on — Paul Simon, *Fifty Ways to Leave Your Lover*. Chris opened his door and got in. 'Do you want the radio on?'

'Yeah, I like this one.'

He started the car and reversed out of the parking bay, changed gear and edged out on to the main road. He accelerated sharply. Tina felt herself pushed back into her seat.

She said, 'Oh, you're a good driver. I really like your car. Is it very powerful?'

'It's not bad. I can get it up to ninety if I push it a bit.'

Tina was nervous. No, she was excited.

He said, 'I didn't think you'd say yes.'

'Why?'

'Oh, I don't know. I suppose with the investigation into Brian Abbott's death and all that. Yesterday must have been very upsetting. Anyway, the point is, I'm really glad you're here.'

'Me, too.' They sped along. Tina sniffed. 'What's your aftershave?'

'Gillette, do you like it?'

'Yes, it's very — um… manly.'

'What's your perfume?'

She had hoped he wouldn't ask; it had slipped out of her head. She said, 'Oh, I can't remember. It's either Chanel or Rive Gauche, or maybe something else. It's pink, if that helps?'

'I don't know anything about perfume. It smells nice, that's all I know.'

They were dashing up Shenley Road. She said, 'Are you allowed to drive at any speed, you being a detective and everything?'

'Don't worry. If I get stopped I'll flash my badge. We'll be all right.'

'What about drinking? Are you allowed to drink and drive?'

'We have to stick to the laws but the funny thing is that, if I have a few, then I'm a much better driver.'

'Really?'

'Yeah, I never go mad. I might have three or four pints and then call it quits. Most of the blokes I work with drive when they've had a few, but we know when to draw the line. I find my reactions are much quicker when I'm more relaxed.'

'Well, as long as you're not too drunk when you drive me home.'

'Don't you worry about that; I'll get you home safe and sound.'

Tina saw the pub come into view. She'd been here quite a few times before. It wasn't one that Kev came to: she definitely didn't want him turning up and ruining everything. She asked, 'Do you come here much?'

'Not really. It's all right, though.'

He got out and opened her door. They walked towards the lounge bar. 'Is this one all right for you?' he asked.

'Lovely.'

When they went in, it was busy but not packed. He led her to a small table in the farthest corner. She sat down with her back to the wall. He said, 'What would you like to drink?'

She said, 'Well, I'm not used to drinking alcohol, but I do like vodka and orange. Is that all right?'

'Of course.'

'What are you going to have?'

'Hmm… Because I'm on my best behaviour, I'll have a lager and lime.'

'Oh, and what would you have if you weren't on your best behaviour?'

'I like Bacardi and Coke.'

Tina said, her eyes bright, 'Oooh, why don't you treat yourself? Go on, go mad. Actually, can I change my mind? Can I have one, too?'

Chris smiled. 'Sure! Your wish is my command. Do you want ice in it?'

Tina considered. 'Um, do you have ice in yours?'

'Yeah, definitely.'

'Oh, you obviously know what you're doing; can I have ice, too, please?'

'Of course. Anything you like, sweetheart.'

She smiled at him, meeting his eyes. 'Chris, one other thing, can I have a straw please? I know it's a bit girlie, but I always have a straw.'

'Bacardi and Coke coming up, with a straw for the lady.'

As she waited, blokes around her were gawping in her direction; one winked knowingly at her. She ignored them all.

Chris came back. 'Here we are.' He pulled out a packet of salt and vinegar crisps from one pocket and pork scratchings from the other. 'Now don't say I don't know how to show a girl a good time.'

She smiled. 'No, I won't. You're really pushing the boat out.'

'Cheers, Tina. It's lovely to see you.'

They clinked their glasses.

Tina smacked her lips. 'Mmm! Ooh, that's delicious.'

Chris swigged. 'Yeah, I like it. I like to try all the drinks. I like all kinds of whiskeys, especially with coke. I enjoy brandy too, but if I'm honest, I prefer Cognac. Sometimes, when I'm out with my boss — you know, DS Nott — we have a pint of lager and a whisky chaser. He's a terrible drinker but it's good fun getting wasted with him. I'm lucky, I can drink loads before I get drunk.'

To emphasise the point, he took another pull.

Tina said, 'I'm not very experienced at drinking but I love this. I think I'm going to have it again.' She sucked hard on her straw.

He said, 'I suppose that, living in the fast lane, I've had loads of experiences. When I was your age, I could drink eight pints, no trouble. I started smoking when I was twelve. I was a bit of a lad, to be honest. I got up to all sorts. If you knew me then, you wouldn't believe I'd become a copper one day.'

Tina smiled. 'Well, you've done very well. Do you mind if I smoke?'

'Here, have one of mine.' Chris pulled out a new packet of Dunhill. He undid the cellophane, opened the packet, removed the foil, and with his thumb, expertly slipped out a cigarette for her. He took one himself. Reaching into his pocket, he brought out a petrol lighter, flicked a long flame and lit Tina's cigarette, then his own. Sucking deeply on his cigarette, he looked at Tina. She smiled back.

He asked, 'Everything all right?'

'Lovely, thank you.'

They picked up their glasses and swallowed in tandem.

She said, 'Gosh, I hope you didn't make mine a double. I'm already getting a bit giggly!'

He smiled, 'Well, actually, I didn't mean to, but up till eight they're doing doubles for the cost of a single. I hope you don't mind?'

She laughed, 'No, it's a really refreshing drink. If I'm not careful I'll have to have water for the next round.'

'I've been in the force for three years now. I started as a copper on the beat, then I applied to be a detective. It's a great job.'

They drank again. Tina swished ice around her glass then knocked back the rest. 'Yum, delicious.'

Chris leapt up, 'Same again?'

'Let me pay.'

'Don't be silly. Stay there. I'll be back.'

'Hi, Tina. Who's that?'

Tina smiled at Lynn and Marie. 'Oh, his name's Chris. We're just out for a drink. I wasn't going to come but he suggested it.'

'He's dishy!'

Tina smiled.

Marie said, 'You're looking amazing; I love your lipstick. What colour is that?'

'Oh, I got it in Boots today. It's "Crushed Raspberry".' Tina looked over to the bar. Chris was turning to come back. She said, 'I'll see you in school tomorrow?'

'Yeah, sure. Good luck.' They grinned at her as they walked back to where they'd been sitting.

'Who's that?' Chris asked as he put the glasses down.

'Some friends from — just friends.'

Chris took a long swallow. 'Great news!'

'What?'

'I sneaked in one more double.'

'Ooh, triffic!' She sipped, too.

'Anyway, where was I? Oh, yeah. So you like my car, then?'

'Of course, it's — er, good.'

'I got it at a really good price. When I told the dealer I was a detective, they let me have it cut price. I can do nought to sixty in — er... hardly any time at all.'

'Really?'

'Another fag?'

'Thank you, Chris. You're being very generous. My other boyfriends expect me to pay half and, to be honest, Kevin Abbott never paid for anything.'

Chris lit their cigarettes again. 'Well, I'm glad you got rid of him. Er... have you had many boyfriends then?'

Tina blushed. 'Oh, no. I haven't had many. Oh, my goodness, no. I'm rather inexperienced with boys.'

Chris smiled hungrily. 'I don't suppose you're short of interest though, are you?'

Tina smiled, 'Well, I don't know, really.'

The pub was getting noisy as people got through their drinks. Chris's voice was particularly strident as he told her about his flat, his friends, his ambitions. She kept up with his drinking.

She said, 'I hope I don't make a fool of myself, Chris. I'm not very experienced at being out with blokes and certainly not drinking double Bacardis! What is Bacardi, anyway?'

'It's — um, I think it's a sort of spirit; something Italian, probably.'

'Ooh, how romantic. I am beginning to feel quite drunk.'

Chris smiled. 'Don't you worry, you're fine with me. Wanna crisp or a pork scratching?'

Tina opened the crisps. 'I think I'd better eat something. I don't want to get too drunk. What would you think of me?'

Chris laughed. 'I'd think you were a good sport.'

She found herself giggling hysterically now. She looked into his eyes; he looked back, smiling. He lowered his gaze. She'd been right, the pendant hadn't been necessary.

Chapter 49

Gary couldn't get Tina out of his head. She'd said she would ring when she had some news. Why didn't she let him know? Maybe they hadn't rung her, after all. This was a right fucking mess. For all he knew, she could have told them everything and they'd be arrested any minute.

He said, 'Mum, I'm going to ring her; I can't stand it.'

'She'll ring us, won't she?'

'Maybe, maybe not. I dunno.' He got up and rang her number.

'Hallo?'

'Oh, hello, Mr Castleton. I was wondering if Tina was there?'

'Who's calling?'

'It's Gary Abbott. You know, we met yesterday?'

'Oh, yeah. Well, I'm sorry — she's out.'

Gary thought — *out?* Where on earth could she be that was so important that she couldn't ring him. 'Oh. Do you know what time she'll be back?'

'No.'

'Um, do you know — I mean, it's… I was wondering if you knew where she was?'

'Yes, I do know.'

Gary waited. Silence.

'Will you tell me?'

Tina's dad sighed. 'Listen, son, you might not be as bad as your brother, but as far as I'm concerned, you're trouble. I know where she is, and I know who she's with. That's all you need to know.'

Gary was ashamed to be an Abbott. 'Yeah, of course; I'm sorry. Will you ask her to ring me when she comes in?'

'I'll let her know you rang but I won't ask her to ring you. You understand, don't you?'

'I do. Thank you.'

Gary slammed the phone down.

'You all right, love?'

'Yeah, it's just that Tina's out. She could be anywhere.'

'Hopefully she's having a nice time somewhere.'

Gary needed to get out. 'I'm going for a walk, Mum. I'll be back soon. If Tina rings, tell her I'll call her back.'

He went straight to Anthony's house. Mrs Alexander opened the door.

'Good evening, Gary. It's very nice to see you. I am so sorry — Anthony told me the awful news of your father. Please accept my sympathies.'

Gary shuffled on the doorstep; he wasn't sure how to reply. He said, 'Ta. Um, I'm sorry about — you know, Anthony's dad and everything.'

She smiled. 'Thank you, that's kind of you. Do you want to come in? I'm sure Anthony will be pleased to see you. Anthony, you have a visitor.'

The skinhead that sounded like Anthony appeared in the hall. He smiled broadly, 'Well, how lovely. My favourite gorilla.'

Gary grunted. 'I was wondering...'

Mrs Alexander turned and went into the sitting room. 'I'll leave you to it.'

Gary went on. 'You got a couple of minutes? Also, I was wondering if Frank...'

Anthony said immediately, 'I'll ring him right now.'

A few minutes later, they watched Frank running towards them across Meadow Park.

'Fuck!' said Gary.

'Golly!' said Anthony.

Frank sat down beside them on the bench, puffing loudly. He smiled, 'It's nowhere near there yet, but it feels good to be able to run a bit.'

Anthony said, 'Honestly, Frank, I know you can run, but that wasn't running. It was more like flying.'

'Fuck Steve Austin: you're the new bionic man.' Gary was grinning. He already felt better. He turned to Anthony. 'Anthony, any news on your dad?'

'The police think he killed himself.'

Frank looked at Anthony. 'When did you hear?'

'They rang this afternoon. There's no sign of foul play.'

'I'm really sorry. You too, Gary. It's all unbelievable.'

The three boys sat and thought about their own and the others' situations.

Gary said, 'Listen, do you mind if I tell you what's been going on? I told you some of it last night, Anthony, but so much has happened I just need to get it out of my head.'

The other two nodded.

'Right, so my mum clonks my dad over the head when she sees him — well... he's molesting... molesting? Is that the word? Molesting Tina. Tina's my brother's ex-girlfriend. Anyway, my dad is knocked out. I set up the kitchen, where it happened, to make it look like it was an accident. I get Joe around to check it over. He does, then legs it. I ring the ambulance and the police. Why I rang the fucking police, I don't know. Then, in hospital, my dad dies in front of our eyes: me, my mum and Tina. The police are really suspicious and they've been after us ever since. I don't know what the big deal is; I mean, he's dead for fuck's sake. Does it matter how? Anyway, they come around again this afternoon, this time with their boss, Detective Chief Inspector Flanagan. He's just a little old man — well, not little. Tall. But definitely an old man. The other two cops are suddenly bricking it, as if he's something special. He's not. He's more like your grandad, or your grandad's grandad.

'Oh, I forgot to say, thirteen years ago my dad's dad, my grandad, goes missing. He was living in our house, then he disappears. This bloke, Flanagan, investigated his disappearance and here he is, sniffing around again. Okay, then there's the newspaper. I went to the newspaper office — Frank, the place we went the other day? They remember you, by the way — I talk to this really nice reporter, Nigel Philips, and he helps me find the articles about my missing grandad in the old files. When I get home this afternoon, the coppers tell me that Nigel rang them up and that he'd told them I'd been in looking at the old papers. Honestly, I'd have brained him if he'd been there. Then, one of them tells my mum that they're going to talk to Tina next. She's great, but she ain't Mastermind. I'm really worried that, when they get her by herself, they'll trick her into telling them everything. You see? A right bloody mess!'

He looked at Frank, then Anthony. He went on. 'Oh, and I nearly forgot: three weeks ago, my dad attacked someone halfway along Theobald Street. The police had been looking for whoever did it, and they realised on Sunday night, when we were in hospital with my dad, that it was him. So, they were already waiting to arrest him, only he died — and that was before all this other stuff blew up!'

Anthony said, 'Anything else?'

Gary's laugh was a bark.

'Did your grandad ever turn up?' Frank's voice was calm and thoughtful.

'Nope.'

Frank said, 'That's probably why the man from the newspaper rang the police. Do you think he was trying to investigate the story? I mean, I know it's messed up things for you but, as far as he was concerned, he's following up a missing person story.'

Gary thought for a minute. 'Yeah, maybe. I was really surprised he'd done it. I thought he was a good bloke but then, when he called them behind my back, I thought he was just a prick. The other funny thing, though: I was up in this old attic place there, looking through all the old newspapers, but this Nigel bloke managed to find the information about it much quicker than me. I don't know: do newspapers keep records in different places or something?'

Frank said, 'They keep old papers on some kind of microfilm. I think it's called microfiche, something like that. He could probably look something up on it much quicker than you could.'

Gary spat. 'The crafty bastard.'

Frank asked, 'What I don't understand is why you made up the complicated story? I mean, if your mum was defending Tina, wasn't it reasonable for her to use force to stop him?'

Anthony said, 'True. I wondered that.'

Gary put his head in his hands. 'I know. I've been regretting it ever since. The thing is, I've seen stuff on the telly when people get banged up for self-defence. I saw one where a woman stabbed her husband; she got sentenced for murder, when all she was doing was stopping him hitting her. I couldn't let my mum go to prison. I'm not going to let that happen. Then, once we'd told them what had happened, we were stuffed. If we change our story now, they'll think we were covering up the truth before. It's all a right fucking mess.'

Frank asked, 'Have you talked to Joe about it, since before…?'

'Yeah. He says just stick to the story and it will all blow over. I think the real problem was that they wanted to arrest my dad for attacking this bloke the other day, and they were really pissed off when he croaked.'

Anthony said, 'What do you know about what happened to your grandfather?'

'Yeah, that's another thing. That whole business was new to me. I only found out about him yesterday. No, jeez, it was this morning. God! I'm losing track of time. Everything's all over the place. I didn't know anything. Then I discover a letter from my aunt. And then my mum told me all about it — she didn't want to, though. I'm planning to go and visit my aunt tomorrow.'

Frank said, 'Listen, Gary, this is getting really messy. I'm a bit worried about it. It all sounds like it's out of control. What can we do to help?'

Anthony chipped in. 'Yes, we can help you.'

Gary felt a wave of relief.

Chapter 50

Tina looked around the pub; it had got very busy. The hubbub had increased to a racket. Despite Chris shouting, she had to lean towards him now, to make out what he was saying.

'When you're a policeman, it's really hard to leave the job behind at the office.'

'I bet it is. You're having to deal with so many important things — people's lives and everything.'

'Exactly. You know, you're a pretty clever girl. I hadn't realised that you were, but you are.'

She smiled at the compliment and leaned a bit closer. Glancing into his eyes, she saw they were shiny; glassy even. She picked up her drink — the third of the night — and took long sips through the straw. 'I tell you what, Chris: this is my favourite drink ever. I bet it's really expensive, isn't it?'

'Nah. Anyway, I get paid a shit-load.'

Tina saw her friends grinning at her from the other side of the bar, Lynn giving her the thumbs-up. She smiled back at them: a stupid, drunken smile.

Chris said, 'Who are you smiling at?'

'Oh, just those friends. They were terribly impressed that I was with you.'

Chris turned around to the other girls; they looked away. He smiled at Tina, then let his eyes move to her chest. He grinned. 'You're much prettier than your friends, you know.'

She said, 'Have you got a girlfriend, Chris? You must have loads of girls after you.'

He glugged down his drink. 'Not really. I don't have time, you know, with my job and everything.'

'Oh, so, do you mean that — Oh, that's a shame. I thought that maybe…' She gulped her drink down, too.

He opened the pork scratchings and handed them to her. 'There you go. You get on the outside of them, and I'll get the drinks. Same again?'

'Lovely. Are you sure I can't pay for this round?'

He leaned across and patted her face. 'On me, sweetheart.'

She watched him edge his way through the crowded bar. He was staggering slightly. One of the blokes he bumped into didn't look very pleased. Chris seemed oblivious. She nibbled on the scratchings as she looked around the bar. Her friends were in the middle of a huddle of blokes, clearly enjoying being the centre of attention. Another group of young people were laughing and shouting. Every table was full, with more people standing between, chatting, having fun. She reflected that it must be brilliant to be part of a lively group of people, part of a gang.

Chris plonked himself down opposite. 'Sorry about the delay; it's packed at the bar.'

'Didn't you tell them you're a policeman? I bet that would clear the way.'

He laughed. 'Tempting but I don't like to flash my importance around. Wanna 'nother fag?'

'Ta.' She inhaled deeply and blew a long plume of smoke into his face. He smiled through it, his face red and sweaty.

She said, 'Is this my second or third drink? I've lost count.'

Grinning, Chris said, 'So have I. Actually, I think it's our fourth. I'm lucky. I don't get drunk. I started drinking when I was twelve and I'm... Also, I get better and better at driving when I've had a few. You've got to be good at driving to be a copper.'

'I bet you do. I mean, you must have to race after burglars and crooks all the time.'

'Tina?'

Smiling, she leaned towards him, her eyes on his. 'Yeah?'

'I know I said I wouldn't talk about that thing with Brian Abbot and his family, but—'

Tina held up her hand. 'Hang on. If you're going to ask me about that, I need a bit of Dutch courage first.' She took three long pulls on her straw.

Chris took his cue and gulped from his own glass.

She smiled. 'Actually, I wanted to ask you something, too. Who's going to go first?'

Chris mopped his face with his sleeve. 'Phew! It's really hot in here. Are you hot?'

'Boiling.' She stubbed out her cigarette.

He picked up his packet of Dunhill and tried to pull out a cigarette; several fell out onto the table. He said, 'Oops! Wanna 'nother one?'

'Ta.'

She took the lighter from him and leaned across the table to light his cigarette. Her hand was unsteady. They both laughed.

He said, 'Come here. Let the expert do it.'

She leaned towards him, her eyes on his. She noticed that his hand was even more unsteady than hers.

Chris drained his glass and smacked his lips. They sat inches apart, their elbows on the table, fags between fingers.

'You're not bad for a copper.'

'You're not bad for a — um...'

'Yes? A what?'

'Er, not sure what I was gonna say. Anyway, you're pretty tasty, is what I think.' She smiled. He said, his eyes rolling, his voice thick. 'What were you going to ask?'

She giggled. 'You go first.'

'No, fadies lirst. I mean, lalies lirst. Fuck! You know what I mean.'

She giggled again. 'I know what you mean but maybe I'm not a lady!'

He chuckled, then leered. 'I was hoping you'd say that.'

'Chris, you're cheeky.'

'Yeah, well — I can tell when a girl fancies me.'

Tina licked her lips and looked deep into his eyes. 'And...?'

He sat up straight, sucked in a deep breath, leaned right forward and said, 'I'm sorry, Tina, I hope you don't mind. Thing is... I was wondering — Well, my boss was, really... Thing is — I mean... You know the other night...'

Tina put her fag out, and slipping off her right platform, started to rub her foot against Chris's calf. His eyes popped; he grinned.

She said, 'Listen, Chris, I know I'm really pissed, but you know that thing that doctors do when someone dies? Is it a post-office mortuary, or something? Well, has there been a result yet?'

She continued to stroke his leg with her toes, her eyes on his, her lips parted. She felt his foot against her shoe, pressing, insistent.

He slurred, 'Don't tell anyone, will you? We got it this morning.'

She stroked his hand. 'Anything interesting?'

He shook his head. 'Nothing. Apparently the fucker bashed his head. The report said...' Chris looked off into the distance, 'that the injury sustained was consistent with the witness's testimentary. That's all.'

Tina stared at him. 'So, that proves it, then.'

Chris looked around him before saying, 'Acksherly, my boss thinks you're all full of bullshit but he can't prove it. He told me to see if I could get you to say anything different.' Chris wiped his red face. 'I told him I would, but thing is — I like you, Tina. I think you're really nice and... Anyway, for God's sake never tell anyone that.'

Tina smiled. 'Don't worry, Chris, I won't tell anyone. Now, is that it? I'm really drunk, so maybe I shouldn't say anything, in case you want to take it down in evidence. That's what you say, isn't it?'

Chris smirked, 'Well, it's not your evidence I want to take down, if you know what I mean?' he sniggered.

Tina giggled. 'Chris! I'll ignore that, if you don't mind. I haven't got anything else to tell you. What I said happened is exactly what happened. Honestly, Chris, you believe me, don't you?' Tina gazed into his eyes, her lips, once more, parted. He gaped back at her stupidly, nodding. 'Is that all you wanted to ask me?'

Chris wiped his face. 'Thing is... I wanted to know — Jeez, I've forgotten...' He burst out laughing. 'I've forgotten! Can you Adam and Eve it?'

Tina encouraged him. 'Come on. You can do it. Just relax.'

Giggling, he said, 'I bet you've said that a few times.'

Tina's voice was severe. 'You're a very naughty man, Detective.' They laughed and laughed.

'I know: I 'member... Bloody hell! I think I might be a bit pissed myself. Yeah... I was going to ask if any of those Abbotts had ever talked about the old man disappearing?'

Tina stared. 'What old man?'

He was giggling again. 'It's coz my big boss is fucking obsessed. 'Pparently... Well, anyway, doesn't matter. Jeez, my fucking glass is empty. Wanna 'nother one?'

'Actually, I need to have a wee. Do you mind?'

'No, course not. Go ahead. I'll go myself in a minute.'

Tina got up and wriggled her way through the crowd. She felt her bum get pinched a couple of times as she went.

'All right, sexy?' came from a bloke at the bar. She smiled at him then stuck up two fingers. He said to his mate, 'Tasty. Wouldn't mind giving that a good seeing to.'

Instead of the Ladies, she went into the public bar, through the boozing blokes to the coin box by the cigarette machine. She squeezed her fingers into her pocket and pulled out a ten-pence piece and dialled.

'Dad, it's me.'

'What's up?'

'Nothing's up. I need a lift home.'

'How come?'

'My plans have changed a bit. I'm in the Mops and Brooms. You know where it is, don't you?'

'On the road to Shenley?'

'Yeah.'

'I wish you'd told me you'd need a lift.'

'Well, I'm telling you now.'

'Okay, okay, I'll see you soon.'

'Thanks, Dad.'

More bum-pinching as she pushed her way back. Chris's head was flat on the table, his arms outstretched across the sticky surface. Was he asleep? Squeezing past him, she settled back into her chair. Tina felt sorry for him. He was a big kid really, trying to be the big man. She said quietly, 'Are you all right, Chris?'

He didn't answer. Curious, she reached over and picked up his empty glass and sniffed: it smelled of neat alcohol.

She lit a cigarette and waited for her dad to arrive.

Chapter 51

When Edward rang she held her breath: would he come home late, or not at all?

He explained, 'I'm really sorry...' She crossed her fingers. 'There's a massive panic on, up here. There's a clause in someone's contract that needs resolving before they're prepared to turn up tonight. Honestly, these people, Gerry, they're like children. I bet your pupils could get on better than this lot. Anyway, I've decided to stay at the club; that will take the pressure off me, and I can be here early in the morning to sort out all the ruffled feathers.'

'Oh, poor you. Will you get something to eat?'

'Don't worry, I'll be looked after. Do you want me to call you later?'

She didn't want him to ring. Now that she'd decided to relax properly, it was better that he left her to it. She said, 'If you get the chance; it's always nice to hear from you. I'm going to have a really early night. So, if you do ring, can you make it before nine p.m?'

He said, 'All right. What are you planning, apart from an early night? Something nice to eat?'

Geraldine looked at the cold Riesling in front of her. 'I was going to open a bottle tonight. Do you mind if I have half a glass with my dinner?'

'Please do. Don't go mad though, will you?'

'Of course not. I'll only have a little. Right, I'm off to eat some gruel. You enjoy your feast and try to get a good night's sleep.'

''Night, Gerry. See you tomorrow evening,' then, as an afterthought, 'if not later tonight.'

When she put the phone down, a wave of relief washed over her. There would be time for phone calls, a leisurely supper, a glass of wine. She might even treat herself to a luxury bath with essence, scented candles. She giggled: she might even drink some wine in the bath! What decadence! Edward would be very sniffy about it all.

She checked in on her mother, enjoyed her meal, and resisted, with all her might, the Arctic Roll. And she basked in the deep, warm luxury of her essence-filled bath, with the chilled Riesling by her side.

Sitting in her fluffy dressing gown, she emptied the remainder of the bottle into her glass and settled down to watch the *News*. The log-effect gas fire made the sitting room beautifully cosy. Altogether, life felt extremely comfortable indeed.

The headlines were full of strikes and demonstrations. She got up and changed channel: a dramatisation of *Tess of the d'Urbervilles* — that was more like it!

She slid out of her slippers and with a frisson of naughtiness, stretched out on the sofa, her head on the arm, burying her feet under the cushions. The miserable luck of Tess was getting on her nerves. Geraldine got to her feet and snapped the television off. Next to the set was the drinks cabinet. Smiling, she unlocked and pulled down the walnut door and studied the bottles. This was Edward's domain. She felt like the little Geraldine again, going through her parents' drinks. Edward had far more in his cabinet than her parents' Bristol Cream and Stones Ginger Wine. She edged out the bottles on to the flat surface: Talisker, Glenlivet, Laphroaig, Martell, Captain Morgan, Martini — Dry and Rosso — Dubonnet, Campari, Gordons, a vintage port, Smirnoff and, yes, Harvey's Bristol Cream, as well as two other sherries. Underneath the cabinet was a vast array of mixers, an ice bucket and tongs. She went out to the kitchen, rinsed her wine glass, and filled it with the port she'd been denied that other time.

Her gaze was caught by the box of cigars on top of the cabinet. She lifted the lid. There they all were, like princes waiting to be crowned. Although tempted, Geraldine thought it best not to light up one of his pride and joys: the smell would last, and he'd never forgive her.

She flipped through the record collection, chose Chopin, and went back to her sofa. The gentle, soothing piano, the syrupy warmth of the port and the constant hiss of the fire were lulling her into a trance: she must get Edward to stay out more often. She'd let him instil a life of rules and regulation. They suited him and that was fine; she was happy for him. Subtly though, without her noticing, they had wrapped themselves around her like barbed wire and their confining pressure was starting to hurt.

Perhaps one evening a week might be a good idea — a time for her, for her own identity? What could she do? Maybe there was a club or society she could join? Her mind immediately jumped to the prospect of meeting new people, new men. She brushed the idea away. She had allowed herself to have a childish crush on Daniel and nearly made a ludicrous spectacle of herself.

Why on earth would she want to meet a man? She was married to a successful and, she had to admit, attractive man.

Edward was a cold fish, but he still had his looks. Maybe it was all the golf he played? Whatever it was, he looked good: fit, trim, nearly all his hair and plenty of it. This was the problem: he was still in good condition, yet she was a "walrus". She looked across to the mantelpiece. There he was, smiling across at her.

She smiled back and lifted the port to her lips, calling out, 'To Edward and Geraldine, and happiness!' She tilted back her head and emptied the glass. 'Delicious.'

She was about to get up and refresh it, when Edward's face caught her attention again. This time he didn't look so pleased with her. In fact, now she looked more closely, there was a hint of disapproval in his expression. 'Sorry, darling, I'm having another one. When the cat's away and all that.'

This time, Geraldine filled the glass to the brim, and turned back to her sofa. She caught her foot in the sheepskin rug and lurched. Watching in fascination, she saw the crimson splosh form into the shape of a fish, or was it a butterfly, on the cream carpet. She giggled.

'Oops! Oh well, never mind.'

Concentrating hard, she tip-toed back to her sofa and placed the half-full glass on the coffee table. She was halfway through the tricky process of finding the perfect position to recline, yet still reach her glass, when the telephone rang. Edward's face, now cold and haughty, looked across at her: he was looking extremely serious. She rubbed her face to get some reason back into her head, then weaved her way to the hall. 'Hello, Edward?'

'Hallo, Gerry.'

'Everything all right?' Her mouth didn't seem to be working as it should. She realised she must sound pretty drunk.

'Fine with me. I've finished sorting out all the contractual small print. I'm off to have a drink.'

She could hear drunken laughter in the background and the thump-thump-thump of bass-heavy music. 'Absolutement, ma cherie.'

'What? Are you all right?'

'Certainment. Et toi?'

'Geraldine, what's wrong with you?'

She wasn't sure herself. She never spoke French. What was wrong with her? She coughed. 'Sorry about that. I've been listening to Chopin.'

'He's Polish.'

'I know that, Edward; I'm not an ignoramus.'

'Gerry, are you drunk?'

Geraldine was swaying — goodness, she must be. She leaned against the wall. 'Not drunk, just a bit tipsy. I had a glass of that nice Riesling. Don't worry, I've saved most of it for you.'

She could hear a voice in the background. Edward answered, 'Please, brandy and soda; yes, a large one.' Then, 'Gerry, you sure you're all right? Do I need to come home?'

'No, no, don't be silly. I'm perfectly fine. I'm off to bed in a minute. No, you enjoy your drink with your friends. You deserve it.'

'Oh, all right then.' He sounded relieved.

'Good night, Edward. See you tomorrow evening.'

'Good night. Go to bed. You know you need your beauty sleep.'

Geraldine wanted rid of him now. She said 'Bye' again and put the phone down. She meandered back to the sofa and slumped into its welcoming embrace. She picked up her port, toasted her husband's health once more, then drained the glass.

Chapter 52

Terry struggled into the Imp. This time, it was even more difficult. Sitting in front of the telly for two hours had not been a good idea: he had completely seized up. Mind you, he hadn't expected to be going on another outing this time of night. He shook his head. *Bloody Tina!* He turned the key: the old engine coughed, spluttered, then slowly came to life. The fuel gauge caught his eye — damn! Red. He'd noticed it was nearly empty earlier, but without his wallet he was stymied. Shit — still no wallet! He certainly wasn't going to be able to get to Tina and back without filling up somewhere. Sighing deeply, he clambered out and trudged heavily back up to the flat.

Puffing even more than usual, he opened the front door and looked for the telephone directory. He flipped to the Ds, hoping against hope that there wouldn't be too many Duttons. He was in luck: only two. Even better, one of them was in a posh street, the other one was in the council estate. He dialled. It rang and rang. 'Come on!'

'Edward?'

'Er, no. I'm terribly sorry to disturb you. Is that Geraldine Dutton?'

'Yes, who is this?'

'I'm so sorry. This is Terry, Terry Castleton. I'm the caretaker at the school.'

'Oh, Terry, what a relief! I thought you were... Anyway, how are you?' She sounded really peculiar.

'I'm fine, thank you. Are you all right? You sound — Is everything all right?'

He heard snorting laughter, then, 'Oh, I'm fine, thank you, Terry. I meant, are you all right after I gave you that hideous eyeful today?'

'I can assure you it was nothing of the kind. No, I'm ringing to see if I can collect my wallet. I've got to go and fetch Tina and I'm almost out of petrol. I think my wallet is in my jacket?'

'Oh, I see. Well, if you tell me your address, I'll bring it over. The only thing is I've had a tiny glass of Vimto and I'm a bit squiffy.'

Terry now understood, 'Ah, I see. It's very kind of you. Actually, I think I've got enough to get to your place. If I pop over now, can I get my jacket?'

'Shertainly. I'm 4 Priory Lane. Do you know where that is?'

'I do — well, roughly. I'll be with you in five minutes.'

He put the phone down, tossed the directory on to the kitchen worktop and did his best to dash down the stairs. Starting up the car, he prayed there would be enough fuel to get to Priory Lane and on to the Esso on the roundabout.

Terry whistled when he saw Number 4.

'Very nice.'

The detached, double-fronted house had a wide, gravel drive, an 'In' and an 'Out'. There were two cars outside the front door: a Jag and Mrs Dutton's Rover. He got out and rang the doorbell.

The hall light came on at last; he could see her approach the glass door. To his embarrassment, she was wearing a creamy dressing gown, nothing on her feet, possibly nothing else — blimey, this was really awkward. She opened the door.

He said, 'I'm so sorry. Please forgive me. It's just that Tina has rung me to collect her from a pub and I don't want her to be waiting around with a bunch of — well, you know.'

Geraldine smiled. 'It's fine, Terry. Do come in. Come into the sitting room. Come on. Come and sit down. Have you got time for a drink?'

'Well, thing is, I'm against the clock a bit. I just need my jacket.'

Terry now realised that Geraldine Dutton was more or less legless. As well as a delicious coconut oil fragrance, there was more than a whiff of booze in the air. She was unsteady on her pins and her speech had the hallmarks of a comedy drunk.

She said, 'Of course, Terry. Sorry. Now, where did I leave it?'

He watched her swishing coats along the coat rail in the hall. She said, her hand to her head, 'I can see it in my mind... Where is it? Ah, of course. It's upstairs. Come and sit down, Terry; come on. It's nice and warm by the fire. I've poured you a drink — I hope you like port?'

'No, honestly, I couldn't possibly come in. You and your husband are obviously having a cosy night in. I'll wait here. It's fine, really it is.'

She waved at him airily. 'Come on, in you come. It's just me. Edward's away for the night.' Reluctantly, he followed her into the sitting room. 'There you are: take a seat. At least have a drink. Don't leave me to do all the hard work.'

He saw a large wine glass full to the brim. 'I'm sorry, I don't drink and drive. You have it.'

'If you're sure? I shouldn't — but waste not, want not.' She wobbled towards the coffee table, bent down and in one, long glug, emptied the glass. Giggling, she said, 'Mmm, delicious. I haven't got a headache or anything. Edward should put that in his pipe and smoke it. Now, let me see. Sorry, Terry, what am I looking for?'

'My jacket?'

She scratched her head in mystification. 'Er... um, oh yes. Stay there. I won't be a mo.'

Standing with his back to the fire, Terry watched her weaving towards the stairs. She bumped her hip on an armchair, then ricocheted against the door jamb.

'Won't be a minute,' she called. He heard her unsteady steps disappear upstairs.

Terry looked around the room; it was all very good quality: lovely furniture, plumped up cushions, paintings, lamps, rugs; and a recent accident with what might be port. He wondered how many she'd knocked back. There was a tremendous crash on the ceiling above. He looked up — bloody hell, that was a real bump! He dashed up the stairs and followed the landing to the end room. Terry peered in. There she was, on her rear end, wedged between bed and bedside drawers.

'Are you all right?'

She looked blearily up at him. 'Oh, Terry, what must you think of me? I was getting your jacket and then... I think I had a rush of blood to my head.'

Terry saw that his jacket was on the floor next to her. He was tempted to grab it and make a dash for the safety of his car but pushed the idea away. He bent down, picked up and put on the jacket, then looked down at Geraldine. She was motionless, eyes closed.

'Er... are you all right?'

'I think so. Anyway, you know what they say: "drunks don't hurt themselves when they fall."' She slapped her face. 'What am I saying? I'm not a drunk, Terry. Really, I'm not.'

'Don't worry about that. Let's get you up and then I can... Can you get up, do you think?' Geraldine started giggling. 'What? Why are you laughing?'

'Oh, Terry, it's only a few hours since the last time we did this! We're making something of a habit of it.'

The irony hadn't escaped him. 'Can you get up?'

She wriggled ineffectually. 'Oh. I think I might be stuck.'

Terry looked away: the dressing gown, now agape, had ridden up, revealing smooth, white thighs. Her voice was determined. 'Come on, Geraldine — heave ho.' Her hands sought purchase on locker and bed. She bent her knees to push up from the floor. She let out a great groan of effort then collapsed back, giggling.

Through tears of hysteria and, Terry guessed, embarrassment, she said, 'Sorry, Terry, you're going to have to haul me up. I hope you're strong!' She noticed her dressing gown had opened fully. 'Yikes, I'm sorry; thank goodness I'm wearing a nightie.'

Trying to ignore the inadvertent display, Terry said, 'Of course, madam, it will be my pleasure to assist you. Oh, and it hardly needs saying, strength won't be required.' When she'd belted up her dressing gown securely, he put both his hands down towards her. 'Grab hold.' Geraldine grasped his hands.

He said, 'No, that's far too feeble. Get a good grip.' He tightened his grip around her soft hands. Planting his feet in front of hers, he said, 'Ready to weigh anchor, First Mate?'

She giggled again, 'Aye-aye, Cap'n.'

'Okay. After three: ready? One, two, three, and — heave!'

Terry had been confident that he would find it easier to pull her up than it had been for her to get him upright in the shed. In the blink of an eye, she was on her feet. Geraldine clearly hadn't been quite as ready for being in the vertical.

She shrieked, 'Oh, my goodness! Ooh!' She started reeling and threw her arms out wildly. She grabbed hold of his jacket, then over she went again. Terry caught her. She wrapped her arms around him for ballast; he held her. 'Oh, Terry, I'm so sorry. This is utterly humiliating. I can't even stand up, I'm so drunk.'

Terry hadn't held a woman for six years. The warm, scented femininity of Geraldine Dutton was simultaneously exquisite and excruciating. He wanted to let go and run away, yet couldn't bring himself to do anything other than hold her to him. Her shampooed hair was in his face, her arms were tight around him. She wasn't giggling anymore; she was still, silent.

Finally, he made himself say, 'That's it. Well done. Can you step back? That's it. Now sit down — there you are, you're on your bed. Well done. You've done it.'

Geraldine let go of him. Reluctantly, he stepped back. He looked at her. She was sitting still, her hands in her lap, head down.

Kneeling down in front of her, he asked, 'You all right?' She looked into his face; there were tears on her cheeks. She nodded. 'You sure? Can I get you anything?'

'I'm so sorry, Terry. What must you think of me? It's just that I'm... I'm... Anyway, please forgive me?'

He took one of her hands in his. 'May I?' She looked at him, wondering. He brought her hand to his lips and kissed it tenderly. 'You're a beautiful person, Geraldine. I feel honoured to have been on hand to assist you in your hour of need. Now, sweet lady, I must jump aboard my steed and sally forth to the aid of an even younger damsel. Please will you excuse me?'

'Sir, you are a splendid knight and I do indeed excuse you. Thank you, Sir Terry Castleton.'

Terry let go of her hand. 'Why don't you get into bed and doze off? I'll turn off everything downstairs.'

'Will you help me?'

He stood back, holding out his hand. She took it and got to her feet, swaying precariously. Keeping her steady, he pulled back sheets and blankets then steered her back on to the bed.

'Shall I take your dressing gown?' She started to undo the belt. 'Hang on, let me switch the light off first.'

Once the room was dark, he heard the dressing gown being opened and thrown on to the floor. The bed creaked slightly as she got in. He picked up the dressing gown and hung it on the open door, then tenderly pulled first sheet, then blankets up over her shoulders.

'Goodnight, Geraldine.'

'Goodnight, Sir Terry.' Her voice was a mumble.

He couldn't resist stroking her hair. He said, 'There you are. Good girl. Sleep tight, now.'

'Thank you, Terry. Thank you so much. Thank you for more than you realise.'

A thought suddenly struck him: was his wallet even in his jacket? Yes. Phew! He hurried down the stairs and back into the sitting room. Quickly, he picked up both glasses and took them in to the kitchen. Next to the sink was a damp cloth. He went back to the table and wiped it clean. The port stain on the carpet called out to him. He searched the kitchen: yes, a large tub of Saxa. He sprinkled it liberally over the stain: it would either work or it wouldn't. He switched off the kitchen light and walked through the sitting room. What was on? Lamps, fire, and a red light on the record player. As he bent down to turn off the gas fire, the photographs on the mantelpiece caught his eye: Geraldine in her twenties? Wow, what a dish! Next to her was… Terry felt a wave of nausea rush through him. He dashed for the door, into the hall and flung open the front door. White, hot bile erupted from his mouth over the long, sleek bonnet of the Jaguar. Unable to stop retching, Terry slumped against the body of the car.

After a minute, he stood up, his heart racing, lungs heaving. He pulled out a handkerchief and mopped his face. Shaking his head in disbelief, he tried to calm himself. *Slow down… deep breaths. Count to ten.* His jangling nerves began to ease. *Damn!* He'd have to go back in and sort things out; he couldn't let Geraldine down. He went back in, turned off the fire, record player and lamps, averting his eyes from the photographs. In the kitchen, he got the cloth and ran it under the tap. He took it, dripping-wet, out to the Jag and swished puke off the shiny bonnet. He opened his own car boot, grabbed a plastic bag and shoved the cloth inside it. Finally, returning to the house, he switched off all the lights and shut the door. Getting into the Imp, he leaned his head against the steering wheel and counted to ten, very slowly.

Chapter 53

Tina felt like touching the comatose form in front of her, just to let him know she was still here. She felt conspicuous, sitting with a drunk man whose head was lolling, arms spread out in front of him, on the table. She moved his glass out of the way, in case he knocked it to the floor and drew even more attention to their corner.

The two blokes at the table to her right were looking first at Chris, then at her. One of them, who was wearing a blue tank-top, said, 'Do you want to join us, darling? He ain't exactly charming company, is he? Now us, we're a bit more fascinating — don't you think?'

Tina laughed, 'Yeah, well. It must be my electric company: I've obviously electrocuted him!'

They looked her up and down. Tank-top said, 'Nah. It's because he's a pillock.'

'You're too much for the poor boy,' said the other bloke, his large, protruding teeth catching the lights of the pub.

She laughed. 'If only.' She looked around the bar. *Where was he? Come on, Dad.*

Lynn and Marie were coming over. Tina groaned inwardly. She smiled at them, pointed to her companion and held a finger to her lips.

Lynn whispered, 'What's wrong with him?'

Tina shrugged and shook her head.

Marie ventured, 'Is he asleep?'

Tina couldn't help herself. 'Well spotted.'

'No, I meant, perhaps he's had a heart attack or something?'

Tina hadn't thought of that. Maybe he was dead?

Tank-top said, 'No, he's pissed out of his head. I was watching him: his face was like a beetroot, and he was sweating buckets. He can't hold his booze; some blokes can't.'

Tina was sorry for poor Chris. She leaned across and patted his shoulder. She felt the need to excuse him. 'He's a copper. He hasn't had any sleep for days.'

Goofy leered, 'Oh yeah? Do you keep him busy at night then, darling?' The men sniggered.

'What are you going to do?' Marie asked.

'My dad's on his way. He'll sort it out. Don't worry about us.'

Lynn said, 'You know, Steve Bellingham is quite nice, Tina. I bet he wouldn't fall asleep.'

Tina snapped. 'He's a prick and a wanker! Will you stop going on about Steve 'Knobhead' Bellingham.'

Lynn said, 'Well, actually, he's my cousin. Come on, Marie. Let's leave her ladyship to her pissed constable.'

'I'm sorry! Please don't go. I'm sorry. I'm really wound up, to be honest. I'm sorry about Steve. I'll think about him. Yeah, maybe he is quite nice.' To Tina's relief, the friends looked mollified and stayed where they were. Having them with her meant that she didn't have to sit here and be gawped at.

Tank-top said, 'Never mind Steve Bellingham, what are my chances?'

Again, Tina was grateful. The two lads, drunk and ugly as they were, also provided some cover. She turned to him, smiled, and said, 'Okay, shall we run through your qualifications?'

He grinned. 'Well, I've got a massive advantage over other men.'

'Oh yeah, what's that then?'

Goofy said, 'He's lying. It's a miniature and it's never seen any action.'

Tank-top was indignant. 'No it ain't — and yes it has!'

Lynn and Marie were giggling. They stood there, flicking back their hair and sticking out their chests. Tina saw her dad pushing his way towards them.

'Sorry, guys and girls, I've got to go now.' She stood up as her dad came close.

Her dad looked down at Chris then up at Tina. 'You all right, love?'

She nearly threw her arms around him. 'Fine! Just fine.' She squeezed out between the two tables.

A bloke said, 'I'll take that seat if I may.'

Tina looked up and saw Joe waiting to take her place. He smiled at her, then winked. She looked down at Chris, then back to Joe.

He said, 'It's fine. I'll make sure he's all right.'

She smiled her thanks, then said, 'Come on, Dad, let's go. Bye, Lynn. See you, Marie.' She took her dad's arm and let him guide her out. They got into his car.

He said, 'I'm sorry it took me so long. I had to get some petrol and that wasn't as straightforward as I'd thought. Anyway, home, me lady?'

Relief, at last. God, it had been hard work! Part of her had enjoyed it: she'd felt like a spy or something. The acting had been exhilarating, but keeping it up had exhausted her.

Her dad said, 'What was going on?'

'Oh, Dad, I'm so pleased to see you.'

'Who was the drunk lad?'

'Oh, just a bloke. He's a copper; a detective, in fact. Lynn, Marie and me were talking, and he came over. He was feeling a bit dodgy, so we offered him a seat. He just crashed out in front of us.'

'I hope he's not the one you said was interested in you?'

She'd forgotten they'd talked about Chris. 'Oh, er, well — hmm… yeah, but don't worry, Dad; he's out of the picture.'

'Glad to hear it.'

They drove along in silence. She was beginning to feel really tired, and a bit shaky.

Her dad said, 'That Gary Abbott rang.'

She looked across at him, 'What did he want?'

'He didn't say, but he was a bit arsy. I told him that I'd tell you that he'd rung, but I wouldn't ask you to ring him back. That's fair enough, isn't it?'

'Thanks, Dad. I will ring him. I've got some news. He's much nicer than his brother, by the way. I think you might like him if you gave him the chance.'

They turned into their block's car park.

She said, 'Flip, I'm so tired; you might have to carry me up the stairs.'

'Sorry, Tina, I was going to ask you that.'

'I tell you what, Dad. As soon as I've got a good job, shall we move to a house in the country?' They were trudging up the echoing flights.

He said, 'Definitely. I'm sick of this place.'

He unlocked the door, went into the kitchen and put the kettle on.

Tina said, 'I'm just going to ring Gary. Can I have a cuppa please? First things first — I'm busting for a wee!'

As she emptied her bladder of all the Coke, it occurred to her that it would be quite likely that one of the other Abbotts would answer the phone. She could hardly ask Kev or Derek if she could speak to Gary. It would be all right to ask Jenny, but she might say something that would give the game away. She stood next to her dad, who was looking through paint charts as the kettle heated up.

'What are you looking at?'

'I thought I'd paint your bedroom at the weekend. What do you think?'

'Oh, that would be great. The only thing is, we'll be moving out soon, won't we? Shouldn't we wait until we've bought our mansion before deciding on colours?'

The kettle boiled. 'Hmm, good point. But just in case we don't move for a few days, what kind of colour would you like?'

She thumbed through the pages of bright, light and summery colours and slowed down as they darkened to the gloomier.

He peered over her shoulder. 'No, I'm not allowing miserable colours.'

'Dad, will you do me a favour?'

'Don't tell me: you want black walls.'

'No, yellow would be lovely. No, it's something else. I want to ring Gary back, but I don't want to talk to his brother. Will you ring and ask for Gary for me? If it's him that answers, then you can hand over the phone; if it's anyone else, you can say you're — um, someone else.'

'Who?'

'Er... um, you could say you're — oh, I don't know — Harold Wilson?'

'Ha, so let me get this right. You want me to ring up a family of low-lifes, pretending I'm the recently-resigned Prime Minister? Tell me, why would Harold Wilson be ringing the Abbotts?'

'Oh, Okay. Jim Callaghan?'

'Tina!'

Tina wondered if she were making a meal of things. She knew Gary would be wanting to talk, and so would Jenny. She needed to talk to both of them: she had great news. The phone rang.

She rushed to it. 'Hello?'

'It's Joe.'

'Thank God!'

'How did you get on?'

'Oh, Joe, it was awful. I had to work really hard. I thought he was going to realise what was going on. Honestly, it was awful. But I got it: I got what we wanted!'

'Go on.'

'Near the end — just before he fell asleep — I asked him if they'd had the report back from the doctor. They had. He said that the injury was consistent with what we said. And he said that that was all.'

'Oh, Tina, you're a marvel!'

She laughed. 'I nearly leapt up and yelled "Yes!"'

'You've done something amazing tonight. I think you're incredible.'

She said, 'How is he? I feel so sorry for him.'

'I managed to get him back to his car. He was still really groggy. I had to ask your friends to help me.'

'What, Lynn and Marie?'

'No, the lads.'

'Oh, yeah, of course. He didn't drive, did he?'

'No, I got his keys out of his pocket and stuck him in the passenger seat. I drove to the police station car park and left it there. He's fast asleep there now, as far as I know.'

Tina laughed. 'Oh, the poor bloke. How many did he have?'

'Well, I hadn't bargained on the free doubles. So, let me see. He had four drinks, two of them were doubles plus your double each time; that's eight. Then two more doubles, plus your two drinks. I think he may have had sixteen in the end. I began to lose count.'

'How did you do it?'

'I asked the barmen to make sure that he got all the shots. I had to pay a few quid to make it worth their while but — you know, needs must. It was a bit tricky, because they had to do it without him seeing. Your idea of having a straw was brilliant; they always knew which one was the one without the booze.'

'What did you tell them?'

'I said it was a practical joke. We were getting him back for one he played on us.'

Tina thought through the evening. She said, 'When you nodded to me at the beginning, I nearly waved to you!'

'I know, sorry about that. I wanted you to know I was around, but not in the way.'

She thought of poor Chris, asleep in his smart Avenger. He wasn't a bad bloke, just an arrogant one. 'You weren't horrible to him, were you?'

'I promise I was very gentle with him. I made sure he had his cigarettes and lighter in his pocket.'

'What about his seat belt?'

'"Clunk click, every trip."'

'Sorry, Joe, I feel like we stitched him up, that's all. Anyway, here's something else I found out.'

'Yes?'

'He said that his boss was obsessed by something. Apparently, Gary's grandad disappeared ages ago — I think he said thirteen years ago. Chris wanted to know if I knew anything about what had happened.'

Joe was quiet for a while. He said, 'Do you?'

'No, nothing; it was new to me.'

'Have you spoken to Gary yet?'

'No, I'm desperate to, but I can't ring his house.'

'I'll ring him now and get him to call you. Is that all right?'

'Thanks. That's perfect.'

'Tina, I owe you. I really needed your help, and you haven't let me down. Thank you so much.'

Tina laughed. 'I think you could have started me on my new career. I'm not sure if it's acting or spying!'

He said, 'Listen, my money's going to run out in a minute. Let me ring Gary now. Speak soon, Tina. Well done — you're amazing.'

She put the phone down and went into the kitchen. Her dad was at the table, head in his hands.

'What's wrong, Dad?'

'Your tea's on the counter.'

She carried it over and sat opposite him. He looked done in.

She said, 'What happened tonight? You said it hadn't been straightforward?'

He sighed, 'Oh, it was nothing really. My wallet was in my jacket; I'd forgotten that Mrs Dutton had it. So I had to go to her place before coming to you. There was a bit of a delay… Anyway, I got stuck there for a few minutes and — it's all fine now.'

Tina said, 'I'm going to get another call in a minute. When that's done, why don't we look at the paint colours? We can do up my room together on Saturday.'

'That's a lovely idea. To be honest, I think I'm going to turn in. It's been a hell of a day.'

'Fine, but let's decide on the colour tomorrow.'

'Good idea. I'll feel more able to argue the toss with you after a good night's sleep.'

Chapter 54

Gary was conscious that all they'd talked about was the shit he was in. He looked at his friends. 'I'm sick of all my stuff — what about you?'

Anthony said, 'Well, I've been at school preparing to take over the world.'

Gary laughed. 'Knob. How about you, Frank?'

'Yep, I've been at school. I had a chat with Mr Wilson today. Do you remember he suggested that I might do a bit of after-school training? Well, I thought maybe I'd give it a go. He was pretty good actually. We've got a session planned for tomorrow evening — some fitness routines. I'm so out of condition, I need to build myself back up again. I'll have to go slowly though; I don't want to do any damage.'

'That's great. What's made the difference?'

Anthony said, 'Was it everything that happened over the weekend?'

Frank thought for a while, then said, 'Yes, it was all of that. There was something else, though. I came here Sunday evening, to have a bit of a jog around. I had this idea that, maybe if I did some running, I would feel closer to my dad and brother. I've been trying to bring back their memories all the time, rather than get on with life — you know, the present and the future. So, I started to run, and before I knew what was happening, I felt them with me again, like they were still here. I guess it sounds a bit fanciful, but I think that's the answer. I was doing the wrong thing by trying to bring them back; they're with me all the time.'

Gary did think it sounded like a load of old guff, but he really respected Frank and said, 'If it works, then it must be true.'

Anthony asked, 'Will you get to the Olympics, then?'

Frank smiled. 'I doubt it. I'll take it day by day!'

They gazed towards the streetlights on the far side of the park.

Gary said, 'How's your mum coping, Anthony?'

'It's hard to know. I mean, she's had to deal with a terrible, manipulating man all these years. The fact that he's taken his own life and, basically, removed his presence from hers, is sort of a relief, I think? It's funny though:

I feel bad about him. I saw him four days ago and he was absolutely foul and evil. Then, when I heard he was dead, I felt sorry for him. I think that maybe my mother might feel a bit mixed up too. What about your mother?'

'I can't work her out. She's getting on with funeral arrangements and that stuff. She supported him for all those years. I don't know, maybe she loved him? It's hard to understand that, though. He used her as a punch bag, as far as I can see.'

Frank said, 'Maybe she thought she had no choice? I think that sometimes we can get into a sort of prison existence?'

Gary said, 'Yeah, well, my house feels like a prison right now, not to mention the bloody police everywhere you look. By the way, Frank, you told me your brother used to do work at your local newspaper; is that right?'

'Yeah, he used to go in and make a nuisance of himself. Why?'

Gary thought about Karen. 'Oh, well, apparently, the newspaper here takes on apprentices. I know I'm hopeless at school, but I thought I could try my luck. Anthony, what do you think?'

Anthony took a long time to answer. Finally, he looked at Gary and said, 'You're an extremely ugly, brutish and ignorant person, Gary Abbott. You've got the manners of a caveman and the intelligence of a single cell organism. If I ran a newspaper, I'd avoid you like the plague. I'm almost tempted to ring them up and warn the proprietor that you're planning to make an approach. I don't think I have any further thoughts on the matter.'

Gary looked at Anthony. Then he stood up, bent down, grabbed him by the ankles and pulled hard. Anthony landed heavily on his back and was hauled fifty yards across the mown grass of the park. Throughout his treatment, Anthony was yelling in outrage. Gary strolled back and sat down next to Frank.

Gary said, 'What do you think?'

Frank said, 'I think you'd be good at it. You may need to keep your temper under control. I suppose that to be a good reporter you have to be like a dog with a bone — never let go. Also, I don't know, but I imagine you would need to be driven by the truth rather than personal preference.'

'You what?'

'Well, I'm not sure, but I think people might want something to be true or false; but what we want isn't relevant. Truth is not about what we want or like: it's something in itself.'

Anthony was trudging back to them. 'I'll get you, Abbott.' He sat down again.

Gary said, 'Are you thinking about that bastard Nigel and him going behind my back?'

'I don't know anything about him. He might be thinking that your grandad going missing is an interesting story. He might like you. He might not. The story remains interesting, anyway.'

Gary said to Anthony, 'We're talking about truth.'

'Yes, so I understand. So, the point is, Gary, you are an ugly, brutish caveman, whether you like it or not.'

Gary held up his hands, 'Okay, Okay, I get it. I'll try and do better.' He looked at his watch. 'I'd better go home; I've got to be in when Tina rings.'

They went their separate ways.

Gary thought about Tina: where would she go on a Tuesday night? He didn't really know much about her. She'd only been going out with Kev for a couple of months. She'd come round and join in with the banter, but mostly they went out. He didn't blame them for that. Why would they stay in their shithole of a house? Gary had thought of her as a bit of a scrubber. He had to admit she was sexy, all right but, he realised now, she was a lot feistier than he'd have guessed. He'd like to get to know her much better. It was a shame that she'd gone out with Kev; that spoilt things a bit. He thought about Karen Mitchum; she was really nice, too. He wondered why he'd never been able to get a girlfriend. Maybe Anthony was right — What was he thinking...? Anthony was definitely right.

Somehow, he would try and make himself more like... who? He thought about some of the boys who always had girlfriends. What did they have? They had trendy haircuts and fashionable clothes. They had something else, though: they weren't thick bullies. He was nearing his house. Looking at it flattened his spirit instantly. He unlocked the door and went in.

Derek and Kev were watching the telly; his mum was writing a letter. He sat down next to the hall door, ready to grab the phone.

'Who you writing to?'

'A letter to one of Dad's cousins.'

Derek looked over. 'Mum, Gary was asking me about that time we stayed at Auntie Maureen's house. I'm right, aren't I? That was when Grandad went missing?'

Jenny didn't look up, 'It was all around that time. The actual dates have got really cloudy now.'

Kev said, 'I can remember it. I didn't want to come back coz I thought he'd still be here. When we got here and he'd gone, it was like Christmas.'

'Now, come on, Kev; he wasn't that bad.'

Derek laughed out loud. 'Not that bad? He was horrible. Honestly, Mum, what planet are you on? We were all scared of him, even Dad.'

Jenny couldn't help smiling. 'Well, all right. He wasn't exactly sweetness and light.'

Gary said, 'I can't remember him, except his voice. What was so bad about him?'

'Nothing if you didn't mind getting whacked for no reason or being told you were a useless waste of space,' Derek said.

Kevin said, 'Yeah, but Del, you were a useless waste of space.'

'Fuck off.'

Jenny looked up, 'Shush, now!'

Gary asked, 'What do you think happened to him?'

They all looked at their mother.

She put her pen down, took off her glasses and polished them with her sleeve. 'I've never said this to anyone, but I think your dad did away with him.' They were silent, waiting for more. 'He always said he didn't know what had happened. They certainly had a terrible relationship. The old man only came to live with us because he'd been evicted from his own place for non-payment of rent. When he was here, Dad and him had terrible arguments... Really terrible — fighting and everything. We sent you off to stay with Maureen, to get you all away. I'm sure the police thought that it was Dad, but they couldn't ever prove it. Mr Flanagan wouldn't leave us alone. That's why he was here today, I'm sure of it.'

Derek whistled. 'Well, that was one good thing Dad did.'

'Hang on — he produced me; that was his greatest achievement,' Kevin protested.

Derek and Gary snorted. The phone rang. Gary's heart leapt. Keeping his cool, he got up without rushing and went into the hall, shutting the door behind him.

'Hello?'

'Gary?'

'Yeah?'

'It's Joe.'

'Great, any news?'

'We're in the clear. Tina's done it.'

'What? Why? How?'

'I can't tell you. She's got all the news. Give her a ring as soon as you can.'

'Okay. Thanks, Joe.'

'Bye then.'

Gary put the phone down. He listened at the closed door. The telly was still on; the others were talking. He dialled her number.

Chapter 55

'Oh, Gary, thank God! I've been dying to talk to you!'

'What's happened?'

'Okay, it's all been mental. After you rang me earlier, that copper, Chris Armstrong, called me. He asked me if I wanted to go out for a drink.'

Gary blurted out, 'No! What a tosser. I hope you said no?'

'No, that's the thing. I told him I'd have to think about it. He said fine. But then I rang Joe, and he said how about I go out with him and maybe we can use him to our advantage?'

'How?'

Tina couldn't help laughing. 'By getting him really pissed.'

'How?'

Tina related the events of the night.

Gary scoffed, 'He was really drinking Bacardi and Coke?'

'It's a really trendy drink.'

'It's a bit poncy, isn't it?'

Tina tutted. 'No, it's what sophisticated people drink. What do you drink? Don't tell me — fizzy lager?' She heard Gary pause, then sniff. She smiled; her guess had been right.

He said, 'Go on.'

'By the end, he's out of it. The thing is, Gary, he set it up himself. He was trying to get me drunk so that I'd tell him stuff. I got him drunk and he told me stuff.' She paused, keeping him dangling.

'What?'

'He told me that they had the report back from the doctor, you know, about your dad and his injury?'

'Yeah, the post-mortem?'

'That's right. Guess what?'

'I don't know — just tell me!'

She paused again. Then she burst out, 'Chris can't help himself blabbing... The injury is consistent with the witnesses' testimony!'

'God, what a shit detective!'

217

Tina was irritated. 'Aren't you forgetting something?' Gary was silent. She said, 'It was my brilliant skills that made it all work. And Joe, of course.'

'I'm sorry, Tina. You're right. Bloody hell, you stitched him up like a kipper.'

That was more like it. 'I know. I had to appear to get more and more drunk to make him think that he could trick me into giving him information.'

Gary said, 'So, let me get my head around this. He asked you out to get you to do the blabbing. But he already knew we were telling the truth?'

'Gary, you thick-head! He asked me out because I'm a beautiful woman and he fancied me.'

'Oh, yeah. That's true.'

She laughed. 'It's all right. No: he said his boss didn't believe us, but they can't prove it. But listen to this: what he was really interested in was your granddad!'

'What? What about him?'

'Well, apparently, my boyfriend Chris — you know, the really handsome one —' she giggled, 'sorry… I can't help it. No, the thing he wanted to know was whether I knew anything about your grandad going missing. I said I didn't… well — because I don't. He said that his boss — not the one we know but another one — is obsessed by it. What does it mean?'

Gary said, 'I don't really understand it myself. I only found out this morning that he disappeared. He's right though: the main detective was around here this afternoon.'

Tina said, 'So, that's it now. Joe thinks we're safe.'

'Yeah, he told me.'

'Gary?'

'Yeah?'

'I did the right thing, didn't I?'

She heard Gary breathing as he thought. Finally, he said, 'I think you took a big risk. What if Chris had also wanted a straw?' Tina hadn't thought of that. Gary went on. 'If he'd had a lager, what would have happened? Or if he realised that his drink was incredibly strong?'

She thought about all the possible ways it could have backfired. Maybe she had been a bit reckless? Joe had seemed confident; and he had been there, making it all work out all right.

She said at last, 'But don't you think I did a good thing?'

'Tina, I wish you hadn't gone out with that — your new boyfriend.'

She was deflated now. She had been sure that he'd be pleased, even delighted with her. Suddenly her adrenalin drained away and all she wanted to do was cry.

Gary said, 'Listen, I'm being a miserable bastard. What you did was amazing. I don't know how you managed it, but it's a fucking miracle. I'm sorry. I was thinking about all the dangers, and I was worried about you and suddenly felt — well, you know. If you want to know what I really think, I think you're absolutely, fucking fantastic.'

Elated again, Tina let out a great sigh. 'Oh, good! Phew!'

Gary said, 'Yeah, you're brilliant, Tina. I'm sorry I didn't trust you. I should have had more confidence in you. Oh, by the way, I'm sorry I swore. I'm trying to be less of a caveman.'

Tina smiled at this. 'You're much nicer than some I could mention: no names, no pack drill.' She waited for his response. He was silent. Had she said something stupid? 'Are you still there?'

'Sorry, yeah. What are you doing tomorrow?'

Tina thought she ought to go to school. What was the point, though? There was no chance of her getting any qualifications — well, apart from Art. She'd be better off trying to get a job. Better still, she could try and find a make-up course or something like that.

She said, 'I haven't made up my mind. Why?'

'Oh, I was going to find my aunt. I think she might know something about what happened to my grandad. I was wondering if you wanted to come along?'

She was starting to really like Gary; he was so much nicer than his brother. With all they had been through together, she actually felt quite close to him. Her dad, she knew, hated the Abbotts and wanted her to mix with better company. What company did he have in mind? She didn't have any proper friends, and the blokes she'd previously hung around with had been mostly wasters and creeps. Gary was, in fact, a lot nicer and more caring than every other bloke she'd known.

She said, 'Thanks, Gary, I'd like to, but I'm not family. I don't know if I'm the right person.'

'I'd really like you to come along. I need someone sensible to make sure I keep my mind straight. Also, I think... You see — we're in the same team now, aren't we?'

'Yeah, we are: you, Jenny, Joe and me.'

'Brill! I'll meet you at — when do you want to meet?'

'Ten?'

'Okay.'

'Gary, there's something else I wanted to say.'

'What's that?'

'Well, you know you're trying to be less like a caveman? Well, I sorted out my room today. It's now tidy, everything's clean; it's much, much better. I was ashamed when you were here. I'm sorry you had to see it like that.'

'Oh. Um… nice one. I'd tidy up my room, but there's something really horrible in it: it's dirty, smelly, a massive waste of space, and it's disgusting.'

'Kev?'

'Yep.'

She laughed.

Chapter 56

When Terry had discovered Diane with the man — her client — he hadn't known what to do, apart from run away.

He careered down their street, across the main road and on and on. In the end, he simply ran out of breath. He looked around, uncertain where he was: a recreation ground with some benches, a slide, roundabout and swings. A mother was pushing her toddler in one of the swings. The little creature was laughing and screaming for more. The innocent image helped him calm down a bit. He sat on a bench and tried to get his breath back, waiting for the hammering of his heart to subside. He focused on the small child — was it a boy or girl? He would like it to be a girl, then he could imagine it being Tina. She loved swings. He shut his eyes as he remembered once seeing her fall off and the empty seat crack her head on its return swing.

He whispered to the child now, 'Please be careful. No risks, please.'

The mother was helping the child off the swing, gentle and loving. *That's it, take care of her.* The idea of any harm coming to that beautiful, precious thing was unbearable to him. He watched them go, the toddler in its pushchair, mother chatting to it as they wandered away.

Terry gingerly lifted the mental bandage he had pressed to his injury as he'd left the house. The wound was a horrible mess. He covered it up immediately. Behind him, a blackbird was going through his vocal gymnastics; a chaffinch hammered out its repetitive rhythm; a bad-tempered crow was shouting the odds. From far away came the sound of a train; it got closer and closer and then rushed by, very close. Terry looked along the path and realised that it must lead to a bridge over the railway.

He wondered how long Diane had been doing it? It had never occurred to him to ask about the money she always had. Her job was a good one, but it didn't pay more than any other secretarial role. She did always have cash, that was now screamingly obvious. She was generous with it: surprise presents for him and lovely clothes for Tina.

What was he going to do? He'd have to do something: kill her? Kill her clients? Kill himself? All options seemed like the right answer. He would have no trouble with any of them. There was just one problem: Tina. He got up and walked along the path. Yes, sure enough: a wooden bridge. The handrails were chest high. He could easily vault that.

Looking north, he saw the tracks converge far into the distance. A train coming at the speed of the last one would be doing possibly seventy or even eighty miles per hour. He would need to time it perfectly to make sure the driver didn't have time to react or, better still, have any awareness of what was happening. Terry thought that to kill someone like that would be unbearable; he wouldn't do that to a train driver. Perhaps the best option would be to leap off on the other side of the bridge so that the driver wouldn't ever know that he'd even hit someone? He crossed to the guardrail opposite. Yes, it was the same height. He leant against it and waited. Two women came on to the bridge; they stopped talking as they passed him. He saw one of them glance in his direction as they stepped off the bridge. He heard a hooter in the distance. Turning back, he saw a train approaching; it was going too fast; he wouldn't have time to jump. It flashed underneath him. Damn! He would have to be much faster next time

Tina's face appeared again. He returned his gaze to the horizon, his little girl next to him in his mind's eye. What would she say when she heard her daddy wasn't coming home anymore? What would she say when she was old enough to hear that he'd topped himself? How would he feel if he were with her when she was told? No, he'd have to be brave and keep going; tough it out. He could never inflict such pain on her.

Shakily, he walked back to his bench in the rec. So, what should he do? First, he'd have to get through the rest of the day. Should he tell Diane what he'd seen? Maybe it was best to pretend nothing had changed? A sudden, sickening image blasted through his head — how could he go to bed, in that bed? How could he touch Diane? How could he even look at her? Another question, this one the worst: if they separated, would he ever see Tina again?

He cried out, 'No, no, no! Please, God… Not that.' Through his sobs, he became aware that someone was sitting next to him on the bench. Embarrassed, Terry wiped his eyes on his sleeve. 'I'm sorry, please forgive me, I've had some bad news.'

'Don't be sorry; I'm sorry I've disturbed you,' the voice was gentle, kind.

Terry didn't dare look at the stranger; he kept his head in his hands.

He said, unsure why, 'I don't know what to do. I'm up shit creek. I haven't got a paddle, no canoe, and to make things worse, all I can do is shit myself.'

The kind voice said, 'Shit!'

'I've got a little girl. She's only ten. She's all that I've got, and I can't lose her. No matter what, I can't lose her.'

'That's right. She wouldn't want to lose her dad, either.'

Terry wondered about that. Maybe his whole life was a fantasy? He'd thought they were a happy, loving family: Diane, Tina and him, especially him and Tina. Was it all a lie? No, that wasn't right. Their adventures, the books they read together, building camps in the garden, sitting side by side whilst they watched telly: no, that was all real.

He said, 'I've discovered that my wife has been doing something awful. I can't tell you what. I can't live with it, though. I've got to get away from it, and from her. How do I do that?'

'I don't think I know the answer to that. I'm sorry. Is it possible to talk to her about it?'

'The thing is, I'm not sure I can control myself. I'm scared of losing my temper and going mad or something. I've done it before and… it can't happen again. '

Terry felt the man grip his arm. 'Do you want to tell me more about that?'

Did he? He'd got over it; at least, he thought he had. The first time he'd lost his rag was with the other squaddies. It had been in a place where violence and aggression were encouraged and, although he'd been disciplined, it hadn't ended his career. The subsequent times he'd been lucky; he knew that luck would run out one day. If he lost it to the same extent in a domestic setting, it would be prison for a long time.

He shook his head. 'No, I'm all right. I've got myself back under control. Thank you.'

The hand was removed. 'If you like, I'll hang on for a minute. It's nice here; all the birds, and flowers and stuff.'

They sat in silence. Terry heard people walk past. He kept his eyes closed and let the world spin around a few degrees. He said, 'I think I'll ring Diane up and tell her that I know what's been going on. I'll tell her that I'll pack a bag and move out until we can sort things out. I think I'll do that. I can't see her. I'm sorry, I can't go near her.'

The stranger said, 'Sounds sensible.'

Terry hadn't realised he'd voiced his plan. Surprised, he opened his eyes and looked at the man: a uniformed policeman looking off into the distance. Noticing that Terry had opened his eyes, the man turned and smiled. 'Hello, my name's Martin.'

Terry rubbed his eyes with his sleeve again, 'Hallo, Martin. I'm Terry.'

223

Martin stood up. He put out his hand. Terry shook it. 'Thank you, Martin. You're a bloody angel.'

Martin laughed, 'That's not what I normally get called.'

Lying in bed now, Terry wondered where Martin was these days. He hoped he'd progressed through the ranks. That kind voice had often sounded in his head when things were getting on top of him. There was a small number of people, places and events that Terry had in his locker for when he couldn't sleep, which was most nights. Today, Geraldine Dutton's rescue of him had been added to the repertoire. Her need for his help, later the same day, had filled him with love for humanity all over again. He had to admit to himself, however, that those few seconds had been more than just human contact. As she'd wrapped her warmth around him, and he'd rested his face in her hair, he had felt a surge of something long forgotten. Then the horror of seeing that photograph had smashed all loving images out of his head. If he hadn't had the pressure of needing to collect Tina, God knows what he might have done. Somehow, he didn't think Geraldine would thank him if she came downstairs tomorrow to find a smashed picture frame and her husband's face torn to shreds. On the other hand, her husband had been happy to shred Terry's life, presumably without a second's thought. Had Terry's life been ruined, though? Maybe for the first time since that fateful day, Terry wondered if it might have been for the best? When he'd rung Diane, to tell her that he knew, she either hadn't been in, or had decided not to answer. When he'd gone home, meaning to collect his things, she had beaten him to it. Her note was clear.

Dear Terry

I should have told you before but I'm a coward as well as a bitch. I couldn't do it. I can't tell Tina. Will you tell her for me? Make something up if you like. I'll come back for my stuff another time. I guess you'll want a divorce. I won't fight it. I hope you do okay. I know you'll look after Tina. She always loved you more than me anyway.

Diane

Since then, he and Tina had gone through some rocky times. He was pretty sure he'd been a terrible father when it came to her education — far too wrapped up in himself to think about her growing up. He didn't know her friends or her boyfriends, apart from that little shit, Abbott. Today, however, they had been so close. He had felt such a strong wave of certainty that, together, they were going to be all right. Her face this afternoon had been the epitome of determination. He smiled now as he heard her say, 'You watch, Dad. You and me — we're on our way!'

He thought again about Geraldine Dutton. How could he look her in the eye when he knew that her husband, with all his money and success, paid other men's wives for sex? Would she want to know the truth? No, of course not. He must never tell her.

Wednesday

Chapter 57

The face was just a mask of blood, but McGregor was still defending himself, still swinging wildly, in fact. By contrast, Terry's punches had been frenzied, but now he was picking precise parts of the head and body. Around them were half a dozen of their fellow squaddies, forming a natural ring as the uneven fight continued. Terry feinted a knockout blow with his right. When Jamie ducked, Terry's left upper cut caught the point of his chin, and over he went.

The lads cheered and went to pull Terry away, but he wasn't finished. He bent down, pulled McGregor up by his ear and smashed his right fist into the side of his head.

Len Sammons held Terry's arm and said, 'Okay, Tel, you've got him now; let's leave him.'

Terry didn't hear. Again, he grasped his fellow soldier by the ear and bashed his head savagely back into the floor of the pub.

'Tel, leave it now.'

Some of the boys were trying to pull him away; he shrugged them off. Kneeling on McGregor's chest, Terry began to pound the half-conscious man's head against the floor. Finally, Len, Ray and Andy wrestled him off his opponent and dragged him away.

Terry roared, 'Get your fucking hands off me, you cunts! I'm going to kill that bastard.'

As he was manhandled out of the pub by his mates, he took one last look at the figure on the floor. Through the blood and broken teeth, he saw Dutton's face looking back. The bastard still wore that haughty expression: 'I can fuck your wife any time I like.'

Terry roared at him, 'I'll kill you, Dutton. I will kill you.'

Dutton smiled at him through his smashed-up face. 'I can fuck her any time I like and what's more, she'll enjoy it with me. You can't hack it, Terry — you know you can't.'

The landlord was banging a glass on the bar. Terry's head finally cleared. He opened his eyes: what was that banging?

'Hello?' he called.

'Dad, it's me. Are you all right?'

At last, consciousness returned. 'Sorry, love. Yes, I'm fine. Sorry to wake you.'

'Get back to sleep, Dad.'

'Yes, sorry, love. Good night.'

Her door closed. He rubbed his face. God, when was he ever going to get over these awful memories? The fight with Jamie McGregor might have been the end of his army career, if the lads hadn't pulled him away. He had been determined to kill him: when he'd seen that Scottish wanker touching up Diane, by the bar, he'd lost it. It had meant getting hauled over the coals by the Commanding Officer, then seven days locked up with nothing to do but polish fucking boots, thousands of boots. Even now, nearly twenty years later, the compulsion to beat the shit out of McGregor was just as powerful. It was that photograph which had brought it back. Dutton's face rushed into his mind again; with it came the thumping heart and impotent fury.

He looked at his clock. It was just after four. The chances of going back to sleep were low; he might as well make a cup of tea and have a cigarette. Damn, no cigarettes. Maybe that was partly why his nerves were so frayed. Talking of chances, what were the odds of Geraldine's husband being the very man Terry had seen with Diane? Poor Geraldine, she'd suffered the same fate as him; although, he presumed, she didn't know about it. Mind you, he wouldn't have known, if he hadn't come home at the wrong time.

Terry wondered what Dutton did for a living. Judging from the flash car and big house, he was successful at whatever it was. The man in the photograph exuded self-assurance and authority. The man he'd seen in his bedroom, in his wife, had appeared just the same. As Terry once again picked at the festering wound of that afternoon, he pictured getting Dutton by the neck. He saw that smooth, self-satisfied face begin to lose its colour; its eyes were bulging, the tongue beginning to protrude.

'Yes, your Lordship. It's your turn to get fucked. This time I'm going to ruin your fucking life. Yes. When I've killed you, I'm going upstairs to fuck your wife. That's right, lovely Geraldine Dutton: everyone's favourite teacher.' Terry watched as the life went out of Dutton's face.

Gasping for breath, Terry shot up in bed. God, had he slipped back again? This was getting dangerous. He pushed Dutton out of his head, got up and made a cup of tea. Yesterday's resolution to give up the fags had seemed like a good idea. Boy, did he regret it now. Still, it was something positive — something to show Tina that she could still look up to him. He drank his tea then went for a shave and a bath. When he emerged, Tina was up and buttering toast.

'Have you had something to eat, Dad?'

'Yes, I had half a grapefruit, some mixed nuts and seeds, a glass of distilled water with some oriental herbs and spices plus an assortment of vitamins and minerals prescribed by my team of specialist advisers.'

'No breakfast then?'

'That's right.'

She said, 'I heard we're supposed to eat breakfast like a king, have dinner like a prince and tea like a pauper. You're doing it all back to front.'

Terry watched her load a ton of jam on to her toast. 'Which king has that much jam on his toast? Anyway, I bet they eat caviar, kedgeree and truffles for their breakfast. I can't imagine our dear Queen sitting at our table wolfing down Mother's Pride, can you?'

'Not yet; but when we've got our new place she'll be popping around all the time.'

Terry put on his jacket, folded up his overall and put it into a carrier bag. 'What are you doing today?'

'Well, I thought I'd look for a job and maybe see if there're any courses I could do.'

'Good girl. I'm going to have a word with Miss Ratcliffe today; I missed her yesterday. I think she'll have some good ideas about you.' He looked over at her: she wasn't pleased.

She said, 'Dad, I don't need people sticking their noses into my life. What does she know about me? What does she know about anything?'

Terry knew better than to argue with her. 'Sure, I won't if you don't want me to.'

Tina munched her way through her jam mountain. Swallowing the last mouthful she said, 'That was one hell of a dream, Dad.'

'Was I shouting?'

'Hmm, put it this way: I wouldn't want the vicar to hear you.'

'Oh, sorry. Was it French or German?'

'Fishwife.'

'Ah.'

'Dad, are you very friendly with Mrs Dutton?'

Terry looked at Tina sharply. 'Why do you ask?'

'You were shouting about her... er — um, doing something to her.'

Terry had forgotten the dream the moment he'd woken, but Tina's words brought back, with hideous clarity, what he had been picturing.

He said, 'She's lovely. She was really kind to me yesterday. Then, with her being the referee of the Castleton Cup; then my late trip to her house last night, I saw more of her yesterday than I have in the last five years.'

'I assume she's married?'

'I assume so. Don't worry. I'm not after her or anything dodgy.' He glanced at her. She was pulling a cigarette out of its packet. 'Now, Tina, why don't you give up with me? We can back each other up.'

Tina replaced the cigarette and looked up at him. She said, 'Dad, do you think you might be able to be friendly with Gary?'

'Do I have to?'

'No, course not. It's just that he's my friend and it would be nice if you could be a bit less horrible to him. I know Kev was awful — *is* awful — but Gary is much better, and I think he'd like you if you gave him the chance.'

'I don't mind who you have as your friends as long as they treat you properly. If you want to be his friend, that's fine. I shall be civil to him. If I find he's done you wrong, I will cut his balls off and shove them up his arse. I think that's reasonable, don't you?'

She smiled, 'You're full of hot air, Dad. I don't believe you could ever hurt anyone.'

He pictured his life of violence. That was good: she needn't know what was really going on in his head. 'You're right. I'm everyone's favourite school caretaker.'

He put his flask into the bag and lifted his keys from the hook beside the door. 'See you this evening. I'm going to have a quiet day: no shocks, no surprises.'

'Yeah, me too. I don't really mind if you want to talk to that teacher. But do you mind if I talk to my friend about you?'

'Gary Abbott? Don't make me laugh!'

'No, silly. No — I know a bloke who's really nice and helpful and I think he might be able to give some good advice.'

Terry couldn't imagine Tina having a friend who could possibly have anything helpful to say, but he realised he'd walked into her sucker punch. 'Fine. Let me know what he says.'

She smiled at him. 'Good boy. Bye, then — see you later.'

He parked outside Harringtons just before nine. There were lights on but the 'closed' sign was still showing. As he waited, he wondered whether it was time to think about moving away. Now that Tina's school life had come to an end, there was nothing keeping them here. There were so many ghosts waiting for him, queueing up to knock him back down. Tina didn't seem to have a circle of friends that were important to her. If the best she could do was a bloody Abbott, then it was high time she started afresh, too.

He saw the nice assistant unlocking the door. Terry ambled over to the shop. She saw him coming and opened the door as if he were royalty. He smiled, 'I wish I had this sort of respect from others I could mention.'

Bowing slightly, she said, 'Enter, your Excellency.'

'That's enough. You're making me feel uneasy.'

'Sorry about that. We've got your trophy here. What do you think?'

She handed him the cardboard box. With great reverence, he lifted lid, flaps, then tissue paper, and eased the gleaming cup out.

'Blimey, it looks amazing.'

The assistant said, 'He's done a lovely job, hasn't he?'

Terry admired the handiwork. 'Brilliant.'

She said, 'I could tell it was important to you, so I gave it a good polish last night. It's come up really well.'

He slid it back in, carefully replaced the tissue paper and looked at her smiling face.

She said, 'You don't recognise me, do you?' Terry studied her: forty-ish, shoulder-length, light brown hair, smiley, large glasses, comfortable figure. She said, 'I thought I recognised you, but it wasn't until you gave me the words for the inscription that I was sure. I nearly said something, but I was too shy. It is you, isn't it? Terry Castleton?'

Terry stared. Did he know her?

She went on. 'I used to work with Diane. We trained together at Rawlings. We started on the same day and worked in sales for a while; then she went into marketing, and I moved to the corporate admin team. It was such a shame she left. I remember her saying she'd got an amazing job in some agency or something. I stayed on at Rawlings for a few years before coming here. I really like this job; it's much more my kind of thing — you know, dealing with the public. How is she? We used to have such a laugh together. You wouldn't believe what we got up to back then! Of course, we were a lot younger. I don't think I've seen her for… hmmm, maybe five years. Even more. I remember you from a couple of Christmas parties. Is she still beautiful? I bet she is, the cow. All the men used to go weak at the knees when they were around her. God, Terry, you really pulled a plum with her.'

Terry switched off. He mumbled, 'Ah, yes, I think I...'

'I'm Jean. Jean Richmond.'

She was looking at him, expectantly. He had to say something; what could he say? A minute ago, he had been so cheerful: his gleaming cup waiting to be presented; little Patricia Whiting's happy face; this attractive woman seemingly liking him. Now, as usual, he felt his life crumbling.

He pulled himself together. 'Sorry, Jean. Yes, of course, I — er... I recognise you now. Now: you need paying, and I need to get to work.'

She looked disappointed. He felt wretched.

'Right. £19.99, please.'

He reached into his pocket and pulled out the two tenners he'd had ready. Keeping his eyes down, he said, 'Jean, I'm sorry. Diane and I separated a few years ago.'

She took the notes from him, then took his hand in hers. 'Oh, I'm sorry, Terry. Me and my big mouth!'

Terry tried to pull his hand away; she held it tight. 'I'm sorry about Diane. We were good pals for a while. If you speak to her, will you let her know I was asking about her?'

He extricated his hand and backed away to the door, the box under his arm. 'Thank you, Jean. I don't have any contact with Diane. I'm sorry.'

She was looking dejected. 'Oh, that's a pity. I don't speak to my ex, either. We got divorced last year. We're a right pair, aren't we?'

Terry opened the door. He was about to leave when she called out, 'Terry, before you go...'

He stood still and waited for whatever was coming to be over. She came out from behind the counter and walked towards him. Aware of his flinching posture, he stood tall, ready for action.

'When I got home from work, my son, Graham, told me about the football match yesterday. He was in the Crackerjacks. Apparently, the captain was the best player he'd ever seen. He said he was like — er, sorry, um... well, he said... like Bobby Charlton, only bigger and... um, sorry... fatter, and — oh dear — balder. That wasn't you, by any chance?'

Terry couldn't help himself — he burst out laughing, 'Balder? Than Bobby Charlton? Bloomin' cheek! Still, I'll accept the compliment.'

She laughed, too. 'Will you forgive me, Terry? I put my foot in it, like I always do.'

Terry felt sorry for her. She was a nice woman. How could she have known?

'Jean don't worry. It's all water under the bridge. I've moved on and life's — well, life's not so bad. I hope you're doing all right?'

She nodded, 'I am, bit by bit.' She held out her hand. 'Bye for now, Bobby.'

Chapter 58

It was the incessant throbbing that woke her. No, not throbbing exactly. It was the on and off squeezing of her skull: side to side, back to front. Then she became aware of her sour mouth, sweaty, acrid skin, gritty eyes. She tried to go back to sleep — but that was madness: this was only going to get worse.

Geraldine couldn't remember ever feeling like this. She didn't drink very much and, if she did, it would only be wine. Drinking a whole bottle was unheard of; washing it down with her nemesis — the port — was sheer folly. To do so on a weekday was the act of a lunatic.

She glanced at her alarm clock through a slitted eye. As she tried to focus, it began its dread toll. At least Edward wasn't here to scoff and make her feel even more pathetic. It was because he wasn't here that she'd gone to pieces. Like it or not — and she didn't — he did make her behave more sensibly. What had got into her last night? She must have been drunk as a skunk. She couldn't even remember getting to bed.

With a weak effort, she pushed the bedclothes away to let some fresh air replace the fetid stew in which she'd slept. The evening had been fun. As the alcohol insinuated itself into her head, Edward had slipped away; so had her embarrassment with Daniel; likewise, the preposterous display she'd given Terry in his shed. Instead, she had found herself laughing out loud at the comedy character she had become. She'd thought that she might even go to work in the morning showing off about it all. Now, as was always the way after she'd had too much, life was grey and grim.

With a huge effort, Geraldine hauled herself to her feet and waited to see if the intense throbbing would increase. It did. She sat back down on the edge of the bed and put her head in her hands: bad idea. Gritting her teeth and screwing up her eyes, she lumbered to the bathroom, taking care to avoid the image of the bowed, old woman who could just be glimpsed out of the corner of her eye. She turned on the shower and waited for it to warm up. Before getting in, she gulped down three glasses of water. Geraldine knew that rehydration was critical for recovery, but the sudden influx of fresh water made her innards feel decidedly unstable. Oh, God, no! Please, no… She just managed to lift the lid of the lavatory in time. She stayed kneeling over the bowl until she was sure there was nothing left to come. Last night she'd been glad Edward hadn't been home; she was doubly glad now.

Geraldine flushed the loo, put the lid down and pulled her nightie over her head. It smelled rank. She balled it up and shoved it deep into the laundry basket. Unsteadily, she stepped over the edge of the bath, pulled the shower curtain across and let the rushing, hot water cleanse her. After five minutes, she squeezed out a handful of shampoo and covered her head and body with it. Again, she stood still and allowed the water to purify her. As the seconds, then minutes, went by, she began to feel better. She squeezed another shot of shampoo into her cupped hand and lathered her whole body — God, not only drunk, with a thundering hangover, but to complete the misery, more wobble than the wobbliest jelly! At last, however, it was feeling good to caress some love back into her damaged body. She turned to let the water rush against the back of her head: that helped, too. She stood still and let it do its good work, closing her eyes, willing her head clear.

Geraldine screamed as the hot water ran out. Frantically washing away the last of the lather, she turned off the shower. Her mind focused, at last, on the school day ahead.

As she reached the hall, the smell of booze hit her. She went into the sitting room to open the curtains. On the floor beside the sofa was a puddle of something white. Puzzled, Geraldine bent down to examine it: *salt?* She stood up straight and thought through the brain-fog; the head-squeezing had also returned. Events were starting to come back to her — the call from Terry, his arrival, her going upstairs to get something — yes, his jacket. Then... had she fallen over? *Yes, you stupid old fool! Tottering around like an old toper.* Had he come up to help her? Yes, he had. He'd pulled her up and helped her into bed. She shut her eyes with embarrassment.

What a sweet man to try and save her carpet. She opened the patio doors to let in some fresh air, then went quickly to the kitchen for some strong coffee. After forcing down a slice of toast, she got out the vacuum cleaner. Was Terry's trick going to work? A few seconds later, the answer was clear: no. Although the salt had drawn out much of the stain, there was still a large, rusty smudge in full view. The evidence was damning. Geraldine cursed herself. Never mind. She'd have another go at it before Edward got home.

She scurried upstairs to brush her teeth, and to face the grotesque figure looking back at her in the bathroom mirror. What a sight: blotchy, pale skin, red-rimmed, puffy eyes, shame-faced expression. She thrashed a brush through her hair, put on some pink lipstick and stuck her tongue out at the hideous old bag. As she rushed back downstairs, the idea of ringing in sick popped into her head, then straight out again: she'd feel fine as soon as she got there — although the thought of a classroom full of ten- and eleven-year-olds was not an enticing prospect. She unzipped her bag and slipped in the packet of Phensic, retrieved her driving glasses and opened the front door. What was that? On the gravel next to the Jag was… what was it? It looked like vomit. It was vomit. Geraldine hurried back into the house and grabbed a plastic bag. Putting her hand inside it she scraped the mess into a pile and picking it up, she turned the bag the right way out again then tossed it into the dustbin. She cursed under her breath, stomping back into the kitchen to wash her hands.

The whole sorry tale was making her tearful. What she wanted right now was someone to tell her she was lovely, kind and attractive. Edward would be the last to express any such sentiments, but he was all she had. Geraldine picked up the phone and rang his club.

Chapter 59

'You look nice.'

'Yeah, well. I thought I'd better make an effort.'

'Why? What's happening today.'

Gary wasn't sure quite how the day was going to work out, but he thought looking a bit smarter than usual might be a good idea. He had washed his hair for the first time for... well, weeks. He was wearing the trousers his mum had bought him which, although he was sure made him look like a wanker, were probably more suitable for his plans than baggies.

'Those trousers suit you. Why haven't you worn them before? I saw John Wright with exactly the same ones only the other day.'

'Mum, John Wright is at least sixty! What a crumbly old git like him wears is hardly going to suit me.'

His mum smiled, 'Well, that's where you're wrong; you look very nice. That shirt looks reasonably clean. What about a tie?'

Gary was not going to wear a tie. There was something about ties that made him feel sick.

He said, 'I don't think a tie is a good idea. I don't want to look like a creep or a swot.'

'Stay there. I'll see if Dad has any.'

'Don't, Mum, I don't want...'

She'd pushed back her chair and was already up the stairs. Gary looked inside her bag: there it was. He flicked through the pages until he found the details.

'Here you are. Which ones do you like?'

Gary did not want his dad's tie. When he saw the selection, he was even more certain: hideous kippers.

'Er, they're... um...'

'The wide ones used to be rather trendy; perhaps not so much now. How about a smart jacket?'

'Don't worry, Mum. I'll be all right.'

'You haven't said what you're up to?'

'Well, I'm going to the newspaper office in case there's any chance of some work as an apprentice. I probably haven't got a hope in hell but it's worth a go. What do you think?'

Jenny Abbott smiled at him. 'A journalist! You'll be brilliant. Oh, Gary, what a fantastic thing. I think you could easily get a job in Fleet Street, or anywhere. You're a fantastic writer, and now that you're wearing glasses, well… I think it's amazing!'

Gary shook his head. 'No, Mum, there's not an actual job and definitely not in Fleet Street. I'm just going to ask about some work experience, that's all. Anyway, what does wearing glasses have to do with it?'

'Well, you look so clever.'

'Even though I'm not?'

'Well, that doesn't matter, as long as they think you are.'

'Jeez, thanks, Mum.'

He thought she might be right. He had noticed that his glasses had smoothed some of his rough edges. Maybe it was his height, his angry stare or just his threatening way of walking, but people usually kept out of his way. It was the effect he had cultivated. Since he'd started wearing his glasses, Gary the Gorilla had melted away.

'I'd better be off. I don't know what time I'll be back today. I might go to school later. I've got sod-all chance of getting any qualifications, but maybe I should try.'

'Listen, Gary. It's been terrible recently, I know. Losing Dad is awful. I still can't quite get my head around it. Life wasn't easy with him, but it was our normal. Now we've got to start again. I'm going to try. If you can too, that would be great.'

'I am trying, Mum. Honest.'

She smiled and nodded. 'I know you are. Now that we know the police aren't after us, we can begin to breathe again.'

When he'd told her what Tina had found out, his mum had closed her eyes and puffed out a long sigh of relief. 'Oh, thank you, God. Is she sure?'

'Well, she sounded definite. She and Joe stitched up that young detective and got him to blow the gaff. Apparently, they don't believe us, but they haven't got any proof, so they're going to have to drop it. Anyway, they fingered Dad for the attack on that bloke, so it's not like they haven't got someone to arrest, even if he is dead.'

'She's a nice girl. It's such a shame that she and Kev split up.'

Gary hadn't answered that one.

He got ready to leave. He pulled on his leather jacket and looked in the hall mirror. His hair did look better clean. The shave had made him look cleaner, too. Yes, the shirt, his best one, did give him a cool look — bright blue with wide, white collar. Gary looked down at his trousers: sharp crease, not flared enough, really, but definitely smart. His shoes looked scruffy. He ran upstairs and tried on Kev's: nah, even worse than his. He went into Derek's room; he always had good stuff. He found a pair of two-tone wedges, very nice. Gary put them on: a bit tight but not bad. He went back down and looked again at the whole package: Yeah, not bad.

'Bye, Mum. See you later.'

'See you later. Good luck, love!'

He slammed the door and walked up the street. The new trousers made him feel older; cleverer, even. He stood up straight and walked like a journalist: confident, alert. He took his hands out of his pockets and swung his arms. He knew that he could adopt a physical appearance to assert his personality. He had always worked on how he looked: thuggish, sullen and with maximum menace. He would now try to present a new image, see if it made any difference to his luck.

It was just after nine. He pushed open the door.

'You again?' It was the older receptionist.

'Yeah. Watcha.'

'You're looking different. What have you done to yourself?'

'Nothing.'

'Well, how can we help?'

Gary had been hoping Karen would be here but didn't want to say so. In the large office, he could see the old farter and two other blokes and, in his back office, Rob Mitchum.

He said, 'I was wondering if Nigel was free for a quick chat?'

'He's around somewhere. Hang on, I'll ask.'

She went through into Mitchum's office. The editor looked over at Gary, then back to the woman. He pointed to the interview room.

The receptionist walked back over. 'Nigel's got someone with him, but he won't be long. Do you want to wait?'

'Thanks. Yes, please.'

'Take a seat. I'll let you know when he's free.'

Gary sat down on the plastic chair and picked up a copy of this week's paper. He flicked through the articles. He wondered about the people featuring in the reports: their lives, homes, relationships. The door opened and Karen came in.

She saw Gary, 'Well, look who it isn't! It's Gloves. Big Gloves.'

'All right?'

'Not bad. You?'

'Yep, ta.'

'Are you waiting for someone?'

'He's waiting for Nigel.'

'Ah, have you got some news for him?'

'No, why?'

'Oh, he was talking about you last night. Very interested he was.'

Gary thought about Nigel. He was still pissed off that he'd gone to the police, but Frank had been right: maybe he was sniffing a good story. He thought that reporters 'sniffed' stories; he would ask Nigel. Gary looked at Karen — very tasty; not big tits like Tina. Taller, slimmer. She grinned at him; he smiled back.

'Morning, Gary. Back again?'

Gary turned to see Nigel at the counter. 'Hello, yeah. I just wanted a quick chat.'

'Come on, then. We'll go into the interview room. Our friend hasn't been in there yet, so we won't have to gasp for air.'

Gary got up and followed him.

Karen said, 'I really like your shoes, Gloves. Where did you get them?'

'Oh, I'm not sure. Somewhere in London. Um… Camden, I think.'

She said, smiling, 'Are your feet big, as well as your hands?'

'Of course. You know what they say: big feet…'

'Mmm?'

'Big feet — er, big…'

'Yes?'

'You know — big feet, big footprints.'

She laughed, 'You're good!'

Gary went on into the interview room. Nigel shut the door. 'What's up?'

Gary had given this chat some thought: it could go either way. It was up to him.

'Okay, this is what I think happened. I gave you enough of an idea that there was something interesting about my dad. You connected the fact that he'd just died with my interest in my grandad disappearing. While I was looking for a needle in a haystack in your storeroom, you were looking through files down here: microfilm or something? I don't know if you contacted the hospital or if you went straight to the police but, anyway, you speak to our friendly Plods and get them all excited. Then, when I get home they're there, asking a load of questions. Is that about right?'

Nigel held up his hands. 'You got me, bang to rights. The only other thing I did was contact the Missing Persons Department to see if Bertram Abbott was still listed. He is. I'm sorry, Gary. I feel bad about it. I should have told you what I was doing. Will you forgive me?'

Gary wanted to tell him that if he'd met him last night he would have kicked his head in. Instead, he said, 'My friend says that sometimes a reporter has to find out what's true, not just what he wants to be true. Is that true?'

'Who's your friend? Gandhi?'

Confused, Gary said, 'No, Frank Gordon.'

'Well, he's right. The thing is, reporters are just like anyone else. We want to get a good story and be the first to get it. I thought that if I went straight to the police, I might squeeze something out of them before they noticed.'

'But I don't get it. What makes you think there was a story, anyway? The old man was never found. My dad dies. What's the story?'

'You're right. Maybe there's no story. I just thought it was odd that you should start making your own enquiries. You obviously thought there was a story, otherwise you wouldn't have wasted two hours rifling through a load of boring old papers. I was just following a hunch.'

Gary wanted to ask him if he had been sniffing out a story. 'So, did you find anything out from the police?'

Nigel shook his head. 'No, they didn't tell me anything. They were, however, very interested in you and what you'd told me. I spoke to a Detective Constable Armstrong: he was interested. He put me on to Detective Sergeant Nott: he pretended not to be interested. Then, five minutes later, Detective Chief Inspector Flanagan, no less, rings me up: mildly interested. What does this all add up to, Gary?'

'I reckon it adds up to something interesting, something worth sniffing around a bit more?'

Nigel grinned, 'That's what I thought. Have you got any theories?'

Gary wanted to have an honest chat with Nigel. He just wasn't sure he could trust him. 'I've got one or two ideas. Thing is, I don't want to say anything if you're just going to rush off and do things behind my back. It's my family, my story.'

Nigel was looking at him. What was he thinking?

Gary took a chance. 'I'm not very good at school work. I don't think I'll get any CSEs, except English possibly. I'd really like to be a reporter, but I don't know if I can even do it, never mind persuade anyone to give me a job. I was thinking that maybe I could work with you, as your assistant or something, and then if I'm any good, we could talk about a job. I know it's a cheek and all that, but what do you think?'

'Interesting proposal. You do realise that being a reporter means spending all day writing about missing cats, old people falling down holes in pavements, what a town councillor said at a meeting that no one was interested in, who died, who didn't, and that's just the fun stuff. I don't want you to imagine that we spend all our time with film stars.'

Gary hadn't actually given much thought to anything. But he wasn't going to be put off, not now he'd opened his big mouth.

'I know. Most of it's everyday life. Now and then there'll be a crime, a celebrity or an event. I'm just interested in finding out the truth, that's all.'

Nigel smiled. 'I think you're a bullshitter, Gary. It doesn't matter; so am I. Maybe we can sort something out. I'll have a word with Rob and see what he says. Tell you what, why don't you say what you know and then we'll see what we can do?'

Gary wasn't going to be tricked again by this crafty bugger. He said, 'I tell you what: how about you speak to Rob first. I'll wait here.'

Nigel pulled out his fags, lit one and gave Gary the packet. 'Hang on, I'll be back in a minute.'

Gary thought through his plan. He should have told his mum what he was going to do. It wasn't fair for all this dirty laundry to be washed in public. He wondered if he could make a quick phone call. There was a phone on the desk in the corner. He stepped over and lifted it to his ear. It had a funny dialling tone: it didn't sound right. He put it down again. He opened the door. Nigel was talking to Rob Mitchum, beyond the closed office door. Gary walked round the corner to Reception.

'Excuse me, can I make a phone call, please?'

The older woman was still there.

'Sure. Use the phone in the interview room. Just dial nine for an outside line.'

He went back and closed the door. Feeling self-conscious, he rang home.

'Mum, it's me.'

'Hello. Any news?'

'I've just been talking to one of the reporters about possibly working here. I don't know if they're interested, but I need to be able to offer something. I mean, I'm just a big, thick bully without a CSE to scrape together.'

'Stop that. You're very clever.'

'Well, anyway, I want to know if you're okay for me to tell them about Dad being involved in the — er, incident — you know, when he headbutted that rich bloke. The thing is, the police know, so it's going to come out anyway. I just thought that it would show them that I was prepared to put my neck out for them.'

'Oh, Gary, do you have to? Can't we just keep out of trouble for once? Honestly, people think we're bad enough already.'

'I know, Mum. You're right. It's just that I think that the paper is probably going to do a report on Dad, anyway.'

'Why?'

'Coz the police will report that the attack on the bloke was by Dad; that Dad is now dead; and that the mystery of the missing grandfather is still unsolved. I dunno, something like that. They're going to do it anyway so I think we might as well get something out of it.'

'I don't understand. If they already know, what is there to tell them? How on earth can we get something out of it?'

Gary hated himself. 'Well, I can give them all the details of what happened before anything else comes out. And...' he took in a deep breath, 'it might mean they give me a job.'

He heard her sigh. 'Oh, go on then. It doesn't matter if it's going to come out anyway.'

'I'm sorry, Mum. I know I'm being a bastard. I want to get on, and this might be my only chance.'

'I know, love. Maybe it's right that something good comes of this whole mess.'

The door opened.

Gary said, 'Thanks, er — Mr, er... Mr Chivers. Thanks very much.'

Chapter 60

There he was, leaning against the bus shelter. She waved. 'All right?'

'Yeah, not bad. You?'

'Fine. You're looking pretty good, Gary. I like the trousers. Wow, look at your shoes! They look just like Derek's. Same shop or same shoes?'

'Well spotted. Nothing gets past you, does it?'

When she'd been going out with Kev, Tina had always thought Gary was better looking. Now, scrubbed up a bit, he actually looked quite handsome. She was glad she'd made an effort with her own appearance.

He held out his fags. 'Want one?'

Her dad's comment, about girls who smoked looking tarty, had worried her more than she'd let on. 'Actually, Gary, I'm thinking of giving up smoking.'

'Why? We all have to die sooner or later.'

'Yeah, I know. I'd rather later. Also, I smoked so many last night: you know, with my new boyfriend.'

'What, that wanker?'

Tina smiled. 'I didn't know policemen were so cool. He was a total gentleman, too. He spent the whole evening asking about me, complimenting me on my appearance, holding doors for me and letting me take his arm. Honestly, Gary, he made me feel like a lady.'

Gary sniffed.

'Yes, it's so rare for men to treat me with respect. I'm going to give him a call later to arrange another evening out.' She glanced at Gary: he was almost eating his fag. She elbowed him. 'I'm joking. He was a complete and utter idiot, completely selfish. All he did was talk about himself and try and impress me. He was just a big kid. To be honest, I was expecting him to be clever and, you know, crafty. Joe told me to be careful and not get myself into any difficult conversations. The way it turned out, even you could have outwitted him.'

Gary threw his cigarette butt on the ground and trod on it. 'Thanks very much. Thick as that, was he?'

'Seriously, I was nervous about it all. It would have been good if you'd been there, somewhere in the background, so you could have seen what was going on.'

'So, was Joe there the whole time?'

'I don't know. I saw him right at the beginning; after that I didn't see him 'til the end, when pretty boy crashed out.'

Gary lit another fag, 'I can't believe it — did he just fall asleep?'

Tina couldn't help telling it from the beginning. Gary's concentration was absolute. She liked it.

In a final burst, Tina announced, 'Then, I went off to the bogs — well, to ring my dad — and when I came back, he was out cold, head on the table.'

Gary laughed, 'That'll serve him right, arrogant bastard.'

They saw the 107 appear over the bridge. Tina reached into her pocket for change.

Gary said, 'Allow me. This trip's on me.'

'Oh, Gary Abbott, you are a true gent.'

They went upstairs and sat at the back. Tina was enjoying being with Gary. He wasn't just good-looking, he had brains, too. She said, 'So, what's the plan today?'

'I looked around my dad's shed yesterday. We'd always wanted to get in there, but he kept it locked. I didn't know where he kept the key and Mum asked me to wait until she'd had a look around. So, point is, I had this sort of crazy idea of getting in, seeing what was in there and getting out with no one the wiser. Trouble is, the only way I could get in was by smashing the window. I managed to do it but, still, it'll be obvious that I done it.

'Doesn't matter now. Anyway, it was full of shit: fishing tackle, old newspapers, loads of magazines, cigarette cards and stuff — just a load of crap, really but, in a steel box, there was an envelope with some photos and a letter. The letter was from my auntie telling my dad that, now that their father had gone, she'd had enough and was going to keep away. I didn't even really know I had an aunt — or maybe I did. I wasn't sure. I asked my mum when my grandad had died and that's when she told me he'd gone missing years ago, in 1963. So, that was what made me start poking around to see if I could find out what happened. I spent all afternoon in the newspaper office looking up old copies and found out about it all. Then, later in the day, the cops come around and, well — you know the rest.'

Tina liked listening to Gary. He had a way of talking that made it more like listening to a story.

'So, no one knows what happened to your grandad?'

'Not that I know. This old copper, Flanagan: he was investigating the disappearance back then. He was the one that your lover-boy told you about. I reckon he suspects Dad of killing him off. My mum said last night that she thought Dad had probably done it. The other thing that makes me suspect Dad is that, in the envelope with the photos and the letter, was this.'

Gary reached into his inside pocket and pulled out a tie. She took it from him. 'That's a regimental tie, isn't it?'

'How do you know that?'

'My dad was in the army and he's got a tie a bit like it.'

'I didn't know he was in the army.'

'Yeah. Anyway, thing is, what's the point of the tie?'

'Oh, well, it belongs to my grandad. I've seen a few photos of him and he's wearing it in all of them. The fact that he went missing is weird, but I thought: if he was going to disappear deliberately, then wouldn't he want his special tie? The fact that it's locked away in my dad's shed with some photos and a letter made me think that Dad knew what had happened and wanted to keep a souvenir or something.'

Tina had known that Gary was clever. The way he'd handled everything the other night in the kitchen — and then the hospital — had proved that. This new bit of thinking was further evidence.

She looked at him. 'It's those specs, isn't it? They give you special powers! You're not really Clark Kent, are you?'

'Who?'

'You know, Superman in disguise.'

'Oh, yeah. No, sorry, Lois.'

She laughed. 'You think your dad did the old man in, then?'

'Looks like it. I thought it would be interesting to talk to my auntie and see what she knows. My mum said that when our grandad was staying with us, we all went to live with her for a while. Apparently, he was horrible and she thought it was best to get us out of the way. I don't remember it, but Del and Kev do.'

'Why are you so bothered about it? Does it matter?' She looked at him as he thought. He really was nice-looking.

He turned. 'What are you looking at?'

'You.'

'Why?'

'Coz.'

'Coz what?'

'Just coz.'

'Hmm.'

'Go on, then!'

'What?'

'Why are you so bothered about it?'

'Oh, yeah. Well, I suppose it's because I want to find out the truth? That's why I want to be a journalist.'

She couldn't help herself. 'A journalist! But I thought you had to be really — well, I dunno.' She saw his face fall.

'Really what?'

She'd been so enjoying being with him and now her stupid, big mouth had ruined it all.

'I'm a stupid cow, Gary. What do I know about anything? I don't know about journalism. I know you're really clever — and if you want to be a journalist, then I'm right behind you. I want to be a make-up artist in the West End, or something like that. I'm sorry I pissed you off.'

His face cleared. He was even better looking when he smiled. Normally he was scowling, as if he was looking for trouble. Through the lens of his glasses, she saw his deep, dark eyes. They were shining.

He said, 'Never mind doing the make-up! I think you should be a model.'

'Oh, you're just saying that.'

'Why would I?'

Tina was tempted to say what she thought: that, in her experience, blokes' compliments were what they said when they wanted to get their ends away. Maybe Gary really did think she was nice-looking... But he hadn't given any indication that he fancied her. She thought he was going to kiss her when he had been in her bedroom the other day. She had hoped he would. In fact, right then, she had wanted to pull back her bedclothes and get in, pulling him in after her. The state of her bedroom had stopped her; it had obviously not exactly turned Gary on, either. She was glad now. What she wanted, more than a boyfriend or sex, was a close friend, someone to confide in and share laughs with. Maybe Gary was the one.

She patted his hand. 'Thanks, Gary.'

He said, 'I think we need to get off at the next stop. We've got to catch the Finchley bus.'

Ten minutes later, they were travelling south. Back on the top deck, Tina asked, 'What's your auntie like?'

'Believe it or not, I don't know. I haven't seen her since 1963. I was only three; I can't remember her. I rang her this morning and asked if I could come over with a friend. She seemed friendly. Here...' he reached into his pocket. 'I've got a picture of her.'

Tina looked at the photo closely. 'She looks cheerful, anyway. Blimey, look at your mum! She's so young! I didn't know she was such a stunner. You definitely take after her. I don't mean you're pretty — just that you look more like her. Is that old bloke your grandad?'

Gary studied the old man. 'Yeah. What do you think?'

Tina thought he looked horrible but said, wanting to be kind, 'Not really my type.'

Gary laughed, 'That's the understatement of the year.' He opened the letter he'd found in the box and showed it to her.

She said, 'What do you think it's all about?'

'I dunno. That's what I'm hoping to find out. I hope she's not too much like my dad. I mean, not as — um, bolshy.'

Bolshy! Tina thought about Brian and his attack on her.

She shivered. 'There's an awful lot of nasty stuff, isn't there? Not just your family, but everywhere. Actually, there's some nasty stuff in my family. Sometimes I wonder if it's best to leave it hidden and just pretend it never happened. Other times I think that's stupid: it is there and it's best to deal with it.'

Gary thought about all the shit he'd shared with Frank, Anthony and Katy Walker. He said, 'Well, if you want to talk to someone, why don't you talk t—'

Tina cut in, 'I bet you're going to say Joe!'

Gary smiled. 'Wrong, clever-clogs! I was going to say you should talk to your policeman boyfriend! I bet he's a good listener.'

'Oh, shut up. I might talk to Joe. He is terribly nice and — mind you, I think he might be better off talking to my dad.'

'I think this is our stop. Yeah, that's her street. Come on.'

Chapter 61

Louise Ratcliffe came into the staff room. 'Morning, Geraldine.'

'Morning.'

The younger woman looked at her properly. 'Are you all right? You look a bit peaky.'

'Don't ask.'

'Out on the town?'

'If only. Out on my feet, more like.'

Louise laughed. 'There's me thinking you experienced teachers go to bed with a mug of cocoa and get your eight-hours' beauty sleep.'

Geraldine was still queasy. The coffee had got her to work but its miracle effect was wearing off. She said, 'Have you seen Terry this morning?'

'No. Wasn't the match yesterday brilliant? I saw Jim in a different light. My God, he's so competitive!'

Geraldine smiled wanly. 'It was fun. I don't think I'll continue with my refereeing career, though.'

'So, what were you up to last night — out on the town with hubby?'

'Ha, if only, again! No, a big night in without hubby. I treated myself to a glass or two, and then a few more. Never again. I'm not built for it.'

Jim Dixon limped in. 'Morning, ladies.'

'Morning.'

Louise said, 'Not another walking-wounded?'

'Ah, well, my playing days are over, I'm afraid. I woke up with more muscles twanging than I thought I possessed. Good heavens, Geraldine! You look like you've seen a ghost!'

'Thank you for your concern. I am struggling with a serious condition and need sympathy but, most of all, I need to be left alone.'

The door opened and Terry came in. Geraldine felt herself blush as he studiously avoided her gaze.

'Excuse me, folks. I just wanted to — well, I don't know. I thought it would be nice... perhaps you'll think — here you go, anyway.' He handed a box to Jim, who set it down on Louise's desk.

'May I open it?'

Terry was smiling, bashful. 'If you've got time?'

Jim picked up the box and shook it gingerly. 'Chocolates?'

Terry shook his head. 'Not even close.'

'Louise, you guess.'

Louise took the box from Jim. She weighed it in her hands, then, unaccountably, sniffed it. 'Not another injured soldier?'

'No. No more casualties, I'm pleased to report.'

Geraldine took the proffered box. 'I hope it's a miracle cure for — never mind. May I open it?'

She looked up. Terry was studying her closely; his expression was... what? Was he disgusted by her? She must have sickened him last night; so much so that he'd thrown up as soon as he was out of the house. She shut her eyes. The shame of it...

Jim said, 'Come on, Geraldine. We've got work to do.'

Fingers fumbling, she lifted the flaps on the box to reveal tissue paper. She looked up at Terry; he nodded to go on. She drew out the tissue-wrapped object. As the paper fell away, gleaming silver appeared. She set the cup on her desk. Jim read out,

'The Castleton Cup Star Player 1976 — Patricia Whiting'.

Geraldine couldn't help herself: she started crying. 'Oh, Terry, what a lovely thing!'

Louise came over and read the inscription. 'You are such a dear, Terry.'

Jim said, 'Right: we're going to have a ceremony. Thank you, Terry. What a splendid idea!'

Terry's face was beetroot. 'I feel a bit embarrassed. I shouldn't have put my name on it. It's not about me.'

'Nonsense. It's all about you.'

Louise said, 'Actually, I'm not sure Patricia did very much to win the match. All she did was cry. Terry, you were the best player — isn't that right, Jim?'

'Well, I'm not sure about that — ahem! We'd better get on. I'll think of doing something to mark the event.' He sped off.

Terry said, 'Me, too. I've got work to do.'

Louise called, 'I'm sorry I missed you yesterday. I'll come over in a minute.' She turned to Geraldine, 'What's wrong?'

Still wiping her eyes, Geraldine said, 'Oh, it's nothing. I'm just hungover. I'm sick of being the way I am. I'm just a laughing stock.'

'What are you talking about? Everyone thinks the world of you.'

Geraldine wanted to tell her how Edward couldn't hide his contempt for her; that their dinner party guests thought her little more than a skivvy; that her crushes on young men were humiliating; and that she knew herself to be fat, ugly and still drunk. 'Nothing. It doesn't matter.'

Chapter 62

Terry wasn't sure what to say about Tina. The last couple of days had shown him that he needed to be careful not to underestimate his girl. He had to admit he was finding it difficult to come to terms with the fact that she was more-or-less a grown-up and probably better able to cope with life than he was. However, his abilities were not the benchmark he was looking for. Tina could do very well if only she got going in the right direction. Until now, he had been sure she was travelling inexorably down a blind alley into somewhere bad.

He shielded his eyes against the sun to see if Louise was on her way. Yes, there she was, with Geraldine Dutton. As they stepped on to the grass, they separated. Louise waved to him and went to the far side of the field, and Geraldine kept coming towards him. He watched her get closer. He had always liked her — she was so kind and cheerful. He realised with a jolt that his liking for her had taken on a different aspect. She had a beautiful, open face, no lines, no wrinkles. She was curvy in all the right places, and he could see that she definitely still had a spring in her step. For understandable reasons, he knew, right now, she wasn't looking at her best.

'I'm sorry, Terry. I know you wanted a word with Louise, but I asked her to let me take her place.'

'Don't be silly. It's very nice to welcome you to my humble abode. Would you like to come inside? You know your way around the establishment.'

She blushed. 'Oh, Terry, you must think I'm an absolute — don't answer that. I will pop in: what I have to say is probably best said in private.'

Terry stood aside to let her in. She sat down on the folding chair; he took his old armchair.

He said, 'You don't need to say anything at all. I don't know what's in your head but, honestly, we both helped each other out yesterday and that's good. I wouldn't want either of us to feel we owed the other something.'

She nodded. 'I have to say two things. First, thank you very much indeed for…' she ticked off on her fingers, 'taking my empty glass out to the kitchen; doing your best to get rid of the port stain — ninety per cent successful;

hauling me out of what I suspect would have been an incredibly uncomfortable night wedged in a corner; and saying nothing about it all this morning. I'm sorry you had to see me like that last night, but I'm glad it was you, because of all the people I can think of, you're the most kind and thoughtful. Thank you, Terry. I may have put you through other hideous experiences, as well as the spectacle I made of myself in here, but fortunately I can't remember them.'

'I was happy to help out, even if it was only a little. I told Tina how lovely you were to me yesterday afternoon — and you were! I was glad I could repay the compliment. Oh, by the way, you did nothing at all on the spectacle side of things.'

She smiled. 'Well, as you're a gentleman, you wouldn't tell me, anyway.'

Terry looked at her pale face. He'd love to make her feel better. 'You've got a lovely house. I mean, I didn't case the joint or anything like that; I could tell it's — well, a beautiful house. I always think a drive with a 'way in' and a 'way out' is the first measurement of a quality home.'

He saw at once that his comment hadn't been well judged. She turned her sad face towards him. 'Terry, may I ask you a question?'

Terry knew what she was going to say. He stayed bright, though. 'Of course, anything you like. Fire ahead.'

He watched the struggle in her mind through her expressive face. Finally, she blurted out, 'Do you have a dodgy tummy?'

It was his turn to redden; he'd been right. Shit!

'I'm so sorry. I don't know what came over me. I was in a bit of a tizz. I was rushing to get to Tina to pick her up from a pub. I was running late because I needed petrol but didn't have any money; that was why I had to pick up my jacket. I must have eaten something funny; I don't know. For whatever reason — maybe it was the fresh air — the moment I left your house, I felt queasy. I couldn't really see what I'd left behind. Oh, blimey, was it awful? I'm so sorry — was it terrible? Please forgive me?' He watched her scanning his face.

'The thing is, Terry, I was worried that I — Oh, this sounds so selfish and childish and... well, pathetic, but I was scared that it was you seeing me like an old drunk that made you sick.'

'What? No! Oh, no! Of course not!' Terry had to resist the urge to pull her to him in a hug and comfort her. 'No, on the contrary. I thought you were lovely last night. No, definitely nothing like that. Anyway, I've seen dozens of drunk people over the years, and they've never made me feel sick. Especially not lovely — ahem. You know...' He got up and patted his pockets. Damn, still no fags.

She said, 'I thought the Castleton Cup was lovely. I think Jim is organising some kind of ceremony. You will present it, won't you?'

Terry laughed, 'Hardly. No, I think the school caretaker has had his quinquennial day in the sun. You should hand it over. You were the officer in charge.'

She looked at her watch. He didn't want her to go yet. 'Geraldine, may I ask you a question? Well, two actually.'

'Of course.'

'What does your husband do for a living?'

She looked at him, surprised. 'He's a lawyer; he does contracts — for people in show business, mostly. Why do you ask?'

'Oh, it's nothing really. I thought I'd seen him before but couldn't quite place him.'

'Before what?'

'I saw the photographs on the mantelpiece last night — yours and his.'

'Oh, of course. Well, we're a lot older now. He looks the same though; it's me that's aged.'

Terry was beginning to understand Geraldine a bit better. But why was she so low on self-esteem? Maybe it was her husband… The dream of last night exploded in his head: the arrogant face, the eyes popping, then the life draining away.

'Are you all right, Terry?'

He shook his head. 'Yes. Sorry. Where was I?'

'You had two questions.'

'Ah, thank you. And secondly, the reason I wanted a chat with Louise was Tina. She's sixteen now, quite a handful; I'm sure you can imagine. I think I mentioned that she's about to leave school and I'm desperate for her to have a good start to her career. The trouble is that she's not academic in any way and I doubt she's going to get any qualifications. She is clever, don't get me wrong — I think that if she could get a foot in the door of something, she could do really well. I don't know anyone or anything and I thought Louise would be able to help. She's not here — you are. Have you got any advice?'

'It's sweet of you to ask me. I don't really know her. I remember her being a lovely little girl — lots of fun, rather volatile. She was, and I presume still is, a very pretty thing.'

Terry smiled. 'You're right on all counts. She's very keen on appearance — her own and other people's. I think she'd like to get a job in the beauty side of life: hairdressing, make-up, clothes maybe. That kind of stuff isn't really my area of knowledge.'

'Well, Louise knows much more about that sort of thing than me. There is one thing I could offer. Our neighbour across the road is David Gainsborough. I could have a word with him. He's terribly nice and friendly.'

Terry searched through his empty head: nothing came to him. 'Who?'

'Sorry, he's a hairdresser — terribly well known.'

'Not famous enough for me. Mind you, I stopped worrying about hairstyles a few years ago.'

'He does famous people's hair.'

'Such as…?'

'Er, Joanna Lumley, Jasmine Honeysuckle, Lyndsey de Paul and, he told me the other day, Suzi Quatro.'

Terry whistled, 'Lucky boy.'

'Shall I ask him if he'd be prepared to talk to Tina? He might say no. He might tell her to go off and sweep up hair in Dazzle. He is nice, though; he'll do what he can, I'm sure.'

Terry pictured telling Tina that he'd managed to get her an interview with a famous hairdresser. She wouldn't believe him. 'Thank you! If you're sure?'

'I'm sure. I'll pop around to their place this evening.'

'Thank you. I can't wait to tell her I know so many famous people.'

The bell clanked. Geraldine got up. 'Time to face the wild beasts again. I'm actually beginning to sober up, at last. Terry, thank you so much for everything. It's been a most peculiar day or two. I'll have a chat with David tonight, if he's in, and I'll report back tomorrow.'

Terry held the door for her. 'Thank you! See you tomorrow. Make sure you get an early night, won't you?'

'You bet your bottom dollar. Don't you worry about that.'

Chapter 63

Auntie Maureen had sounded really nice on the phone. 'Gary? How wonderful... I'm so sorry for you — about your dad, Gary... Yes, of course... When would you like to come over? Today? Well, yes... this morning? Okay, fine. Sure! Yes, the 263 from High Barnet... Get off at Totteridge and Whetstone Station and take the first road on the left, and I'm down a little snicket on the right. See you later. Eleven a.m.?'

'Wow, what beautiful houses; I bet they cost a bomb!'

Gary had been thinking the same. Totteridge was a nice area, trees lining the roads. The houses were bigger, smarter, cleaner than any houses he'd seen before. The gardens were leafy and tidy — so unlike his front yard.

'It must be down here?'

They walked along the quiet lane; there were only three houses on it. They paused opposite Autumn View: big, wooden door with brass letterbox and knocker, white window frames, daffodils in the lawn.

'Come on, let's go.'

'Gary?'

'Yeah?'

'I don't mind waiting. Maybe you should see her on your own? I mean, you'll want to talk about family stuff and I'm not part of that, am I?'

He looked at her. His heart flipped: she was so pretty. 'Will you come with me? I could do with back up.'

'If you really want me to. I'll keep quiet, though.'

'That'll be a first.'

She punched him.

When the door opened, Gary wondered if he'd got the wrong house. The woman was not big, or fat, and certainly did not look like his dad. He was about to stammer an apology when the elegant woman pulled him into an embrace, exclaiming, 'Gary! Oh my gosh, is it you? Yes, it is! Look at you! You're so tall, so handsome, so... You're an absolute smasher! Come in. I can't believe it. Oh my! Come in, come in.'

Gary, now released from the unexpected show of affection, got a better view of his aunt. She was tall, slim and, he guessed, what people referred to as refined. Her floaty dress was not like anything his mum ever wore; it was a creamy, silky thing that seemed to be made of air. He sniffed. Yes, perfume — unlike any he'd ever smelled. Although Maureen must be in her late forties, Gary noticed that her hair was a rich, dark brown, with no grey or silver to be seen. Unlike her brother's face, which was always hard and challenging, her expression was friendly and cheerful. She stood back and looked him up and down.

Shaking her head, she said, 'When I last saw you — Oh, put it this way: you've grown!'

She saw Tina. 'Oh, you've brought a film star with you! Who is this?'

'Er… this is my friend, Tina.'

Tina held out her hand, 'Hello, nice to meet you.'

The proffered hand was ignored, and another hug delivered.

'Oh, Gary, you look like Cary Grant, and you've brought Grace Kelly with you! Come on, let's go through. I was thinking, as it's such a nice day, why don't we go into the garden? Come on, keep up.'

Gary looked at Tina; she looked back. They smiled at each other and followed their hostess through large rooms and down onto the patio.

'Here you are — take a seat. I'll be back in a minute.'

They sat at the wooden table on cane chairs. In front of them was a long lawn with borders down each side and circular beds cut into it. Gary didn't know anything about gardens, but he could tell that this one was how they were supposed to look: neat edges, shaped bushes and colour dotted everywhere. At the far end was a greenhouse. There were some trees near it, covered in blossom.

'What a lovely garden! This is the kind of place my dad and I are going to buy soon.'

'I don't blame you. This would suit me, too.'

'You any good at gardening?'

'What do you think?'

'Nor me. We'll have to employ a gardener. Maybe my dad is good at gardening. We used to have a nice house with a garden when I was a kid.'

'What happened to it?'

'Oh, we had to leave.'

Maureen came out with a tray, crockery and cutlery rattling.

'Here we are. Isn't this nice?' She put the tray down. Gary wasn't used to a tea tray. For a start, there were cups and saucers; his family preferred chipped mugs. There were iced fairy cakes, a chocolate Swiss roll, pink wafer biscuits and yellow and pink square slices.

'Go on. Help yourselves.'

Gary was about to pick up a plate and scoop something of everything on to it, when Maureen said, 'Tina, you first. What would you like?'

He watched as Tina delicately selected a slice of the pink and yellow thing.

She said, 'Mmm, I love Battenberg cake.'

Maureen smiled. 'Good girl. Now, Gary, what are you going to have?'

He took some, too, and stuffed it whole into his mouth.

Tina squealed, 'Gary! Honestly, your manners.'

'What? It's what it's there for, isn't it?'

Maureen said, 'I remember you being a good eater. I'm glad nothing's changed. Tea, Tina?'

'Yes, please.'

'Gary?'

He'd been about to say 'Ta,' but corrected himself in time. 'Yes, please.'

Their tea was poured. Gary wasn't sure if sugar was allowed. He could see a silver sugar bowl, but maybe that was just for show. Taking a chance, he leaned over and picked up a couple of lumps.

Tina huffed, 'Gary, what do you think the tongs are for?'

'Eh? Oh! Um, sorry.'

He wasn't sure how Tina had become such an expert on posh behaviour. Nevertheless, assuming that she was, he followed her lead. He lifted the teacup with his finger and thumb and sipped. It didn't taste like tea to him, but he was buggered if he was going to say so and make himself look even more stupid.

Maureen smiled at him. 'Gary, it's lovely to see you. I'm really sad for you, of course, and dear Jenny. I didn't like to fire loads of questions at her yesterday. Is she bearing up?'

'She's doing all right. We're still trying to get used to things, you know.'

'She didn't really say what happened, only that he'd fallen over and banged his head.'

'Yeah, that's it. We were with him in the hospital, but he didn't wake up.'

'Gosh, how awful.'

Gary had expected some resemblance between his dad and Maureen, and maybe there was some facial similarity. But he could already tell that their personalities were opposites. Her voice, though! She sounded like a newsreader. It wasn't that she was posh exactly — more well-spoken. Everything about her — the house and garden, her appearance, the china cups and everything — shouted 'class'. Gary looked at her closely again. She was definitely the woman in the photo, but five stone lighter, and there was something else he couldn't put his finger on.

He said, 'I was talking to Mum about the time I stayed with you and Uncle Ray. I don't remember it at all. When you opened the door, I was expecting to get a load of memories flooding back but I didn't. Did we have a nice time?'

She said, 'I think so. We enjoyed having you all to stay.'

'It wasn't here though, was it?'

'No, we lived somewhere else in those days.'

'I'm sorry, I don't really remember Uncle Ray.'

'He and I went our separate ways a long time ago.'

'Oh, sorry about that.'

'Don't be. We had some good times and then it was high time to go our own ways. More tea?'

When Maureen went back inside, Tina said, 'What a lovely lady.'

'I know! I can't believe she's my dad's sister.'

Maureen came back with the pot and some books. 'I've brought some photographs. Tina, you want to see Gary when he was a wee, little fellow?'

'Of course. Oh, there he is! Gary, you're such a sweetie!'

Gary saw a toddler with fair hair grinning at the camera. Blimey! He had to admit, he'd been a nice-looking kid.

Tina said, 'Listen, I'm going to wander around the garden. I'll leave you two to go down memory lane.'

Gary watched her walk away. He couldn't help gawp at her beautiful arse as she meandered down the garden.

'What a lovely girl. You've done very well for yourself there, Gary.'

'She's not my girlfriend. She's just a friend. Actually, she was Kev's girlfriend.'

'Oh, pity. I'm backing Cary to get his Grace, though.'

Gary hoped she was right.

They flicked through the black and white snaps. There were pictures of the three boys and a man with a beard, as well as a younger Maureen. She looked more like the woman in the earlier photo — a bit hefty, but still cheerful-looking. He couldn't remember playing football but there they were, mid-action. The garden was much smaller than this one: a few yards of lawn rather than the small field which lay in front of them now. The pictures showed them having fun. As they turned the pages, other people and places emerged, including photos with his dad and mum in their own house. There was one in particular which caught his attention: his dad, mum, Maureen, Derek, Kevin and him.

Gary turned to Maureen, 'Where's this one taken?'

She looked over. 'That's in your garden. Don't you recognise it?'

'No.'

Maureen studied it. 'Ray must have taken it. Let me think… He must be standing with his back to the kitchen window. I suppose that hedge behind you is probably much higher now. Maybe it's not there at all? I think that must be the time we came to get you for your holiday with us; it was certainly around about that time.'

Gary pictured his back garden. The photograph showed a very different place. He looked across the long lawn at Tina; she was peering into the greenhouse. Gary felt his heart lurch: the fucking greenhouse!

He remembered Flanagan staring out of the window yesterday, as he'd asked his questions. Almost immediately after that, he'd given up his interrogation. What had he said? 'I think I've got everything I need.' When had Dad built that greenhouse? It definitely wasn't before Grandad had disappeared, otherwise it would have been in this photo. Gary had never known his dad ever do anything in that greenhouse, except fill it with shit.

He turned to his aunt. 'Why did you and Dad never keep in touch??'

'Ah, I thought you'd want to know. I'm sorry to say that we didn't get on very well. Right from our earliest childhood, we fought like stray cats. I think our father probably had a hand in that. He was a very hard man to live with; it probably rubbed off on us. When your lovely mum came along, things got better but it was never great. I found your dad very difficult company. He wasn't nice to me, or Ray; and the way he treated Jenny was — put it this way: I didn't like it. So, when our father went wherever he went, I took the decision to say goodbye. I'm sorry. I felt bad at the time. I sort of left poor Jenny to deal with everything. Ray and I got on so well with you boys but, honestly, Gary, I had had enough of being an Abbott. I hope you don't hate me for it.'

Gary had been watching Tina stroll around the garden. She looked up; he smiled at her. She started walking back. He turned to Maureen, 'Course not. I'd have legged it, too.'

'Thanks, Gary. That means a lot to me.'

Gary asked straight out. 'Do you think my dad got rid of him?'

Tina was near them now. Out of the corner of his eye, he saw Maureen's mouth open — close — open. 'I'm sure of it.'

Tina sat down. 'I'm going to get a garden like this. Do you have to spend all your time looking after it?'

Maureen sighed, 'I'm ever so lucky, Tina. I have a little man who comes in and does all the hard work. All I have to do is tell him what I want, and he does it.'

'That's how all men should behave. Don't you think, Gary?'

Gary nodded, 'Yeah, definitely. Can I have a look around?'

'Help yourself; see if you can get some ideas for when Tina employs you to do her garden.'

Gary heard their chit-chat as he wandered around the edge of the lawn. Could his dad have topped the old man? Was the body underneath the greenhouse? Maybe the time he and his brothers had been with Ray and Maureen was to give his dad the opportunity to build the greenhouse and bury the body, without the interference of little boys? He thought back to the conversation with his mum last night. She'd said she thought Dad had done it, too. He reached Maureen's greenhouse: it was clean and tidy. There were trays of little plants, bags of compost, canes, watering can, a table with those sharp scissor things, packets of seeds, some kind of heater. He thought back to their shithouse of a greenhouse. When he got home, he'd ask his mum about it. He was pretty sure she'd tell him the truth. As he neared the patio, Maureen and Tina stopped talking.

He looked at them. 'What?'

They answered in unison, 'Nothing,' then giggled.

He sat down and stretched out his legs.

'Maureen was telling me what you were like. She said you were a sweet little boy. What happened, Gary?'

'Ha, ha.'

Maureen said, 'What do Derek and Kevin do?'

'Del's a van driver at the big place down the road, the same place that Dad works — worked. Kev's training to be a fitter there.'

'What about Jenny? Does she work?'

'She works part-time at the chemist near us.'

'And what about you?'

'He's going to be a journalist.' Tina's voice was bursting with pride.

Gary could have brained her but, at the same time, it did sound good.

'No, that's what I would like to be. I doubt I could ever do it, but I am interested in working for a newspaper.'

Maureen looked impressed. 'Well, that's interesting. You know there's literary ability in the family?'

Gary's laugh was derisive. 'Don't tell me my dad was a playwright or something?'

'No, that would be a work of fiction. No, my mum — your nan — wrote poetry. Her father — your great-grandfather — wrote the most beautiful letters. I've got a box of old papers in my loft. I'll hunt them down and let you have them the next time you visit.'

Gary said, 'I know my mum used to write stories, too.'

Maureen looked dejected, 'Oh, poor Jenny. I sometimes wonder what she did to deserve the Abbotts. I imagine she could have been a very different person if only... Do you think she'd want to meet up, now that — Now things have changed?'

Gary thought about his mum and her life. Surely she would want to mix with nice people in better places. He could see her really enjoying coming over here and having tea with Maureen.

'I think so. I hope so.'

Tina said, 'I'll come! Well, if that's all right, of course?'

'Oh, that would be wonderful, Tina. You'd be so welcome. You can bring Gary with you, if you want. Mind you, he might be too busy investigating stories and publishing articles.'

'Look, I'm not a journalist. I'm not even working for the local newspaper. I'll be back here, don't you worry.'

Chapter 64

Tina had really enjoyed herself. The journey over had been fun; Gary was so much nicer than Kev. Auntie Maureen had been absolutely lovely. One day, Tina had thought on her wander around the garden, she would be like Maureen — so glamourous and sophisticated. She had enjoyed the tea and cake, the chat... And seeing all the photographs had been fun. Gary really had been a lovely little boy. All those golden curls!

They were back on the top deck of the 263. Gary was quiet, gazing out of the window, aggressively chewing gum.

'What a nice lady!' Gary didn't answer. 'Wow, what a house! I can't believe she's an Abbott. Sorry, Gary, I don't mean to be horrible, but you know what I mean. Her clothes are beautiful: she looks a million dollars. I wonder where she gets her hair done? I should have asked — maybe she could put in a word for me. She must get it dyed; there's no way it's her natural colour. Still, who cares when you look like that? She reminded me of Diana Rigg in The Avengers; older, obviously, but sort of like her. Did you think there was anything funny about her face? I mean, she was wearing a lot of makeup, but I wondered if — Gary?'

'Sorry. Yeah, she was nice, you're right.'

'You all right?'

'Yeah.'

She thought about all the shit that had happened over the last few days. Maybe it was getting to him? She wondered how she'd feel if her dad died suddenly. The very thought of it brought tears to her eyes. At no point since it had all exploded had she given any thought to Gary losing his dad.

On impulse, she put her hand on his. 'Are you sad about your dad?' She felt his hand grip hers; she liked the feel of it. The blokes she'd been out with never wanted to hold hands. She said, 'I'm sorry, Gary. It must be awful for you. I know he was — you know, quite — er, well, but he was your dad and I know that if my dad... passed away, then I'd be devastated.' She squeezed his hand again.

He said at last, 'You're right, he was awful. I grew up thinking he was brilliant. I thought everything he did was great. When he got drunk, I thought it was funny. When he swore at people in the street, I laughed. Del, Kev and me always wanted to be with him when he went fishing, or playing snooker, or just going down the boozer. You won't believe this but it's only in the last few weeks that I even realised that he's been beating up my mum! I suppose he always has, but I was too stupid to notice. She never said anything but, even so, I should have realised.'

He stopped talking and looked out of the window again. She wasn't sure whether to say anything.

Hesitantly, she said, 'I thought he was quite funny, sometimes.'

'Oh, yeah, he could crack jokes; and most of my life I've thought he was a great comedian. I don't think he ever said anything to make us feel good. It was always about him.' She squeezed his hand.

He went on, 'I don't understand how it's possible to be scared of someone, hate them, want to kill them, and at the same time miss them when they've gone. He can't have been all bad, can he? I mean, we thought his sister was nice, so maybe he might have been nice, too, if we'd given him the chance? I don't blame my mum for bashing him; I'd have done the same thing. I wanted to do it — and I really wanted to do it when I saw him attacking you.' She felt his hand hold hers tightly.

'I don't get it, Tina. If he was in when I get home, I'd be... er, disappointed. No, it would be worse than that: it would be like a holiday had come to an end. Right now, life feels like it's starting properly. I'm glad he's gone. Why do I feel so sad?'

Tina didn't know what to say. She sort of understood. 'I remember something like that when my mum left home.'

Gary turned to her, his eyes wide. 'I'm so sorry. I didn't know about your mum. I'm such a selfish bastard. All I do is whine about me. How old were you when she left?'

'Ten.'

'Blimey, that must have been hard.'

Tina knew it had been awful t these days, the detail of it wouldn't come back. Although she couldn't put her finger on it, had there always been a sense of waiting for it to happen? She did remember the moment her dad had told her. She hadn't felt shock: it had been more a protective wave that had swept through her.

263

She shrugged. 'Well, like I said, sometimes I think it may be better to leave things, rather than dig them up.'

He was looking at her. There was concern in his face and something else… She thought, for a minute, he was going to kiss her. No, he let go of her hand and pulled out his cigarettes. She was sorry: she wanted to kiss him. They lit up.

He said, 'Tina, I'm pretty sure my grandad is under our greenhouse.'

'What? You're having a laugh!' He nodded. 'Why, what — how come?'

'Well, when the old copper was at our house yesterday, he was staring out of the kitchen window. He was the detective who investigated the disappearance all those years ago. My Auntie Maureen showed me a photograph of us all standing in the back garden. That picture must have been taken around the time the old man went missing. There was no greenhouse there in the picture. I know, you're going to say — well, there's nothing wrong with building a greenhouse — and that's true. But my dad didn't do gardening. Why would he put up a greenhouse? If he was going to build a greenhouse, why would he do it after his father went missing, unless…?'

'But how do you know it was built then?'

Gary thought for a minute. 'I don't know for sure. But it's been there for as long as I can remember, so it must have been around the right time.'

Tina felt cold as she thought about the horrible old man lying under the greenhouse. 'But, Gary, you're forgetting something.'

'What?'

'Well, if you're right, your mum must know about it.' She watched his face: he didn't look shocked.

He said, 'Hmm. But I don't believe she was involved in him being bumped off, do you?'

Tina thought about Jenny Abbott — the sweetest woman she had ever met.

'I don't mean she was involved. I only meant that she would have known what was going on. It would be hard for your dad to bury a body under your greenhouse without her knowing about it. Anyway, she would have asked him what he was building a greenhouse for, especially when he wasn't interested in gardening.'

Gary nodded. 'Fuck! Oops — sorry, Tina. What a mess. Come on, time to get off.'

They sat down on the wooden bench to wait for the 107. Tina picked up a tattered *Evening News* and turned to the classified ads. There was a load of jobs for high-flyers; she skimmed past them. The sales jobs didn't appeal to her, nor did the admin and secretarial vacancies. There were loads of ads for recruitment agencies, offering jobs that were for ordinary people — she flicked past them. Her heart leapt as she read the next one.

She nudged Gary in the ribs. 'Listen to this, what do you reckon? "Gorgeous and adorable girls wanted for high class opportunities. Minimum £100 per week guaranteed. Ring 01 580 1212 for details."'

'What about it?'

Tina was disappointed; she'd hoped Gary would have shared in her excitement. This was exactly the kind of opportunity she'd been looking for.

'Oh, it's a central London number. I bet it's in show business or — I don't know — mixing with stars or something.'

He looked at her. There was pity in his expression. 'Tina! What's in your head? Anything?'

'What do you mean? There's plenty in my head! What's in yours? You've spent the last half hour persuading yourself that your dad is a killer, your grandad is under a greenhouse, your mum is an accessory to a brutal murder and God knows what else. Anyway, if you can be a journalist then I can be a — well, earn a hundred quid a week, thank you very much!'

He was smiling at her; a stupid, patronising smile.

'And don't you smile at me like that, you — you — well, just don't smile at me like that, that's all!'

'Okay, okay! Calm down!'

Tina flung the paper back on the bench, stood, and stormed off down the road. Bloody cheek! Why couldn't he be interested in her career? She'd been so encouraging about his stupid newspaper ideas. As if Gary-flaming-Abbott could ever be a journalist! It was so typical: as long as you stroked their egos, told them what they wanted to hear, let them have sex whenever they wanted, then they were happy. As soon as she ever wanted anything, then they got stroppy or lost interest. Also — and this really wound her up — blokes thought they knew best about fucking everything. How could Gary Abbott know anything about work in the West End, with famous people and that kind of thing? It was absolutely ridiculous. His stupid face came back into her head: pity. Then, telling her to calm down! He wouldn't be saying that if people treated him like he was a thick bimbo. She carried on walking. That was it! That was the last time she would have anything to do with the fucking Abbotts. Her dad was right: she shouldn't have anything to do with rubbish like them. Her dad was always right about stuff.

She looked around. The 107 went sailing past her on its way back home. She clenched her fists. There he was, looking at her, his face like thunder.

With great satisfaction, she yelled, 'Up yours, Gary Abbott!' and flicked two fingers at him as she marched on.

As she stomped along the footpath, stacks clacking, she imagined the excitement of her new world. The house in Totteridge had impressed her, but it was a bit too far from her job. Maybe a flat in St Johns Wood might be better for this stage of her life? Or perhaps an apartment? She wasn't sure what the difference was, but apartments always sounded bigger and more luxurious — they were more likely to be in higher-class parts of London than flats. She smiled as she thought of her dad coming to visit.

He would look around and whistle. 'Not bad, Tina. You've done very well for yourself. Thank you — yes, I'll have a Martini. On the balcony...? Who's coming later? Photographers, other models? Oh — isn't he on the telly? I'm very proud of you.' She laughed as she pictured Gary sweeping roads, his dirty old clothes ragged and shapeless.

'Hi, Gary. I'm going out with a journalist. Who are you going out with? Your broom?'

She opened the wardrobe door. Now, what should she wear to the party? Who else would be there? Maybe models, singers, fashion designers? One thing was certain: road sweepers wouldn't be invited! After the party, maybe she'd go to a trendy disco? Actually, now she thought about it, people in showbiz went to night clubs, not discos. Where did her type go? She brought front-page pictures to mind with beautiful, well-dressed people emerging from Tramp, Annabel's, The Ritz... She smiled at the commissionaire who clicked his heels as she sashayed past.

'Gary Abbott, is it you? My, your uniform looks smart!' Tina pressed her smooth cheek against his and said, 'How lovely to see you! You're looking great.'

His eyes were wide, his mouth hanging open as he stammered, 'An' you, Tina. Wow, you look gorgeous!' She walked past him, her arm through Sacha Distel's — or was it Omar Sharif's? No, it was David Bowie's. There were photographers everywhere. Tina stood up tall, her face aglow with the confidence that comes from others' adoration. Now, the images vivid in her head, she walked with elegance and self-assurance; her head high, back straight, chest out, happy that she looked great and was in control.

'Nice tits, darlin'.'

She looked up at the bloke leering from the top of his ladder. The compliment hadn't quite fitted her daydream, but since it was the only one available, she smiled regally and called out, 'Thank you. Would you like my autograph or a knee in the balls?'

'Oooh! Get you, sweet'eart.'

Her clumpy, great shoes were beginning to pinch her feet. She'd have to get the next bus; there was no way she could walk the rest of the journey. One of these days she'd have enough money to hail a taxi home to her penthouse apartment — was that the right word? Or better still, she would have her driver pick her up. For now, a bus would do. A long way up the road, she could see a request stop. Cursing silently, then loudly, she stooped to slip off her shoes and carried on along the pavement in bare feet. When she had her holiday in the Bahamas, or Benidorm, or one of those foreign places — no, The Riviera — she'd walk along the beach in bare feet. Maybe she'd be invited out on to one of those white ships, to sip cocktails with film stars…

The pavement was increasingly broken up, sharp stones and scattered gravel cutting into her feet. She gritted her teeth and carried on towards the bus stop. Why wasn't it getting any closer? Tina forced her mind to keep the dreamy images alive, but this self-imposed punishment was not the sun-drenched stroll across white sands she was trying to envisage. Behind her came the sound of a heavy diesel engine, changing gear. Spinning around, she saw the 107 making its inexorable way towards her. Shit! Only a hundred yards back. She started running, holding her hand out to catch the driver's attention. She gasped with relief: someone at the stop was sticking out a hand.

Chapter 65

Gary watched Tina stumbling towards him. Behind her, loomed the bus; then it sailed past her to pull up at the stop. The doors opened. Gary looked back along the road. Tina was still fifty yards away, frantically waving. What was she carrying? Stupid girl — her shoes!

The driver called, 'Are you getting on, mate?'

'Yeah, I'm waiting for my friend; she's on her way.'

'I've got a timetable to keep; this ain't a taxi service!'

Gary kept his temper (it must be the glasses, he thought). 'Sorry. Here she is.'

She almost collapsed into his arms. 'Thanks, Gary! Phew!'

They boarded the bus. Gary paid and started up the stairs to the top deck.

She called, 'I'm sorry, Gary, can we stay downstairs? I've had it.'

They sat at the back. He looked at Tina. She was slumped against the window, her eyes closed, struggling to get her breath back. Despite her dishevelled appearance, she looked beautiful.

He went straight to his prepared speech. 'Listen, Tina, I'm really sorry. I should have been more excited about your job. You're exactly what they're looking for, I'm sure. You deserve a good job, and you'd definitely get it. I know you wanted me to be happy for you. I let you down. I'm sorry. The thing is—'

She held up her hand, opened her eyes and said, 'It's all right. I was being childish. They're probably looking for topless waitresses, or prostitutes, or strippers. I know, Gary. I'm really not stupid; I just get stupid ideas.'

Gary blurted out, 'I didn't mean you wouldn't be good at those things! I mean… what I mean — The thing is… You're pretty and… I didn't want you to get into funny stuff, that's all.'

'I know. It's all right. You were being a gentleman and I was being a spoilt child.'

Gary rather liked the idea of watching Tina doing a strip-tease, but he didn't say so. Right now, it was probably best to stay quiet on the matter.

He did say, 'Also, you're right about me getting carried away. But you've got to admit that the idea of my dad growing anything is unbelievable.'

She nodded agreement. 'I'd like to work up in London, in the West End. I'm sick of everything around here. My life is so boring. The trouble is that I can't see a way out of it. I wish I'd worked harder at school.'

Gary thought exactly the same. Why had he been so determined to be a stupid, ignorant yobbo? For years, his only ambition had been to succeed in being a failure at school. Maybe he was thick after all? When he thought about Anthony and Frank, he realised what brainy people were really like. But Joe didn't think he was a thicko and, of all the people Gary knew, it was Joe's opinion that meant most to him. He thought about Tina; she wasn't thick either. In fact, the way she'd dealt with that copper last night had been incredible. She had completely outwitted him without him even realising. Gary smiled as he thought about the slimy bastard.

'What are you smiling at?'

'I was imagining your boyfriend waking up this morning with a world-record hangover.' Her smile was a little sad. 'Oh, I was also thinking that you're really smart, too.'

'Do you think so? Do you, Gary? I get boys telling me nice things, but it's always coz they want — you know — sex. Sometimes I want someone to say a nice thing because it's true.'

Gary wanted to say that it was true — but that he'd also like to have sex with her. Once more, he thought better of sharing this.

'No, I mean it. You're clever, all right. The other thing is, you've got a lovely personality and that's more important than brains. It's not that you haven't got brains, and I don't mean I wouldn't want to — er… um, I don't know. Point is, you're nice. That's the point.'

'Thanks, that's nice.'

They sat in silence as the bus neared their stop.

Gary looked down at her bare feet. 'You in agony?'

'I'm crippled for life.'

'Shit, sorry.'

'Don't be. I'm the one that flounced off.'

'I'm the one that made you.'

'What are you going to do now?'

'I'm off to get a letter from Victoria Court.'

'Who's she?'

'The headmistress of my school. I've got to get a letter from her to say she's happy for me to do a work placement at the newspaper.'

'Get you — Victoria!'

'Yeah, well, she's a sort of friend… I'll tell you about it another time.'

The bus pulled up; they got off.

'I'd come with you, but I want to catch my dad when he comes home from work. Thanks for the trip; it's been fun.'

He looked down into her eyes. Could he kiss her? Would she slap his face? Maybe a hug would be better? She was still holding her shoes; they'd get in the way.

He said, 'Yeah, ta to you, too. See you.'

'Bye, then.'

They turned away and went in their different directions. Gary looked around and saw her limping across the main road. He sucked in a long breath; why hadn't he said something deep and meaningful? Anything to make her feel good…

Gary had never been out with a girl on her own before. He wasn't sure what the rules were or what was expected of him. She'd made it pretty clear that she didn't want a boyfriend, and certainly not an Abbott. He didn't have anyone who he could talk to about it, either. He was going to have to work it out himself.

As he walked up Cardinal Road, he thought about the chat he'd had in the newspaper office earlier. Nigel had whistled when Gary told him that it had been his dad that had done in the posh bloke.

'What, John Eustace? You're having me on!' He got up, threw open the door, went out for three seconds then came back clutching newspapers. He held one up for Gary to read.

Ex-mayor assaulted

Nigel read it out aloud. "'John Eustace, owner of Eustace Electronics, was brutally attacked on the evening of March 20th. Eustace, 53, who stood down as Mayor in 1974, was attacked by an unknown assailant on his journey home from a business function. Mr Eustace was headbutted by a large, middle-aged man. The incident took place on Theobald Street at approximately 10 p.m., between the junctions of Gateshead Road and Oakley Avenue.

"His wife, Elizabeth, said, 'We were waiting for a temporary traffic light to change when the driver of the car behind us became aggressive. When John asked him to stop sounding his horn, the stranger got out of his own car and savagely headbutted John. He then got back into his car and drove off.'

"Mr Eustace remains in hospital with serious injuries to his head and face. John Eustace, whose company employs nearly three hundred people, has been a major supporter of the town and the local community. Police are asking for any witnesses to come forward to help with investigations."'

Nigel looked at Gary, eyebrows raised. Gary nodded. Nigel put the first paper down then picked up the next.

"'Ex-mayor discharged from hospital. John Eustace, owner of Eustace Electronics, was discharged from hospital yesterday after a recent assault. The local businessman and ex-mayor was attacked on Theobald Street on the evening of 20th March. After fears of brain damage, John Eustace, 53, was well enough to go home but remains poorly. Police are asking for anyone who was in the area to come forward with information. Elizabeth Eustace, the victim's wife, described the attacker as a large, middle-aged man who was obviously extremely drunk. He was driving a Ford Cortina. There were several other people in the car..." Blah blah blah.'

Nigel looked up. Gary nodded again.
'You're telling me that it was your father?'
'Yep.'
Nigel shook his head. 'And you're telling me that he's the son of Bertram Abbott — it's the same Brian Abbott?'
'Yep.'
'And he died in hospital three days ago?'
'Yeah.'
'Having received a crack on the head when he fell over in his own kitchen?'
'Yes.'
'Phew! No wonder our friendly bobbies were trying not to lick their lips when I rang yesterday. Hang on a minute, you're not going to tell me where the old man's body is, are you?'
Gary shook his head. 'No, I don't know anything about that.'
Nigel was silent. He sat looking at Gary. Gary looked back, unsure but alert.
'So, what do you want to tell me about the death of your father?'

'There's nothing to say. He fell over in our kitchen and bashed his head against something hard. He died in hospital on Sunday night. That's it. I'm sorry.'

'Don't be sorry. I'm sorry. No, I was wondering if there was a little bit of extra that you might want to add. Anyway, we've got until five p.m. today to sort out the story. As you can see, the last couple of editions have covered the John Eustace story. Are you and your family prepared to allow us to report that it was your father who attacked him?'

Gary thought about his poor mum: she was going to have to face her friends and neighbours with the truth. It would come out, anyway, and at least this way they would have a bit more control.

He said, 'Yeah, we're ready. Will you let me see what you write before it's printed?'

'Of course. I'll be chatting to the police this morning. I'll want to get a quote or two from them. If you can get back here later, say around two p.m?'

'Okay. Er, what about me working here? Is there any chance?'

'Rob says he's happy for you to have a try out. He wants a letter from your school and one from your parents — well, mother. If they can say they're in support of a work placement, that would be brill. It's not going to be glamourous, Gary. We'll be getting you to do all the crappy jobs, and at the end of it we'll probably say "on your bike".'

Gary looked at him: was he taking the piss?

'Great, thanks very much. When do you want me to start?'

'Get those letters to me and you can start straightaway.'

Now, as he approached school, the excitement was building. He was going to work! Not any old work: he was going to work for a newspaper! He knew that it could all end up in failure; he might be shit and get sacked on the first day. Nevertheless, he had a job; and it wasn't a thicko's job with a load of thickos.

As he walked up the main drive into school, kids were looking at him strangely; what were they gawping at? He remembered: he was wearing his glasses. Sod it, he was going to keep them on and if anyone laughed at him, he'd beat their fucking heads in. He went straight for the three steps into the corridor with the school offices; he was here on business, after all. He knocked on the secretaries' door and waited. He heard a distant, 'Come in.' He opened the door.

Mrs Chalkley turned round and, looking up, said, 'Yes, may I help you? Oh, Gary, is it you?'

'Yeah, it's me. I was wondering if I could see Miss Court?'

'I'll check with her. You're looking very… different?'

'Yeah?'

'Hang on there. I'll go and see if she's free.'

Gary felt different. In his mind, he'd left school years ago. Here he was, about to meet with the headmistress on a matter of important business.

Mrs Chalkley came back. 'Go through; she's got a few minutes.'

'Thank you, Mrs Chalkley. Nice to see you.'

'And you, Gary.'

Pleased with his newfound refinement, he walked across the corridor to the open door. He went in.

'Gary! It's so lovely to see you. Come in. Sit down.'

As he walked in, he remembered the last time he'd been in this office — with Steve, Phil and Paul and a copper whose face looked like it had been slapped. He couldn't quite believe what had happened since. Then, Victoria Court had been severe and uncompromising. Now, she was smiling at him.

'Gary, I'm thrilled to see you but I'm also so sorry about your father. I'm wondering if it's a bit soon for you to come back to school. I know you're a tough guy and everything, but it's only been a few days… How are you coping? Your mother? Brothers?'

'Everything's all over the place. The police have been sniffing around. I think things are going to settle down now, though.' She was looking at him closely. He remembered that Joe had told her all about it. He added, 'Joe told you what happened?'

'He did. I'm sorry about it all. It must have been so frightening and upsetting. I understand that it's been straightened out now; is that right?' He nodded. She said, 'I'm glad to see you're wearing your glasses. Didn't the contact lenses work out?'

She'd been responsible for getting him those the other day, so he didn't want to disappoint her. 'I need a change now and then. Thanks for your help with them. But I need another favour.'

'Yes?'

'I know there's exams coming up and I haven't finished school, but I've got a job arranged at the newspaper office and I need a letter saying that you support me. You wouldn't write something for me, would you?'

He'd been a bit nervous even saying the word 'job'. Would she laugh, be angry or disappointed? She'd been so nice to him at the weekend; maybe she'd be back to normal today.

She beamed at him. 'Gary, you're amazing! Well done, you! I'm so impressed and, if you don't mind me saying, proud too. I'd be delighted to write something. What shall I say? Hmm… Gary Abbott is violent, always angry, is disruptive in lessons, shows no aptitude for anything other than intimidation and adopting a surly demeanour?'

She looked at him, a very serious expression on her face.

Gary didn't smile. 'Is that what you think?'

'Yes.'

'What about my other skills and talents?'

'Which ones are they?'

'Do I need to spell them out?'

'No. How about Gary has great potential, has a fine, analytical mind, is a trustworthy team-player and takes responsibility in difficult situations?'

'Is that what you think, too?'

'Yes.'

'Oh.'

She smiled, 'When are you going to start?'

'As soon as I get your letter and my mum's written one — maybe later today.' She picked up a pen. He said, 'Er, could you say that I can write? I don't know but it might help a bit.'

Still smiling, she began writing.

Chapter 66

Tina crossed the road and went straight into True Form. Just inside the door was what she was looking for: a basket of crappy shoes at reduced prices. She picked out a pair of shapeless, rubbery slip-ons, and went to the counter.

'Do you want to try them on?' asked the assistant.

'No, thanks. Whatever they're like, they'll be better than these things.'

'Wanna bag?'

'Yeah.'

Tina handed over a pound note and waited for the penny change. She sat on a bench and put the shoes on. They were better than her stacks and bare feet, but not by much. She put her old shoes in the bag and hobbled out. The church clock was chiming — one o'clock. Shit! She'd missed her dad: now what was she going to do? Their conversation of that morning came back to her. She walked down the main road to the library. The grey-haired woman behind the counter eyed her suspiciously.

'Yes? Can I help you?'

Tina groaned inwardly: not another mean old bag. She adopted her best, celebrity manner, 'Why, yes, thank you. I wonder if you can give me some information?'

The prune was not impressed. She sniffed, 'Yes?'

Tina wanted respect, not disapproval. Haughtily, she said, 'Thanks, I've changed my mind. Good day to you.' As she turned, her foot slipped out of its newly acquired rubber slip-on; she stumbled.

'Oh dear, does madam need assistance?' The librarian's voice was dripping with false concern.

Fuming, Tina hobbled out.

Back on the street, she saw a telephone box down the road on the far side. Without looking, she crossed over; a car horn sounded angrily. She flicked the Vs.

There were two teenage kids in the phone box, one was speaking into the handset, the other smoking. Huffing, Tina turned around to survey the scene. God, this place was a shithole. Boy, was she desperate to get into London. She pictured the heady atmosphere of Soho, Shaftesbury Avenue, Oxford Street: everything was colourful, people were younger, better dressed, exciting. Tina knew that it was there that opportunities awaited her, not here in this dump. She turned back to the phone box: the smoker was staring at her, weighing her up. She stared back. He kissed the inside of the glass, his eyes on hers. Without thinking, she whacked her heavy bag of shoes against his face. He reared back, cracking his head into his friend's.

The friend shouted angrily at his mate. 'What did you do that for, you prick?'

Tina smiled sweetly at them. The call had obviously ended prematurely; they tumbled out of the box and shambled off. Tina quickly opened the directory for R to Z: no mention of The Beeches. Annoyed, she thought hard, then tried A to D: there it was. To her surprise, The Beeches was only five minutes' walk away.

She'd never been to an old people's home and felt a bit conspicuous as she walked through the gates. It was a large, concrete building, more like a prison than a home. The gardens were nice and tidy, though; she made a note to tell him. The entrance was straight ahead of her; she walked towards it.

'Tina!'

She looked round; Joe was walking towards her, smiling. She waved. As he approached, she took in his appearance again: average height, strong-looking, friendly face. She noticed that he had a springy sort of walk, like he was about to start running. His eyes were on her: they were friendly and kind, though watchful.

'Hello again, Tina — the star of our show.'

When he reached her, she realised that he was bigger and taller than she'd thought; maybe it was that she'd taken off her platforms?

Shyly, she said, 'Yeah, hello. I thought I'd come and see you. Um, the gardens are very tidy by the way.'

'Thank you — they'd better be! Would you like to sit down? We can occupy Gary's bench, since his Lordship is elsewhere.'

She followed him to a bench next to some bushes and sat down. Although he'd agreed to her talking to someone, she felt a bit disloyal to her dad. How should she start? She looked at Joe. He was opening a penknife. She watched his hands and fingers moving; they held her attention. He started scraping dirt from under his thumb nail. Satisfied, he carefully folded the blade back into its casing. Then he pulled out a handkerchief and blew his nose. He looked off into the bushes; got up and pulled up some weeds, threw them on to the edge of the border then came to sit down next to her.

He said, 'The trouble is, once you start weeding, you can never stop. I think it may be better not to start in the first place. What do you think?'

Tina knew nothing about gardening but guessed that he didn't say stuff for nothing. What was he getting at? 'I don't know; I'm sorry.'

'Any news?'

'Nothing since last night. Gary and me went to see his aunt in Totteridge this morning; that's all.'

'Nice time?'

'Yeah, it was.' She made up her mind to speak and to trust him to help her. In a rush, she said, 'My dad's not very happy. He does his best to look after me — my mum left us six years ago. He needs to lose some weight — I don't think he's very healthy. He's pretty clever... not brainy but capable, you know. I want him to be happy but I don't know how to help him. Since my mum left, things have been pretty difficult. He does his best. We live alone, and I feel responsible for him — it's silly I know but, thing is, I think he should find a girlfriend — well, lady-friend, but he never goes out or meets anyone. He stays in, goes to work, stays in again. Since my mum left, he's become a recluse, really. I'm sure he went out more, when we were all together... We had to move house — we used to live in a nice house but when she left we moved out — we now live in a flat in the town centre. He'd do anything for me and I want to help him but I don't know how... I miss my mum but it's much worse for him. The thing is...' She paused. Should she tell him? Turning slightly, she tried to catch a quick glimpse; he was very still. His eyes glanced back at her.

He said, 'Tell me if you want. Don't if you don't.'

Tina felt her heart start to bump and a sudden heat rush through her. She'd always thought that if she started talking, she'd never be able to handle whatever came out. What would her dad think if he knew she was talking to a stranger about their lives, their secrets? She didn't know Joe at all — why should she trust him? He had helped her last night. Gary trusted him and she trusted Gary, but apart from that...?

Joe said, 'I tell you what. Sometimes it's very difficult to decide what to do. Whichever way we look at something, there seem to be too many reasons for not doing it. On the other hand, not doing something isn't going to get the thing moving or changing. I've got a little trick I use; it sometimes helps. This is what I do: I decide that option A is heads, option B is tails. I toss the coin and whichever one it is, I register whether I am relieved or disappointed. Does that make sense? It's a way of clarifying what I really want to do. Even then, you don't have to be led by it; it's only a guide. Want to try it?'

Tina rehearsed what she might say when the coin came down. Could she even say it? What would it sound like if she talked about her dad's screams and shouts — the terrible violence he was obviously experiencing. Maybe her suspicions about her mum were just a product of her wild imagination? Could she tell someone, even someone like Joe, about the writhing, sickening dread she had that her mum hated her so much that she'd had to run away from her? Did she think it would ever be possible to tell another person that when her mum had gone, she'd been pleased; that she'd always wanted to have her dad to herself? What kind of monster was she, anyway? How could she say any of this out loud?

She looked at Joe again. What was so special about him? Why would he be able to help her, or her dad? He was an ordinary bloke, not a priest or anything special.

He said, 'Sometimes it's a little bit helpful to say one tiny thing, to get the ball moving — something small. Then, if it still feels all right, saying something else becomes possible.'

Tina pictured the evening she'd seen her mum kissing a strange man. She had been visiting her friend Deborah Peacock and when Mr Peacock had driven her home, she'd glanced at the couple in the car at the end of the road. When she'd got indoors, her dad had said her mum was out with friends. Tina had almost told him that she'd just seen Mum with a man in a car, but, despite her age (how old had she been? Maybe eight?), she'd known it was better to keep it a secret. From that day, the signs had become more and more obvious, even to her younger self. It was only recently that Tina had pieced it all together: the constant phone calls, wads of cash; her mum telling her that, to get on, she should give men what they wanted; her mum lying to her dad the whole time; him believing her.

Maybe if she, Tina, hadn't been in the way, her mum and dad would still be happily married... Tina knew that she used to really annoy her mum: she was always telling Tina to leave her alone and stop asking stupid questions. She never read stories to her or took her on picnics. All her friends had birthday parties, but her mum was never interested in that sort of thing.

Tina screwed her face up, 'Oh, Joe, it's all so horrible; I can't bear it.'

'I'm so sorry. Let's leave it. You've told me loads of things already. I know it's all going around in your head; you can tell me anything you like, whenever you like.'

She sighed with relief. It wasn't time to say anything. It had been the closest she'd ever come to sharing it all. Thinking it through had made things clearer.

She said, 'I've got one question.'

'What's that?'

'Do you think it's possible that a mother can hate her child?'

Joe thought for a while. She looked intently at his face.

His eyes turned to her. 'Yes, I'm sure mothers — and fathers — feel all the usual emotions towards their children but, whatever they feel — and it's always going to be a mixture — it can't be the child's responsibility or, if you like, fault. What do you think?'

'Yeah, I guess that's right. It's just that I can't get it out of my head that if I'd been different, then maybe everything would have been all right.'

'How could you have been different? To be different, you'd have had to be an adult, with years of experience upon which to draw, and — this is important, too — a different genetic make-up. So, bearing in mind you're who and what you are, I can't see that you could have been different or done anything differently.'

'But that doesn't mean I can't change, does it?'

'Do you want to change?'

'God, yes; I'm a total mess.'

Joe smiled at her. 'Total?'

'Well, maybe not total — more, "mostly".'

'I'm sure you can change if you want. Don't change too much, though.'

Tina sat up straight, drew in a deep breath. 'Phew, too much nasal gazing for me. Will you help my dad though? He needs to change, too.'

'Just so you know, it's navel. Of course. I'd like to meet him. Can you arrange that?'

Chapter 67

'Afternoon, Terry.'

Striding out across the field was Jim Dixon; he was waving and beckoning at the same time.

'Hallo.'

'Can I talk something through with you?'

'Sure, I'm nearly done. I'm removing some — ahem, a critique of primary school leaders and their loved ones.'

Jim Dixon peered at the sanded-down goalpost. 'What did it say?'

'It was in French; well, some foreign language. It was double-Dutch to me.'

'Don't tell me: someone thinks I'm a twit?'

'That kind of thing.'

Jim was looking out across the pitch. Terry followed his gaze. What was he looking at?

He guessed, 'Remembering all those lost chances and wondering about ifs, buts and maybes?'

Jim turned back to him. 'Of course. I can't help it, Terry. Also, I was wondering where to have our award ceremony. I was thinking about where the winning goal was so luckily scored?'

Terry laughed. 'You mean the perfectly timed header-volley that shot past the hapless goalkeeper?'

'Hmm. Anyway, I was wondering if you could set up some kind of makeshift podium? We're going to end lessons early this afternoon so we can have a little ceremony. I'd like you to hand over the cup. If we're all out here by three p.m., does that give you enough time?'

'What, you give me ninety minutes to set up what takes Wembley weeks to plan and execute? I'll do my best.'

'Good man. There's something else I wanted to talk about. It's absolutely up to you, but I wondered if you'd think about organising a school team. You're not in my league, of course — I don't think I mentioned that I had a trial with Orient — but you've got a bit of talent and I think you could help us

compete in the local schools' league. I'd have to add the finishing touches —
you know, put the icing on the cake — but I reckon you could do the donkey
work. What do you think?'

Terry liked the idea but knew, from his recent experience, that discipline
might be an issue.

'The thing is, I'd love to do it, but my background is in the army, where
you do what you're told. You know what some of these little bleeders are like.
They'd eat me for breakfast, dinner and tea. How will I keep discipline in the
ranks?'

'I'll make sure there's a teacher present at all times. I'm going to win that
league; no little bleeder is going to stop me!'

'Well, let's try it out. I won't do it if it's not working. What are you
thinking: during dinner break or after school?'

'I haven't decided yet. What would suit you?'

'I don't mind. You decide.'

Jim Dixon nodded and strode off again. Terry thought about how he might
arrange the podium. He walked into the school hall and picked up one of the
dining tables. On his way back to the field, his eye was caught by the pile of
breeze blocks waiting to be formed into an outhouse for the rubbish bins. He
positioned the table on the penalty spot, then went to get his wheelbarrow.
Five minutes later, he had three secure steps up to the dais. How could he
make it look more ceremonial? He brought the vast dust sheet from its place
in his shed and stretched it out on the field. It was, unsurprisingly, dusty and
paint-stained — but principally whitish and, if he could fold it neatly, it would
dress the table and blocks to give an impression of pomp and ceremony.

He stood back and admired his handiwork — rough and ready but
passable. At the far end of the field, in the little woodland area, there were —
yes — a few daffs. He picked them, and finding some rubber bands in his
shed, made two bouquets which he positioned at the base of the steps. Again,
he assessed the suitability of his official setting — not Wembley but good
enough.

He pictured the handing over of the FA Cup. What happened there?
Dignitaries, that was it! They'd need some officials behind the podium. There
were a few minutes before playtime: he'd go and ask Jim Dixon to ensure
some teachers were on hand to add a bit of gravitas to the ceremony.

Chapter 68

Gary had been sorely tempted to open the letter from Victoria. She hadn't sealed it, but something told him to trust her to do what was best for him. Despite his run-ins with her over the last couple of years, he had grown to like and respect her, and he reckoned she'd do her best for him.

His mum had got into a right state. 'What shall I write? I don't know anything about newspapers. What if I say the wrong thing and you get sacked?'

'Mum, they can't sack me: I don't even work for them. Anyway, all they want is for you to say you are happy for me to work with them. I don't think they want your journalistic advice.'

She scratched her head, looked agonised, then wrote:

To whoever it concerns

My name is Jennifer Abbott. Gary Abbott is my son. I think he'll be a very good reporter if you give him the chance. He isn't great at school but this is because he's la ('la' scratched out) lacks discapline. He is a good writer and I think will work much harder if he has a job than he does at school.

I hope you will give him a chance.

Yours very truly

Jennifer Abbott

Gary read it.

'Mum, why do you have to write negative stuff! And you've spelled discipline wrong. Look at it, it's obvious you were going to write "lazy".'

'I wanted it to be a true statement. Okay — sorry about discipline, but they're employing you, not me. Anyway, you saw it was wrong: that shows you're a good writer.'

'Have you got an envelope?'

'Yes, who is it for?'

Gary thought, maybe it should go to the editor? 'Robert Mitchum.'

'If only! Somehow I can't see him working in the local newspaper office.'

'That's his name; he's the boss.'

Jenny addressed the envelope. She looked into Gary's eyes as she handed it to him. 'Here you are. Good luck! I'm so proud of you. What we've gone through has been awful, but you've been amazing. I don't know if you're going to be a reporter, or a journalist, but I'm sure you're on your way to a better life. You deserve it, Gary.'

Gary sneered at kids who cried. In fact, to see kids crying compelled him to give them even more to cry about. As he absorbed his mother's words, he didn't try to stop the tears running down his face.

'You silly boy, don't cry. Here, let me—'

Gary ducked, seeing the hankie coming his way. He took off his glasses, wiped his face with his sleeve, and put them back on.

'Wherever I'm going, Mum, you're coming, too. We're both getting out of here.'

He put her letter into his pocket with Victoria's. Checking himself in the hall mirror, he nodded. Still okay; hair a bit straggly, though. He pulled the steel comb from his back pocket and parted his hair in the centre, then combed it back. Who did he look like? Maybe the lead singer of Mud? Only thinner.

He shouted, 'Bye, Mum,' and opened the door.

'Wait a minute — let me look you over.'

He stood still as she undertook her assessment. 'What's this pink stuff on your shirt?'

Knowing it was Battenburg jam, he said, 'Oh, I dunno. Maybe it's from… er, something I ate?'

'Come on, back to the kitchen.'

As she wiped it clean, he wondered when he'd ever be able to stop lying about everything. Was it normal to lie? Why didn't he say he'd been to see Maureen? He looked over his mum's head, into the garden beyond — the greenhouse — could there be a body under there? He shivered.

'You're not cold, are you?'

He looked down. There was a damp patch on his shirt for everyone to see now.

'I'm going. Thanks, Mum. I'll be back soon.'

This time he shut the door softly. Once again, he walked like a top journalist: tall, confident, determined. No one was going to stop him getting his big scoop. Was that the right word? He'd have to learn a load of stuff pretty quickly.

The older woman was behind the counter. She smiled at him. 'We can't keep you away, can we?'

'I'm here to see Nigel; is he around?' Gary could see him in the main office. He was on the phone, his pen busy on his pad. Gary liked the energy of that pen, as if it had a life of its own. Nigel looked up, saw Gary and beckoned him over. 'He's waving to me. Can I go through?'

She turned around to check. 'Sure, go through.'

As Gary went in, he asked, 'Is Karen around?'

'Yes, she's tackling a serious journalistic project; it's what they all have to do to learn the ropes.'

'What's that?'

'Washing up the cups.'

Gary remembered what Nigel had said: he'd better get used to the menial work. He didn't mind. Just being in this place gave his dreams a touch of reality.

Nigel put down his phone, stood, and beckoned Gary after him into the interview room. They pulled out their fags. Nigel looked at the packet of Number 6 Gary was opening.

'If you're going to work with me, you'll need to smoke better ciggies than that. I'm not going to nick those coffin nails off you. I want decent fags.'

Gary saw the Piccadillys and made a mental note.

'Any news from the police?' he asked.

Nigel beamed at him. 'Thanks to you, we've got ourselves a nice little story for the front page. I'm halfway through writing up the sorry saga of the Abbotts — long-lost Grandad, assault on John Eustace, fatal accident of perpetrator and something else which I don't quite get yet.'

'What's that?'

Nigel inhaled a lungful. 'I spoke to DS Nott. Do you know him?'

'Yeah, I think you mean Scunt.'

Nigel smiled. 'I can guess. Yep, well, him. He was like a cat on a hot tin roof when I spoke to him a few minutes ago. He was almost cracking jokes. I don't know what was going on, but he was cock-a-hoop.'

Gary asked, 'Can I see the article yet?'

'I'll have it done in a few minutes. I should have asked you before if you had any photos of your old man? It would be good to have him alongside your grandad's picture from before.'

Gary nearly reached for his pocket.

'Nah, we lost all our photographs in a fire a while ago.'

'Pity. Never mind. Have you got the letters?'

Gary handed them over. Nigel read them quickly. Gary liked the way he seemed able to read and absorb stuff so easily. He'd try and read more, and see if he could get quicker at it.

Nigel said, 'Your headmistress thinks you're shit hot.' He smiled at Gary's mum's letter. 'Mother not so sure?'

'Yeah, well, she doesn't like to boast about her children.'

'Hang on. Stay there. I'll show these to Rob.'

Karen looked in. 'All right?'

'Oh, hello. Yeah, fine. You?'

'I'm fine. What are you smoking for? You look like a right div.'

'Everyone smokes.'

'I don't.'

'Oh. Well... Maybe you should.'

'What, and look like a div?'

Nigel came back with Rob. Gary sat up and put out his fag in the full ashtray.

'Hallo, Gary, my name's Rob. It's good to meet you.'

Gary got up and shook hands.

'You, too.' He examined Rob Mitchum. He looked pretty good: tall, big shoulders, white shirt with sleeves rolled up, tie and braces.

'I'm sorry about your dad, Gary. It's a terrible thing you've had to experience. You've been very generous with your help on this story. We're really grateful. Nigel thinks you're a good candidate to be an apprentice and so does your headmistress. Would you like to join us for a week or so — so you can make up your mind about us? We can see what we think, too?'

For a second Gary wondered if he was on the telly: Rob was talking to him as if he was an adult. He was offering him, Gary Abbott, a job. Gary broke into his own head and shook himself,

'Er, yeah, yes. Thank you. Yes, please.'

Rob smiled. Nigel was smiling, too. Karen was grinning. Gary felt his face go red.

'You'll be pleased to know that I've got a job for you straightaway. It's a good test of your reporting skills. You do have good reporting skills, don't you?'

Gary had absolutely no idea. 'Very good. They're my best skills, I'd say.'

'Okay. You've got thirty minutes to get to Aycliffe Road Primary School. There's some kind of award ceremony going on and they've asked for it to be reported in *The Post*. Unbelievably, we have a crack photographer available to go with you. Now, Gary, think carefully: have you got a pen with ink in it? Do you have a notepad? Have you got official Post identification?'

'Yes. All three.'

'Great. See you later.'

Rob went back into his office. Gary looked at Nigel, who shrugged and walked off.

Karen said, 'I'll get you a notepad. You can take a business card with your name on it.'

'Thanks. Great. Where's the photographer?'

She went into Rob's office. Gary could just make out her voice. Rob opened a filing cabinet, pulled out a camera and handed it to her.

He raised his voice. 'If it doesn't come back pristine, you're out of here.'

Karen returned, her smile wider than ever. 'Come on. Let's go.'

Gary stopped at Nigel's desk. 'Thanks, Nigel. I won't let you down.'

'Make sure you don't.'

'Er, Nigel?'

'Yeah?'

'Have you got a case or a folder or a something I can borrow, you know, to put my stuff in? I don't want to look like a div.'

Nigel pulled open a drawer and rummaged. He couldn't get any purchase on the piles of stuff that were jamming it shut. Cursing, he got off his chair, bent down and pulled everything out. In amongst all the papers, he found a clipboard. He flicked through the pages attached to it, removed them and handed the clipboard to Gary.

'Don't lose it. If it doesn't come back pristine, you're out of here.'

Gary laughed and took it. 'Thanks, I'll treasure it.'

Karen was waiting for him at the front door. She handed him a notepad.

'Thanks. Actually, now I've got my clipboard I need some blank paper to, er… clip on to it.'

'You're very fussy, aren't you?'

'Well, I need to get it right. I am a top journalist.'

Tutting, she went back behind the counter and opened a drawer. She re-emerged with a wad of foolscap paper.

'Can I get you anything else? How about a stapler to keep all your articles neat and tidy? I know. Here, have this bulldog clip.'

Gary was so pleased with his new job and assignment, he didn't mind being teased, especially not by Karen.

'Yeah, I'll take that. And I'll need some paper clips.'

Karen looked at her colleague, 'Eve, can we spare paper clips for the great man?'

The older woman said, 'Hmm, ordinarily I'd say no but since we're in the presence of greatness, I think we can make an exception.'

Karen rejoined Gary and handed him his stationery. 'I'm going to call you Bulldog Abbott, ace reporter.'

Gary quite liked the sound of it. 'Bulldog by name, bulldog by nature.'

'What, slow-witted and ugly?'

'No, determined, and what's that word, ten... ten — er...'

'Um, tenterhooks?'

'Here you are, you'll need this.' Eve was handing something to him. He looked at the card — Gary Abbott, Cub reporter, *The Post*. He felt his heart thump. He was a journalist — on his way!

He opened the door and held it for Karen. As she passed him, he stepped back towards Eve and whispered, 'Um, can I borrow a pen?'

It took Gary thirty seconds of fumbling to get his sheaf of blank paper into his clipboard. Nigel leant against the counter, watching. Gary looked at his smiling face, embarrassed. 'Any advice?'

'On how to clip paper onto a clipboard?'

'Well, yeah. That. And I meant the story?'

'Write down as many facts as you can establish. You can make it perfect when you get back here. You'll need to find out all the usual stuff: what it's all about, why, who's involved, where, when and how — that kind of thing. It will be good to get the human interest, so see if you can identify some main characters. I'd go for the pupils rather than the teachers, if I were you. Get Karen to take pictures of people, not buildings.'

Gary had his paper neatly squared off now. 'Ta. How long will I have to write it up?'

'We're 'off stone' at five.'

'Huh?'

'It's got to be with the sub-editor — that's Alan — by four thirty.'

'What, today?'

'Yeah? When did you think?'

Gary said, 'But that only gives me a few minutes!'

The door opened. 'Are you coming?'

Eve called out, 'Stand back! Bulldog Abbott's on his way.'

Gary put the yellow Bic in his inside pocket and puffed out his chest, 'Hold the front page!'

Nigel and Eve clapped and cheered as he strode out.

Chapter 69

'Miss?'

Geraldine hadn't felt as bad as this for a long time. She had only herself to blame; that made it even worse. She'd tried to eat something at lunch but had managed no more than a digestive biscuit. When William Edmondson had informed her, very kindly, that she smelled like his dad, she'd let the comment go. The fact that William's father ran a pub told her everything she needed to know.

Now, with the school day nearing its end, she did not want any further hassle. A strong coffee, fifteen minutes on her own, and then the last session. She already knew that she would get them to plan the set project on Holland. That shouldn't require too much effort on her part.

'Yes, what is it, Barbara?'

'Stuart Nelson says I smell.'

'Did he, indeed? What a rude little boy.'

'I don't smell, though.'

Geraldine leaned towards the little girl to check. 'No, you don't smell. You're very nice and fragrant.'

'Why did he say I smelled?'

'Perhaps he was trying to be funny but being a rude little boy, he said the wrong thing. When I see him next I'll have a word with him. Now, come on — let's go. Are you going outside?'

'Miss?'

Geraldine groaned to herself. Her few minutes of calm were seeping away. 'Yes, Barbara? You do ask a lot of questions, don't you?'

'I know it's not very nice, and I really don't want to be rude, but did you know that you smell?'

'Come on. Let's skedaddle.'

Barbara Jacobs looked up, tears in her eyes. 'I'm sorry, Miss. My mummy told me that it was important to tell the truth. Stewart told a lie when he said I smelled. You smell, and I thought it would be a lie if I said you didn't. Did I do the wrong thing?'

Although acutely conscious of her foul state, Geraldine couldn't help bending down to the little girl. 'Thank you for telling me. I'm sorry I don't smell as nice as you. When I get home, I'm going to have a lovely, hot bath and when you see me tomorrow, I shall smell as nice as you.'

Barbara's eyes shone. 'Do old ladies have baths too?'

Geraldine smiled. 'At least once a year.'

'Will you use Matey? That's what my mummy puts in my bath.'

'Yes, and maybe some Harpic too. I think I'm going to need it.'

When she got to the staff room, Jim was in full spate: 'Ah, Geraldine, in the nick of time. Right, this is how it's going to work. At three p.m., all children need to be on the field with all teachers. I want you, Geraldine, behind the podium. Louise, you can be there, too. Geraldine will probably need instruction on the finer points of cup ceremonies. I want another three teachers to be on hand — Daniel, Joyce and Edna — you're all dignitaries. Terry is going to hand over the trophy. I'll do the announcing. Is everyone clear?'

Louise called out, laughing, 'Will the press be here?'

Jim smiled. 'You can laugh, Louise. The answer is a resounding yes. *The Post* is sending around a reporter and — get this — a photographer, too.'

Geraldine groaned. *Oh no.* All she wanted was to get home, purify her sullied body and then go to bed.

Jim called, 'Terry?'

She looked over to Terry. He was at the back, evidently uneasy. She smiled: he was such a nice man. Despite his bulky shape, there was something of the little boy about him.

'Yes, Jim?'

'You're happy with all the arrangements?'

'Well, put it this way: as long as no one tells the reporter that it's a table, six breeze blocks and a dust sheet, he'll assume we borrowed it from Wembley.'

'And you're happy to hand over the trophy?'

'Ah, no. I don't want to do that. I'll keep out of the limelight, if you don't mind.'

'But hang it all man, it is The Castleton Cup!'

'No. I'm a 'behind-the-scenes' kind of chap.'

Sadly, Jim looked around the room. 'Oh well, I'll have to do it myself then. Now, we need Patricia Whiting to be on good form. She'll be in the picture receiving it so, please, no repeat of yesterday's temperamental issues. Geraldine, you're in charge of making her as cheerful as possible.'

'Me?'

'Yes — come on! You can make any child smile if you put your mind to it.'

'Hmm. We'll see about that.'

'Right. See you all out there in twenty minutes.'

Geraldine made a coffee and sat down at her desk. So much for a quiet last lesson. Still, at least now it would be outside and perhaps she could get away without any further candid revelations as to her 'aura'. Elbows on the desktop, fists in her eyes, she allowed herself to drift off for five minutes. What time would Edward be home? It would be good if he were late: she'd have time for a bath and even an hour's nap.

'Are you all right?'

Without moving, she mumbled, 'If by 'all right' you mean half dead, then the answer is yes.'

Louise pulled a chair over. 'Not recovered yet?'

'No.'

'Poor you. I thought it was only young cats like me who went out and got drunk during the week.'

'Dear Louise… as you can see, I'm more of an old dog than a young cat.'

'Listen to me, and listen good. In fact, follow me. Come on, get up and follow me.'

Geraldine pushed herself heavily to her feet, drained her cup and did as she was told. The younger woman marched down the corridor to the art room. Geraldine followed her in and looked questioningly at her colleague. Louise shut the door and pointed to a chair. Geraldine sat down.

'I'm sorry: I feel bad about this and maybe it's not my place to say anything, but I'm going to. I'm tired of hearing you putting yourself down. Every opportunity that comes along, you say something horrible about yourself. It's not funny and it's not clever. You are far and away the best teacher in this school. I've learned so much from you. Your pupils all think you're wonderful. We all look up to you. You're so kind and helpful. Honestly, Geraldine, we love you. I know, you're going to say something like 'yes, but who wants to be a highly-respected and cherished fatty?' Am I right?'

Geraldine was taken aback by the younger woman's outburst. The compliments were lovely to hear but, yes, she had been about to say something like that. She nodded.

'But, you silly thing, you're not fat! You're an extremely attractive woman. If I look like you do when I'm your age, I guarantee you — here and now — I shall be delighted. You've got it into your head that you're overweight. Maybe we've gone along with your own version of yourself. You are not fat and nowhere near it. God, Geraldine! You've got lovely skin, beautiful hair and you have a sexy, curvy figure. Where has this false idea come from? You're lovely in every way. If I hear any more of your nonsense I shall — well, I'm not sure what I'll do, but I'm sure I'll do it.'

'But —'

Louise put her hands up to block the denials. 'No, I don't want to hear it. Do I make myself clear?'

Geraldine nodded and hung her head. 'Yes, Miss.'

'Good girl. Now cut along and pull your socks up.'

'Thank you, Miss.'

They heard the bell clanking.

Chapter 70

'Did you go to this school?' Karen asked, as they strode along Brook Road.

'No. You?'

'No. Which one did you go to?'

'Abbotsbury. You?'

'We moved here three years ago.'

'Oh. Where from?'

'Slough.'

'Oh. Why did you come here?'

'My dad is a cameraman; he got a job at EMI.'

'Yeah? That must be exciting.'

'Not anymore. It's closing down. He was made redundant.'

'Oh, sorry.'

'It's all right. He's been working with 20th Century Fox on some kind of space film. Apparently he might have a job in Hollywood if the film takes off.'

'Wow! What's the film called?'

'Star Wars.'

'What's it about?'

'Um, wars... stars? I'm only guessing.'

'Oh, yeah. Like Star Trek?'

'I'm not sure. I can't be bothered with science fiction.'

They had been walking for a few minutes. Gary usually left people behind when he really strode out. Not Karen: she was keeping up easily.

He gestured to the camera around her neck. 'Do you know how to use that thing?'

'Of course I do!'

'Sorry. I didn't mean I thought you didn't. I was just interested. I'm sure you're really... Well, sorry. I didn't mean anything.'

Clearly still cross, she said, 'Do you know how to use a pen?'

'Yeah, but it's not the same thing, is it?'

'No. Sorry.'

When Nigel had said it was Aycliffe Road Primary School, Gary hadn't been surprised. This was how his life was working out these days. He paused at the front gate, where he'd waited for Tina's dad the other day.

He turned to Karen. 'Listen, I'm a bit — you know. I've never done anything like this before. If you think of anything I should be doing, just whisper it.'

Karen smiled. 'Same for me. This is my first professional assignment and I've got absolutely no idea what I'm doing either.'

They smiled at each other.

'Good luck, then' Gary said. 'Listen, I've been thinking. Do you think I should wear a tie? I hate ties; I always have. But I wonder… maybe it will make me look a bit more professional?'

He watched her examine him. She screwed up her face, shook her head with a sad expression, 'Oh dear, oh dear, oh dear, oh dear.'

'What?'

'Nothing. I was saying it, you know, to wind you up.'

'Cow.'

Smiling broadly, she said, 'Have you got a tie?'

'Well, yeah. It's… Well, I don't know if it's suitable, but…'

'Let's see?'

He pulled out the old army tie.

'Hang on to this, will you?' He passed her the clipboard, and fumbling, did up the tie. 'Jeez, I hate ties.'

She stepped back and assessed him again. He looked at her closely. Really pretty. She was wearing shiny, black, plastic boots and black trousers tucked into them. She had a big grey overcoat on with a bright pink scarf. He really liked her face. It was sort of — well, she looked as if she found everything a bit funny. Her big, brown eyes were crinkling now, her white teeth showing.

'You look pretty good, Bulldog. Are you ready?'

They marched into the main entrance.

'Are you from the newspaper?'

Gary looked towards the middle-aged lady coming towards them. 'That's us.'

'Er, I think you have some identification?' With a flourish, Gary produced his business card. The woman glanced at it. 'This way, Mr Abbott.'

He blinked: was she talking to him? Aware of Karen beside him, he told the woman, 'This is my colleague, Karen Mitchum. She's the photographer.'

The woman smiled. 'I guessed. I'm quite quick on the uptake.'

Gary blushed. He'd have to be a bit sharper. He gripped his pen and held it over the clipboard. 'Can I ask your name, please?'

'Mrs Sullivan.'

'Your job here?'

'School secretary.'

'Thank you.'

She said, 'Follow me.'

As they walked behind her along a corridor, Karen whispered, 'Thanks for introducing me.'

Gary was pleased. He'd done a good thing: a promising start.

They went through a fire door and out into the school field. It was full of children, many of them clustered around some kind of white stage. Excited chatter, squeals and laughter were in the air. Teachers were clearly trying to get the children under control. A whistle was blown repeatedly. Slowly, quiet descended.

Mrs Sullivan walked up to a tall, thin, grey-haired man. 'These are the reporters, Mr Dixon.'

Dixon looked across to Gary and Karen. 'Ah. Welcome to Aycliffe Road Primary School.' He stuck out his hand; they shook.

Since leaving the newspaper office, Gary's stomach had been full of flittering butterflies; surely no one was going to take him seriously. How was he going to make anyone believe he was a reporter? Mr Dixon seemed genuinely pleased to see both him and Karen; he was showing no sign of doubt as to their right to be here.

Nerves melting away, Gary said, 'Nice to meet you, Mr Dixon. My name is Gary Abbott. I'm a reporter with *The Post*. This is my colleague, Karen Mitchum. Are you the headmaster?'

'That's right.'

'Okay, tell me all about what's going on today.'

'Excellent. Well, today is the inaugural presentation of a football trophy. Our caretaker, Terry Castleton, has been with us for five years. Actually, where is Terry?' Dixon turned away from Gary and shouted, 'Terry, over here please.'

Gary watched Tina's father come over; the big bloke was looking embarrassed. As he neared them, he recognised Gary. 'What are you doing here?'

Dixon said, 'This is Mr Abbott. He's a reporter with *The Post*.'

'Hallo, Mr Castleton. Nice to see you again.'

'Ah, you know each other. Splendid! So — Terry here has been at the school for five years and yesterday we had a football match to commemorate the excellent service Mr Castleton has given the school. Today we are going to present the Castleton Cup in his honour.'

Gary was writing as fast as he could. He looked up, 'Who played who?'

'Two teams of top-quality players: the Crackerjacks versus the Dynamites. Terry, here, captained the former, I led the latter. It was a close-run thing, but I think that it's safe to say honours were even.'

Dixon had been walking slowly towards what Gary had thought was a stage but, up close, was clearly a table with a cloth on it. In the middle of the 'stage' was a silver trophy.

'Honours even? Mr Dixon, the Castleton Crackerjacks thrashed the Dynamites.'

Gary looked towards the voice: a young teacher was standing with her hands on her hips, looking crossly at the headmaster. Beside him, Gary heard Karen taking photographs.

'Er, hmm — well, a narrow victory. Anyway, we'd like you to write it all up and get it in the next edition. We're going to present the cup in a minute and if you can take a few snaps that would be excellent. Now, where is our star player? Mrs Dutton, is Patricia with us?'

Gary walked over to the young teacher; she was absolutely stunning. Pen poised, he asked, 'What's your name?'

She smiled at him. 'I'll tell you mine if you tell me yours.'

His face reddened. 'Come on — for the story.'

'Louise Ratcliffe.'

'What was the score?'

'The Crackerjacks won two-one.'

'Here we are, Mrs Dutton. This is Mr Abbott,' the headmaster announced.

Gary looked over. Walking towards him was a teacher holding the hand of a nervous-looking little girl. The teacher — nice looking, like Hannah Gordon in Upstairs Downstairs — didn't look very well, but still managed to smile at him.

'Mr Abbott, this is Mrs Dutton. She was our referee yesterday. With her is Patricia Whiting, who scored the winning goal. Isn't that right, Patricia?'

Gary smiled at the girl; she did not have the appearance of a natural striker.

He asked, 'Are you very good at football?'

She stared back at him, silent.

He tried again. 'Who's your favourite footballer?'

Mrs Dutton knelt down next to her. 'Don't you have a favourite player, Patricia?'

The goal-scorer's face contorted into fierce concentration; then it cleared. Looking up at Gary, she said, 'John Noakes.'

Everyone laughed; Karen's camera clicked.

Dixon said, 'Patricia isn't one to blow her own trumpet, are you, Patricia?'

The little girl looked even more confused.

Gary saw Karen's camera pointing at the ill-looking teacher; she held up her hand to fend off its attention.

Dixon clapped his hands. 'Okay, everybody. Silence please. Terry, where are you going to stand?'

Gary watched Tina's dad edging away. 'I'm fine here, Mr Dixon. I have a good view.'

Dixon called out, 'Rubbish. Come on! It's your cup. However, to ensure some authority is evident, I should really be in the picture. Right: Mr Jenkinson, Miss Davies and Mrs Jackson, please stand behind the podium and look important.'

Gary watched a poncy-looking young man sidle reluctantly to his designated place; two older women went with him.

Dixon said, 'I'll stand here by the steps. Patricia, when I say your name, you come along, up the steps and stand on the top of the podium. I shall then hand you the Castleton Cup. Is everyone ready?'

Gary saw Karen edge her way through the crowds of children lined up in front of the table. He scribbled.

Dixon picked up the gleaming trophy and called out, 'Ladies and gentlemen, may I have your attention?' The excited hubbub continued unaltered. 'Silence!' roared Dixon. When, at last, there was quiet, he continued, 'Thank you, everyone. It is my absolute pleasure to welcome you all, together with representatives of the media, and all of you from around the world, to our ceremony today. It is with great delight that I welcome our very own celebrity caretaker, Terry Castleton. Come on, Terry; come and join the proceedings.'

Applause broke out and Karen swung her camera towards the red-faced man trudging towards the podium.

Dixon went on, 'Terry Castleton, our favourite caretaker, has been with us for five years. He looks after all the needs of the school and its grounds.

We are very grateful to him for his hard work. He deserves our thanks and a big round of applause.'

Everyone clapped.

'Yesterday saw the inaugural playing of the Castleton Cup and we are here to present it to the player who scored the winning goal.' Dixon lifted the cup and proclaimed, 'The 1976 Castleton cup goes to the Castleton Crackerjacks and, here to collect it today is their star player, Patricia Whiting. Up you come, Patricia.'

The little girl walked nervously towards the headmaster. He encouraged her up the steps on to the tabletop. Handing her the gleaming trophy, he called out, 'Three cheers to the Crackerjacks!'

Everyone yelled 'Crackerjack!' with all their might. Patricia took the cup and looked inside it. Finding nothing, she gave it back to Mr Dixon and ran back down the steps to join her friends.

'Hold on, Patricia! Come and have your photograph taken.'

Reluctantly, the little girl came back to the podium but, without the helping hand of the ailing teacher — who, Gary saw, was stumbling back into the school — tripped on the last step and sprawled across the tabletop. The crowd cheered even louder than before. Despite tears beginning to run down her cheeks, after persistent encouragement, Patricia grasped one handle of the cup whilst Dixon, beaming proudly, gripped the other. The camera clicked.

The headmaster called, 'Right, everyone. Time to go home, I think.' He turned to Gary, 'Do you want to interview me now?'

'Any details of the match?'

'Yes, I played for Orient many years ago so, of course, I was head and shoulders above the rest. I was able to engineer the match to ensure the other players could perform at their best.'

'Ahem. Mr Dixon, Terry was far and away the best player.'

Gary felt his face flush again as the sexy teacher pushed past him.

'Miss Ratcliffe, you probably need to make sure the pupils are ready to leave.' Dixon was pointing her back towards the school.

'I'm stating the facts for the reporter, that's all.'

Gary watched her rear retreat. He dragged his attention back to the headmaster, 'Did she say Terry? Not Terry the caretaker?'

'That's right. He was above average, I'd say. Though not in my league, you understand.'

Gary said, 'Anything else you want to include in the article?'

'Only that Aycliffe Road Primary School will be making a charge on the District Schools Football league next year.'

Gary jotted this down and looked around the field for Tina's dad: there he was, going into the big shed on the far side of the field. Where was Karen? There — talking to the poncy teacher as he tried to pacify the star striker, now wiping her streaming nose on her sleeve.

'Karen! Come on! We've got to get a picture of the caretaker.'

Gary jogged across the field to the shed. As he neared it, Mr Castleton came out, something in his hand.

Gary pulled up, 'Oh, hello, Mr Castleton. Can I ask you a couple of questions?'

'Er... well, not really. I've got to... Go on, then.'

'I hear you're a brilliant footballer, is that right?'

'Who told you that?'

'The pretty teacher, Miss Ratcliffe?'

'Not really.'

Gary persisted. 'Did you use to play football for any particular team?' Karen joined them.

'Listen son, I don't want to be a spoilsport, but this isn't about me. I've got work to do. Do me a favour; will you give this to the little girl? She's not having much luck.' He held out a Penguin.

'I'll give it to her,' Karen said.

Gary asked again, 'Any football experience, Mr Castleton?'

'All right. No photos, though.'

Gary nodded and turned to Karen.

She said, 'I'll deliver the Penguin.'

They watched her run off. Gary turned back to Tina's dad, pen at the ready.

'Do you really work for the newspaper?'

'Yeah, this is my first article.'

'Where did you get that tie? It's Royal Engineers, isn't it?'

Gary had forgotten it. He looked down. 'Yeah, it was my grandad's. It was the only tie I had with me.'

'Listen, Gary. I'm sorry I've been a bit cold with you. I didn't like your brother, but I can tell you're made of different stuff. I did play football a bit. I played for the UK Armed Forces a hundred years ago. I never got a trial for Orient — that's the big time.'

Gary smiled. 'He told me he played for them!'

'Ah, well. Let him have his moment of glory.'

Gary said, 'Did you win anything, as a footballer?'

'Only a few things. Nothing really.'

'What was your position?'

'Oh, mostly prone.'

'If you don't tell me, I'll have to make something up.'

'Is that what they tell you to do?'

'Who?'

'Your editors?'

Gary guessed he was right, but said, 'You know — a little something. Something juicy.'

'Okay, you win. I scored the goals in the 1958 Army FA Challenge Cup. There. That's it.'

'Where was that?'

Tina's dad smiled. 'You bloody journalists! You're all the same. Aldershot Military Stadium. We beat First Yorkshire two-one.'

'Who's we?'

'Last one. Royal Artillery.'

'Were you in the war?'

'You cheeky bugger. That's it. I'm going back into my shed and not coming out till you're gone.'

Putting his pen in his pocket, Gary held out his hand, 'Thanks, Mr Castleton.'

Chapter 71

On her way home, Tina popped into *Martins* for the *Evening News*. She was tempted to buy some fags — but if her dad could give up, then she definitely could. Reaching into her pocket, she remembered Joe's money: her dad still owed it to her. She looked forward to seeing Joe again; he was the kind of bloke you could look up to. A proper man. She loved her dad more than anything, but he was her dad and that was different. Every other man she knew was a complete, dead loss. She'd thought that Chris Armstrong might be better: he was a policeman, after all. The vision of him slumped over the table at the Mops came back to her. Poor Chris: he hadn't stood a chance. Maybe Gary was the right one for her. There was no doubt he was good-looking. Since he'd started wearing glasses, his whole personality had changed. She'd always thought he was tasty — nice and tall, lovely eyes — but the glasses had given him a more sensitive side.

Turning into the carpark of their block of flats, she saw someone waving to her. *Oh no.* She slowed as he approached.

'Hallo, Tina.'

He looked terrible. His face was a sickly, greeny-white, his eyes, deep, dark hollows; his clothes rumpled. She could smell him from two paces.

'Hello. You look... Are you—? Hello.'

'I've come to say sorry.'

Tina couldn't help feeling sorry for him. She smiled. 'What for?'

'I made a total fool of myself last night. What you must think of me! Are you all right?'

'I'm fine. Don't worry. I was worried about you. I asked my dad to come and collect me. I tried to wake you up but — anyway, I'm glad you got home safely. Er, you have been home, haven't you?'

He shut his eyes. 'God, I'm so sorry. I don't know what happened to me. I must have had a bug or something. I remember us talking, then... Well, I don't remember anything. Are you all right? I mean, you look fine, great. You weren't... Did you have a hangover, even?'

'Did I? My head was hammering like a pneumatic drill was trying to get out. I'm going to keep away from Bacardi from now on. Honestly, Chris, don't worry about it. I only got home coz my dad came to get me. Um, how did you get home?'

He shook his head. 'Don't you know?'

'No?'

'Jeez, nor do I. In fact, to be honest, I haven't been home yet. Listen, don't tell anyone this, but I woke up in my car this morning. Someone put me into it and drove it to the station carpark. I'm on my way home now. I wanted to come here first and say sorry and to check you're okay.'

Despite him being a copper and a bit of a tosser, he was a nice bloke really. 'You didn't get into trouble at work, did you?'

'Ah, well, I'm not in anyone's good books right now. DS Nott — you know, my colleague — told me to go home and come back tomorrow.'

'Poor you. Still, you can put your feet up and recover a bit.'

'Yeah. Trouble is, I can't go home. The thing is, you know I said I had a flat and all that? Yeah, well, that was a bit of bullshit. I live with my parents and they're out. I'm locked out.'

Tina had to stop herself giggling; the poor boy's glamorous lifestyle was crumbling in front of her. 'Oh, sorry about that!' He was kicking at the ground, hands in his pockets, face down.

She said, 'Do you want a cup of coffee? How about something to eat? I can do you some toast or something?'

He looked up, his face grateful. 'Well, if you're sure you don't mind? I mean, after last night, you probably think I'm a complete waste of space.'

'Oh, come on. You're exaggerating. You're all right. You should have seen me this morning: I looked like death warmed up.'

He smiled. 'I doubt that. Anyway, a coffee would be triffic.'

She led the way up to the flat. Despite her sore feet and new shoes, she reached the top floor long before him. As he joined her at the door, he gasped, 'Bloody hell, I'm out of shape.'

'It's the booze. You'll be back to full strength soon. Come on — come in and sit down.'

She led the way and pointed to the table. He sat down, his head in his hands.

Filling the kettle, she said, 'Stay there. Don't move an inch. Get your breath back. I'm just going to put my shoes away.'

Shoving them into the wardrobe, the thought came to her that it had been a good thing she'd tidied up her room, that she'd changed her sheets. *What are you thinking, you idiot?* She flushed at the thought of putting Chris into her bed, soothing his brow, tucking him in. A sudden jolt of desire shot through her as she imagined slipping off her clothes and getting in to press against him. His grateful voice whispering in her ear, telling her he was sorry and how beautiful she was. *'There, there. Don't cry, Chris. You're all right now. I'll look after you. Come on, let me help you feel better. That's it. Now, that's more like it.'*

Chris coughed then called, 'Are you there?' Phew, she'd got lost in her own daydream. Tina went back into the kitchen. He was still sitting there, looking miserable.

She said, 'Tea or coffee?'

'Coffee, please. This is terribly nice of you.'

'Don't be silly. Do you want some toast?'

'Lovely.'

'I've got marmalade, Marmite or jam — blackcurrant, it's my favourite.'

'Can I have marmalade, please?'

'Coming right up.'

'Tina?'

'Yes?'

'Do you have any idea who drove me back last night? It wasn't your father, was it? I only ask because — well, it's embarrassing — but I wouldn't want him to think that I was unsuitable.'

Although she guessed what he meant, she couldn't resist. 'Unsuitable for what? The police force?'

'Well, yeah, that. But also unsuitable to take his daughter out.'

'Oh, I see. No, it wasn't my dad. I don't know who it was. Have you asked the pub? Maybe whoever it was worked there?'

Chris was silent. She looked at him; what was he thinking?

He said, 'It doesn't matter. Whoever it was looked after me. There was nothing missing from my pockets or anything. Bloody hell, I must have been out of my head.'

Tina spooned instant coffee into a mug. 'I'm going to give you sugar, whether you take it or not.'

'I do. Three please.'

She pulled out the grill pan, turned the slices of Mother's Pride over, and slid the pan back in. Bringing two mugs back to the table, she sat down opposite him.

'My dad and I have given up smoking but, to be honest, I could do with one now. If I have one, will you? If he says anything, I'll tell him the police made me have one.'

Chris groaned. 'Actually, I decided to give up as soon as I woke up. Honestly, Tina, I feel as sick as a parrot and my mouth is like the bottom of its bottom. You go ahead, though.'

She smiled. 'No, I'll resist. You're inspiring me.'

She smelt the toast was close to burning and got up to rescue it. Conscious of his gaze, her erotic thoughts returned. *Stop it!*

He said, 'I know I made a mess of everything last night, but do you think we could try again? I realise you're probably thinking that I'm a loser but, I promise you, I'm not like that normally.'

She brought his toast over. 'Here you are. Get that down your neck.'

'Thanks very much.'

'The thing is, Chris, I'm a bit off blokes at the minute. I've got my own plans and — realistically — men just seem to let me down all the time.'

She looked at his face: no interest, typical. He was as selfish as all the other men.

He looked up. 'Tell me about your plans. I'm bored of me. What are you going to do?'

'Oh, are you really interested? There was me thinking all men were selfish bastards. Well, I'd like to get a job in the beauty business. I don't know, maybe in make-up, or modelling; maybe hairstyling? I really want to be involved in something exciting up in the West End. I know it's childish, but I want to be part of the glitz and glamour. I'm so bored of life around here. Everything's so grey and grimy. Anyway, I'm looking in the papers and I might even do a course or something. That would be a good start, don't you think?'

He was shovelling down toast like there was no tomorrow. His lips were covered in crumbs and marmalade. He swallowed, picked up his mug and slurped noisily. 'Sorry, go on. This is lovely by the way.'

'Good, you need a bit of something inside you. Have you any idea how much Bacardi you drank last night?'

He had been about to put the last piece of the first slice of toast into his mouth. Instead, he looked at her, his eyes narrowed, 'Same as you. We had the same.'

Tina kicked herself; she'd been getting cocky. 'I've absolutely no idea how many I had, dummy. I thought you might remember.'

He resumed scoffing. 'No, I lost track. The trouble was that we started with doubles. I think that was what got me. I think I must have a touch of something else. I don't usually get drunk. I mean, normally I can drive home even if I've had a few.'

She wondered if it might be wise to introduce another possibility. 'You don't think our drinks were spiked by someone?'

Again, he looked at her sharply. *Damn!* Why couldn't she button her lip? 'Like who?'

She'd have to be careful. Chris wasn't an idiot. 'I dunno. You're a policeman. Maybe you have enemies?' She watched him think.

He shook his head. 'Nah, I would have noticed something going on. Thanks for the toast, Tina. I feel much better already.'

'You're welcome. Any time.'

Putting elbows on the table and resting his chin on his clasped hands, he said, 'Will you give me another chance? I really like you and I owe you one. I won't let you down next time.'

She felt her heart begin to bump. He did have lovely green eyes. And it would be nice to go out with a proper bloke, one with a real job and career prospects.

She smiled. 'Thank you, I'll think about it.'

He got up. 'Listen, I know it's a cheek, but may I use your bathroom. I'd really like to have a quick wash and brush up. Do you mind?'

'Sure, it's in here. I'll get you a towel.'

She opened the airing cupboard door; he stood behind her waiting. Was he going to press up against her? What would she do if he did?

She turned around and handed him the towel, 'Take your time.'

'Thanks, Tina. You're a real gem.'

She looked at the kitchen clock: nearly three. Her dad wouldn't be back until half past four at the earliest. She hurried into her room and checked herself in the mirror. Yep, she looked all right. She pulled back the bedclothes: clean and tidy.

'Come on, let's pop you away.' She carried the giraffe over to the top drawer of her dressing table. She looked in the mirror again: a bit of lippie? No, it would make her look too keen. She went and listened outside the bathroom door; she could hear splashing. Would he take a bit of toothpaste to freshen up his breath? Excited at the prospect of what was to come, she went into the kitchen to wait.

Chapter 72

They ran back to the office. Gary was rehearsing his story. He tried to think of something special about the whole event — what was the story? No one was interested in the school except parents of its pupils. The fact that a caretaker had been working there for five years didn't seem particularly amazing. The little girl didn't have a single thing to say that was of any interest and Gary was doubtful that she even knew what scoring a goal meant. The headmaster had been interesting; his determination to prove that the school was special was obvious, but he seemed more concerned about how he came across than about the school. When it became clear that he'd only ever had a trial for Orient, Gary had dismissed it as a non-story. Anyway, who gave a damn about Orient? Three things had caught his attention: the sexy teacher, the ill teacher and the fact that Tina's father was not only ex-army but had also been a really good footballer.

They ran into Shenley Road before slowing to a fast walk. Gary started to take off his tie: God, he hated them.

'Don't take it off; you look good with it.'

'Do you reckon?'

'Yeah. Sort of... well, quite impressive.'

Pleased, Gary left the tie on, but loosened it and undid the top button of his shirt.

'Do you think you got some good pictures?'

Her face was pink, her hair all over the place. 'Blimey, I haven't run that much for years.' She took a few seconds to catch her breath. 'I think I got a few... phew... bloody hell... phew... What's going to be your angle?'

'Well, we'll keep the headmaster out of it, I think. He's only in it for his own publicity.'

'I agree.'

'I thought the little girl was kind of sweet but, to be honest, the best bit was when she tripped up on the steps.'

'Oh, you bastard! That poor little girl — she didn't want to be in it, anyway.'

'Yeah, I know. I think the caretaker is the interesting part. When you went back with the Penguin, he told me he played in a big cup final for his regiment and scored the winning goals. He was the player they all said was the best yesterday. I think he should be the focus. Did you get any pictures of him?'

'I'll have to see when they're developed. He was doing his best to keep out of it. I think I got a few when Mr Pompous presented the cup. By the way, she didn't want her Penguin.'

'Why not?'

'It was a blue one and she only likes the red ones.'

'Spoilt brat. What did you do with it?'

'I gave it to one of the teachers. Did you see her, the sickly one?'

'Yeah, I think she might be really ill. I remember our next-door neighbour used to look like that. She died of jaundice.'

They reached the office and went inside. Eve clapped and cheered, 'Ah, here comes Bulldog — and Linda McCartney.'

Gary looked at Karen. 'I don't get it. Isn't she the crap one in Wings?'

'She's really a photographer.'

'Oh, yeah. I knew that.'

They walked past Eve and into the office. Rob waved them over.

'Right, let's have it. Is it the big one? Are we going to have to fight off the nationals?'

'No, it's only a little story. Shall I write it up?'

'Yep, you do that. Can you get it into two hundred words?'

Gary had no idea but said, 'Easily.'

'Get any decent pictures?'

Karen said, 'We think we know what we want to select. I'll go and develop them straightaway.'

'Right, come back to me in...' Rob looked at his watch, 'fifteen minutes.'

Gary gulped. Could he do it? 'Where shall I sit?'

'You can go into the interview room.'

They went their separate ways. Gary strode into the interview room and sat down. His heart was pounding. He wondered if this was what it might feel like to do an exam. He pulled a blank page from his clipboard and hunched over it. What now? *Come on*, he urged himself. He'd lost a minute already. Unsure of what was right or wrong, he began writing. He'd need a headline first.

War hero shows his class

No, that wouldn't do. For all he knew, Tina's dad might have spent the war in prison. Also, he hadn't checked how old he was. Damn! Stupid mistake. He guessed he wasn't old enough. He sucked the end of his pen...

Sharp-shooting school caretaker captains cup winners

He wasn't sure about it, but it would do for the moment. He remembered doing alliteration in Wilson's class; apparently it was a good thing. How to start? He needed to set the scene.

Aycliffe Road Primary School saw the other side of its caretaker — Terry Castleton is a brilliant footballer. Yesterday, headmaster, James Dixon, called children and teachers together to see who was the best footballer in the school. To everyone's surprise it turned out to be Terry, who, before working at the school was a soldier in the royal artilery.

Two teams were pitted against each other — the Dynamites, captained by headmaster Dixon, and the Crackerjacks with Terry as skipper. After a tremendous battle, with the result always in doubt, The Crackerjacks won 2–1 with seven year old, Patricia Whiting, scoring the winning goal in the last minute. Patricia said her favourite footballer was John Noakes but the other kids thought that caretaker Terry was the best.

Headmaster Dixon said that the school was really grateful to Terry for his hard work as caretaker but teachers and children were more interested in his footballing abilities. The school is going to put a team together and compete in the District Schools Football League later in the year. If the team can take advantage of Terry's soccer skills the other schools had better watch out!

Gary quickly counted up — it was about right. He jumped up and dashed back into Rob's office. Alan was already in there.

'Hallo, son. I'm about to get my hands on your perfectly composed piece and make mincemeat of it.'

Gary looked at Rob.

'Alan's our sub-editor. Everything we brilliant reporters write gets wrecked, torn apart and then greatly improved by him. Let's have a look at what you've done.'

Gary handed it to him. Karen came in waving a couple of photographs in front of her.

She showed them to Gary, 'What do you think?'

The black and white images were drying and lightening before his eyes. The first one showed Dixon in the middle, handing the little girl the cup. Terry Castleton was on the edge of the picture, smiling broadly. The second one had Terry more in the centre with only Dixon's arm showing as Patricia accepted the cup.

He looked at Karen, 'Great. They're brilliant. I reckon the one with Terry in the middle, and Dixon's arm just showing.'

Smiling, she said, 'I thought that, too.'

Rob handed the page to Alan. 'It's pretty good. If you sort out the spellings and punctuation, we can use it.' He looked at the two prints. 'I think the girl and the caretaker should take the centre stage, don't you?'

Alan grunted and went back to his desk.

'Well done. Not bad; not bad at all. Do you want to come back tomorrow?'

Gary grinned. 'Ah, brill! Yeah, thanks. What time?'

'Be here at eight-thirty. It's out tomorrow and it'll be busy — people like to ring in with complaints and corrections. You can take some of the calls.' He turned to Karen. 'Good pictures. I hope my camera is in good nick?'

'Pristine.'

Gary followed Alan back to his desk. 'Um, Alan?'

Without looking up, Alan grunted, 'Yeah?'

'Can I have the article back when you've finished with it?'

'What, for posterity?'

'Well, not really, I'd like to check for mistakes. Do you think you could point them out for me?'

Alan smiled. 'There's far too many, son. It would take me hours.'

Gary looked at the older man's face: he was almost smiling. 'Bastard! I'll get you back. Is there anything I can do to help?'

'Nah. I'd get off home if I were you. See you tomorrow, all being well.'

Gary left the clipboard on Nigel's unoccupied desk and called goodbye to Rob. The editor had the phone to his ear but waved back.

Eve said, 'Looks like you're in then? Well done. I would have given you nul points when I saw you the other day. It shows you can't judge a book by its cover.'

Gary handed her the pen. 'Thanks for that. I'm going to buy myself a few pens and pencils right now. Anything else, do you think?'

'Apart from your bulldog clip?'

'Yeah, don't worry. I've still got that.'

'Don't bother buying anything; we'll give you what you'll need — tea towel, rubber gloves.'

Gary smiled. 'Jeez, thanks. See you tomorrow. Say 'bye to Linda for me.'

He strolled down the high street wondering whether people could tell he was a published writer. What a day. What a week! What was happening to him? Only a few days ago, his life had been as full of shit as a full-up shithole. Now, he had a job, nicer friends than he'd ever had before, a pretty colleague, a sexy best friend and — a bulldog clip. As he passed Studio Stationers, he peered in. There were pens, notebooks, tons of smart gear. He'd been planning to pop into *Woolies*, but maybe he'd treat himself to some decent stuff. He checked his pockets: hmm, not much. He went in, anyway.

The smell of the place conjured images of great articles — his writing starkly black against the clean, white sheets of — what was it? Basildon Bond? The rows of fountain pens called him over — Parker, Platignum, Sheaffer. No, he'd get ink all over the place. He turned to the biros. The silver Paper Mates looked good — no, too expensive. He wandered around the rest of the shop, breathing in its air. There was something about stationery that gave him butterflies. Why? What about? Might it be the promise of success? He checked out the pads: all too expensive.

Dispirited, he was about to leave when the display on the back wall caught his eye: briefcases! He walked down the aisle towards them, their shiny black, brown, and even red faces smiling at him. His imagination was fired by the thought of those glittering brass catches and locks keeping all his neatly-arranged documents safe and secure. As he got closer, the smell of leather reached him — blimey, these were for serious journalists. They were expensive. Looking along the rows he could see only one that was affordable; he lifted it off its hook. Gary held it to his nose and inhaled deeply — no leather-smell. Disappointed, he inspected it. It was plastic, with no lock, and there were only two sections inside. He'd been hoping for secret compartments and pockets for business cards. Closing it, he put it back. He'd pop into *Woolies* and see what cheap crap they had.

'Can I help you?'

He started. 'Er, not really; I was only looking.'

The woman, in her thirties and glamourous, smiled at him. 'Is it for work?'

Gary reflected that only days before he would have scoffed at anyone buying a briefcase. What's more, shop assistants would have assumed he was here for shoplifting which, to be fair, would probably have been his reason.

'Yeah, I started today.'

'Oh, well done. What's the job?'

He reached into his pocket for the 'cub reporter' card but changed his mind: he wasn't a kid.

'Oh, I'm... It's nothing really — a job at the newspaper.' No, he was going to let people know that he'd made it; this wasn't a time for modesty. 'Actually, it's a top job. I've... er, filed a massive story.'

The assistant, really quite tasty for an oldie, widened her eyes, 'Golly, you have hit the big time. My, my — a top reporter in my shop! No wonder you're looking at the briefcases.'

She looked along the rows of polished beauties; Gary followed her gaze. He sighed. He'd love one of the black ones, with a lockable, shiny clasp. He'd have to nick some cash from somewhere before he could afford one of those. The assistant looked at him; he looked back, disappointment in his eyes.

She said, 'They are a bit pricey, aren't they?'

Gary took his glasses off and wiped the lenses with the end of his tie. As he did it, he looked into her eyes for a couple of seconds.

Then, putting the glasses back on, he said, 'Look, how about we do a deal? If I pay half now and the other half next week, will you let me take it away today?' He pointed at one of the black ones, slim, shiny, 'You'd be doing me a big favour; honestly, you would.'

The woman looked up at the one he indicated. Gary sneaked a look at her chest, very nice. She reached up and took the case off its hook.

She said, 'Hmm, how about we do a different deal?'

'Yeah. Name it.' He was pleased with himself; his charm and confident manner had obviously won her over.

'I'll make it half price, if you get me a half-price ad in next week's paper.'

Damn! She had outwitted him. He didn't know how much ads cost to put in the paper, but he was pretty sure he couldn't persuade Rob to do a deal just so his new recruit could have a briefcase. She was looking at him, half smiling, waiting.

Embarrassed at shooting his mouth off, he shook his head. 'Nah, I doubt I could swing that. I'm sorry. Never mind. I'll leave it.' He was disappointed. For a few minutes, he'd actually believed that whatever he wanted could be his.

'Oh, what a shame. I'd have thought your salary would easily cover the cost of a briefcase. Maybe you're not quite as successful as I'd thought.'

His confidence dribbling away, Gary wanted to get out. Why had he bullshitted like that? Mind you, why did this old bag have to make him feel like shit?

'Yeah, well, don't worry about me. I'll be all right, you watch.'

'I'm sorry,' the assistant relented. 'I was being horrible and snarky. I was only joking. I'll do you a deal. I've got one that's slightly scratched. I'll do it for half price. What do you think? Any good?'

He smiled; she was pretty tasty, after all.

Chapter 73

From the kitchen, Tina heard Chris pull the chain. The idea of soothing him, tending to him, was giving her a warm flutter. He was so obviously out of his depth, pretending to be a tough guy. What he needed right now was kindness and care. It would be nice to help him into bed and stroke his hair. She would tell him that he shouldn't feel bad about last night. It had been her fault that he'd made such an exhibition of himself; it was up to her to make things right for him. Despite his sickly appearance, he was still good-looking. She'd have no problem being seen out in public with him, especially once he'd got his colour back a bit. She tip-toed to the bathroom door. He was gargling: good. She went back to the kitchen, her heart thudding with excitement.

What was that? Some kind of rustling sound? She looked around at the front door: an envelope was emerging through the letterbox. Tina got up, pulled the envelope out of the flap, then opened the door.

Kev Abbott said, his voice meek, 'Oh, I didn't know you'd be here.' He was holding out a bunch of flowers, his face hopeful.

'What do you want?'

'I've come to give you these and the card. I don't want anything, just — you know.' He pushed the flowers at her.

'Kev, I thought we'd agreed: we're over.'

'Yeah, I know. I've been a wanker and I wanted to say I'm sorry, and to give you these.'

Conscious of Chris about to emerge from the bathroom, she said, 'Well, thank you. They're lovely flowers.'

'Can I come in?'

'No.'

'Why not?'

'Because.'

'It's all right; I won't stay. Let me put these flowers in some water.' He pushed past her and went into the kitchen. Dumping the flowers into the sink, he stood and looked at her. Smiling, he said, 'You look great.'

Cross now, she stayed by the front door, holding it open for him.

He said, 'Don't you want to open the card?'

Quickly, she tore open the envelope and scanned the card: the picture was of an old-fashioned racing car. She looked at him: he was smiling, eager for her to read it. She looked inside: Dear Tina, Sorry I'm such a wanker. Your lovely and your special. Luv Kev.

'Why the racing car?'

'Oh, well, I — I thought it was... er, interesting.'

'Was it the first one you saw?'

Kev's face was getting flushed. He looked around, his attention caught by the table. 'Is your dad around?'

'No. Listen to me, Kev; I want you to go, now.'

'Why are there two mugs on the table?'

'Kev, I want you to go. Now.'

He smiled at her. 'No, I think I'll stay a little bit. We've got so much to catch up on.'

Tina's temper flared. She wanted to care for Chris; he needed her to make him feel better. Having this little, weasel-eyed creep in her face was making her mad.

'Go! Just go!' She kept her voice under control, but she knew she was going to blow if he didn't get out.

'You've had a bloke here. God, Tina, you're a fucking scrubber. I'm out of the picture for two days and you're already screwing someone else.' He looked at her, his eyes accusing, 'If it's Gary, you're dead and so is he.'

'Who are you?'

Kev spun around. Chris was standing there, doing up his shirt. 'Who the fucking hell are you?'

Tina said, 'This is my friend, Chris. It's time for you to go, Kevin.'

Kev's face contorted with rage. 'You're a dirty, fucking whore. How much is he paying you?'

He turned to Chris. 'Whatever she's charging, it's not worth it. She's fucking useless in bed; it's like fucking a sack of potatoes.'

Chris, shirt now done up and tucked in, said, 'Look mate, I don't know who you are, but you don't want to be talking to birds like that.'

Kev's lip curled. 'Oh yeah, and how exactly should I be talking to birds? You're hardly an expert; you have to pay to get your end away.'

Chris's face reddened. 'Hang on a minute, you take that back.'

Tina blew. Taking two steps to the sink, she grabbed the flowers and shoved them into Kev's face. Tearing up the card, she flung the pieces at him.

'Get out of here. You disgust me! Get out!'

'You going to make me?'

Chris said, 'I don't know what's going on here, but—'

Tina pulled open the kitchen drawer and snatched up the first weapon she could find. She raised the scissors above her head and approached Kevin. 'If you don't get out, I swear I'll...'

Chris came into the kitchen and shrugged on his jacket. He turned to Tina. 'Listen, um, I think maybe I ought to leave you two. Er, you know...'

Kev's laugh was contemptuous. 'You're right. She's a fucking low-life. You're better off out of it. Believe me. I've been there, and it ain't worth it.'

Tina ran at Kev, the scissors ready for a downward plunge. He darted out of the kitchen door and sped to the top of the steps. She turned to Chris. 'Get out, I'm sick of you all.' Chris kept his head down as he dashed after Kevin.

Tina put the scissors back in the drawer. Tears were pricking her eyes. All she'd wanted was for him to feel better; to feel nice; to make amends. Now he thought she was a tart. Still, maybe it was better this way. She would have had sex with him and, afterwards, the usual depression and disappointment with herself would have taken hold, like it always did. Then what would she have done with him? Her dad would have come home, and she'd have had to explain away a strange man. No, it was definitely better this way.

God, Kevin Abbot was the biggest mistake of her life. What an arsehole! Fancy giving her flowers! What was he thinking? And that card? He'd probably nicked it. He'd come round for a bit of slap and tickle; he couldn't give a monkey's about her, about what she might want.

Tina put the kettle on again. Smiling, she wondered what her dad would have said if she'd stuck a pair of scissors into an Abbott? Maybe he'd say 'well done'. No, not her dad: he hated violence. As the kettle heated, she washed up Chris's plate. He was probably all right, but not for her. Any bloke that either wanted sex, or to show off, was from now on already out of the picture. She made up her mind: no blokes, no sex. It was time to concentrate on her career.

Chapter 74

The field was empty apart from the table. Terry picked it up and walked back to the side door into the hall. After the hullabaloo of a few minutes ago, the school was calm. Most of the children had been picked up, only those waiting for the coach were still in the playground. He added the table to the stack and straightened it with the others until their edges were aligned.

'Ah, there you are, Terry.'

Terry turned around to see Jim Dixon walking across the hall.

'I thought it all went well; how about you?'

Terry had been thoroughly relieved to get the whole thing out of the way. 'To be honest, it's not my kind of thing.'

'It's absolutely my cup of tea. I'll pop in and pick up *The Post* tomorrow on my way in. How do you know the reporter?'

Terry hadn't believed his eyes when Gary Abbott had shown up. For a minute he'd been about to tell him to clear off, but he'd apparently been legit. Terry would have bet money that the Abbotts couldn't read, never mind write an article for a newspaper. Still, he'd find out tomorrow.

'He's my daughter's friend.'

'Well, he was a bit rough and ready, but he seemed to grasp that I was the star of the show.'

Terry smiled. 'What, with your long career at Orient?'

Dixon looked penitent. 'Well, maybe I over-egged that bit. Actually, Terry, don't tell anyone — I was going to have a trial with Orient, but I fell off my bike on my way there and didn't make it, in the end. Obviously, I would have made the big time but for that one small hiccough.'

'Don't worry, I won't tell anyone.'

'Good man. Thanks for all your help with everything. It's been a very positive exercise. You will help with our team, won't you?'

'I'd love to.'

Dixon strode off. He called, 'Bye, Geraldine. Try and be on better form tomorrow, won't you?'

Terry turned to see her walking towards the car park. He hurried to catch her up. As he approached, she was fumbling the car key into its lock.

She looked up. 'Hello.'

'You all right?'

'What do you think?'

'I don't know. You look all right.'

'Liar.'

She was right. The normally healthy Mrs Dutton had been replaced by a very poor imitation.

'Are you going home to have a lie down?' Terry blushed at his own effrontery: what was it to do with him what she did in her own time?

'That's exactly what I'm going to do.'

'I'm sorry; it's nothing to do with me. You will have something to eat though, won't you?'

'If I can get anything down that will stay down, it will be a miracle. I might mumble on a rusk.'

'I'm sorry. By the way, don't worry about Bobby Goldsboro. It's nice of you to think about Tina, but please look after yourself.'

Geraldine laughed. Despite the sickly pallor, her face was transformed into its usual sunny beauty. 'Oh, Terry, you're not really with it, are you?'

'What did I say?'

'It's David Gainsborough, not Bobby Goldsboro — he's a pop singer.'

Terry smiled sheepishly, 'Well, Goldsboro, Gainsborough — it's all the same to me! I admit it: I'm a dinosaur.'

'Anyway, putting your ignorance of popular culture to one side, if I see him, I'll ask about Tina. I've got something for you.' She dug into her handbag and pulled out a blue Penguin.

'Not wanted by our star player?'

'Apparently she only likes the red ones.'

'That's funny. I only like the green ones. You have it — to go with your rusks.'

She looked sad.

'Go on. It would make me happy.'

'All right, I will.'

She unlocked her car. 'Thanks again for looking after me last night. I'm sorry I let you down so badly.' She pulled the door before he could answer. It didn't shut properly.

He opened it again. 'Mind your fingers, darling.'

He closed it firmly. He felt his face go beetroot; what had he just said? How embarrassing! What was he thinking? The only person he'd ever called "darling" was Diane. He was about to open the door again, to say sorry — or at least admit his mistake — when she turned the ignition. What could he say, anyway? He stood back and watched the car move off. Time for him to go home and put his feet up. What he wanted more than anything else was a quiet night watching the telly.

Chapter 75

'Darling!' For a moment she nearly opened the door again to say something: what, though? He was such a kind man it would be churlish to embarrass him. Anyway, the prospect of her bed was so powerful, Geraldine wasn't going to let anything get in its way.

Without knowing quite how, she steered the car back to her house. Someone was waving to her: surprise, surprise, it was David Gainsborough. She slowed and wound down her window. 'Talk of the devil!'

'Charming! All I wanted to do was say goodbye, and I get insults thrown at me!'

'Sorry — no! I was talking to someone about you, literally fifteen minutes ago.'

'Anything good?'

'Of course. What else is there?'

'That's true. Anyway, tell me all.'

'Oh, I said I'd ask you a favour. My friend's daughter is very interested in getting into the beauty business and I thought, with all your contacts, you might be able to give her some advice.'

'I should think so. How old is she?'

'Hmm, sixteen, I think. I used to teach her. She's a real character and, I suspect, she's an absolute beauty. She certainly was pretty when I knew her.'

'Does she want to get into hairdressing?'

'I'm not sure she knows. I suspect she needs a bit of help finding some direction. Terry's a single parent and he's feeling a bit out of his depth with a teenage daughter.'

'I'd love to help, Gerry, but we're off on our holiday tomorrow. Then I've got work in New York straight after. Is she local?'

Geraldine racked her brain. She remembered the Castletons had moved, but couldn't remember where to. They must be pretty close, though. 'I think so.'

'Well, if she wanted to pop around in the next couple of hours, I could have a quick chat. If not, then it will have to be next month.'

'Thank you, David. That's so kind of you. I'll see if I can reach them. Are you okay for me to give her your number?'

'Sure. Are you all right? You look a bit... not your usual picture of health and beauty.'

'Don't you start! Thanks, David. You might be hearing from her. If not, then it's because I couldn't get hold of her.'

She turned into the drive and parked up. Peering towards the windows, she whispered, 'Please God, don't be in yet.'

She got out of the car and walked across the gravel to the front door. Very relieved, she saw there was no sign of Terry's vomit. What had got into him? The poor man. She let herself in. Sort Tina out first, then a cup of hot water, a tin of Ambrosia — then bed. Pulling out the directory, mindful that Terry must have done the very same thing last night, she found one Castleton, at 33 Hertsmere Court, Manor Way. She dialled the number.

'Hello?'

'Good afternoon, is that Tina Castleton?'

'Yeah?'

'Hello, Tina. This is Geraldine Dutton, your old teacher. Do you remember me?'

'Of course! How are you? Dad told me that... Anyway — of course! How are you, Miss?'

'I'm... Anyway, is your father there?'

'Not yet. He'll be here soon. Shall I ask him to ring you?'

'Well, actually it's you I wanted to speak to. I have some information for you.'

'Really? Do I need to write it down?'

'Probably a good idea.'

'Hang on.'

Geraldine heard the phone clunk on something solid, then Tina's distant voice, 'Paper, paper, paper... ah, that'll do.' Then, 'Pen, pen, pen... ah, pencil, that'll do.' The phone was picked up. 'I'm ready.'

'Your father told me you were interested in working in the beauty industry.'

'Did he? I thought he was going to talk to another teacher... um, a young one.'

Geraldine smiled. 'Well, he chose an old one, instead. Actually, that's not quite right — I stepped forward.'

'Oh.' Tina sounded disappointed.

Keen to show that she wasn't entirely without connections, Geraldine said, 'Don't despair, I've landed a big fish for you. Do you know David Gainsborough?'

'Um… er, well — not really.'

'What about Suzi Quatro? Britt Eklund?'

'Yeah, of course! I really like Suzi Quatro.'

'Well, he's their hairdresser. He does famous people from all over the world.'

'Wow! What about him?'

'Well, if you can give him a call in the next few minutes, he's happy to talk to you about your career.'

'No, I don't believe it! How come?'

'He lives over the road from us. I've just been talking to him and he said I can give you his number.'

'Stop it, Miss — I don't believe you!'

'Well, it's up to you. Are you ready for his number?'

'Where does he live?'

'His house is called The Hollies; it's in a little cul-de-sac opposite us — Clarence Close. If you go down Rectory Lane, it's on the left, about halfway along. His number is 953 3396. Now, it's up to you. I'm off now, Tina. Good luck. He's a very nice man and his wife is lovely, too. Say hello to your father for me. Bye.'

'Thank you so much. Bye, Miss! Thank you.'

At last: time to recover. Geraldine put the kettle on and looked for a tin of rice pudding. She opened the lid and poured the contents into a bowl. She'd never eaten it cold before but couldn't be bothered to heat it up. She spooned it into her mouth as quickly as she could. Halfway through, she switched off the kettle and poured half a mugful of the hot water. A few more spoonsful, then a few gulps of warm water and that would be it. Time to collapse.

On her way to the stairs, the stain glared at her. No, she'd sort that out later. What time was it? Glancing at the clock on the mantelpiece, she saw Edward's face smiling at her. He wouldn't be smiling if he could see her in this state. It was four-twenty; he probably wouldn't be back till eight. If she could have two hours of solid sleep, a cold shower and a walk around the block, maybe she could get herself and the house shipshape before he got home. With a heavy tread, she climbed the stairs, unbuttoning her shirt as she went. She drew the curtains in her bedroom, then pulled down the bathroom blinds. She splashed cold water on to her face, had a wee, then stripped off her clothes and dumped them all into the laundry basket. Finally, with a tremendous sigh of relief, she fell into bed and let exhaustion overwhelm her.

Sleep slipped over her head like a silk cloak. Terry Castleton was still on the floor of his shed. As she helped him back to his feet, he put his arms around her and bent to kiss her. The picture was intensely arousing. Her half-befuddled head was fuelling her imagination. As Terry whispered to her, she felt him tenderly stroke her breasts. Covering his hands with hers, she gasped out loud, 'Oh, Terry, that feels so good.' She felt his big, bulky body pressing against hers as she opened her mouth to receive his. Trembling, she moved her hands to her thighs and then between them.

Chapter 76

Certain that everyone was looking at him, Gary swung his new briefcase as he sauntered down the road. The sales assistant had put in a large notepad and a packet of pens; not top quality but not shit ones either.

'Anything else?'

'Nope, that's all I need. Cheers, thanks, you've been brilliant.'

As he neared his house, he wondered whether he could ask out a woman like that. Maybe she'd prefer it if he came around to her house for dinner. They could share a few cans — no, wine would be better. What was that fancy stuff people drank? Mateus Rose? She'd be so impressed by him that she'd be certain to ask if he'd like to have sex with her. He shook his head; life wasn't all about sex. Remembering how she'd outwitted him, he wondered if she'd teach him how to persuade people to tell him what they didn't want to reveal. As a top journalist, the Bulldog, he needed to get a reputation, not just for 'sniffing out' a story but for getting his teeth into it. He rather liked the image — what the fucking hell!

Outside the house were two police cars and a black van with darkened windows. A large, uniformed policeman was standing outside the front door.

'Sorry, son, you can't come in here.'

'What's going on?'

'No one's allowed to come or go.'

'But I live here.'

'What's your name?'

'Gary Abbott.'

The copper said, 'Hang on,' and shouted into the house, 'There's a Gary Abbott here.'

Seconds later, Dickie Davies came to the door. Smiling, he said, 'Ah, hallo, Gary. I was wondering when you'd turn up. Do come and join the party.'

Frightened now, Gary followed the shabby detective into the house, through the hall and into the kitchen. His mum was sitting at the table.

'Mum, what's going on?'

Before she could answer, there came the sound of glass smashing. He looked out of the window — the greenhouse was being dismantled.

He turned to Dickie. 'What are you doing? What's happening?'

Dickie opened the kitchen window and called, 'Mr Flanagan? Gary's here.'

The old man turned around. Although his face was still kind and gentle, there was a new intensity in his eyes. He walked away from the greenhouse, round the side of the house and came in.

'Good evening, Gary.' The voice was different, too — an edge of excitement? 'Have you filled Gary in, Detective Sergeant Nott?'

'No, sir.'

Flanagan smiled. 'Good. Let me update you. Your mother knows it, but I would like to tell it all again; it helps me get matters straight in my head. You don't mind, do you, Mrs Abbott?'

Gary looked at her. She shook her head at Flanagan.

The old detective sat down at the table. He stared at Gary. He just sat there, staring. Then, with an apologetic, yellow-toothed smile, he leant back and opened his mouth to speak. They heard another crash of glass and a cheer from the men outside.

Flanagan shook his head sadly. 'So, Gary, this is it, in a nutshell. Thirteen years ago, your grandfather disappeared. Despite our best attempts, he was never found. I was unable to find anything at all. I couldn't understand it. An old gentleman goes for a walk and is never seen again. No one sees him. His family, friends and neighbours have nothing to say about it, except how much they miss him. A shocking tragedy. That poor, kind and dignified war hero — gone. Just like that, as Tommy Cooper might say. As you can imagine, I was troubled by it all. What troubled me most was that everyone expressed their sadness, but I knew that dear Mr Abbott senior was not a popular man. He was not a nice gentleman; in fact, he was a thoroughly bad lot. Why, then, Gary — why was everyone so upset? It didn't ring true.'

Gary sat down next to his mum. 'You all right?'

She took his hand and squeezed it. They turned their heads as a rumbling sound came down the side of the house, past the door and out into the garden. Gary got up and looked out: a wheeled generator. Behind it was a bloke with a pneumatic drill. Gary sat down again.

Flanagan said, 'As I was saying: it didn't make sense to me. I smelled a rat — that was the apposite expression then — and it has stayed with me ever since. I've always wondered what had happened and yesterday things became clear. I had to do a bit of checking, of course, but it didn't take long. Any ideas, Gary?'

Gary knew perfectly well but shook his head.

Flanagan said, 'I was looking out of this window yesterday and saw the greenhouse. For a second it didn't register with me, but then I thought: I don't remember there being a greenhouse out there. I came several times, didn't I, Jenny?' She nodded. 'I was very familiar with house and garden and there was definitely no greenhouse. What's more, the greenhouse wasn't full of plants and flowers; no, it was full of — well, put it this way, not your usual horticultural paraphernalia. I said to Detective Sergeant Nott, "I wonder when that greenhouse was constructed", didn't I, Nott?'

'Yes, sir.'

'So I have spent today finding out. First, I chatted with the neighbours, Mr and Mrs Lincoln. They weren't sure — maybe ten years ago? Mrs Ross, on the other side, moved in five years ago when Mr Gray died; she wasn't able to assist me. I didn't give up. I got in touch with all the companies in the area that sell greenhouses. You see, it's what the police do: check things out. When I was here yesterday, I noted the design, size and shape. I rang up Pigotts, Dewers, Salisburys, Smith and Arnolds and Woodlands. Guess what? None of them can remember selling a greenhouse to anyone called Abbott thirteen years ago.' He smiled, regretfully. 'Don't worry, Gary, there's a happy ending to this sorry tale. Mr John Hamilton of Hamilton Garden Supplies informed me that a Mr Brian Abbott bought a ten-foot greenhouse, with beech panels, steel frame and door at front and rear, on the 24th October, 1963. He told me that, when the greenhouse was delivered, all he had to do was erect it over an existing concrete base. I said to him, "It's thirteen years ago: how can you be sure of the date?" He keeps records; he had his invoice at the ready! I said, "Mr Hamilton, how can you remember that the concrete base was already there? It's a very long time ago." He told me that — get this, Gary — he told me he remembered that Mr Abbott and he had had a great joke about it. Do you know what the joke was?' Gary and Jenny were silent. 'I'll tell you: Brian said to Mr Hamilton, "It's where I buried the bodies."'

Flanagan smiled and shook his head. Dickie was almost choking on his laughter.

His wheezing was suddenly drowned out by the generator growling into life; then came the hammering racket of the pneumatic drill. Flanagan got up and watched. There was an intense air of expectation on his face. He turned back to Gary and Jenny.

He shouted, 'Of course, what I don't know, is where Mr Abbott senior's body was in the period between his disappearance and his burial. Jenny, you'll be telling me that shortly, I think?'

Gary didn't dare look at his mum.

Flanagan turned again to Gary, his sad smile resumed. 'We had a very good look around your father's shed, Gary. Apparently, he kept it locked at all times. Have you ever been inside it?'

Gary swallowed. He could deny it but maybe they'd taken fingerprints. Anyway, why shouldn't he have been in his dad's shed? Could they tell how recently he'd been in there from fingerprints? Sod it — tell the truth for once.

'Yeah, I was in there yesterday.'

'Ah. And how did you get in?'

'I broke the window and climbed in.'

'Ah, thank you. That clears that up. Now, Gary, this is an important question. Tell me the truth — no need to worry: everything's sorting itself out at last.' Gary got ready. Whatever it was, he'd protect his mum. 'Gary, you're wearing your grandfather's tie. Where did you get it?'

The drill stopped. The silence was immense. His mum turned towards him, her eyes met his.

'I found it in the shed. I took it. I... dunno, I thought...'

Flanagan's eyes were boring into him. He said, 'Did you find anything else, Gary?'

Gary could feel the photos and his Auntie Maureen's letter in his inside pocket. Should he pull them out and hand them over? The drill started up again.

He shook his head. 'No, I didn't find anything else. There was a load of mags, fishing stuff, football programmes, stuff like that.'

Flanagan kept staring at him. Gary stared back.

'Why are you wearing the tie, Gary? I didn't have you down as a tie wearer.'

'Coz I had an interview and it was the only tie I had, apart from my school tie.'

'Really? How did you get on?'

'All right.'

The drill cut out again. They heard a shout. Flanagan got up and looked out.

'Ah, excuse me please. Nott, you'll stay with our friends?'

'Yes, sir.'

Gary shifted in his seat. 'I'm going to take a leak. I'll be back in a minute, Mum.'

Dickie said, 'Don't be long, Gary. We don't want you missing all the fun.'

Gary dashed up the stairs and into his room. He pulled out the envelope — where should he hide it? The wardrobe was the obvious place, but Kev might find it in there. What about inside a book? There was no chance of his brother finding it then. No, the book might get knocked off the shelf and the envelope would be right there in full view. Gary lifted his mattress and thrust the envelope underneath as far as he could. He had a pee and dashed back downstairs.

Dickie said, 'That was a very long leak, Gary.'

'Jeez, I didn't know you were going to time me. If you must know, I decided to have a dump. Do you want to know size, shape, smell?'

His mum, horribly quiet up 'til now, said, 'Gary, that's enough of that.'

Dickie smiled. 'Thank you, Jenny. I don't like that kind of language, either.'

Gary sneered at him then looked out of the window. He could see Flanagan with the other men. Two of them were shovelling away the broken-up concrete. Gary stared at Flanagan: he stood still, hunched and ready, like a heron Gary had once seen on the bank of the reservoir. They heard the copper at the front door shout. Dickie got up and went to investigate. Seconds later Kev came in: he was red-faced with fury.

'What the fuck is going on?'

Dickie said, 'I'm Detective Sergeant Nott. You're just in time.'

Gary looked at his brother; there was something wild about him. Apart from the crazed look on his face, he had pink petals caught in his jumper and a stalk sticking out of his hair.

'What's going on out there?' Kev was staring at the police and the devastation in the garden.

Gary said, 'They're digging up the greenhouse. They think Grandad's under it.'

'What?'

Flanagan was walking back towards the house. The kitchen door opened.

'Gary?' Gary looked up. 'I'd like to take that tie; do you mind?'

With great relief, Gary undid it and handed it over. Flanagan pulled out a see-through, plastic bag and put the tie into it. They heard a shout. Flanagan dashed outside. Gary, Kev and Nott crowded next to each other at the window.

One of the coppers handed his shovel to a colleague and knelt down at the edge of the hole. He was scraping soil away from something. His movements became careful, then delicate. Flanagan knelt down beside him, blocking the view.

Dickie hissed, 'Shit! Move, you old fool.'

Gary watched in fascination. Were the crumbling bones of his grandad about to be hoisted out of the grave? The situation was more like a film than real life. Suddenly he remembered his mum. Again, he felt so sorry for her: violent, recently-dead husband, ignorant sons, and now this excavation of her own back garden for her father-in-law's body. He turned around to mouth 'sorry', or at least look sympathetic. He gaped: she was winking at him.

Chapter 77

Tina's heart was in her mouth but, as soon as she heard the man's voice, the nerves left her.

'Ah, Geraldine was telling me about you. It's very nice to hear from someone keen to get into my world. Well, my wife and I are off on our holiday tomorrow so I'm a bit short of time... Yes, Antigua... in the Caribbean. Yes, should be warm and sun, sun, sun! No, it's okay. If you were able to pop around shortly... I don't mind. Geraldine's a very good friend of ours... Sure. Lovely. I'll see you soon.'

She dashed into her bedroom: what should she wear? Their high street had no trendy boutiques. There were clothes shops for oldies, but she wanted height-of-fashion, cool, trendy stuff. She looked out of the window. It was bright, probably quite mild still. She decided on a cornflower-blue, sleeveless dress, just above the knee. It had buttons down the front; she could undo a couple. If she took a jacket, it would be all right to keep it on or take it off, depending on how things worked out. She didn't want to look as if the meeting was a big deal for her; on the other hand, she should let him know that style came easily to her. What shoes? Platforms didn't go with the dress; she'd try on her sandals. They had a heel, to give her that bit of extra height. Time for her raspberry crush again, plus the good old French perfume.

Satisfied with her general appearance, she squeezed some toothpaste straight into her mouth and gargled it around. Remembering how, earlier, she'd waited outside the bathroom for Chris, she spat it out quickly. Blimey, what a horrible scene! She was sorry it hadn't worked out well, but it was probably for the best.

Back in her room, she took the giraffe out of his drawer and put him on her pillow, pulling the bedclothes up to his head. 'See you later. Wish me luck.' Picking up the pencil again, she pulled the folded Daily Express towards her and scribbled along the top margin.

I'm seeing someone about a job. I'll be back soon.

How best to get there? Twenty-minute walk? Or two stops on the bus, then five-minutes' stroll? She looked along the street. Brilliant! A 292 was in sight. Speeding up, she reached the stop with a few seconds to spare, unlike her frantic dash on the way back from Totteridge. She smiled at the driver as he opened the doors, his eyes looking her up and down.

She put ten pence down. 'Springfield Wood, please.'

'Going somewhere nice?'

'Wouldn't you like to know.'

'Yes. Can I come, too?'

'Hmm, not where I'm going, you can't.'

'Ah, never mind. Next time, maybe?'

She smiled again, took her ticket from the machine and strolled to the seat nearest the middle doors.

'Hello, Tina!'

She looked towards the back. It was Steve Bellingham and another boy she didn't recognise.

'Hallo, Steve.'

'You look nice.'

'Thanks.'

Steve whispered theatrically to his friend, 'That's Tina — you know, the one I was telling you about?'

Tina heard his friend whisper back, 'You haven't got a chance, Belly. She's way out of your league.'

Steve said loudly, 'Yeah, you might be right. I'm thick, ugly, I'm covered in boils, I stink like a blocked bog, I've got stumps instead of teeth, even my mum hates me but, hey, at least I'm modest.'

Tina looked around. 'Don't forget your breath, Steve. You could strip wallpaper with it.'

The friend laughed. 'What about me? I'm available.'

She rang the bell. 'What as? A scarecrow?'

Steve said sadly, 'She'll see the light, when everyone else lets her down.'

The bus slowed. Tina got up to leave.

'Good evening, gentlemen. Enjoy your dreams.'

As she left, Steve's friend called, 'My number's 953—' and the doors closed.

She waved to them. They waved back. Crossing the road, she felt nervous. Impressing teenage boys was one thing: could she make a famous, celebrity hairstylist think she was anything special?

The little streets around this area reminded her of Totteridge this morning. The houses were detached and set back from the road. Each one was a different size and style to its neighbours; they all reeked of money. The gardens were beautifully kept: lovely bushes and trees; expensive cars parked outside garages. The sound of the neighbourhood — quiet, subdued, private — was so different to her own. She came to Clarence Close. Pausing on the corner, she looked. There were two whacking great houses. On the drive of one was a gleaming white boat perched on a trailer and, beyond it, a gold Rolls Royce: were they his? As she approached, a wooden sign in the lawn announced the house as The Hollies. Wow, this was it! She walked up the gravel drive to the front door.

'Hello? Ah, you must be Tina?' From behind a large holly bush came a middle-aged woman, holding out her hand and smiling. 'Hello, Tina, my name's Judy; I'm David's wife. Come and join us.'

Tina followed the shapely figure, dressed in a cream, linen dress, around the bush to a wrought-iron table and chairs.

'Do sit down. David's getting drinks.'

Tina, doing her best to be elegant and poised, sat down and surveyed the scene. What was before her looked like a photograph from a high-class magazine — Vogue or one of those. The lawns around them were more like carpets than grass. She gazed at the boat and wondered if it was one of those she'd been imagining only yesterday. There were nuts and olives on the table and folded linen napkins. Although it wasn't sunny, the white parasol was hoisted high.

Judy Gainsborough looked like a film star with her bright, red lipstick, glittering earrings and a large sparkler on her ring finger.

She said, 'I love your dress, Tina. Where did you get it?'

Not wanting to say it was left by her mother when she did a runner, Tina said, 'Oh, my aunt bought it — somewhere in London, I think.' Encouraged by the compliment, she stood up and took off her jacket and put it on the back of her chair.

'Oh, you're here. How lovely.'

Tina turned to see a little old man trotting towards them. He was carrying a silver bucket in one hand and three tall glasses in the other.

Tina stood up, 'Hello, Mr Gainsborough. I'm Tina Castleton.'

He put bucket and glasses down and stood back to look at her. Whilst he sized her up, she checked him over: short, plump, pink-faced, with long, bright, yellow hair. He might be a great hairdresser but, she thought, he ought to do something with his own barnet.

He said, 'Mm-mm, you're an absolute dish. Do sit down. Will you have some fizz?'

She looked at the table, unsure. Seeing him pull a bottle out of the bucket — a Champagne bottle — she smiled, 'Well, if you insist!'

He'd been concentrating on peeling a strip of foil from around the top of the bottle. Pausing, he said, 'Oh, sweet angel, I most certainly do insist; don't I, Judes?'

'Yes. Tina, sweetie, he's a most insistent man, as you'll find out.'

He unwrapped the wire and seemed only to caress the cork. 'Thar she blows!'

Tina tensed, waiting for the pop. Instead, there was a long hiss and then the glasses were being filled. He put the bottle back in the ice bucket, picked up a glass and handed it to Tina, then one to his wife and finally took his own.

'To two, exquisite young women.'

Huffing, Judy said, 'Davie, you are preposterous. However, I shan't split hairs. Cheers!'

Holding out their glasses, the Gainsboroughs leaned towards Tina. She followed suit: they clinked. Wrapping her fingers around the stem of her glass as they were doing, she sipped carefully: sour — acid.

Davie said, 'Mmm — ambrosia!'

Confused, Tina smiled and sipped again. It was no better.

She said, 'Yes! Ambrosia, all right.'

'You see, Judes? I can tell a goddess a mile away: Aphrodite has come to visit us.'

'Tina, don't pay any attention to him. Thank you for popping over at short notice. Do you live nearby?'

Fearful that they'd ask for details, she said, 'Yes, very near.'

Judy spoke again. 'Will you have an olive? They're terribly tasty. Or perhaps a nut — olives aren't to everyone's taste.'

Tina had never had an olive, but knew that you had to like them if you wanted to be posh. She saw that a few of them had little sticks poking out. She picked up a stick and popped the glistening, green olive into her mouth.

Judy said, 'Good choice. I love the anchovies, too.'

Doing her best to smile through the urge to gag, Tina lifted her glass again and threw down enough champagne to wash away the disgusting taste. The olive had been hideous, but the champagne tasted much better than it had only minutes before. Maybe she could get to like it.

Davie looked at her, his scrutiny open and unembarrassed. She wondered if she ought to be saying something. If he asked her what she wanted, what should she say? Imagining this scene, she'd anticipated him doing all the talking and her doing the listening. It occurred to her, maybe too late, that she should have prepared more for their meeting. What should she say? Why was she here? Up until this minute, she had only had a vague notion of her future life — a child's view, with princesses, celebrities, glamour, colour, bright lights and a backing-track. What she needed were abilities, skills; some talent might be helpful! Did she want to be a hairdresser, or was she only really interested in hanging around famous hairdressers' famous clients? Feeling her face colour, she took another sip of her drink. It was nice, after all.

Davie said, 'How tall are you, Tina? You're taller than me, but then everyone is.'

Surprised, Tina said, 'Five foot seven — well, I was the last time I checked.'

He nodded. 'You're a bit too busty to be a traditional model. Any good at singing?'

Tina laughed. 'I can do "Wanderin' Star" like Lee Marvin, only deeper.'

'Pity. Dance?'

'I like dancing — you know, at discos.'

He nodded and knocked back his champagne. 'Drink up, girls; I'm gasping for the other half.'

'Davie, it's not a race!' Judy raised her eyebrows at Tina and shook her head sadly. Tina smiled back. What a nice lady.

He said, 'Geraldine is one of our best friends. She and Edward are such dears, don't you think?'

Puzzled, Tina looked across at Judy for help.

'Geraldine and Edward Dutton?'

'Oh, of course. I'm such a dimmo! I only know her as Mrs Dutton. She was my teacher when I was at primary school. Yes, she's lovely; the best teacher I ever had. All of us loved Mrs Dutton.'

Judy emptied her glass. Tina followed suit. She was surprised; it was tasting better and better. Davie refilled the glasses.

Tina, although a little light-headed, recognised that now was the moment to change her life. If she left it any longer, she'd be talking rubbish and would come away with regrets.

She said, 'It's very kind of you to meet me. You don't know me, or anything, but you've given up your valuable time to talk to me. I'm really grateful to you both. You're probably wondering what I want? Well, I'm not sure; that's the honest truth. I'm ambitious. I want to get on and out of here and into London. I'm not very good at academic stuff, but I think I can do plenty of things. I'm good at art and I can make stuff. My dad has taught me how to sew and draw and, you know, think up ideas and stuff. I think I might be good at hairdressing, but I also like make-up and beauty and —'

The memory of running out of words in front of Father Christmas in Selfridges all those years ago crowded into her head. Why couldn't life be a bit simpler, sometimes? This had been a golden opportunity to get her foot on the rung of a ladder. Instead, she was digging herself into a hole and looking increasingly childish as she did it. Leaning forward for her drink, she saw Judy smile: was she trying to encourage her or to sympathise? Tina put her glass down and tried again.

Looking directly into Davie's eyes, she said, 'You don't know me. I have no right to ask for anything from you. You have already been incredibly kind to me. But I want to get somewhere in life. I have something that is driving me on, and I can't ignore it; it won't let me. I need a chance, Mr Gainsborough, just one chance to see what I can do. Can you help me? If you can't, I understand. But if you can, I wouldn't let you down.'

This time, she did drink: a long swig. She risked another olive, too: really, they weren't as bad as she'd thought.

Davie said, 'If I gave you a pencil and paper and asked you to design a brand-new hairstyle for me and you only had five minutes to do it, what would you say?'

Tina giggled. 'I'd say it would look like a total mess, but I'd give it a go.'

'Right, stay there. I'll get you a pencil and paper, and while I'm at it, I'd better see if there's any fizz left in the fridge.'

'He likes you, Tina. Don't worry.'

'Oh, I'm so embarrassing sometimes. Honestly, just when I want to make a good impression, I come across like a stupid kid.'

'Listen: this is important. Do you know how many girls turn up at his salons asking for opportunities? Hundreds and hundreds. All of them are probably brilliant hairstylists. What he's looking for are characters; people who are different and who stand out because of it. You're lucky, you're a lovely-looking girl, as well as a character. If you can do a half-decent design, he'll be interested in you. Don't get me wrong: whatever happens, you'll have to work very, very hard. You may not like the work, nor the people you'd be working with, but at least you could say you'd done your best. Here he comes; don't have another drink until you've finished your design.'

Whistling, the bumbling little man tottered back, bottle in one hand, pad in the other.

'Here we go — another slurp, and a pad and pencil for you, my dear. Judes, Edward's coming over for a drink in a few minutes. Tina — you probably know — Edward really is in show business. I'm sure he'd love to meet you too.'

Chapter 78

'Hallo?'

'Can I speak to Gary Abbott, please?'

'That's me.'

'Watcha, Gary. It's Nigel from *The Post*. How you doing?'

Gary tensed. 'Er, you're not sacking me, are you?'

'Don't be silly. No, I'm ringing to read you the final copy about your father and everything we talked about.'

'Phew! Oh yeah. For a minute… Yeah, sorry. I'm all ears.'

'Okay, it's going to be mostly about John Eustace. He's what people are interested in. You know he's a councillor, former mayor, and big employer?'

'Yep.'

'Right. But we are going to say something about your father and grandfather. This is it…'

Gary listened carefully. It all sounded reasonable to him. He'd promised his mum that there wouldn't be any mention of other members of the family, or of the fact that he'd been in the car when his dad had attacked the posh bloke.

He said, 'I think that sounds all right. How long before you send it off, or do whatever you do next?'

There was a pause, then Nigel said, 'Well, actually, it's already — um, in the next five seconds. I need your approval. Why do you ask?'

Gary thought about what was about to emerge from its thirteen-year-old grave. 'Well, I think there might be some more news on the missing person story.'

'Yeah?'

'I can't say now. I reckon I'll have more information in the morning. Thanks, Nigel. Thanks for everything. I've really enjoyed today.'

'You're welcome. I've seen the final copy for your story. Old Alan tore it to pieces. I don't think you'll recognise it, but well done on it, anyway.'

Gary was disappointed; he thought it had been all right. Never mind, he'd done something, even if it was crap. 'See you tomorrow.'

He put the phone down and went back into the kitchen. The men were gathered around the hole at the site of the erstwhile greenhouse. Flanagan was on his knees still; he looked as though he was praying to whatever it was they were all staring at. Clearly exasperated by his exclusion from the excitement, Dickie said, 'I'd better go and help. Stay here.'

As soon as he was out of the door, Kevin snarled, 'Can someone tell me what the fuck is going on? Who was that on the phone? It had better not have been Tina.'

'For God's sake, Kev. Leave it alone. It was my boss.'

'Boss? What boss?'

Jenny looked up at her son, her eyes alight. 'Did you get it Gary? Well done.'

Kev fumed. 'Get what?'

'I got a job at the newspaper. I'm an apprentice. They're running a story about Dad attacking John Eustace. They were all over the thing, so we had to let them run it in tomorrow's edition. Nigel — he's one of the main reporters — read it out to me.'

Kev was spitting feathers. 'How can you have a job with a newspaper? You're not even literary.'

Gary said, trying not to laugh, 'I think you mean literate.'

'I'll give you fucking literate! Anyway, now we've got our family being dragged through the shit by the newspapers.'

Gary said, 'Mum, what's down there? Is it Grandad, or not?'

Jenny got up and joined them. Dickie was now standing on the far side of the hole. He looked over at them and smiled; a horrible, leering smile. One of the men went into the shed and came back with the pickaxe. He bent down, levered one end underneath something, then leaned on the handle. Opposite him, another man stuck his shovel into the hole and leaned back, too. Two others slid a plank underneath whatever was being forced up to ground level. Through the gaps between legs, they could see a rectangular shape emerge.

Gary said, his voice shaking, 'Mum, tell us. What do you know? Quick, before they come back in: what is it?'

'I don't know. Dad never told me. He said he wanted to start growing tomatoes and that was it. The only time I ever said anything about it, he lost his rag, and I left it.'

Kev said, 'I don't remember Dad putting up the greenhouse. Where were we? Were we even here?'

She said, 'No, we were on holiday. I took us to Clacton for a week; it was half term. We hired a caravan with Grandpa and Grandma. When we got back, it was up and it's been there ever since.'

'Yeah, I remember that holiday, just about,' Kev said.

They watched in silence. Flanagan was standing now. He was pointing downwards. A policeman was taking photographs, several were writing in notebooks. Dickie was talking into his walkie-talkie, his face shining with excitement. Cigarette packets were being opened and handed around, lighters and matches proffered. Flanagan swivelled to face the three Abbotts peering out of the window; he was expressionless. Turning back to what Gary could glimpse was a steel box, like the one in the shed, Flanagan pointed at one of the officers, who leaned forward. They could see the hammer and chisel in his hands. Seconds later they heard heavy blows — metal on metal — a lock being smashed. The lid of the box was lifted, and the men surrounding it leaned forward as one.

Gary said, 'Mum, if there's anything we need to know, tell us now. We can cover up for you; we'll say whatever you want us to, won't we, Kev?'

'Course, I'll lie my head off, if that's what you want?'

They looked at their mum. She was shaking her head. 'There's nothing to say; I don't know what's out there.'

The men out there were wide-eyed. Gary saw their mouths 'effing and blinding'. One officer bent down and seemed to be rummaging and repositioning. Almost as one, they looked at Flanagan. He turned towards the window again. His face was white. He looked up at the sky for several seconds then came walking back to the house, Dickie trotting behind him. They disappeared from view, then the back door opened quietly.

Flanagan stood in the doorway. 'Excuse me, Jenny, boys. May I have a bit more of your time?'

Jenny said what she always said, 'I'll make us a nice cuppa.'

Gary couldn't help himself: he laughed, 'Cor, lovely! Thanks, Mum.'

She said, 'Mr Flanagan, would you like one?'

Gary looked at him: he was looking around the kitchen, searching for something. Behind him, Dickie looked nervous.

Flanagan stepped into the kitchen. 'Thank you, Mrs Abbott; I think I will join you.' Dickie came in and shut the door behind him. Flanagan said, 'Jenny, did you know that's what was buried out there?'

'Until you tell me, I've absolutely no idea. It's not Grandad? You seemed so sure a few minutes ago.'

Gary watched Flanagan's eyes flicker. He was evidently trying to stay calm.

Dickie said, 'Jenny, you know what's in that box. Why didn't you say earlier? You must have known we'd ask you.'

Gary saw Flanagan's eyes clear. The old man coughed, wiped his face and said, 'Thank you, Nott. Mrs Abbott, were you here when the greenhouse was erected?'

'No. The boys and I were in Clacton. We were on holiday with my parents. We had a caravan. When we got back, the greenhouse was built and that's all I know about it. Brian said he wanted to grow tomatoes and that was that.'

Flanagan said, 'Clacton eh? Hmm. Nott, I'd like you to write down everything that Mrs Abbott says about Clacton; is your notebook at the ready?'

'Yes, sir.'

Gary felt his stomach twist; Flanagan was clearly a clever bastard. Was he going to try and trick his mum?

'Mrs Abbott — Jenny. Is the beach at Clacton sand or shingle?'

'Sandy.'

'Is there a pier — yes or no?'

'Yes.'

'Are there amusements on the pier?'

'Yes — well, there used to be.'

'What sort of amusements?'

'Um, one-armed bandits… you know, an arcade. There was a café, and public toilets.'

'Was your caravan overlooking the sea?'

'No.'

'What was the name of your caravan site?'

'Um, I can't remember.'

'Who organised the holiday?'

'My mother.'

'Is she alive?'

'No.'

'Your father?'

'No.'

'I'm sorry to hear that, Jenny; I really am.'

Gary watched his mother. She was so calm, she must be telling the truth.

'Did you have fish and chips on your holiday?'

'Yes, I'm sure we did.'

'Where is the fish and chip shop in Clacton?'

His mum looked off into the distant past. 'I think it was on the sea front.'

'What did you and the boys enjoy most about your holiday?'

She smiled. 'That's easy. There's a funfair on the front — at least, there used to be. We went there every day. The boys loved the roller-coaster.'

Kevin exclaimed, 'I remember that. Yeah, she's right. Do you remember, Gary?'

Gary shook his head.

Kev scoffed, 'That's because you were scared of it probably.'

'No, I was not.'

'Well, you were scared of most things. You still are.'

'No I'm—'

Flanagan cut in. 'Thank you, thank you. Jenny. One more question, if I may?' She nodded. 'Can you tell me why there is a large box buried in your garden?'

'No.'

'Can you tell me—'

Kev cut in, gleefully. 'That's two questions.'

Flanagan's voice was little more than a whisper. 'Thank you, Kevin.'

Kev looked triumphant.

'Jenny, can you tell me anything at all about the contents of that box?'

Gary watched his mum carefully. She seemed genuinely unaware of the box's existence and its contents.

'I'm sorry, Mr Flanagan. I wish I could help you. This whole business is rather a shock to me. To be honest, I'm finding it all very upsetting. I don't know anything about it.'

Flanagan turned to Kevin. 'I don't suppose you know anything?'

Kev shook his head.

Flanagan raised his eyebrows in Gary's direction.

'I was only three.'

Flanagan's irritation got the better of him. 'I know that. I meant, do you have any idea subsequent to your being a toddler?'

'No.'

'Thank you. We'll continue with our search. We shall, of course, want to ask you further questions, so please don't leave the house for the foreseeable future.'

Jenny asked, her voice neutral, 'Do you want a cuppa, Mr Flanagan? Mr Nott?'

They went back out into the garden. The three Abbotts breathed out noisily. Kev was the first to speak.

'Fuck, Mum, you're amazing.'

'Stop that swearing. All I did was tell the truth.'

Gary said, 'Kev, why have you got pink petals in your jumper?'

Kevin looked down. 'Er, I dunno. Bloody hell, what are we supposed to do now?'

They stood close together and stared out of the window. Now that the box was out, the men went back to their digging. The whole devastated area was chaotic. Sitting on a beer crate, face impassive, Flanagan was staring into the hole. Gary tried to think what must be going through his head. He'd obviously never been able to let go of the mystery of Bertram Abbott and had come along today convinced that, at last, he had uncovered the truth. That another truth had materialised might be important for the old policeman, but it was not the one he wanted. Maybe whatever was in the box was a clue to what had happened all those years ago?

Behind him, his mum was pouring boiling water into the pot. Kevin had gone upstairs. Gary looked at Flanagan; he was deep in concentration. Then, suddenly, he put his hand in his jacket pocket. Seconds later, the plastic bag with Grandad's tie in it emerged. Flanagan looked up, and stared straight at Gary.

Chapter 79

Tina loved drawing faces and hairstyles, designing clothes, shoes, jewellery. During lessons, she spent more time sketching out what was in her head than she ever did on the subject under discussion. Art was the only lesson that motivated her and even that became boring when all they did was learn stuff that she could already do. When David Gainsborough had suggested she sketch him a new hairstyle, off the cuff, she'd been excited. Five minutes was a bit tight, but not an impossibility. Seeing her excitement, he'd smiled back.

Then he turned to his wife and said, 'Let's make it more interesting; what do you say, Judy?'

She looked severe. 'Nothing too demanding, please. What have you got in mind?'

'Tina, this is the challenge. You have five minutes to draw me and give me a new hairstyle, and in that five minutes, I'll do the same for you. We'll compare notes afterwards. What do you say?'

Tina considered his ridiculous hair; was he really giving her the opportunity to improve it?

'Okay, say when!'

Four minutes on, she looked at her page. Though tempted to give him a short-back-and-sides, she'd gone for something trendier. There he was, David Gainsborough, now sporting a 'George Best', with layers. Ideal for the West End. Content with her effort, she became aware of his busy pencil. She looked across at him.

He smiled. 'Give me thirty seconds.'

Tina watched him work. He was entirely focused on his pad. She thought he probably wasn't the theatrical old fool he'd been portraying earlier: you didn't get to be top in your field if you were an idiot. His expression now was quite different. The twinkling, bumbling manner had disappeared, replaced by deep concentration. Checking her drawing one more time, she saw that her David's expression was amused; she put a tiny crease between his eyebrows to suggest a more serious air.

'Right, time's up.' He gurgled, 'I'll show you mine if you show me yours.'

He tore off the page he'd been working on and passed it over. Embarrassment flared in her: it was extraordinary. Hers was pathetic. He'd sectioned his page into three frames, each with a different view of her — front, profile and from behind. Her face wasn't in any of them, just her hair and head shape. He'd given her a 'Purdey' in the front-on image, an urchin in profile and a bob from behind.

'Oh, Mr Gainsborough! You are amazing.'

She handed her page to him. Picking up his glass, he assessed her pitiful effort. Tina looked again at his drawings and realised that he'd gone about the exercise quite differently to her. His pencil strokes were minimal, their effect great.

'Tina, what you've done here is good. You're much better than I was when I was sixteen. I think you've been rather flattering with the youthful appearance: so thank you for that. Don't worry. It's only a little game. How's your drink going? Gosh, you haven't touched it. Come on, drink up! Ah, here comes Edward.'

Grateful to shift attention from her childish performance, Tina took a long swig and turned to see Judy coming back, a tall, handsome man at her side. As they approached, the man caught sight of Tina and she saw his eyes widen, a smile spread over his face.

'Hello, hello! Who do we have here?'

Judy said, 'Edward, this is our new friend, Tina. Tina, this is Edward, Geraldine's husband.'

'Oh, hello. She used to be my teacher. Nice to meet you.'

They shook hands. He was looking at her closely, weighing her up. Tina was used to this. She assessed him in return. Mrs Dutton was an attractive woman — well the last time she'd seen her, she was — her husband was also very handsome. He was tall, slim, had dark hair greying at the temples; there was a dark curl over one eye. He looked like her idea of a secret agent: half Sean Connery, half Roger Moore. This man had that kind of cool composure, but instead of a humorous expression, wore a cold, judgemental look.

He said, 'Nice to meet you, Tina. Now, Judy, where's my champagne?'

Judy went off to get a glass. Edward Dutton picked up the picture of David.

He laughed, a short bark. 'Very good.'

Tina flushed. Okay, so maybe it wasn't great, but he didn't have to laugh like it was shit.

David took it out of his friend's hand. 'Why are you laughing; it's very good.'

Edward turned to her. 'Did you do it?' She nodded. 'No, I'm laughing because you've done something with his hair and, if I may say so, you've greatly improved matters.'

'Oh, do you think so? Thank you.'

He smiled at her. Maybe he wasn't so cold, after all.

Judy came back and handed him a glass. She looked at Tina's drawing. 'Wow, brilliant! Well done, Tina.'

Embarrassed again, this time for different reasons, Tina gulped the remainder of her champagne. She decided that it was a very nice drink indeed.

David said, 'So, Edward, how did the big bash go last night? Were any of my victims there?'

Judy explained, 'Some of Edward's clients were at a big event last night. Where was it, Edward?'

'Café Royale.'

'Really? Ooh, sounds fab!'

'Edward's a lawyer. He represents people in show business.'

Edward said to David, 'Lyndsey was there. She's a real sweetheart. I've tried to get her onto my books but no go, so far.'

Judy said, 'That's Lyndsey de Paul.'

Tina said, a bit giggly now, 'Was there dancing?'

Edward frowned, 'There was, as it happens.'

'I hope someone danced with her?'

He looked puzzled; Judy and David burst out laughing.

She said, 'You're a natural entertainer, Tina.'

Edward drained his glass, 'I'd better go and wake up Sleeping Beauty. Honestly, I get home from a busy day's work and there's nothing on the table. What do you think of that, Tina?'

Buoyed by the success of her last funny, Tina said, 'I think you should give her a detention. Or maybe a hundred lines?'

He looked at her closely. 'Do you know, I think this girl does have something.'

David said, 'I'm absolutely sure she does.'

Dutton pulled out a packet of St Moritz from his pocket and offered them round. David and Judy shook their heads; Tina took one. As the flame of

Edward Dutton's gold lighter neared her cigarette, she smelled his expensive cologne.

Chapter 80

Terry finished the heated-up pastie and washed up his plate and mug. He had his television sorted for the evening and, with Tina out, there wouldn't be the usual squabbling over what they should watch. Tonight, it was a repeat of *Whatever Happened to the Likely Lads* followed by *Pot Black*. Then, after the *News*, *Sportsnight* had the highlights of Arsenal versus QPR, a feature on Princess Anne's preparations for the Montreal Olympics, plus an interview with James Hunt. After that, it would be bedtime and another day out of the way.

He reflected on events — not your usual sort of day at all. Jean Richmond's kind face smiled at him again; he remembered her now. It had been a Christmas do. Diane had got pissed and was draping herself over one of the company's directors. Jean had helped Terry get her into the car — she'd been really kind that night. Maybe it would be nice to see her again. If he did, it would provide the opportunity to box her son's ears for being cheeky. For the hundredth time, he reached for his tobacco: when would the craving go away? He wondered how Tina was getting on without the fags. She'd never do it. As soon as someone offered her a cigarette, she'd capitulate. He went into the lounge and put on Coronation Street. The harsh, northern haranguing really got on his nerves, but at least it used up thirty minutes without requiring any effort on his part.

Before sitting down, he opened Tina's door. Yes, there he was. Knowing how loved the old boy was, Terry handled him gingerly. He collected his sewing kit on the way and took the giraffe with him into the lounge. In a soothing voice, Terry told it, 'You poor old chap; you're in a bad way. We might be different shapes but we're both more or less fucked.'

With Hilda Ogden's shrill voice in the background, Terry considered how best to keep the giraffe in one piece. He'd need to make some kind of sleeve for the entire length of its neck, both to support it and keep the stuffing from spilling out any further. He called out, 'Why do you stay with her, Stan? Don't let her walk all over you.' Then thought of Diane and said, 'Hang on to her, Stan. At least Hilda's not open for business.'

There was a knock at the door. Terry carefully put his patient down, turned off the television, and went to answer it. As he walked through the kitchen, he found more scraps of paper and pink petals. What had Tina been up to? Grasping the door latch, he briefly wondered would it be Kevin Abbott? If so, he would pick him up and throw him over the bannisters. Opening the door, he saw a stranger — solidly built, maybe early forties, friendly face.

'Yes?'

The man held out his hand, 'Terry Castleton?'

'Yes?'

'Hallo. I hope you don't mind me popping around. My name is Joe Marshall; I'm a friend of Tina's. She and I had a chat today. I don't know if you're expecting me? She said you might be.' Terry looked at him. How could this man be a friend of Tina's? He was shaking his head, when the man said, 'You're wondering how Tina and I are friends?'

Terry nodded. 'Ten out of ten.'

'Well, it's a long story. It all happened over the last couple of days. It came about as a result of Brian Abbott's death. She and I had a couple of conversations and we met up again today. Don't worry: I'm not here for any other reason than to have a chat about life. If you don't want to talk, that's fine by me. She's worried about you and thought that you might appreciate a chinwag.'

Terry was pissed off. Tina had tricked him into this. On the other hand, she'd said she was going to talk to this bloke, so it wasn't as if it was behind his back. The man — did he say Joe? — was waiting. He looked all right: respectable, intelligent, maybe ex-military. Not wanting to be discourteous, he stepped back.

'Do you want a cup of tea?'

The man smiled, 'Thank you, that's very civil of you.'

Terry led the way into the lounge. As they walked through the kitchen, Joe said, 'Someone's been doing a bit of gardening?'

'Yeah, I don't know what was going on here before I got back. You wouldn't believe I've already been over it with the Hoover. Take a seat; I'll put the kettle on. I'd offer you a beer, but Tina's banned me from the booze.'

'No, I'd prefer a tea.'

Terry filled the kettle and lit the stove.

'So, what's this about Brian Abbott's death?'

'Oh, it's all over now. I'm a friend of Gary Abbott and his mum, Jenny. When Brian died, I had a chat with them both and they mentioned Tina had been present when he'd had his accident. I bumped into her at the launderette, and we had a bit of a talk; then a phone call yesterday about something I checked out for her. And today, she popped by where I work and mentioned that she thought you could do with a friend. I'm sorry, Terry. I realise that it's an imposition and maybe the last thing you want is a friend. All I'm doing is doing what your daughter asked me — to come along and have a chat.'

Terry looked at the stranger; he did seem all right. He had picked up Giraffe and was inspecting the surgery.

'This boy has done some service…'

Terry wasn't sure why, but the other man's tender treatment of Giraffe was bringing tears to his eyes.

'Yeah, he's been around the block a few times. We gave him to Tina for one of her Christmas presents.'

The man looked up. 'It's funny how we attach so much meaning to inanimate objects, isn't it? I suppose they have all those associations. Childhood toys bring with them happier times. Innocence?'

Terry filled the tea pot. He thought about the treatment he'd had yesterday.

'I work at a school; I'm the caretaker. I see kids every day. Believe me, some of them aren't what I'd call innocent.'

The man nodded. He looked sad.

Terry liked the look of this bloke. He could see why Tina thought he was all right. He asked, 'What do you do?'

'I'm a caretaker, of sorts. I work at The Beeches: odd jobs, gardening, that kind of thing.'

Terry laughed. 'Look at us — high-flyers or what! Do you want sugar?'

'No, thanks.'

Terry spooned sugar into his own mug and poured the tea.

The man said, 'Tina said you were in the army?'

'Yep, Royal Artillery. I was in for twelve years.'

'I did my two years National Service. I quite enjoyed it once I got over the brutal treatment by the NCOs.'

Terry smiled, 'Well, I daresay you deserved it. What regiment were you in?'

'Signals.'

'Overseas?'

'Germany.'

Terry passed over the mug. He noticed Joe's hands were scratched. 'You've been pruning, or digging up brambles?'

'Well spotted. Yeah, I've been trying to clear a bit of waste ground. Are you a gardener?'

'I used to be. We had a nice garden before…'

The man put his mug down on the pine table in front of him. With calm deliberation, he reached into his pocket and withdrew a folded handkerchief. Apparently fascinated by it, he slowly opened it up, examined both sides, then wiped his nose with it. He put it back in his pocket.

Looking across at Terry he said, 'I'm going to have to come clean, Terry. Tina is worried about you; that's why she asked me to come over. The thing is, though, I need some help. I'm sort of here under false pretences. I was wondering if you might be able to help me, rather than the other way around.'

Terry reached for his tobacco: shit. He was still irritated by Tina talking to strangers about him. It wasn't that he didn't need help — far from it: he knew he was in a mess. Maybe it was just male pride, but the idea of a strange man knowing that he was a physical and emotional wreck wasn't doing anything for his self-esteem. But this man wasn't making him feel pathetic. In fact, he was revealing his own weakness.

Terry said, 'Well, Joe, I'm not exactly Marje Proops, but I'm happy to listen.'

The man smiled, 'Thanks, Terry.'

They drank their tea. Terry watched Joe. He didn't look like he was struggling with anything. In fact, he looked like he was in complete control of himself. Terry remembered his favourite officers. They had been like this: calm, authoritative.

Joe looked at him. 'I have a real problem with anger. I've got into some serious trouble with it in the past. I don't know if you've ever had the experience, but every now and then, total rage so overwhelms me, I go a bit mad. It scares me, Terry. I've done some bad things in the past and I never want to do anything like that again. I can't afford to. You're an army man. What do you do to keep your temper under control?'

'You're probably asking the wrong man. I've got something of a track record in that department.'

Joe looked up, interested. 'Really? How do you contain it?'

Terry thought about it. 'I just bottle it up. I'm scared to let it loose. It feels like a giant that I've got to keep behind bars.'

Joe nodded. 'Yeah, that's the same for me. I'm scared it's going to get the better of me, one day. This is how I feel sometimes, Terry: I start to dwell on what someone has done to me. It gets under my skin. Bit by bit, I find myself building up a picture of the other person: what they've done, what they look like. I picture them smiling as they dream up their next despicable act. I can't help myself: I start to imagine my revenge. All sorts of scenarios come into my head; all of them involve me getting the better of him, or her. The trouble is that the images get more and more violent. I have a feeling this is all very familiar to you, Terry. Do you ever feel like hurting someone? I bet you imagine getting your own back in a big way. When someone kicked you when you were down? When someone fucked with your life, with the people you love?' Terry gave an involuntary nod. Joe nodded back. 'I'm right, you're like me: you want them to hurt like you do.'

Kevin Abbott flashed into Terry's head. That little shit had it coming to him. First, the idea of him being with Tina was unbearable. Then, the bastard had had the brass neck to throw a punch at him, out of the blue! Since then, Terry had imagined getting hold of him, walking to the stairwell and hurling him over the rails. What made the scene really satisfying was the pathetic cry of 'No, no! Please, not that! Please, Mr Castleton — No, no!' before Terry loosened his grip. Then, the screaming wail of terror cut off by a single, heavy splat.

Joe was saying, '... but the trouble with revenge is that it always brings consequences. The gratification of the moment is gone, and the real shit starts to kick in — that terrible regret and the constant 'why was I so stupid?' It's never worth it. I know the pleasure of getting my own back isn't going to last. The people I love are going to have to pay for it. They'll look at me with their eyes wide and they'll say: why did you do that to me? It won't matter that I was wound up, that I was driven to it. The fact remains: I lost control, and my life and theirs is ruined. I can't allow that to happen: they're too important to me! I'm going to have to prove myself stronger and bigger — I am stronger and bigger! I'm going to discover that there is a huge, deep reservoir of extra strength in me that I didn't know was there. When the time comes, it's there and I know I can rely on it. I don't know when that time will come, but it's there and I can find it when I need it. It will be like a switch that I can click on. It will shine a bright, clear light on the situation — it will help me see clearly. The darkness will clear, and the fog will lift. That swirling, red mist has gone. I've realised, in time, that the right thing to do is stay strong and keep control. Before I flicked that switch, I was going to punch, stab, shoot, break, maim, smash, snap, wreck, ruin, devastate. I was going to enjoy destroying! Now when I switch on the light, I realise that I would only have destroyed myself and the people who love me. Instead, I shall take control. That light will be there for me. Terry, you have helped me find it. You did that, Terry. You showed me the light and how to use it. I know I can switch the light on, and you can, too. The relief of knowing that I'm on top of things is amazing! I'm on top of the situation, no matter what comes my way. I feel like I've grown bigger, stronger. I'm more powerful in every way — the power is the ability to control what happens. I'm in control; from now on, I'm in control. You're in control, Terry — you have it, too.'

Terry opened his eyes.

Joe picked up Giraffe and handed it to Terry. 'Here you are. You've sorted me out. Can you help your next patient, too?'

Terry took it. 'Yeah, I think so. I'm going to fashion some kind of sleeve to wrap around the entire length of his neck and stitch it into his body. He won't feel a thing.'

Joe nodded. 'I think you're very resourceful. You've got those practical skills that are so useful. The way you can sort out a problem, just like that.' Joe clicked his fingers. 'Now, I'd better go. I'm so sorry. I was supposed to be a listening ear and I've done all the talking.' He got up. 'I've taken up your time. I'm sorry. Don't tell Tina I talked about myself, will you?'

Terry watched him walk to the door of the lounge. For some reason, he was finding it difficult to get up. All he wanted to do right now was nod off.

He heard himself say, 'Thanks for popping around. I'll see you again.'

Joe paused at the door, 'It's getting a bit murky. Shall I put the light on?'

Terry looked up; the light had begun to dim. 'Thanks, yeah. Good idea. Ah, that's better: I can actually see the patient now.'

Joe had reached the front door.

He called, 'I hope we do meet again; I've really enjoyed our chat. Take care.'

Chapter 81

'Mum, I'm going to have a word with Kev. I'll be back in a minute. Whatever you do, don't talk to that Flanagan: he's trouble.'

Gary ran upstairs. He pushed open the door into their bedroom. Kev was lying on his back, his hands over his face.

He said, 'What do you want?'

Gary sat on his own bed. He needed to retrieve Auntie Maureen's letter before Flanagan started asking awkward questions.

He said, 'It's fucking mental down there. I had to get away from it.'

'Yeah, me too.'

Until the last few weeks, Gary had looked up to his big brother Kevin. He considered him now: slighter, shorter, thicker. Gary felt sorry for him. He saw tears seeping out from under Kev's fingers.

'You all right?'

'No.'

'What's up?'

'Everything. Every fucking thing is shit.' Gary didn't know what to say. Kev dragged a sleeve across his eyes. 'I went to see Tina today. I put in a load of effort to make things right. I went into *Martins* and bought a nice card — well, nicked a nice one, anyway. I nipped into the graveyard and picked up some flowers. I even wrote lovey-dovey stuff in the card. Guess what? She only had a fucking bloke in there with her.'

'No! I don't believe it.'

'Fucking did. I was there, saying how much I loved her and that I'd do anything for her. Then, out of the blue, the bathroom door opens, and a geezer comes out, like he owned the place! He didn't have a shirt on. Jeez, they'd obviously just been fucking. Tina goes all furious, the way she always does. I try to reason with her. I even thought that maybe I was jumping to conclusions, but she goes off on one and before I know it, she's slashing at me with a massive carving-knife. I tell you something: that girl is a total nutter. Anyway, even the bloke realised he'd picked a loony. I get to the door before she can stick this great, fucking machete into my ribs, and the cunt is there before me, yelling to get out of his way. We leg it down the stairs, and she's at the top, screaming at us. I'm telling you — that girl is mental.'

Gary didn't believe his brother. It was probable that Tina had told him to fuck off, but there was no way she'd been with another bloke. At least, he didn't think so.

He asked, 'Who was it? Do you know?'

'No, he looked like a wanker, with a stupid, fucking, Kevin Keegan bubble perm.'

'What?'

'Yeah, I know: what a tosser.'

Gary's head was reeling. What was she doing with the fucking Filth?

'And, he really didn't have his shirt on?'

'Well, I can't quite remember. Does it matter?'

Gary shut up. Tina wasn't his girlfriend. He liked her, but she obviously wasn't interested in him. He had no right to be upset. But Kevin Keegan! That really was unbelievable. It must have been him: Kev couldn't have made that up. His brother was crying openly, now: hideous, racking sobs. Gary felt like crying, too. Everything was such a mess.

Kev wailed, 'I want my dad back. I miss my dad. Oh, Dad, why did you have to leave now?' Through snuffling tears, he choked, 'Bloody hell, Dad! Why did you have to leave me right now, when I needed you? Fuck me! Fuck you. Fuck you, you selfish fucking pig! The one time I needed you, you decide to fucking die.'

Gary was missing his dad, too. He was pretty sure that any advice given to Kev would be the same as the wise, fatherly words offered to Del when Sally Morris had dumped him. 'Don't worry, Derek, you'll slip another bint a length before you die.' But despite everything, Gary knew that their father would have made them feel better, by being his belligerent, 'fuck 'em all' self. There was a soft knock on their door.

Their Mum called, 'It's only me.' Kev rolled off his bed and got up.

'I'm going out. I might stay at Dean's house tonight. Anything to be away from here.' He opened the door and pushed past Jenny, 'See you, Mum. I'll be at Dean's.'

Jenny came in and handed Gary a mug. She sat down on Kev's bed and sipped from the other one. They heard Kev's heavy feet go downstairs, two treads at a time.

'How did you know it wasn't Grandad under the greenhouse?' She sipped again, and again. 'Mum?'

'Because.'

'Coz what?'

'Because I remember Dad burying it.'

'What? But — where? I mean — who? What's in the box?'

'When Grandad turned up, we knew he was in some sort of trouble, but he didn't say what. He was really cagey; we could tell he was scared of something, or someone. Anyway, he had two cases with him; one he kept in his room and the other he put in the shed and told Dad to put a lock on the door. When he went missing, Dad looked in the case and said that whatever happened we must never talk about it. That night, Dad took it and hid it somewhere — I honestly don't know where. Then, when we went to Clacton, he built the greenhouse and buried the case underneath it. I don't know why he thought a greenhouse was a good idea, but he did. I suppose he might have wanted to try growing tomatoes. Mr Hale across the road always used to grow them, so that's where Dad must have got the idea. Anyway, that's what happened.'

His mum was all hunched up, like a little bird. What a terrible life she'd had with the fucking Abbotts.

He said, his voice quiet, 'You didn't think of telling the police?'

'I would have done, and I wished I had. But you know your dad: his mind was made up.'

'But, Mum, a minute ago you looked so innocent. I believed you. How did you manage to fake it so — I dunno — believably?'

'I'm not sure. I don't like lying. I wish I didn't have to but, Gary, I really do not know what's in the case, so I'm not really lying, am I?'

'Why didn't you tell Kev?'

'He's a sensitive boy. I'd rather he didn't know anything that would upset him. Him and his dad were always close.'

'And do you really not know anything about Grandad? I mean, was he in trouble with someone? Or more than one? Was he mixed up with gangs, the Mafia — I dunno — the IRA?'

She shrugged. 'I don't know. To be honest, I was so scared of him. I wanted everything to be back to normal. Well, normal for us, anyway.'

They heard a diesel vehicle pull up outside. Gary stood and looked out: another police van had arrived, its back door open. From the side of the house, two coppers were carrying out the box, one at either end. There was a tarpaulin draped over it. It wasn't as big as he was expecting. Somehow, he had imagined it would be like a coffin but he realised that was because of all the talk of Grandad being buried down there. His mum must be right: it was more the size and shape of a suitcase. Gary sat down opposite his mum. He looked at her intently. She looked back without blinking.

'Mum, I think I'm only beginning to get to know you. I thought — well — I don't know; I thought you were a bit... Put it this way: I thought I would have to look after you but, the last few days, I realise you're — amazing.'

She put her finger to her lips. 'Listen, Gary, I trust you to keep as strong and silent as you can. We'll look after each other.'

Dickie called up the stairs, 'Mrs Abbott?'

She said, 'I'd better go down. We're going to have to sit and answer their questions all over again. I'm sorry, Gary. I wish you didn't have to go through all of this.'

'Me? I don't care. I'm sorry for you, Mum. Don't worry about me. I'm a professional journalist!'

'Really? Did it go well today?'

Gary smiled. 'I've only written my first story. It's going to be in tomorrow's edition.' Gary saw his mother's face light up: she looked like a Hollywood film star.

'Well done, Gary. Oh, my! You're going to make it. I knew it.'

She touched her hair into shape, took his empty mug and went back downstairs. Gary quickly lifted his mattress and pulled out the letter. What should he do with it? He read it quickly.

Brian

This is my last letter to you.

Thank you for your recent help. It's worked out nicely, everything's under control.

Now that Dad and Ray have gone, I can see no need for us to have further contact. We've got nothing in common. You can live your life how you want. Your way isn't my way and I want to get away from all the horrible memories.

I send best wishes to Jenny and the boys and hope that you all do OK.

Remember, this is my final word. I'm sure you understand.

Maureen

He tore it into tiny pieces, went quickly to the bog and flushed them away. He knew what he had to do.

Chapter 82

Tina was having a ball. This was the kind of life she wanted: champagne, intelligent, adult company, glamour. She tilted her head and knocked back the last of her champagne. Even the glasses felt sophisticated — long, smooth and elegant. She had slipped her sandals off; the clipped lawn was cool and comforting to her lacerated feet. Edward Dutton's St Moritz made her feel like a film star, with the gold band and menthol taste: she decided she'd make them her first choice from now on.

Just then, bright light turned the lawn, wrought iron furniture and sparkling glasses into a scene from a film.

'Gosh, how did they know when to come on?'

David said, his voice grave, 'I've spent years training them to come on when dusk falls; this is the first time they've done it. You must be a good influence on them.'

Tina knew he was teasing her, but said, anyway, 'Oh, I'm not surprised. I do tend to bring a bit of electricity to a party.' The Gainsboroughs laughed.

Edward said, 'You've certainly made an impact this evening, Tina. I have a hunch you're going to go a long way. Where would you like to be in, say, five years?'

'Oh, sitting on a beautiful boat with my friends David and Judy.' The white boat was shimmering at the bottom of the lawn. 'Maybe on their boat?'

David smiled sadly, 'I'm sorry to disappoint you, dear Tina. It's not our boat. It belongs to Rex and Miranda, next door. Anyway, I'm scared of water. Would you join us on Concord? I'm determined to get a flight on that beautiful bird before the end of the year.'

Judy said, 'I'm sorry to break up the party, but we've got to start packing; we're off early tomorrow. Come on, David — get your arse in gear. You two stay here if you like.'

Edward picked up the bottle and shook it. 'We'll guzzle down your fizz if you don't mind?' Without waiting for an answer, he filled Tina's glass, then his own.

David looked sadly at the bottle. 'Well, bloomin' cheek! Still, I suppose I've helped myself to enough of yours over the years. Tina, darling girl, will you excuse me?' She was about to get up, but he put his hand on her shoulder. 'Don't get up, sweetie. It's been lovely meeting you. I'll call you when I get back. I'm sure we can sort out some work for you. That is, if we fit into your five-year plan?'

'Oh, of course! How lovely. Thank you ever so much. Oh, my dad is going to be so proud of me. Thank you.'

She did get up, and hugged him with all her strength. Judy came over and kissed Tina on both cheeks. Not sure how to respond to this, Tina embraced the older woman.

Edward said, 'I hope I get the same treatment when it's my turn.' She looked at him. He was only half-smiling. 'Come on, Tina. Let's enjoy our brief time together.'

She sat down and took the proffered cigarette. Again, his expensive fragrance was in her face.

'So, you're going to be a hair stylist?'

'I'd love that. I've always wanted to work in the beauty business.'

'I could introduce you to some beautiful people. You say the word, and I'd be happy to set something up. Now — er, let me see, um… What about Jane Seymour, or Olivia Newton John? Or maybe you'd like to meet some chaps? Do you know Dennis Waterman, or — I know: how about some musicians? Er, I'm sorting out contracts with Rod Stewart and Elton John at the minute.'

Tina looked into his eyes. Something was making her feel a bit uncertain. Why was he trying to impress her? Geraldine Dutton popped into her head.

Tina smiled, 'All those people are interesting, I'm sure but, to be honest, I think your wife is the nicest person I know. She's very beautiful, too. When I was in her class, I wanted to grow up and look like her. She was the prettiest woman in the world — well, apart from my mum.'

Edward sat back. He lifted his glass to his lips and sipped. Then, he took a drag of his cigarette and blew a long plume of smoke towards her.

'You, young lady, are a cool cucumber. I wonder where you'll be in five years. I hope I'm around to find out.'

'Don't hold your breath. I'm ordinary really. I'm full of bull — ahem — big talk, but really I'm just a girl with big ideas and nothing to back them up.'

He leaned towards her, his eyes on hers. 'Not just big ideas, my dear. If you want my opinion, Tina, you've got plenty; more than enough.' He looked at his watch. 'I'd better go and wake up my wife. May I give you a lift home? I assume you're local?'

The very idea of him seeing where she lived made her shudder: what would he think of her?

'Ah, you're terribly kind. Actually, I'm going on to meet a couple of friends near here. It's only a short walk to their house.'

'Good, I'll come with you. There's some awful people living around here, you know. The Gainsboroughs are a dodgy lot, and as for the Duttons!'

She laughed, 'No, I'm fine. Thanks for offering. I'll quickly say goodbye to David and Judy and then I'll fly.'

She got up, tottered slightly, grabbed the garden table, then righted herself. She glanced at Edward. He was eyeing her up, a knowing smile on his face.

'Are you sure I can't offer you my arm?'

Slipping on her sandals, she shook her head. 'No, thank you. I'm ready to go.'

He stood and walked beside her towards the open door into the house. Tina didn't feel quite so elegant; in fact, all her poise had left her. This man was making her edgy.

She called, 'Thank you, David. Judy, thank you for everything.'

A high-pitched voice came from a long way off, 'Don't rush off, angel; I'd like to give you something.' Ten seconds later, David appeared; he was puffing. 'Ah, here's a little giftie from me, until we meet next time.' He was holding out a book. Tina took it — I Love Your Hair by David Gainsborough.

'Wow, thank you very much.'

'Open it.'

She opened the front cover and saw: 'For Tina, crackling electricity.'

'Oh, how lovely. That's the nicest present I've ever had.' She flung her arms around him.

David's squeaking voice could hardly be heard, 'Stop it! You're strangling me!'

She let go. 'Sorry, I think I might be a little tiddly!' Although pink-cheeked and breathless, David was beaming.

Judy appeared. 'It's been lovely meeting you, Tina. Looks like we're definitely going to see you again next month.'

Edward said, 'Bye, Jude, I'll see you the moment you get back. Have a lovely time.'

Tina wobbled down the drive. As she reached the road, Edward caught her up.

'Goodnight, Tina. I wonder if I might take a liberty?' She peered at him in the gathering gloom; his look was unreadable.

'Er... um, maybe?'

Before she knew what was happening, he had taken her hand and brought it to his lips. She felt a dry kiss on her fingers.

'Thank you, Tina. I shall treasure this moment for a long, long time.'

Flustered she stepped back. 'Sorry, I must go now. My Da — my friends will be wondering.'

He smiled — teeth but not eyes. 'Goodnight, my fair lady.'

She turned and hurried away.

Chapter 83

Only vaguely awake, Geraldine wiped saliva from her lips. She snuggled deeper into bed and let the soothing darkness cloak her again.

'I think it's time you woke up.'

She shrieked. Struggling to a sitting position, she put a hand on her chest. 'Edward, you shocked me.'

He was sitting in the cane chair by the wardrobe, his legs and arms crossed.

'Well, I'm sorry about that.'

'What time is it?'

He shot back his cuff and looked at the gold watch. 'Eight thirty.'

'What! I'm — well, goodness! Where on earth has the time gone? Honestly, I only dropped off for a few minutes. Well, that's what I meant to do. How long have you been home?'

Edward looked at his watch again. 'An hour or so?'

Geraldine was beginning to wake up properly. At least the awful, thick headache had gone.

'I'm so sorry, Edward. You must be starving. What would you like to eat?' She looked at him; was he furious with her? He didn't move. There was something going on. 'What's wrong?'

'Nothing.'

'Come on, Edward. You're thinking something. I can tell.'

He stared at her. She didn't like the look on his face: a hard expression. It frightened her. She pushed back the covers to get up.

'Stay there; don't move. I am going to ask you a question. Look at me.'

'Edward, you're scaring me. What's this all about?'

He lit a cigarette. Whatever was wrong, she wasn't going to let him lord it over her. She started to get up.

'I said, stay there. Geraldine, you're not going anywhere until you answer my questions.'

Angry now, she snapped, 'Well, ask your questions, then. What is wrong with you?'

He got up and opened the window. This was not like him, not at all. His face was white, eyes hard. Flicking the cigarette out of the window, he asked, 'Who was here last night?'

'No one. I was on my own.' He looked into her eyes. Stammering, she said, 'I had a night on my own. Honestly, I don't know what's eating you, Edward.'

'What's eating me, my sweet, innocent, little wife, is the knowledge that as soon as I'm away for one night, you get up to all sorts. I am not a stupid man, Gerry. At least, I didn't think I was. I trusted you to behave like a decent, faithful wife and I now realise that I've been mistaken. How long have you been at it? Every afternoon? Do you enjoy a little bit of 'how's your father' whenever you get the chance? No wonder you don't want to have sex with me anymore. God, how naïve can I be? My dear wife is having rumpy-pumpy with someone else and it didn't even occur to me. Maybe it's not with someone else; maybe it's with lots of men. Is that it? Maybe you're selling yourself and making a few quid on the side? Mind you, I don't think you'd make much money, not the way you look. Still, perhaps there's some ugly bastards out there who aren't choosy.'

'Edward, what an awful thing to say! What is wrong with you?'

He mimicked her, 'Edward!' Then in almost a whisper, 'Don't play the innocent, Gerry.' He was moving erratically, jabbing his finger at her with every word. His face had gone red, eyes half-closed. He was spitting. 'I have spent all these years trusting you. You're supposed to be a decent human being. You're a pillar of the community. Children grow up believing everything you say. I've just met one of your ex-pupils. She said she wanted to be like you when she grew up. I hope to God she doesn't turn out like you — a disloyal, lazy, drunken whore.'

'Edward! Stop it. What's wrong with you?'

He bent down in front of her, his face twisted in fury. 'What's wrong with me? What's wrong with me? You. You! What's wrong with you?'

She got out of bed and put her arms around him.

'Please stop, Edward. I don't know what's wrong, but please stop being like this. There's obviously been some sort of misunderstanding. Come on, sit down. Tell me what's happened.'

He pushed her back on to the bed. 'Don't touch me. Keep away from me.'

She felt tears prick her eyes. What was this all about? She wanted to get really angry with him, but his own violent fury was stopping her. Edward was a detached, clinical man. He never lost his temper. It was as if an imposter had turned up in her room. Acutely conscious of her nakedness, she got up and pulled on her dressing gown.

'Thank God! At least I don't have to look at that!'

Unsure that she'd be able to keep upright, she sat down on the edge of the bed.

'Edward, tell me what you think has happened. I don't know what you're talking about.'

He returned to the chair, his breathing back under control.

His voice was now the usual cold drawl. 'You had a man here last night. I know you did. There are two glasses downstairs. You were drinking port with him. You came up here with him. You presumably had sex in our bed together. Why are you pretending you don't know what I'm talking about?'

At last she understood. 'Oh, Edward, is that all? Gosh, I was really worried for a minute. I did have a drink last night. I had too much. I had the Riesling. I had a glass of port.' For some reason she didn't want to mention Terry coming around. Why bring him into it? It would only make things more complicated. 'Then, I was going to go to bed and thought one more glass wouldn't matter, so I poured another one. That's it. Why on earth would you think that two empty port glasses should mean all that other stuff. Honestly, dear, please don't get so upset. I would never be unfaithful.' As soon as she said the word, Daniel Jenkinson's pert buttocks, encased in his nylon flares, flashed into her head, only to be replaced by Terry Castleton's big strong hands. She blushed. She looked at Edward; there was a shocking, knowing smile on his face.

'You see, Gerry, I knew you were lying. And you've proved it again.'

What was going on? All that had happened was that Terry helped her up off the floor and into bed. Surely they hadn't done anything more than that? He hadn't taken advantage of her: no, she remembered him being such a gentleman. But — was it conceivable that when she had fallen asleep he had…? No, that was ridiculous! Anyway, how would Edward know if he had? Was there something on the sheets, some evidence? No, that wasn't possible. The bedclothes had been covering her.

He said, his voice awful, insinuating, 'Gerry, you're so transparent. I can see your mind spinning through what you did last night. You're trying to work out what I can see, or maybe what I can deduce. I'm a lawyer. I know how guilty people think.'

He was right: she had been working out all the possible ramifications, but of what? She wasn't guilty of anything; she was sure of that. Her indignation rose to the surface.

'Edward, you are a contract lawyer. You've never done litigation. As for my guilt — well, I am not a lawyer but two empty glasses of port is not what I'd call "beyond reasonable doubt" or even "on the balance of probability".'

'Oh, aren't you clever? Well, what about this?'

He put his hand in his pocket and drew something out. Geraldine blinked: what was it?

'What? What about it? It's just a button.'

'It's a button from a jacket. It's not a button from any of my jackets. Why, my dear, faithful wife, would a button from a man's jacket be on my bed?'

Chapter 84

'Well, goodnight, Jenny. I'm so sorry we've had to take up your time. What an awful mess we've made of your garden, too. Please forgive me. I'm afraid we shall have to come around tomorrow as soon as it's light and carry on our investigations. You do understand, don't you?'

Gary marvelled at Flanagan's manners: he was so dignified and respectful. Why were the other coppers so scared of him? Gary made a note to adopt a similar manner in the future; it seemed to give a bloke real authority. When Gary's mum had insisted she knew nothing about the box, the building of the greenhouse, nor anything about Grandad going missing, Dickie had snorted, 'Oh, jeez, come off it!' But Flanagan had turned to his junior colleague and said, 'Detective Sergeant Nott, please try and remain civil in front of Mrs Abbott.' Gary had sniggered out loud. Dickie had looked like he could stick a knife into him.

Now they were gone. Kev hadn't come back. Derek was nowhere to be seen.

Gary said, 'Cor, I'm starving. Shall I go and get some fish and chips?'

'Good idea. Hang on, I'll get my purse.'

'No, Mum, they're on me. We need to celebrate my first day at work.'

'Oh yeah, I want to hear all about it. Much better to talk about positive things; not all this horrible stuff.'

As Gary walked down to the High Street, he thought back over the day. Too much had happened for him to remember, never mind make sense of it all. He was looking forward to another day at work — especially if it was with Karen Mitchum. Karen had been a good laugh. Yeah, she was really pretty, but it was her spiky cleverness that he liked as much. If today's visit to the school was anything to go by, then working alongside her would be bloody brilliant.

As usual, Tina too wasn't far from his thoughts. Had she really had that creep Kevin Keegan in her flat? It must have been him. Kev didn't know him from Adam. Gary thought back to the disgusting state of her bedroom. His was a mess, but hers was like a pigsty. Maybe she was the kind of girl who didn't care who she screwed or in what kind of shit she did it. He was surprised though: he'd thought she was a decent girl, really. Her dad certainly was a respectable bloke. Ex-army and all that.

Gary had enjoyed his trip to see Auntie Maureen this morning. Tina had been great company — well, most of the time. Jeez, did she have a temper on her! Thinking about his aunt now, he couldn't quite see how she could be so different to his dad. After all, they had the same parents and grew up together, but there was no doubting the fact that she was a lovely lady. He'd really quite like to get to know her better. Also, he needed to ask her about the letter.

As he neared the chip shop, the door to the Indian opened and the smell of curry rushed out. Since the time they'd stopped the Indian bloke being beaten up, Gary had thought that maybe he should have a go at eating a curry. He went in. The smell of the place was overwhelming; it was weird and nice at the same time. There was odd music in the background: crazy instruments and not much tune. A couple of tables were taken by older people.

'Hello again. How are you?' It was the same kid; was his name Haroon or Sadiq? Gary couldn't remember, it had all been a blur.

'Wotcha. Yeah, I'm fine. You?'

'Very well. I'm really pleased to see you. How are your friends?'

Gary thought back to the evening. It had been Anthony that had saved the day with his quick thinking. Katy and Susan Walker had been there, and Frank. 'They're all fine — well, yeah. Fine, ta.'

'What would you like?'

'Um, do you do takeaway food?'

'Yes, sir. Here is our menu.'

'Ta. Listen, sorry, remind me of your name again. We got it all a bit arse-over-tit the other day.'

'It is Haroon.'

'Triffic.'

Looking at the menu, Gary realised his mistake. Somehow, he had imagined there would be ordinary food but with spicy gravy on it. In vain, he scanned the unfamiliar words for anything that looked halfway recognisable.

Haroon said, 'May I make a recommendation?'

'Good idea. I can't decide.'

'How about some tandoori chicken, and perhaps an onion bhaji? Would you like some rice? Pilau, perhaps? I recommend a little sag, too? Do you like papadums? What about some naan bread?'

Gary didn't know what the fuck he was on about, but keen to get out without making an arse of himself, he said, 'Yep, yep, yep — they're all my favourites. Can I have enough for two people please?'

'Certainly, sir. Come through and take a seat. Please will you have a glass of lager while you wait?'

'Er, Indian lager? Do you make — I mean, is it like proper lager?'

'Oh, yes, very proper.'

Gary followed the young waiter through some swing doors into a smaller, private-looking dining room. There was one central table with a dozen or so chairs around it. He sat down and waited for his drink to arrive. A minute later, his new friend brought him a tall glass, full of what looked like proper lager.

'Thank you. Very nice.' He took a tentative sip. It tasted like ordinary lager. He gulped down the top half.

'Sir, may I ask you a question?'

'Sure — fire away.'

New voices arrived in the restaurant. Haroon looked exasperated, 'Excuse me, sir, I must look after our customers.'

Gary swigged from his glass. 'Don't worry, I'm not going anywhere.'

Through the swing doors, he heard Haroon welcoming in the new customers, then the reply from one of them. 'At the back, out the way of people. Yeah, over there, in the far corner.'

Gary knew that voice. Ten seconds later, Dickie's voice was only feet away.

'Ta very much. Now, I'm gasping for a pint. Get us two lagers.'

'Certainly, sir. Right away.'

The waiter came in through the swing doors; Gary leaned back out of sight. He could hear cigarettes being lit. Dickie carried on, his voice a hoarse whisper.

'Fucking Flanagan — he's getting on my tits.'

'What's been going on?'

'You toe-rag, Armstrong. If you hadn't got slaughtered last night, you'd have been in the thick of a massive coup today. You owe me a big favour, by the way. When I found you this morning, you looked like you'd been buried under a greenhouse for thirteen years!'

'Yeah, well, thanks for getting me out of trouble. What happened then?'

Gary wondered if he ought to let them know he was there. They'd realise as soon as his food came, but maybe it was worth hearing a bit more?

'So, Flanagan spends all day ringing up the Abbott's neighbours, all the local greenhouse suppliers, even a load of local builders. He wouldn't let me help him with it. Honestly, he was like a man possessed. Then, he gets a warrant to dig up the garden — he's convinced himself that old man Abbott is under their greenhouse. So we all go down there — Flanagan, me, Billy Shotton, Dan Willcox, Danny Jeavons, Steve Cox, old Uncle Tom Cobbly an' all. Flanagan tells us to raze the greenhouse and dig up the concrete foundations. I tell you what, that greenhouse was full of the shittiest pile of God knows what; it took us hours to empty it. So, we pull it down and then the hard work started. The whole time, Flanagan sits there like fucking Buddha.'

'Were the Abbotts there?'

'Yeah, the Mrs; then that wanker Gary. Then his brother turns up: he's an even bigger wanker.'

Gary wished Kev could hear this!

'Well, go on. Was the old man underneath it?'

Dickie laughed wheezily. 'Not even close! No, there's a steel box down there.'

'What's in it?'

'A suitcase.'

'Come on! What's in that?'

Gary had to lean towards their whispers.

Dickie said, 'Two handguns, a fuck-off big knife, an old set of clothes, boots, maps, drawings, train timetables, notes and a load of photographs.'

'So — no body, then, after all that?'

'Yeah. Flanagan was fizzing like a fucking firework. He was convinced it was going to be old man Abbott. Anyway, he calms down when he realises what it all is!'

'What is it?'

Gary was tempted to edge closer and even poke his head out. It was too risky. He could hear Dickie wheezing his smoker's laugh, then Keegan say, 'Come on! I can't stand the suspense.'

Dickie was coughing now. Finally he got his breath back, 'God, I need a pint. Where is fucking Sinbad? Well, it's big, Chris; it's fucking huge.'

'You bastard, you're just winding me up.'

Dickie's whisper almost disappeared. Gary got up and stuck his ear next to the hinge of the swing door. The kitchen door opened, and the waiter came through the private room with two full glasses. He grinned. Gary sat back and puffed out his cheeks. This was unbelievable.

Keegan said, his voice back to normal levels, 'Thanks. Jeez, I need this. I got seriously hammered last night.'

Gary wanted to call over, 'What were you doing in Tina's flat?'

Dickie did it for him, 'You're looking a bit better; where did you hide out today?'

'Oh, I slept it off at my girlfriend's place.'

'Which one?'

'The one I was with last night.'

'I thought you were with the Castleton girl?'

'Er — well, yeah, I was to start with; then I called up Julie.'

'Did you get anything out of her?'

'Who?'

'Tina fucking Castleton! Who do you think?'

'Oh, I thought you meant Julie.' He sniggered, 'I got plenty out of her.'

'You bullshitter. Never mind her. What about Tina?'

'Yeah. Sorry. Not really. I got her pissed — you know, like we planned — but she didn't know anything about old Abbott disappearing. I asked her, without her realising, about Brian Abbott and what had happened. To be honest, I put her through a full-scale interrogation. She didn't even notice what I was doing, for God's sake: honestly! No-go, though. Even with a load of Bacardi down her neck, she kept on saying the same story. I think they probably are telling the truth.'

Gary heard Dickie snort again. 'Chris, you're a bullshitter. She's a bullshitter. They all are. We've had trouble with that doctor before. You know they did Abbott in; I know they did him in. Why can't a trained doctor prove it for us? Still, it doesn't matter now. Okay, what happened then?'

'Well, I drove her home, then went on to Julie's.'

'So, what happened?'

'I'm sorry, boss. I got wrecked, spent the night with her, then drove straight to work from her place. I was there early and thought I'd have twenty minutes kip. Put it this way, I didn't get much last night, know what I mean? Anyway, next thing I know you're hammering on the window and that was that. Just as well it was you. Imagine if it had been Flanagan!'

'Yeah, the end of your short-lived career. Ah, at last! Here comes Ali Baba.'

Gary listened to them ordering their food. That Keegan was a solid gold knob. Maybe he hadn't been with Tina today... It was none of his business, but he wanted to look after her. She was part of his team now.

The waiter came back through the swing doors and smiled again, 'Your food will be ready in a second. Wait one minute, please.'

His voice back to a whisper, Dickie said, 'Flanagan's in a huge paddy; the case is going to be—'

'Here you are, sir, with the compliments of the Golden Bengal.'

Gary looked up: Haroon was standing with a paper bag, smiling at him. Gary knocked back the pint and stood up.

Haroon gave him an envelope. 'Will you be kind and give this to your pretty friend for me?'

Gary had to think for a minute: somehow he had managed to gather quite a few pretty friends. 'Er... um — Oh, do you mean Katy Walker?'

'Yes, do you mind?'

'Course not. Consider it done.'

He took the bag, winked at Haroon and pushed through the swing doors. Looking across at Dickie and Keegan, he gave them a cheerful wave.

'Evening, lads! Enjoy your meal.'

Their heads swivelled in his direction, their mouths agape.

He turned back to his new friend, 'How much?'

'Nothing, sir. It's our treat to you. You are always welcome here and you are always our special guest.'

'Oh, ta very much. Well, I look forward to the next one.'

As he left, Gary smiled broadly at the grim-faced policemen.

Chapter 85

Geraldine stared at Edward. He looked back at her, his eyes unblinking. She wasn't sure what a snake looked like when it was about to eat its prey but that was the image that came into her head now.

The truth was so simple and ordinary: why hadn't she told him? A few seconds ago, she'd thought it easier to say nothing, to avoid all the embarrassment of the buttons in the shed, her awful state last night, Terry helping her into bed. Although that was all hideous, it was nothing compared with the mess she'd got herself into. If she told him the truth now, he'd assume she was making it up to avoid the more obvious explanation. What should she say? Her temper flared: why should she have to justify herself? This was ridiculous. She opened her mouth to protest then, seeing his cold smile, she closed it again.

'Yes, Gerry? I can see you working out a suitable lie. I'm all ears: let's hear it.'

She felt tears seep from her eyes. This was so unfair. Nothing had happened. Everyone had behaved impeccably. Yet, because of Edward's horrid mind, she was having to face up to this… kangaroo court.

'This is so unkind of you, Edward. I've done nothing wrong but you're treating me like a dirty criminal.'

'I never said you were a dirty criminal. All I want to know is why you were drinking with a man when I'm out of the way, and — rather more seriously — why his jacket button is on our bed? Surely it's reasonable to expect an honest explanation? That's not unfair of me, is it?'

She sniffed back her tears. As usual, Edward's cold logic made her feel like a naughty child.

'No, it isn't. But — after all these years — why don't you trust me? I've told you that there's nothing to tell you; why don't you believe me? I'm your wife, Edward. We've been married for a long time. Why would you think me capable of doing anything that wasn't entirely appropriate?'

The hardness in his face was horrible. She knew him to be a brilliant negotiator, but she'd never seen him properly in action — certainly never with her on the other side of the deal, the wrong side.

'Edward?'

'Gerry?'

'Please don't be nasty to me. I wasn't doing anything bad.'

He held out the button. 'All you need to do is tell me who this belongs to.'

Swallowing hard, she said in a whisper, 'The school caretaker.'

'What!'

'Yes, Terry. The caretaker came round last night.'

Edward got up and went to the window; he stared out. She could see his face in profile: clenched jaw jutting, eye slitted.

He turned back to her, 'I don't believe you, try again.'

'It's true. I don't know why I didn't tell you straight up. I was embarrassed, Edward. Please believe me. It's all so shameful. I was in his shed yesterday afternoon—'

He held up his hands, 'Stop! I don't want to hear about you having it off with the school caretaker in his shed. Gerry, you're forty-three, not a teenager. What on earth...? How old is this caretaker? Don't tell me. I don't want to know. I can't believe this: my wife is having sex in a shed with a school caretaker. How do you expect me to react?'

'Listen to me, Edward. We were not having it off. He collapsed in his shed. I tried to help him. He couldn't get up. I tried to pull him up. He's rather large and the effort made my buttons all pop off. When he finally got up, he lent me his jacket to save my blushes. Then he said I could wear it home. I mean, I couldn't be seen in public with my — Well, I wasn't properly dressed. I didn't realise, and he didn't say, but his wallet was in it and he needed it to get some petrol. So he came around here and got it. When he arrived, I was already drunk. I poured him a drink but he didn't want it, so I drank it. I had hung his jacket up here, so I came up to get it; he stayed downstairs. When I was up here, I was so drunk I fell over and got wedged into the corner. Down there. He must have heard a commotion, so he came up and — Well, not to put too fine a point on it, he helped me into bed. The button must have been torn off when he helped pull me up. Nothing else happened, honestly. That's all.'

Geraldine heard her pleading voice echo around the room. She looked into his face: the snake's eyes were still on her.

'Please believe me, Edward.' Slowly, she began to relax. Although he hadn't spoken, she could see his face starting to soften. Gradually, the thumping in her heart was slowing. Wiping her face with the fluffy sleeve of the dressing gown, she said, 'I wish I'd told you the truth straightaway. You can see why I thought it was better to say nothing. I feel so stupid. I mean, getting drunk is bad enough. Having to get the help of a strange man in my own bedroom is utterly humiliating. You told me not to wear that blouse yesterday and you were right. You're always right, Edward. I've let you down. How can I make things up to you? I'll make you a lovely dinner. Maybe you'd like me to do something nice in bed tonight for you? Anything you want, please say.' He was smiling now; she smiled back. 'Thank you. Oh, thank you, Edward.'

'Gerry, I wish you'd told me the truth. Really, you should always tell me absolutely everything. There's nothing else to tell me is there?'

'No, honestly, that's everything. I mean, isn't it bad enough?'

'Are you sure?'

Geraldine felt uneasy. What was going to happen now? His eyes were crafty; something awful was about to happen.

In a tiny voice she said, 'Yes, I'm sure.' There was a tremendous stillness in the room. She was struggling to breathe as the seconds ticked by. What was he going to do? He got up from the chair and came around to her side of the bed. The possibility of relief began to trickle and then, as he knelt down beside her, it swept through her in a rush. 'Oh, Edward, I'm so sorry.'

She waited for him to take her in his arms. He didn't.

Instead, he reached down beside the bed and said, 'I suppose school caretakers always carry these around, just in case of an emergency?'

She looked at his outstretched hand — an opened packet of Durex.

Recoiling, she said, 'But, what? Where? How? I don't—'

Edward looked inside the packet. 'Interesting. Two missing. Gerry, you really ought to clear up after you. Or — as I'm sure he's a gentleman — maybe he should?'

Chapter 86

'I think I might be a size six. What size are your feet?'

Terry looked over at Tina: her feet were in the washing-up bowl. She'd burst in, eyes shining, voice squeaking. He'd managed to keep her quiet until the end of *Pot Black* — John Spencer had beaten Eddie Charlton with a clearance of eighty-seven — but now it was the *News*, and he couldn't bear all the usual misery. He got up, switched off the television and went to fill the kettle.

'Go on. Let's hear your big news.'

'Oh, it's not that amazing. You're right, Dad: watching a couple of penguins poking balls with sticks is much more important than the rest of my life.'

'Want a cuppa?'

'Yeah.'

'I'm all ears.'

She wrapped her feet in a towel and called, 'I've got the chance to work with a world-famous hairstylist! I met him this evening — David Gainsborough. He was so nice. His wife was there; she's lovely, too. Oh, Dad, I've had an amazing time. We were drinking champagne, eating olives — they are horrible by the way — me chatting with them, can you believe it? We were sitting on their garden chairs. They've got an amazing house and their garden is like something you only see in films. They were so nice. He's going on holiday tomorrow but, when he comes back, he says I can be a trainee in his place in the West End. Honestly, I can't believe it myself!'

The kettle boiled. Terry filled the pot.

He came back into the lounge. 'Is this the bloke Mrs Dutton knows?'

'Yeah.'

'Wow, that's fantastic. But how does he know you can even cut hair? Please don't tell me you said you cut your bald father's hair?'

She laughed. 'Hardly! No. He got me to draw a picture of him with a new hairstyle. It's funny, but even though he's a famous hairdresser, he's got awful hair. He looks a bit like Mickie Most, only not at all trendy.'

'Who on earth is Micky Most?'

'You know him!'

'No?'

'The long-haired judge in New Faces.'

'Oh, him.'

'Well, it doesn't matter. He gave me a pad and a pencil and asked me to draw him, but with a different hairstyle.'

'Mickie?'

'Dad! You're being really annoying.'

'Sorry, sorry — and did you?' He looked at her; she was absolutely glowing.

'Yep. I gave him a sort of shaggy look, with layers, and other stuff you wouldn't understand. I have to admit that it looked pretty good.'

'So, all that practice on my hair stood you in good stead?'

'He did me at the same time. Well, not really me. He did three different views of my hair, all done up like a — well, like a star's hair. I should have asked him if I could keep it.'

Terry got up and poured the tea. Glancing back at her, he thought his heart might burst. 'So, you think he's kosher?'

'Definitely. Also, his wife, Judy, she was so nice too. I think they quite liked me; I hope so, anyway.'

'I'm sure they did. How could they fail to like you?' He put her tea in front of her on the stained, old coffee table. 'Well done, love. Actually, I've been busy, too.'

'I can see. He's looking good. Thanks, Dad. I've been a bit worried about him, but you've done a brilliant job.'

'Get your hands off him; he's still in a critical condition. I haven't done his stitches yet. No, I had a visitor.'

'Oh, God, not Kev Abbott?'

'No, why?'

'Oh, he came around earlier. What a pillock! He brought me a load of old flowers and—' she shuddered, 'I sent him packing.'

'Ah, that explains the foliage. Well done for getting rid of him. By the way, his brother turned up at the school today. Did you know he works for *The Post*?'

'What, Gary?'

'Yes.'

'Oh, no, I didn't. I knew he was interested. Was there a big story, then? There must have been, to make them send their top reporter!'

'No, it was only the headmaster trying to get some publicity for the school. We had a ceremony to hand over the Castleton Cup to the little girl who scored yesterday.'

'Dad, are you going to be in the paper? Wow, you're more of a top celebrity than all of them put together!'

'Hardly! Anyway, he interviewed me, and I think there might be a picture or two. He had some girl photographer with him — a pretty thing. Yeah, Gary. I thought he was all right, actually.'

'Yeah, he is. Anyway, if it wasn't Kev, who did come round?'

'Your friend, Joe.'

'Really? That was quick. How did you get on?'

Terry recalled the man's visit. He'd only left an hour ago, but their conversation was already a blur.

'I liked him. Yeah, he's a pretty good bloke.'

'I knew you would. He's been terribly helpful to Jenny, and I know Gary likes him.'

Terry sipped his tea. 'Did you know he was a caretaker, too?'

'I thought he was a gardener.'

'Well, that as well. I do the school gardens, don't I?'

'Yeah, I suppose you do. What did you talk about?'

'Oh, this and that. Nothing much.'

'Dad?'

'Yeah?'

'Er... Was it helpful talking to him? I mean, I thought he would be good at — I don't know... sort of — you know — doing what people do to help people who might need a bit of... You know what I mean?'

Terry was about to say, 'What, help emotional cripples, like me?' but could feel Tina's anxiety. 'Well, actually, he did help me.'

Tina beamed. 'So, we've both done all right tonight. Time for a toast.' She held out her mug and announced in a grand voice, 'Three cheers for the Castletons! Celebrities and hairstylists to the stars!'

Terry clunked his thick mug against hers. 'Well done! You're on your way.'

'Oh, I nearly forgot the best bit. You never guess what! Mrs Dutton's husband joined us. He's very good friends with David and Judy. He's very nice, too — a bit scary — but you never guess what? He's in show business.

He is an agent or something for singers and actors and all sorts. He said he could introduce me to—'

Terry smashed his mug down on the table.

'Dad, what's wrong? Are you all right?'

He roared at her, 'What did he do? Did he touch you? What did he say? Tell me what happened. Tell me everything he did. Tina, now! Tell me!'

'Stop it, Dad. He was just being friendly, nothing else, honestly.'

He didn't see her shocked face, or hear her confused, plaintive voice. He felt knifing pain in his chest, but he didn't care. Terry jumped up, ran to the hall, grabbed his jacket, opened the door and slammed it shut behind him. As he pelted down the stairs, he wished he'd said goodbye.

Chapter 87

Terry put his hand on his chest: blimey, could it beat any harder? His lungs, too, seemed to be well past safe operating-level. He sagged to his knees and waited for his vital signs to return to normal. After a couple of minutes, he got heavily to his feet, sucked in his breath and knocked on the door. She opened it, hesitant: still frightened. He went inside again.

'Come and sit down; we need to have a serious talk.'

Tina followed him into the lounge. Terry slumped into his chair and thought back over the last two minutes. He had got as far as the car, unlocked it, opened the door and then... Something had clicked in his head: thank God! Up until that point, he was going to kill Mrs Dutton's husband. He'd had it all planned out: smash the door down, grab him by the throat, stove his head in against the nearest wall. He hadn't given any thought to right or wrong; the idea of life imprisonment hadn't entered his head. His only thought was of watching that man's skull being crushed — with himself doing the crushing; Dutton's momentary realisation that he was about to die, and that it was Terry Castleton killing him. The compulsion was overwhelming. Terry had pictured Geraldine Dutton there, trying to save her husband, grabbing at his hands, pleading with him to stop. Then his head had cleared.

'Jeez, Tina, I lost it badly. I came close to the edge. Oh, thank God I looked over it. I don't know what stopped me. I was so sure that it was the right thing. I've never told you before, but I've got a bit of a temper. I've tried to keep it under control and, to be fair to me, I have more or less managed to. Tonight — I lost it. I'm so sorry.'

'Do you want a fag, Dad? I think you might be having withdrawals. I've heard people go a bit mad when they give up smoking. It's got a name... um, old turkey, is it?'

He shook his head. Her lovely, kind voice was calming him down. In a minute, he'd be able to make another pot of tea and watch the end of Sportsnight.

'Cup of tea?' she asked, her voice hopeful.

No longer able to control himself, Terry started crying; first quietly, then he broke down with awful gasping sobs.

'I'm sorry, Tina. I'm so sorry. I've let you down again. Please, please, ignore me. I'm all right really.'

He felt her sit down beside him and her arms go around his shaking shoulders.

'It's all right, Dad. It's fine. Don't worry. I've got you. Come on, you're all right now. I've got you. Shussshhh. You're making me cry now! Come on, we're going to get through this. I've got my prospects all sorted out. You're going to get fit and strong again. We're both giving up smoking. I'll never, ever, ever speak to him again if you don't want me to. Even Giraffe is feeling better. That's it, Dad. That's it, let me hear you laugh again...'

He extricated himself from her limpet-like reassurance and got up.

'I'm okay. I've pulled myself together now. I'll make the tea. Before I do though, there's something I have to tell you. It's the right time. You probably always wondered why your mum left us. Well...'

Tina held up her hand to shush him. 'It's all right, Dad. I don't—'

'No, I've got to tell you. You see, Mum—'

'Was a prostitute.'

Terry felt the floor move; he sat down again.

'What? How do you... but Tina, you were only...'

'I didn't know then, but I've worked it out since. There were clues and it's only recently that they made sense. Did you chuck her out, Dad?'

He shook his head, 'No, I didn't get the chance. She left the day I found out. She said she wasn't happy, and we'd be better without her.'

Tina took his hand, 'Was Mrs Dutton's husband involved?'

'Yeah, I didn't know 'til last night. I saw a picture of him and...' Terry shut his eyes as the grotesque picture rushed back at him.

'Was he a pimp or a client... or something?'

Terry didn't want to talk about it. It was too awful even to find the words, let alone use them in front of his daughter. Something in him knew that he should get it out of his system, but not with Tina.

'I've said enough for now. I'm so sorry even to have told you this much. You don't deserve any of this awful mess and I don't deserve an angel like you. However... we do both deserve a nice cuppa.' He got up again and went into the kitchen.

She called after him, 'Thank you, Dad. I'm glad it's out in the open now. We can begin to clear the air and really start to plan our future.'

'That's right. We need a battle plan. No — let's go for the big one: a full-scale strategy.'

'You're on, Sergeant Castleton.'

Terry thought about Tina. Only minutes ago, she'd been full of her exciting news and influential new friends. He shouldn't ruin it all for her; this was a big day in her life.

'Tell you what — well done on making friends with Bobby and Julie! They sound like nice people and if they can give you a leg up, then that's fantastic.' As he said it, an awful thought bit into his mind: surely the hairdresser wasn't one of Diane's fucking clients? He shoved the idea away.

She said, 'Yeah, I know. They were so lovely. They weren't like that oily, old man, Dutton. Honestly, I can't believe they're even friends with him. They probably like Mrs Dutton, that's why they talk to him. Oh, by the way, it's David and Judy; not Bobby and Julie.'

Terry made the tea. 'Have you had something to eat tonight?'

'An olive — yuk! And some nuts. What's in the pantry, Parker?'

'I can warm up a pastie for you; that's what I had.'

'Now, that's what I call proper food.'

He turned the oven on, unwrapped the cellophane and popped in the pastie. A wave of relief had replaced the boiling rage he'd felt a few minutes ago. Thank God he'd seen reason in time. He couldn't believe that Tina had known about her mum; the poor kid. What had she seen for her to have been so sure? He would ask her tomorrow, or maybe another day. Right now, he wanted nothing more than to sit in silence with Tina: him trying to watch *Sportsnight*, whilst she chugged her way through a pastie.

'Dad?'

He braced himself. 'Yes?'

'I need to practice hairstyles — you know, designs. If I get a pen and paper, can I see what I can do with you? What do you reckon?'

'Er, I'm a bit short of the raw material.'

'Don't worry. It's more about what's in my head than on yours.'

'Fire away. See if you can turn me into Paul Newman.'

She went off to her room. As he heard her opening and closing drawers, he thought about Geraldine Dutton: what would she say if she knew about her husband and Diane? Presumably that episode hadn't been his only time with a prostitute? Terry didn't have a problem with blokes paying for sex. Plenty of his mates had gone off for light relief over the years. He probably would have done, if he hadn't met Diane and then married her so quickly. The only problem he had with paid-for sex was when it was his wife doing the charging. He guessed that for a wife to discover that her husband paid another woman for sex would be about as shocking for her as his own experience had been. Anyway, it would be a cruel and loathsome act to tell her. Poor woman. What a thing not to know! He couldn't help himself: the picture of drunk Geraldine Dutton wouldn't leave his head. She had looked after him in the shed; he would make sure she was all right, too.

Tina came back in with pencil case and tattered drawing-pad.

'Now, sit still. Look straight ahead. Pretend I'm not here.'

'Yeah, in a mo. I'll pour the tea, prepare your feast, and then that's it, I'm not moving a muscle.'

He opened the oven and checked the pastie. He called, 'Five minutes.'

'Thanks for talking, Dad. I'm glad.'

'Me too, sweetheart. Thank you.'

Chapter 88

'Frank, have you ever had a curry?'

'A few.'

'You, Anthony?'

'No, I'd love to try one. Why?'

'Me and my mum had one tonight. I dunno, I thought it would be different to how it was. I loved it. I always imagined it would be like eating proper food but with a load of spicy sauce. It wasn't like that at all. We had this kind of orangey chicken that was really lovely. Then there was oniony things and some green stuff — spinach, I think. My favourite were the papadums; they're like the biggest crisps you've ever seen and you get pots of stuff to dribble onto them. Honestly, it was all lovely. There was rice an' all, but not like the rice my mum makes. It had a really nice, um — er, smell — er, flavour.'

Anthony said, 'Watch out, Egon Ronay!'

'Who's that?'

'A food critic.'

'Anyway, I've been saving the best bit 'til last. I still can't believe my luck. I was in the restaurant, waiting in this private room. Your friend had given me a pint of lager — you know, Haroon. Anyway, who do you think comes in?'

Frank and Anthony shook their heads and waited.

'Dickie Davies and Kevin Keegan! They don't know I'm there, listening to every word they say, and they blab out everything I wanted to know. All the stuff about the doctor and the post-mortem — it's unbelievable! Anyway, your friend, Anthony — Haroon — comes along with my grub. I stand up and our boys in blue look at me as if I'm Eamonn Andrews about to say: "Dickie Davies, Kevin Keegan, this is your life…" So, I smile and wave and walk out. It takes me about ten minutes to get home and I'm laughing all the way. Jeez, you should have been there. So, I tell my mum and even she can't help herself laughing. I'm telling you, they're going to be spewing for weeks.' Gary started giggling all over again then coughing took over.

When he finally got his voice back, he told his rapt audience about Tina's escapade of the night before, then, without a pause, the scene of destruction in his back garden. 'Fucking hell, I can't believe this is all happening! Oh, by the way, there's a couple of other small items. I work for *The Post*! I'm on a trial. I had my first assignment down Aycliffe Road Primary School. I had to attend the handing-over of a cup and do some interviews. I wrote it up and it's in tomorrow's edition! Can you believe it? Me, a journalist! Anyway, you two got any news?'

Anthony said, 'Well, I did my maths homework. How about you, Frank?'

'I went running.'

Gary spluttered, 'Hey, what do you think they call me at the newspaper?'

'Gary Abbott?' Anthony hazarded.

'Half right. Frank, any ideas?'

'Er, Bob Woodward or Carl Bernstein?'

'Who?'

'They're famous journalists. Watergate.'

'Nah, you're both wrong. I, Gary Abbott, am officially known as Bulldog Abbott.'

Anthony whistled. 'Impressive. Is it because when it comes to a big story you're like a dog with a bone? A bulldog, in fact?'

'Sort of. Mostly though, it's because I've got a bulldog clip.'

The three of them collapsed into uncontrollable, wheezing laughter.

Anthony said at last, 'I'm missing the arrangements for Grace's party. Do you think we can get it going again? I think Joe probably assumes we're out of commission — you know, with everything that's happened.'

'I'd like to get things going again. I feel like we're letting her down if we don't.' Frank said.

Gary said, 'Have you seen Katy and Susan at school this week?'

Anthony said, 'Yes, quite a bit. I know they want to carry on arranging it. Although Katy is rather excited about something else she's doing.'

'Yeah, what's that?'

'I don't know what it's all about but apparently she's auditioning for something called *Grab the Headlines*.'

'Wow.'

Anthony said, 'What is it?'

'Don't you know anything, Anthony? I thought you were supposed to be clever. It's on the telly, every Saturday night. It's like *Opportunity Knocks* but much better. You know, Bruce Buick?'

Anthony looked to Frank. 'He's the presenter,' Frank explained. 'Smarmy, terrible jokes, sings a bit.'

'Hmm, well, sorry, I'm afraid Mr Buick has evaded my attention.'

Gary sympathised. 'Never mind, Anthony. One day you'll catch up with the twentieth century. Are you and Susan, you know…? Um — you know?'

'Would you like to be a little more specific, Bulldog?'

'Yeah. Are you getting your leg over?'

Frank laughed, 'Ah, I see you go for the subtle interview style.'

'Well, he asked for it. Anyway, I hope you are, Anthony. She's a brilliant girl, and even though you're a prick, you deserve a nice girl.'

'Thanks for your approval. It means a lot. Susan and I are continuing our liaison, but I wouldn't describe it quite in those terms.'

'Frank, you got any birds lined up?'

'Well, there is someone; but I'm a bit tied up with my running, right now.'

'Yeah? Did you train with Wilson again?'

'Yep. It's going pretty well. Come on, then. Your turn to update us on the romance in your life.'

Gary thought about his morning with Tina. He'd loved being with her. Then the hour or so with Karen Mitchum had been brilliant, too.

He said, imitating Anthony's voice, 'Put it this way: I've not been without charming company!'

Anthony said, 'What, Dickie Davies and Kevin Keegan? By the way, who are Dickie Davies and Kevin Keegan?'

Gary tutted. 'Anthony, don't you know anything? Honestly, you've got the intelligence of a single-cell organism! I don't think I've got anything else to say on the matter.'

Anthony laughed. 'Touché!'

Frank helped out. 'One's a sports presenter; the other's a footballer.'

Gary said, 'Anyway, I haven't told you the main news yet. The Old Bill turned up at our house this afternoon and they knocked down the greenhouse and dug up under it. I guessed it: they were after the body of my grandad. The old copper, Flanagan, has got this obsession that we killed him off and buried him. So, they dig this massive hole and guess what they found down there?'

'Your grandfather. And he's still alive?'

'Anthony, you're such a knob. No, a big, steel box with a suitcase in it.'

'Is that it?'

'Yeah, but listen. When I was in the Indian, Dickie and Keegan spilt the beans!'

'Go on, then: spill them again.'

'Well, Dickie starts whispering so I have to stick my head really close to these swing doors. The steel box — it's got a whole heap of information about the Great Train robbery in it! Also, get this one small detail — a couple of guns an' all.' The other two whistled in unison. Gary went on, 'Dickie's whispering so quietly I nearly tell him to speak up! Apparently, all the papers in the box were about it, the robbery I mean. I can't remember the details and, to be honest, I couldn't hear everything, but basically it's all in my grandad's suitcase: maps, stuff about trains, photographs… um, what else — shit, I wish I could remember. Dickie sounded like he'd won the pools. There was one thing in particular that he kept on going on about; listen to this: there's a notebook with loads of names and addresses one of which is…'

Anthony urged him on. 'Yes, who?'

'Only Ronnie Fucking Biggs, that's who! Get this! Apparently there's pictures of him and some of the others.'

'Jeez, bloody hell!'

Gary was pleased, even Frank was impressed.

'Yep, that's right. Grandad must have been part of the gang. Mind you, he was pretty old then — um… sixty-eight, I think.'

Anthony said, 'When did your grandad go missing?'

'I'm not really sure. Around the beginning of August, 1963.'

'When was the Great Train Robbery?'

'My mum can't remember. She's pretty sure it was that year.'

They looked at each other. Frank said, 'Has anything not happened to you today?'

'Well, yeah. It's mental, isn't it? No, I think that's everything — so far, anyway!' He got up. 'Same time tomorrow?'

Chapter 89

'Well?'

'Well, what?'

'Well, what do you have to say?'

'I don't know what to say.' She didn't. Geraldine was pretty sure either madness had taken hold, or she was in the middle of a nightmare. Terry must have dropped the packet last night. Why she hadn't seen it when she came home from school mystified her but, on the other hand, the state she'd been in, her senses were definitely not fully-functioning. There was something horrible about the packet. Terry's behaviour to her, last night, had been so kind and compassionate; he could not have been more of a gentleman. The evening was now really blurry, but his kindness was clear in her mind. The thought of him having a packet of condoms in his jacket didn't fit with her idea of him. Terry Castleton was the caretaker: big, gentle, shy. It had never occurred to her that he might have a girlfriend or, more than that, sexual relations. The grappling session she'd had with him in the shed, and again last night, suddenly took on a different complexion. She reddened at the memory of her arousal when she'd got into bed. It hadn't been her intention to fantasise about Terry; he'd popped into her mind, unbidden. Now, a couple of hours later, his packet of Durex turns up. It was all insane.

However, irrespective of any of that, she knew that they had not had sex last night. She looked up at Edward: he was waiting.

'I don't know. I don't know anything. I think I might be going mad. I did not have sex with Terry. He must have dropped that packet when he hauled me up. That's the truth; I've got nothing else to say. There is nothing else to say.'

'Was he here when I rang you last night?'

'No, of course not.'

'He was! I know he was. That was why you were behaving so strangely. It didn't occur to me. Why should it? It's all clear now. I remember you hanging up very abruptly. Was he pawing at you? I bet he was. I bet he had his hands all over you, whispering to you to get me off the phone? Honestly, it never crossed my mind that you were a slut, Gerry. I've been taken in, like everyone else. We all thought you were lovely, kind, thoughtful Geraldine. You're always so keen to make sure everyone is happy and looked after. All my friends in the golf club tell me how lucky I am to have you. I always smile and tell them they're right. God, how many of them have you had in my bed? I'm only now realising the full extent of this. That's why they all like you: you've been giving them exactly what you don't give me anymore.' He was getting more and more worked up. He turned to her, his face stricken, 'What am I supposed to do now? You've ruined my life in a matter of minutes. I was happy, fulfilled and altogether comfortable with my lot — my job, my home and, most of all, my loving wife. Now, it's all gone. All gone, Gerry. You've taken everything from me. Everything.'

He went back to his chair and sat down, head lolling, shoulders slumped. What was going on? Was this really happening?

Remembering her phone call this morning, she said, 'Edward, where did you stay last night?'

He looked across at her. 'Why? What on earth does that have to do with the fact that you have destroyed our marriage?'

'Just tell me, Edward.'

'Well, if you must know, I stayed at a different club to my normal one.'

'Oh? Why was that?'

He leapt to his feet, fury in his eyes. 'I hope you're not going to try and wriggle out of your shocking behaviour by attacking me? Geraldine, you have been rutting with a school caretaker in my bed. Where I stayed last night is hardly relevant, is it?'

She got up and went into the bathroom. For the first time since they'd been married, she locked the door. Standing in front of the brightly-lit mirror, Geraldine saw a stranger.

The handle rattled. 'Open this door.'

The woman in the mirror was still. Why didn't she react? Geraldine waited for her to do or say something, anything.

'Gerry, open this door. Now!'

What was she going to do? Geraldine was genuinely interested to find out how this would develop. She didn't like horror films, but whenever she and Edward had watched one together, she couldn't tear herself away from it. The man hammered on the door; he was getting hysterical. Would he carry on shouting and swearing? Would the woman give in and open the door? Maybe he'd become so enraged he would smash the door down, come in and kill her?

'Right, that's it. You're impossible. I'm going out. When I get back, you will tell me everything — and I mean absolutely everything. You are in serious trouble, Geraldine Dutton. You will tell me everything; unless you're gone, of course.'

The woman looked back at Geraldine: she was impassive, utterly still. The front door slammed. A car started up; the scrunch of its tyres receded, was followed by silence. Geraldine shut her eyes and made herself count — first to ten, then twenty. She knew breathing was going to be an issue, so she moved to thirty. At last, she caught her breath, then heaved in great lungsful of air. Still with her eyes screwed shut, she put the plug in the sink and ran hot water. Gingerly, she put her hands in and let them flounder there. Bending down, she immersed her face. The calm, steady warmth of the water felt safe. Finally, she reached for the hand towel next to the basin, and coming up for air, enveloped her whole head in it. Still scared to open her eyes, Geraldine sat on the edge of the bath and allowed her mind a tiny glimpse into what had happened. Immediately shutting it out again, she shook her head — no, not yet. She was reminded of that instant of certainty that comes between the stubbing of a toe and the subsequent pain. She was going to defer the moment of agony for as long as she could.

Downstairs, the phone rang. Time had stood still; had she been asleep? She unlocked the door, yanked it open and rushed to silence the insistent shrilling.

'Hello?'

'Geraldine, it's Brenda Stubbs.' She was whispering.

'Er… Oh, hello, Brenda. This is a surprise.'

Brenda's whisper became a little louder. 'Yes, sorry.'

'Is everything all right, Brenda? You're sounding a little…'

'Well, things are fine here — well, mostly. I was wondering if you're all right?'

Geraldine wanted to tell someone everything. She liked Brenda, but Jack Stubbs was one of Edward's best friends: could she trust her?

'Why do you ask?'

'Oh, it's probably nothing. Edward's here; he's rushed into Jack's office.'

'Oh?'

'Nothing strange about that: Edward often turns up, and they disappear together. Anyway, he comes straight in, and they go into the office and shut the door but, the thing is, he didn't shut it properly and I heard a bit of what he was saying.'

'Ah. And?'

'I overheard him say something a bit peculiar. It's probably nothing, but I thought I'd better check.'

Geraldine paused for a second, then, trying to sound casual, 'Oh? Sounds intriguing.'

'I'm not one hundred per cent sure, but it was something like "I've done it, Jack. Remember, this is your doing; you made me." Then, Jack said something, but I couldn't hear it. Edward comes back with, "Does it matter? I got the opportunity and it's done. Gerry did it for me, and that was it." I didn't hear any more, because he shut the door properly. I thought it was a bit odd, so… Is everything all right, Gerry?'

With her free hand, Geraldine dug finger and thumb into her eyes: *please could life stand still and be normal for a few seconds?* What had Brenda said?

'I'm sorry, Brenda, you must think me a bit dense; could you say that again, please?'

There was a long pause, then, 'Sorry, I was trying to listen to them, but they've gone all quiet. Um, what did he say…?' Brenda paused, then went through it again. 'You see, it was him saying, "Gerry did it for me" … And he was so agitated. I thought… I'm sorry, I'm wondering now why I even rang you. He's probably organised a fantastic holiday, or a new car, or something. Ignore me, Gerry.'

Eyes throbbing from her manic eye-massage, Geraldine tried to compose herself. What did it mean? One thing for sure: it wasn't a holiday, or a car.

'Thank you, Brenda. You're a brick. All's well, thank you very much indeed. I won't mention this call to Edward; we'll keep it to ourselves.'

'Good idea. Take care. See you soon.'

Geraldine slapped her cheeks hard. Something sinister was going on. Edward's behaviour upstairs hadn't been right. His reaction to the 'evidence' had been far too dramatic. They'd been together for a long time: she knew him — well, she thought so, anyway. He was not behaving normally. Her mind and body, she knew, were seriously smashed up — the alcohol, the craziness of the last two days, Edward's accusations and reactions, plus the incredible hunger she was only just acknowledging. She had to be very careful what she did next. Food: she must eat. Then, she would try and unravel what on earth was going on.

Chapter 90

'Oh, hello, Mr Castleton. Er — this is Gary Abbott here. I wanted to thank you for giving me the interview today, at the school. I think the article is going to be in the paper tomorrow. I wanted to let you know.'

'Oh, that's all right, son.'

'Yeah, and I think there's going to be a picture, too — you and the little girl.'

'What, my horrible face ruining it? Is the editor mad?'

Gary laughed. 'Well, I've seen worse.'

'Thanks, pal.'

'Anyway, I know it's late, but I don't suppose Tina's there, is she?'

'I'll see if she's receiving phone calls. Tina, it's the ace reporter. Are you in...? Yes, you're in luck. Here she comes.' Gary heard the phone being handed over. Tina's dad said, 'Don't be long: I'm waiting for a call from Don Revie.'

'Hello, Gary.'

'Wotcha, Tina.'

'You okay?'

Gary pictured her at the other end of the phone. He liked the image.

'Yeah, I wanted to tell you the latest news.'

'Good. Is there some?'

'Yeah, it's all gone a bit... well, mental ain't the word. You know what I was saying about our grandad being buried under the greenhouse? Well, you were right: he isn't. That didn't stop the cops smashing it down and digging up the concrete and everything. They were convinced he was down there, but no — Tina Castleton knows best. There was no body, but — get this.' He lowered his voice. 'A case full of stuff about the Great Train Robbery!'

'No!'

'Anyway, they're coming back first thing tomorrow morning to carry on digging. Then, if that's not mad enough, the next thing is even madderer. I was in the Indian and the two cops, the normal ones, you know, your boyfriend and the other one, they come into the Indian and start talking but they don't know I'm there. They're blabbing like, well, I dunno — blabbers — they say out loud that the post-mortem lets us off the hook, like you said.'

'Brilliant!'

Gary had to play the next bit carefully. He wanted to know what had happened between her and Keegan this afternoon. Who was telling the truth: Keegan or Kev?

'Thing is… Listen Tina, I'm sorry. I know it's none of my business, but what happened this afternoon? Kev came home and said he'd been at your place and that Keegan — I mean that copper, Chris — was there and… but Keegan told Dickie Davies that he was at his girlfriend's house all day. Anyway, it doesn't matter and it's not my business, but I thought you'd want to know.' He listened hard. There was a long pause. He heard her take in a sharp breath.

'I hate blokes. They're all total tossers. Your brother Kevin is the lowest form of pond life. He came around here with flowers and a card. Honestly, Gary, the flowers were nice, but why he thought I'd want a picture of an old-fashioned car, I do not know. That copper — what do you call him? Kevin Keegan? Yeah, he does look like him. He came by, sniffing around. I have to admit I did feel sorry for him: I didn't treat him very well last night. The funny thing was that he said he'd come around to say sorry about getting drunk. Actually, I think he was probably hoping to get his leg over; that's what blokes usually want. Well, he was here when Kev came around. I lost my rag with both of them.' She laughed. 'Actually, Gary, I threatened Kev with a pair of scissors. I went a bit over the top, but honestly — an old car!'

Gary wanted to laugh. He was also tempted to tell her that Kev had pinched the flowers from the graveyard, but thought it might be a bit disloyal.

He said, 'Kev said Keegan didn't have a shirt on. I mean, it's nothing to do with me but—'

'Honestly! Of course he had a shirt on. What's wrong with Kevin? Um… Chris had been in the bathroom; I think he might have had a wash. He definitely had his shirt on. You believe me, don't you, Gary?'

'Like I say, it's nothing to do with me. Thing is, I was wondering why Keegan said to Dickie that he was at his girlfriend's house if he was round your place?'

She was impatient now. 'Haven't you got it yet, Gary? Blokes are liars, cheats, wasters. They're just in it for one thing. Well, two: their pricks and their pride. I don't know why he said that, except he probably needs to save his face in front of his boss. I'm sick of them all. You're the only bloke I know who is half-way decent. I trust you, Gary; you're the only one except my dad. Oh, and I trust Joe. I nearly forgot — I trust David Gainsborough, too.'

'Who?'

'He's a world-famous hairdresser and he's given me a job as a trainee. What about that?'

'Bloody brilliant! When did all this happen?'

'Oh, this evening. I'm still flying high under the influence of fine champagne, don't you know.'

'I've got a job an' all.'

'I know, Dad told me. Trust you to pull off the big one.'

'Ta.'

'We're doing all right, aren't we?'

Gary thought that they were. He wanted to be with her right now. He liked being trusted. It would be really nice to be with Tina and know that she trusted him — maybe in her bedroom or, even better, she could trust him in her bed.

He said, 'Listen, I've got to go to work tomorrow,' he liked the sound of that, 'but I've got to do something in the evening. I was wondering... I mean, you're probably busy, but if you're free for a couple of hours, would you help me?'

'What is it?'

'Well, I need to check out a couple of things first. I'll tell you more tomorrow when I'm sure about it all.'

'Hmm, I'll need to consult my team and see what else I've got on.'

'Yeah, I know: you'll need to make sure you're not needed up the West End.'

'That's right. Let me see... I've got a bit of a break between appointments. I could be ready at — When do you need me?'

'Say, five thirty? I'll call for you.'

'Any clues?'

Gary told her, said goodbye then put the phone down. Life was pretty good. He still couldn't get used to the idea of having a job — for a newspaper! He hoped Karen would be in. He would need to make his phone calls at lunch time. Mind you, were journalists allowed a lunch? He'd better take a sarnie in case he had to work all day. Then there were the police: what would they be doing tomorrow? Were they going to be digging up the whole garden? He knew enough about old Flanagan to know that he wasn't going to leave their house until he'd found every piece of evidence available.

He went into the kitchen. His mum was at the table, hunched over a piece of paper.

'What are you doing?'

She put her pen down. 'Oh, I thought we should write to John Eustace and apologise for everything.'

'Mum, it's nothing to do with us! It was Dad that did it, not you.' She looked at him with a funny expression. 'What?' Gary said. 'It really isn't our fault.'

'I feel bad about it. Dad's not here to say sorry to that poor man. If someone had attacked me for no reason, wouldn't you want them to apologise?'

'I'd want to go round and smash their heads in.'

'Would you feel better if someone from the family wrote you a nice letter? I think I would. Anyway, my conscience is telling me to do it, and I usually listen to what it says. Trouble is, thinking about it and doing it is a bit different. What should I say?'

It occurred to him that it should be him who wrote. After all, he'd been with his dad when it happened. Maybe if he wrote a letter to say sorry, it would impress Tina. She'd trust him even more, then. His mum was right: it was the right thing to do. He'd be impressed if someone told him they'd done that.

'I tell you what, Mum. I'll write a letter from all of us.'

'Will you? Thank goodness! I didn't get very far. You're a good boy, Gary.'

'Nah, it's nothing. I'll knock something up tomorrow.' After he'd had a chance to talk to Joe, he would, anyway.

'The police are really upsetting me, Gary. I don't mind Flanagan but that awful, little one makes me shudder. I've got to get out of the house. I know Dad has only just gone, but I think I'll go back to work tomorrow. You don't mind, do you?'

'I don't blame you, Mum. Don't go to work though, how about a trip to—'

They heard the front door slam. Derek came in. 'Phew, what's been going on in here? Is the bog blocked?'

'We had a curry,' Gary said, ready for his brother's clever comments.

'Well, if the bog ain't blocked yet, it soon will be.'

Jenny said, trying not to laugh, 'Derek, it was quite delicious. Gary bought it and we ate every morsel.'

'Oh, morsel, is it? I suppose you had your punkah wallahs fanning you as you nibbled on your succulent, spicy morsels?'

Gary said, 'We need to tell you what happened today.'

'I know. Kev came and told me down the pub. What a fucking mess.'

'Must you swear, Derek?' Jenny's voice was tired.

'Sorry, Mum. So, did they find Grandad?'

Irritated, Gary said, 'Didn't Kev tell you? They didn't find Grandad. Mum doesn't know anything.'

'Shut it, four-eyes! I can talk to my own mother when I want to.'

Gary got up. 'I'm off to bed. I'm up early, Mum. Any chance of a sarnie to take with me?'

'I expect so. What do you want in it?'

Derek snapped, 'Give him a slice of humble pie; he's getting too big for his boots. Hey, you're wearing my fucking shoes, you little shit!'

Gary walked away. 'They're really uncomfortable. You need a new pair.'

In bed, Gary renewed his pledge to his mother: he would get her out of this dump. When he was a famous journalist, he'd buy her a house in Totteridge — one of those near Auntie Maureen, but nicer.

Thursday

Chapter 91

Her mother had held the door open saying, 'Straight upstairs. Come down when you're ready.'

Geraldine collapsed on to her childhood bed, in her own room, surrounded by the oh-so-familiar smells and sounds: where else would she go? Where else could she go? She cried her eyes out, head buried in pillows. Then she dragged herself to her feet and went downstairs.

'Want to tell me about it?'

For a second, Geraldine wondered if she could climb onto her mother's lap, just for a minute, just long enough to feel absolute love — real love. 'Oh, Mummy, not tonight. Tomorrow. I'll feel better in the morning.'

An hour and one or two glasses of ginger wine later, Geraldine had got into bed. She found a hot-water bottle already in it: she'd known it would be there.

Now, Thursday morning: a workday, and routine beckoned. Geraldine issued herself a command: *Right, come on! You're pulling yourself together, young lady.* She ran a shallow bath — that was the rule, in this house. She lathered up a sponge with Pears soap and rubbed hard at every inch of her body. With no heating in the bathroom, the idea of luxuriating in warm water was never an option. After five minutes, she was out and back in her room. Flapping her clothes to get out the creases, she dressed quickly. On the rickety dressing table was her old hairbrush; she counted out the regulation fifty strokes. Although a bit puffy-eyed, the reflection in the mirror showed a different person to last night's apparition. She put on a little lipstick and mascara, and reckoned she looked half-human again. She ran down the stairs like a schoolgirl.

'You're having a cooked breakfast; I don't care what you say. How do you want your eggs, fried or boiled?'

Geraldine smiled. 'Hmm, let me see… What about scrambled, or poached, or coddled? Perhaps an omelette? Maybe eggs Benedict? No, I know! I think I'll have a soufflé.'

'Is that fried or boiled?'

They laughed. They always laughed.

'Mummy?'

'Hmm?'

'I'm sure everything will be back to normal tonight, but just in case, would it be all right if I came here again? I mean, it's highly unlikely but…'

'Of course you can. This business with Edward — is it…? There's nothing…? You haven't done anything you'd regret, have you?'

'Why do you ask that? Has he been in touch?'

'Certainly not. He and I are not exactly bosom buddies, are we? No, I wouldn't want you to feel responsible for anything untoward. If there is something you're worried about, you must tell me. You know that your father and I have always backed you up, no matter what.'

'Thank you. I know you have. This will blow over; don't worry.'

After much encouragement, she had two poached eggs on toast and two cups of tea. As she drove to work, she wondered how she should approach Terry. The button was in her handbag and the sight of the Durex was seared into her memory: the poor man would be so embarrassed. It had crossed her mind that in her drunkenness, Terry had indeed taken advantage of her. The image of it popped into her mind now: not whether he had, but what it would be like, if he had. Blushing, she dashed the thought away.

What was wrong with her? Every morning, she spent most of the drive to work imagining sex with her colleagues. What never came into her head was any kind of intense enjoyment with Edward. What would life be like without him? Certainly, much less comfortable. But did central heating and all mod-cons equal happiness? Surely there was plenty in their life together that, once gone, she would miss horribly, wasn't there? But nothing came immediately to mind. She knew that all couples became accustomed to the same old way of being. She and Edward didn't share any particular interests or hobbies. He had his golf and work; she had her work and… What? What did she have? They often ate together, watched the same television programmes — was that all they did? She tried to remember the last time they'd had sex. Was it even this year? Maybe she wasn't giving him what he needed. That horrible barb about his golf friends getting what he wasn't must have come from somewhere. Terry and the condoms appeared again. What kind of life did

Terry have? He was probably very happy with his home and was certainly not wealthy, as she and Edward were. Mind you, it was principally her inheritance that had made them so comfortable. She shook her head. What on earth had Terry Castleton's life got to do with hers?

What would Edward be thinking now? Was he regretting his awful accusations? Maybe he had got drunk with Jack Stubbs and had let off all that unhealthy steam… He had certainly been drinking before the terrible scene in their bedroom. Brenda's call had been really odd. What on earth could Edward have been talking to Jack about? What was the 'opportunity'? Maybe she should ring Brenda and find out how long he'd been at the Stubbs' house. Edward and Jack had been close for a long time. They weren't colleagues, but she knew they did a lot of work together. The flood of thoughts and images ricocheted around her head as she drove. Nothing was making sense.

The car behind her flashed its lights. She looked in the rear-view mirror: Daniel Jenkinson. She waved in reply. At least she wasn't lusting after him anymore. That memory brought her up sharp. Only two days ago, she had been close to dragging him into a stock room, pulling off all her clothes and insisting he have sex with her. Her face burned with shame. That poor boy: what must he have thought of her ridiculous antics? What would she have told Edward if her fantasy had come true? *Er, Edward, darling, we've got lamb chops, peas, carrots and mashed potatoes. I thought it would be nice to have a bit of apple pie and cream for pud. Oh, by the way, Daniel Jenkinson — you know, the young teacher? Yes, him. Well, after school, he and I fucked in the stock room.* No, she wouldn't have told him. But when Edward had accused her of doing something that she hadn't done, what had her reaction been? Outrage. It had only been the lack of opportunity that had stopped her.

Surely, she wasn't unique? Everyone had their fantasies and many lived them out. Edward must have done plenty that he wouldn't want to tell her about. It had never occurred to her that he might have secrets, possibly even unsavoury ones. He had everyday dealings with rich and famous people, many of them were young, pretty and, she had to admit, sexy. Maybe he had been unfaithful to her — many times. She shook her head. This was getting her nowhere.

Mrs Rumney, the lollypop lady, waved to Geraldine as she turned into the school carpark. At least the working day would be familiar, with no unexpected shocks or surprises.

'Good morning, Geraldine. You're looking more like yourself.'

Geraldine locked the car and looked over to Daniel. 'Thank you, I feel much better.'

'Thanks for the advice on the big surprise. It's all arranged; cross your fingers for me, won't you?'

She smiled. Daniel's earnest face was so endearing. He most certainly was not sexy. What had she been thinking? It was loneliness, plus a sharpening belief in her inadequacy, that had driven her fantasies. No prizes for guessing the source of those feelings.

'Don't you worry, Daniel, dear. She won't be able to refuse; you'll sweep her off her feet.'

'Morning, you two,' Louise joined them as they walked through to the staff room. 'I've got *The Post*. We've got a really good write up. Jim will be hopping mad: he's not in the photo.'

Geraldine said, 'I hope I'm not, either. Let's have a look.'

Louise spread the paper open on her desk; the three of them leaned over it.

'Oh, poor Patricia: she looks dazzled by it all. Daniel, that's your dignitary's hand behind her head. Terry looks good — I've never seen him with a grin like that.'

Geraldine peered past Louise's pointing finger. Yes, Terry looked as proud as punch as he smiled broadly at Patricia. He really was a very nice man.

'It's a shambles,' snapped Jim Dixon, when he saw them looking at the article. 'I hardly get a mention and — honestly! — I'm not even in the frame.'

Louise looked sad on his behalf. 'I can't believe it; there's not even a mention of your trial for Orient!'

'Hmm. Exactly!'

Geraldine said, 'I'm off to the salt mine. See you later. We can discuss Jim's glittering football career then.'

'Me, too. By the way, did you see the story about the man who attacked John Eustace?' Louise flipped back to the front page: in large letters...

John Eustace Attacker Dies in Freak Accident

Chapter 92

'Here he is! It's the Bulldog!'

Gary smiled sheepishly as he went into the office. 'Watcha. You all right?'

Eve saluted him. 'Wow, nice case! I bet that set you back a few bob.' Gary tried not to smile. 'Have you seen your article?' She held the paper out for him. He leaned against the reception counter and read it. Seeing his words in print, in a real newspaper, wasn't quite registering with him. He read it again.

'Pleased with it?'

Gary nodded; he was thrilled. Alan hadn't changed any of it. Gary Abbott, a journalist! Trying not to look too pleased, he said, 'Thanks, Eve. It's not bad. I can't say it's going to win any awards, but, well… what do you think?'

'I think it's, um — let's say, reasonably acceptable. I like the way you got the human story into it, rather than reporting on an impromptu football match. Yes, well done.'

'It's my photograph that turns it into a major story of course.'

Gary saw Karen in the office beyond Eve. She was looking even nicer than yesterday: hair tied in a pony tail with bright red ribbon, emerald green shirt, black, flared trousers, broad grin.

'Yeah, you're right. After all, you've had much more experience than me. Er… remind me, how long have you been in the business?'

'Oh, I've lost track! Anyway, overall, I think we did a good job.'

Gary flicked to the front page and read.

John Eustace Attacker Dies in Freak Accident

In an incredible twist of fate, the perpetrator of the brutal attack on local businessman and politician, John Eustace, died in hospital, early on Monday morning. Brian Abbott, resident of Carlisle Road, suffered brain injury when he tripped and fell in his own kitchen and died from the injury only a few hours later.

Police have been searching for Mr Eustace's attacker since the captain of industry was assaulted on the evening of Thursday 20th March. Mr Eustace was savagely headbutted at 10pm in Theobald Street. The unprovoked attack resulted in a serious head injury to Mr Eustace, who is only now recovering.

In a separate incident, ambulance and police officers were called to Carlisle Road on Sunday night where Brian Abbott, 49, an employee of the London Bus Overhaul Works, was found unconscious on his kitchen floor, having tripped over an electric cable. Mr Abbott was rushed to casualty at Edgware General Hospital where he received urgent treatment. It was there that detectives noticed that Mr Abbott had a tell-tale tattoo which matched that sported by Mr Eustace's attacker. It was later confirmed that Mr Abbott had indeed been in Theobald Street at the time of the attack. Mr Abbott, married with three sons, died before police were able to charge him for the assault.

Police declined the opportunity to comment.

Turn to page 3 for full story.

Gary looked at the pictures. The one of his dad was old — it might even be from when grandad had disappeared. He was wearing one of the kipper ties his mum had tried to get him to wear yesterday. He looked up; he was being watched by Eve, Karen, Nigel, Alan and Rob, plus two other blokes he hadn't met before. He folded up the paper. 'What's going on?'

Rob said, 'Gary, we're all really sorry about your father. It's such a terrible business. We also want to thank you for sharing your news with us, and with our readers.'

'Yeah, well, put it this way — nothing gets between Bulldog Abbott and his readership.'

Karen laughed. 'Boy, am I regretting we ever called you that! If only Eve had given you something else from her drawer. I don't know... um, well, we could have called you... er — I know: Pinhead Abbott!'

Eve said, 'That's right. Or Paperweight Abbott.'

Not to be outdone, Alan went behind the counter and rooted through Eve's drawer. He produced an open safety pin.

He guffawed, 'We could call him That Prick Abbott!' They looked at him in silence. 'Okay, so it's not that funny. I thought it was appropriate, though.'

Gary did think it was funny but wasn't going to let Alan know. He looked at them all: they were smiling at him.

'Thanks, everyone. I appreciate it. Now, I need to talk to you about something else.'

Rob held his office door open. 'You've got thirty seconds. After that, you've got all day to get used to proper newspaper work — cups need washing, Alan's ash tray is full, we need someone to go and get some doughnuts and I definitely need some cigarettes.'

Gary sat down on the swivel chair next to Rob's desk and told him what Dickie had said the night before. At first, Rob was only half listening. Then he stopped cleaning his glasses, put them on and looked closely at Gary.

'You're not making this up?'

'No, it's all true.'

'Don't move an inch.' He leaned to his office door and opened it. 'Nige, in here. Now!' He waited for Nigel to come in and close the door. 'Go on, Gary: say it again. Slowly, this time.'

When he'd finished, Nigel shook his head. 'Gary, you're a walking headline.'

Rob opened his door again. 'Alan, in here. Now!'

Gary watched him through the glass wall. He'd been sitting back in his chair, arms crossed, eyes closed. When he heard his name barked out, he jumped, and struggled to his feet. Evidently reluctant, he came to the door, his eyebrows raised.

'Alan, what was the date of the Great Train Robbery?'

Gary was excited. He had known that the discovery was important, but Rob's urgent interest was even greater than he'd expected. Alan looked into the distance.

'Hmm, I reckon July or August '63; I'd have to check.'

Rob looked at Gary, 'When did your grandad go missing?'

Nigel piped up, '1st August.'

Rob, Nigel and Alan stared at Gary.

He nodded, 'Yeah, I reckon my grandad was part of it.'

Alan came in properly and shut the door behind him. 'Want to tell me what's going on?'

Rob said, 'The police dug up Gary's greenhouse yesterday. They thought his grandad was going to be under it. He wasn't. However, what they did find seems to connect the old man with the Great Train Robbery.'

Alan puffed out his cheeks. 'Your grandad was a train driver, wasn't he, Gary?'

Gary nodded. He looked at Rob.

Rob said, his voice slow and deliberate, 'One of the Great Train Robbers was a man called Ronnie Biggs. His part in the whole affair was simple: to bring in a train driver to take over once they'd put the actual driver out of commission. The man he brought in was never arrested, and as far as I know, has never been identified. That's right, isn't it, Alan?'

'Yep.'

Rob went on, 'Anyway, the funny thing about the whole business is that the driver Biggs brought in hadn't ever operated what was then a new-style locomotive. So, it transpired that he wasn't able to do the very job he'd been engaged to perform.'

Gary didn't know much about The Great Train Robbery, but he knew that name.

'Isn't Ronnie Biggs the one that escaped from prison? Is he in Brazil or something like that?'

'That's him,' Rob said.

Gary shook his head. 'I can't believe this. This kind of thing doesn't happen to my family.' As soon as he'd said it, though, he realised that what had happened to his family in the last few days was exactly like this — something out of a television drama.

Rob said, 'Did he leave anything in your house before he cleared off? I don't know... clothes, shaving tackle, papers, passport?'

'My mum said he had two suitcases. One he kept in his bedroom and the other one was kept in our shed; that's the one that went under the greenhouse.'

Nigel said, 'So, maybe the old man didn't go missing. Maybe he went off with Biggs and the rest of them to lie low before the big job? But what doesn't make sense to me is why he'd go without his case. Also, by disappearing like that, he was drawing the attention of the police to what was about to be a massive news story.'

Rob looked at Gary. 'Any thoughts?'

'Well, the one thing that I wondered was whether he knew all about the robbery, but wasn't actually involved in it himself. Maybe he knew the train driver who was part of it... I mean, Grandad was old in 1963. He'd already retired from the railway. Maybe he thought: *I know, I'll blackmail Biggs and the gang with all this information I've got.* So, what would they do? They'd knock him off, wouldn't they?'

The four of them were quiet as they considered it all.

Nigel said, 'Yeah, good theory. The trouble with that is that they'd want to get hold of any and all of his stuff. I mean, he had a caseload of incriminating evidence. They wouldn't get rid of him and leave all that to be discovered, would they?'

Gary thought about that: it was true. Then he said, 'But it wasn't discovered, was it? Even though the police were crawling all over our house, they didn't find it. It does look as though my dad was involved in some way. He was the one that hid it under the greenhouse. Maybe he thought he'd hang on to all the evidence and blackmail them with it?'

Gary looked past Alan's head to see Karen sticking her tongue out at him. He looked away. Glancing back, he saw her gurning instead.

Rob lit up a Benson. Nigel pulled out his Piccadillys. Alan shook out a Players Navy Cut. Gary had run out of fags. He looked hopefully at Nigel and he proffered his packet. Rob's lighter went around the room.

Rob stood and opened his door. 'Karen, instead of pulling stupid faces, how about you make four coffees, three sugars in each?'

She tutted loudly, stuck her tongue out at Gary and disappeared.

Rob said, 'Whatever we're doing or thinking, the police will be ahead of us. I imagine your mum is going through the mangle as we speak, Gary. Do you think you ought to be with her? Is there anyone with her?'

'No, she's on her own. I—'

Rob said, 'We owe you, Gary. We'll have our coffee. Then you'd better go home and back her up. You might even learn something, just by following the direction of their questions. When they ask anything, think what might lie behind it. Old Flanagan will come at it from all sorts of funny directions.'

Gary was disappointed. He knew he should go home, but being with the blokes and trying to work it all out was like watching a film, with him as the star. He saw Karen approaching with a tray. He got up and opened the door.

'Four coffees for the important gents,' Karen announced in a Barbara Windsor, cockney voice. She put the tray down on Rob's desk and looked around for thanks and information. There was silence. She stood still and waited.

Rob gave in. 'Thank you, Karen. Here's a quick resumé of what's going on.'

His phone rang. 'Eve? Yes… Ah… Right. Thanks.' He turned to Gary, 'Sorry, you've been summoned: the police want you home now.'

Gary took a glug from his mug: too hot. 'Sorry, I'd better go.' He handed his mug to Karen and stood up to let her have his chair. He turned to Rob. 'I'll ring later. What are you going to do?'

'We'll read up on all the facts of the case and check if there's anything that could connect it all with your old feller. Good luck with Flanagan.'

'Thanks.' As he left the office, he added, 'If this is my last day at work, can I say "Thanks very much"? I've enjoyed being Bulldog.'

'You'll be back, I'm sure of it. That's right, isn't it?' Rob looked around the little office.

Alan grumbled, 'Yeah, and I'm sorry I called you a prick.'

Gary saw Karen looking at him, her eyes questioning: was she sorry to see him go?

He called, 'Bye!' and went through into Reception.

Eve was there. 'I'm sorry. It was your mum; she was really insistent. She says the police are at your house. You haven't robbed a bank or something, have you?'

Gary smiled. 'Nothing so simple.'

She said, 'I can't say it's been dull since you arrived!'

Gary put his case on the counter, opened it and pulled out the bulldog clip. 'Look after this for me. Promise me you won't give it to any apprentices. Promise?'

Smiling she put it in her handbag. 'I'll guard it with my life.'

Gary waved as he went through the door, then legged it. As he raced past the stationers, he glanced in: the tasty woman was there talking to a customer. Maybe he would go in again later. The way he was feeling, he reckoned he could pull any bird, even classy ones. He didn't have time to think about that now. He belted up the alley that came out near the back way into The Beeches. Hurdling the low fence, he looked around the gardens: was he here? No. Shit. Gary ran around the front of the concrete building and peered in through the doors to Reception.

'Ah, Gary Abbott. Fancy meeting you here.'

Gary spun around. 'Phew! Brill! I need your help, Joe.'

Chapter 93

'Watcha, Tina.'

'Watcha.'

'You all right?'

'Yeah.'

'It was a right laugh last night, weren't it?'

Tina knew why she would never go out with Steve Bellingham: he was as thick as pig shit and twice as ugly.

'Come on, Belly. She's never going to give in to your charms. Watcha, Tina. You all right?'

Tina looked at Steve's friend: three times uglier, possibly only half as thick.

'Yeah, I'm all right.'

She walked quickly to her first lesson. It was nearly a week since she'd been at school and she had only come in today for art. Down the corridor, she saw Lynn going into the art room.

Tina called, 'Watcha, Lynn. You all right?'

Lynn turned to her. 'Oh, watcha. Yeah. You? Been out with your copper friend again?'

Tina tutted, 'God, no! Wasn't that a dead loss?'

Lynn said, 'I thought it was terribly nice of that man to drive him home. Who was he, do you know? I thought he was quite dishy, for an old man.'

Tina thought about Joe; yeah, he was sort of handsome.

'No, I've never seen him before. I won't be seeing Mr Plod again, either.'

'I didn't think we were going to see you again. You planning to do your 'O' level?'

'Probably. I haven't decided yet.'

Miss Lewis came in; the room went quiet. She looked around.

'Right, I thought it would be useful to talk through your portfolios, to make sure you've all got good work under your belts and, if you haven't, we've got time to do something about it.'

Tina did have good work in her portfolio but, right now, she needed advice. When it was her turn to go up to the front, she opened the large cardboard folder and pulled out her drawings of last night.

She said, her voice low, 'I'd really like to get good at designing, 'specially, stylish things. I've got a chance to do an apprenticeship at a hair salon up in London, but I'm not sure I've really got what it takes. I did these last night. Forget the model — he's my dad — but do you think I've got anything? I mean, you know — what should I be getting better at?'

She watched the teacher's face carefully. Miss Lewis was quite an old lady but, despite that, Tina respected her opinion.

'Tina, I really do wish you'd put a bit more effort in. These are very good drawings. In fact, all your work is excellent. The trouble is that there's not very much of it. I don't know if I can help you. I think the best thing you can do is go and spend a day or two in a hairdresser's and just see what you can pick up. You've got an excellent eye; your perspective is good and your shading really is effective. There is just one thing worth bearing in mind.'

'What's that?'

'I'm not sure your father looks good with all those layers and highlights.'

Tina laughed. 'That's amazing! He said exactly the same thing. Maybe he should be an art teacher, too!'

When she went back to her desk, Lynn said, 'Let's have a look at your stuff.'

'Nah, it's rubbish. I won't even bother putting it in my portfolio.'

Lynn grabbed at the pad and plucked it out of Tina's hand.

'Tina, don't tell me you did these? I don't believe you.'

'You're right, my — um... my friend did them.'

Lynn was turning the pages. 'My God, you're a genius. Look at my efforts — pathetic.'

Tina was gratified. It was true that Lynn's drawings were awful but, even so, getting the compliment was encouraging.

Lynn turned to Julie Nicholls next to her and showed her the drawings, 'Look, Tina's done these.'

'Oi! Give me that back! Who said you could show them? Give it back here, now!'

It was too late. Julie had taken the pad and flipped it over to Caroline Hughes who whistled and told Tracy Crocker, 'Look, Tina's done these.'

'Girls, settle down now. Tracy, give Tina her pad back.'

Miss Lewis's feeble request had no effect. Tina's blood boiled over. She got up and walked over to Tracy's desk and snatched the book away. 'I'm off. You're all a bunch of cows and bitches.'

She went back to her desk, picked up her bag and portfolio and stomped out of the room.

Behind her she heard Lynn's voice, 'Ooh! Little Miss Muffet's in another strop.'

Tina marched down the corridor to the main exit. Why did she bother coming to this dump? It had been the same all through her time at secondary school. She tried her best to get on with people but there was always a point at which someone would piss her off and then — BAM! — she'd lose her rag. Was it her fault? What had happened this time was nothing to do with her. Lynn, the little cow, had not respected her or her property. Was it such a big deal, though? Now she thought about it, Lynn had genuinely seemed to like her drawings. The others had been impressed, too. Why had she been so indignant and then infuriated? As usual it was she, Tina Castleton, who had come out badly. All the others were in there now, laughing about her, rubbishing her.

'Miss Castleton, are you going somewhere?'

She looked around to see the headmaster coming out of his office.

She said, 'Yes, I'm off to get a job. Good day, Mr Sanders.'

'Ah, good day and, I suspect, goodbye.'

'Indeed, I suspect your suspicions are correct.'

'Well, good luck. Perhaps you'll come and visit us when you're rich and famous?'

'Yes, perhaps I will.' Tina looked at the shambling, old man. Although he was the headmaster, she had always felt a bit sorry for him. He was rather ridiculous, with his dusty, old-fashioned clothes, glasses without rims, bowed posture. Worst of all though — and the subject of everyone's ridicule — was his 'syrup'. 'Mr Sanders?'

'Yes, Miss Castleton?'

'I hope you don't mind but can I ask you a favour?'

'Yes?'

'Well, I've noticed that you wear a wig. I'm pretty sure I could design you one that suits you better. Would you be prepared to let me try? The thing is, the one you've got doesn't even fit your head properly.'

He looked at her; was he going to blow up?

'Well, I wasn't expecting that. It's a very civil offer. I'm rather busy at the moment, but perhaps it would be feasible. I tell you what — if you get grade A in your Art, I'll grant you the once-in-a-lifetime opportunity to design my — what I believe those in the profession refer to as — coiffure. Now, that's a reasonable bargain, isn't it?'

Tina smiled at him. He wasn't such a dinosaur after all. 'Yes, sir, that is a good bargain. I'll do my best. Right now, though, I do have to see if I can sort out an apprenticeship.'

'Well, good luck. I hope it's just *au revoir*, after all.'

As she hurried down the road, it occurred to her that it was people her own age who wound her up. She had got on perfectly well with Gary's aunt, with David and Judy, Joe, and with Miss Lewis this morning. It was the silly little girls that got on her nerves. Oh, yes, and the stupid men who couldn't keep their pricks in their trousers.

Over the road she saw *Dazzle*. She'd been in a couple of times and had enjoyed it. The girls there were chatty and friendly, and the old bag who owned it was a good laugh, too. Tina darted through a gap in the traffic and walked up to the salon. On the window was a sign.

Models needed for our students — more information inside

She pushed open the door. Tinny pop music was coming from a transistor propped on one of the window ledges. There were two women having their hair done and behind the counter was the old girl.

'Hallo, darling. How are you?'

'Fine, thanks. I was wondering if I could be one of your models. I don't know what's required — but what do you think?'

The woman put out her fag and looked closely at Tina's hair.

'You'll do. All you need to do is come in and have your hair cut by a student. Are you available this evening between five and seven?'

'Er… yeah, but it depends on how much it is.'

'Well, it's a quid. The only thing is we can't guarantee you'll be delighted with the result. It'll be a student, you see.'

'Oh, hmm. Well, that's all right. I just want to… Well, good! I'll come along at five.'

'Name?'

'Tina Castleton.'

'Right you are, dear. See you later.'

Now what could she do? There wasn't much point in going back to school. She walked along the high street, looking for inspiration. She decided on the library again. She glanced into the shops as she went: *Harringtons* — that was where Dad got his cup; *Boots*; *Martins*; *Studio Stationery*... She'd pop in and pick up a decent pad and some pencils.

'Hello, can I help you?'

Tina looked at the woman: very nice make-up, classy jewellery, clothes well cut.

'No, I'm all right, thank you. I'm only after a pad and some pencils.' Tina took her time. She very rarely bought good quality paper. She looked at the prices of the cartridge pads: no wonder! They were way out of her price range.

The woman came up to her. 'It's rather expensive, isn't it?'

'Hmm.'

'I tell you what, if you come back when it's quiet, I'll have a look in the storeroom. I might be able to make you an offer.'

Tina looked at the woman: her glossy lips were parted, there was invitation in her eyes.

'Well, that's terribly kind of you. I think I'll probably find what I'm looking for in *Woolies.*'

'You won't find what I'm offering you at *Woolies.*'

'Yeah, but at least I can nick something from pic 'n' mix when I'm there. I don't suppose you've got that in your storeroom?'

'No, but... I'm sure I can find something sweet for you.'

Tina wanted to giggle but kept herself together. 'No — thanks for the offer, though.'

'Oh, shame. Never mind.'

Tina resisted the urge to run out of the shop. She'd never been propositioned by a woman. It hadn't even occurred to her that it was a possibility. She couldn't wait to tell Gary later; he wouldn't believe her!

Thinking of Gary made her slow as she approached the newspaper office. She peered inside; there was a tall girl behind the reception counter. Beyond her, Tina could see an office with some men sitting at desks, but no sign of Gary.

The girl looked up at Tina, her eyes questioning. Tina looked away and hurried on to *Woolies*. As she'd hoped, there was a lovely big pad of cartridge paper, half the price of the one in *Studio Stationery*. She picked up a box of coloured pencils and a packet of charcoal sticks, then got in the queue to pay. From her position, she could make out half of the record and cassette section.

One of these days, she'd persuade her dad to buy a cassette player. Glancing at the make-up counter, her gaze was caught by the tall, slender woman rearranging the lipstick display. There was something about the way she moved which appealed to Tina: she was composed, rather elegant for a *Woolies* assistant. Tina's queue moved; she shuffled forward. Looking again at the striking assistant, Tina could now see that the woman was older than she had initially thought. Her bright, blonde hair must be dyed and her face, now visible, was lined, its expression pinched and — No! It couldn't be! It was.

Chapter 94

Gary looked at the coppers: Flanagan was perched on the old pouffe; Keegan, looking nervous, on the edge of a kitchen chair; Dickie Davies was standing up. The week's events, or maybe it was the curry last night, hadn't done him any favours. Gary wondered whether he might fall over before this 'interview' ended.

Everyone was smoking, except Flanagan. Even his mum had lit up; she normally only smoked when her friends came around. Gary was pleased to see that Dickie and Keegan couldn't meet his eyes when he'd arrived. He wondered if they'd told Flanagan that their hot news was broadcast around the local curry house. They were shit-scared of the old man, and he'd probably flip his lid if he knew they'd been so unprofessional.

At long last, Flanagan spoke. 'Thank you all for making yourselves available at such short notice. I know that the last few days have been terribly upsetting and traumatic, so the last thing I want to do is add to your ordeal.' The Abbotts sat in silence. 'As you know, we found some material buried under your greenhouse. I fear we shall have to continue to search the premises. I wish it weren't the case, but again, as you know, we are sticklers for detail. Isn't that right, Detectives Nott and Armstrong?' Gary had to stop himself laughing out loud, as he saw them nod with false enthusiasm. 'What we found yesterday is of some interest and may well help us with our long-standing investigation into the disappearance of Bertram Abbott. Regrettably, however, we are having to hand over the matter to the Flying Squad.'

'The Sweeney!' exclaimed Derek, Kevin and Gary in unison.

Flanagan ignored them. 'However, before those officers become involved, I have one or two further questions. I hope that is all right, Jenny?'

Gary was on his guard. He glanced at his mum; she was nodding.

Flanagan pressed on. 'Thank you. Now, I know it's a long time ago. You young men will probably have little or no memory of what was going on, but one never knows what sticks in a child's head. I want you all to think back to when your grandfather was here. With whom was he most friendly? Derek, was it you? Kevin? Gary? Jenny, did you and he talk much? Perhaps he helped with things around the house? I wonder if he might have bought any of you a little present? I know — maybe he took you to the park for a game of soccer? I'm going to be silent for a few minutes, whilst you bring to mind those few weeks that he was here.'

Gary found himself thinking through this evening's trip. He was looking forward to another outing with Tina. Would they be able to spend more than two hours together without her doing her volcano impression? Fancy The Sweeney getting involved in their little lives! He hadn't any real idea about the Great Train Robbery, but the very fact that he knew about it, and it was still in the news now and then, showed that it must have been a massive story. In a way, he wasn't surprised that Grandad had mixed with serious villains. The way Del and Kev spoke about him, and his mum's memories, made it clear that he really was a bad man. Gary thought about the times his dad had mentioned him: never a good word and usually something horrible.

Flanagan looked around. 'Now then, who's first? Jenny? Tell me about the nice things that your father-in-law did with you?'

She said, 'Well, I think he may once or twice have gone through the day without swearing at me or the boys. I can't be sure about that, though.'

The three brothers sniggered. Even Dickie and Keegan cracked smiles. Flanagan nodded his understanding.

'Derek, how about you? I bet he used to read you a bedtime story or talk about his time being a train driver? Did you want to grow up to be a train driver? Did he talk much about trains or, possibly, his fellow train drivers?'

'You're having a laugh. I kept out of his way. He was a right shit. I'll tell you what he did: he used to threaten to show me his willy.'

Gary and Kevin were giggling now. Jenny shushed them.

Flanagan continued. 'Kevin, come on. You and your grandad had a close bond, I'm sure. Did he tell you about his friends? Maybe he talked about his work friends?'

Kev's shoulders were shaking. 'I'm sorry, it's not funny. I used to hide from him. I was shit-scared of him. I've got a vague memory of having a fight with him, but I can't really remember it.'

Derek scoffed, 'You didn't, you liar. He'd have beaten you black and blue and eaten you for breakfast.'

'Well, all I'm saying is that I've got this memory, that's all.'

'You're talking through your arse, as usual.'

'No, I ain't.'

Flanagan ignored them. 'Gary?'

'Sorry, I can't remember him.'

Flanagan nodded. Silence returned.

Gary wanted to get back to work. He knew there were all sorts of jobs to do; he wasn't sure what, but impression was important and, right now, his contribution to the paper was zero. Mind you, what was going on in front of his eyes and ears might turn out to be important. Rob's excitement about the story had been infectious. He concentrated.

Flanagan said, 'You see, I'm wondering something. I understand that Mr Abbott Senior was perhaps, um, not such a jovial fellow, but I imagine he must have had a friend or two. Jenny, did anyone come to visit him? Did he go and see people, do you know? Did he get telephone calls from anyone in particular? I have an idea that he might have been friendly with some specific people, and it would be extremely interesting to know about that.'

'I'm so sorry, Mr Flanagan. I can't remember him having any friends. He wasn't someone to chat with the neighbours. We didn't get many calls, back then. In fact, I'm not even sure that we had a telephone.'

The old man nodded sadly. 'I thought you might say that. Oh well, never mind. By the way, I imagine you might be surprised to learn that the large box we found under your greenhouse contained something extraordinary. Would any of you like to hazard a guess as to the nature of the discovery?' His eyes were hawklike as he looked into their faces. Gary glanced at Dickie and Keegan. They looked shifty.

Del said, 'Don't tell me — a lead pipe? No? What about a candlestick, a revolver, a rope, a dagger and, um… what was the other one?'

Kev said, excited, 'Wasn't it a spanner or a wrench or something? By the way, I remember Grandad used to ring someone up all the time!'

Flanagan looked warily at him. 'Yes?'

'Yep, I'm sure of it.'

Flanagan remained patient. 'Please do tell us, Kevin. What you tell us may very well assist us with our enquiries.'

Kev was silent for a long time, then burst out, 'It was Colonel Mustard.'

Everyone was laughing, except Flanagan. He turned to Dickie, who shut up immediately.

'I'm sorry that you find heinous crime so amusing. I shall leave you all to think about the extent to which you have assisted the police with their enquiries or, indeed, whether you have fulfilled your duty to the public in any way that might be considered honourable. I'll leave you now. However, if you think I'm determined, you had better watch out for the officer about to take over the investigation. I would advise you not to be quite so flippant with him.'

The Abbotts shut up. Dickie leaned down and whispered something. Flanagan wafted Dickie's breath away. 'Thank you, Nott. Before I leave, Gary, may I take a look in your bedroom, please?'

Gary started. 'What? Why?'

Flanagan's voice was as sharp as a razor. 'Because I want to, that's why.'

'Well, it's Kev's room, too.'

Flanagan looked at Kevin, who said, 'Can I stop you?'

'No.'

Gary got up and led the way upstairs. Kev and Flanagan followed. The detective went into the untidy room and said, 'Wait downstairs, please. I shan't damage anything. Anything that I find that is perfectly legal is of no concern of mine. If I find anything that requires you to answer a question, I shall ask you to come upstairs. Now, please leave me to it.' He called downstairs, 'Nott, please come up here.'

Gary and Kev waited for Dickie to brush past them before they went back downstairs. Keegan did not look happy. He smiled uneasily. 'All right?'

Kev's voice was trembling. 'What were you doing with Tina yesterday? Don't tell me, you were taking down her particulars!'

'Well, thing is, I was — um… you know, asking her about the case.'

'You're full of shit,' Kev spat.

Gary was sorely tempted to ask Keegan what his curry had been like last night. Like Kev, he also wanted to know what the fuck he'd thought he was doing with Tina yesterday afternoon. Instead, he bit his lip and waited. Boy, was he glad he'd flushed away Auntie Maureen's letter! He was pretty sure they were looking upstairs because Dickie had remembered Gary had spent too long going to the bog yesterday afternoon.

Keegan pulled his fags out of his pocket. Before he could light up, Del said, 'No smoking in the house.'

Keegan looked pissed off, but did as he was told. Derek immediately lit one of his own; so did Kev. Gary followed suit.

Their mum said, 'Would you like a nice cuppa?'

Keegan looked at Del.

Del shook his head. 'No thanks, Mum. We're all okay.'

They sat in silence.

Finally, the two detectives came downstairs. Keegan looked up, clearly desperate to get out.

Flanagan said, 'Thank you very much. We're going to leave you now. As I say, you will be in the hands of our colleagues very soon. Don't worry, though. I shall remain interested in you and your affairs.'

Everyone got up. Keegan couldn't get away quick enough.

Jenny said, 'Will you be clearing up all the mess in our garden?'

Del said, 'Yeah, that garden was my dad's pride and joy. He put a lot of work into that greenhouse.'

Flanagan looked at each of them in turn. He said, his voice level and without emotion, 'Remember your public duty? Well, I can tell you, none of you has fulfilled it. Not at all.'

Gary looked at his mum; she seemed really upset.

Jenny said, 'Um, Mr Flanagan... um — if anything comes to light... er... um... is there a number I can ring you on?'

Flanagan face was impassive as he took a card from his pocket. 'Here you are, Jenny. Ring me any time, any day. I'd love to hear from you. Of all the people I'd like to hear from, it's you.'

With that, he left, followed by a shambling Dickie Davies and a sweating Kevin Keegan.

The front door closed.

Derek rounded on his mum. 'What the hell is going on? I don't know much about the police, but the fucking Sweeney don't turn up looking at greenhouses for no reason. What's it all about?'

Gary said, 'Whatever they found must be really serious. I can't believe old grandad could possibly be mixed up in anything. He was nearly dead, anyway, wasn't he?'

Derek ignored him. 'Mum, come on! You must know something?'

She shook her head. 'The thing is, Dad didn't want any of us to know about whatever he'd buried. I tried to get it out of him, but he started to lose his rag. I wasn't going to aggravate him, was I? You know your dad, Derek.'

Kev started giggling again. 'That was a brilliant one, weren't it?' They all looked at him. 'You know — Colonel Mustard?'

Derek snapped, 'You knob! This is serious.'

'Hey, hang on a minute — you were the one that said all the Cluedo weapons.'

'Shut it.'

'I will not. You shut it.'

'You going to make me?'

'Yeah.'

'Come on then, you tosser!'

Kev pushed Derek in the chest. 'I wouldn't waste my time with a loser like you.'

'You what? You're the fucking loser. You can't hang on to a girlfriend more than a few minutes; not even that slag, Tina Castleton.'

'You bastard! Come here and say that.'

Grinning maliciously, Derek pushed his face into Kev's. 'I gave the fire a few pokes and, put it this way, she was gagging for more.'

Kev swung a fist. He missed.

Gary turned to his mum. 'I'm going to work, Mum. You all right?'

'I'm fine, Gary. You go. I'll ring you if anything happens.'

The two of them looked hard at each other for the briefest of moments.

Gary nodded. 'Bye, boys. You're like a couple of cartoon characters.'

Kev snapped, 'What?'

Derek spat, 'Come here and say that!'

Laughing, Gary left.

Chapter 95

'Oh, hello, love; I wasn't expecting to see you.'

She didn't reply. He put his keys down on the table and looked at her.

'You all right?'

'I've just seen Mum.'

His stomach flipped. 'What?'

'In Woolies.'

'What?' His heart lurching, Terry pulled out a chair and sat down. 'You're having a laugh. What was she doing in there?'

Tina's face had a frozen look. He guessed his was the same.

She said, 'I don't know, do I?'

He tried to stay calm. What was the woman doing, coming back from the past? First, the picture of that bastard, Dutton, now Diane herself? He got up and filled the kettle.

'Are you sure it was her?'

Tina nodded.

'Did you talk to her?'

A shake.

'Did she see you?'

'I don't think so.'

He noticed her uniform. 'Been to school today?'

A nod.

Apart from last night, they'd never talked about Diane. He tried to imagine what Tina might be feeling; he couldn't. He warmed the pot. Poor girl — life was such a roller-coaster for her!

She said, 'I'm sorry, Dad. Life keeps on bashing us over the head. I wish I hadn't seen her.'

'I'm supposed to say I'm sorry to you. I am, by the way. What was she doing?'

'She must be working there. I looked over at the make-up section, and there she was. I didn't believe my eyes at first, but when I looked again, it was definitely her. She didn't—'

He turned to look at her. 'Didn't...?'

She was rubbing her eyes. 'I'm sorry, Dad: she didn't look very good. I know it's six years since we last saw her but, blimey, she hasn't aged well. I mean — oh, it doesn't matter.'

Terry pictured Diane. The last time he'd seen her — well, before the time... he shut his eyes... before that, she had looked like a million dollars. She'd been thirty-two, then. What had she been doing in the meantime? If she was working in *Woolies*, then life hadn't worked out for her in the way she'd hoped. Had prostitution been a short-lived career? Why on earth would she want to hang around here, anyway?

He put the teapot down between them. 'Blimey, what a shocker.'

Tina nodded. 'I couldn't get out of there fast enough. I sort of wanted to wave and then all I could do was leg it out of there, like I was being chased. I didn't even have a chance to pocket some sweeties for you!'

He reached across and tousled her hair. 'You're an angel. Best not get mixed up in serious crime; not even for me.'

'What are we going to do about her, Dad?'

He'd been thinking the same. Why did she want to come back and haunt them? They were getting on just fine on their own. If she was thinking of sailing back into their lives, he'd tell her what was what.

'What's in the bag?'

'Oh, it's why I was in there. I've bought myself some decent paper. I'm going to get an A in my 'O' level art.'

'Brilliant! That's great — well done! Blimey, you kept that quiet. Oh, Tina, well done! When did you hear?'

'Steady on, Eddy. I haven't done it yet. I'm predicting it, that's all. I did a deal with the headmaster. I've got to do some work, though.'

'What kind of deal?'

'I'm designing his new wig for him. I'll work on yours, too. In fact, you two can share wigs: weekdays for him, weekends for you.'

'What do I want a wig for? I've got a great big head of hair.'

'Dad, you make Kojak look hairy!'

Terry was relieved they'd managed to lighten the mood. This was exactly why Diane was not welcome back in their lives. Tina and he had a way of being that suited them and only them.

'Want something for lunch?'

'I suppose. What have you got?'

'I was going to have a sandwich. Want one?'

'Yeah, go on. What are you having?'

'Sandwich Spread.'

'Go on, then.'

Terry busied himself as he thought about Diane. What should he do? He turned around, steeled himself.

'Do you want to see her?'

'Definitely not. It's the last thing in the world I want to do.'

He studied her face: no, she wasn't sure. Damn!

She said, 'Miss Lewis liked my pictures.'

'Yeah? I bet she thought your model could be a professional.'

'Well, funny you should say that. She thought you might suit a more avant-garde look. By the way, I might be out a bit late tonight. I'm going to have my hair done and then I'm meeting up with Gary.'

'Don't be too late. Top students need their beauty sleep, you know.'

'Ha! The same goes for you. You haven't forgotten you're a top wig-model now, have you? Don't worry about Mum, Dad. We won't be seeing her again.'

He opened the cupboard door, picked out two plates, loaded them and brought them over to the table. 'Thanks, Tina. I'm sure you're right.'

Chapter 96

'Have you got a minute, Jim?'

'Of course! Come in.'

Geraldine watched as the headmaster attempted, in vain, to keep the ball in the air.

'Um… Jim, do you think it would be easier to do it out on the field?'

'Much easier. The trouble is, Terry would see me, and I don't want him to know that I'm polishing my skills.'

'I see. With the greatest respect, you've managed two so far. Is that what you call polished skill?'

Jim sighed and sat down behind his desk. 'How can I help you?'

Geraldine shut the door and sat down opposite him.

'I need to get some legal advice. Do you know any local solicitors?'

Jim looked surprised. 'I thought your husband was a lawyer?'

'He is but, the thing is, he's involved in a different field and, well — I need to check something out and he's away at the moment.'

'There's the firm the school uses — Chinnock and Tewson. I think they cover a wide range. What's the issue?'

'Er, hmm… It's…'

'Sorry, none of my business. Sally and I used Jefferies when we bought our house; I don't know what else they cover. We were more than pleased with them. Apart from the fee, of course.'

'Thank you, I'll give them a call. Would you mind very much if I rang from here?'

'Fire ahead! I'm off for my lunch now, anyway.'

She thought through the conversation she was about to have. Was this absolute madness on her part? They would ask all sorts of personal questions that, right now, she definitely did not want to answer. Also, even if they weren't personal, the questions she'd need answers to were in Edward's head, not hers. Her insides fluttered and wobbled as the look he gave her flashed back — contempt. Even loathing. She shut her eyes to expunge the image; it wouldn't go. As he looked at her, she — again — found a dissociative awareness. There was something else in his look: knowingness. She watched him closely: he was weighing her up, gauging her reactions. Was she imagining it? Edward was a very clever man. She had lost track of the times he had been able to outwit her, shepherd her thinking towards his held-back intentions. How could she be sure of her ground? Facts were needed. One certain piece of information was the condoms; they sure as hell weren't hers. They must be Terry's or — she gulped — Edward had 'planted' evidence to incriminate her. But that couldn't be right: he loved her! Why on earth would he do such a thing? No, she must get a grip on herself. The best thing to do right now was ring him up and make everything all right again.

'Bright Star Entertainment, may I help you?'

Geraldine didn't recognise the voice. 'Oh, hello. No Katherine today?'

'No, I'm new. May I help you?'

'Thank you. May I speak to Edward Dutton, please?'

'May I ask who's calling?'

Should she say who she was? Maybe he had told this receptionist not to put her through. No, she really needed to play everything straight. If there were any fault, it must not be on her side.

'It's his wife, Geraldine.'

'Hold the line.'

How was this going to go? She expected the new girl to come back and tell her he wasn't available. Maybe he would take the call and apologise for the awful mistake he'd made? That couldn't happen, though: for him to admit a mistake would require him to explain why he had an opened packet of Durex with him.

'Gerry?'

She jumped. 'Oh, Edward, is that you?'

'What is it, Gerry?'

'I wanted to… I've been wondering… I'm frightened, Edward.'

Silence, just his breathing. She fought to get a sensible thought out; nothing emerged. She heard him light a cigarette.

She said, at last, 'Um, about last night…'

'Yes?'

'Oh, Edward, I have no idea where those — ahem — things came from. I suppose they might be Terry's, but we certainly did not… Oh, this is awful. Edward, you must believe me, please!'

Cigarette smoke being exhaled.

'Edward, what is going on? Please explain it all to me?'

At last he spoke. 'I still can't quite believe it. I don't know why, but I've always thought of you as a loyal and loving wife. I now realise that you're a scheming woman who takes opportunities to have what you want, when you want, with whom you want it, and damn your husband.'

'What! What are you saying? Why are you saying all this, Edward?'

He snapped, 'Face the facts, Gerry. Stop pretending. Maybe — just maybe — if you come clean, we can get things back on track. I don't know; it's all too much for me to comprehend.' His voice was cracking. Why was he so upset? He was doing this to her!

Her voice shaking, 'There's nothing to come clean about. I've done nothing wrong. Nothing.'

'That's a lie, Geraldine. The evidence is black and white.'

'Evidence? There's been no crime; there can't be evidence.'

'No? First, a button from a man's jacket is on my bed. The button is not from any of my clothes. Second, there is a packet of Durex on the floor next to our bed — no, on the floor on your side of the bed. Third, your lovely silk blouse that you wore to school yesterday morning, has been ripped so forcibly it has lost its buttons. Fourth, the bra you wore yesterday is more suitable for a Soho streetwalker than a primary school teacher. Fifth, you told me that no one had been in our home but when presented with evidence to the contrary, you tell me that a caretaker — yes, a caretaker — came to help you into bed. So, Gerry, at best you are a liar; at worst, you are fucking other men in our bed.'

The venom in his voice made her reel. No one had ever spoken to her like this.

'Stop it, Edward! Stop it, stop it, stop it! This is terrible of you. I don't know what you're doing or why, but please stop it. It's not fair.'

Silence.

Eyes streaming, nose dribbling, Geraldine put the phone down.

Chapter 97

'Hello?'

Terry was confused, 'Oh, hello. I was expecting the headmaster?'

'I'm sorry...' The woman's voice was so full of cold, he couldn't quite hear what she was saying.

'Er — I'm sorry, I didn't catch all that?'

There was a load of blowing, sniffing, more blowing, 'I do apologise; that's better. No, the headmaster is at lunch at the moment. He'll be back soon, I'm sure. Would you like to leave a message?'

'Mrs Dutton?'

'Yes, who is this?'

'It's Terry. Terry Castleton.'

'What?'

'Don't sound so surprised — I am a trusted employee and part of the fabric of the school!'

'Of course, I'm sorry. Gosh, you surprised me, that's all. Er — are you in school at the moment? No, of course you're not. Sorry, Terry, I'm a bit bemused.'

'It's all right. The thing is, I'm going to be a bit late back from lunch, and I wanted to let Jim know. Well, actually, I wanted to ask him if that was okay. I don't suppose you'd let him know, would you?'

'Yes, of course.'

Terry realised that it wasn't a cold; she'd been crying. What should he say? What can have happened to her? He'd kept out of everyone's way during playtime this morning, so hadn't seen her, or anyone else. Thinking back to her appearance yesterday, he wondered if it had been more than too much port that had left her so low? He judged it would be best to keep a bit of social distance right now, especially from Geraldine Dutton.

'Right, thank you. I'll be off now. Actually, my money's about to run out. Bye, then.'

He waited for her to respond: more snuffling and blowing.

He put the phone down and looked out through the grimy panes of the phone box. The plate-glass windows of *Woolies* revealed people milling inside, but not their identity. As soon as he'd registered what Tina was saying, he made up his mind: he would see Diane immediately. He must make it crystal clear that there was no room for her in their lives and, whatever she was planning, Tina was not to be approached. Also, he knew himself well enough to know that if he didn't deal with Diane now, she would start to grow in significance: before long he'd be fixated about her all over again.

He pushed open the phone box door and crossed the road. It was ridiculous, he knew, but he was reminded of going on his first manoeuvres more than twenty-five years ago. He found himself looking around to see where possible danger might lie. Starting with the far left-hand aisle, furthest away from make-up, he pretended to examine the range of hardware: nails, screws and screwdrivers, brackets, hammers, saws… yards and yards of cheap stock that he wouldn't touch with a barge pole. He moved around the far end and into stationery, peering around him as he went. Up ahead, he could see the sweets and chocolates aisle was busy, so reversed and went into cards, wrapping paper and board games. Standing in front of Cluedo, he stood on tiptoe and peeped over the top of the display. There she was, serving a customer.

Tina had been right: she looked much older. Her hair had been a beautiful, honey colour, now it was an unnatural blonde. Conscious of his shifty behaviour, he walked to the end of the aisle and around into the next one — paint, wallpaper, brushes. What was he going to do when he reached her counter? It was hardly appropriate to tell his estranged wife to leave him and his daughter alone, not in the middle of FW *Woolworths*, anyway. He kept moving. He was going to do this, no matter what. He was about to round the corner when he heard quick, clicking footsteps on the other side of the display. Terry peeped around the kettles and saucepans at the end of the aisle and saw her speed past cricket bats, tennis racquets, snorkels, masks and flippers, then disappear through the 'Staff Only' door, beyond lamp-stands and shades. He looked at his watch: one p.m. He knew what she'd be doing.

Turning on his heel, he marched out of the shop. Taking a sharp right, he sped the ten yards to the alleyway which ran to the service road at the back of the shops. There were three youths lounging against the wall; one of them handed a bottle to another. Terry slowed to let them move out of his way; they didn't.

'Excuse me, lads.' They looked surly and stood still. Terry raised his fists, 'If you don't get out of my way, I shall beat your fucking heads to a pulp.' The youths scarpered.

He ran down the dark, dank path and out onto the road at the end. He zipped back along to the loading bay at the rear of *Woolworths* and looked around. Three people were standing smoking; one of them was Diane. She looked at him; their eyes met.

'Hallo, Diane.'

'Hello, Terry.'

They stood staring at each other. The two girls with her were looking on, intrigued. Terry turned to them. 'Excuse me, ladies. I wonder if I might have a quick word with... er, your colleague?'

They didn't move or speak. 'Sorry, I didn't make myself clear: sling your hooks.'

They looked at Diane; she nodded. Muttering, they moved away.

Close up, she did not look good. Her face was heavily and, Terry knew from of old, skilfully made up, but it wasn't covering the deep lines or the hard expression. Even her body looked like an older woman's.

He said, 'Sorry, Diane, I didn't mean to interrupt you.'

'Nothing new there, Terry.'

He ignored the barb. 'Do you have two minutes?'

She looked at her watch. 'I've got twenty-eight minutes. I've got enough time to smoke five ciggies, have a coffee, then get back to my high-level role in the glamour business.'

Terry had wondered what he'd feel; pity had not been on the list. She looked like her own mum, only a much sadder and scrawnier version.

'I'm really sorry, Diane. I hadn't planned this. Maybe I should have warned you. How are things?' He wasn't sure what made him ask that. She was clearly not very well.

'As you see. You?'

'Yeah, I'm fine. We're fine.'

'Good.'

'Listen, I don't quite know what to say. All I really want to say is that we're fine and I hope you are, too. Shall we keep ourselves separate? You know, our lives are separate; we're different people now. There's no need to pick up where we were or anything, is there?' He noticed, to his great irritation, that he had immediately returned to his old ways: asking, even pleading.

'You scared I'll come back and ruin your love nest with Tina?'

He felt a flash of anger: what a thing to say! He did his best to keep his temper.

'We're doing all right. I'd like it to stay that way.'

'Don't worry, Terry. I'm out of your lives. I'm almost out of my own miserable life.'

'Meaning?'

'Well, I'm only back for a few days, a week or two at most, so I can get myself sorted out. Then I'm off to Australia — forever.'

He breathed a sigh of relief. 'Oh, right. How come you're working here?'

She flicked away the butt of her fag. 'I need a few quid, just for expenses. Sylvia knows the manager. I'm getting cash in hand for a couple of weeks.'

Every now and then Terry had spotted Diane's sister in the streets; he did his best to avoid her. She was a first-class bitch.

Diane said, 'You look the same, Terry; more or less. Well, now I look closely, mostly more. I'm glad I didn't ruin your life.'

'Me too. You did a pretty good job.'

'If it's any consolation, I ruined mine, instead.' Six years ago, and every day since, this is what he'd wanted to hear. Now, he felt sad for her: this wreck of a once-beautiful woman. She opened her bag and took out a packet of *Silk Cut*. 'Want one?'

'Er... no, ta. I don't smoke.'

'Bully for you.'

Terry wanted to get away; she was making him edgy. He'd made himself clear, more or less; she was off soon. What else was there?

She said, 'Wanna know what happened?'

It was not what he'd come for but, despite himself, he felt a ghastly fascination. 'Only if you want to tell me.'

'I want to tell you, Terry. I want you to know that although I fucked your life up, I did a better job on my own.'

She lit her cigarette and blew the smoke away as if trying to get rid of something poisonous. He waited. The two other women were slinking back into the building, both casting surreptitious looks over their shoulders.

'I got a plush job, running girls for a high-class agency. I hardly had to do any work myself.' She smiled at him. 'Yes, I know you know, Terry. I'm an evil bitch. I knew you were there, and I carried on. I was getting a fuck-load of money and I wasn't going to risk it by apologising to my husband whilst I was in the process of making it, was I?' He watched her. Was she mad? 'So, I ran the girls, checked them out, kept them clean. I booked hotel rooms, I took orders, I looked after the interests of our top clients. It was easy money and suited my particular skills down to the ground. I even attended nice events where the girls were working, making sure they did their bit for the enjoyment of rich, famous and filthy fucking low-lives. Dukes, earls, kings and queens… I've looked after the lot. Trouble is, all that glossy lifestyle has its downsides. Do you know what they are?'

'Not really.'

She was inhaling with a vicious hatred.

'Being abused whenever it suits other people. I became a slave, Terry. A slave to money, to drugs, a slave to the whim of anyone who had enough money to fuck me. Oh, by the way, I was not cheap. You wouldn't believe what I could make in a night. What was it worth? Nothing.'

A Bedford van pulled in next to them. Its rumbling diesel engine drowned out all other noise. Terry and Diane watched the driver light a fag before switching off the engine.

'It had to end; I knew it would. I began to lose my looks and, boy, did they go fast. I suppose it was all the hard living. Anyway, the big boss turns up and tells me to get out and not come back. He gave me five hundred quid and left: no thanks, no goodbye, no nothing. What a cunt! Terry, what do you think of that? Oh, by the way, I was living in a flat paid for by him. My home went with my job; what you might call a tied cottage. He gave me four days' notice. Still, what did I expect? He never promised me a pension, four weeks holiday a year, luncheon vouchers. No, I knew it would end and it did.' She chucked away her cigarette butt and pulled another fag out of its packet. 'The only good thing to come of it all is the knowledge that his little empire is going down the shitter.'

'Sorry. Sorry… I don't know what else to say.'

She laughed — a harsh, derisive sound. 'How about it serves you right?'

'No, that's not what I think. I am genuinely sorry.'

'You were always too nice, Terry. That's why I got bored of you. You treated me like an angel but I'm really a devil.'

He didn't want to hear this. Tina was the daughter of this woman; she should have a nice, kind and beautiful mother. 'No, you're not, Diane. You've had a run of bad luck.'

'You poor, pathetic man. I'll tell you how rotten I am. When I—'

He held up his hands. 'No, no more. I'm going to leave you now. I hope things work out well for you in Australia. I'm sorry that you're… Good luck, anyway.'

She came up close. He thought she was going to kiss him or give him a hug: something affectionate. He stepped back to avoid any contact. She kept coming.

Leaning into him, she whispered, 'Terry, sweetie, my big, strong soldier. I don't know if you've got any spunk left in you…' She looked into his eyes. 'Hmm, doesn't look like it. Never mind, I'm glad you're here; you saved me the effort of finding you. You see, I want you to do something for me.'

He stood still, dreading what she was about to say.

'If you can, will you do what you used to do best? Will you protect me? Will you do that for me, Terry, for old times' sake?'

He swallowed. What was she going to ask him to do? Her face had taken on a hard, uncompromising aspect.

He said, 'Er… I shouldn't think so. I'm a school caretaker. I'm not in security anymore.'

'Please, Terry. It won't come to anything. I'm going to need a little bit of company during a discussion I'm having; that's all. All you'll need to do is wait in the car; but it would be so lovely of you… You know — reassuring to have someone nearby.'

'No, I can't do that; I'm sorry. All that stuff is behind me. I don't get involved in anything like that. I can't afford to.'

She smiled: a parody of sweetness. 'Oh, Terry, you're such a teddy bear. I'm not really asking you. I'm telling you. If you don't, I shall come around and tell Tina all about her daddy and his previous life.'

God, she really was evil. How could he ever have got mixed up with someone so rotten? He swallowed again. 'You must know lots of blokes that are better than me at that kind of thing, with your connections.'

'What, other losers like me?'

Terry didn't answer.

She puffed on her fag. 'I don't. I'm what they call 'persona non grata' these days. I know you're not an intellectual — it means no one will touch me with a fucking barge pole.'

Irritated by her condescension, but drawn in as usual, he said, 'What kind of meeting is it? Who with?'

She lit another cigarette. Looking up at him, her face triumphant, she said, 'Thanks, Terry. It's with my former employer. He owes me a little bit of money, not much. It's for my ticket to Sydney. He'll definitely give it to me. He wants me out of the country.'

'Hang on, I didn't say I would. Jeez, Diane, I'm a tired old man. Look at me, for God's sake!'

Without warning, she slashed at his face with a clawed hand. Before he could stop himself, Terry blocked it.

She smiled horribly. 'You're made to fight, my dear Terry. You can't help yourself.'

'But—'

'Stop, I don't want to hear it. As soon as I get that money, I'm off. You and little Tina will never hear from me again. You'll be guaranteeing my disappearance forever.'

'When is this meeting?'

'As soon as I can get it in my busy diary. Are you fully booked, or do you have any availability in the next few days?'

God, this woman was such a cow. What had he ever seen in her? He knew: it had been lust, and her shameless ability to manipulate him. Could he do it? There was no way he was up to any serious security work, but he could probably pretend to be threatening if really pushed. If it meant he and Tina would never see Diane again, it was definitely worth it.

'Well...'

'Honestly, it's a quick chat and him handing over a brown envelope.'

'Who are you meeting?'

'No one you know.'

The arrogant, supercilious face of Dutton was insinuating itself into Terry's head. 'I want to know who it is. Tell me, Diane.'

She smiled. This time she did get close enough to kiss his cheek.

'Oh, thank you, dear Terry. I knew you'd help me. His name is Stubbs. Jack Stubbs.'

Chapter 98

Gary had guessed that his idea of journalism wouldn't be entirely accurate, but playing delivery-boy to churches, undertakers, council offices, the fire station — collecting names, addresses, handing out a variety of forms — was a long way from what he'd imagined. Two hours after the interview with Flanagan, it was only now that he was permitted to sit down and write some articles.

Rob was putting on his coat in the reception area.

He said, 'It's the tradition to have a couple of pints at lunchtime every Thursday, to celebrate another acclaimed publication.'

'Really? Great! Hang on, I'll drop these forms off, then I'm right there.'

'Sorry, you interrupted me. The tradition is that the newest reporter stays behind to hold the fort whilst we're out.'

'Oh!'

'Eve will show you how the phones work and, well — that's it. You're in charge.'

Gary didn't mind. Normally he'd be the first down the pub and keen to show off his drinking skills. Today, the very fact that he was at work, away from the police and, for the first time in ages, not having to duck, weave, dodge or lie was a great relief.

Eve joined them. 'Here you are: I've kept it under lock and key.'

'Thanks. I was worried that I might begin to lose my powers.' He took the bulldog clip from her and put it in his pocket. 'Right, talk me through it all.'

She explained the telephone system and how the plugs for different phone numbers got pushed into the switchboard. 'You're the only one here, so you won't need to transfer any calls. In future, you can take over from me during lunchtimes.'

'What about Karen? Doesn't she stand in for you?'

'Yeah? Why would that be, then? Because I'm a girl?'

'Oi! Stop doing that. You're always turning up when I'm not ready for you.'

Karen grinned at him, 'Well, you shouldn't keep saying things you don't want me to hear, should you?'

'Hmm.'

'Watch out, I might ring you up from the pub and be a nuisance caller.'

'You try it, mate.'

She and Eve went out. Nigel, two other blokes that he'd seen but not yet spoken to, Vic Kitchen, the classified ads man, and Rob, all went through the door Alan held open. Each one said goodbye to Gary and saluted him.

Alan grinned, called 'Cheers!' then left a fat, wet fart hanging in the air.

Despite his abandonment, Gary was happy. He was in charge. He took off his jacket and hung it on the back of Eve's chair. He took out his cigarettes. Looking at the packet, he thought about changing his brand. He only smoked Number 6 because they were cheap. It was time to present a different Gary Abbott. What would the Bulldog smoke? When he'd been to see Jaws last year, the Marlboro advert had impressed him. There was no doubt that they were a bloke's fag and he'd look pretty cool pulling those out of his pocket. They'd be much more expensive than Number 6 but how he came across was important. He certainly wasn't going to smoke poncy fags like Dunhill.

The phone rang.

'Hello, *The Post*.' He thought he sounded pretty good.

A strong accent — Welsh? 'Is that *The Post*?'

Gary could hear voices in the background, laughter, a shrill woman's voice in the distance.

He'd been expecting this. 'Yeah, I said it was, didn't I?'

'How dare you? Your manner is most uncouth. There is no need to be so rude.'

'Why not? You are?'

'Well, really!'

'Come on, then: what do you want?'

'What's your name?'

Gary wasn't sure which of them it was; it didn't really matter. This was a chance to get his own back on that farting old bastard, Alan.

'It's Alan.'

'Alan who?'

Gary didn't know. He looked around Eve's desk. Yes, there was a list of names and extension numbers; there he was. Alan Cook.

'It's Alan Cock.'

Gary heard spluttering, then, 'Right, well, Alan, I want to make a complaint.'

'There's a surprise.'

'Are you trying to aggravate me still further?'

Gary was enjoying this. He could last all day if necessary. 'Why, what are you going to do about it?'

'Put me through to the editor; I can't believe your attitude.'

'He's down the boozer, getting pissed.'

'Do you know who I am?'

'No and, what's more, I couldn't care less.'

'Mr Cock, if that is indeed your real name, I am the Reverend William Thomas. I am the rector of St Michael's church. I am going to write to the editor expressing my extreme disappointment in his staff and the attitudes of the paper. I simply rang to point out that the date of the fundraising event at the parish hall has the wrong month — it says June and it should be July. However, bearing in mind your attitude, sir, I shall instead write a very stiff letter, a very stiff letter indeed. Good day to you.'

As the man was speaking, Gary began to think he might have misjudged the call.

He said, 'Er, sorry — um... I... Could you hold the line for a minute?' Gary reached for the newspaper and flicked through it as fast as he could. There, page twelve, an article about a concert on the eighteenth of June. He put the phone to his ear again. 'Er, I've found the right page. Um, should it be the eighteenth of July, then?'

Through the earpiece, he heard wheezing, then gasping laughter.

'Got you, Bulldog! You can't beat me! I'm the king of wind-ups.'

'Alan, you bastard!'

'Bye, sucker!'

Smiling, Gary put the phone down. Soon after, it rang again.

Cautious this time, he said, 'Hello, *The Post*?'

'Hello, my cat's disappeared. I haven't seen him since Tuesday. He normally comes home at six every night for his supper. I've been giving him Whiskas chicken and rabbit; he really likes that. I'm so worried about him. Has anyone reported anything to you?'

'I'm very sorry. What colour is he?'

'Stripey, but he's got some spots too.'

'What's his name?'

'Mr Tibbles.'

Surely this was another joke. 'Is he large or small?'

'Well, he's got a large head and a small body.'

A figure caught his eye outside: Joe! 'May I take your name?'

'It's me, Eve. Well done. You've passed. See you later.'

He waved to Joe, got up and opened the door.

'Thank God! Some sanity. Have you found anything out?'

Joe pulled an envelope out of his inside pocket. 'I don't know if it's what you want or expected. It's the best I could do.'

The door burst open. Karen was there, smiling broadly. 'Come on, Gary. The jokes are over. Your drink's on the bar.'

Gary took the envelope, stood up and held out his hand. 'Thanks, Joe. I owe you, again.'

They shook hands. Joe went to the door. He turned back to Gary. 'Keep in touch, won't you?'

When the door closed, Karen said, 'Who was that? He looked terribly, um — you know.'

'Terribly what?'

'I don't know. Is he a soldier? Spy? Secret agent or something?'

'No, just my friend.'

'Hmm, you've got some interesting friends. Now, come on: time to lock up and get a drink down your neck.'

She locked the door behind them. 'We're next door. You did very well, by the way. When they tricked me, I didn't have a clue what was going on. I wrote a great long message about the Pope and had to read it back before Nigel broke down. You're a natural.'

They went into The Crown. Gary's colleagues cheered as they saw him.

He charged up to Alan. 'You've picked on the wrong bloke, Alan. I'll get you back.'

Nigel handed him a pint of lager. 'There you are. Get the other side of that. Some of us thought you might prefer a Babycham but I decided you'd want some fizzy piss, so here's your Heineken.'

Gary took the glass and knocked half of it back. 'Thanks. Lovely.'

Alan said, 'You did very well, Bulldog. I think you're going to fit in nicely.'

They sat around a large table in the corner, Gary sandwiched between Rob and Alan. Everyone was laughing. He felt about as happy as he could ever remember.

Rob leaned in towards him. 'Just so you know, it looks like your grandad was a near neighbour of Ronnie Biggs, back in 1963.'

'No! Bloody hell, can I ever escape from the flippin' Abbotts? Flanagan told us that the case is being taken over by the Flying Squad. Apparently, there's some big bloke coming in. Even Flanagan was impressed by whoever it is.'

Rob nodded and looked at Alan. 'Slipper?'

'Sounds like it.'

'What's that?'

'Jack Slipper: he's the copper who's been after the Train Robbers all these years. He went over to Rio to get Biggs but couldn't get extradition for him. It was only a couple of years ago; the papers were full of it.'

That must be how he knew the name. Gary drained his glass. Surely his mum must know some of this? Mind you, if this Slipper bloke was as big a fish as Flanagan was suggesting, then maybe they'd all be in the nick before the end of the day.

He said, 'Well, thanks for the background info. This afternoon I'm going to concentrate on missing cats and fundraising events, if that's all right?'

Alan got up, patted Gary on the shoulder and called, 'Same all round?'

Chapter 99

After her dad went back to work, Tina dug out their photograph albums. Most of the snaps were of her as a baby, then a little girl. When her mum had gone, they'd stopped taking pictures. It was her mother who she wanted to see now. The difference between the two faces was incredible. Diane Castleton had been a stunner: long, thick hair, like curtains of honey; huge, brilliant blue eyes; wide, smiling mouth with exquisite full lips. She had a lovely slim figure, but curves, too.

In pictures with her mum and her dad, there was a stark contrast between them. Her mum hogged the camera; her dad was awkward, often not looking in the right direction and sometimes only half in the frame. Early pictures of her dad showed a handsome man, tall and well built. It appeared to Tina as though he had been so besotted by his wife that he had deliberately put himself in her shade.

The woman Tina had seen today was a haggard imitation of the beauty in the photographs. She was, what, thirty-eight? She looked more like fifty-eight, with her poor skin, pinched mouth and narrowed eyes. Also, there was very little left of the curvaceous figure. She had looked bony and a bit ill. What had happened to her? Obviously, the career of prostitute wasn't the way to achieve a dream lifestyle.

When Tina had seen her mum, her first thought had been to rush home and tell her dad the wonderful news. A second later, she knew that it wasn't good news, at all. In fact, she had wrestled with the problem for nearly an hour before deciding to tell him. She was glad that it was out in the open, but hoped that the subject was now closed. She certainly wasn't going to make contact with the woman, not after what she'd done to them.

Conscious of the time, Tina put the albums away and got out her new pad and charcoal sticks. Bringing Mr Sanders into her head, she started sketching his craggy, old face. She paid no attention to the exercise, but let the image emerge. As his features started to appear, she saw that, although it was a goodish likeness, it was as much her mum's worn face as the headmaster's. She swapped charcoal for coloured pencils to apply some thick make-up and add blonde, stringy hair. Sitting back, she examined the finished product — could be either mother or headmaster. She got up and found a picture of her dad in uniform: he did look smart. Fifteen minutes later, there he was on her next page, smiling back at her. She tore out both her creations, went into the lounge and stuck them on the wall, above and either side of the television set. Would he be pleased with them?

She looked at the kitchen clock; nearly time to go for her haircut. Gary would be here to collect her at five thirty p.m. It wasn't going to work out: damn! She changed out of her school uniform and into jeans, white T-shirt, denim jacket, baseball boots. Before shutting the front door, she thought again about her drawings; maybe it wasn't a good idea, after all. Looking from the door into the lounge, the two images were striking: the hideous face of her mum and the clean-cut, hopeful young man. No, it wasn't appropriate. She'd took down the one of her mum and put it into her portfolio. Better make sure old Sanders never saw it!

She decided to leave a message for Gary at the newspaper office. He could meet her at Dazzle after he finished work. She could see a woman behind the counter and men beyond her in an office. There was no sign of Gary. She went in.

'Can I help you?' The woman was friendly.

'Yeah, I'm a friend of Gary's. Is he in?'

'You don't mean the famous Bulldog Abbott?'

'What?'

'He's our ace reporter.'

'Really? Already? He only started yesterday.'

'Oh yes, he's taken over the place. I think the term used is "red hot".'

'Wow! Mind you, I'm not surprised really; he is very clever.'

'Hallo, hallo, hallo: who's this lovely lady?'

Tina looked up to see a tall bloke, tasty-looking, eyeing her up.

'Watcha. My name's Tina. I'm here to see Gary.'

'He's up in the attic, sorting out clippings. My name's Nigel.'

'Oh, hallo. Can I speak to Gary?'

The door opened behind her.

'There's a load of police activity outside Gary's house, still. I got some shots.'

Tina turned around to see the tall girl again; she had a massive camera-case hanging around her neck.

'Really? I'm a friend of Gary's — what's going on there?'

The girl looked over at Nigel, her eyebrows raised. 'Oh, I'm not sure. You'd better talk to Gary. Anyone know where he is?'

Nigel said, 'He's doing the clippings.'

Tina was watching the girl. There was something odd about her behaviour. One thing though — she was very pretty; a bit thin maybe, but a real looker.

The older woman said, 'Do you want to leave a message for the Bulldog?'

'Yeah, thanks. Have you got a pen and paper?' Tina wrote, *Dear Bulldog, I'm having my hair done at Dazzle. I'll meet you there.* She folded up the paper and gave it to the lady. 'Thanks. Bye then.'

Nigel put out his hand. 'Bye, Tina. It's been a pleasure.'

She shook his hand, 'And you. See you again, maybe?'

Tina glanced at the tall girl; she didn't say anything.

Chapter 100

Geraldine could hear him working behind the closed door. What was … a filing, grinding sort of sound. The day had been such an up-and-downer. Starting it in her childhood bedroom, then having breakfast with her mother. The innocent and natural atmosphere, sights, sounds and smells had almost pushed last night's horror into the background. But the lunchtime conversation with Edward had put paid to any relief from the nightmare. Whatever Edward was doing, she must establish the facts. There was no getting away from it: she must be sure that Terry had not dropped that packet. If it wasn't Terry's, then she knew that Edward really was up to something sinister.

Poor Terry. She knew that he had endured some very upsetting marital difficulties himself. Should she impose her private affairs onto his gentle nature? After all, none of this was anything to do with him. His only involvement was that he had hoisted her drunken hulk into bed; done so gently, and with such respect. Nevertheless, she must sort this out.

Hesitantly, she knocked on the door. The filing stopped. She heard a chair scrape backwards. The door opened. They looked at each other.

He said, 'Hello, Mrs Dutton. To what do I owe this honour?'

'I'm sorry to bother you, Terry. Can I come in for a minute?'

'Er… um, yes, of course.' He stepped out. 'The thing is… I tell you what: why don't we talk out here?'

Geraldine did not want to talk outside, in full view of anyone watching, nor indeed, within earshot of eavesdroppers.

'I know it's a cheek, but do you mind if we talk inside?' She could see he wasn't keen. She guessed that her drunkenness the other night was repulsing him, but the facts had to be established whether he liked it or not. 'Listen, Terry, I can imagine that you find me really quite repellent, but I must check something with you. Please will you help me?'

His face was horror-struck. 'Repellent? What are you talking about? No! The thing is, I've got something in my shed that is — ahem… Let me see; hang on there just for ten seconds.' She watched him retreat into the shed and close the door. A drawer was opened and something heavy was put into it.

438

There was some coughing and some moving around, then he reappeared. 'Okay, sorry about that. Do come in. I'm afraid I can't offer you anything.'

She went in and shut the door behind her. Terry was standing up, gesturing to the folding chair he'd pulled out from behind the tools, hanging from their hooks. 'Here, have this splendid item of luxury furniture; it's got your name on.'

She lowered herself on to the seat. Terry sat opposite. How was she going to start? First, it had to be the button. She glanced across at him; was he looking at her? No, he was studying his hands. With his sleeves rolled up, she saw how big his forearms were: massive. Terry was obviously powerful and used to physical work. Compared to Terry's hands, Edward's were like a boy's; his fingers delicate, not like Terry's bananas. She wondered what damage Terry could do with his hands.

He said, 'What is it that Rick says in *Casablanca* — "We'll always have Paris"? Well, maybe we should say "We'll always have the shed".'

She blushed. Rick and Ilsa were lovers; what was he suggesting? Could he tell somehow that she'd fantasised about him last night? Not knowing how to reply, she stared at him.

He said, 'I'm terribly sorry, Geraldine. I don't know why I said that. I wanted to say something light-hearted, you know, to ease the tension. The last time we were in the shed together we — ahem, well... I don't know. It was a shared moment. I'm such a great berk; I always say the wrong thing.'

'You're not a great berk, Terry. It's up to me to talk, not you. I'm afraid I'm going to have to worry about the consequences afterwards. You see, I've got myself into a right old pickle. It's a personal matter and, like the other night, I'm afraid I must turn to you for help. It's not that you're not a good person to turn to — on the contrary. I'm afraid I am making rather a habit of it.'

'Well, if I can help, that's a good thing. I'm touched that you think of me as a friend. Whatever it is, I'll do my best. Whatever it is, I'll keep it to myself. I'm quite a trustworthy person.'

'Oh, I'm sure of that. It's more that the awfulness of the situation shows me up to be — oh, I don't know. Put it this way, I don't think I come out of it very well.'

He turned towards her, his elbows on the little table between them. 'Best to say it. Then it's out and we can talk it through. I'm ready: hit me with it.'

The time had come. She counted to three in her head. 'Thank you. Right, first things first. Do you recognise this?' She held out the button.

He took it from her hand. She noticed that despite the size of his fingers, the way he picked the button off her palm was gentle, tender.

'That looks like it might come from my jacket? I'd say it was from the sleeve. Did you find it at your house?'

'No, I wish I had.'

He looked at her, puzzled.

'I'm afraid my husband found it. When he came home last night, it was on our bed.'

'Ah, I see. Let me guess: he wondered how a man's button came to be on your bed? He was a bit put out?'

She nodded. 'It's worse than that. When he asked me if a man had — um, visited me when he was away, I said no. Well, that was true, in the way that he meant. I don't know why I said no. I think it was because I was so embarrassed about being drunk and I thought he would think I was a slattern or something. The thing is, he didn't say he'd found the button until after I said no one had been around. So, he immediately caught me in a lie.'

'I see.'

'So I had to say that I had been visited by a man and that he — I mean, you — had helped me into bed. He didn't believe me. I know it probably did sound rather far-fetched, especially as I'd already lied about you coming around.'

'I'm so sorry. How awkward for you.'

Geraldine felt tears rushing into her eyes. Terry's kindness was such a contrast to Edward's accusations. She wiped them away.

'It gets much worse, I'm afraid.' She glanced at Terry. His chin was resting on his hands. He was looking at her, concern and sympathy all over his face. She noticed that his hands were bunched into fists, as if they were ready to punch someone. She drew in a deep breath. 'Now, this is where it gets really bad. He was waiting for me to tell him that he's right, that I've been with another man. I denied everything. Of course, I did, there's nothing to admit. But he kept staring at me — clearly, he didn't believe me. Oh, by the way, I'm sorry, Terry: I told him that it was you who came round to get your jacket, that it was you who helped me. I shouldn't have done that, but it didn't occur to me not to.'

'That doesn't matter. We didn't do anything wrong, did we?'

'Didn't we?' Her voice was a whisper.

'No, nothing. You might have been drunk, but I wasn't. Anyway, I wouldn't have done anything even if I had been.'

'I don't blame you; I must have been an awful sight.'

'No, I don't mean that. Definitely not that. It's just that taking advantage of someone — you know. Anyway, it doesn't matter about me.'

The moment had arrived. 'Right, I'm so sorry, Terry. I'm going to have to ask you something very personal. It's rather awkward. Just thinking about saying the words is making me feel embarrassed. You have to promise me you won't be angry with me.' She looked at him. He opened his eyes wide and nodded. 'Oh, God, I'm sorry… Did you drop anything when you helped me into bed? I mean, is it possible that you did?'

For a minute he didn't react. Then he said, his voice calm and guileless. 'No. Not that I know of, anyway.'

'I'm sorry, Terry; I've got to ask you. Is it possible that you dropped a packet of Durex? Could it have been in your jacket? When you helped me up, could it have fallen out?'

'No, I think I'd know if — Well… Definitely not. Also — I'm sorry to be crude — I've been rather inactive in the romantic department in recent years.'

So Edward was making it all up. She had been ninety-nine per cent sure, but Terry's reaction proved it conclusively. What a terrible thing to do to her. Now, with Terry's clearcut reaction, Edward's plot was exposed. She was glad that madness wasn't overwhelming her. Instead, the realisation that her marriage had ended so catastrophically was dawning.

She looked across at Terry. 'I'm so sorry. Thank you. You've told me everything I need to know.'

She wasn't sure what to do now: sitting here in Terry's shed, having had a discussion about lies, accusations, French Letters and, with her head full of the horrendous implications, she simply did not know what to do.

Terry turned in his chair and looked towards the ceiling, clearly embarrassed. She ought to do or say something to put him out of his misery. What, though?

He said, 'I'm not exactly Einstein, but I'm guessing that he found the Durex and has accused you?' She nodded. 'So, to be clear, your husband believes you were intimate with another man and has produced the packet of Durex as evidence. The packet does not belong to you or me. That must mean, unless someone else has been in your room, that he put them there himself, with the intention of proving you've been unfaithful? I'm sorry, I know I might be stating the bleeding obvious, but that is right, isn't it?'

'Yes.'

She noticed that his jaw was clenched and fists tightly bunched again.

Sod it, she was going to tell him everything. Who else was there? Maybe she would tell her mother half of it, one day, but right now she needed to get it out of her system and share it with someone who would take her side.

'Terry, there's more. I got a phone call from Brenda last night. She said Edward, my husband, had come around to her house — well, their house — and had rushed in to see Jack. She said she'd overheard Edward say something weird about him not wanting to do something, but that Jack had made him and that I'd done it for him.'

Terry's demeanour was worrying her. Surely he wasn't going to have another attack? He was fidgeting, crossing and uncrossing his arms, fists clenching tighter and tighter.

She said, anxious now, 'I'm sorry, am I making you feel ill again? It's all been so ghastly, I had to tell someone. Are you all right, Terry? Shall I call an ambulance?'

He got up, opened the door and went outside. She watched him walking around in circles, shaking out his arms and hands. He was muttering, 'Calm down, calm down, get a grip on yourself.'

After a minute he came back in, shut the door and sat down.

'Right, I've pulled myself together. You must think I'm a lunatic. Right, back to what you were telling me. It does all sound unbelievable. I mean, I believe you but surely there's no possibility of...? There must be another explanation for it all. Has your husband been ill recently? Does he suffer from stress? I bet that's it — he's under a lot of pressure at work?'

Geraldine, too, had calmed down. Terry's agitation, and hers, had been relieved by the fresh air. Could Edward be ill? She didn't know if he were stressed at work or not. It was possible.

'Maybe you're right. There could be all sorts of things going on that I don't know about.'

Terry's smile was funny. Not really a smile at all.

'What is it? Why are you smiling like that?'

'You don't want to know. Listen, perhaps you should go home and talk to him. That's always the best thing to do, don't you think?'

The conversation she had with Edward at lunch today made her shake her head now.

'The more I think about it, the more certain I am. It was what Brenda said; it all makes sense now. He went straight around to their house — right after he pretended to find the packet — accusing me of adultery.'

Terry's voice had a horrible quality: very quiet, but there was something hard there, too. 'Who's Brenda?'

'Brenda Stubbs. Her husband, Jack, is a close friend of Edward's. Terry! What is it?'

Terry turned towards her, his face contorted with rage. She tried to get to her feet, but the look of wild fury made her freeze. 'Terry, don't hurt me, please don't hurt me!'

His face cleared. 'Oh, God, what on earth... Sorry! Sorry. What am I doing?'

Geraldine pushed her chair back from the table. Whatever had got into Terry had turned the soft, gentle man into a savage. For a moment it had been like a film, where a kindly character turned, in a split second, into a demonic figure.

She coughed, nervous. 'I think it's time for me to go. Thank you for listening; you've been very kind to me.'

'Don't go yet. I need to explain. You think I'm mad. I'm not. I didn't ever want to tell you what I know, but I think you need to know now. All I can do is apologise in advance. Actually, before I say anything, you'd better give me permission. I know something about your husband that will be very difficult for you to hear. It's why I was sick outside your house. I know that by saying what I'm saying now means that you probably can't say no. Still, I need you to give me permission.'

He was looking into her eyes now; his face was calm and he was clearly back under control.

'It's your turn to tell me, Terry. I've put you through it; now it's my turn to listen.'

She watched him. Whatever he was about to say must require a great effort. What was it going to be? How could Terry know anything about Edward? Again, she found herself dissociating. The shed, with all its tools, pots, brushes, petrol and oil cans, dust sheets, tins and boxes, was around them — everything so practical and normal. Trees poked their swaying heads above the windowsill. Outside, she could hear a crow shouting at something. Apart from its raucous cry, the only sound was her heart thumping.

Terry coughed, cleared his throat and said, his voice flat, 'I discovered that my ex-wife was a prostitute. I came home one day and found her in bed with a man. That man was your husband. I recognised him in the photograph on your mantelpiece.'

The world outside her fell away as she absorbed the words. She swayed in her chair; was she going to faint? She looked across at Terry, to check he wasn't grinning with his poorly-gauged joke. He had his head in his hands.

'Oh, Terry, I'm so—' What was she? In the space of a day, her whole life had been turned upside down. The man she thought loved her, and whom she loved in return, had shown himself to be a monster. She didn't know what was going on in Edward's mind, but the evil intent was obvious. The man in front of her now, a kind and gentle caretaker, had himself been badly treated by his wife and Edward, her own husband. She looked at him again: head in hands, tears on his cheeks. 'What are we going to do, Terry?'

He wiped his sleeve across his face. 'I'm sorry. I've let you down. I vowed that I would never tell you and I've broken my own rule. I think you had better go and be with people you trust, and who love you. I'm the last person you should be with right now. I'm part of the situation; you should go and be looked after.'

'But I don't want to leave you now. We've got to look after each other. I'm worried about me and how I'm going to handle whatever comes next. I need you, Terry. I want to help you, too. Don't you see? We need each other.'

She was surprised by the vehemence she felt. She wanted someone close, someone reliably kind and decent.

Terry looked up and said, 'I'm not the man you think I am. I'm not good old Terry Castleton. You need someone else, believe me.'

She didn't believe him. Why wouldn't he want to be her friend? It was obvious: she was a pathetic creature who could only bring him further sadness and, worse than that, a reliving of a terrible trauma. Now it was her time to cry. She tried not to. Covering her face with her hands, she did her best to breathe slowly and deeply; instead, her breaths got more and more shallow until she wasn't breathing at all. Gasping sobs from deep inside her escaped, then erupted. She was vaguely aware of wailing and moaning but couldn't do anything to stop it.

'Breathe slowly, Geraldine. Slow down. Listen to my voice. Breathe again... that's it... and again, and another one. That's it. Follow me — in... and out... in again... and out... That's it. You're doing well; there's a good girl. Slowly now, nice and slow. That's it.'

As her breathing returned to normal, she leaned into the embrace of the man kneeling in front of her. She felt him pull her close.

'I've got you, Geraldine. You're safe now. I won't let you go.'

Time stood still for her as they clung together. She didn't dare move; he might leave her.

'Geraldine?'

'Yes?'

'I promise you I don't want to let you go, but I've got to.'

'Yes, of course, sorry, Terry. I understand, you find me—'

'No, it's not because I want to. It's because my flippin' knees are killing me.'

She laughed, 'You silly man, you should have—'

The door burst open. A man stood there, a camera in front of his face. She heard several clicks.

'What the hell?' Terry clambered to his feet and moved heavily to the door.

The man with the camera ran off.

Chapter 101

Whoever it was could run like greased lightning. The man, already fifty yards away, was now jumping over the wooden gate at the top of the gravel track to the main road.

Geraldine joined Terry as the figure — jeans, jacket, short hair — disappeared. Twenty years ago, Terry would have run him down, broken his fucking fingers by way of encouraging a quick explanation as to what, who and why. Alas, those days were long gone.

Geraldine said, 'I don't suppose you know who—'

Terry shook his head.

'I can't bear this. What on earth is going on, Terry?'

'Let's go back into our strategic nerve-centre and work things out.'

They retook their seats, elbows on the table. Terry wondered if he should tell her about his meeting with Diane. He had spent all afternoon reliving the conversation he'd had with that ghastly apparition. It wasn't just her appearance that shocked him; her whole personality seemed to have gone through a hardening, even blackening, transformation. His Diane, or, rather, the woman he had thought was his, had been sunny, saucy, full of life. Yes, she had also been capable of volatile mood swings, and even physical violence, but the woman he'd met today could have been another person altogether.

'Terry, I'm so sorry about Edward and your wife; I genuinely am.'

Terry flinched at the memory but then, just as quickly, it was replaced by a new image: Geraldine on all fours, like Diane all those years ago but this time it was he, Terry, in control, not Dutton. He swallowed noisily, coughed, then said, 'Come on, Geraldine, you're the one who's taking the hit this time. I got over all that years ago. It's you that needs consoling. I mean, what has happened to you is... I don't quite believe it. As for that little sh — er, rascal with the camera... What's that all about?'

He watched her face; she was clearly wrestling with the grisly nature of it all.

Looking up at him, she said, 'I've been trying to work out why he would be doing such an awful thing to me. I'm slowly putting two and two together and it's all pointing in one direction: our house. Shortly after we got married, my godfather left me a very large amount of money in his will. Edward and I bought our house with it. I think Edward used the house as a guarantee on a loan for the start-up of his business. I'm not sure about that; all that kind of thing is his domain. But I'm wondering if he's worked out some kind of scheme to raise money on the house. Or maybe his business is in trouble and he needs to find some quick money? Oh, gosh, I don't know. This is all so awful, so unbelievable.'

Terry heard himself say, 'His little empire going down the shitter?' He looked up, ashamed of himself. 'Sorry, that's an awful thing to say. It's a quote. I think it might be true, though. You see, I met my ex-wife today; she works at *Woolies*. Tina saw her and I got a few minutes with her. I think your husband and this chap Jack Stubbs have been running an agency — prostitutes. She said that the business was going downhill — that's my word — and, well, maybe it all fits together?'

She put her head in her hands. 'No, this can't be right. Edward is a respectable man; he runs a successful business. Are you sure?' She looked up at him, a glimmer of hope in her eyes. They dulled, 'No, it must be true. Oh, God, I can't believe it. This is too awful to be true.'

Terry wanted to get up and cuddle her, to make it all better. He was also dying to get the cosh he'd been working on, go and find those cunts and smash their fucking heads in. Surreptitiously, he put his hand against his heart: pounding again. He must try and calm down. The thought that came next stopped his heart completely.

'Terry, what's happening?'

He closed his eyes, breathed deeply and exhaled slowly: again... again... another one. He felt his right hand being held, then his left. Her fingers stroked his knuckles. He was going to be all right.

'Thank you. Phew! Thank you. I had this awful thought again — I had it last night. Tell me — be honest — is the famous hairdresser part of this Jack Stubbs crowd? I need to know. I must know.'

Her hands tightened on his. 'Oh, Terry, of course! No, I don't think so. Edward and David are friendly but, as far as I know, they are not in business together. I've never seen Jack with David. Oh, God, I hope I'm right!'

'She was so happy when she came home last night. Apparently, they'd all got on like old friends. I couldn't bear it if she — I'd have to kill him.' He looked at Geraldine; would she be shocked?

'It's all right, Terry; I'd help you.'

Terry heard a new sound in the distance. 'What on earth is that?' He stood up and peered out of the window. 'I don't believe it. Of all the…'

Geraldine stood next to him. She had to go on tiptoes to see out. Jim Dixon was at the far end of the field, practicing his keepy-uppies.

Terry said, 'He's actually quite good, for an Orient man.'

Geraldine couldn't keep her balance. Terry felt her lean against him. He pressed back towards her to provide a firm buttress. They stood together and watched their boss's childlike performance.

'What are we going to do, Terry?'

'I've got two ideas. The first, a simple one, regrettably results in me going to prison for the rest of my life. The second, less straightforward, involves us using our brains.'

'Are you sure you don't want to take the first option? I'd support you if you did.'

Terry felt a wave of something so warm sweep over him, he wanted to snuggle into it forever. Whatever it was, it filled him with such joy he had to take immediate avoidant action, or start blubbing.

'Excuse me, Geraldine, I need to show that lad how to play football.'

Before he could move, she put her arms around him and hugged him hard.

'I know I'm being a baby, but you will look after me, won't you? I'm going to really try hard to be strong and pull myself together but I'm going to need you to help me.'

Once more Terry pressed his face into her hair and breathed in the coconut fragrance.

'Me look after you? You're having a laugh, Guv. I need you more than you need me.'

'No, you don't.'

'Yes I do.'

'No you don't, times a million.'

'Yes I do, times a million million.'

'Is that a trillion?'

'You're the teacher.'

'You're the caretaker. You have to take care of me.'

Terry would love to take care of Geraldine Dutton. The trouble was that, right now, he couldn't even take care of himself. Plus — and this was more pressing — he was going to take care of two little laddies down the road.

'Um — you know this bloke, Jack Stubbs? Is he a local chap?'

Chapter 102

Geraldine felt safe holding on to Terry. She'd never known what it was like to be enveloped like this. Her father had been the only man ever to show her physical affection. Edward was a cold fish. Compliments did not come naturally to him; he would be more likely to tell her that she hadn't done too badly rather than say 'well done!' As for sympathy, he'd explain to her why she was feeling the way she did, rather than express concern or kindness. Their physical contact was confined to their sex life and, as Edward had pointed out so cruelly last night, that had decreased dramatically.

Now, holding a large, warm man and being held in return, was making her cry all over again.

'It's all right. We'll get through this. I'm sure we'll be... I'm sure.'

His voice rumbled through his chest and into hers. What a dear man. How long could she stay like this, being looked after with kindness and love? The time was up.

'Right, I'm officially pulling myself together. I'm sorry, Mr Castleton, please forgive me. Let's work out what we're going to do.'

In unison, they wiped their eyes. 'Cor blimey, I must look a right mess; I bet my make-up's all over the place.'

Geraldine inspected his face, 'Hmm, you might want to touch it up a bit. What about mine?'

'You're looking quite delightful, ma'am.'

She heard the tap-tap-tapping of Jim Dixon keeping up his ball. 'I don't particularly want to go out and see Jim right now; do you mind?'

'Not at all. To be honest, I'm not in the right frame of mind for top soccer skills. The only thing is, he knows our cars are here so will realise that we're somewhere on the premises. I suggest we go soon. I'll tell him that you were giving me some advice about Tina. By the way, did I say? She's over the moon about John Galsworthy.'

'I'm learning about you all the time. Thank you, Terry. You're making me feel better, despite everything.'

'Well, that's good. It's all part of a caretaker's duties. Where are you going next?'

'Oh, I've got an appointment at five thirty. I'd better go and prepare for it.' Thinking through the details of her meeting, she turned to Terry. 'Do you think he's building up a case of adultery?' Terry didn't answer. She pictured the young man with the camera running away. 'He must be. God, how sordid can you get?'

Terry nodded. He sat back down at his little table. 'You'd better go now. Go and be with someone who'll look after you. I'm off in a minute. Tina will want her dinner.'

'Yes, I must get off. I'm going to stay with my mother tonight. If I can pluck up my courage, I shall probably go home and get a few things. I've got to face Edward sooner or later.'

She watched Terry from the door. He sat still: was he waiting for something? 'Terry, are you all right?'

'Sorry, sorry…Yes — sorry. I was just waiting for you to go. I have one or two things I have to finish off. Um… See you tomorrow?'

'Oh, I'm sorry. I'd better go. Yes, see you tomorrow. May I say sorry one more time? I'm something of a liability, aren't I?'

Without looking up he got to his feet, came over to her and took her hands in his. Still with his eyes downcast, he said, 'I never, ever want to hear you say anything horrible about yourself again. Now, you must cut along young lady.' He opened the door for her, 'Go on — 'op it.'

She walked past him and out onto the field. Could she say something nice to him? What would be appropriate? She wanted to let him know that if it weren't for him, she'd have gone mad. More than that, he had, in a couple of days, become the most important person in her life. Jim Dixon saw her and waved. Ten paces away from the shed, she turned back to tell Terry how she felt, but before she could, the shed door closed firmly behind him.

Jim ran over, his long limbs flailing. 'Perfect timing, you can go in goal whilst I practise my penalties.'

'Actually, Jim, I've got one or two things to deal with. Perhaps tomorrow?'

'Fair enough. Terry will be better opposition.'

Geraldine walked back to the school; what should she do next? If she went home, would he be there? Part of her, the main part, wanted to fill a suitcase and run away forever. There was also a powerful drive to stand up to him: to say that she knew what he was up to and there was no way he could

ever get away with it. Edward was not a man to take on in a battle of wills —
and definitely not wits — the idea of it was enough to make her run a mile.
She wondered how much Brenda knew about her husband and his business
affairs? Should she tell her? All the teachers' cars were gone except hers and
Jim Dixon's. The cleaner's car was parked next to her Rover, but that was it.
Glancing over her shoulder, she saw that Jim was pulling a reluctant Terry
into the field. She walked quickly into Jim's office, picked up the phone and
dialled.

'Hello, 953 4418?'

'Brenda, it's Geraldine; have you got a couple of minutes?'

There was a pause, then a slow 'Yes?'

'I don't quite know how to start. It's all rather awkward.'

Geraldine waited for Brenda to make it easier: she didn't.

'Brenda, you may have picked up that things are a little strained between
Edward and me.'

'Hmm?'

'Yes, you know you rang me last night to say Edward was around at your
place? Well, I think there might be something going on between him and Jack.
Do you have any ideas or thoughts or… anything?'

'I see… hmm… interesting. The thing is, Sandy, I'm rather tied up for
the next day or two, so the chances are pretty slim, I'd say.'

'Ah, Brenda, you are a dear. I'm guessing that "you know who" is there?'

'Exactly.'

'Thanks very much. So, before I get off the line, are you able to say if
anything is striking you at present as being worrying?'

'Yes, that's an excellent idea and I do agree with you. It's probably best
if we catch up another time? Yes? Okay, thanks for calling Sandra.'

So, there was something afoot. Good old Brenda. If Edward was at Jack
and Brenda's, maybe there would be enough time to get a few things and
possibly even have a quick sneak around Edward's office. It would be risky
but might be worth taking the chance.

Chapter 103

'I'm not really up for a game, Jim.'

'Come on, Terry: where's that Crackerjack spirit?'

'Honestly, Jim, I've got things to do.'

Jim fired another rasping shot, this one fizzing low into the bottom corner. Terry stooped, blocked it and hurled it back over the ex-Orient man's head.

What was he going to do? Dutton was clearly a full-scale shit, and Stubbs sounded even worse. Terry knew how to sort out their type; he'd smashed up plenty of jack-the-lads in the past. But the heavy-handed methods of yesteryear weren't really appropriate for a man in his forties with what felt like a dodgy heart and lungs full of a lifetime's tar and nicotine.

Despite plenty of reasons for taking a calm and measured approach, he had enjoyed the adrenalin rush that swept through him as he'd considered what he'd need. To start with he'd picked up the old knife he used to cut wedges and tapers for fixing 'stuff'. Testing the blade with his thumb he knew he'd inflict little more damage with it than bruises. He found the carborundum stone and started sharpening the knife blade. After Geraldine's visit, he'd gone back to the task only to notice that the stone itself was compactly heavy and would fit easily into his pocket. Hefting it in his hand, the thought of whacking it against Dutton's temple filled his head: the adrenalin rushed back. What about smashing it against the back of his neck? Or slamming it into the small of the man's back. No, kneecaps! As he pictured the scenes, he gripped the stone tighter and felt his heart bang harder. Then Jim Dixon had knocked on the door and sanity had returned.

'I'll go in goal, Terry; see if you can slot any past me.'

Dutifully, Terry dribbled the ball to the edge of the penalty box and waited for the headmaster to get into position. The silly idiot was reaching up to tap the cross bar, windmilling his arms, leaping up, then crouching down: what did he look like?

He called over, 'Ready! Do your worst, Mr Castleton.'

Terry curled a shot into the far corner. Dixon leapt high and punched dramatically; Terry headed it into the other corner.

'Hey, Terry, that's not fair!'

As Jim ran to get the ball, Terry saw Geraldine's Rover speeding down the drive. He knew he was caring far too much for and about her. He was so long out of the saddle, the idea of having any kind of relationship with a woman was ridiculous, especially one as lovely as her. She needed him to be strong and kind; she most certainly would not appreciate inappropriate advances from any man — and definitely not a dead loss like him. Anyway, although her husband was clearly a bastard of the highest order, she was married to him, and Terry knew from his own experience that it didn't do to get mixed up in other peoples' marriages.

'Right, no clever headers or attempts to outwit me. Try your luck again.' The ball rolled out to the D. Terry lashed it past a stationary Dixon. 'Terry, I wasn't ready! Hmm. Maybe it's time to pack up. Same time tomorrow?'

'Sure. Perhaps you'll be ready then.'

They walked back towards the school. 'You and Geraldine were having quite a chat.'

Despite Dixon's comic persona, Terry realised that nothing much escaped his attention. 'Yes, we were having a chat about my daughter. She used to be a pupil here and Mrs Dutton was one of her teachers. Tina is thinking through what she might do, and I thought I'd get some ideas.'

Dixon nodded. 'See you tomorrow. You will let me know if Geraldine needs any help with anything, won't you, Terry?'

Dixon was even sharper than he'd realised. 'Yeah, I will. I don't imagine that I'll know though. She seems all right to me.'

Dixon stopped and turned to him. 'Listen, it's got nothing to do with me, except that it's on school property but, you and Geraldine — you will be adult and professional, won't you?'

'Cor, of course! Now, hang on, there's nothing like — No, I don't know what's in your head, but honestly! No, no, no. Oh, cripes! Nothing's going on in that department.'

'Thanks, Terry. I'm relieved to hear it. Okay, I'll see you here after school tomorrow. Good night, old lad.'

Old lad! Who did he think he was? Still, it had obviously been noticed that there'd been a bit too much contact between teacher and caretaker. It was definitely time to leave poor Mrs Dutton to sort out her own affairs. Was it possible to attend to his own problems without involving her, though? Answering Diane's plea for help with Jack Stubbs had seemed vaguely doable. That Stubbs was a business partner of Dutton made it a million miles more complicated. What was he, Terry, going to do, anyway? A heavy implement over the back of a head in the dark was tempting all right, but it was a childish fantasy.

Terry walked back to his shed, picked up his overall and shut and padlocked the door. He was going to leave his weapons in there, out of the way of his foolish hands.

Chapter 104

'Are you awake, Sleeping Beauty?'

Gary opened his eyes. Where was he? The dusty, musty smell of all the back copies filled his fuddled head.

'Ah, you are alive, at least. I was beginning to wonder if I should call for an ambulance, or possibly the undertaker.'

He coughed and sat up. How long had he been asleep? Karen's slim shape was framed by the open doorway. 'What's the time?'

'Twenty past five.'

'Blimey, I've been out of it for ages. Not a good impression on my second day.'

'Well, you were the best at knocking back pints. After all, that is what top journalists do, isn't it?'

'How many did you have?'

'I don't drink alcohol.'

'Why not?'

'I don't want to be...'

'I know — a div.'

'No, a waste of space.'

'Like me?'

'Well, what do you want me to say?'

Gary wanted Karen to say she liked and respected him. He got up. 'I'd better get going. I'm already late.'

'Your friend popped in.'

'Yeah? Which one of the many thousand?'

'The ugly, blonde one.'

Gary kept a straight face. 'What did she want?' Karen handed him Tina's note. He looked at it quickly. 'Ah, that's good.'

'You'd better hurry and find her; Nigel couldn't keep away from her.'

'Thanks for the warning. She's not my girlfriend, just a friend.' He put away the cardboard folder with today's clippings. 'What happens on a Friday?'

'Probably plenty of skivvy work for me; tidying for you.'

'Good, I'm sure I'll mess up anything complicated.' They stood together by the door. He wasn't sure what she was waiting for. 'What is it?'

'Oh, it's nothing really. I wanted to let you know that I think you're doing well here, that's all.'

'Yeah? Oh, ta. That's good. Yeah. Thanks.'

'My pleasure. Now, you'd better get off and look after the sex-bomb. Oh, by the way, you got a message from your friend Joe.'

'Yeah? What was it?'

'He left a message with Eve.'

'Right. Great.'

Gary called goodnight to the others as he left the office. What a day. He shouldn't have had three pints for lunch. But they kept on buying them, and he wasn't going to say no. He felt a bit rough now though and he guessed his breath would strip paint. He nipped into *Martins* and bought some Polos and a packet of Marlboro. He'd have to watch out for money: it was slipping through his fingers like water. Lighting up, he strolled along the high street, swinging his case, glancing into the shops as he went.

He flipped the butt of his fag into the gutter, zipped into *Woolies* and walked to the far end where the bags and cases were displayed. The few on show were crappy compared with his lovely new case. It was a shame about the long scratch on the corner, but no one would notice. He thought again about the woman in the stationers; he'd have to pop in and say hello. She certainly was sexy, and a bit of young rough might be right up her street.

He walked up the long central aisle to the sweets and chocolates. What was the right kind of thing? Something a bit special? There were a few foreign-looking boxes. That was what classy ladies liked, wasn't it? Damn! Too much choice. He decided on a box of Meltis Newberry Fruits: absolutely horrible, but his mum liked them. Perhaps all older women did?

The girl on the till said, without looking at him, 'Seventy pence.'

Gary rummaged in his pockets. As he sorted out his change, he became aware that the girl was looking at him. He glanced at her, 'Yeah?'

'It's Gary, isn't it?'

'The one and only.'

'Don't you recognise me? It's Shaz, Kev's old girlfriend.'

Gary looked closely at her; yes, he did recognise her. She was a nice girl. Kev hadn't been with this one for long. What any of them ever saw in Kev was beyond him.

He said, 'Watcha, Shaz. Yeah, of course.' Conscious of his glasses, he said, 'I'm surprised you recognised me.'

'Really? Well, put it this way, you stand out in a crowd.'

'Do I?'

'Definitely.'

'How you doing?'

'Great, now that I've got rid of you-know-who. I'm sorry I don't see the rest of you, though. How's your mum?'

Conscious of people behind him he said, 'Fine, ta. We're all fine, except... Anyway. Here you go.'

She took the money. 'You're looking good, Gary. Very good indeed. If you were a bit older... Anyway — good to see you.'

'Cheers. See you around.'

He sauntered out of the shop clutching his briefcase. Outside the main door was a bench. He sat down, opened the case and put the box in with his copy of *The Post*, the new notepad, pens, spare matches, business card, Polos, and his trusty bulldog clip. He thought about Shaz; she was tasty all right. The idea of seeing her again quite appealed to him. Mind you, he didn't want to keep on hanging around with Kev's old birds. It was time he met his own girlfriends, like Karen Mitchum or the woman in the stationers. What would Kev think if he turned up with a nice bit of crumpet like that!

He stood up and stretched. The Bulldog was ready for action.

Gary walked past Dazzle most days. He knew it was where the girls at school went. His mum got her hair done at Monsieur Le Roy; she always came home smelling like something out of the chemistry lab and, as far as he could see, looking much worse than before she went in. The girls who came out of Dazzle looked like they'd been freshened up; it wasn't just their hair that looked better, but their faces, too. He looked in through the grubby window: there she was, in the far chair. Reluctant to go into a women's hairdresser, Gary leaned against the window and waited. Keen to look like a cool, Marlboro-smoking kind of bloke, he took his time selecting his next fag. Picturing Clint Eastwood, or maybe Carter from The Sweeney, he looked up and down the street with an alert, cagey sweep of his eyes. Yep, he looked cool all right.

'Gary, you great ape, what are you standing there for? Come in. It's your turn.' Tina was holding the door open for him. She looked stunning: eyes bright, wide smile, hair all airy and shining: like gold! He gulped — jeez, she was utterly gorgeous.

'What do you mean? I'm not having my hair cut.'

'Yes, you are matey boy; I've already paid. It was only a quid.'

With great reluctance Gary threw his half-smoked fag away, picked up his case and went inside.

The place smelled, as his dad used to say, like 'a Turkish bath with a load of Turkish tarts getting ready for some Turkish delight'. The chair Tina had occupied was now empty; a girl in her twenties was standing at it, smiling at him.

'Is this your boyfriend, Tina?' cackled an old bag by the till. Gary thought she looked more like a Turkish tart's grandad than a hairdresser but he did his best to smile in her direction.

Tina said, still smiling at Gary, 'Nah, I don't bother with blokes anymore; they're all mouth and trousers. Now, Gary, your stylist today is Tracy — Tracy, this is Gary; Gary, this is Tracy.'

Gary mumbled, 'Watcha,' and sat down.

The young hairdresser said, 'Okay, Gary, this is your lucky day; your hairstyle dreams are about to come true.'

Before he could answer, Tina said, 'I think you should give him a Ziggy Stardust; he'll look absolutely fantastic. What do you think?'

Tracy eyed up Gary's hair, 'Hmm… Yeah, great idea.'

Gary complained, 'I am here, you know. Doesn't it matter what I want?' The girls laughed.

Tina said, 'Um, no?'

Actually, Gary thought that maybe the Bowie cut might look pretty good. He took his glasses off. 'Go on then; since I'm not paying.'

Glad that he'd washed his hair recently, Gary watched Tracey as she first examined her subject's head, then start snipping and combing. Tina stood close by, studying her every move.

She said, 'If you like it, I'll dye it red; you'll look like Ziggy's twin brother. What do you think of my hair?'

Gary thought it was amazing. He said, 'Well, put it this way: I hope they didn't charge you for it.'

'You cheeky bugger.'

As Tracy worked on his hair, Tina started sweeping up around them.

The old hag called over, 'You don't have to do that sweetheart; that's why we get the students in — to do the menial work.'

'Yeah, but I want to be a hairdresser. So the more sweeping I do, the better I'll be at haircuts. Isn't that right, Trace?'

Tracy said, snipping the whole time, 'Actually, I think the best thing you can do is get a really good pair of scissors. I'm using my dad's garden shears on Gary. That's why he looks like a… a film star.'

Tina weighed up Gary's emerging look. 'Yeah, you're right; he looks like that actor in that film… what's it called? Oh yeah — Planet of the Apes!'

Gary glanced at the clock on the wall: twenty to six. They'd better get a shift on.

'How long are you going to be?'

'You'll be out of here by six o'clock.' She saw Gary's face. 'You in a hurry?'

'Well, we have to catch a bus at five to. Any chance you can speed up a bit?'

Tracy said, 'Going somewhere interesting?'

Gary was wondering the same thing. Joe's note had told him what he needed to know but the 'think carefully before you take your next step' had made him pause for thought. Still, however it turned out, it had to be done.

'Nothing, really. Just an errand.'

Tina said, 'You're doing a great job, Trace. Listen, Gary. I'm going to nip around the corner and buy a couple of things. I'll see you at the bus stop. Bye, Tracy. Thanks very much. Bye, Doris. Thanks ever so much.' Gary watched her reflection swish out of the door.

Tracy said, 'Phew, she's like a tornado!'

Doris called over, 'You wanna get yourself sorted out, young man; she'll be someone else's before you know it.'

Gary didn't answer; he knew it was true. David Bowie looked back at him — well, a strange imitation thereof, anyway.

'What's this haircut called, apart from a Ziggy Stardust?'

'A mullet; it's really fashionable.'

He wondered what Karen would say when she saw him in the morning — definitely a sarcastic comment. He'd try and think up something clever, a Bulldog type of reply. 'That's about it. What do you think, Mr Bowie?'

Putting his glasses back on, he inspected the person in the mirror: a brainy-looking rockstar stared back.

'Not bad. Not bad at all. Thanks very much.'

'You're welcome. Come back any time. If I pass my exams, I'm hoping Doris will take me on properly.'

Gary glanced at Doris; she was lighting another fag. He wondered if he ought to point out to Tina that smoking wasn't good for women.

'Well, good luck. See you around.'

Doris came over, 'I'd better check the work, Mr Bowie. Now, let's have a look. Hmm, not bad. Tracy, you're getting better. Scissor-work a bit erratic — look: this side is longer than that.' Gary felt, and smelled, her smoky fingers tugging at his hair. She went on, 'Look at this, you've got straggly bits behind the right ear, neat bits on the left. Now, come on — there's a giant bald spot here!'

Tracy said, 'Oh yeah. Sorry, Mr Bowie; it'll grow back in a year or two.' They lost it: old bag and young girl started giggling, the old crow hacking up a lifetime of grollies.

'Oh, bloody hell! I'm going to kill myself if I'm not careful.'

Gary got up and moved towards the door.

Doris called, 'Bye, darling! If Tina doesn't want you, I'll be next in line!'

Her cackling laughter chased him out of the shop.

Chapter 105

'How're your feet?'

'Never mind my feet. Where did you get the briefcase? It's fab.'

She watched Gary's face light up. 'You like it? I got it at Studio Stationers. It's got all my important documents in it.'

'Hey, guess what! You know the woman who runs it? Well, I'm pretty sure she was after me today.'

'What? No...! Rubbish!'

'Believe me, I can read the signs.'

'But she was after me yesterday.'

'Well, maybe she's one of those who can't make up their minds?'

'Is there such a thing?'

'Apparently. Anyway, what "important documents"?'

He opened the case and pulled out *The Post*.

'Here you go. Front page news.'

Tina read the article then turned to page three.

'Did you write all this?'

'No, it was Nigel, the reporter who I met. He's the one that got me in there.'

'Oh, I think I met him; what's he look like?'

'Tall, thin, glasses, blond hair — why?'

'Yeah, I met him today. He's really tasty.'

'Hmm.'

'I can't believe all this stuff about your family is in the paper. Didn't you say you had an article printed?'

'I did. Page twenty-seven.'

Tina flipped through and read it. 'It's great, Gary. Dad looks like he's about to burst a gasket. I wonder if he's seen it.' She jabbed him in the ribs with her elbow. 'Wow, you really are a journalist! I thought you'd be doing boring stuff, you know, 'til you'd been there for a few years.'

'What, like sweeping up hair at Dazzle?'

She laughed, 'That's right. Serve your time, put the hours in.' Tina looked again at the front page. The picture of Brian Abbott brought back all the horror of him attacking her in the kitchen and then those awful hours in the hospital. 'I'm sorry, Gary; I'd like to tear it up and chuck it out the window. I think I'm going to have nightmares about that day, and night, for a long time. What about you?'

'Yeah, too right. It's funny, though: it was also a good time in a weird sort of way.'

She thought, *Yeah, but no one attacked you.* Instead, she said, 'How?'

'I dunno. I suppose it was when my life changed, and it's got better ever since. I mean, I've got a job; I've got rid of some wanky friends; I've got some much better friends; I like having Joe as my friend, and Victoria; you're my friend and you weren't before — loads of things.'

'Your dad died, though.'

'I know but maybe that's part of the good stuff.'

'I wonder if your dad dying is that thing people say: you know, a catapult is it? No, something like that though. What's that word? You're good at English.'

'Um, cata... er, cata... hang on — er, cataclysm? Yeh, I think that's it. Want a fag?'

'Ooh, get you with your Marlboros! I would have one, but I've got my own.' With studied assurance she unpeeled the cellophane from her St Moritz and looked at the white filter-tips. 'Hmm, which one shall I start with? Yes, this one, I think. I'm supposed to be giving up, but I reckon cutting down is better. Anyway, a better-quality cigarette is called for, don't you know?'

'What are those? They look like something... Blimey! I bet they cost you an arm and a leg.'

Tina smiled at him. 'They look like something a film star might smoke?'

'Er, no — they look like the kind of fag a tosspot would smoke.' He looked away, then, 'Tina, I probably shouldn't say this, but do you think cigarettes are good for you, if you want to be in the beauty business? I wouldn't mention it, but that woman in Dazzle looks like she's at least a hundred and sounds even older. I bet that's because she smokes.'

'Don't you start. You're worse than my dad.'

'I'm only saying. You're nice-looking now and I wouldn't want you to look like that old hag.'

'Jeez, thanks very much.' She was pleased though. 'Right, what's the plan tonight, then?'

'Well, do you remember Maureen said she had a load of papers in her loft?'

'Yeah?'

'Well, I thought I'd go and take a look through them.'

'Yeah? What are you looking for?'

'Oh, this and that. I'm not sure, but I thought I might find out a bit about what went on when — er, you know, in the old days.'

'Go on, out with it.'

'Hmm, I dunno really. I've been wondering a bit about my Uncle Ray and what happened... I'm not sure. I thought I'd just play it by ear.'

Tina glanced at him: he looked away. What was he hiding?

She said, 'As long as we get some nice grub. I could eat a horse, and its jockey.'

'Don't you think you ought to be careful what you eat? You know, you being in the beauty business. You don't want to become a fatty.'

'Listen mate, unless you want your flashy briefcase shoved up your arse, you'd better stop worrying about what I put down my gullet. What about you? You smell like a brewery. Don't tell me your second day at work was spent in the boozer?'

'Actually it was. I know! Unbelievable isn't it? They do it every Thursday after the paper's come out. Anyway, I was only joking: you're lovely and slim.'

Kev had never said anything like that to her. He used to comment on her tits and arse and boast about his own tackle — that was it. Gary was such a gentleman in comparison. It was a shame that she was giving blokes the old heave-ho: Gary would make a nice boyfriend. It wasn't going to happen. Although she thought he liked her and said she was nice looking, it was obvious that Gary only wanted to be friends.

She said, 'I met some of your other colleagues today.'

'Yeah, which ones?'

'Well I don't know who they were; we weren't exactly introduced. There was a nice lady behind reception — middle-aged? There was a scruffy bloke in the background, beard, glasses. Then there was a skinny thing, a bit of a clever-cloggy look on her face.'

'Eve, Alan and Karen. I don't know why you thought that about her; she's really tasty, a stunner.'

'Hmm.' Tina thought that the tall girl was very pretty, but she wasn't going to encourage Gary to take up with smart-arsed birds. 'Oh, yeah, I nearly forgot. She said that the police were outside your house still.'

'Yeah, I need to tell you about all that. Here we are — our stop coming up.'

They had ten minutes until the next bus. Gary read *The Post*; Tina picked a copy of the *Evening Standard* off the ground and went straight to the classifieds. A lot of the ads were the same as two days ago in the *Evening News*, including the one that had caused all the trouble. It was ridiculous but she couldn't help imagining her first day in her new role — gliding through a marble-pillared, hotel reception hall to a dimly-lit room with PRIVATE on the door. There was a loud cheer as she entered. Beautiful faces were illuminated by glittering chandeliers. Everywhere she looked were elegant men and exquisite women. 'Ah, here she is, the talk of the town, Tina...' No — she'd change her name: Katarina Castleton. No — 'Katarina Chateau, our brightest star.' She offered her cheek to be kissed by the tall, handsome man. 'Oh, hello, Warren, how lovely to see you again!' As she scanned the table, she saw David Gainsborough smiling at her. Next to him was Jane Fonda; Robert Redford was sitting opposite. 'Don't you dare sit next to me, sweetie, you'll put me in the shade!' Everyone laughed as Bianca Jagger warded Tina off. 'Don't be silly, you're the most beautiful woman alive!' Tina lifted the glass of champagne pushed towards her by David Cassidy. He said, eyes gazing into hers, 'I hear you're off to do a shoot in the Caribbean?' 'Yes, Patrick Lichfield and I are flying out tomorrow. Yes, Concorde to JFK then a private jet down to—'

'Here it is.'

Tina looked up, momentarily confused. The rackety bus was slowing down. She shook her head: this dreaming thing had to stop. She had no chance of living in that world and the sooner she started sweeping hair the better. They got on and went to the back of the bus.

'Gary?'

'Yeah?'

'Do you think you'll get away one day?'

'I bloody hope so! What about you?'

'Same. I'm worried that I'm too much of a dreamer. I mean, I'm not good at anything; I want to be better and for life to be good, but the chances are so slim. You're a brilliant writer and you've already cracked it. What if I never amount to anything? I'd be so depressed.'

'You'll get somewhere.' Gary ticked off on his fingers: 'You're not bad looking. You're good fun. You can draw and stuff. You're not stupid. Plus, well — that's loads, isn't it?'

Although it wasn't enough to cheer her up, she nodded her thanks for his encouragement.

He went on. 'Also, I haven't cracked it. I've worked for two days in a local newspaper. I probably won't last for a week. Honestly, everyone thinks you're gorgeous and adorable.'

She laughed out loud. 'Okay, Okay, I know! I was being a complete pillock. Thanks for cheering me up. I wonder what we'll get for tea? I'm famished.'

Chapter 106

Thank God, his car wasn't in the drive. Parking in Ashley Close, Geraldine was sure the Rover couldn't be seen from the house. With no idea how long it would be before Edward came home, she went straight into his office. Where to start? They'd lived in this house for fifteen years, but she thought this was probably the first time she'd been in here on her own. Predictably, everything was in strict order. The top of the desk was empty, apart from three stacked filing trays containing papers clipped together like manacled prisoners. Glancing around the room she saw the filing cabinets, full bookcases, shelves crammed with volumes of all shapes and sizes, journals, boxes. There was an armchair in front of the desk and Edward's padded swivel-chair behind it. The drop-front drinks cabinet was open against the wall, bottles and glasses lined up awaiting orders.

Quickly, Geraldine tried all the drawers of the filing cabinets: locked. She sat down behind the desk and tried the drawers: all locked. The documents in the filing tray were entirely unremarkable: blank forms, typed letters with his business letterhead — Bright Star Entertainment. She flicked through the trays: envelopes, new and used, a receipt book and a bundle of receipts, stationery, an A-Z of London: nothing that drew her attention. Edward was a lawyer. His clients were private people. She knew he would be careful with his paperwork.

The thought of him catching her here gave her the shivers; she got up, went out and hurried upstairs. She pulled a suitcase out of her wardrobe and gathered items for her immediate needs: everyday clothing, make-up and toiletries. Keeping an eye on the gravel drive outside, she wondered how her life could have degenerated so completely, and in such a short space of time. As she worked, the expected dejection didn't materialise. Instead, a sense of something else started to seep into her consciousness which, at first, she couldn't identify. As the case filled, and the feeling became more insistent, Geraldine began to smile: she was excited. Was this what escape from a dungeon felt like? The bedroom she and Edward had shared all these years had become a cell. The controlling, all-pervading personality of her husband

467

was in these walls and furniture. She was about to break out and it was making her light-headed.

She leaned on her case and clicked the catches shut. A quick look out of the window: nothing. Geraldine did not expect to find anything informative amongst Edward's drawers and personal effects, but it was worth a quick look. Like hers, his bedside locker had three drawers. The top one had a hairbrush, combs, tie-pins, cufflinks, reading glasses, a black bow-tie, nail scissors. Next one down was socks and handkerchiefs: she knew, she put them there. Final drawer was pants — again, no surprise. Turning to his wardrobe, she swished through his coats and jackets, checking all pockets as she went. What was this? In his grey suit inside pocket? She drew out the small cardboard packet: the box of Durex from last night. She shuddered.

At the bottom of the wardrobe was his old leather briefcase. She pulled it out: locked. Judging by its weight, there was plenty in it. Was it worth trying to pick the lock? Geraldine was not confident in her ability to open a locked case, and time was definitely against her, but maybe it was worth risking a few extra seconds. She stood up and put the case on the bed, reached for a hairpin from her dressing table, and without knowing what she was doing, wiggled the pin inside the lock. After a couple of minutes of fruitless effort, it felt to her as if she could feel some movement inside the mechanism. Applying a bit of pressure, she felt more give — a possible breakthrough! Her fingers slipped and the pin sprung out of the lock and away. Damn! She'd almost done it. Standing up quickly, she peeped out. Still nothing. She pushed the hairpin back into the lock, positioned it against the moving edge and levered hard: a click. Had she done it? She tried the catch. It opened.

Thrilled by her success, Geraldine wrenched the case open and scanned the contents: papers, a small book, folders. Did she have time to go through everything? Heart fluttering, she checked the book first: an address book. Edward's writing, lots of names, phone numbers, but no one popped out who she recognised. The first folder was full to bursting with property particulars. She saw office accommodation in central London locations, principally around Soho, Regent Street and Leicester Square. The next folder was crammed full of brochures displaying shiny, luxury office furniture. Another had surveyors' reports on more commercial property. A fourth was full of menus, hotel and club brochures and, incongruously, rugby match programmes from the 1960s. There was a 1970 Wisden and a load of cards and leaflets from people and businesses unfamiliar to her.

Geraldine put everything back in the same order, pausing with the address book. On a whim, she flicked through to the Cs. No! There she was: Castleton, D, 57 Fairfax Road, 207 9158. Oh, Edward. Oh, dear Terry! She wondered who the other names were. There were only surnames and accompanying initials. Surely they weren't all prostitutes? Were they all wives of decent, innocent caretakers? She shoved the book back in and snapped the case shut. There was no way she could waste more time attempting to relock the briefcase, so she returned it to the bottom of the wardrobe, picked up her own case and fled downstairs.

She looked out through the glass front door, Geraldine's heart missed a beat: the long, black bonnet of the Jag was turning into the drive. What should she do? It was her house, her home; she had every right to be here. If she wanted to put a few things in a suitcase and go away for a day or two, then that was entirely reasonable and nothing to be ashamed of or embarrassed about. The trouble was that she was scared of Edward. He had the power to control her and, whatever she might know was reasonable, he would be able to twist and turn it into guilty actions or motivations. She couldn't go out the front. The car was already parked outside the house. Quick! Out the back door and into the garden. The patio doors were locked; fumbling with the key, she opened the right-hand door as the front door slammed shut.

She heard him call, 'Are you in?'

As quietly as possible, she closed the patio door behind her and ran around the side of the house, trying not to bang her case against the wall. She ducked low as she passed the window of his office. Again, she heard him call. As she moved quickly to the side gate, the office window was pushed open behind her. Geraldine froze, then pressed herself flat against the wall. The gate was noisy; she would have to wait until the window closed. How long would it take before she could safely unlatch the gate? She heard a filing cabinet being unlocked, the drawer pulled out then slammed shut. A key turned in a drawer. A lighter clicked and smoke was sharply inhaled, then exhaled with equal force. The handset of the phone was picked up and a number was urgently dialled.

His voice was harsh, 'Come on, come on! What are you doing?'

The phone was slammed down. Pages were turned. Another call: clearly no answer.

The dial was rapidly spun again. 'It's me — Edward, for fuck's sake … What do you think? … I don't know. Did he get anything … He's your man, not mine … Where did you find him? … Jesus … Yes, I'll wait.'

Geraldine realised that she wasn't breathing properly. Desperate not to gasp, she tried to take in a long, slow breath; it made things worse. The silence from the office seemed to be amplifying the sound of her shallow intakes of breath. Surely he could hear?

'Yes, I'm here ... What did he get?... No — I don't believe it! No, not Gerry! ... With a man, in a shed? What man? ... What do you mean a bald man? ... Is he — I don't know, old? Young? Fat? Thin? ... You're telling me my wife is fucking a bald, middle-aged man in a shed? I — This is unbelievable ... Well, is she fucking him or not? ... You can't be sure? Well, have they got their clothes on? ... Well what can you see? ... Yes, I know that, but I didn't for one second think there was anything — God, it looks like she's been ... Well, what else is she doing in a shed with a man? My God! So I've been fucked good and proper ... Right. So, what's the deadline? ... What! You're fucking joking. How the fuck — Well, I know, but that's not enough time ... Yeah, I've got it all set up ... No, seriously, all she needs to do is sign — I know, I know! I just thought I'd have a bit more time ... Look, Jack, don't you threaten me. I'm trying to get ... Are you mad? I know they mean business. I've been working with them long enough ... You decided to take on the extra — Don't shout, Jack ... What? ... No! That bitch? I told you she was trouble ... No, for fuck's sake ... Five grand? You're not taking her seriously? Come on Jack. She's full of shit ... My God — to think I used to — You're going to have to sort her out, Jack. I don't care how you do it ... You've got to get rid of her ... Of course I've got it all ... I'm a fucking lawyer. What do you take me for?'

Geraldine had never heard her husband like this. He was raving down the phone: this was the time to go. She crept to the gate. If she could click it open while he was ranting, she'd be through and out. Putting the suitcase down, she gripped the rattling latch. The suitcase handle gave a loud tap as it flipped flat on the body of the case. She held her breath.

'I know all that ... She's not having a bean ... Sort her, Jack, once and for all ... Hang on a minute ... Yes, yes. Just hang on for a fucking minute...'

Geraldine lifted the latch and slowly opened the gate towards her. Putting her foot against it to hold it open, she took the case again and edged out into the front garden. Once through, she put the case down and closed the gate behind her. Right, time to get out of here. She picked up the case and sprinted around the front of the house. Ducking under the level of the front room window, the case gripped tightly in her right hand, Geraldine looked across the gravel drive. It was at least thirty yards to the pavement: would he hear her footsteps? If she took a circuitous route along the grass border, it would be longer but quieter. The thought of any contact with him was so repellent, she decided on speed. Right. After three… one, two, three! She ran as fast as she could, straight into Edward's arms.

'There, there, Gerry. You're safe now. Come on, come back to me.'

Chapter 107

'Hallo?'

'Hello, Terry. It's your dearly beloved wife.'

Terry swore under his breath. He had hoped, even prayed in a vague way, that he wouldn't hear from her again. Here she was, only hours after their meeting that lunchtime.

'What do you want?'

'It's tonight.'

'What is?'

'Don't be annoying, Terry. The meeting is tonight. I need to be there at nine p.m. Will you pick me up at eight thirty?'

'Look, I've been thinking. I can't do this, Diane. I know what you said, but I'm a coward.' He was shocked by the sound of that word; was he a coward? He certainly wasn't going to risk anything for his ex-wife; someone he despised. The trouble was that, somehow, she still seemed to have a hold over him.

'Terry, we've been through this. There's nothing to be scared of, and everything for you to gain. Look, if it makes it easier, I'll give you a few quid: what about five hundred?'

'Money! I don't want your dirty money. Jeez, you don't know me at all.'

'Okay, don't get all hoity-toity. I get it: me leaving for ever is your incentive. If you help me, I'm gone. How about that?'

'Where is this meeting?'

'That's better. He doesn't want me coming around to his house and I certainly don't want him anywhere near my sister's place. So we're meeting in the car park at the top of Woodcock Hill. There'll be no one around. Everything will be straightforward.'

'Hang on, I thought it was only handing over some cash. Why all the cloak and dagger?'

'You're being melodramatic. He doesn't want to be seen with me: I'm filth. I don't want to be seen with him: he's shit. A private place with no one around is ideal.'

472

This did not sound right. What if this Stubbs bloke brought a load of heavies with him?

'Will he be alone or... I bet he'll have some protection.'

'Don't worry, Terry; it's not that kind of meeting. He knows he has to give me the money. I've got so much on him; he can't risk not paying me. The thing is, he can't hurt me coz he knows I've got my insurance policy in place — you know, a little bit of information tucked away safe and sound. You see, Terry, I've got one or two contacts that I can rely on; you're one of them.'

'What do you want me for? It sounds like you've got it all sorted.'

Her voice softened; the hard-edged confidence was gone. 'Oh, Terry, I know I've been an evil bitch and, of all the people I've been horrible to, you're the one that got it worst. I know it's unfair to ask you to help. I completely understand that you would rather run a mile than do anything for me. To be honest, if I was you, you wouldn't see me for dust. The thing is that I can't trust anyone else. You're so dependable and decent, I know you'll look after me. Even though I'm sure you hate me, and I know I don't deserve it, you'll look after me.'

Terry knew she was playing him. She was simply going through her act; a performance he'd seen a hundred times. He also knew resistance on his part was impossible.

'All I need is a lift there and back. That's it. Please, Terry. Please help.'

What could he do? He knew that he'd fallen in love with trouble all those years ago. Diane had flirted outrageously with other men during their courtship, but he hadn't cared. All he'd wanted was for her to be his wife. The pride he had felt on their wedding day, and every other day, had been like a glittering medal on his chest, given for valour, gallantry, outstanding conduct and only ever given to one person: him. Now, although that medal was no longer shiny, he couldn't help pinning it back on his chest. There was that other motive, too. He wanted her gone; for himself and Tina to be free, once and for all.

'I tell you what. How about I drive you there? I'll wait until he comes along, then leave you for five minutes, then come back and collect you. That'll do it, won't it?'

He heard the smile in her voice. 'Oh, Terry, I knew you wouldn't let me down. Thank you so much. Will you pick me up? You remember Sylvia's address?'

Already regretting it, but now committed, Terry said, 'Yeah, I'll be there. Listen, Diane, I'm not getting into any funny stuff. I'm just your taxi driver: that's all.'

'Don't worry, I understand. Thank you, Terry. I don't deserve you.'

He put the phone down and raged out loud, 'Shit, shit, shit! You bloody idiot! You total and utter berk, pillock, idiot!'

Still, it was decided now. Whatever was going to happen tonight, he would be ready for it. He was going on a mission and — he couldn't pretend otherwise — he was excited. The adrenalin had been missing from his life for too long. It had been the football match that had done it. He wasn't just a big, fat, caretaker, he was Terry Castleton: big, strong, capable, soft as butter but, when he wanted to be, hard as fucking nails.

Chapter 108

For a second, the relief was so powerful she almost collapsed: at last she was safe. Edward, her Edward, was going to take care of her. Then, everything that had happened, that she had discovered, swept away the relief and replaced it with horror and repulsion.

'Get your filthy hands off me!' She heard the shrieking tone in her voice and, sensitive even now to what the neighbours might think, hissed, 'Get away from me. You're a monster!'

Edward's voice, by contrast, was calm and measured, 'Come on, Gerry, let me take your case. I owe you a massive apology and an explanation. Come inside. Sit down and hear me out. I know I was horrible last night, but I can explain everything.'

She felt him take the case and usher her into the house. All her strength had gone and, like good, little Geraldine Dutton, she did what she was told. The front door closed, its solid weight sealing her back into captivity.

'Come and sit down, Gerry. I'll take your case back upstairs; you won't be needing it now.'

She slumped into an armchair and listened to his steps going upstairs. The sound of his feet disappeared, then became audible again as he went into their bedroom. The case thudded down. What must poor Terry have thought as she had crashed on to the floor two nights ago? Oh, how she wished Terry were with her now. He'd look after her. Whatever Edward was going to say, she knew it wouldn't be true. He didn't know what she knew. On the mantelpiece were the two photographs. There he was — smiling, young and handsome — the face that Terry had seen with his wife.

Looking past the photograph of Edward, she saw the drinks cabinet: would a drink help her manage the next few minutes? Although her resolve did need stiffening, alcohol wasn't going to do it. She wondered what Edward was doing up there? Would he check his old briefcase to see if she'd been looking through it? No, he'd be looking through her case! Well, that was only right — quid pro quo and all that. She pulled herself together. The next few minutes would need a huge amount of determination; her future depended on whatever she could summon up right now. Their bedroom door closed followed by his quick steps.

'Ah, good, you're sitting comfortably. Shall I begin?'

Again, Geraldine found herself watching the scene as if from the outside — why did this keep happening? The man sat opposite her. His face had a sympathetic expression, even a sad look. She wondered what the woman was going to do or say to whatever preposterous stories he was about to produce. He would progress through various phases, starting with shamefaced admissions, on to wide-eyed justifications then, after she had acknowledged his awful predicament and that everything had been an understandable mix-up, he would smile and tell her how lucky he was to have her as his wife. He would probably pop in something about going temporarily mad but that he now had his senses back fully under control.

Before he could start, she held up her hand. 'Edward, you don't need to explain anything. I fully understand. You're under a lot of pressure. Things have been going badly with the business and you need a large injection of money to shore things up. Why you couldn't have said so in the first place, rather than go about the ridiculous gaslighting campaign you've embarked upon, I simply don't know. Don't look horrified, Edward. I know now that it's been going on for some time. You're a terribly clever man; I'm not very bright. However, when badness is illuminated by goodness, everything becomes clear and obvious. Now, the question is, what is to be done about it all?'

Whilst she'd been talking, Edward's face had gone through the expressions she'd expected: hurt, denial, realisation, shame, slyness, and now indignation.

'Oh, Gerry. I hold my hands up to much of what you say but — please believe me — it's all because of Jack Stubbs.'

Geraldine's brain whirred: how should she react? 'Jack? What on earth has he got to do with it all?'

'He's got everything to do with it. That man is pure evil. He has been extorting money from me for months and months. You see, he knows one or two things about my clients that, he says, he'll take to the papers if I don't invest money in his affairs. Those clients will bring me down. So, you see, he is effectively blackmailing me. I couldn't tell you about it because, to be honest, I don't come out of it very well. I'm sorry, Gerry. I know you don't want to hear a load of sob-stories, so I shan't demean you or me. Suffice it to say, I'm in a horrible mess and only money will get me out of it — us out of it.'

As expected, he'd leapt at the chance to blame someone else. Honestly, he was not only rotten, he was a coward, too. 'How much do you need?'

His stricken face cleared for a second. 'Oh, Gerry, after everything I've done, are you really going to help me?'

'All I want is the truth, Edward. There has clearly been a terrible breakdown of trust that has led to your actions: you didn't trust me enough to tell me what was going on. I'm sorry about that. I've let you down badly.' Was she laying it on too thick? He was as sharp as a pin: would he see through her tactics?

Edward stared at her; his eyes narrowed then opened wide. 'I'm sorry, I can't lie to you: we're talking five figures.'

Like one of her least able pupils, Geraldine found herself doing mental arithmetic. Five figures. How much was that? 'That doesn't tell me very much. Is that ten or ninety thousand?'

'Ninety? No, nothing like that.'

'How much, Edward?'

'Oh, it doesn't matter; it's a lot, that's all you need to know.'

She almost burst out laughing. How he could sit there and treat her like one of her pupils. The arrogance of the man!

'Honestly, Gerry, things aren't that bad. All I need is a bit of a financial injection.'

How could he claim that things weren't too bad? She mentally ran through the list: he'd committed adultery at least once and probably many more times; he'd had accused her of being adulterous and had planted evidence; he'd been complicit in the man photographing her with Terry; and — the icing on the cake — he was trying to wangle tens of thousands of pounds from her. She stared at him: he looked back, penitent.

At last, she said, 'I haven't got any money, Edward. How can I help you?'

He let out a long sigh. 'Thank you, Gerry. Oh, thank you. I knew you'd help me once you knew what was going on. I suppose I haven't been clear with you. I'm afraid there's only one way out of our fix: we need to use the house. I need to arrange a loan on the value of the house to release some capital.'

Geraldine knew their 'heart to heart' would conclude with this moment but, now that it had arrived, she was unsure. The time had come for her to say no. Did she dare? Putting off the moment she said, 'But, is the house worth enough?'

He smiled indulgently, 'Oh, yes. It's worth more than enough, sweetheart.'

For a split second, she was tempted to leap up and punch that awful, smug face.

Instead, she said, 'Oh, that's good. I don't really understand these things, as you know. Help me understand, Edward. I don't see how I can help with this horrible mess.'

Seeing Edward, a man who loved control, wriggle in front of her was momentarily gratifying. His head drooped towards his hands; they seemed to be wringing themselves.

He looked up at her. 'I need you to sign the application for the loan, Gerry. The house is in your name.'

'Ah, I see.' She wondered how long it would take him to press her to an answer. He was a professional negotiator; there was no way she could beat him at his own game. Still, there was no need to help him. She looked over at the clock and decided on a minute. Until now the stately, old grandfather clock had been silent; its ticking had suddenly become deafening.

He got up and went over to the drinks cabinet. 'Would you like a drink? I'm going to have one.'

'No, thank you.'

'Are you sure? Everything's been so stressful; I think you deserve one. I've been an absolute bastard to you. I'm so sorry.'

She knew he was a bad lot but how could even he pretend that a drink, given to her as if he were treating a little girl, could in any way compensate for the evil he'd committed?

'No, I'm fine, thank you.'

Options raced through her head as she heard the sounds of Edward pouring his drink — a cork being pulled, bottle clinking against a glass; then splashing, followed by the heady fragrance of brandy. This might work in her favour: brandy made him argumentative, irritable. He sat down in the chair next to her, within arm's reach. The clock showed that two minutes had passed.

She said, 'Edward, how do we know that Jack won't want more and more money from us? I mean, if he's as bad as you say, won't he milk us forever?'

Edward took a long drink from his balloon glass, then another; then he drained it altogether.

'Sorry. God, I'm in a dreadful state, Gerry! I'm going to have another one. Come on, have one too, won't you?'

'Edward, never mind a drink. Answer my questions.'

'I'm sorry. Yes, you're right. Jack has prepared a document that sets out the terms of the deal. He is getting it signed by affidavit. That document will set out the termination of any further matters between him and us. After that, we'll be in the clear.' She heard a can being opened and the hiss of an effervescent drink. Edward sat down again, his drink in one hand and a highball glass in the other. 'Here you are; I know you said no, but a brandy and ginger might help you calm down a bit.'

Calm down! Fortunately, she was now so calm that the urge to smash something hard against his head was quickly suppressed. 'How soon do we need the money?'

He eyed her; his look was crafty again. He nodded towards the door of his study,

'How much did you hear?'

'To be honest, all I heard was you shouting and swearing.'

'Ah, sorry about that.' He drained his glass again.

'So, how long do we have?'

Her cool, collected, in-control husband fumbled for his cigarettes. He lit one and angrily snapped the lighter shut. 'End of next week.'

'Next week! But why does he need it so quickly? Can't you ask for an extension?'

Inhaling irritably, he handed her the glass, 'This isn't school homework, Gerry. He's an absolute shit, and he's given me an ultimatum. Why do you think I've been behaving so badly? Please have a drink, Gerry. I'm going to have another one; don't make me drink alone.'

'No, I'm fine, thank you.'

He got up and went into his study. She heard his case being opened then shut. There was a document in his hand, a pen in the other.

'We have no other money. We have to use the house; it's our only source of funds. This document states that you are authorising me to undertake certain transactions in relation to the house and its contents. All you have to do is sign it, and our future is safe. Please will you do it, Gerry? Say you will, for us?'

Us! Surely he was insane? Geraldine read through the single sheet: it was exactly as he'd described. She thought about her conversation with Mr Leigh, her new solicitor. He had been confident that Edward's recent behaviour was suggestive of duress and any agreement she entered into would be voidable. Nevertheless, her nerves were getting the better of her. The earlier determination to fight him at his own game was ebbing away as all her years as Edward's wife queued up to remind her of her lack of power in this relationship. Shaking her head, she clenched her teeth: no! She was damned if he was going to beat her. He would be expecting her to put up some resistance.

'I'm not sure, Edward. I don't understand any of this.'

He was lighting another cigarette. 'It's simple, Gerry. I can take this to a bank or building society in the morning, and secure a loan to pay off that bastard Stubbs. Once he's off our backs, we can get back to where we were and start enjoying our lives again.'

'But won't we have a terrible financial burden?'

'Of course not. This house is worth a lot of money. Anyway, the point is that, as soon as I've got Stubbs out of the way, I can start to build the business back up again.'

'Will you keep me informed of all the details from now on? I'm so out of my depth. Don't keep me in the dark.'

He smiled, she guessed it was his reassuring smile — the smile that sealed a deal — all she could see was the devil.

'Of course, darling; I shan't let you down. Here you go, let's drink to us bouncing back — back to how things used to be.'

She was going to beat him. He was so arrogant and dismissive, the idea of getting one over on him was enough to make her laugh out loud. She would sign his silly document and pop back to Mr Leigh first thing and tell him that Edward had coerced her into signing the document.

'Do you know, I will. I feel as if I've got something to celebrate.'

As she put the tall glass down, half of its contents sliding deliciously down into her stomach, Geraldine felt euphoric: she — poor, stupid Geraldine — had got the better of him. She took another long swig and smiled.

Looking greatly relieved, unaware that he'd been out-manoeuvred, he said, 'Here you are, Gerry; sign here. Let's get the whole thing done and dusted.'

She glanced at the single sheet of paper; words danced in front of her 'in the event ... assign to my spouse ... value of the property ... release funds in relation to ...' It was all gobbledygook to her. Already feeling drunk, she focused her attention on the paper, but the meaning of its words kept slipping out of her grasp. The insurance policy of her solicitor's advice, and the statement both she and he had signed, gave her security: she picked up the pen.

'That's it ... And date it ... Perfect. Well done, Gerry. You've just saved us — well, me, anyway.'

She saw his cunning eyes. Suddenly not so sure of herself, she said, 'What's up?'

His voice had taken on a flat, matter-of-fact tone. He was no longer trying to encourage, appease or mollify.

'You're going to start feeling sleepy soon. There's no point fighting it. You've had enough to put you out for a little while; you might as well enjoy it.'

For a second, her eyes did close; she blinked rapidly, fighting to bring back sense. What had he done to her? Her mouth had gone incredibly dry. She reached for the drink.

He said, 'Good idea, that will speed things along.'

Before she could pick up the glass, her eyes closed again, and this time she let sleep sweep over her. As she disappeared into the blackness, she heard, 'Don't worry, Gerry. Everything will be alright when...'

Chapter 109

Cursing Diane, and his own weakness, Terry turned the key in the ignition: a feeble cough, then nothing.

'Don't you start causing trouble.' Praying that the old car was going to make the decision for him, he turned the key again: another wheezing cough. He pictured Diane's face as he told her his car wouldn't start. She'd be absolutely furious: would tell him to stop pissing around and to get there anyway. He tried again. The engine cleared its throat, then reluctantly spluttered into life. Was he relieved? Yes.

Terry manoeuvred out onto the main road. What was he playing at? Tonight's mission had the hallmarks of a pantomime. The idea that Jack Stubbs would give Diane any money for anything was surely fantasy? She may have all sorts of information about him but that didn't mean he was going to hand over a wad of cash. What he — fat, old Terry Castleton — was going to do about anything, if it all got hairy, was a mystery to him. Okay, he could push a broom around and, if pressed, still kick a football, but he was hardly a crack commando. However, as had always been the case, where Diane was concerned, he went where she said.

She was a bad person; he knew that now. He also knew Diane could ruin his and Tina's lives and, if pushed, she would. Damn! If only he'd been strong enough to keep out of her clutches all those years ago. How could he have known, though? At the time it was obvious that he should intervene: any decent bloke would have done so, especially one who enjoyed violence so much.

It had been a Sunday lunchtime in the garden of the Plough; he'd been there enjoying a raucous few pints with his mates. It was the day before he was off to Germany for six months and he was determined to have a bloody good laugh. The bloke, a big, mouthy shit, had started giving her a load of verbals in front of them. Big Mouth had grabbed hold of Diane and dragged her towards the gate leading out of the garden. She was yelling blue murder and flailing wild punches. Terry had been eyeing her up for the last thirty minutes: surely she was the sexiest girl he'd ever seen. He was very happy to jump in to the rescue.

Terry called across to the scrapping couple, 'I'd take your hands off the young lady if I were you.'

Big Mouth turned on him and barked, 'You fuck off, mate. When I want your advice, I'll ask for it.' With that he fended off a further scratching swipe from Diane and slapped her hard.

Terry got to his feet and approached the melée. 'Listen, sir, pick on someone your own size.'

Big Mouth turned to Terry and eyed him up, clearly not used to being challenged.

He sneered, 'Fuck off, you wanker, or I'll give you a good slapping, too.'

Terry moved closer: he loved this feeling, 'Come on, then. Let's see what you're made of, although I already know: you're pure shit.'

Big Mouth's face went dark with rage. He charged, his head aimed at Terry's face. Leaving it to the last moment, Terry stepped to the side and the hulking man careered past into a rosebush.

Terry's mates cheered and called, 'Get him, Terry.'

His temper now white hot, Big Mouth scrambled to his feet and lumbered towards Terry, his fists bunched. Terry didn't waste any time. He darted forward and brought his right fist up hard into the man's chin. Big Mouth went over and lay still. There was a ghastly silence amongst the onlookers as they watched in fascination to see what would happen next. Terry stood over the inert body, unsure how best to continue the attack. He was tempted to stamp on his neck but the idea of smashing his foot on a kneecap also appealed. His friends came over, nervously, familiar with Terry's love of doing serious damage.

Ronnie Shepherd put his hand gingerly on his friend's arm. 'Come on, Terry, time for a pint. Leave him now.' Terry looked up; his eyes were clearing. Aware of the commotion in the garden, and now feeling self-conscious, he nodded, went back to their table and sat down.

The pretty girl came over and stood in front of him. 'Thank you. I was all right, but it was nice of you to help me. Maybe we'll meet again, one day?' He looked into her blue eyes and was lost forever.

Here he was, nearly twenty years later, getting ready to do battle for her again: this was definitely going to be the last time.

He looked at his watch: eight fifteen p.m. Pulling into a space a few yards from Diane's sister's house, he reviewed his reconnaissance. He'd driven up to the car park at the top of Woodcock Hill on his way here. It was a flat, gravel expanse surrounded by large trees. At the far end was the edge of the steep escarpment, which fell to a gravel pit a couple of hundred feet below. There had been no other cars there, and it was unlikely that any would come along after nightfall. It was probably a good place for lovers to have some unobserved rumpy-pumpy, but that would be an issue for Stubbs and Diane to sort out.

He had chosen his clothes carefully: black donkey jacket, his favourite dark blue jersey — what Tina called his Cap'n Haddock — Levi jeans, black gloves, a black balaclava in his pocket for when he got up there. In the end, he had decided not to have any kind of weapon to hand; why would he? He was going to do everything in his power to avoid involvement in tonight's arrangements: he was simply a taxi driver.

Before leaving home, he'd jotted a note. Out for a bit, back later, help yourself to any delicacies you can find, otherwise I've left you a deluxe cheese and pickle in the fridge. All being well, he'd be back before Tina, anyway.

Checking his watch again, Terry felt the adrenalin singing in his blood: he had to admit it, he was excited.

The front door of number forty-five opened and closed. He watched Diane hurry down the path and out on to the pavement. She, too, was wearing all black. Terry turned the key: a feeble whirring, then it caught. He flashed his lights; she walked towards him. Leaning across, he opened the door.

Her voice was derisive. 'Jesus, Terry! What are you doing in this thing? It's not much bigger than a roller skate.'

'If you don't like it, you can walk.'

Terry put the car in gear and his foot on the accelerator to pull away. The car stalled.

'Oh dear, she's not liking your manner, me lady.'

'Get on with it! Let's get this fucking mess out of the way.'

This time, Terry encouraged the little car out; they sped along the residential street. He noticed Diane's smell: fags and booze, like an old tramp. He flashed back to that first meeting. She had been so pretty: an exquisite English rose.

He said, 'Listen, I've worked it all out. When we—'

She held up her hand. 'No, you listen. You'll do everything I tell you. I don't want anything to go wrong. If I leave it to you, there'll be bodies all over the place and I'll come away without my money. This is what's going to happen. You park at the edge of the car park. You get out and hide somewhere

— hmm… behind one of the big trees up there? When Stubbs comes along in his Roller, I get out and go over to him. The only reason for you to do anything is if I tell you I need help. The way I'll do that is by taking off my hat.' She pulled off her bobble hat to reveal her long, blonde hair. 'I'm certain you won't have to do anything; I've got so much dirt on Stubbs, he won't risk any kind of harm to me but, just in case, be ready to come over and say that you were passing and would I like any assistance. Don't worry, he'll give me the money. I'll walk back to the car. He'll drive off. You drive me home and we say goodbye forever. Is that clear?'

She was as crafty as a box of snakes.

'I don't like this. It's too risky.'

'You're not at any risk. All you've got to do is stand by and be attentive.'

'I don't get why I'm even involved at all. If all you need is a lift, then anyone can do that.'

'Terry, you knob; I need someone there I can trust. Who do you think I can trust in my life?'

'What makes you think you can trust me? I'm sorely tempted to let you get what you deserve.'

'Oh, Terry, you're full of shit. You'll do anything for me. Even after I've screwed you so badly.'

He gritted his teeth: she was right. 'What kind of bloke is this Stubbs?'

'He's a malicious bastard who couldn't give a fuck about anyone or anything. The only person he cares about is himself. I made a very big mistake getting involved with his sordid business, but that's all history now. After tonight, I'll never see him again and he won't see me. Even better news for you, Terry dear: you'll never see me again, either.'

This was good news.

The little car's under-powered engine was beginning to complain as they zig-zagged up Woodcock Hill. He glanced at his watch.

'Still got it? I'd have thought you would have flogged it off at the first opportunity.'

He wondered about that, too. The watch was certainly the best one he'd ever had, and it had been his pride and joy, just like she'd been.

'Yeah, well. It keeps good time.'

She lit a cigarette.

He heard his voice whine, 'Do you have to smoke in here?' God, what did he sound like?

'Hey Terry, do you remember when we used to do it in the car?'

The memories rushed back; he slammed his mind shut to them. They were not what he needed right now.

'Come on, Terry, join in the game. We had some fun, didn't we?'

The car struggled over the brow of the hill. He turned into the car park; it was empty.

'When this is over tonight, do you want one, for old times' sake?'

'Diane, I can't think of anything worse. Now, please shut up and let's just do it.'

'Dear Terry, you're such a sweetie. You didn't deserve an evil bitch like me. What's Tina like? You or me?'

He was not going to talk to this devil about his angel. One more check of the watch — eight forty-seven.

'Right, I'm out of here. I've already lined up my tree. I know what my orders are. I'll keep to them. When I get out, you sit behind the wheel. If you're in the passenger seat, he'll know you got driven up here.'

She inhaled deeply on her cigarette. 'Thank you, Einstein, I had worked that out. See you later, alligator.'

Terry got out and, without looking back, walked thirty yards to the edge of the car park. A large oak provided a screen between him and the Imp. Peering around the vast trunk, he saw her get out and move to the driver's seat. The flame of her lighter flared again. He thought briefly of Tina chiding him for smoking; he'd have to drive back with the windows open. He felt the urge to pee — jeez, what kind of soldier was he? How many times had he told his men that only dead soldiers pissed? Too many to remember. Shit, he couldn't wait: he unzipped his jeans and let a torrent splash against the sturdy trunk of the tree. Hot urine bounced back against his legs — for fuck's sake! He was a disaster waiting to happen.

What was he doing here? The flat, and all it represented — failure, depression, a place to use up time — suddenly seemed desirable. What was on the telly? He was already missing 'When the Boat Comes In', his favourite programme. *Terry Castleton, you great waste of space, what are you playing at?* Another flame in his car. Maybe he could walk home and leave her to it? It was at least two hours' walk but he'd rather do that than stand here waiting for trouble to turn up. Would Tina be home when he got back? He hoped so. They could talk about their futures again: her celebrity lifestyle and his plans for the renovation of the old manor house he was going to buy.

Chapter 110

'Cor, I love this house. How much, do you reckon?'

Gary sized it up: long front garden, wide, solid door, big windows and, he could see from where they were standing, high ceilings. The light was on in the front room — well, more like a chandelier than a light. 'I don't know much houses cost; I bet it's a lot.'

'One day I want a house like this. Maybe in Kensington? I'll have a butler and a maid and definitely a gardener. I wonder how much your aunt pays for her gardener... Where does she get all her money, do you know?'

Should he say? It was probably all fantasy. He knew from the cop shows that his 'evidence' was what they called circumstantial. Although his hunch about Grandad hadn't worked out as he'd thought, what had emerged made his latest theories at least possible. Could he talk to Maureen about it? Would she blow a gasket? He would make it clear that he wasn't interested in the rights and wrongs, only that he wanted to know the truth.

'Come on, let's get some decent food.'

Again the door was opened wide. 'Gary? Well, this is... I wasn't expecting you back so soon. I thought I said to ring me? Well, come on in; it's wonderful to see you. But — you naughty boy — you should have let me know you were coming. Anyway, lovies, come in, come in. How wonderful. Let's go in here: it's nice in the evening.'

Gary followed Tina into the large room. On the walls were pictures: a massive painting of hills and trees; there was one of a bowl of fruit, and one of some flowers. There was a huge, fancy mirror over the fireplace. He saw Tina glancing at herself in it: she looked fantastic. On the mantelpiece was a big, old clock with heavy, silver candlesticks either side. There were logs piled up beside the fireplace and, next to them, a shiny, copper shovel, then a collection of copper-handled brushes and a stubby poker. The armchairs and sofa were covered in dark green, velvety material.

'Do make yourselves comfy. Gosh, what a lovely surprise! I wish you'd let me know you were coming. I could have got ready... Never mind. Now, to what do I owe this pleasure?'

'Well, you know you said you had letters and papers and stuff? I wondered if it would be possible to look through them? I don't want to take up your time: just a quick flick through would be really interesting.'

She smiled. 'Oh, you are keen. Well, before that, how about something to eat? Tina, dear, would you like a little something? I'm sure I can rustle up some sandwiches.'

'Ooh, yes please. If you're sure it's no trouble?'

Maureen's high heels clicked away down the corridor to the back of the house.

'She's so elegant and — I dunno — sort of like aristocrats must be like. She's got lovely taste, don't you think?'

Gary had to admit his aunt was several classes above his own branch of the family. How could she be his dad's sister?

'Yeah, she's done all right for herself.'

'Gary?' Tina was whispering.

'What?'

'Have you noticed that there's something funny about her face?'

He had. Auntie Maureen's eyes seemed to pop out of her head and her face was sort of stretched.

'I know what you mean. Do you think she's had an operation or something?'

'I'll tell you later.' Gary put the box of Newberry Fruits on one of the armchairs and sat down on the luxurious sofa. Tina carried on exploring the room. 'Blimey, this must be what the Queen's sitting room is like. All these things… They're so classy. I mean, look at this ash tray: I bet it's made of something expensive.' She handed him the shiny, black bowl.

'Flip, this weighs a ton; what's it made of? I bet my dad wouldn't be impressed. He'd call all this a load of expensive crap, just here for show. I wouldn't mind stuff like this, though.'

'Don't worry, Gary; we'll have this kind of house one day.'

He wondered if, maybe, there would come a time when he would be married, with a wife, maybe a couple of kids. What would life be like? A wife like Tina would be lively, and the sex would be amazing, but would he be able to cope when she went off pop?

'Different houses though, yeah?'

'Oh, yeah. I didn't mean the same house.' She laughed, 'That would be weird: you and me married!'

'Do you want to get married one day?'

'I'm not sure. Sometimes I see married people and they're happy — like David and Judy Gainsborough. Most couples seem miserable. I mean my dad and my mum got divorced. Your parents... Well, you know what I mean. On the other hand, it might be nice to have a special person.' She lowered her voice. 'What happened to your aunt and her husband, do you know?'

Gary was about to answer when the clicking heels returned, this time accompanied by the sound of a loaded tea trolley.

'Here we are. Ooh, are those for me? Mmm! My favourites.'

Gary was pleased; he'd never bought a box of anything for anyone.

'Well, it was the least I could do; actually, they're from both of us.'

Auntie Maureen parked the trolley by a big, mahogany sideboard and came over to him. Before he could escape, she'd enfolded him in a swamping embrace of perfume and silky blouse. He fought the urge to wrestle himself free and waited for her to release him. She let go at last, ruffled his hair, then went over to Tina to deliver the same treatment. Gary was having second thoughts about everything — had he let his imagination run away?

Maureen said, 'I bet you're hungry? Tina, you look like you could manage a morsel or two? Gary, you look as if you could eat two or three horses; look at the size of you!'

'Lovely, Auntie Maureen.'

'Dig in, both of you. The quiche is broccoli and stilton, my favourite. The sandwiches are smoked salmon and cream cheese on brown and the white are cucumber. I hope they're to your liking.'

Gary looked at the pastry thing; he decided to risk it. Grabbing a plate, he put a slice of the quiche on it and then piled up a load of sandwiches. Should he wait to be given permission to eat? Yes, he thought that must be right: he'd be accused of being vulgar if he went first.

'Tuck in, Gary; don't stand on ceremony.'

Pleased that he'd done the right thing, he didn't wait any longer. He put a whole sandwich in his mouth and got ready to feed in the next one.

'I'm sorry, Maureen; Gary's not exactly Mr Manners, is he?'

'Don't worry, Tina; he's like his dad.'

Gary immediately slowed down; this was not a description he wanted. He watched Tina eat her sandwiches like a lady; where did she learn how to act? Her dad was only a bloody caretaker after all. Mind you, he had been a soldier and there were high standards in the army. Maybe Tina felt guilty about teasing him.

She said, 'Gary's got a brilliant new job.'

Maureen opened her eyes wide. 'Really, do tell.'

Gary glared at Tina. He wished she'd stop bragging about him.

'It's nothing really. It's a trainee job at the newspaper office.'

'Oh, I'm so pleased for you. When do you start?'

Tina cut in. 'He started yesterday. He's already had one article published. Why don't you get it, Gary?'

Maureen smiled. 'Don't tell me: it's in that executive briefcase?'

Embarrassed, Gary went into the hall and came back with it. Tina and Maureen whistled.

'Stop it, you two. Honestly, anyone would think I've won an award or something.' He turned to page twenty-seven and handed it over.

'The man in the picture is my dad; he's a caretaker, but he used to be a brilliant footballer and he was a soldier.'

Maureen read the article. 'Goodness, you're a very good writer, Gary. Your father looks like a nice chap, Tina. He's rather handsome in a large kind of way — my sort of fellow.' She shut the paper and handed it back. The front page caught her eye, 'Hallo, what's this?' Gary watched her expression as she read the article. Shaking her head, she said at last, 'Oh, Brian, you stupid, stupid man.' She looked up at Gary. 'You drew the short straw with him as a father, didn't you?'

'Well, you had him as a brother.'

'Come on, you two: if you've finished with the sandwiches, will you have a slice of cake?'

Gary crammed down the last sandwich. 'Mmm-mm. Yes, please.'

Maureen loaded the tea trolley with empty plates and wheeled it back up the wood-tiled corridor.

Tina whispered, 'Hey, guess what?'

'What?'

'I've just realised something.'

'What?'

'She's… I'll tell you later.'

Gary sat back and looked at his aunt as she came back in, this time with a sponge cake, jam and cream oozing from between its layers. She smiled at him, her white teeth starkly contrasting with the vivid lipstick. What had Tina noticed?

Maureen pushed luxuriant, chestnut hair out of her eyes as she deftly wielded the long knife to cut them large slices. 'Tina, will you go first?'

'Yum! Thank you.'

'Gary?'

'Not 'alf.'

Maureen poured more tea.

'How about you, Tina? How are the plans for your glittering career coming along?'

Gary said, keen to get his own back, 'She's very high up in the beauty business. She's David What's-his-face's right-hand woman.'

'Idiot! I'm going to be a hairdresser. David What's-his-face is David Gainsborough — you know, the famous hair stylist. I met him last night and he said I could train with him.'

Maureen's eyes popped even more. 'What — Davie? Oh, Tina, he's utterly divine! I've been going to him for years. I'm terribly impressed; he doesn't take on anyone, you know. Oh my, you two: you really are a couple of high-flyers.'

Gary wondered when he'd get his chance to talk to her on his own. He was unsure of himself: had he gone up a wild-goose chase? Or was it a blind alley? Whatever it was, should he let sleeping dogs lie? But he'd taken in what Frank had said about the truth: this wasn't about what he wanted to be true, it was about what was true.

'Er, Auntie Maureen — you know you said you had old letters and stuff?'

'Ah, you're keen to dig around in the family archives, are you?'

He studied her face; she looked all right about it. If she had anything to hide, she'd hardly be so encouraging, would she?

Maureen said, 'Tina, will you excuse us for a few minutes? We're going to nip upstairs for a jaunt down memory lane.'

'Of course. I'll read my book.' She opened her shoulder bag and pulled out *I Love Your Hair*.

Gary followed Maureen upstairs. He had been wondering how on earth she'd be able to clamber up into the loft. He was good at climbing, but even he found it difficult to get into their loft at home. Maybe there was a ladder or something.

She said, 'Up one more flight.'

He now saw that he wouldn't need to shimmy up into a hatchway; there was a complete staircase winding up out of sight. He followed her up. Although the steps were not steep, she was beginning to puff.

'Gosh, Gary, I think I might need to lose a bit of weight. What do you think?'

Actually, Gary thought she had a pretty good figure for an old lady. He'd clocked her long legs as they'd sat in the garden the other day.

'Er... no, you look fine to me.'

'You charmer! You didn't learn your manners from Brian, did you?'

Too right!

At the top of the winding flight was a small landing with two doors off it. She unlocked the first one and pushed the door open. Gary had never seen an attic room before. He was expecting a dark, if not black, room with cobwebs and a load of rubbish; that was what was in their attic. Not here. It was light, clean, tidy. There was a desk, a couple of comfortable chairs, and shelves all around the walls. There was even a telly in the corner. The light was coming from a window in the roof.

'Wow, what a great room.'

'I very rarely come up here these days. I send our cleaner up now and then to dust it. Now, where to start? You said you had some questions; what would you like to know?'

So, the time had come. What would be her reaction? She sat down, crossed her legs and smiled at him, inviting. He didn't want to upset her — she was such a nice lady — but he had to know the truth.

'Well, it's like this. I was thinking about Grandad going missing and all that. When I — Well, the thing is, yesterday the Old Bill came to our house and they — Look, are you sure you don't mind me asking you some questions?'

'Of course not. Ask away, dear.'

She looked genuinely unbothered. Was he making up a load of childish rubbish? He sat down opposite her. He decided to approach it indirectly.

'Right, the police decide that they have to dig up our greenhouse. They've got it in their heads that Grandad is under it.'

She was smiling. 'Don't tell me they found him? I don't believe it.'

Gary pressed on. 'They completely trash our garden — well, it was a dump anyway, but now it looks like a bomb hit it. They don't find Grandad. It's all right, Auntie Maureen, he hasn't turned up out of the blue. No, they found some stuff in a case. I only know coz they let it slip when they thought I wasn't there. Anyway, the point is, um — er... they rang up a load of companies who sell greenhouses and found the one that sold us ours. So, the thing is, well...'

'Gary?'

'Yeah?'

492

'Apart from Tina, does anyone know you're here?'

'No?'

'Sorry. Do go on.'

He was sweating; this was much more difficult than he'd expected. He'd had this idea that it would be easy to say, and they'd be able to laugh about it all. Gary didn't mind what the truth was; he just wanted to know what it was.

He started again. 'Right, I did a bit of research, too. I found out — well… yeah, I found out that you put a greenhouse in your garden the year after Grandad went missing. I put two and two together and thought… do you see…? I thought that Grandad might be under your greenhouse. Look, I don't care either way. I was wondering, that's all.'

'You have been a busy boy, haven't you? No wonder you're a journalist. You're pretty good at sniffing things out.'

He smiled. She was right about that.

'Well, Gary, congratulations on your research. However, I'm afraid your enquiries have led you up the garden path, if you'll excuse the pun. My father is not under our greenhouse. I have no idea what happened to him. Ask the police. They wouldn't leave us alone when he went missing. Ask Mr Flanagan: he couldn't find anything. Is he still involved? Ah, yes, he was digging around your garden yesterday, I presume? Anyway, as you say, our greenhouse came some time after we lost Dad. Now I think about it, I'm certain. It must have been, because we didn't move into this house until at least a year later.'

Gary swallowed. He might as well blurt it all out now. 'Yeah, I realised I'd been going up a blind alley. But I discovered something else. In the case that they dug up yesterday, there was a load of information to do with the Great Train Robbery…'

Maureen's smile was even wider. 'No, stop it! You're not going to tell me that my father was involved in serious criminal activity, are you?'

'Well, I was wondering, that's all. The thing is, apparently the gang had a train driver who drove the train to where they could unload all the money. I thought it was Grandad who did that — he was a train driver, wasn't he? But he was really old, so it wasn't very likely to have been him. Then, my mum told me that Uncle Ray was a train driver, as well. Anyway, what I wondered was… The thing is — Look, it doesn't matter to me, but I thought that maybe Uncle Ray was the train driver — you know, the train driver in the robbery?'

Her laugh was so delighted he found himself chuckling too. It did sound unbelievable.

She said, wiping her eyes, 'You want to know if my ex-husband was involved in the Great Train Robbery? Are you having me on?'

He pressed on; he might as well.

'Well, yeah, I know it's all a bit... Also, apparently the police never discovered who the train driver was. So that's what made me think. I thought, hang on a minute, why don't I remember Uncle Ray? I asked my mum when you and him were divorced. She couldn't remember exactly because you cut off contact with us. The thing is, the company that did your greenhouse said it was in 1964, a year after the big robbery. They sold it to a Mrs Cross, not Mr Cross.'

'Gary, what is this all about? You seem to be building up to something.'

'Okay, so I was thinking, you've got this lovely house; you've got a gardener, a cleaner. Where did you get the money for it all? Then, I thought that if Uncle Ray was involved in the robbery, he'd have got paid a load of money, you know, for his work. Then, I thought, maybe it's him under your greenhouse?'

Her laughter was infectious.

He started to giggle, 'Oh, blimey, have I made a tit of myself? I dunno. In my head, it all made sense. I mean, you used to live in south London, in a little house, and now... And another thing, what happened to Uncle Ray? I found out that there's no record of you ever getting divorced. So, you know, I pieced it all together. Okay, Okay, so I got it all wrong.'

She laughed again. 'Oh, Gary, you ought to be writing for the films, not a newspaper.' She got up and walked to the door. 'It's terribly dark up here. Let's have a bit of light.'

Chapter 111

Gary realised that he'd let his childish imagination get out of control. When he'd been working it all out, the facts had clicked nicely into place: Auntie Maureen's evident wealth must have come from somewhere. The clear connection that Grandad had had with the Great Train Robbers and the fact that her husband had been a train driver, these couldn't be denied. Then again, she and Uncle Ray 'going their separate ways' at the very time when she moved into this amazing house was, at the very least, something that needed an explanation. Where was Uncle Ray now? Joe's dash up to Somerset House hadn't revealed any information about their divorce. Surely Uncle Ray must be under the greenhouse.

Now, with his crazy theory still hanging in the air, he realised that it was just fantasy. He had scoffed at Tina's ridiculous dream-world; her head was in the clouds. Clearly, so was his. Auntie Maureen was such a lovely lady. As he'd explained and suggested the 'truth' to her, he'd expected her to change expression: to look disappointed in him, or even get angry. On the contrary, she had shown interest and even amusement throughout. He'd been ready to fend off her fury as he'd done so many times with his dad. He looked up as she walked to the light switch by the door.

'I'm sorry. I've got it all wrong. I dunno… I think I must have got carried away. The police coming around yesterday and finding all that stuff…'

'It's all right, Gary. I understand.'

Instead of turning on the light, she opened the door, went through and shut it behind her. A key turned. What? Gary jumped up and rushed over, grabbed the handle and pulled. The door was definitely locked. Gripping the handle tight, he turned it and pulled with all his might. The door was heavy; he couldn't budge it, or the lock. Turning back to the room, he wondered what he could use as a battering ram. Nothing obvious. Surely there was something here he could use? The chairs were big and squashy. The coffee table was too fragile. What about the window? It was built into the pitch of the roof. He unclicked a couple of catches and pushed hard. It wouldn't budge either. Shit! The angle of the window made it impossible to look out, but he could tell that this room was at the back of the house; he must be above the concrete patio. Fuck, fuck, fuck! He was fucked.

So, had he hit the nail on the head? Was Uncle Ray the train driver? Was he now mouldering away under his aunt's greenhouse? He really didn't want to start shouting for help but what else could he do? Tina's face popped into his head — was she in danger now? What would Maureen do? With him locked up here, she'd have to do or say something — Tina was sure to ask where he was. Fuck, fuck, fuck! He started shouting, hesitant at first, then at the top of his voice. All he heard was his own panic, echoed back at him. He went to the window again and considered the possibility of smashing it, then slithering down the roof and beyond. No chance; he'd break every bone. Then he remembered Maureen had asked if anyone knew that they were there. Fuck, fuck, fuck! What had he been thinking? If his theory had been right — that she was a killer — why had he thought they could come around for tea and have a cheerful chat about her murdering her husband? Not to mention living off the proceeds of the Great Train Robbery. Even if he'd thought it was reasonable, why had he brought Tina with him? What was happening down there right now? How had she killed Uncle Ray? Did she stab him? Strangle him? Poison him? Was she going to have to kill Tina now? Tina would realise that he was locked up here; she'd ask questions. Maureen would have to kill her too... Fuck, fuck, fuck!

There was nothing for it: he'd have to scream the house down.

He sucked in a huge breath and bellowed 'HELP!'

Was the room soundproofed? His voice had a deadened sound to it. He tried again, and again. He picked up the coffee table and smashed it against the locked door. The table broke in his hands; the door didn't move. This was fucking hopeless. What was he going to do? A few minutes ago, he'd been eating cakes and sipping tea with his lovely, gentle auntie. Now here he was: imprisoned, his gorgeous Tina about to get killed.

He started banging on the door, 'Help! Help! Please help! Let me out of here!' A heavy silence returned his frenzied cries. The futility of his efforts and the growing fear were making him cry. Wiping his face with the back of his hand, he tried again. This time, his shouting was hysterical. 'Please help me! Please, someone, help me! Help Tina!'

Chapter 112

Tina closed the book. She liked the pictures, but David Gainsborough's writing skills were not up to his drawing. She acknowledged that her reading ability wasn't too hot but, right now, she preferred to daydream. Reclining on the sofa, shoes off, legs stretched out, the images of her new lifestyle came easily to her.

'What will you drink, Davie? Of course! You name it, I've got it. Judy, how about you? … Let me introduce you to some friends. This is Alan Alda — yes, the one in MASH. That's right. Over there is Patrick Mower: he's been working on a new series … That's right. Him? Erm — ah yes. He's with Anoushka Hempel; they're filming a new series of Whodunnit. Oh, which one? The tall one? … Yes, the dishy guy? Yes, that's the famous journalist, Gary Abbott … That's right, Bulldog Abbott. Oh, we've been friends for years … I know. He is, isn't he? You should have known him when we first met … Still, ugly ducklings and all that!'

The clock on the mantelpiece struck its silvery chimes. She must have dozed off for a second, or maybe a few minutes. Still nothing from upstairs. She wondered if it would be good manners to clear up all the plates and take them out to the kitchen? Maybe she could pile it all on to the tea trolley.

'Don't worry about all that, sweetie. You can leave it to me.'

Tina jumped. 'Oh, blimey! You startled me.'

Maureen, smiling broadly, came into the room.

'Gary's looking through some papers upstairs. He'll be down in a minute. Now, Tina, while he's upstairs, I can find out a bit more about you.'

'Oh, well, there isn't much really. I'm rubbish at school, apart from art. I love pretty things — you know — hair, make-up, style: that sort of thing. I met David Gainsborough yesterday. Oh yeah, I told you already.'

'My… yes, you really are on the way up. Now, Tina, sweetheart, I was wondering something. Gary was telling me about his theories, and it occurred to me that you might have talked about them and maybe even agree with him?'

Tina wasn't sure what theories she was talking about. 'Well, I'm not sure. Gary and I have only been friends for a few days. I used to go out with Kev... you know that already. Gary and I have only just—'

'So, you didn't talk about the police or anything else?'

'Oh, I see. Well, Gary did have his theories about the greenhouse and your—'

'Thank you. That's what I thought. Now, I want to show you something. Come on. You'll never guess what I've got for you.'

Putting on her shoes, Tina picked up her bag and waited.

'After you. Into the hall and along to the kitchen.'

Tina did as she was told.

In the distance she heard a shout, 'Goodness! Whatever is that?'

'I'm so sorry, sweetheart. I'm afraid my next-door neighbours make quite a lot of noise. They have a handicapped child and this is his bedtime. He creates a terrible shindig every night, crashing around, shouting and screaming. It's an awful shame; his parents are such lovely people. I do my best to help them whenever I can, but what can you do? I think that a little bit of tolerance is the least I can offer. Don't you agree?'

'Definitely. Poor people.'

Tina could hear more distant shouting; blimey, the boy was making a hell of a racket.

'This house has got a lovely big cellar. While Gary goes through his old photographs, I want to show you my collection. I can tell you're very keen on clothes and fashion accessories, and all that kind of thing. Over the years, I've collected lots of memorabilia: hats, jewellery, shoes from past generations. All sorts of things. Will you come and take a look at it all?' Maureen opened a door, switched on a light to reveal steps winding down and around a corner. 'Here you are, Tina. After you.'

Tina paused at the top of the steps as she heard the poor kid's shouts and screams get more and more frenzied. She wondered how his parents resisted the urge to smother him. She grasped the wooden handrail and went downstairs. The door closed behind her.

Chapter 113

Gary's voice was already hoarse. Surely someone would wonder why there was a madman screaming his head off? What was happening to Tina? If she were still in the house, she'd be up here. She'd have found him by now. Had Auntie Maureen killed her? He felt hot tears of rage and frustration running down his cheeks. Why had he been so fucking stupid? What did he think he was playing at? Was he going to write some kind of exclusive article about his own family being murderers and train robbers? Jesus, he was a stupid, fucking idiot! Now, just when he'd found Tina and wanted to look after her, he'd led her to — what? Her death?

He screamed again, 'Help! Someone help! Please help! Anyone. Someone, help me! Help us!'

He sat down in one of the armchairs and breathed hard. He must keep a clear head; getting hysterical wasn't going to help him or Tina. Once more, he looked around the room; was there anything here that he could use? He looked through the desk drawers again: a load of papers and folders. What he needed was a sharp and heavy implement to smash against the locked door. Snarling with rage, again he considered breaking the window and seeing if he could climb out onto the roof. No, that really was insane. The tears ran down his face; this was a fucking nightmare. He roared for help, over and over again.

Chapter 114

Maureen's lovely, friendly voice followed her down the stairs. 'Now, what do you think about all this?'

Tina looked around the brilliantly lit room. She'd been expecting a dark and dingy place with creepy-crawlies. What she saw was an Aladdin's cave of clothes rails hung with coats, dresses, skirts and blouses; festoons of scarves and sashes; hats hanging on pegs; racks and racks of shoes of every shape, size and colour. Bags were piled high, and in gaps between the racks and rails, were mirrors on stands and on walls at every level; there were even mirrors on the low ceiling. Tina wandered around the cellar, picking up articles that caught her attention.

'This is amazing, Maureen! How long did it take you to collect all this stuff? Oh, there's so much lovely stuff. I could spend hours down here. I bet you do, don't you?' She went up and down between the rails, pulling out clothes that caught her attention, holding them against her, finding a mirror to study the effect each garment was having. She picked up a scarf and wrapped it around her neck. 'This is lovely; it makes me feel like a film star.' She reached up and took a broad-brimmed, duck-down hat, placing it casually on her head. Stepping up to one of the mirrors she pushed the brim up slightly to show off her blue eyes to best effect.

'What do you think, Maureen? Could I pass for a starlet, do you think? I mean, not a top one, of course — maybe a small, semi-starlet?' In the mirror, Maureen was staring at her. The smile had gone, replaced by a look of pure hatred. Tina spun to face her. 'What's wrong? Have I said something stupid? Auntie Maureen, what is it?'

The woman's face had changed out of all recognition. Her eyes were hard and narrowed, her teeth seemed to be bared.

She said, her voice little more than a whisper, 'You're a nice girl and I really do not want to have to do this, but you and Gary have left me with no choice.'

In disbelief, Tina looked at the long, thin knife Maureen was holding, its blade caked with cream, jam and crumbs.

'No, please, no… What are you doing? What is this? Please, Auntie Maureen; is this a joke or something?'

The woman moved slowly forward; there was something demonic burning in her eyes.

Tina cried out, 'Leave me alone. Stop it! You're mad. Please, don't be silly. It's me, Tina. I'm nothing — no one.' Maureen kept coming; she raised her knife. Tina shrieked with terror, 'No, no! Please stop it! I'm nothing; I'm your friend!'

As the monster moved inexorably towards her, Tina realised that she wasn't going to be able to reason with her. She darted to the right, pushing through assorted coats. As she emerged on the other side of the rail, the crazed woman appeared in front of her, the knife slashing through fabric. Screaming now, Tina ducked and dashed through another aisle of hanging clothes but a table beyond them blocked her way; she crashed into its edge. Crouching behind a rack of coats, she tried to weigh up her next move. Before she could take stock, the ankles of her pursuer appeared. Tina, on her bottom, pushed back and away. She tried to stay calm — panic wasn't going to get her out of this nightmare. What was wrong with this hideous woman? Why wasn't Gary down here to save her? Where was her dad? *Please, God, find my dad! Please.*

'Come here! Tina, come here!'

The voice was cold and clipped: an order that was not to be disobeyed. Tina hurled herself back further, on her backside, pushing away through a jumble-sale mess of dangling clothes, past feet and corners of stands and shelves. What could she fight back with? Was there anything?

'Tina, come here now! I won't tell you again.'

Tina's back hit a wall. Shit! She'd got as far as she could. Standing up, she faced the woman who was shoving through the clothes towards her. The knife was in her white-knuckled hand, its blade rising for a downward strike. Tina held her bag in front of her, wrestling to get it open.

She couldn't keep the sobs out of her voice. 'Auntie Maureen, please don't be angry. Don't hurt me, please. I don't know what I've done, but I didn't mean it. Tell me what I've done, and I'll make it up to you. Please, Maureen! Please, no. No, please…'

As the arm was raised high, Tina felt a warm gush of liquid saturate her jeans. She shrieked in terror — then saw the figure rushing down the stairs beyond her attacker.

'Gary! Oh, thank God! Gary. Gary, here! I'm here! Quick, quick…!'

But, just as she thought she was safe, Gary's frantic descent into the cellar was brought to a crunching standstill as his head whacked against a massive rafter: he went down in a heap.

Maureen spun around. At the sight of Gary's crumpled body, she screamed with rage and barged her way towards him through the clothes-racks. At last, Tina managed to unzip her bag. She reached in, pulled out her brand-new steel scissors and rushed after Maureen. Fighting off hanging garments that clung to her, shoving aside clothes racks, she found the madwoman on her hands and knees, her knife raised above Gary's chest.

Tina screamed, 'No!' and threw herself forward, plunging her scissors hard into Auntie Maureen's silk-clad bottom.

Maureen screamed in agony. 'You bitch! You bitch! Come here — I'm going to kill you! Come here, you bitch!'

Tina sprang back, her scissors, now bloody, ready to thrust home again.

Suddenly there were footsteps, strangers' voices. Maureen's screams were competing with other shouts. Tina lost track of how many people were now in the cellar. The only constant was Maureen's shrieking as she flailed around with her knife, hacking and stabbing at everything in her way. Then, total silence.

Chapter 115

'Gary... Gary, are you all right? Gary... Gary, can you hear me? Oh no, he's dead! Gary, please wake up. Come on, Gary! Wake up, please!' He opened his eyes. 'Yes! Come on! You're alive. Oh, thank God! Thank you, God.'

Tina's eyes were looking down at him. He wondered what colour they were. Blue wasn't quite enough; they were sea and sky and some sort of wildflower or something. He'd have to ask her what that colour was. Whatever it was, her eyes were the most beautiful sight he'd ever seen. Her hand was on his forehead. Her face, so worried and loving, was making him cry. He wanted to just lie there and gaze up at her.

'Oh, Gary, are you all right? I thought you'd... Phew! Blimey, where were you?'

Where had he been? Had he been unconscious?

'Er, I was here.'

'Not here, you idiot. Where were you before that — when I needed you?'

The last few minutes were coming back to him.

'I was locked in a room upstairs. Maureen must have gone mad or something. What's happening?'

'Mad? She's an absolute, fucking lunatic! She tried to stab me. It was only coz you turned up that she didn't. Then, she was going to kill you, but I got her first. Then, your mum arrived and... Thank God, you're safe.'

He tried to sit up.

Tina wrapped her arms around him. 'Oh, God, Gary, it's been absolutely, bloody crazy. She was trying to kill me. She had this long knife — it was the cake knife. I thought she was going to... Jesus! It was like some sort of horror film.'

Gary was enjoying being hugged by Tina. Even in his stupefied state, the press of her breasts against his chest had pushed everything else out of his head. Her tear-stained face was close to his. For a split second, he thought of kissing her. But as he began to reposition himself, his hand pressed against her leg. It was wet, soaking wet.

'What's happened?' She burst into tears. He held her tight. 'Shush, it's all right. Whatever's happened is over now. Come on. It's all right now.'

She moved away from him, wiping her face with her sleeve. 'Sorry, I'm being a baby. I pissed myself, that's all. I'm alive... and so are you.'

He groggily got to his feet, then went down again. A man hauled him up and began more or less carrying him up the staircase, out of the cellar.

Tina's voice came up the stairs, 'She's out cold, thank God.'

The man spoke. 'Everyone in the kitchen. Let's stop and think for a minute.'

Gary recognised the voice but couldn't place it.

Tina said, 'But Joe, shouldn't we leg it?'

At last. It was coming back to him. He'd decided to try and smash the attic's high window when the door had opened and he was ready to charge at whoever appeared. But it was the slight figure of his mother who came in, clutching — something? The hefty poker from the fireplace.

'Mum! Thank God! What on earth are you doing here?' In the distance, they heard a scream of terror. 'Tina! Where is she?'

He barged past his mum, vaguely aware of someone else in the other attic room, and bolted down the stairs to the ground floor. He paused to work out where the screams were coming from: the kitchen? Dashing through, he looked around. No one. Then he saw a door, heard Tina's petrified cries behind it. He wrenched the door open and hurtled down the steps beyond. As he careered round the turn in the staircase, he glimpsed Tina's terrified face, his Auntie Maureen about to stab her.

Now, he was back in the kitchen. Joe sat him down on a chair and ushered Tina to sit next to him.

She carefully put his glasses back on his face. 'There you are. We can't have you bumping into things, can we?'

'I'm sorry, Tina. What a total mess I got you into. I tried to get out, but she locked me in the room at the top of the house. I was shouting and yelling but no one heard me.'

'I thought you were a handicapped boy.'

'Jeez, thanks very much!'

'No, that was what she said. She told me that the next-door neighbours had a handicapped child and he got really wound up at bedtime. I heard all the screaming and shouting but I didn't realise it was you.'

'But we're nowhere near another house. How could you hear a child screaming? Honestly, Tina, sometimes I wonder if you've got anything in—'

'Oh, yeah, I forgot that. Hang on a minute — you were the one that got us into all of this. I mean, for God's sake! What the hell did you say to her, anyway?'

Joe appeared from the cellar again. He was holding Gary's mum's hand; in his other hand was the poker.

He said, 'Here you are, Jenny. Come and sit down.'

Gary watched his mum do as she was told. Her face was white. She looked like she had the other day, after she'd cracked his dad over the head. Joe sat down at the table.

He said, 'I think she's dead. Let's take a minute to think what to do.'

Tina, holding Jenny's hand, reached out and grabbed Gary's.

She said in a rush, 'Let's get out of here. This house is like the worst nightmare I've ever had. I've got to get out. I've just had an evil witch trying to kill me; then I've had to watch her try and kill you. Let's leave while we can.'

Gary looked at Joe, then his mum.

'I don't get it. What are you two doing here, anyway? How did you know we were here?'

Tina joined in. 'Yeah, how did you know?'

They all looked at Jenny. In a flat voice, she explained, 'When you came into the shop, I heard you say you were in a hurry.'

Gary said, confused, 'What? What shop? Where was this?'

Jenny said, 'Tina came into the chemist. I was stacking shelves out the back, and I heard her talking to Pat at the counter. Pat asked her where she was rushing off to and Tina said a place called Totteridge.'

Tina said, 'Oh, yeah, that's right. Is that where you work?'

Gary looked at his mum. 'But, why did you come here, too? I mean, thank God you did, but —'

'I couldn't take the risk. When I got off work, I rang Joe and told him everything. We came up here straightaway.'

'What risk? What do you mean 'everything'?'

'Dad told me to keep away from her. He said she was a nutter, and that Uncle Ray was mixed up with all sorts of bad people.'

'I don't get it, Mum. If she was so bad, why did you send us off to stay with them when we were kids?'

'It was when you were there that Dad found out what was in Grandad's case. That's why we asked them to bring you all home early.'

Gary tried to fit together the pieces of the jigsaw in his head. He remembered Maureen's warning in her letter. Had his dad tried to blackmail her and Uncle Ray? The letter had sounded nasty — what was it...? *Remember, this is my final word. I'm sure you understand me.*

'But, shit! This is all crazy. How did you get in? Did you just knock on the door? No, you can't have done.'

Joe said, 'I was about to, when we heard you shouting. I went around the back and was able to climb over the back gate. Luckily, the patio door was unlocked.'

'Gary, what did you say to her? When you went upstairs with her, she was as nice as pie; the next time I saw her she'd turned into a psycho.' Tina's voice was shaking.

He covered his face. 'I'm sorry, I made a mess of everything. I was so sure she'd killed Grandad. Then I'd convinced myself she must have topped Uncle Ray. I wasn't going to tell the cops or anything; I wanted to know the truth, that's all. Next thing I know, she's locked me in the room and... I'm really sorry.' He turned to his mum. 'So, do you think Grandad's under her greenhouse? Or is It Uncle Ray?'

'What? I didn't even know she had a greenhouse.'

Gary scratched his head: ouch! It really hurt. How had he got everything so wrong? Why would Maureen get a greenhouse if it wasn't to bury someone underneath?

'But I don't get it! Why did she go mental when I suggested that he was under there? I mean, she went completely round the bend; she tried to kill Tina and me! Why? I still think someone's underneath it. It must be Uncle Ray.'

Joe said, 'Listen, we need to decide what we're going to do—'

Tina's wail cut in. 'I don't believe this... Not another body! This is all a nightmare.'

Joe went on, 'And what we need is to decide what to do regarding the police.'

Gary sat up straight in his chair. 'We're telling them everything. We've done nothing wrong. We have to tell them what happened; there's no point in lying. This time, though, we tell them everything. I'm sick of lying. I'm going to ring up Flanagan. I bet he'll want to dig up the greenhouse; I'm sure Uncle Ray is under there. I mean, there's no way Auntie Maureen could afford this massive place; he must have made a load out of the train robbery — I bet she done him in.'

Joe's voice cut in. 'Let's work things through before we do anything hasty. If we call the police, they will be digging around trying to get an arrest, and a conviction. We know that we did nothing wrong; they don't know that. They will want to apportion blame and motive for a woman's death. We're their only suspects. They already suspect your father's death was more than an accident. Even if we can persuade them that Jenny — or I, or any of us — acted in self-defence, there is a real risk of a manslaughter charge. That means a substantial prison sentence. Any of us going to prison, or even having to go through a trial, with all that aggro, is not going to bring back your aunt. It's not even going to make her feel better about dying. What is the value of going to the police? Honestly, what will anyone gain?'

Gary didn't want to lie again. In fact, what he really wanted was the feeling of doing the right thing. But Joe was making sense. The person who would get it in the neck was his mum and he'd vowed he would look after her — not have her sent to prison.

Tina said, 'You're right, Joe. The thought of being interviewed by those horrible detectives again gives me the heebie-jeebies. I'm scared, though. When someone finds her body down there, it will be obvious that she was killed. And we've probably left loads of fingerprints everywhere.'

Gary said, 'Yeah, that's true. But don't forget we were here two days ago, so we would have left them here anyway.'

Jenny said, 'I know this sounds awful, but maybe she isn't dead. Shouldn't we check on her first? I think that, if she's alive, we ought to ring the police, and an ambulance. But if she's dead, we leave her to be found by someone else.'

They looked at Joe; he sat back in his chair and stared at the ceiling.

At last, he said, 'There's quite a bit to sort out here. We don't want to get ourselves caught in our own lie. I agree, the first thing is to check on her. Let's go down and take a look.'

No one moved. Gary really didn't want to go and look at his aunt again, especially not her corpse. But he knew what was the right thing, 'I'll come down with you. Mum — you and Tina stay here.'

Tina got up. 'No. I'm not letting you take all the responsibility. I'll come too.'

Jenny said, 'I'm sorry. I can't go down there again. You go and look. I'm sorry. I'll stay here.'

They went down in single file. When Gary got to the bottom of the steps, he saw the shape of his auntie crumpled up, in amongst a load of dresses and coats. Her sightless eyes, even more popping than before, stared up: she looked disappointed in him. He saw that the wig was half dislodged, revealing a grey, waxy skull. The knife, with its long, thin blade, was next to her. He shivered at the thought of it going into him, and into Tina.

Joe put his fingers against Maureen's throat; he shook his head. Blocking their view with his body, Joe lifted the dead woman's head. He hissed, 'Shit.'

Gary tried to work out how long it had been since he'd seen his dad in the same state: was it only four days! Fuck. Up until then, life had been sort of predictable.

He said, 'I know we've done this before, but could we set it up to look as if she fell down the stairs?'

Joe went back to the steps and started prodding the treads. 'They're all solid and stable; why would she have tripped or fallen?'

'Well, it's quite steep. Maybe she lost her balance?'

'Yeah, but it's her cellar and she's obviously used to it. Just look at all the stuff down here.'

'I smacked my head against that beam. Maybe she did the same thing?'

'It's a good idea but I'm guessing you're much taller than her.'

Tina said, 'Maybe she's got a funny shoe? I don't know, perhaps the heel's broken or something?'

They looked at the dead woman's feet: her high-heeled slingbacks were intact.

Gary said, 'I know. Okay, this might be a bit unbelievable, but how about the bulb blew the moment she came down the stairs and — er, she lost her balance and... um... um, well — toppled over and smashed her head against... um, what? Er, the—'

'It's all right. I've sorted it out.'

They turned towards Jenny's voice.

Chapter 116

The glow of Diane's cigarette had him gagging for a roll-up. When he got home, he'd have a chat with Tina: if she was still smoking, he would, too. He cursed his weakness. He was supposed to set a good example. Not that he'd done too well in that department over the years. Maybe he should give parenting up as a bad job.

Terry looked at his watch again; the luminous dial picked up the faintest glimmer of light still in the sky. Nine p.m. Removing the watch from his wrist, he took the balaclava and gloves from his jacket pockets and put them on. Again, he wondered what kind of comic character he must resemble.

He whispered, 'Come on! This is getting ridiculous.'

Mind you, all being well, Stubbs would fail to turn up and, after dropping Diane off, he could go home and forget all about this pantomime. Oh, for fuck's sake: now his bowels were cramping. No — surely he wasn't going to need a crap behind the tree, as well?

He saw lights flickering through the trees, then heard the engine of an expensive car. Light flooded the car park. Terry kept still behind the oak and waited for darkness to return. What if it didn't? If those lights stayed on, not only would he be blinded by them, he'd be spotted the moment he looked around the sturdy trunk. Thank goodness! The whole scene was plunged into dark again, a much deeper darkness than before. Terry opened his eyes wide and looked hard into the tree trunk, his hands cupped around his eye sockets to remove all extraneous light. After ten seconds, he slowly knelt, then stretched forward onto his stomach and peered around the tree. His first thought was inner fury — why had he pissed behind the very tree where he was hiding? Ignoring the wetness, he focused ahead. There was a long, dark car parked next to the Imp — a Roller? The car's interior light was on, revealing a man's shape. Diane's door was opened; she got out and walked the few paces to the big car. Terry could just about hear her voice, which sounded questioning. The other driver leaned across and opened the passenger door. Diane got in and closed it behind her.

Terry got to his feet but kept his gaze on the car. The urgent need to move his bowels had gone, and his quickened breathing was returning to manageable levels. So far, it was as she'd said. A flame flared in the car; two red tips appeared.

He muttered, 'Come on, Diane, don't just sit there smoking. Get your business sorted and let me go home.'

All he wanted right now was a mug of cocoa and to sit in front of the telly. The Sweeney had already started; it would be halfway through by the time he got home. There was a repeat of Fawlty Towers after the nine-o'clock news. Maybe he'd be back in time for that.

What was that? He strained his ears: yes, a car engine. No light, though. It changed down and edged its way on to the gravel. This one wasn't swanky. What was it? An Escort? Why no lights? This wasn't part of the plan — at least, not Terry's plan. He was properly alive for the first time in years: on edge, the thrill of potential violence pulsing through him. He watched the new, dark car move towards the stationary 'Roller'. Had Stubbs and Diane seen it yet? Yes, their heads turned towards it. The Escort was manoeuvring to face the other car. What was he up to? Terry loosened his shoulders and prepared: for what? He wasn't sure, but his love of a fight was edging him forward.

The posh car's interior light illuminated Stubbs and Diane as they stared, seemingly entranced, at the car now facing them. Suddenly, its full-beam headlights blazed. They held up their hands to fend off the dazzle. Diane tugged at her hat as the stranger got out; there was something in his hand. Terry started running towards the man but was miles too slow: several shots shattered the silence. Stubbs' windscreen frosted over. The pounding of Terry's feet alerted the gunman, who whipped around, pistol in hand. Terry, at full pelt, smashed shoulder-first into the man's chest. Both went down, the gunman's head crashing onto the bonnet of the big car, Terry landing heavily on top of him.

In the stillness of the moment, Terry was profoundly aware of the gentle sighing of swaying branches and the distant hum of traffic. Another sound caught his attention — a slight creaking; something was shifting the gravel. Was someone in the Roller? Had Diane survived those shots? Terry got heavily to his feet as the Escort's engine roared.

Spinning to face the blinding lights, Terry glimpsed a shape behind the wheel. There was a squeal of tyres and gravel spurted as the car sprang forward. Terry leapt high — higher than he'd ever managed in any football match he'd ever played — and crashed down onto the windscreen of the

Escort, the bonnet of which had piled into the grille of the Roller and whose front wheel bumped over the gunman on its way.

Although badly winded, Terry knew he had to get off the car: he was a sitting duck if the driver had a gun. As the car was thrown into reverse, he slid off the passenger's side and rolled away behind the bigger car. Somewhere, there was a gun on the ground; was it next to the gunman still? How could he get to it? The Escort engine howled, accelerating in reverse. What was the driver doing now? Terry, crouching low, his knees screaming, peered around the Roller. The Escort was gathering speed, the driver hunched over the wheel — was he wearing a white hat? Then it was gone.

Aware of a sudden, sharp pain in his chest, Terry shook his head; this was no time for aches and pains. Breathing hard, he stood and opened the big car's passenger door. In the dark now, the man and woman lolled together like lovers. Light — he needed light. Maybe they were still alive.

With a heavy heart, Terry got into the Imp and turned the ignition: nothing.

'Come on! Don't piss around.'

He tried again and the engine caught. He manoeuvred the car to turn its headlamps onto the scene, then got out and bent over the man on the ground — a young man: jacket, jeans, crew cut, clean-shaven. Was it the one who'd taken the photographs at the shed? The poor kid didn't look alive, but Terry's medical expertise was limited to toy soldiers. Anyway, he'd always been better at hurting people than treating them.

He took a deep breath and looked into the big car. For a second, he stood and stared. His beautiful wife, his Diane — half of her face missing. In her left hand was the bobble hat.

Next to her, Stubbs was casually holding a pistol in his right hand; his head was a bloody mess. Even if Terry had known what Stubbs looked like, he wouldn't know him now. Terry had seen dead people before; he'd killed some of them. This was different.

Shivering violently, he turned back to the man on the ground: a seemingly lifeless shape. Terry pressed his fingers against the neck — was that a pulse? He stood and looked again at Diane: the poor girl. She'd wanted so much more than he could offer.

Out of respect, he quietly closed the door. Something about it caught his attention: it wasn't a Roller; it was a Jag! He looked carefully at the car, its occupants no longer able to tell him who they were. Was it Dutton's? Was the man with no face Geraldine's husband? Shit! Life was tumbling out of control.

He scanned the number-plate — KMR 148P — but he hadn't clocked the registration of the car on the Duttons' drive. He was tempted to open the driver's door, see if there was anything to identify the dead man. What was the point? What would he gain?

Terry looked around once more. What now? He'd have to find a phone box and get an ambulance up here pronto: even if the kid were alive, he wouldn't be for much longer.

Terry got into the Imp and began to reverse from the ghastly scene. On impulse, he stopped and drove slowly back towards the still body of the young man — there it was. He got out, picked up the gun, looked around one more time, then accelerated away.

The little car had not been built for speed; ten years on, and its days of even sluggish acceleration were long past. Terry urged it forward, but it was not playing ball. What's more, his over-revving was causing an ominous rattle; he slowed down. Whatever happened, he must get to a phone box, even if it were slowly.

The events of the last few minutes whirled chaotically through his mind. The gun shots were echoing still; the bloodied corpses were there but, thankfully, already blurry. It was the young man who was driving Terry forward now. There was something personal about being in a physical fight; he felt a responsibility for him, whoever he was.

He press hard on the accelerator; the engine roared and seemed to lose power — *fuck, fuck, fuck*! He pulled off the balaclava and stuffed it into the glove compartment.

'Come on, come on! Please don't fuck around!'

He recovered speed and drove as fast as he dared down the long, winding road and back towards town. Every now and then a car came towards him, lights blazing into his shielded eyes: any car seeing him might connect the Imp, and its bald driver, with the scene of carnage up the road.

What should he say to the Emergency Services? There was no way he could give his name: Diane being there, and murdered, would immediately implicate him. If it were Dutton in the car, then he, Terry, was going to be a suspect. The photographs that the young bloke had taken might make an appearance at any point. Maybe he should drive away and let the kid live or die. Someone else might find him up there. But what if a few seconds were enough to save him? Terry saw a phone box ahead, at the junction with the main road. He made up his mind.

'Which service?'

Terry wiped his face, pinched his nose, and with classic RP Pathé News diction in his mind's ear, said, 'Ambulance.'

'What's the problem, caller?'

What to say? Maybe it would be better to call Geraldine first, to check on the Jag? The crushed body of the kid up there was too much.

'Woodcock Hill. I heard some shots up there.'

'What's your name, caller?'

He put the phone down. What was her number? Cursing his stodgy brain — why wouldn't it work anymore? — he pulled up the A to D directory. It was missing.

He hissed, 'Fucking vandals!'

What was the time? He extended his arm: not there. Where was it? Oh, yeah, he'd taken it off before the mayhem started. He reached into his trouser pockets: not there; jacket — nothing. Terry felt his heart start to hammer: surely the watch wasn't up there? Telling himself to stay calm, he began to stroll casually back to his car. A couple were walking towards him. He continued on past the Imp for fifty yards before glancing back: they'd turned the corner. Terry stooped to tie a lace; he couldn't see anyone else around. He stood, shrugged his shoulders and returned to the car. Now for the next call.

Two minutes later, he saw another phone box. Occupied. He parked up a side street and got out. Jeez! He could do with a fag. As he waited for the phone box to be vacated, he scoured his sluggish brain for Geraldine's number but nothing came back to him. He looked towards the phone box; would its directories be there? So many of them had been vandalised recently. Oh, for fuck's sake! The couple in the phone box were necking. Terry turned around and got back into his car; he couldn't wait for them to finish, nor could he afford for them to see him. Where was the next one? There. He slowed. It was empty. Again, he strolled: mustn't draw attention to himself. Great! The directories were intact. He dialled, then waited.

What would he say if Dutton answered? Stupid! If he did, then there was the answer. Terry knew that what he wanted was to hear her voice, to be with her, to hold her and make sure she was all right. The phone rang and rang. Maybe she and that bastard had made up and gone out to an expensive restaurant; or, worse, they might be in bed together right now! He shut his eyes at the thought of it. Get a grip, Castleton! All he needed to do was check whether it was Dutton's car, and that Geraldine was all right — that was all. Once he'd got that out of the way, he could dash back to the scene and find his watch before the ambulance got there. He'd have to be bloody quick though.

Maybe he'd misdialled. He tried again.

Chapter 117

What was that sound? Why wouldn't it stop? Stop it, stop it! Why wasn't Edward doing something about it?

The delicious, heavy blackness was nearly within her reach; could she claw it back? Please come back — don't drag me away. That awful noise was still going, and going, and going. What was it? Oh… the phone.

Now that consciousness was returning, Geraldine became aware of her physical state. What on earth was going on? Her head cleared: enough to feel the hammering headache. She grimaced. It was like the awful hangover she'd had the other day. Which day was that?

The phone stopped, thank God.

Where was she? Geraldine cudgelled her wits — what was going on? She was lying on the sofa in the sitting room, her hands behind her back. She tried to rearrange herself but for some reason her arms wouldn't obey her commands. Was she bound? Yes, her hands were tied. There was something strapped across her mouth. Feeling panic begin to build, she counted to twenty: elephant-one, elephant-two… She opened her eyes to find the room in almost total darkness, only a light somewhere outside providing a glimmer.

The phone started again. Why didn't Edward answer it? Then it all came back. Edward, the man she had loved with all — well, nearly all —her heart, had become a monster in the last two days. Now, here she was, trussed up like a chicken, presumably drugged out of her mind, and unable to do anything about it. Maybe the person calling might be able to help her — at least, untie her. Geraldine tried to get up but discovered that her ankles were also tied. As she struggled, the extent of Edward's monstrous behaviour began to fully dawn. He might think of her as silly, naïve Gerry, but she would show him: there was no way he was going to beat her.

Rolling off the sofa, Geraldine landed heavily on her side; she wriggled on to her front and writhed towards the hall. Damn! The door was closed. Straining every muscle, she levered herself into a standing position, banging her head against the doorjamb as she did so. With her back to the door, she managed to hook a little finger around the door handle. Not sure if her finger would take the pressure, she sagged down on to the floor, the door handle opening as she went. The moment her bottom hit the floor, the door closed again. Tears of rage and frustration ran down her face. This was impossible.

The phone stopped ringing.

Sitting there, her tied hands jammed uncomfortably against the door, Geraldine thought through her options. Could she wriggle into the kitchen for a pair of scissors? Yes, but how would she use them? What else was there? A violent hatred swept over her. She screamed, 'Fuck you, Edward!' All that came out was a mumbled whine and a load of spittle.

The phone began ringing again. There was light coming from somewhere — there, from the other side of the room. The door from sitting room to kitchen was open! Cursing her own stupidity, Geraldine felt a pang of hope: if the kitchen door was open, the door from it into the hall might be, too. Rolling back on to her stomach, she set off again. The kitchen floor was cold and hard, but it made her progress quicker — this slithering was easier than against the friction of the carpet. Was the door into the hall open? Thank God, yes. Could she get to the phone? Nearly there — but how was she going to answer it? Inching closer she decided: there was no other way. She pushed her head under the telephone table and lifted. The vase, with the daffs in it, the ash tray and the telephone crashed to the ground. Was the caller there? Geraldine twisted her head around in search of the handset. Was that it? She listened hard: silence. Could she make a sound loud enough to be heard, if the caller was even there? She took a deep breath and shouted through barely-parted lips; it was a pathetic sound. She tried humming, but that was hardly better. What about a high-pitched shriek? Again, she emptied her lungs and sucked in hard, then squealed for as long as she could. Exhausted, she put her ear to the ground and listened: was that a tiny voice? She squealed again. The voice, like a mouse's, was squeaking something. Then came the familiar sound of the line being disconnected.

Chapter 118

'What do you mean, Mum?' Gary looked up at her. He didn't like the look on her face. 'What have you done? Oh, no. What have you done?'

'I rang Mr Flanagan. I've told him what happened.'

'Mum, no! We can sort this out.'

Gary felt Joe's hand on his arm. 'Actually, Gary, I don't think we can sort this out. I think we're in it too deep.'

Gary knew he was right. The more he thought up possible explanations, the more unbelievable they became. 'Okay, maybe. Yeah, it's better we tell the truth.'

Tina climbed the stairs; Gary followed. They went back into the kitchen and sat down to wait.

Jenny said, 'I didn't say I told the truth. I'm afraid I told a little lie.'

Joe said, 'Okay, tell us exactly. Then we can get the story straight.'

She said, 'I'm sorry, Gary; I had to do it. I know you wanted to tell the truth all along, but I think this is best. In fact, I'm feeling much better about it now.'

'What, what did you say, Mum?'

'It's simple. I came here after work on the bus. I decided that I needed to have it out with her after you and Tina were here. You told me about her greenhouse. I confronted her about it and said that I thought she had killed grandad and that he was under the greenhouse. She just laughed. She said she needed to show me something in the cellar and then when I went down, she tried to stab me. I picked up the nearest thing I could find and hit her with it. You see, exactly what happened. The only lie is that I was on my own. So, you'd better all get going as soon as you can.'

Gary cried out, 'Mum, you're being stupid; you're going to go to prison. For fuck's sake! This is terrible.'

'Stop that awful language now. I'm so sorry, Tina; please forgive him.'

'It's all right. I don't know what to say, Jenny. I'm scared: you're going to be in awful trouble. Joe, is she in trouble?'

Gary fumed, 'Of course she's in trouble, you thicko!'

'Don't you call me a thicko! You're the one that got us into this mess in the first place.'

Joe said, his voice calm, 'Jenny, this is a very generous act. Are you sure it's what you want?'

She smiled. 'Yes, it's the right thing to do.'

Joe said, 'All right. In that case, we must get ourselves sorted. First, fingerprints: Gary — you and Tina. If the police ask, you need to tell them that, when you were here the other day, Maureen showed you around the whole house and that you went into every room you've been in tonight. Have you got that?'

They nodded. He went on, 'Jenny, where did you find the poker?'

'In the sitting room.'

'No, that's not going to work. Why would you take the poker downstairs to the cellar?'

'Oh, well, in that case, I found it in the cellar.'

Joe picked up the poker from behind Jenny's chair and went into the sitting room.

Coming back, he said, 'That's not going to work. It's part of a set: there's no way she'd have this poker down there. Come on, Jenny. Come down and let's see if we can find something suitable.'

He went down the stairs, Jenny followed him.

Gary said, 'She's amazing.'

Tina nodded, 'Absolutely fucking amazing. Oops! Sorry about the language.'

'I'm sorry I got you into this. I was stupid. I'm the thicko. I wish I hadn't said that to you. You're amazing, too.'

'Gee, thanks. You're a gent, and no mistake.'

He looked into her eyes again. If only he were brave enough to hold her hand or, better still, take her in his arms and cuddle her, or even kiss her. Would she shout at him to get his dirty hands off? Anyway, if they didn't leave soon, Flanagan would be here. All he could manage was a muttered, 'You're the nice one.'

Joe and his mum came back.

Joe said, 'We found something, but I won't tell you; you don't need to know.' He took the poker to the sink and washed it under the tap, dried it with a tea towel, then took it back to the sitting room.

Jenny sat down at the table, 'Thanks Joe, thanks to you two, as well. It's time for you to go. I think Mr Flanagan is going to be so excited at discovering where grandad is, he won't be so bothered about...' she pointed to the floor. She smiled, her face mischievous. 'Also, with any luck, your Uncle Ray is under the greenhouse, too.'

Chapter 119

At last! A car crunched into the drive. Geraldine had barely moved since the phone call. She was lying on her side, the only position that wasn't excruciating. Please come back, Edward. Please be nice to me again. She listened hard: it wasn't the Jag. Even after everything he'd done, she was disappointed. The car stopped. Nothing happened. Who was it? Was there any point in her screaming for help? The gag rendered every noise she made almost inaudible, and whoever it was hadn't even got out of the car. Was the driver waiting for someone?

The question of whether she could open the front door went through her mind again. She wriggled across the floor and on to the coconut matting. How could she arrange herself to turn the knob whilst taking the lock off the latch? It wasn't possible; they were at least a foot apart.

What was the person doing out there? Thank God, a door opened; it didn't close. She heard rapid footsteps. They approached the door.

She yelled, 'Help! Help me! Help me!'

The voice that emerged was pitifully quiet. The flap of the letter box opened above her head. Again, she cried out. The flap closed and the quick steps went away. Was he going around the house? No, back to the car. Another door was opened: the boot? A few seconds more and it was closed again. The urgent steps came closer then moved away. Yes, he was going around the house. Geraldine's scrambled wits cleared as she remembered that earlier, she had unlocked the patio door to escape from Edward. Was it still unlocked? Gritting her teeth, she again shoved herself headfirst back to the kitchen. Her face was already burned from the carpet, but it was her only hope. Hang on — maybe she'd do better to make enough of a racket to let whoever it was know she was here? What could she crash? The hall mirror? There was a standard lamp; would that make a racket if she could get it to go over? How long ago had the footsteps died away? Maybe thirty seconds? She would wait for a minute then do it. There was no choice. As she prepared for the inevitable pain, the hellish reality of her situation hit home: her marriage was disastrously over. Her beautiful home, with all that it contained and represented, was now a horrible prison. How could she ever live here again? But where would she live? Where could she go? The very idea of going back to school seemed ridiculous. How could she face innocent little children or, come to that, innocent, decent colleagues.

Her time was up. With a supreme effort, Geraldine scraped herself along the carpet to the closed hall door. If the person was in the house, then he must be there: that was the only way in, assuming Edward hadn't locked the patio door. Steeling herself for the sickening impact, if not concussion, she counted to three then stretched her neck to its full extent and headbutted the door as hard as she could. A tremendous, echoing sound reverberated around the hall, then absolute silence.

What more could she do? Through her tears, she became aware of movement in the kitchen. Was the intruder coming through from the sitting room? She groaned, moaned, yipped and cried: surely whoever it was must hear her.

A torch beam flitted, illuminating the walls, pictures, hall mirror, the floor... then moved towards where she lay. Geraldine screwed up her eyes against the dazzling beam and again pleaded for help. The light flashed around the hall. For an instant, she glimpsed a white head in the mirror. The torchlight went back into the kitchen, followed by quiet footsteps.

At least she knew who it was. She cried out in desperation, 'Jack! Jack, help me!' But Jack did not help her.

Geraldine gave up. Someone must find her eventually: Edward would realise the monstrosity of his actions and come to his senses. Maybe Jim Dixon would drive over when she didn't turn up for work in the morning? Terry's bulky shape flashed into her head — he'd save her! He was the one person who knew that she was in serious trouble. When he didn't see her tomorrow, he'd put to and two together. In the meantime, all she had to do was cope with an indefinite period of extreme discomfort. 'Come on, Geraldine! Where's your Dutton grit?'

What was that? Footsteps skittering on the gravel. There was something else trying to catch her attention — petrol. Yes... Definitely. The stench of petrol was filling the air. The steps outside were close now. A door was opened, then slammed shut. Three or four more steps, another door opened. Then it struck her. *Petrol! No! No... Please!*

Chapter 120

The closer Terry got to the Duttons' house, the further he was from safety. His reference to shots when he rang for an ambulance would mean that police would be called seconds later. They might be there already: swarming over the crime scene. His goose was cooked: the watch would glitter like gold in the blaze of all those headlights. But he'd made up his mind and that was that. Would he be able to see Tina one more time? His poor girl: what had she done to deserve such parents? He often wondered if she would have been better off had the kindly copper not calmed him down that day. Sure, learning that your dad had thrown himself under a train would have been agony, but maybe she would have recovered from even that — definitely by now. Having a father in prison for killing his ex-wife — Tina's own mother — would mean such shame that she'd never shake off. How could she ever become famous with her father in a maximum-security prison?

Right now, though, he had to deal with the priority: Geraldine. He'd been about to put the phone down when the receiver was picked up at the other end. He slid home the ten-pence piece, prepared to say something vacuous, and heard the distant, high-pitched sounds. What was going on?

He waited for a gap then said, 'Is that you, Geraldine?' More nonsense sounds then another gap. 'Geraldine, are you being attacked?' His voice was gentle, what could he say to help her answer? This time a load of hysterical yipping sounds. He said, realising now that she must be gagged. 'Don't worry, I'm on my way.'

He indicated left and turned down the leafy lane towards the house. How far along was it? Although it was only two days since his visit to the Dutton's luxury home, the events of that night had already blurred. There it was: those white-painted gate posts. A car outside the front door — not a Jag: a dark Escort!

He drove slowly past and parked the Imp in the next close. *Okay, stay calm.* The next few minutes needed clear thought. Reaching over to the glove compartment, Terry pulled out the balaclava. Should he wear it? No, he'd look like a housebreaker. He picked up the gun and weighed it in his gloved hand

— idiot! Why court trouble? He was in enough already. Winding down his window, he listened: breeze-ruffled trees, the M1 a long way off, nothing else. Who was the driver of the Escort? Maybe it was Dutton? Was he in the house with Geraldine now? Were they making up? Eating together? Were they in bed together? Why did his brain keep doing this? He got out of the car and walked quickly to the entrance to the gravel drive. He paused. The front windows were dark. There was the sound of a gate latch: Terry ducked behind one of the Duttons' shrubs and waited. A man appeared in the light of the nearest streetlamp: he was tall with dark overcoat and white hair. Terry watched him dash around the Escort, open the boot, put something inside, then slam it shut. He sped to the driver's door and opened it.

Terry stepped out of the shadow. 'Excuse me?'

The man froze, then turned. Terry grabbed the white hair and wrenched the man's head back. The streetlight lit his Adam's apple. Terry chopped hard. Stepping back, he let the body collapse at his feet, then stooped to examine the crumpled form: whoever this person was, the only sign of life was a dry crackling coming from his open mouth.

Turning his attention to the house, Terry could see no sign of life. Nothing. He rang the doorbell. No answer. He crashed the heavy, brass knocker several times against the front door. Nothing. Jogging along the front of the house, Terry peered in through the front windows: everything was dark. He retraced his steps to the high wooden gate at the side of the house from which the man had emerged.

Terry looked around: did other houses overlook the property? Were people watching him? He guessed not and, anyway, what did it matter now? Clicking open the latch, he went through and shut the gate behind him.

There was just sufficient light to see the flagged path leading down the side of the house to lawn, stretching into darkness. The light was coming from a side window: a strange light, a flickering light. Then he smelled it — fumes… and burning. He raced to the window and looked in. Fire blazing. Fuck! That bastard had set the house on fire. Was Geraldine in there?

He sped around the side of the house to the patio door — shit! It was locked. Should he smash it open? He mustn't cause a draught, feed the flames. Maybe it would be best to go back to the front? He'd be more conspicuous, but what did that matter?

Dashing back to the dark front of the house, he looked around. The streetlamp picked out a row of heavy-looking plant pots. He picked up the nearest one and ran it straight into the kitchen window. With his gloved hands, he beat away jagged remnants of glass, reached in and lifted the catch. The open window was too high. Terry turned the pot upside down, stepped onto it, then pulled himself in, over the sink and onto the floor. There was the stabbing pain in his chest again. As he righted himself, the stench of petrol and burning fabric filled his nostrils; then he heard the sound of the fire — crackling, whooshing.

He bellowed, 'Geraldine, can you hear me?' He moved towards the door, feeling for a switch. The kitchen was flooded with light: no sign of her. Finding the next switch, he went into the sitting room; the fire was in the office off it, the flames were still contained.

He rushed to the office door and gently closed it.

'Geraldine, it's Terry. Can you hear me? Are you here?' Maybe she was upstairs? He hauled open the door into the hall and almost fell over her. 'Oh, God, you're here! Thank God! Okay, I've got you now. You're safe now.'

He knelt beside her. She was bound and gagged with tape. 'Listen, sweetheart, I need to cut all this off; I won't be able to undo it. I'll get you out first, then nip back for a knife or scissors. I've got you now. Hold tight.'

He put one arm under her head and the other under her knees and prepared to heave her up. She was making a keening sound in his ear as he began to lift. With the image of hoisting a joyfully-shrieking Tina high into the sky, he sang out, 'Hooray and up she rises!'

Carrying her with great care to the front door, Terry reached awkwardly for the latch and felt the sickening, sharp pain in the left side of his chest: this time it wasn't a flash of pain, it stayed. He willed it to go away — no, no! Not now. Not now!

'Sorry, Geraldine, I've got to rearrange things.' He lowered her down, the pain excruciating, opened the front door, picked her up again, and ignoring the jabbing in his chest, rushed out. Where could he put her? 'Sorry, sweetheart, I'm going to have to put you down on the grass. Here you go. Now, stay there — only for a minute. I'll be back.'

He dashed into the house again, shutting the door behind him. He must keep that fire down! Into the kitchen, which drawer? There were so many. There: a knife block; next to it was a pair of kitchen scissors.

He rushed back to Geraldine. 'Here you are, my lovely girl. It's all right now. A little snipping… There you are! Hang on, hang on! Don't say anything yet. Breathe properly.'

She was gasping for air and trying to cry out. In his awkward kneeling position, the sharp pain came again *Don't you dare let me down now!* Doing

524

his best to ignore the insistent stabbing, he gently snipped the tape away from her ankles and then her wrists.

'There you go, right as rain.' She was sobbing; gasping, and shuddering. Words were clearly beyond her. 'Geraldine, try and get some life back into your wrists and ankles. I'm going to call the fire brigade. I'll be right back.'

At last she spoke, her voice cracked and guttural, 'Don't go back in, Terry. Don't worry about the house.'

'It's okay, don't worry. There's time. I'll be right back. I... I'll be quick.'

For the second time in thirty minutes, Terry rang 999. 'Yes, please, it's an emergency — Fire, Ambulance and...' he couldn't help pausing, 'Police.'

Chapter 121

Terry put down the phone and dashed back outside. Geraldine was getting to her feet, weaving and wobbling, about to go over.

He reached her. 'I've got you; I've got you now.'

'Oh, thank God, Terry! I was so scared. I thought I was going to die. I was going to die…'

She buried her face in his chest and let herself be held. Terry gripped her tight, as tight as he could. He ignored the shooting pain.

'You're safe now. The fire brigade will be here in a minute. The police are coming, too. The man who did this to you is…'

He paused, who had done all this? Who was the white-haired man? Where was Dutton? Was he the man in the Jag, his head blown away? Maybe Dutton's hair had gone white — had he gained revenge, after all?

He felt Geraldine shaking against him. 'Oh my God, this is a nightmare. I can't believe what's happening to me.'

Terry gripped her tight. 'I know; it's unbelievable.'

'What's that?' She had pulled away.

'What's what?'

Geraldine wiped her face and touched his chest. 'That.'

Confused, Terry put his hand on his coat and felt a hard object — what was it? He reached into the inside pocket; his fingers closed around the bulky, metal strap. For a second he felt his heart really leap, out of control: was he going to be in the clear? He pulled out the watch and showed her.

'It's my watch. See…? On the back?'

She looked, but the light was too dim. 'What? I can't see it.'

Embarrassed now, he said, 'Oh, it doesn't matter; my name is engraved on the back of it. It was a present from someone.'

As he spoke, the image of Diane came into his head, followed by the shocking realisation of everything that had happened. Now that there was no evidence of him being up there, maybe he could keep out of it altogether? What did he need to do? First, his car: he had to bring his car onto the Duttons' drive. If he had come along to see what was wrong, he would hardly have parked down a side street. Looking around the drive, he realised hers wasn't here either.

'Where is your car?'

'Um, I can't remember. Er… does it matter?'

Terry only had a matter of minutes, possibly seconds.

'I'm really sorry — I've got to go and get my car. I'll explain everything later. Right now, I've got to leg it and get my car back here. I'll be back in one minute. Will you be all right? Can I leave you?'

She hugged him, 'I trust you, Terry, more than anyone.'

He kissed her hard on the mouth then hurtled, knees protesting, out of the drive, down the road to the close. As he ran, the image of Diane's limp body resting against the man — was it Dutton? — blurred into those of them fucking, all those years ago. Terry had dreamed of revenge but not like this.

Was he out of the woods? Would anything connect him with the butchery in that car park? Maybe the white-haired man would regain consciousness and remember the large man in dark clothes who had overpowered the gunman. Terry unlocked the boot, whispering, 'Please be here, please, please! Ah, phew!' A quick look around: everywhere was quiet. Thank God for wealthy people in their secluded homes on leafy side streets.

Taking off his donkey jacket and Cap'n Haddock, Terry put on the caretaker's uniform so beautifully laundered by Tina. He thought about his gloves: why would he have gloves on a mild, spring evening? He took them off and put them into the pockets of the donkey jacket. He opened the passenger door and carefully folded up jacket, jersey and, adding the balaclava, placed the bundle on the seat. A glint of something white was caught by the dim interior light: a long strand of hair. He picked it off the passenger seat and blew it into the night.

He got behind the wheel: would it start? It didn't. Terry kept his cool and tried again. After prolonged resistance, the Imp spluttered into life. Terry drove it sedately back to the Duttons' and parked behind the Escort. He looked around for somewhere to hide his 'commando uniform'. Over the road, a short way up the cul-de-sac, was a boat on a trailer — would that do? How could he be sure? Dashing across to the boat, he peeled back the tarpaulin and shoved the bundled-up clothes inside. He'd come back later, much later, and retrieve them. Terry sped back to his car, reached in for the gun, crossed to the nearside of the other car and placed the murder weapon into its glove compartment. Then, shutting the door, he breathed a sigh of relief. Fuck, prints! That was close. He reached back in, pulled the gun out, and holding it with a corner of his overall, polished it clean with the other. He stretched in and carefully replaced the gun, making sure to wipe the compartment, and finally, the door handle.

Now, where the hell was Geraldine? Horrified he turned back to the house — no! *Don't be in there, please.* Why would she go back in there?

He called, 'Geraldine, where are you? Where are you? Geraldine, come out of there, now!'

'I'm here, Terry.'

He whirled round. Her face appeared over the roof of the Escort. He ran to her. She was looking down at the body.

Terry stood beside her. 'Who is it, do you know?'

'Yes, it's Jack Stubbs.'

Terry bent down to him: he was still unconscious. His breathing hadn't changed. The man was wearing gloves — great: that would explain the lack of prints on the gun. There was also a strong smell of petrol emanating: this boy was stitched up good and proper.

'Did you hit him or something, Terry?'

'Well, I — The thing is. Well, yes, I'm... Yes, I did.'

For a moment, Terry thought she was going to do something violent herself.

Instead, she turned to him. 'I'm glad. He's a very bad man.'

'Yes.'

'Why did you park around the corner?'

Should he tell her everything? No, not now. There would be plenty of time later. Maybe it would be better never to speak.

'For some reason I thought it would be wise to park down the road. I just had a hunch something bad was going on.' Terry took her hand and led her back to the grass, well away from the house and injured man. He said, 'You're safe from them now; that's the important thing.'

She shuddered, 'I don't know what's happening, Terry, but whatever's going on, please look after me.'

Terry held her close again as the sound of sirens cut through the night air.

Chapter 122

As the fire engine turned into the drive, the wailing of the siren was suddenly cut, replaced by a shattering silence. Terry whispered, 'I know you don't need me to say this, but I have to: just tell the truth about everything. I don't have anything you need to protect me against. Everything we've talked about — you know, in the shed — it's fine by me.'

Bright lights starkly illuminated the men piling out of the fire engine. Terry walked quickly over to them and spoke, gesturing towards the gate. Two of the crew moved purposefully to the side of the house, leaving two unrolling the hose from the side of the vehicle.

Terry came back to Geraldine's side. She gripped his hand hard. 'Will you stick around for a while?' She searched his face. He was suddenly a stranger to her. This was Terry Castleton, the school caretaker. Why should he be able to look after her? 'Terry, I'm confused. I'm not even sure what's happening right in front of me. What did you do to Jack? What if the police find the photographs of you and me? I mean, after Edward's accusations…'

'You can tell them everything, sweetheart. You've done nothing wrong. You told me that your husband was being horrible, and I did my best to sympathise with you. There's nothing for you to feel bad or guilty about.'

Another siren was approaching, then another. She felt his hand tighten around hers as, first, another fire engine pulled up just beyond the driveway, then a Panda car crunched onto the gravel. Two uniformed officers got out: a man and a woman. They walked over. Terry squeezed Geraldine's hand again, then let go.

Bracing herself, she stepped forward. 'Thank God you're here. My name is Geraldine Dutton. I—'

The policewoman interrupted, 'Thank you, Mrs Dutton. Before we go any further, may I ask if your husband drives a black Jaguar?'

'Yes. Why?'

'Do you know the registration number?'

'Er, yes… It's KMR 148P. Why?'

The policewoman looked at her colleague; he shook his head.

'Perhaps we'd better start with clarifying what has been happening here?'

Terry said, 'Listen, there's a bloke on the ground over there who needs urgent attention. I socked him one. I think he's badly hurt. I called for an ambulance, but I'm really worried about him.'

'Who are you, sir?' the policeman had a notebook out.

'I'm Terry Castleton. I don't know what's been going on, but when I got here, the bloke on the ground, over there, had just closed the boot of his car. I asked him if Mrs Dutton was at home and, out of the blue, he started throwing punches at me. Well, as you can imagine, I defended myself. The next thing I know, he's down.

'I came over because I was worried about Mrs Dutton. I rang her, but I could hardly make out what she was saying. I guessed she must be gagged or something. Anyway, I got here as quickly as I could. When I got into the house — I had to smash a window — I found Mrs Dutton in the hall, bound and gagged. Then I realised I could smell petrol and burning and I heard this crackling and roaring and when I looked through, the office at the back was on fire. I shut all the inner doors to stop the draught. It was pure luck that I rang Mrs Dutton. I had a hunch that she was in trouble because when she left school today, she told me that her husband had been saying horrible things and she was a bit scared. Anyway, I'll shut up now.'

Geraldine had been watching Terry talking. Up until the police had arrived, he had been bigger, stronger, more authoritative than Caretaker Terry. Now, she noticed that he had put on the other persona. His caretaker voice and demeanour had returned: slightly subservient, a bit rough around the edges. Why hadn't she ever realised that he was much more than the downtrodden, old-before-his-time caretaker?

Another siren. She looked up the lane. This time it was an ambulance followed by two cars. Thank God David and Judy were away; she'd be so ashamed if they were here. The scene was pure chaos: the pumps of the fire engines were making a hell of a racket, the ambulance's blue light was flashing, there were uniformed officers everywhere. The ambulance men knelt beside Jack Stubbs. Almost immediately, one of them returned to the ambulance for a stretcher. With infinite care, he and his colleague began to lift the motionless figure onto it.

'Mrs Dutton?'

Starting, Geraldine turned to the new voice; it came from a dirty little man with a white streak in his hair. He had a crafty face; his knowing eyes darted around the scene, then came to rest on her.

'Yes?'

'I'm Detective Sergeant Nott. I'd like you to come down to the station.'

'What? Why? What for?'

'I'm sorry, madam. Normally I'd say let's go inside, but in view of...' he nodded at the fire engine and the ambulance. He turned to Terry. 'Who are you?'

'I'm Terry.'

'Terry who?'

'Terry Castleton.'

The ratty little detective did a double take. 'What? Not Tina Castleton's father?'

For a second, Geraldine thought she saw the other Terry reappear — big, hard, frightening.

Terry said, meek again, 'Yeah, that's right.'

Ratty called to his colleague, 'Oi, Chris! You'll never believe it! Guess who's over here? Pretty little Tina Castleton's daddy.'

She watched the other detective walk towards them. He was young, tall, flashy.

Glancing nervously at Terry, Geraldine said, 'Er, Detective Sergeant Nott, are you going to take my statement? I have been drugged, tied up, gagged, and left to die in a conflagration. Whether you or your young colleague know Terry's daughter is neither here nor there.'

'Thank you, Mrs Dutton. Quite right. Let's get on with it. We want you to come with us to the station. Tina's dad, you're coming, too.'

A new car slowed to a halt. It was Rex and Miranda. Rex got out and walked over. The two detectives intercepted him.

Ratty said, 'Name?'

'I'm Rex Willoughby; I live over there.' He gestured across the lane.

'Who's with you?'

'My wife, Miranda.'

'Where've you been tonight?'

'Out for a meal.'

'Where?'

'Piccadilly.'

'When did you leave your house?'

'I was at work all day. Miranda joined me around five p.m. She must have left here around lunch time; she went shopping before meeting up with me. She had tea with a friend and—'

The ratty little detective snapped, 'I'm not interested in your wife's life story. Listen, here's some advice. Go inside, lock the doors and don't come out 'til tomorrow. Seriously: keep out of our way. One of us will be over tomorrow. We can find out all about the exciting lives of the Willoughbys then.'

Rex was indignant. 'I'm sorry, officer. We're off first thing tomorrow. It's a tradition of ours: Easter hols, we meet up with friends — you know, old university pals, sailing—'

Ratty held up his hand, 'Shut it. You're not going anywhere until you've helped us with our enquiries. You play ball, then you can join your friends for Swallows and Amazons.'

Geraldine waited for Rex to take control; he wasn't someone to push around.

'Now, you listen to me. I want your name, number, name of your superior officer and, by the way, I'm a personal friend of Sir Jack Humphreys. In case you're not one of his friends, he's the Chief Constable.'

Ratty was silent, then said, 'Hmm, well, if you'd like to pop over to your house, one of us will be with you shortly.'

As Rex got back into his car, Ratty sneered under his breath, 'Poncy wanker! Who does he think he is? Lord Fucking Snooty?'

The Willoughbys' car slowly turned into the cul-de-sac. As it approached their house, the security light blazed white. For a split second, Geraldine saw Terry's face in detail: he was staring at the Willoughbys.

Geraldine was getting panicky; what was going on? 'Sergeant Nott, please will you tell me what this is all about? Do you know the whereabouts of my husband? I can tell you now that he is the person who drugged me and left me tied up in our house that has been set on fire. That man being put into the ambulance is Jack Stubbs; he is the person who set fire to the house. I don't know what is going on, but they're both guilty of the most appalling crimes. If Terry hadn't come along, I'd be—'

The Willoughbys' security light went out as one of the ambulance men came over and whispered something to Ratty, who snapped, 'Well, what are you doing here? Get him to the hospital.'

'All right, all right! Keep your hair on. I just thought you'd want to know, that's all.' He marched back to the ambulance. Geraldine heard him say to his colleague, 'What a shithead! Let's get going.'

As the ambulance reversed carefully onto the lane, its siren was turned on: the sound made Geraldine reel against Terry. Two more cars pulled up —

more men, plain-clothes. There were now several bright lights harshly illuminating the whole area. One of the new men came over to Nott; the pair walked away, muttering to each other. The others were by the Escort, bending to examine the front bumper. Geraldine felt Terry's hand grip hers again.

He whispered, 'I'm here, don't worry.'

Ratty came back. He said, 'I'm sorry to have to tell you, Mrs Dutton — your husband is dead and' he jerked his thumb in the direction just taken by the ambulance, 'he isn't far off.'

'What? Edward, dead? What happened to him? Oh my God, what's he done? Don't tell me he's — No! I knew he was in a terrible state, but… No, no, Edward, no… This can't be true…'

'Come on, Mrs Dutton; come with me.' It was the policewoman who took her arm and led her to the Panda car.

Geraldine couldn't help herself. 'Terry, will you come with me?'

Ratty said, 'Don't worry, Mrs Dutton. Your friend will be right behind. That's right, isn't it, Terry, old chap? Mind you, I think it might be a good idea if Detective Constable Armstrong has a quick look around your car, don't you? Chris, give it a good going over, you never know what you might find.' He sized Terry up. 'You don't mind, do you, Terry old lad?'

'Of course, officer: whatever's required.'

Geraldine got into the back of the car and put her hands over her face. Edward dead? Jack Stubbs clearly critically injured? Her house was on fire and she had nearly been burned alive in it. Starting to shake, she wrapped her arms around herself. The policewoman got in beside her; the car moved off. Geraldine opened her mouth to speak. Nothing came out. She tried again, but the only sound she could make was the chattering of her teeth.

'Here, hold my hand. That's it. Tight. Well done.'

Geraldine held the woman's hand and felt her hard grip in return.

At last, she summoned the strength to ask, 'My husband, Edward, what…? How did…? Is he…? Oh, God!'

The voice was calm. 'There appears to have been a shooting. I don't know the details, but he was found dead in his car.'

'Where?'

'Nearby. It's probably best to wait until we get to the station. We can have a nice cup of tea and get warm.'

'He's been behaving so strangely recently. I think there's some trouble with his business. He was trying to get me to mortgage the house to bail it out. I wonder if — Oh, was he…? Oh God, this is so awful!'

'Let's wait, Mrs Dutton.'

They were driving up the high street now, past the road to the school. Wouldn't it be wonderful to be in her classroom, with twenty-five children singing along to a BBC Schools programme, all of them unaware of the despicable acts of adults.

Here they were, at the police station. What she wanted right now, more than anything, was to wake up in bed at home, her mother reading her a story: everything safe and innocent.

Chapter 123

'Are you sure about this, Mum?'

'I am. I should have come clean about Dad. I can't keep killing people and pretending it was nothing to do with me. I'll explain everything to Mr Flanagan. Don't worry, love; I'll be home later. Well, let's hope so, anyway.'

Tina looked at them. She'd never seen Jenny so... what was the right word? Contented? Gary, on the other hand, was about to cry.

Joe said, 'Right, we have to go now. Jenny, you're sure you've got all the details straight?'

She smiled. 'I'm sure. It's all fine. The quicker you lot go, the better I'll feel about it all.'

Joe was holding the patio door for them. Tina stepped up to Jenny and they hugged.

'You're a wonderful woman, Jenny. One day I want to grow up to be like you.'

'Silly girl! Promise me you won't ever grow up to be like an Abbott.'

'Mum, ring me if you change your mind. I'll tell them everything the moment you say the word.'

Tina's heart went out to him: he was openly crying now.

'Go on. Get lost! I'll be fine.'

Tina took Gary's hand and pulled him with her, 'Don't worry, Jenny, I'll look after him.'

They stole down the side of the house — Joe first, then Gary; she trotted along behind. Her legs were horribly uncomfortable. She wanted to sit in the back of the car, holding Gary's hand, but guessed he wouldn't want to be near her right now.

Joe was striding along the lane. He reached a car, unlocked the driver's door, then came around to the passenger's side.

'Okay, Tina, where would you like to sit?'

To avoid the embarrassment of Gary choosing to sit away from her, she said, 'I'll go in the front with you, if that's all right?'

Gary got into the back and shut the door. She saw him put his briefcase on his lap, open it and take out a note pad. Getting into the front, she let Joe close the door.

She said, 'You all right, Gary? Sorry, that's really stupid! I just—'

Joe got in beside her. 'Let's go. We need to be nowhere near here when Flanagan arrives.'

Tina hugged herself. What had happened tonight? She briefly pictured the horror of the cellar: the madwoman, with her savage face and wildly-slashing knife.

Joe called back. 'Gary, behind you is a blanket. Would you pass it over?'

Tina wondered if Joe might be a mind reader. 'Thanks, Gary. Are you sure you don't want it?'

'Nah, I'm fine. You need it more than me.'

Rather than pass it to her, she felt him draping it over her. She covered her legs and pulled it up to her face.

Gary said, 'What's going to happen to her, Joe?'

'I don't know. She's made up her mind that it's the right thing to do, so we must support her.'

Gary's voice was cracking. 'Why though? We could have all said what happened. Now, she's got no one to back her up. It's not right she has to take the shit for us.'

Tina wanted to cry too, but that wouldn't be right: Jenny was Gary's mum, not hers.

She said, 'I think she's a saint. She must be a saint.'

They sat in silence as the car sped along the streets. It wouldn't be long before she was home and, in spite of her dreams of moving, the flat, with her grumpy old dad half-asleep in his chair, was the only place she wanted to be right now. Poor Gary, he'd be going home to no mother or father, just a couple of ignorant brothers. She wondered if he would like to stay at their place? Yeah, maybe it would be a good thing to offer. Dad would be pissed off, but Gary was completely different to Kev, and it wasn't as if he would be sleeping with her or anything. She could make up a nice bed on the settee and give him a hot-water bottle and bed socks and everything. He probably wouldn't want to stay, but it was something she could do for Jenny.

Tina sighed deeply. If only her life had sorted itself out! They could be in a taxi coming back from a club. They'd had champagne with some of her friends from the salon and a few of their most famous customers had joined them for a dinner at a classy restaurant. In the club, she had been introduced to Tony Blackburn, Noel Edmonds and Dave Lee Travis. She'd had to thank them but explain that she was taken: she was with Bulldog Abbott, no less. The idea of being in a relationship with him wasn't so ridiculous. There was no doubt that he was good-looking and, despite the broken nose — or maybe because of it — he had a real physical presence. The DJs had looked up at him and accepted that they had no chance. She smiled sweetly and linked her arm through Gary's.

Joe's voice was low. 'Hallo, what's going on here?'

She opened her eyes. Up ahead were a load of flashing blue lights; uniformed police were putting tape around the entrance to the car park.

'Where is this?'

'Woodcock Hill,' Joe was looking out of the side window as they drove past.

She could see several cars, men milling around. 'Blimey, what's that all about?'

Joe said, 'We're lucky: it looks like they're going to cordon off the road. Now, we need to think about where we've been this evening. It probably won't be an issue, but it would be helpful if we can be clear about where we've been and what we've been doing. It's unlucky that someone in the chemists heard you say you were going to Totteridge, Tina but, on the other hand, if you hadn't mentioned it... Well, anyway, Gary: where were you this evening and what were you doing?'

'Um, er... hmm. I could say, er... Any ideas?'

'It's got to be something that can't be disproved. If you say you were at the pictures and then were asked what the film was you'd have to be able to talk about it. It would be better if you could say you were at home; no one could say that wasn't true.'

Tina said, 'What if we said we were together at home? We'd each be able to confirm we were telling the truth.' As Tina said it, she knew it would have to be Gary's house; her dad never went out and he never lied, either.

Gary said, 'That'd mean we'd have to rely on Kev not being at home. Anyway, I don't think you'd come round to our house, would you?'

'God, no. Not if there was a chance of him being there. Any ideas, Joe?'

'I think you're best off saying you were at home; that's what I'm going to say if I get asked. It would be better if you were together, then there's only one story to worry about.'

'It's going to have to be mine, then. I'll explain it all to my dad. He'll do anything for me, including giving me a right old bollocking.'

'I'm more worried about him giving me the bollocking,' Gary said.

The car had slowed down and was entering the car park. The images of West End glamour long gone, here she was, in the shithole of the century.

'Thanks, Joe. Thanks for everything. I never saw you today. I've been in my flat all evening with Gary — poor boy! I was going to go to Totteridge with him, but we decided not to in the end. We — um... we stayed in and played Tiddlywinks. Come on, Bulldog.'

She got out, folded the blanket and put it on her seat.

Joe said, 'Well done, Tina. You won't hear from me again unless I need to tell you something important. You can ring me if you want, but I suggest you ring only if it's an emergency. Same for you, Gary.' He drove off.

'Your dad is not going to be happy with me being here. What are you going to tell him?'

She'd been wondering the same. 'Well, I'm going to take a leaf out of your book, Oh Wise One: I'm going to tell him everything.'

Chapter 124

She pushed open the door and walked towards the stairwell. He followed.

Tina stood back. 'After you.' He started to trudge up the steps, wobbled a bit then lunged for the banister. 'You all right, Gary?'

'Yeah.' He took another step then stopped. She saw his knuckles whiten as he gripped the metal rail. He tried another step, then shook his head. 'Shit! I've lost my balance or something.'

Was he concussed? She'd never seen anyone get knocked out before — well, apart from Brian Abbott in the Abbotts' kitchen, four nights ago. It had been only a couple of hours since Gary had come round after braining himself in the cellar. Maybe this was delayed shock or something.

'Do you need help?' He turned back to her; there was something not quite right about him. He had a faraway look. 'Gary, what's wrong?'

'Nothing.'

'Are you sure?'

'I said I was, didn't I?'

She could see he was not all right. His face had gone white, and he was teetering on the step.

'Come on, let me help you.'

Gary's face went from vacant to blazing fury. She'd never seen him lose his temper before: he was really scary — like his dad.

'I do not need your fucking help! Got it?'

She felt her own face burn with rage. 'Don't you talk to me like that! I don't care who you are; no one talks to me like that!' She ran past him, 'Sort yourself out, Gary Abbott; I'm sick of you and your whole rotten family.'

'Shit!'

She turned to see him weave, then he was over and tumbling down the steps to the ground.

Dripping scorn, she said, 'Enjoy your trip?' He lay at the bottom of the steps, all crumpled up, his hands over his face. 'Gary? Are you all right?' There was no answer. Frightened, she rushed back down, half hoping that he would pull his hands away, grinning at having beaten her: he didn't. 'Gary,

I'm sorry. Are you all right?' He didn't move. 'Gary?' She gently touched his shoulder.

His voice was muffled. 'Sorry. I'm so sorry. I don't know what's wrong with me.'

'It's all right. I was just being a bitch. You know me by now; I'm such a cow.'

She sat on the bottom step, suddenly really conscious that her urine-soaked trousers were not only uncomfortable, they were also beginning to smell. God, no wonder Gary didn't fancy her!

He slowly gathered himself then, with a groan, sat next to her.

'You're not a cow; I'm a bastard. I'm feeling a bit weird. You're brilliant, Tina, really, you are. I think I've got concussion or something. I ran down some stairs into a cellar. I think I whacked my head against a rafter or beam, I'm not sure. Something anyway.'

'I know. I was there, remember?'

'What? Were you? Hang on… Yeah. Bloody hell, this is doing my nut in! Of course, you were there. What happened then? I've gone blank.'

Tina tentatively rewound the horror show in her head: her only thought was to stop the madwoman killing Gary. Thank God her new scissors were sharp-pointed! The shop assistant in the chemist had recommended blunt ones but she'd wanted a pair like Tracy's. The overpowering drive to plunge the sharp steel into Maureen's backside came rushing back.

Shuddering, she said, 'Oh, nothing, really. I managed to distract your aunt long enough before Joe and Jenny arrived.'

'What did you say?'

'Oh, I discussed the finer points of hairdressing with her. She was fascinated.'

Gary smiled at her. 'No, seriously — what happened?'

'Well, if you must know, I stuck my new steel hairdressing scissors into her skinny arse. I'm sorry, Gary. I know she's — well, was — your aunt and everything, but she was trying to kill you.'

Gary was staring into her face. He seemed to be working something out. She felt self-conscious. 'What?'

'What colour are your eyes? I was thinking they were blue but that's not really right. Do you know what I mean?'

'Hmm, yes. I know what you mean. Do they remind you of the shimmering depths of the Aegean Sea?'

'Er, um…'

'Or, maybe you were thinking of gems — half sapphire, half emerald, half… er… half amethyst?'

Gary was still staring at her. 'Well, anyway, doesn't matter. By the way, ta very much for the scissor-work. I owe you.'

She ruffled his hair, 'You're welcome, milord.'

'No: thank you, milady.'

'You sound like Parker.'

'Who?'

'You know, Lady Penelope's chauffeur from *Thunderbirds*.'

'I thought his name was Brains.'

'Brains! He's the clever one that invents things. Brains is a bit stupid-looking, although he's brainy. You're clever, but good-looking, too. Not as handsome as Scott, but not bad.'

He started to pull himself up. 'Remind me, how many flights is it?'

'Don't worry. I'll carry you.'

Gary smiled. 'You couldn't! Unless you're the Bionic Woman.'

'But I am!'

He looked at her intently, 'That's it! I knew you reminded me of someone famous. You do look a bit like Lindsey Wagner.'

'But I am her. I can't believe you didn't realise before. Come on, let's go. We've got to deal with my arsey old dad yet. That's going to take all my bionic powers.'

She took his hand and began to walk slowly up the stairs. Her trousers chafed her thighs, making a slight squelching sound.

'Sorry about my jeans. I don't make a habit of pissing myself.'

'Don't be stupid. Anyway, I've done it, too. Everyone has.'

'Well, let's get upstairs and have a nice cup of tea. I'm gasping for a fag, as well. Mostly, though, I'm desperate for a bath and change of clothes.'

Chapter 125

As he watched her get into the car, Terry wondered if he'd ever see Geraldine again. Although finding his watch meant that he hadn't left any physical evidence, he couldn't be certain that someone hadn't seen or heard something. True, Stubbs was firmly in the frame for the shootings, and the Escort's bumper was clearly the cause of the dent in the Jag. Nevertheless, he, Terry, was a long way from being out of trouble. The fact that his ex-wife was one of the victims meant that the police would want to know everything about his whereabouts and activities this evening. They'd quickly find out that he had been with her behind *Woolies* at lunchtime today. He would just have to answer their questions as calmly as possible and make sure Tina could vouch for him being at home at the time of the shootings.

'Come through, Mr Castleton.' It was the flashy copper.

Terry sat down opposite the badger-weasel cross who, jabbing out a cigarette, snapped, 'Any luck getting hold of Flanagan?'

A voice from further away called, 'No, he's gone AWOL.'

The weasel got up, slammed the door. 'For fuck's sake! Where is he? Typical of him. I bet he's playing bridge or something poxy.'

Flashy sniggered. 'At least he's not breathing down our necks.'

Weasel sat back down and lit another fag. Terry guessed that the tactic would be to intimidate. That was fine by him: he could handle cocky, little jack-the-lads. But had they already made contact with Tina?

'So, Mr Castleton, we're getting to know you and your family pretty well. Did you know Tina was in this very room the other day?'

'Erm — was it to do with Brian Abbott?'

'Yeah, that's right. Did she tell you what happened that night?'

'I understand there was an accident?'

'Oh, that's what you heard was it?'

'Listen officer, I don't know anything. I'll help in any way I can, but I'm not sure I can offer very much.'

Weasel said, 'You good friends with Mrs Dutton?'

'Not particularly. I've been working at the school for five years, but I don't really know her.'

'Why don't you tell us everything that happened tonight: we can compare it with Mrs Dutton's story.'

Flashy wrote as Terry recalled it all.

Weasel sized Terry up. 'Don't forget your meeting with Mr Stubbs. You left that bit out. Did you know him, before your brief association tonight?'

Terry's heart missed a beat. How had they managed to place him in the frame? Then he realised: Weasel meant outside Geraldine's house. But should he say that he knew Diane had worked for Stubbs, that she had told him she was going to meet Stubbs tonight? What if someone at *Woolies* had overheard their conversation? He couldn't picture anyone being within earshot but…

'No, I've never met him before.'

'So, what happened exactly? You arrive, like a knight in shining armour, then you decide to beat up a total stranger. That wasn't very neighbourly of you, was it?'

'I got out of my car, and he starts throwing crazy punches at me. I had to defend myself.'

'Are you good at hitting people, Mr Castleton?'

He had to be up front. 'Well, I suppose I used to be. I was in the army for twelve years. If someone starts throwing punches at me, I know what to do.'

'What, kill him?'

Terry kept quiet.

Weasel turned to Flashy. 'Are you getting all this down? I mean, including Mr Castleton's refusal to answer my questions?'

Flashy licked his lips. He was nervous.

'Yeah, don't worry.'

Weasel turned back to Terry. 'Do you think it's appropriate to use the sort of lethal force you learned in the army on an innocent member of the public?'

Terry wondered what they knew. This was the last opportunity to come clean. If he professed ignorance and was then proven to have been up at Woodcock Hill, it would be much worse for him. What should he do? If he said now, *Listen, I was there. I saw it all. I saw that innocent member of the public drive his car over a man's unconscious body. That man, possibly dead now, had just blown my ex-wife's head off*, would it be better or worse? No, for Geraldine's sake, he must stick to their agreed story. He cleared his throat.

'When he attacked me, I had to defend myself.'

Weasel said, 'Do you know Mr Dutton, Terry?'

Terry wondered how they'd react if he said that he'd seen Dutton fucking his wife and had harboured the desire to wreak violent revenge on the bastard ever since.

He said, 'No.'

Weasel leaned back and stared at Terry. There was something rotten about this man. He was the kind of insinuating shit that Terry felt compelled to avoid — in case he gave him a beating.

Weasel inhaled again. 'Where were you this evening, Mr Castleton? I mean, of course, before you saved the damsel in distress and, oh — let's not forget beat the living shit out of a pillar of the community?'

'At home.'

'Is that right?'

'Yes?'

'What were you doing?'

'Watching television and — well, mostly just watching television.'

'Go on: what else?'

Terry looked at Weasel and Flashy; he had their attention. 'Nothing interesting, really — honestly.'

Weasel leaned forward, his eyes narrowing. 'We'll decide if it's interesting, Mr Castleton.'

'Well, I was sewing.'

'Sewing!'

'Yes.'

The detectives looked at each other, then back at him.

Weasel said, 'And, Mr Castleton, what exactly were you sewing? No, don't tell me! Um... er... a doily? No. Were you stitching up a kipper?'

'The broken neck of an ancient giraffe.'

Weasel got up and went out of the room. Flashy lit a cigarette. Terry watched him. The young copper was avoiding his gaze. There was something familiar about him; where had he seen that face? Weasel came back holding a paper.

He flicked through it, then said, 'Right, Tina's dad, tell us what you were watching.'

Terry was about to list the programmes but thought it through. What were the chances of these two shitheads being called into the station after the bodies were found? Maybe they'd been at home watching television themselves. This could be a trick of Weasel's. On the other hand, he'd already said he'd been watching the telly, so he could hardly change his story now.

'Well, first, it was *Tomorrow's World*, then *Top of the Pops*; then *When the Boat Comes in*, with James Bolam — you know, the bloke from *The Likely Lads*. Then, when the *News* started, I rang Mrs Dutton.'

Weasel consulted the newspaper. 'How did you know her number?'

'It's in the telephone directory.'

There was a knock on the door. Weasel shouted, 'Yeah?'

The door opened. Terry heard a woman's voice.

'Some news.'

Weasel got up and went out. Terry stared at the young detective as he lit another fag: who was he? He'd seen him, or someone like him, in the last few days. Hang on — no, surely not? The drunk bloke in the pub, his sleeping head flat on the table… Was it him?

He chanced an enquiry. 'I hope you don't mind me asking, officer, but did I see you at the Mops and Brooms the other night?'

'Nah, not me. I wasn't there. I never go there.'

It was him: he couldn't meet Terry's eyes.

'Oh, my mistake. You look a lot like someone I saw down there the other day. Sorry, please forgive me.'

'Maybe you need glasses.'

'Hmm, you might be right.'

Weasel came back in and sat down. He looked at Terry, clearly weighing up whatever he had just been told. Terry looked back, indifferent.

Weasel said, 'So why did you ring Mrs Dutton when you did? What was it that made you decide that you just had to check up on a teacher from school — one that isn't even a close friend?'

'Well, it's complicated. She was very kind to me a couple of days ago and I — anyway, none of that matters now. She told me today about a difficult situation she was having at home with her husband. I don't know really. I suppose we've been looking out for each other and I felt a bit responsible. When the *News* came on, I gave her a quick ring.'

The door opened. The two detectives looked towards the newcomer, sat up straight and put their fags out.

The new man said, 'Please excuse me; I wonder if I might have a word with you, DS Nott?'

Weasel said, 'Of course, Mr Flanagan. We were having a chat with Mr Castleton here.'

Terry turned towards the newcomer: tall, older, he looked like the vicar from Dad's Army.

He turned to Terry, 'I'm so sorry; please forgive me.'

Weasel scuttled out after the old bloke, shutting the door behind him.

Terry couldn't work out all the odds: was he up shit creek or not? Boy, what would he give for a fag right now. As far as he knew, there was nothing linking him with Diane and her assignation this evening. The fact that his ex-wife was dead in a car with Geraldine's husband was certainly odd, and maybe even suspicious, but it wasn't evidence of anything. He could really do with establishing his alibi. The only person who could do that was Tina. If he could ring her and get her to confirm that he'd been at home with her right up till nine, then surely he'd be in the clear? He had to strike now.

Flashy pulled out another cigarette. He smiled at Terry. 'Do you smoke, Mr Castleton?'

'No.'

'You don't mind if I do?'

'Go ahead.' The young copper pretended to read through his notes. Terry asked, 'How is Mrs Dutton?'

'I'm sorry, I can't say.'

'I'm worried about her.'

'Yeah.'

'I tell you what. Why don't you tell me how she is, and I'll keep quiet about you being in the Mops and Brooms, pissed out of your skull?'

Flashy's face coloured. 'Listen, you've got the wrong bloke. I don't know what you're talking about.'

How far could he push it? Tina would be able to vouch that the kid had been there that night. If he needed to, Terry could even accuse him of assaulting his daughter.

'Listen, son, let's not get into a debate. The thing is, Tina told me about what happened that night — everything, literally everything. You understand, don't you? We both know the truth. All I want to know is how Mrs Dutton is. I'm very worried about her.'

He put his hands over his eyes and waited. There was a long pause, punctuated by nervous puffing.

Finally, Flashy said, 'Well, er… thing is… I believe she's at the hospital, identifying… Anyway, that's where she is, I think.'

'Edgware General?'

'Yeah. Don't tell anyone I told you, will you?'

'I won't, son. One more thing. Can I make a phone call? I'd like to ring the hospital to check on her.' He nodded at the phone on the table between them. 'If you gave me a couple of minutes, I'll never mention what you did to Tina that night.'

Flashy's face had gone grey. Terry hated himself.

The young copper licked his lips. 'Er, I'd better check if anything's developed. I'll be back in a minute.'

To cement their relationship, Terry put out his hand. Flashy took it.

Tightening his fingers, Terry said, 'We'll look after each other. I won't let you down: you can rely on me.'

Flashy nodded; he looked pathetically grateful. 'I'll try and give you two minutes. I can't guarantee it.'

Chapter 126

'Come in. Go through and sit down. I'll let my dad know we're here.'

Gary went through to the lounge and collapsed on the sofa. He let his eyes close as the image of his mum's defiant face filled his head. Was she going to be all right? Driving off and leaving her in that witch's house had been unbearable. Why had she done that? They should have stuck together and sorted it all out between them.

'He's not here. It's really weird. He never goes out. There's a note and a sarnie but that's all.'

'What's the note say?'

'Back around ten.'

'What is it now?'

'Nearly half eleven.'

'Any ideas?'

'I dunno. Listen, I need to sort myself out. Give me a few minutes, will you?'

'Do you mind if I have a fag?'

'No. Have one for me, too, will you?'

Gary lit up a Marlboro. He was shocked at the way he'd sworn at Tina. What kind of bastard was he? Maybe he'd inherited some of the bad Abbott genes? His dad had been a bastard. Auntie Maureen was obviously round the bend, and everyone said that Grandad had been horrible. He heard Tina open her bedroom door and go into another room.

She called, 'Won't be long, Gary. Will you put the kettle on?'

He heard taps running and her singing, 'Row, row, row your boat, gently down the stream. Merrily, merrily, merrily, merrily, life's a custard cream.'

He smiled. She was such a volcano. He thought about her stabbing her new scissors into Auntie Maureen's arse. Tina had faced up to her own attack and then waded in to save him. Maybe she was the Bionic Woman.

On the way back, he'd tried to write everything down. The poor light and joggling motion had made it difficult, but he thought most of it was in his notebook. He'd have to add Tina's side of it later. What she'd said had triggered a thought, but it wouldn't come back.

The phone rang; he jumped. Where was he? He must have dropped off.

The bathroom door opened a crack, 'Gary, grab that will you? It will be my dad. I'll be out in a minute.'

Gary lurched to his feet and walked through to the kitchen to answer the call. 'Hello?'

'Who's that?'

'Er — is that you, Mr Castleton? It's Gary. You know, Gary Abbott.'

'Where's Tina? Is she all right?'

'Yeah, she's fine.'

'Get her. Get her now!'

Gary dashed to the bathroom. 'Tina, he wants to talk to you now. It's urgent.'

'Shit, what's happening now?' She ran out of the bathroom, struggling to hold a towel around her. 'Dad, what's wrong?'

Gary stood and watched her. As she clutched the phone, her grip on the towel loosened and it fell on the floor. Gary turned away and walked back into the lounge.

'No, Dad, we've only just got back. It's all been mental tonight... No, Dad, you listen to me — What? Stop it! No, not you, too? ... The thing is, you need to help us... Okay, Okay, Okay, I'm listening ... right, yeah, right. Yeah. Yeah, I've got it... Yeah: *Tomorrow's World, Top of the Pops*; yeah, *When the Boat Comes In*. Yeah, then you went out and we watched — um... We turned the telly off. Yeah, I've got it ... yeah: you were here up until the *News,* then you went off, yeah. Now, Dad, you've got to listen to me. Right: Gary has been with us all evening, too ... That's right; yes, that's right. Yeah, the whole time ... I'll explain everything later ... No, no, Dad, it's nothing like that ... Are you all right? ... We're fine ... I've got it straight ...Okay, what time will that be? ... What do you mean? ... What situation? ... Shall I come and get you? ... You sure, Dad? ... Promise me? ... Yeah, I'm fine: safe and sound ... Bye, then. Good luck! ... I love you too, Dad. Come home soon, won't you?'

Gary lit another cigarette. He was gasping for a cuppa, but he could hardly go into the kitchen now.

'Thanks, Gary.'

'What for?'

'Looking away.'

'Well, it wasn't that I didn't — well... you know.'

She came into the lounge, towel in place. 'That was my dad.'

'Really? I thought it was Mike Yarwood.'

'This is important, Gary. He's got himself into some kind of trouble. He needs us to say that he was here all evening, right up to the *News*. He went out when the *News* started. I told him that he's got to say that me and you were here the whole evening, too.'

'Yeah, I worked all that out. What's he done?'

'Dunno.'

'Is he all right?'

'I hope so. I'll be back in a mo. How's that tea coming along.'

'Er... sorry, I think I must have dropped off.'

He went to put the kettle on. Returning to the lounge, he saw a toy giraffe on the coffee table. It was wearing a sort of stocking thing from its head down to its saggy body. There was precise stitching holding the whole thing in place.

'Ah, look! Dad's mended Giraffe. Oh, my lovely boy! Look, Gary, he's been to the hospital!'

Tina, wearing tiger-striped pyjamas, was cradling the giraffe in her arms, kissing its face with exaggerated love. Gary pictured his tiger at the top of the bedroom wardrobe — stuffing everywhere. Could he bring him over for some treatment? The kettle started to whistle.

'Tea, Milady?'

'Thank you, Parker. And Parker?'

'Yes, Milady?'

'Perhaps you'd bring me a cheese and pickle sandwich?'

'What did your last slave die of?'

'You can take your jacket off, if you want. Even slaves are allowed that in this palace.'

He took his fags and matches out of his pocket and chucked them on the table next to the giraffe and all the sewing stuff. He slipped off his leather jacket and slung it over the back of one of the armchairs. As he walked into the kitchen, it hit him. Turning, he went back into the lounge and stared at the scissors lying next to the giraffe.

'Tina, fucking hell! I've been so stupid. Damn! Shit! Fuck!'

'What? What is it?'

'We've left my mum there, on her own. Oh no, no, no... Shit!'

'Gary, what's wrong? We knew that. We all agreed.'

He turned to look into her frightened face; his must look the same.

'We agreed that my mum was going to tell Flanagan that she'd cracked Auntie Maureen over the head when she went mad with a knife.'

'That's right.'

'Jeez, Tina, I'm so stupid. How is my mum going to explain why Auntie Maureen has got a great, fucking hole in her arse?'

Chapter 127

'Are you sure you're well enough, Mrs Dutton?'

'Yes, honestly — I'm fine now. Thank you so much. You've been terribly kind and helpful.'

Geraldine was desperate to get away. She hadn't wanted any attention and definitely no treatment. But the policewoman had insisted. Now, with ill and injured people all around her, Casualty was the last place she wanted to be.

'How are you getting home, Mrs Dutton?' The nurse was looking worriedly into her face.

'I'll get a taxi. Please don't worry about me.'

Actually, the very word 'home' had a rotten sound to it. There was no way she was going to her own home — maybe ever again. She buttoned her coat and stood up straight.

She was a lot stronger after the tea and biscuits they'd forced her to consume.

It wasn't that she'd been ill, earlier: it was seeing Edward's horrific injuries that had done it. Perhaps whatever he'd put in her drink hadn't helped, but it had been the terrible state of what remained of her husband that had toppled her over, in spite of the warnings of the policewoman.

The nurse accompanied her down the long corridor. 'Now, are you absolutely sure you're okay?'

'Yes, you're safe to leave me now. Actually, I can see a friend of mine waiting for me. Thank you again — you've been terribly kind.'

Terry was wedged into one of the plastic seats by the main door, arms crossed, head lolling against the wall. She almost cried out, her relief was so great. At last, someone kind and decent, there for her. Before she could call him, she heard a voice.

'Geraldine? What are you doing here?'

Turning, she saw Brenda waving at her from the other side of Reception. She was with another woman.

'Oh, Brenda!' Not sure what to do, she glanced back at Terry; his eyes were open, watching. Geraldine went over to Brenda and paused in front of her, uncertain. 'Hello.'

'Are you all right, Geraldine?'

'Yes, I'm feeling much — well, I'm fine. Er... are you here because... What's going on?'

'It's Jack. He's really bad, Geraldine. They've done an emergency tracheostomy. I don't know what's happened. He's had a terrible accident, that's all I know.'

'Oh! Well... Actually...'

Brenda went on, 'I don't understand what's going on. He's been put in a room on his own and it's being guarded by the police.'

Geraldine stood still, open-mouthed. What could she say?

Brenda was looking intently into Geraldine's face, 'He went out this evening. He said he'd be back in an hour and the next thing I know the police are at the door. The funny thing is that they wanted to know if he'd been with Edward. Do you know where Edward is? Did he meet Jack?'

'Edward's been shot. He's dead.'

Brenda Stubbs cried out, 'Oh, no, Geraldine, I'm so... Oh no, this is all so awful. What's been going on?' She stood up and wrapped her arms around Geraldine, hugging her tight. 'You poor, poor, dear girl. Oh, here's me whining and you've... Oh, my, I'm so sorry.'

Geraldine let herself be comforted. Brenda was such a lovely woman. She'd always been the one decent friend in their circle. What poor Brenda evidently didn't know was that Jack was not just dangerously ill, he was in very deep water. Geraldine was determined to make sure he drowned.

Brenda loosened her grip and turned to the other woman. 'Geraldine, this is my sister, Mavis. Her son, our nephew Rob, is here, as well. He's been involved in some kind of terrible incident, too! He's — oh my God, I can't even say it... He's been crushed by a hit-and-run driver.'

Geraldine looked at Mavis properly: white-faced, tear-stained. 'I'm sorry, Mavis. I...' she cleared her throat, 'Is he...?'

Brenda said, her voice quavering, 'Crushed pelvis.'

'Oh, what a nightmare!'

Brenda said, 'Is it all connected, do you think? It's got to be, hasn't it?'

Out of the corner of her eye, Geraldine saw Terry get up and head for the doors.

'I don't know anything, Brenda. My head is in a spin. I must go; I can't stay here. I hope... I just hope, that's all.' She turned to go.

Brenda called out, 'I'm so sorry, Geraldine; I really am.'

He was there: bulky, steady, safe.

'Would you like a lift anywhere?'

'Yes, please, anywhere.' She followed him across the car park to his little car. He opened the passenger door and held out his hand to steady her in. She didn't take it. 'Thank you, I can manage.'

He gently shut the door. Hugging herself, she willed the trembling to stop.

'Shall I just drive?'

'Yes, please.'

It took him several attempts to get it going. Not used to a small, under-powered car, she felt vulnerable all over again. Was she going to be run off the road by a black Jaguar?

They puttered along quiet roads, and she began to calm down. What had happened to her? The week had started the way it always did: school, noisy children, sexual fantasies, critical husbands. Four days later, with house ablaze, husband brutally killed, here she was: sitting in a car, inches away from the school caretaker, somewhere around midnight.

He said, 'I saw it all.'

'What? What do you mean?'

'I was there.'

'Tell me.'

As he spoke, she wondered again how she'd failed to see him — really see him. It was his ability to project another personality that was evidently his greatest skill.

She said, 'So, you thought you'd left your watch there?'

'Yeah, can you believe it?'

'But why didn't you go back for it?'

'I couldn't risk it. The young bloke needed urgent care, you were in trouble; and the bodies were going to be found by someone sooner or later, and I weighed it all up and — well, you know the rest.'

'Well, thank God you did, that's all I can say.'

'Yep.'

'Jack Stubbs must be pure evil. I mean — to deliberately drive over his own nephew in order to crush you!

'Yep.'

'I'm so sorry, Terry. Your poor wife.'

'I'm sorry about your husband.'

Was she sorry? Maybe Edward hadn't meant her to be killed in a house fire, but he had certainly done his best to destroy her life and, it seemed, had been doing so for a long time. She just hadn't noticed.

'Were you close to your wife, Terry?'

'I hadn't seen her for six years. She was effectively dead in my head, anyway.' She heard him swallow. 'I wasn't expecting our final meeting to be quite so brutal.'

'I feel terribly dirty and — oh, I don't know — sordid, I suppose. I'd better go back to my mother's house. Will you be kind enough to take me there? It's about twenty minutes from here.'

'I'll take you anywhere, Geraldine.'

'Do you need to let Tina know where you are?'

'I rang her earlier. As soon as I've dropped you off, I'll dash back home.'

'Turn left at the next junction.' Hoping he couldn't see her, she wiped away the tears sliding down her cheeks. How was she going to cope without him?

Chapter 128

'Hello?'

'Yeah, hallo, Miss — I mean, Victoria. I'm really sorry to ring you; I know it's incredibly late.'

'Gary, is that you?'

'Yeah, I'm so sorry about this but I don't suppose you know where Joe is? I mean, I don't mean is he with you or anything like that. The thing is, I need to speak to him about something and he's not at his house and — it's late, I know, but really, the thing is...' he cleared his throat. 'Anyway, that's it.'

'It's getting on for midnight, Gary. What's going on?'

'Yeah, I know; I'm really sorry.'

'He's on his way here; I've just had a call from him. Gosh, Gary, what on earth is going on that you need to speak to him this late?'

As she heard him grappling for an answer, the same old fury she'd had with Joe began to bubble up. What had he got the poor boy into now? It was only days since Brian Abbott had been killed. Joe had managed to get everyone into trouble with the police — including her. She wondered what preposterous lie Gary was going to come up with this time. He'd be sure to protect Joe whatever happened. She would cut him off the moment he started lying.

'I know this sounds unbelievable but—'

'I don't want to hear any fabrications, Gary. Tell me the truth.'

'That's the trouble: the truth sounds unbelievable.'

She heard him gulping for air. 'It's all right, Gary. Take your time.'

'Right, this is it: my Auntie Maureen, Dad's sister, is a total nutter. She tried to kill me and Tina, but my mum arrived with Joe — honestly, in the nick of time — and whacked her over the head with a poker. Tina stabbed her, Auntie Maureen, that is — not my mum — with a pair of scissors — haircutting scissors. Anyway, it's all tied up with my grandad going missing years ago, the Great Train Robbery and Uncle Ray buried under the greenhouse. Well, I'm not sure about that bit but he probably is, although my mum isn't so sure. The thing is, Joe drove Tina and me home and my mum is there still and she's going to tell Old Flanagan everything. But the hole in Auntie Maureen's ar — um... posterior is going to give her away. I think that's it. I need to talk to Joe. We need to do something. Don't you see?'

Never mind Auntie Maureen being a nutter, Gary had clearly lost his mind.

'Gary, have you been drinking?'

'No. I told you it was mental, but it's true, all of it.'

Victoria took a deep breath. 'Right, let me think. Where are you now?'

'At Tina's house.'

'And where is your mum?'

'Totteridge.'

Outside, a car door shut. She inched the curtain aside and peered out: was it Joe?

'Hang on, Gary; this might be him now.'

She put the phone down, went out into the hall and opened the front door a crack. It was him.

Flinging the door wide, she snapped, 'Get in here, now. Gary's on the phone going out of his head with worry. Whatever it is that you've done, you need to look after him. What are you doing now?'

'Taking off my shoes: they've got a bit—'

'Never mind your bloody shoes. Talk to Gary.'

He went into the sitting room and picked up the phone. 'Gary? ... Listen, it's going to be all right ... I know ... I know ... Yes ... Trust me, it's all right. Because ... Because we ... Yep, that's right. Okay, you need to speak to your mother; she'll explain ... No, she isn't: she's at home. I've just dropped her off ... That's right ... Yes, you can give her a ring ... No, she's on her own ... I don't know. Now's the time to ring her. I'm sorry to keep you in the dark but it's ... She needs to tell you ... Yes, well, you could say that ... Ha! Thanks, thanks very much ... Yep, she's here. Of course. I'll pass you over. Cheers, Gary. Good luck with everything!'

Joe held the phone out for her.

'Hello, Gary?'

'Listen, you might not believe this, but we've done nothing wrong. We got caught up in a crazy nightmare. Joe wasn't involved, apart from saving our lives. I wanted you to know that; that's all.'

'Thank you, that's very thoughtful of you. I have to say I'm somewhat flabbergasted by it all. I shall be asking Joe to explain everything in a minute.'

'Good. He'll tell you. Bye, then.'

'Goodnight, Gary.'

'Miss? I mean, Victoria?'

'Yes?'

'Thanks for helping me get that placement at *The Post*; it's going really well so far.'

'You're very welcome. Goodnight, Gary.'

She put the phone down and faced him. 'Gary says you weren't involved until the end, at which point you saved their lives.'

He was standing by the door. 'They were about to get knifed to death by a madwoman. That's the long and the short of it. There's all the detail, but that's the most important fact.'

'I handed in my resignation today.'

'What? Why?'

'Why do you think? Because you have made it impossible for me to undertake a responsible, professional role with any shred of integrity or principle. How can I be the head of a school when I'm mixed up with a man who leaves dead bodies wherever he goes?'

'Mixed up with?'

'Don't get clever with me.'

'I'm sorry to hear about your resignation. I'm even more upset that I'm responsible. If you wanted to retract it, and you feel that I'm in the way of that, then I'll be on my way.'

'Too late, I've made up my mind.' She looked at him closely. Was he genuine? Everything he touched was mired in murk and mystery. Yet her experience of him — and seeing him with Frank, Anthony, Katy and Gary — was of a kind, considerate and empathic man. 'You'd better tell me everything, then I'll know what I'm letting myself in for.'

Friday

Chapter 129

Gary put the phone down and turned back to Tina. 'I don't know what's going on, but she's back home.'

Tina was pouring tea.

She spun around. 'What? What's happened?'

'He wouldn't say. He just said I need to talk to her.'

'Well, don't hang around: ring her up. Want sugar?'

'Yeah, ta.'

She walked to the table with the mugs and the sandwich. As he dialled, she sipped her tea and lit a fag. He was standing in the hall, the phone gripped in his fist, face contorted with worry. The way Gary loved his mum was so touching. What must it be like to have a loving mother? Tina thought back to the haggard-looking woman in *Woolies*: she might have been the person who gave birth to her, but their relationship had never been like the one Gary had with his mum.

'Mum, it's me … Yeah, Joe, that's right … I don't get it … But … Yeah, yeah, we're fine … Yeah, I'm with her now … Yeah, she's fine … Definitely, she's been looking after me.' He looked over at her and smiled. 'Yep, I'll be with you in — er, ten minutes if I run? … Right, right, I'm on my way.'

As he put the phone down once more, Tina stubbed out her fag. What a shame; she'd been hoping they'd have a few minutes together before her dad got back. When she thought about Kev, and the other blokes she'd got off with, shame coursed through her. Why had she been so easy? Gary was a million times better than all of them: six million times, in fact. It was partly that he was tall, and strong and all that manly stuff, but it was more that he was clever, and sensitive, in a rough sort of way, and she knew he cared about her. Kev and that lot couldn't give a monkey's, as long as they were getting their ends away. She'd hoped Gary would have sat next to her on the sofa. She could have snuggled up to him and felt his arm around her as he told her that he — what?

She pushed the tea towards him. 'Here's your tea. I've had my half of the sandwich.'

'Ta. I'd better leg it. She says she's got to tell me stuff before the police get in touch.'

'Drink your tea first. You've had a nasty bump on the head. I know there's nothing inside your skull, apart from important news articles, but you really should have something to eat and drink.'

He picked up the sandwich and crammed it into his mouth. 'Mm, lovely'. He slurped noisily, 'Yum, lovely! Thanks, Tina.'

'Don't mention it. Lucky we're not in my new house: the servants wouldn't be very impressed by your manners. Anyway, what's so important?'

'I dunno. She says she's got to tell me something about Auntie Maureen.'

'When are you going to stop calling her Auntie? That woman was as mad as a box of frogs. And she was pure evil. She was worse than your dad, and he was badder than bad.'

'All right, you don't have to rub it in.'

'Well, they *were* bad. Your dear, departed father was assaulting me, and if your mum hadn't smacked him one, he might have raped me.'

Gary's face was white with anger. She'd gone too far — but, no, she thought, it was totally reasonable: Brian Abbott had been rotten to the core. She looked up at Gary, her face challenging.

Gary looked back at her; he was furious, too. 'That's not right.'

'It is, Gary. I'm sorry, I know he was your dad, but honestly...'

'I wouldn't have let him do anything to you; I'd have killed him myself. I wish I had. I'm sorry my mum got there first.'

'Oh, well. Hmm.'

'I'd do anything for — Ah, shit! I'd better go. Thanks for the tea. Thank your dad for the sandwich, too. Thanks for — you know, all of it.' He went back into the lounge and picked up his jacket.

She followed him. 'Sorry, I didn't mean to be horrible. It must be awful to lose your dad, even—' Gary turned and looked into her eyes. He just stared. 'What is it, Gary? What's wrong? Is your head all right? You're scaring me.'

'I know you'll have loads of boyfriends, or maybe one really good and one and, one day, I bet Steve Austin will come and find you. But if you ever want someone to — I dunno, go for a walk, or see a film, or — I dunno, just have a drink or something, then you could give me a ring, you know, if you got stuck. I wouldn't mind. Look, you're so pretty and funny, and — you know — well, like that advert said, you won't be bothered about an ugly shithead like me but, as I say ...'

Tina could feel her heart banging as he spoke. She put her index finger to his lips.

'Listen, you are an ugly shithead, and you're right, I've got film stars and millionaires ringing me up the whole time, and I had to tell Steve Austin to leave me alone the other day but, right now, you're the gorgeous one, Bulldog.' She reached up and put her arms around his neck and kissed him hard. She felt his arms around her waist.

She had kissed loads of boys but, this time, it was different. She wanted to kiss Gary. It was partly to please him, look after him, make him happy. But it was more than that. She wanted to, for herself.

He broke away. 'Don't tease me, Tina. I couldn't bear it if you were teasing me.'

'You're a pillock, Gary. Don't you know you're really handsome and clever? The only reason Lindsey Wagner hasn't called at your door is because I always block her way. Come here. Let's go and sit down and talk about the future — you in Fleet Street and me in Hollywood.' She took his hand and pulled him to the sofa.

'Shit, I can't. Jeez, I've got to get home and see my mum.'

'Well, I suppose I could go and have a cold shower, to cool down a bit. You're a brilliant kisser, Bulldog.'

'Really? Hmm, not sure how I managed that.'

'Go on, you need to see your mum. Ring me. I want to hear all the news.'

Standing, he bent down and kissed her hard again. 'You're absolutely... you know. I'd better go. Can I see you tomorrow? What I mean is — well, I don't want this to turn out to be a dream. Do you know what I mean?'

'Yes, Gary Abbott, I know what you mean. Don't you worry; it's not a dream.'

Chapter 130

'It's down there.'

Terry turned sharp left into the narrow lane, the Imp's headlights picking out the tangled foliage lining the verge.

'Keep going. I know it looks like nothing's down here… Keep going.'

She was right. They'd been crawling along for a couple of hundred yards and the narrow track was beginning to peter out.

'Here we are.'

'Strewth, how old is this place?'

'Fifteen hundreds.'

Terry pulled up outside the house. They sat in silence. 'You all right?'

'I think so.' He got out and walked around to her door, opened it and stood ready to help. 'It's all right. I'm fine, thanks.'

Terry was about to shut the door when he remembered Diane's long, white-blonde hair. He scanned the seats and footwells and made a mental note to give the car a damned good clean the moment he got home. He shut the door and, not knowing what to do with himself, held out his hand then dropped it.

'Give me a ring if you need anything or — I don't know, you feel like a chat. What you've gone through is beyond belief. You have to look after yourself. Go and see your doctor first thing. You'll need a something or other — a tablet or two, maybe? Anyway, the point is, the shock of what's happened won't sink in immediately: give it time. Believe me, I've seen shock take months, or even years, to hit home. That's all I wanted to say. Well, apart from the fact that I think you're the most wonderful person and I'm sorry about everything.'

She took his hand and squeezed it. 'Don't be a twerp, Terry. You're coming in for a few minutes. You need to think about your shock — you stole all my best lines. Ah — hmm. Now we've got a problem.'

'What?'

'I haven't got a key. It's in my bag; I left it at the house.'

'Is there a spare, hidden somewhere?'

'That's the one in my bag. Damn!'

'Will your mother mind being woken up?'

'She'll be dead to the world. She takes sleeping tablets; ever since my father died. It's the only way she can get to sleep these days. Hang on, sometimes she leaves a window open in the kitchen.' She took his hand. 'Come on, let's pretend we're cat burglars.'

Terry found himself being tugged along a rough path down the side of the house. He felt foliage flicking against his legs, then a thickish branch whipped his face.

'Sorry, Terry. You all right?'

'Apart from being attacked by triffids, I'm fine.' They reached the end of the ancient structure. Terry felt cobbles underfoot. He whispered, 'Can you see anything?'

'Nothing. You?'

'Even less.'

'Great, the window is open. Security has never been my mother's strong suit. Now, if I can just… Ah, brilliant! There we are.' She stood away from the house and pulled open a creaking casement window. 'Now, can I get in there? I'm sure I used to be able to when I was… um, thirty years younger.'

'What's on the other side?'

'The kitchen chair, I think. Let's have a go.'

She took off her coat. 'Will you hang on to this, Terry?'

'It will be my pleasure.'

Geraldine tried to hoist herself up and onto the windowsill.

'Damn! I can't get any purchase. You'll have to give me a bunk-up.'

Terry considered how best to attack it. The window must be four feet off the ground and, apart from the window frame, there was nothing to hold on to. She was going to have to stand on the windowsill and then, if there was space, crouch down and step onto the chair. It was not going to be easy.

'Er… I'd offer to go in, but I think the window's a bit too small. I'm sorry.'

'Don't be silly, this is child's play — literally. Okay, if you stand behind me whilst I try and walk up the wall and if I push back against you, all you've got to do is push me up. It will be easy. Mind you, I'm not exactly Olga Korbut these days. Are you ready?'

'I'm not sure about this. Haven't you had enough adventure this evening?'

'I'm feeling daring. Okay, stand behind me. Here goes.'

She put one foot on the wall and pushed back against him. As he took her weight, she began to walk up the side of the house.

Her voice came in gasps. 'It's working — push me, Terry.'

Terry had been trying to hold her around the waist, but as she went up the wall, the only place he could put his hands was around her chest. 'I'm sorry, Geraldine! I'm so sorry, I can't help…'

Through her panting effort, she grunted, 'Just keep pushing, Terry. This is not the time for chivalry.'

Her full weight was against him. He carried on pushing, his hands now under her armpits, until she had both feet on the sill, then supported her back as she levered herself into a crouch.

'Okay, I'm there. I've got to rest for a minute. Stay behind me, just for a mo.'

He pressed his chest against her back. 'Phew! I'm not made for cat burglary. You, on the other hand…'

'You're such a gentleman, Terry. I'm sorry you had to handle so much blubber.'

This had not been his experience of proceedings.

'I… well — you're… anyway. Are you ready for the final push?'

'Yes, here goes.'

She dangled one leg forward, then the other, and pushed off. There was a stifled 'youch' then silence.

'Are you all right, Geraldine?'

She stood up and leaned her elbows on the windowsill and looked out at him. 'Terry Castleton, how lovely of you to come and call. Would you like a drink?'

Terry was pretty sure Geraldine was hysterical. Although she was not outwardly off her head, he was in no doubt that, now she was safe, the quicker he got away the better.

'Well, that's very kind of you. Let's say goodbye now and I'll come and get you in the morning. I'll take you anywhere you want to go. You'll probably have other people who will come and get you. Goodnight, Geraldine. I'm so sorry for everything.'

'Don't go!'

Her cry of alarm was so anguished he held up his hands, 'Okay, Okay, don't panic, Mr Mainwaring. I'm not…' There was movement from inside the kitchen then silence. 'Hello, are you there?' A light was turned on somewhere; then a distant door was opened. He heard her coming down the path.

'Terry, are you there?'

'Yes, I'm here.'

She grabbed hold of his arm, 'Thank God. Come in for a minute. Please, Terry, don't go just yet.'

He stooped to pick her coat off the ground, then allowed himself to be pulled back down the path.

'Come on. In you come.'

Terry ducked through the doorway, following her into the hall.

Geraldine was speaking softly. 'My mother lives here on her own. She's not good at DIY. You may well find areas that could do with the Castleton touch.'

'Oh, really? Well, I'll submit a quote once I've undertaken a full assessment.'

He followed her down the narrow corridor to the kitchen, the floor sloping this way and that as he walked.

'Right, what would you like? I can do tea or coffee, cocoa, Ovaltine, or maybe you'd like Horlicks? They're all years out of date, but Mother doesn't like to throw anything away. There's also a wide selection of bottles available: all of them ancient.'

'Hmm, they're all tempting. What are you going to have?'

'I'm going to have a bloody big glass of sherry.'

'Oh.'

She laughed, 'Look at your face! Don't worry, I'm not going on a bender. Sit down. Come on, take the weight off your feet.'

He handed her her cast-off coat. As she reached up to hang it on the back of the kitchen door, he saw her cardigan stretch. Shaking his head, he looked away, swallowing noisily.

'What's your poison?'

'How about we both have a mug of Horlicks?'

'That's the oldest one in the larder. I won't even be able to chip it out of its jar. Come on, join me, Terry. Have a proper drink.'

'Thank you, that's very nice but—'

'Do you live in your caretaker's overall?'

'That's what Tina always says.'

'Well, great minds and all that. Take it off; you won't feel the benefit.'

Shyly, Terry unbuttoned his overall.

'I'm sorry, this feels rather indecent, taking off my overalls in a strange woman's kitchen.'

'Strange? Charming, I must say.'

'Well, a strange kitchen.'

'It's an overall, not your trousers.'

'I know. But I'm a caretaker, don't forget. We're never seen out of uniform.'

'That's a nice shirt. Is it from Savile Row?'

'Almost certainly.'

'Don't just stand there — do sit down!'

He pulled out a chair and sat at the table. How was he going to extricate himself? She took two glasses and a bottle from a corner cupboard and poured large measures. 'Here you are. Terry Castleton, I would like to make a toast.'

'Oh, I was going to make one too.'

'Actually… maybe you're really hungry? Would you like some toast? How about a bowl of tomato soup?'

'No thanks, my tummy won't let me eat this time of night. How about you? Maybe you need something hot inside you?' His face burning, Terry coughed. 'Sorry. Right — um, here's my toast. To you — the bravest and kindest person I know.'

'How many people do you know?'

'Hmm, three. Maybe four?'

'So, it's not a great achievement on my part, is it?'

'Yeah, but the other four I know are the world's bravest and kindest people.'

'Okay, let's drink to my credentials then.'

They clinked. She gulped; he sipped.

'Terry, swig it. Come on.'

He took a slurp. 'What's your toast?'

'Hang on. I need a top-up.'

She gulped again, glass clacking against her teeth.

'Right: to Sir Terry "the caretaker" Castleton: easily the most noble of knights in the realm.'

He was not feeling very noble right now. Maybe it was the adrenalin, or the alcohol already racing through his blood. Whatever the cause, he felt an overwhelming desire to stretch across the table and stroke her hair. He hadn't felt like this for years; he had to get control of himself.

'Thank you, that's a very nice toast. Come on, then. Cheers!'

She drained her glass; he took half a sip.

'That's my boy; you're getting the hang of it.'

'Er — you sure you don't want something to eat?'

'Well, I might have something later. I'm enjoying the medicine you've prescribed me.'

Her face was flushed, eyes glittering.

'Geraldine, I'm wondering if a nice cup of coffee might be a good idea. What do you reckon?'

'Oh, goody. Can I have some brandy in it?'

'Hmm. Well, to be honest, that wasn't exactly what I had in mind.'

'Just sherry, then.' She poured another one and topped his up. 'Cheers! You're my hero.'

She cracked the glass back on the table, amber liquid oozing onto the grainy wood. He looked up and saw Bristol Cream dribbling down her chin. She smiled at him as she licked her lips.

'Do you know, Terry, I never realised what kind of man you were until the last couple of days. Can you believe it? I've seen you every day for years and I thought you were just, you know, the caretaker. Will you forgive me for not realising?' She picked up her glass and gulped it empty.

Terry knew what his next mission was: to get her into bed, unscathed.

'Right, I think it's about time for me to get home. Tina will be wondering where I am. How about you? Are you ready for bed?'

'Ooh! Sir Terry. This is a turn up for the books. What a nice surprise!'

'Come on, we've done this before. Do you remember the other night? It's time for me to go.'

She reached for the bottle. 'Stinker! You're not a knight after all. You're going to run off and leave me in mortal peril.'

With relief Terry saw that only a dribble was left in the bottle.

'I am a stinker. Now, are you sure you can manage alone?' She picked up her glass, looked at it, then put it down again. He saw her eyes swivel to his glass; he drained it. 'Geraldine?'

'Hmm?'

'Are you going to be all right?'

Her eyes had dulled. 'Yes, I'm fine. Sorry, Terry, I've let you down again. Don't worry, I'll be all right.' He got up and put his overall on. 'Oh, God, what a day; what a night. What a terrible thing.'

He looked over at her: her elbows on the table, head in her hands. He picked up his glass and held it under the ancient tap. There was a rackety shuddering before a trickle of cold water emerged. He took the full glass to her.

'Come on, get something pure and decent down your neck.' She didn't move. 'Come on, sweetheart: swig it down.' He peeled her hands away from her face and held the glass to her lips. She had a sip, then another, and another. 'That's a good girl. Here you go, you can do it… That's it.' She took the glass from him and glugged it down. He stood close, holding her against him. 'Good girl, that's much better.'

As if she were waking up from a deep sleep, she groaned, 'Sorry, I lost it for a minute. You're making a habit of bailing me out.'

'That's my job. Anyway, you saved me the other day; I was a gonner — don't you remember?'

'I'd better get to bed. I've got school tomorrow.' Pushing her chair back, she staggered to her feet then fell against him, 'Whoa, I'm all over the place! Oh, God, I'm sorry. What a mess. You'd better go now. Don't worry, I'll be all right.'

Terry looked around for the stairs. There was a narrow door with a latch.

'Is that the door to upstairs?'

'Yesh.'

Letting go of her, he sped to the door and opened it: there was a winding, narrow flight disappearing into darkness. This was going to be hard work.

'Yikes, I'm going over!'

Dashing back, he caught her before she toppled.

'Right, we need to think this through. Which room is yours?'

'Er — um… Left at the top, at the front of the house. No… hang on a mo, right at the top. Is that right? Yes, definitely right.'

'Bathroom?'

'Over there.'

'Right, this is the plan; we need to make it a military operation. Are you ready to receive your orders?'

'Yesh, shir.'

'You are going to go to the bathroom, wash your face, brush your teeth, use the toilet. Are you ready?'

'I think sho. I mean, yesh.'

'Come on, then; I'll hold you steady.'

She weaved to the bathroom door, Terry holding her waist from behind. He stopped her, pushed open the door and pulled the dangling string; a dim light illuminated the spartan room.

'Okay, can you manage on your own?'

568

'Yesh, I can.' She lurched into the bathroom and started careering. He took her arm and steadied her.

Giggling, she said, 'Shall we dance?'

'There's no music. Mind you, I reckon you could cut a rug if you got half the chance. Now, come on. Can you manage?'

'I'm not sure. Maybe you'd better stay, just in case.'

As she ran water into the basin, he stood behind her, his hand light on her waist. Her movements — turning the taps, picking up soap, bending forward to lather her face — were giving him an intense feeling of excitement. Then shame swept it away. She leaned over the basin and washed her face: he stepped back. This was going to be a real challenge.

'That's much better; thank you very much.'

He lifted the towel from the back of the door and pressed it into her hands.

'Here you are. Now, teeth?'

'Don't let go of me, will you?'

'No, I've got you.'

She squeezed toothpaste and clumsily brushed. Terry concentrated on keeping her vertical, and shut his mind to the softness of her body moving under his fingers. She rinsed her mouth and tapped the brush on the edge of the basin.

'Don't let go, Terry; I'm very wobbly.'

They stood still, her back to him, his hands on her waist.

She said at last, 'I'm sorry, I need the lav.'

'That's fine; I'll wait outside. Shout when you're ready.'

'I can't move on my own; I'm going to go over.'

'Ah, we-ell…'

'I'm really sorry, Terry — this is so embarrassing.'

'Not for me, it isn't. Don't worry about it. Come on then: let's get on with it.' He held her steady, leaned over to the toilet and lifted the lid. 'Here you go.'

She stumbled across and positioned herself. Lifting her skirt, then pulling down her pants, she sat heavily on the seat.

With a huge sigh of relief, Terry turned his back. 'Now that the eagle has landed, I'll come back when you're done.'

As soon as he closed the door, Terry swarmed up the narrow staircase to the landing. From the back of the house came the steady rumble of a sound sleeper. He went to the front bedroom and switched on the light. It was as spartan as the rest of the house — rickety wooden chest and wardrobe, a "captain's chair", and a wooden, three-quarter bed. He pulled back the floral bedspread and woollen blankets, then quickly went back down, checking out the tricky angled steps. No sound from the bathroom.

'How are you getting on?' Silence. He tapped twice, hesitantly. 'Geraldine?'

'Hallo?'

'How you getting on?'

'Oh, I'm fine. You all right?'

'I'm coming back in, ready or not.' He pushed open the door to find her exactly as he'd left. 'Well done. Up you come!' He took her hands and pulled her up. 'Um, can you pull them up, sweetheart?'

'Sorry, sorry. This is so embarrassing. I'll pull myself together.' She bent and pulled her pants up, Terry's hand on her shoulder, supporting her as she swayed.

'Are you ready for the final push?'

'I'll just wash my hands — sorry, Terry.'

'Quite right, well done.'

She ran the tap. then turned back, weaving precariously, and grabbed his arm with a wet hand. 'Crikey, nearly went again. What's wrong with me?'

'It's the shock, the adrenalin, the sherry. Right, ready for the final, final push?'

'I'll try. Thank you for this, Terry; you're a gem.'

From behind, he steered her out of the bathroom to the first step, 'Here we go... first step. Well done. And the next... and the next.'

His chest provided a solid buttress as they went up. The feel of her body was filling his head, but he kept his focus on her ascent to safety. Suddenly, they were there.

He manoeuvred her to the bed, whispering, 'Here you are, Princess, your bed awaits.' She sat down and stayed motionless. 'Geraldine?'

'Hmm?'

'Can you manage from here?'

'I think so.'

He watched her begin to topple. 'Okay, don't worry. I've got you. Let's sort you out once and for all.'

He held her steady and pushed the door closed. 'Let's start with your shoes; that's it, nice one. Cardigan next? Gosh, what a lot of buttons... fiddly too. Nearly there, that's it, good work. Arms up, slip off... That was easy. Well done. Skirt next — do you want to stand up? That's it... up she rises.

Hang on, let me undo it. That's it, very good girl. Now, tights: allow me. Do you want to sit down? There we go... that was easy, wasn't it? You're very good at this, I must say. Okay, that's the way to do it. Who do I sound like? Mr Punch? You can lie down now.' He tucked her feet under the top sheet then gently covered her with the bedclothes. 'There you are — all warm and cosy. Phew, that was quite an adventure! You can sleep now. It's time to forget everything horrible and dream about lovely things, instead.'

'Thank you. I won't forget what you've done for me.' Her voice was a low mumble.

'Believe me, it's been lovely being with you. It's just a pity the circumstances haven't been ideal.'

'Don't go, Terry. Will you wait for a minute; just until I'm asleep?'

'Sure. Do you mind if I sit down for a second?' He started picking up her clothes from the old chair.

'Why don't you sit on the bed? I won't eat you, I promise.'

'I didn't think you would.'

'I promise I won't ravish you either.'

He'd already guessed that. 'Budge over, give me a bit of room; that's it. Now, close your eyes and think of England.'

'Terry, can I ask one more favour?'

'Ask away. If I can do it, I will.'

'I need some more water, a lot more. Do you mind?'

'I'll be back in a mo. If you're asleep when I get back, I'll leave it on the chest.'

'I'll be awake, don't worry.'

He doubted it. What's more, he'd give her five minutes before coming back up.

Downstairs, he took the opportunity of using the bathroom himself. How long ago had he been desperate for a crap? Jesus, it seemed like years ago. The shocking images were dancing in front of his eyes: that poor kid; would he ever walk again? Would dear Uncle Jack recover? If he did, then there was a pretty good chance of him getting banged up for the killings, not to mention the attempted murder of Geraldine.

Terry knew that he was still in the frame. What if Stubbs recovered? If he did, would he remember the large man with balaclava and black coat at the car park? Maybe Stubbs had got a glimpse of him when he'd socked him one... The weasel copper had recognised Terry to be more than a common-or-garden caretaker. They were sure to look up his history and see the violence in his military career. He got up and flushed the loo. The whole house seemed to rattle. If the old girl didn't get a decent builder into this place soon, it was going to fall down.

Washing his hands, the old man in the mirror looked back. He was glad Tina had challenged him to give up smoking. There was every chance he wouldn't reach fifty if he didn't start taking care of himself. Filling the basin with tepid water, he washed his face. It was comforting. He squeezed some toothpaste onto his finger and scrubbed away the foetid taste of everything that had happened. Rinsing his mouth, he looked up and favoured the stranger with a friendly smile. The old bloke snarled back at him.

He went out to the kitchen, filled Geraldine's glass with water, and tiptoed up the stairs. Halfway, he remembered Tina, and the boat.

Chapter 131

Running through the deserted streets, Gary couldn't help grinning. Tina's mouth on his, her body pressing, her arms around him... Was it real? He'd always fancied her. The first time Kev had brought her home, Gary had thought she was the sexiest girl he'd ever seen.

For as long as he could remember, Kevin had been his hero. Getting a bird like Tina was proof that his older brother really was something special. It was easy to see why girls might find him tasty, in a trendy sort of way. Kev wore cool clothes, had a motor bike, was a brilliant dancer and knew about music and films and stuff but, in the last few weeks, Gary had begun to realise that Kev wasn't quite as heroic as he'd thought. Apart from anything else, he was such a whiner. Everything was someone else's fault... It got on Gary's tits. As he sprinted up Shenley Road, Gary pictured Tina in her stripey pyjamas. When she'd come around that first time, Gary remembered thinking that, one day, he would get a girlfriend like her — and that day had arrived!

His lungs were protesting now. Maybe he should stop smoking; the tightening around his chest was not a good feeling. He reached his street. Slowing, Gary checked for police cars. None, thank God. He let himself in.

'At last! I thought you said ten minutes?'

'Watcha. Yeah, well, I couldn't get away. How are you, Mum?' He flopped down in his dad's old chair, fighting to get his breath back. 'Flip, I'm out of condition. Mum, what about you? Want a cuppa?'

'Thanks, no, I've had one.'

'Where are Del and Kev?'

'In bed, I think.'

He looked hard at her. 'What's going on, Mum?'

'I've decided to tell you everything. Well, Joe said it might be a good idea and he's right. I'm sorry I've had to keep it secret but — oh, I don't know — I suppose I wanted to save you all from it. It's terribly upsetting.'

'I didn't think you'd come back. To be honest, I thought you'd be locked up as soon as Flanagan turned up. What did he say?'

'I didn't call him; that was all just a trick. I'm really sorry, love.'

'What?'

'It was Joe's idea. He got you and Tina down in the cellar so I could pretend to ring. I knew you were determined to call the police; I knew it was a bad idea. I know lying is bad but, sometimes, telling the truth doesn't do any good, either.'

Gary was disappointed all over again. He'd wanted to do the right thing. Still, maybe his mum was right. Was she?

'But how are we going to explain everything?'

'Me and Joe went around the house and wiped everywhere we thought we might have touched. It doesn't matter about your prints, because you'd been there the other day.'

'Hang on — what about all the tea stuff in the sitting room? Those cups and plates and stuff will have our prints on them. The police will be able to tell they're recent. Shit! This is going to go wrong.'

'Calm down. When Joe was driving you home, I cleaned it all up and put it away.'

'But what if someone saw us?'

'Well, we'll have to take that chance. We'll say we've been at home all evening.'

'Tina and me are going to say we were at her place the whole time, with her dad.'

'Good. Is he happy about that?'

'Well, he's involved in something too, so that's what he wants to say. He needs us to be his alibi. I don't know what that's all about. So, come on — spit it out.'

She took off her glasses and stared into the distance. He looked closely at her. She was about forty-five but, right now, the young woman she must have been was sitting there.

'Mum?'

She looked up. 'This sounds ominous.'

'I'm sorry I've treated you so badly. I'm sorry about Dad and — you know. Del and Kev can say sorry for themselves, although they probably won't. The thing is, I know you've been lovely, and I've been a... a selfish idiot.'

'My goodness, Tina's having a positive effect on you. It's a pity she couldn't work her magic on Kev. Still, fifty per cent success isn't bad.'

'What's Tina got to do with it?'

'Well, you two are an item, aren't you?'

'How did you know? I've only just found out myself!' His mum smiled and tapped her nose. Thinking of Tina now, at home, alone, in bed, her pyjamas — he shook his head. 'Come on then, what's the goss?'

'Sorry, love. Right, so... here goes. Uncle Ray and Grandad worked together — on the railways. You were right: Ray was the train driver in the robbery. It was going to be Grandad, but he didn't know how to drive the train coz he'd retired without ever working on the new engine. Actually, as it turned out, nor had Ray, but that's another matter. I don't know what happened to Ray. Maybe Maureen did top him; maybe he is under their greenhouse. They used to have a house in south London and now they've got that great, big place in Totteridge. Once old Flanagan hears that Maureen has gone missing, he'll be digging up that greenhouse faster than a greyhound out of a trap.'

'I knew it!'

'No, you don't. He might not be there at all. All I know is what I've told you.'

'Okay, what about Grandad? How do you know *he* isn't under her greenhouse?'

'Right, this is the important bit. I don't know what you found in Dad's shed, but just in case ...'

'What? Just in case what?'

'In case you found something, and Flanagan asks about it and puts two and two together.'

'The only thing I found was a letter from you-know-who, some photos and Grandad's old tie.'

'What did the letter say?'

'Um... well, she told Dad to stop threatening her and that she didn't want anything more to do with us. The funny thing was, she said, "Now that Dad has gone" and that made me think she must know what had happened to him. That was why I went over there in the first place. It's what made me check out the greenhouse thing. So, do you know what happened to him? Have you known all along?'

'He's in the reservoir.'

'What?'

'It's true, love. We took him down there in the middle of the night.'

'Who? Who's we?'

'Dad, Uncle Ray and me.'

'Bloody hell! What happened?'

'The rowing boats are never locked up. It was about two in the morning. Dad drove, Ray was in the back with the old man. I went along to keep watch.'

'Was Grandad alive?'

'No, he was already dead.'

'So, what happened?'

'Dad and Ray managed to get his body into the boat. Honestly, you should have seen us. It was like some sort of slapstick comedy. Anyway, they got him in, and I pushed the boat off and stayed on the bank with a torch. I was supposed to flick the torch on and off if I heard anyone coming. Anyway, they rowed out to the deep part by the dam wall and shoved him over. They tied a sack of sand to him to make sure he sank, and stayed down.'

'Bloody hell! But why was his case buried under the greenhouse? I mean, why didn't you throw it into the rez with him?'

'Dad decided he'd keep it. He had this stupid idea he'd be able to blackmail the gang after the robbery. I'm glad he didn't; they'd have made mincemeat of him. Mind you — anyway, it's all in the past now.'

'So, old Flanagan was right, Dad did kill him, after all. I knew it.' His mum was looking at him, strangely. He said, 'What? What now...? Didn't he kill him? Who killed him then? Hang on a minute, it must have been Uncle Ray. Yeah, that makes sense. I bet he wanted Grandad out of the story — he was the loose end to the whole thing. He could have blabbed everything to the police, so they needed to get him out of the way. Of course, why didn't I think of it.' His mum was shaking her head. 'Mum — what? Who?'

'Kev.'

'Kev?'

'Yes, love. It was little Kevin. He saved you.'

Gary put his hands over his head — was it about to explode?

'But hang on a minute — how come? He doesn't remember anything; I asked him. Anyway, he was only — what? I was three, so he was only five. Grandad was a giant. How could a five-year-old kid kill someone like him?'

'I think he can't remember because he's blanked it out.'

'Kev! Anyway, what do you mean, 'saved' me? Whatever he did, I bet it was by accident.'

'No, he was terribly brave.'

'Brave? Kev, brave? I don't think so.'

'No, you're wrong about him. He saved you. You knocked a cup of tea into the old man's lap. He went berserk and started throttling you. Kev tried to get him off you. All I could do was scream at Grandad. Then, before I could stop him, Kevin picked up that — and heaved it on to the old man's head.' She nodded towards the fireplace.

Gary looked. 'What — that?'

'Yes.'

Gary leaned over and hefted the brass fish: despite its permanence, he'd never really paid attention to it. It sure was heavy.

'So, did it kill Grandad?'

His mum looked back at him, silent.

'Mum?'

'Well, you have to remember, Kev was only a little chap.'

Gary watched the walls of the room begin to spin. He shut his eyes to stop himself falling over, or was it into, or maybe off? Cautiously, he opened them to meet the blank face of the fish staring back. He carefully returned the fish to its home by the fireplace.

'Why didn't you get rid of it? I mean, it's a bit — er, goulash — no — ghoulish, isn't it?'

'Dad didn't want to. Grandad and Nan gave it to us for our wedding present. Dad said it had sentimental value; can you believe that? I think it's time to get rid of it, don't you?'

'Too right. Was Del there?'

'No, he was out playing with his friends somewhere. So, that's it. Kevin saved your life that day. Grandad's in the rez, with all the fish — the real ones.'

Gary sat back in his chair. The smack he'd taken was giving him one hell of a headache. That moment of dread, when he'd sunk to the bottom of the rez, all those years ago, rushed back. His dad's hysterical laughter echoed, *Meet any other monsters down there?* No, surely not: was his dad really fishing near his own father's dead body?

Shuddering, he said, 'Jeez, this is all mental. I'm going for a leak.'

He trudged up the stairs and into the bathroom. The last few minutes were whirling around and around: Tina's lips, Kev saving his life, the feel of the bottom of the lake... Did his feet touch his own dead Grandad? His dead Grandad — his mum's first victim. Could it all be true?

He brushed his teeth and had a wash. Pausing outside his and Kev's bedroom, he wondered if maybe he'd misjudged his brother, after all. That was stupid: Kev didn't even remember what happened. Mind you, he had said he had a memory of being in a fight with the old man: he'd been right, after all. With extreme care, Gary turned the handle and inched open the door.

Kev's face was half-lit by the luminous clock on the small chest between their beds. Gary looked at his brother sleeping; he felt a wave of aching love for the worthless git.

He silently closed the door and padded back downstairs.

'I'm going to ring Tina. I said I'd tell her what was going on. You don't mind, do you?'

'Well, I do trust her; she's a lovely girl. But maybe she's better off not knowing? If she knows, she'll be part of it all.'

'She isn't part of anything to do with Grandad though. I'm glad you like her. I know she's a bit wild sometimes but she's... well, amazing.'

'She is. She definitely is. She certainly thinks you're amazing.'

'Yeah? Blimey, that's good.'

'Gary?'

'Yeah?'

'Joe suggested something to me and I'm not sure if it's right or not.'

'What?'

'Well, he says that if Mr Flanagan starts getting too interested in us — you know, about Maureen going missing — then I could say that I know where Grandad is.'

Gary thought it through. It was true that Flanagan was obsessed by the mystery; it might go in their favour if they gave him what he wanted.

'I'll do it. When we hear that she's been found, I'll get in touch with him and say that she told me, when I saw her on Tuesday, that it was her and Uncle Ray that did him in. I can even say where they dumped him. Flanagan won't know that it wasn't her — she's not able to put him right, is she? It will be my public duty.'

'You're a good boy, Gary. Don't you worry about it. Let's wait and see. Now, you'd better go and ring Tina. You will look after her, won't you?'

'I will, don't worry.' He got up then sat down again. What had she just said? He rewound the conversation: what was it? Whatever it was hadn't sounded right. 'Mum, you said something a minute ago; it was about Maureen. You said that if Flanagan gets interested in her going missing... yeah, that was it. She's not going to go missing, is she? Someone's going to find her: her cleaner, gardener, friend, I don't know — someone will, won't they?' He stared at his mum. She stared back. 'Mum?'

'Sorry, I forgot that bit. No, she's gone missing, love. We got her into the car, and she's gone.'

'Gone? Gone where?'

'I don't know. You don't need to know, nor do I. Joe wouldn't tell me. Let's just say that she's away with the fairies. Don't tell Tina, will you? She definitely doesn't need to know.'

Gary stared at her: was this woman an imposter? As he tried to absorb this latest revelation, she reached down to the side of her chair and picked up a box — Meltis Newberry Fruits.

'Want one of these, love? They're ever so nice.'

Chapter 132

'You're listening to Radio London. It's one o'clock and here are the news headlines, with me, Mary Jennings. And the main news tonight is of a story developing in a north London suburb. There has been an incident on the A411, five miles west of Barnet, in the carpark of Woodcock Hill, a well-known beauty spot. Police were called to the scene earlier this evening. Details are still sketchy but there are reports of casualties. I think we can hear from our reporter, Robbie Salisbury, who is at the scene now. Robbie, can you tell us the latest?...'

Tina sat up in bed. Despite the radio, the moment her eyes had closed, dreams had started crowding in. It had been the mention of Woodcock Hill that had brought her fully to consciousness. She turned up her transistor radio.

'...Thank you, Mary. I'm here at what the police are describing as "a serious incident". I understand that firearms have been used and, I'm sorry to report, there have been fatalities. The situation is becoming calmer after a chaotic evening. I arrived here at Woodcock Hill, well-known locally for its views and picnic area, to find police and ambulances, with crew swarming around the extensive gravel carpark. A car was found with two passengers, both having sustained serious injury. Another person was rushed to nearby Edgware General Hospital. The identities of those found have not been confirmed. Apart from these scant details, the police are limiting their statement to a request for anyone who might have been in the area between eight p.m. and ten p.m. to contact the incident line immediately. The number to ring is 953 5353.'

Tina rubbed her eyes. What a night! She half-expected the next news item to be that of a Totteridge woman found dead in her cellar! No, it was something boring about another strike. She got up, put on her dressing gown and went into the kitchen to wait for Gary's call. She switched on the kitchen radio and tuned to Radio London. The phone rang; she jumped.

'Hello?'

'It's me.'

'Dad! Where are you?'

'Everything's fine. How about you?'

'Yeah, I'm all right but … why are you whispering? Where are you?'

'I'm — well, I need to keep my voice down a bit.'

'Listen, Dad, I'm in—'

'Tina, listen, whatever happens and whoever asks, you've got to say we were together tonight.'

'Yeah, I've got it, Dad. Now, please listen to me. Remember, you've got to say that Gary was with us all evening, too. You remember, don't you?'

'Er, yes, I remember that, too — just as well you reminded me. I've got it, sweetheart. Everything's all right, isn't it?'

Should she say? No, why worry him? There was nothing he could do.

'Oh, everything's fine. What about you? Where are you? Why are you going on about us being together? You're not in trouble, are you?' Although he was such a softy, he did have another side. The way he shouted in his sleep was terrifying. 'Dad, you haven't done something bad, have you?'

'Nah, don't worry. There's been a bit of a kerfuffle, but it's sorted now.'

'Where are you?'

'I'm at Mrs Dutton's house — well, her mother's house. There was some funny business going on, so I got her out of it. It's all blown over now.'

Was he telling her the truth? Had he finally got his own back on Mrs Dutton's husband? Had it all gone wrong?

'Are you coming back soon?'

'Yeah, I'm setting off in a minute. I'll be back in half an hour or so.'

'As long as you're safe.'

'Yeah, I'm fine. There is one small thing.'

'What?'

'Well, you know you were with David Whatshisname last night, the barber?'

Was it really only last night? 'David Gainsborough, yeah: the nation's leading hair stylist. What about him?'

'Did you see a flashy boat around there?'

'Yeah, on a trailer, parked on the lawn.'

'That's it. Is it his boat?'

'No, it's his neighbour's… er, um — Rex, I think. Why?'

'It's nothing. I was wondering, that's all.'

'Dad, what's going on? You're in trouble, aren't you. Tell me, I'll sort it out.'

'No, it's fine. I needed to check about the boat. It's — er… I'll sort it out tomorrow.'

'Dad! Tell me what's going on? Just tell me and I'll sort it out.'

'Everything's fine. Honestly, sweetheart, everything's hunky dory.'

Chapter 133

'Yeah, I've got it. Don't worry. Honestly, it's not a problem.'

'You sure, Gary?'

'Yeah, no sweat.'

'Remember, Dad says you've got to be careful. If you see anything, or anyone, then just forget all about it.'

'It's fine, really.'

'You're wonderful, Gary. You really are. Dad's going to be so pleased.'

'I'll see you in a few minutes. All I've got to do is find a telephone box and change into my special pants.'

She laughed — was that the sweetest sound in the world? Now, should he tell his mum? As he opened the living-room door, he saw her getting to her feet.

'Gary, what's going on?'

'Er, nothing. Well — something, obviously, just nothing special. It's just an errand for Tina's dad.'

'This time of night?'

'His car's broken down.' He glanced at her: she looked back, suspicious. 'It's important and I said I'd do it. See you, Mum.'

Gary closed the door and shrugged on his leather jacket. He stuck his hand into the pocket of Kev's — yep — bingo! His fingers curled around something else: what a result. This was turning out about as good as it could get.

'No, Gary, you're not taking his bike.'

He spun around: she was standing in the door, hands on hips, face set.

'Don't worry, Mum. I'll have it back long before he even wakes up.'

'No, it's his pride and joy.'

Gary lifted the crash helmet off the hall table. 'I'll be really careful. He won't even know I've borrowed it.'

'Oh yes he will; I'll tell him.'

He opened the door. 'Sorry, Mum, I've got to go.'

'He'll never talk to you again.'

Wouldn't that be perfect? He thought about his brother asleep: a little, lost boy, unaware that he'd saved his brother's life. Gary swallowed and felt tears roll down his cheeks. Wiping them away, he made a promise to Kev: he'd look after him properly from now on. And he would definitely get his bike safely back home.

Gary pushed the Triumph Tiger down Drayton Avenue to the high street. Now, on the main road, he swung his leg over the saddle, turned the ignition and kick-started the bike. The monstrous racket shattered the air around him. No time to worry about that. He let the clutch out and gingerly turned the throttle.

He'd only ridden mopeds before: this machine was a different beast altogether. Within seconds he was past the shops and bombing out into the posher end of the town. For a second, he wondered if he might take it on to the M1 and see how fast it could go, just for a few minutes. No — this was not the time for a joyride. The thought of the Filth flagging him down now made him decelerate to thirty. He had a mission, and he must complete it.

The right-hand turn came into view. Gary cut the engine and coasted to a stop. Tina had said it was where the local millionaires lived: 'My new best friends, in fact.' He'd never been down here before. Why would he? His friends weren't millionaires. Mindful of Tina's stern warning, Gary dismounted and wheeled the bike behind a bush. He took off the crash helmet. He wondered what on earth her dad could have been up to. Ducking through the trees and bushes at the end of the lane, he looked along it. Empty, silent — safe? How should he approach this? If he sprinted, anyone looking out at the wrong moment would wonder what a bloke in a leather jacket was doing running down a rich street like this. But a casual stroll would take ages and he'd still look just as suspicious. He decided on a brisk march but, feeling conspicuous, kept in close to the hedges and walls of the front gardens, ready to take cover if needed. Scenes from secret agent and undercover-cop films flashed through his head as he loped along, his eyes peeled for movement or sudden light.

After a few minutes, his nostrils caught an acrid stench. Bloody hell! What had been going on down here? Then, as the lane bent left, he saw it: on a trailer on the edge of a wide lawn. He'd been expecting a little boat, like the ones on the rez. This was a big, flashy thing: a posh cruiser, or was it a launch? The smell of the fire was getting stronger; it must be from one of the fancy houses nearby. He froze. In the drive of the house over the road from the boat: a fire engine, just its headlights on and firemen gathered around it. Gary slid behind a large bush and peered through its leaves. Two of the firemen were getting into the cab whilst another two were coiling up a hose. Fucking hell! That was close. What should he do? It looked like they were getting ready to go.

Jeez! A car was reversing out of the drive from behind the fire engine. It pulled out onto the road and turned towards him, its lights about to pick him out. Flattening himself down under the shrub's foliage, Gary thought he could feel the warmth from the beam of headlights that swept over him. The car changed gear; the driver gunned the engine. It stalled — silence. Gary peeped towards the road. The engine started; the lights blazed again. This time the driver revved up more cautiously before the car — an Avenger — accelerated up the lane. Seconds later, the fire engine started up; it also reversed out, then powered away.

Gary lay flat and listened. The sound of the fire engine decreased and then, at last, was gone. Everywhere was silent. Slowly, he pushed himself up but kept in, close to the bush and peered around. As far as he could tell, there was nobody else about. Gary looked over to the boat; it was around fifty yards away. What was the best thing to do? It was possible that someone in the boat owner's house had been waiting for the police and fire brigade to leave before coming out to nose around the scene of — what? Mind you, really posh people weren't like that, were they? Perhaps he ought to get the bike, roll down here, get the stuff and get the fuck out. No, just get on with it: there was no other way. To be on the safe side, he waited five minutes longer. Finally, glancing up and down the lane, he marched past the boat and, after checking one more time for signs of life, approached it, keeping its bulk between him and the two massive houses at the end of the cul-de-sac. He reached over the edge of the boat and lifted the tarpaulin. Damn! This was going to be harder than he'd thought: there was a drop to the base of the boat. He looked around again, then hoisted himself onto the side of the boat and reached down as far as he could: shit! Too deep. He took a couple of breaths, then hurled himself over the edge and fell in.

He'd landed on some material; was it what he wanted? Yes. On his knees, he put the coat on, pulled the balaclava over his head, and tied the arms of the jumper around his waist. He peered out from under the tarp. Everywhere was quiet. He was ready: one more heave and he'd be on his way. This time, dispensing with caution, he leapt... What the fuck!

The moment his feet hit the ground, he was sprinting: the brilliant lights must surely be illuminating him in technicolour. Gary didn't wait to find out:

he kept his head down and, arms and legs pumping, hurtled back up the lane. Approaching the junction, he slowed again; it was just possible that the pigs had caught a glimpse of the bike as they turned the corner? No, no sign of anyone or anything. Pulling off the balaclava, he tried to push it into one of the pockets of the donkey jacket: already full: leather gloves. He pulled them on and flexed his fingers. He smiled: Karen Mitchum would be pleased — big gloves. He squashed the balaclava into the right-hand pocket, then tightened the arms of the jumper around his waist. Tina's striped pyjamas and delighted welcome pushed away Karen Mitchum's smile. This was going to be one hell of a night. He wheeled the heavy machine out onto the road, swung his leg over and, taking one more look around, kick-started the engine and blasted away.

Gary had always dreamed of having a motorbike. When Kev had brought home the Triumph last year, Gary watched him race up and down their street. There was no doubt, he looked really cool, like Steve McQueen in The Great Escape. Kev had taken him out for a cruise around the town: Gary had felt like a warrior. Now, the speed of the thing was making him drunk. He could feel the adrenalin gripping his right hand, revving higher and higher. As the long hill down into town bore left, he let the bike go. This was fucking brilliant! He could see Tina's beautiful face: she was waiting for him, the Bulldog! Life was as good as it could ever be. He'd arrived! The sharp turn at the bottom of the hill rushed towards him. He shouted his triumph as he expertly reduced speed, changing down, leaning low into the corner. Suddenly, he was wrenched from the saddle and flung through the leaves, roots and mud of the thicket at the corner of the junction. When he finally pitched up against the now-silent motorbike, he was no longer bothered about its safe return to his beloved brother.

Chapter 134

Excited, Tina looked around her room again. Everything was clean and tidy. He'd be impressed: the last time she'd been so embarrassed. What he was doing for her and her dad definitely deserved the best she could offer.

Where was he, though? Surely it wouldn't take so long to get up there and back. She knew how fast Kev's bike could go; she'd been on the back of it enough times. He'd loved her pressing against him as they'd bombed along the lanes. She shut her eyes to the memory: Kev was ancient history. The phone rang.

'Hello?'

'It's me.'

'I realise that.'

'Is he there yet?'

'No.'

'Tina, where is he? It shouldn't take this long.'

'I know.'

'What a mess! Jesus, that stupid car. I should have got rid of it years ago. Damn, damn! What a bloody mess!'

She felt tears trickle down her face. All she wanted to do was help her dad; that was all she ever wanted.

'I'm sorry, Dad. This is all my fault. I should have gone. I could have—'

'No, sweetheart. This is my fault. I shouldn't have agreed to him going. I'm so worried, love. If this goes wrong, I'm in big trouble and Gary will be, too. Big trouble.'

'What's going on, Dad? What's it all about?'

There was a long pause, then he said, 'I've managed to get caught up in something. Listen, I promise you, I didn't mean to. I thought I was doing the right thing — for you, for us. If I get pulled in, I just want you to know that I'd do anything for…'

'Dad, what is it? Come on, don't cry. Blow your nose or something. Just tell me what's — Hang on. That's the door! Hang on, Dad.'

She put the phone down and dashed into the hall. With heart in mouth, she slowly opened the door. Gary was pulling off his crash helmet.

'Gary, thank God! What's happened to you? You look like you've gone ten rounds with Mick McManus.'

Gary's grin was sheepish. 'Er, I had a bit of an accident. I came off the flippin' bike and — I'm really sorry, Tina — it's bad news.'

'Oh no, I can't bear this. What? Tell me, what's happened?'

Gary held up her dad's jumper. She laughed, a huge, delighted laugh.

'Blistering barnacles! Shiver me timbers!' She pulled Gary to her and kissed him… a long, lingering kiss. 'Oops! My Dad's on the phone still. Have you got the balaclava, too?'

'Yep.'

'Dad, are you there?'

'Yes, what's happened? Is he all right?'

'Yeah, he's here. He's wearing your donkey jacket, and if you don't mind me saying, it looks a lot better on him than you. Mind you, it's going to be going down the launderette soon, if not a trip to the incinerator. I'm holding your very trendy balaclava — hmm, all the rage amongst London's top criminals — and here I am, holding up what used to be your Cap'n Haddock. There's some good news.'

'What's that?'

'He's been promoted. We'll have to call him Admiral Nelson from now on.'

'Never mind the funnies: is Gary all right?'

She called over, 'Dad wants to know if you're all right?'

Gary was sitting at the kitchen table. He looked up, smiling. 'Yeah, all fine. I managed to come off the bike when the sleeve got caught in the back wheel, but apart from that, I'm fine.'

'Did you hear that, Dad?'

'I did. Thank God. Put him on, will you?'

'Hallo, Mr Castleton.'

'It's Terry, son. Thank you so much for what you've done. I owe you one — a big one. It's my car; it wouldn't start. Anyway, that doesn't matter anymore. Now, without giving details, was anything going on up there? Just answer yes or no.'

'Yes, well…' he cleared his throat. 'Yes.'

'Police?'

'I dunno. I saw a car leave just as I got there.'

'Fire brigade?'

'Yeah, it left just after the car.'

'Were you seen?'

'I don't know. There was one moment …'

'Go on.'

'Well, when I jumped out of the… the — you know. All of a sudden, there were bright lights everywhere. I didn't do anything; these lights just came on like — I dunno, like they had a life of their own.'

'Did you leg it?'

'Not 'alf.'

'Sorry, Gary. Fingers crossed, no one was up. If anything happens, I'll take it. You don't need to worry.'

'I'm sorry about your jumper.'

'It's seen better days. Look after Tina — and remember that we were all together this evening up to the *News*. You've got that, haven't you?'

'Yep, don't worry: Tomorrow's World, Top of the Pops, When the Boat Comes In.'

'Well done, son. I was sewing up the old giraffe whilst we watched the telly.'

'Right, got it.'

'Don't say anything to Tina, will you? I'll explain everything in the morning. Don't mention the police, or anything for that matter.'

'Er… okay. Got it.'

'Good lad. Tell her about me doing Giraffe, you know, as we watched the telly. that's important.'

Tina took the phone back. 'Listen, it's me. I know about the lights coming on. It happened when I was there the other night. They've got these lights with a mind of their own. I don't know how it works but—'

'Sweetheart, don't you worry. You just look after yourself now.'

'I will, I promise. You stay and look after Mrs Dutton. Everything's fine here, now. I'll see you tomorrow?'

'Well done, Tina. You're a wonderful girl. I'm so proud of you. I know I'm a terrible dad, but you've turned out to be a… anyway. Let's go and buy that mansion tomorrow, what do you reckon?'

'You bet, Dad. I know I'm a terrible daughter, really, but thanks for saying nice things. You're not a bad father; I'll give you one more chance.' She put the phone down and looked at Gary. He was sitting at the table, head in hands. 'Are you all right?'

His muffled voice was shaky. 'I'm a bit groggy.'

Suddenly, she thought her heart would burst. 'Oh, Gary, you're wonderful.' She stood behind him, and putting her hands on his shoulders, tentatively massaged. 'Do you mind?'

He groaned and leaned his head back against her. She took his face and gently held his classic, mullet hairdo against her chest. As she wept, she felt his tears against her fingers.

Sniffling, she said, 'You're my hero, Gary Abbott.'

'I'm so sorry. I mean, how stupid can you get? I thought you were going to be killed. Jeez, Tina, you would have died tonight. I'm such a cretin!'

'Shush, it's all over now. None of it matters anymore.'

'But—'

'Shush.'

Shuddering, he rubbed his fists in his eyes, then took her fingers and pressed them against his lips.

Snuffling through her tears, she withdrew her hand. 'Stop it, you're going to make me blub like a geyser.'

'Sorry, I just wanted you to know that I — well, I think you're such a — I dunno, a lovely, beautiful, brilliant, um… you know. That's all.'

'Right, that's it. No more of this. Let's get you cleaned up and ready for bed. Stay there. I'm going to run you a bath.'

As she turned on the taps, she wondered if he'd like some of her bubble bath. Her dad didn't bother with anything like that; he preferred coal tar soap. Did all men like to smell like old men? Surely Gary might like something a bit more fragrant… She poured a load in.

She went back into the kitchen. 'Come on. Time for your hot bath and nice clean bed.'

'Your dad says he was mending the giraffe, this evening. He says it's important. Hey, guess what?'

'What?'

'I haven't even told you about my mum yet. You're not going to believe it.'

She took his hand and pulled him to the bathroom.

'Tell me later, when you're all cleaned up. In you go. I'll come and get you in ten minutes.'

Gary was looking confused. 'Er… I think I might be a bit concussed still. Are you absolutely sure I'm not dreaming all this?'

'I dunno. Maybe we both are? Anyway, you need to get cleaned up before you're getting into my bed.'

She pushed him into the bathroom and shut the door. Maybe she'd put a little of her expensive pink perfume on for him? Yes, he deserved the best. She went back to the door and listened; he was taking off his clothes. She heard his furious voice, 'Fucking hell, you bastard!' followed by the sound of something being thrown into the bin.

'You all right, Gary?'

'Yeah, yeah, fine, all good. I'll be quick, don't worry.'

How to play this? Not too pushy. The last time she'd tried it on with Gary, it had gone badly wrong. Maybe she'd get a couple of blankets and a pillow and make up a bed in the lounge? She could pretend to get ready to sleep in there and he'd protest.

She called out, 'Help yourself to toothpaste when you're ready, won't you?'

'Ta.'

'You don't mind the bubble bath, do you?'

'Na, it's — um, very — er, green.'

The makeshift bed in the lounge looked quite appealing. She stretched out on it: yes, really comfortable. Would she be needing it? Going back to the bathroom door, she heard him getting out. Whatever happened she'd let it. Don't force yourself on him, Tina Castleton. He's a nice bloke. Don't ruin everything.

He called out, 'I'm nearly done. Is there anything I can put on?'

'Hmm… Slippers?'

Silence. Shit, she'd gone too far! This was so typical.

'Scrap that. I'll get you something, um… Hang on there a mo.'

She picked up his leather jacket from the back of the kitchen chair. Without thinking, she pressed it into her face: its smell brought a lump to her throat. He could be so surly, annoying, stubborn, arrogant, and so many other things she couldn't think of, but there was something about him. She went back to the bathroom, opened the door a few inches and handed through the jacket.

'Ta very much. Hmm. Hang on a minute, where's the silk dressing gown?'

'Well, what a cheek. Honestly, where do you think this is — the Ritz? Anyway, does it matter? It'll be off in a second or too.' Shit! What was wrong with her? 'Come on, out you come. You're sleeping in my room tonight. Look, I cleaned it all up for you specially.'

Hesitantly, he emerged. She wanted to laugh out loud; his long, white legs sticking out from under the ragged, old jacket.

He peered into her room. 'Wow, looks completely different.'

'Right, get into bed. I'll tuck you in. All right, sleepy head? Then I'll get into my lonely bed on the settee.'

He didn't move.

'What's wrong?'

'I promised I'd get Kev's bike back before he woke up.'

'Gary, the night is still young: there's plenty of time before that lazy toad gets up. Anyway, the quicker you get to bed the quicker. Well, just get into bed, that's all.'

She went into the bathroom and shut the door. Taking her pink perfume down from the windowsill, she dabbed some behind each ear. Remembering, she looked into the bin — a crumpled packet of Durex. She stooped and picked it up: it was empty.

Laughing, she glanced at the mirror — would she pass muster? Steam obscured her reflection. Opening the window, she felt the night air pour into the warm, damp room. Gradually, the mirror cleared. The girl looking back at her wasn't too shabby. Tina smiled. Maybe she did look a bit like Lindsey Wagner.

'Okay, Gary Abbott, let's see if you're worth six million, shall we?'

As she opened the door, the sound of a distant siren cut through the background hum of traffic. She leaned back to the window and pulled it tightly shut.

Chapter 135

She started awake. Thank God! The image of the children trying to escape from the flames had been the most appalling dream ever. Even now, with her eyes open, and consciousness returning, it was unbearable.

'It's all right, Geraldine. You're safe now.'

'Terry?'

'That's right, Terry Castleton, the school caretaker. I thought I'd better check to make sure you were all right? It sounded like you were having a nasty dream.' His voice was a whisper.

'Terry, did it all happen?'

'I'm afraid so.'

'Oh my God.'

Terry whispered, 'Can I get you anything? Your water is there, but maybe you want an aspirin or something?'

She reached out, picked up the glass and gulped noisily. 'That's better, my mouth is like the bottom of a parrot-cage.' As she pulled her arm back under the bedclothes, her lack of clothing caught her attention. Her ludicrous antics, then Terry getting her upstairs and into bed, were coming back. Had he helped her undress? Yes, he had. 'What time is it?'

'After two.'

'Have you been standing there the whole time?'

'No. I've been trying to start my car. It's kaput. Then, I hope you don't mind, but I had to ring Tina a couple of times.'

'Oh good. Is she all right?'

'Yes, everything's fine, I think. 'Til the morning, anyway. She told me to look after you.'

'Did you tell her that you already had?'

'I think we looked after each other, don't you?'

'That's not what I remember, but thanks anyway. Don't just stand there, come and sit down.'

'Thanks. I will.'

She heard him push the door to; her mother's snores receded.

Although it was pitch black, she could sense where he was from the creaking floorboards. He settled into the chair, its ancient, leather upholstery protesting.

The events of last evening were crowding in on her. She shuddered.

'Terry?'

'Yes?'

'I'm so sorry about everything. I know it's not my fault, but I am sorry for you. I mean, your wife and Edward: that's so awful. Then, seeing them tonight... it doesn't bear thinking about.'

'I'm sorry for you, too.'

They were in it together, that was true. There was something horrible dawning on her. But surely it wasn't right? Only hours before, her husband had been killed; other people were dead or, at best, badly injured. Yet an overwhelming sense of relief was washing over her.

'Terry, I'm going to have to own up to someone. You're the only person I can trust in my life. I know my mother loves me, no matter what, but I can't tell her this. I'm glad it all happened. Can you believe that? Does it mean I'm an evil person?'

There was a long silence.

'Terry? Have I shocked you?' She sat up, remembered her near-nudity and lay down again. 'Terry?'

His voice was hesitant. 'I feel the same. I've got something much worse to say. Can I tell you?'

She paused for a second: what could it be? No, it didn't matter. Whatever it was, she could cope.

'Yes.'

'I've been dreaming of killing your husband for the last six years.'

'Ah.'

'Do you hate me?'

'No.'

'That's just for starters.'

'Oh?'

'I love violence. I'm sorry. I always have. I think I might be addicted to it.'

'No, not you.' She pictured him wandering around the school grounds, the epitome of a calm, steady, middle-aged man.

'Can I say another thing? I need to get stuff out of my system. The next one is really horrible.'

'Um…'

'I want to tell you everything, in case I never get the chance again.'

'Er…'

'It's okay, you're safe. Despite what I said, I'm not a crazy killer.'

'Well, of course. I want you to tell me.'

'This is terrible but — the thing is, whenever I pictured killing your husband, I also pictured getting my own back on him.'

'Yes, I can understand that.'

'Can you?'

'Yes, to get revenge on him for doing what he did with your wife. Yes, I understand that. It's not that bad a thing.'

'But, Geraldine, I wanted to do to him what he did to me.'

At last she got it. 'Oh.' She was suddenly very awake. What was he really saying? What was this feeling? There was a rushing sensation in her body. Was it fear or excitement? 'Well, I can understand that, too, I think.'

'It's not what you think, though.'

'Oh? Well, what is it?'

She heard palms on bristles.

'The thing is, it was always a violent, vengeful act. I wanted to hurt him by violating his wife. I'm so sorry. It wasn't an act of desire; it was a drive to hurt. The thing is, I wanted to do that before I knew that you were his wife. It was just someone that existed in my head; not a real person. In fact, I didn't even know if he had a wife. Then, when I found out that it was you, I felt so guilty. The thing is, you're the loveliest person I've ever met. And the thought of doing anything to hurt you is horrible and — I'm sorry. I wanted to say it. I'm sorry; I shouldn't have said anything. Blast! Me and my big, stupid mouth.'

Geraldine turned her head towards him. She could dimly make out a dark shape slumped in the chair. What had happened? What kind of circumstances could possibly have occurred for Terry Castleton, the school caretaker, a man she hardly knew, to be in the bedroom in which she grew up, with her near-naked in bed? 'It's my turn to be honest with you; can you bear it?'

'Anything you want to say to me is fine. You could never shock me.'

'I'm not a saint, either, Terry. You mustn't put me on a pedestal.'

'Sorry, yeah. I understand.'

She knew exactly what she wanted to say but what was the best way?

'I know this is a funny question but — oh, gosh, this is difficult… Listen, will you sit on the bed? I want to hold your hand.'

The old chair rocked slightly as he got to his feet, then the side of her bed sagged.

'Sorry. I'm not sure this antique is built for big, fat, Bobby Charltons.'

'Who said that?'

'Oh, just one of the Crackerjacks.'

'Cheeky beggar. Give me your hand.'

As he shifted his weight, the bed creaked ominously.

'Hang on, this isn't safe. I'm going to kneel down. Hold hard, I'll get the cushion from the chair.' She felt the bed rise again as he stood. Then, knees clicking, he knelt down. 'Right, I'm ready.'

She took his hand in hers. 'So, Sir Terry Castleton, here is my question.' Her heart was beating fast; could she say it? 'Have you ever made love?'

'Sorry?'

'I know. It's a funny question. I mean, I know you've had sex — maybe with lots of women, I don't know. But have you ever made love?'

'I'm not sure I get your drift, I'm sorry.'

'I haven't. I have never expressed tenderness, compassion, generosity, care, gratitude, respect, sadness and joy, gladness and relief, safety and security, absolute trust — with all of my body. I think that is what making love really means, don't you?'

'Um, well... when you put it like that: yes, I think it probably does.'

'Of course, there's desire, too. That's part of it, but only one part. I don't know what was in Edward's mind, but I think it was only ever lust.' He was silent; she guessed that he was thinking about his wife and Edward. Poor Terry, what a terrible thing to see. 'I know it's none of my business, but have you ever made love to someone in that way? You know — all of it, all of those things together?'

She felt his big hand squeeze hers. 'No, Geraldine, I haven't.'

She cleared her throat. 'The thing is — I know it's a funny question, but... do you think you could make love to me, in all those ways?' He was silent. 'I'm sorry, Terry. I shouldn't have asked. It's entirely inappropriate. I just wanted — oh, it doesn't matter. Please forget I even—'

'Yes, I would love to.'

'Now?'

'Well, yes, I would. I can't think of anything I'd rather do right now. But...'

'The bed?'

'Yep. Well, the whole house, if I'm honest. It's...'

In the silence, she heard the distant rumble. 'My mother?'

It was Terry's turn to clear his throat. 'Well, I wouldn't want to frighten her.'

'Anything else?'

'I'm a bit out of...'

'It's going to be a first for us both, in lots of ways.'

'That's true.'

'Would you like me to help you get undressed? It's only fair, after you helped me.'

'I haven't slugged down half a pint of sherry, though. Actually, on that point, will you feel differently when you've sobered up?'

'I'm sober now. To be honest, I wasn't really drunk earlier; I was more — um, off my head. Also, and this is a bit embarrassing, I wanted you to look after me. It felt nice having someone take care of me. You're not angry with me, are you?'

He took his hand from hers and stroked her hair. 'You're such a lovely woman, Geraldine. I don't think you really want a great, ugly bloke to sully your pure mind and body, do you?'

'Terry?'

'Yes?'

'If you could bear to, I would like you to make love to me. Will you?'

He levered himself up from his knees; the floorboards creaked as he moved back to the chair. Geraldine kept her eyes shut and listened to him slowly taking off his clothes: the gentle rustling of shirt buttons being undone, followed by flapping and folding. The old wood of the chair complained as he sat down; laces were pulled, and boots removed. She pictured him picking them up and placing them neatly under the chair. Then a belt being uncinched and a zip hesitantly undone. Conscious of his embarrassment, she pushed back the bed covers.

He stopped. 'What are you doing?'

'I'm sorry, Terry. I thought you might feel like I was putting you on the spot. You know: me warm and comfy in my bed whilst you're having to — well, I don't know — expose yourself in a strange place, with a strange person.'

'Well, it is all a bit strange. But I am ex-army: I'm used to expeditions into uncharted territories.'

'Ah, well, that's one way of describing things. Anyway, I'm in the platoon, is that what it's called? Can a platoon comprise two people?'

'Let's say we're a couple of scouts.'

'Right. Well, the point is, I thought we should both be in the same uniform.'

'Huh?'

She got out of bed, undid her bra and put it on the end of the bed. She slid her pants down, sitting to remove them and put them next to the bra.

'See, I'm ready for action now.'

'Ah, that's very decent of you.' The sound of trousers being removed, folded and set on the chair; then pants. 'Er…'

'Yes, socks too.'

'Geraldine, are you sure about this?'

'Very.' Socks were removed. 'Do you want to get in first?'

'Well, maybe I need to check that the bed will actually take my weight.'

She stood and moved away. As he edged past her, his scent — old sweat; outdoor, manual work; oily machinery — made her smile.

'Terry, you should sell your scent to a Parisian perfumier.'

'What, the Great Smell of Old Caretaker?'

'That's right: "Tout Concierge". Come on — in you get.'

'Look, if this bed is a family heirloom, I'm sorry.'

For a moment, she thought that what had seemed to be a joke was going to backfire: the bed let out a loud groan as he got in. It carried on its protest as he moved to the wall side.

'I'm in.'

'Oh, really? Was that you? I thought it was a feather landing on gossamer.'

For some reason, Geraldine felt confident. If anyone had told her a few days ago that she would be getting into bed with a man that wasn't her husband, the first thought would have been one of disbelief, followed by anxiety. Although her fantasies of late had been carnal, she'd known they would never come true. Now, here she was, about to get into bed with a naked man — and she felt good about it.

'I'm not nervous, Terry. Do you know why that is?'

'Er — because you're ex-army, too?'

'Because it's you.'

'Oh.'

'What about you?'

'Well, to be honest, I am. Just a smidgin. Thing is, I'm a bit like the soldier I saved from the trenches the other day. I'm not sure everything's in working order.'

'I don't care about that. Whatever happens is fine with me.'

Gingerly, she got in beside him. Whatever did happen next would need to be achieved with the minimum of movement: her poor, old bed.

He was right against the wall, lying on his back. She lay on her back, too: there was just enough space.

He said, 'Hallo. Fancy meeting you here.'

'A very nice surprise.'

'I really wanted to join you the other day, you know, in your bedroom.'

'I wanted you to, too.'

'Probably best that I didn't — I'm not sure it's right now, either.'

She knew it was right. In her heart, this was right. Part of her was being driven by the need for comfort and safety, but there was so much more than that going on. It was Terry that she wanted to love. Since she'd got to know him, over the last three days, she had realised that, behind the camouflage of the shambling caretaker, he really was an all-action hero — brave, strong, resourceful, and so loving. He had shown more love for her in three days than Edward had in twenty years. More than anything else right now, she wanted to love him back.

She knew she must take charge of the situation. Terry was such a gentleman, it wasn't fair to expect him to take the lead. What could she do to help him feel safe, secure, the way she felt with him...?

'Will you hold my hand?' She felt him grip hers; she let their clasped hands rest on her thigh. 'I like your hands; they're rather bigger than mine.' He didn't answer. 'Twice the size I'd say.' He sniffed. 'I should think you could probably crush a grape in them, couldn't you?' He sniffed again. 'Want a hankie?'

'I'm sorry, Geraldine; I'm so sorry.'

'Oh, Terry, don't cry. What's wrong? Oh, I'm so sorry. I've been so thoughtless. Please forgive me. Oh, God, I'm so selfish.' She half sat up, resting on an elbow, looking down at the dim form. 'What is it? Is it your wife? Oh, what have I done?'

Through his tears he cried, 'No, no, it's nothing like that. Please, you're wonderful. No, it's that I thought my life was on the way up. For a few days, things seemed possible again. I felt so much better. Being here with you is — well, putting it simply, a flipping miracle. But it's...'

'But it's - what?'

'It's going to go wrong tomorrow. The police will find out I was there.'

'How? Why?'

'Diane's sister.'

'What? I don't understand. What about her?'

'Diane was staying with her sister. If Diane told her it was me picking her up tonight, then she'll tell the police. I'll be banged up forever.'

Geraldine's heart lurched. No. Surely, this wasn't right. Why should Terry have to take any blame for what had happened?

'But would Diane have told her? Maybe — I don't know — maybe she would have kept it to herself?'

He wiped his face. 'Sorry, I just don't know. She's a spiteful piece of work. If she knows it was me picking up Diane, she'll take great pleasure in dumping me in it. Then I've lost Tina, and I'll have lost you.'

'Oh, Terry, you silly man. No, you won't have lost me. Whatever happens next, I'll look after you. Come here, come on.' She lay down, turning towards him, and cradled his head against her chest. For a second, he was reluctant, then she felt his heavy arm wrap around her. The love that swept over her made her head reel. 'That's right, you're safe with me. That's it.'

His bristly chin rasped against her breast as he whispered something.

She lowered her head to him. 'What was that?'

His voice was muffled.

'Oh, Terry, I'm so sorry: what was that?'

He lifted his head. 'I'm sorry, Geraldine, the thing is… your mother's stopped snoring.'

She listened hard — damn! He was right: silence. The seconds ticked by. They lay frozen in each other's arms. Geraldine willed her mother's snoring to splutter back into its steady rhythm. She heard a groggy cough then, at last, the beautiful sound resumed.

'You see, Terry: she approves of you.'

'What a wonderful woman she is; you must take after her.'

Geraldine pressed his head back against her breast. 'Shush, no talking. This has to be what we army-types call a covert operation.' She felt him shaking. 'Are you crying or laughing?' she whispered. 'Whichever, my poor bed's protesting… Oh, dear! This doesn't bode well for the next few minutes.'

The End